Outremer IV

'Who controls the present, controls the past'

D N Carter

Clink Street

London | New York

Published by Clink Street Publishing 2019

Copyright © 2019

First edition.

ISBNs: 978-1-913136-40-6 hardback
978-1-913136-41-3 paperback
978-1-913136-42-0 ebook

Dedicated to
Bob

Author's Foreword

Welcome to the fourth volume of Outremer. As with books one, two and three, I have had cause to refer again to factual research for both religious and historical accuracy, as well as many documents, abstracts and books on a wide range of subjects. I have therefore likewise inserted bibliographic references, all of which are listed at the rear of this volume.

There are many historical accounts of the events portrayed within book four as viewed and chronicled from both sides of the conflict, especially in relation to the assault at Cresson Springs, the Battle of Hattin and then Jerusalem. Consequently I had to review many sources to try and gauge an as near accurate account as possible. This meant sifting through what was clearly propaganda of the time, to documented accounts written by such scribes as Ernoul to Saladin's personal secretary. I have not shown favour or bias to either side but detailed the facts as they happened. Some of the codes and information revealed within Outremer was not established or reconfirmed until the twentieth century. I have therefore added confirmation details in my Epilogue and appendix section so those readers who wish to validate or investigate further may do so.

Acknowledgements

I have already covered my acknowledgements and made my thanks known previously but I again, and at the risk of repeating myself, would like to express my gratitude to those few friends who have gone well beyond what was asked or expected of them over the past few years. They know who they are but without them, book four would not have been completed. Also to the continued support and help of those land owners involved in the codes contained within Outremer. But ultimately, and finally, it really is to you, the reader, who has journeyed through these pages and persevered that my heartfelt thanks must go out to. For giving your time to read what I have simply penned. I hope you have found the journey an interesting one. I also hope the people within Outremer have come to life within you, but more importantly, that you have an understanding that our past history is far more complex and stretches further into antiquity than we are led to believe. By the end of this volume, I hope you will find answers to those questions, such as where do we come from, and where are we going... for the answers to some of the greatest mysteries have been hidden in plain sight all along.

Characters

Conrad de Montferrat

Guy de Lusignan

Mellissa Plantavalu

Arri Plantavalu

Attar (Sufi Mystic)

Nyla

Brother Baldwin (Upside) & Ruth

Armengaud d'Asp

Melissae Inn. Ayleth, Templar, Genoese Sailor, Miriam, Peter, wealthy tailor, Simon, Sarah, Gabirol, old man, Hospitaller, Stephan.

Contents

"Who controls the present, controls the past."

PART XIII

Chapter 73
Annihilation of the Soul

Port of La Rochelle, France, Melissae Inn, spring 1191

"Oh My Lord...columns of smoke...and the Poem and picture are fire damaged,"
Ayleth said, quietly shaking her head.

"Cutting the elm. What does that mean?" Simon asked and shrugged his shoulders.

"I shall explain what cutting the elm means later," the old man replied and looked directly at Ayleth. "You make the connection well, Ayleth." Sarah put her hands to her mouth and sighed heavily with a look of sadness written across her face. "Paul, having seen the smoke plumes, and having learnt to trust his instincts just knew it was Alisha's column under assault. He raced Adrastos harder than he had ever ridden him, and Adrastos seemed to understand the urgency for he galloped through thickets, brush, tall grasses, along dusty tracks and then along the wide ancient part stone corbelled Roman road direct to Pella. He rode completely oblivious to everything else around him nor how far ahead from the rest of his group he was."

"What about enemy patrols?" the Hospitaller asked.

"Paul did not even consider them...he just concentrated on getting to Alisha and Ailia to help defend them. He knew Tenno, Thomas and his men would all be doing everything in their power to protect them but it did not help knowing that, the knot in his stomach turning tighter as the columns of smoke ahead of him rose higher and thicker."

Ayleth covered her eyes, anxious at what she was hearing. Sarah gently clasped Ayleth's forearm reassuringly.

"So please...pray tell us what he found?" Gabirol asked, sensing the sadness in the old man's voice.

The old man paused as he looked across the table at the pictures laid out. He took a deep breath and looked up slowly. Miriam held the Templar's hand tighter as the tension from the old man was almost palpable to touch. Peter gulped hard as the Genoese sailor leaned closer to hear what was about to be told.

3

Old Roman Town of Pella, Principality of Galilee, March 14th 1187

Paul halted Adrastos hard, almost slipping up on the corbelled road, old broken columns on either side marking the original entrance into the old Roman town. Three large fires burned ahead of him sending thick smoke skyward. Small half collapsed walls hid from view most of what was burning. Rapidly he looked around for any signs of life or movement but there was none other than several crows and large vultures circling high above him. The smell of burnt flesh entered his nostrils as a light wind blew across him and Adrastos, who snorted and backed up slightly. Paul steadied him, sweat pouring from both of them. He quickly glanced back as Percival appeared approaching fast behind. Paul dismounted and rushed over to a raised set of fallen stones and jumped up. He drew his sword as he looked forward to see many bodies of men, women and children lying dead in various grotesque positions, flies beginning to swarm. Many caravans were burnt out already with blackened bodies stuck within them, one looking directly at Paul, its face burnt away around its mouth set in a fixed grin of death. There were far too many people and caravans here to be Alisha's caravan, he thought with a sudden sense of relief despite the carnage before him. Then his heart missed a beat as he wondered if Queen Tamar had come further south than she should have. Percival ran up beside Paul and drew his sword covering his nose from the stench by pulling up his sand protector up over his mouth and nose.

"You take that side and I shall take the left," Paul said and started to slowly walk forward into the main area of burning caravans and bodies.

Percival walked toward several poles that appeared to have severed heads upon them. Paul picked his way through the dead, mainly pilgrims by the look of them. Most had been shot with high velocity crossbow bolts. A woman sat propped up against the remnants of a stone wall, having sought cover behind it. Her eyes were fixed open staring upwards, her mouth wide open left in the position of her last scream. She held a baby across her chest but it was pinned to her, just the ends of the crossbow bolt still visible, sticking out of the baby's back, the rest having pierced through to the mother. Other bodies had their throats cut wide. As he stepped forward past a burnt out caravan, the floor littered with empty luggage chests and boxes, a few silks blowing in the breeze, the smoke made him cough. Several black clad men lay dead amongst several dead Templars.

Paul's stomach churned with anguish and he was nearly sick as he moved closer to see them. They had all been beheaded and he could not tell if they were the Templars who had been escorting Alisha or not. Frantically he looked around to see if he could see any signs of Thomas and his men but they were not amongst the dead near to him. A large caravan was a short distance off completely destroyed by fire, its two horses lying dead in front of it, partially burnt. He looked over to Percival, who was just staring up at the severed heads on the poles. The men had clearly given a good account of themselves for Paul had to step over many more black clad men. He knew they were not Al Rashid's men, which left only one other person responsible. Turansha…and he must have left in hurry as they always took their dead with them. Slowly Paul walked towards Percival looking at all the dead. It had been a large caravan of mainly Christian pilgrims. A sugar cart billowed black smoke as the sugar burned away in thick gouts of orange flame. Nicholas and Upside pulled up beside Adrastos and both dismounted as Abi pulled up behind them. Paul looked at them briefly then back towards Percival, who, he could see through the swirling smoke, was now leaning forwards being sick. Paul's heart exploded seeing him like that. Quickly he ran toward him, Nicholas seeing him move started to run toward Percival too.

 11 – 40

"No, no, no, no, no, dear God, no," Paul said as he ran closer to Percival, fearing the worse.

Percival spat to clear his mouth then coughed. He wiped his mouth and looked to his left as Paul approached. Quickly he raised his arm up for him to stop, but instead Paul ran faster. Abi shook her head and dismounted as Al Rashid rode into view behind her.

"No, Paul! Stay back," Percival shouted and stood to face him, tears now streaming down his face. Paul's eyes widened, seeing his emotional expression. Paul threw his sword down and sprinted. "NO!" Percival shouted again as Paul passed him but he just managed to grab his mantle and yank it hard almost stopping him in his tracks. "You must not," Percival cried and tried to wrap both of his arms around Paul's waist as he struggled to move forwards.

Paul's eyes blazed with both fear and rage as he recognised the burnt out large caravan Alisha had left in. Many dead and badly burned bodies were strewn everywhere but he immediately saw the lower section of Alisha's dark green dress still partially visible and un-burnt but the rest of the body was badly burned. Papers and documents, including drawings and writings Paul had done, littered the ground and blew in the breeze. As Paul pushed towards Alisha, Percival could not hold him and he slipped, only managing to hold onto his right leg. Paul fell to his knees just in front of Alisha. His mouth wide and in total disbelief he shook his head, his throat so tight he could not catch his breath and fell forwards on his elbows, Percival still trying to pull him away. Alisha lay upon her left side cradling Ailia protectively. He instantly saw her three bladed dagger resting against her blackened thigh, her clothes being almost completely burnt away. Her blackened right arm was resting around Ailia's charred remains. Alisha's beautiful hair was all but burnt away revealing patches of white bone showing through pink rimmed holes where the flesh had completely gone. Paul blinked and shook his head as he tried to push himself up onto his knees and reached out his hand to touch her. Percival pulled him back hard, but Paul instantly elbowed him violently in the chest, winding him. Quickly Paul jumped forwards and grabbed Alisha's upper arm to pull her over, but as he did, the burnt flesh just pulled clean off in his hand revealing the brilliant white bone of her arm. In shock he dropped the clump of cooked flesh and fell backwards, Percival instantly grabbing him firmly, his arms wrapped around Paul's arms and chest. Paul hit out and swung his arms about to get free as Percival wrapped his legs around him to stop him moving. Alisha's Mother Goddess pendant fell to the floor from where it had been hanging around her neck but stuck upon her shoulder. Paul having tugged at her caused the clasp to fall free, the small wires that had held it closed having melted away. He stretched out and grabbed it in his left hand and stared at it in utter disbelief, his mind refusing to accept or believe what he was seeing. As tears fell from his face, Paul could not speak. He could see Ailia's burnt foot just visible. It was then that he noticed she had six bolts in her back, also burnt with just the ends sticking out. Nicholas ran up and stopped, saw immediately the scene before him and had to turn away his gaze, screwing up his eyes tightly, and gagged as he was nearly sick. Upside had to grab him to stop him from falling over as he nearly collapsed. Paul could see what was left of Alisha's fur hood that had not been consumed by the flames and in that instant all he could see was the last image he had of her beautiful face framed by that fur hood when he had said goodbye. He pushed Percival back hard, and thrust his head against his. Percival instinctively let go as pain shot through his face from the impact on his cheek. Paul jumped up and moved to step over Alisha to see her but as he raised his leg, Upside dived at him knocking him to the side. Instantly Percival and Nicholas jumped upon Paul as he kicked out and fought to get them off his back. Paul moaned and let out a yell of utter pain and frustration.

"Let me fucking go!" he screamed as Upside pushed his face into the blackened and blood covered dirt of the floor.

"No, my friend, 'tis not a sight you should see. If you do it will haunt you for the rest of your days and that is not what she would want," Upside said as Percival and Nicholas held his legs and arms tightly, both with tears streaming down their faces, Nicholas shaking and sobbing uncontrollably, his eyes screwed up shut as he held Paul's legs.

"We are going to let you up but you cannot look…you must not," Percival said as tears kept running down his own face, pained for the loss of Alisha and Ailia but also seeing the pain his friend was suffering.

Upside looked up to his left as Abi approached shaking her head no.

"No…this cannot be…this is not so…it cannot be so," she said quietly and kept repeating it to herself, her voice dry and almost a whisper.

"Ali…," Taqi called out as he dismounted and ran over as fast as he could. He stopped when he reached Abi, who was by now staring down at Paul being physically restrained.

Paul upon hearing Taqi spun over on his side, wrenching his arm away from Percival, then pushed his left arm against Upside, knocking him over. The sheer brute strength of Paul's rage took them by surprise. Nicholas looked up as Paul pulled up his legs fast then kicked away hard causing him to lose his grip upon his legs. Quickly Paul rolled over backwards as Tenno had taught him so many times to do, stood up fast and rushed over to where he had thrown his sword. Picking it up, he raised it and instantly turned to face Percival and Nicholas as Upside stood over Alisha and Ailia's bodies.

"Let me pass to see my wife and child or so help me God I shall force you aside," Paul said through gritted teeth, his tone deep and full of rage. Percival stood up and put his hands out toward him. "I swear it, Percy, if you do not let me pass I shall do you harm."

7

"Then you will have to harm me for I will not let you pass," Percival replied, his face full of emotion. He took a deep breath, clenched his fists and stood up as straight and as tall as he could.

"You cannot beat this," Paul yelled and waved his sword toward him.

"I will not let you pass," Percival replied defiantly and gulped hard.

Nicholas stepped closer to Percival and looked at Paul, the pain and hurt of Alisha's death more than visible in his tearful eyes. He went to speak but words failed him as he held onto Percival. He shook his head no, Paul's eyes narrowing.

"Paul, listen to me," Upside said. "Look at me. You must let us deal with them and prepare their bodies. You know Ali would not want you to see this…you know I speak truth."

Paul looked at them all in turn through tears. He jumped when Taqi placed his hand upon his shoulder from behind.

"'Tis not right you deal with this, Paul," Taqi said emotionally, his eyes looking intently into his.

Abi stepped closer still shaking her head no as Master Douglas walked up to the group. Al Rashid ordered his people to spread out and secure the area whilst others started checking the bodies. Out of the corner of his eye Paul saw movement from among several bodies. It was a black clad figure trying to slowly crawl away into some bushes. Paul lunged towards the man. Within three steps he was over him and flung the man over, his eyes looking up at Paul. Paul put the tip of his blade against the man's throat as he just stared back through the thin open strip in his face cover.

"Who are you before I send you to hell?" Paul demanded as he shook him with rage. "Who ordered this?" he shouted louder and pulled the man up closer with his left arm.

"He will not speak now…but do not kill him for I have ways of making people speak," Master Douglas said calmly as he approached Paul. When Paul looked across at him, he noticed Abi putting her hands to her mouth and tears welling in her eyes. She was looking beyond Alisha and Ailia. Paul followed her gaze. Beside many burnt bodies, she saw the still steaming body of a large man wearing Tenno's armour clearly distinguishable from the others around him. Master Douglas nodded at Paul as Nicholas and Upside rushed up beside him and grabbed the arms of the black clad man and restrained him. Paul slowly stood up. "You make one move to see your family, I will personally gouge out your eyes. Trust me, you do not need to see them. Remember them how they were."

Paul briefly looked back at Alisha and Ailia. If he could die at that moment he would welcome it. Seeing Abi cry made him take a step back. He felt dizzy and sick, his heart beating so fast and hardly able to catch his breath. He watched as Abi approached Tenno. Shaking her head no repeatedly, she fell to her knees just short of him and buried her face in her hands and started to cry. The wind picked up one of Paul's drawings and it wrapped around his right ankle. He picked it up. It was the drawing of Ailia, slightly scorched around the edges but still complete. A tear fell from him, landing on the sheet. With his heart pounding, he could feel the pulse surging through his hand into the sword. Clenching the drawing in his left hand he walked towards several large rocks and boulders just beyond the main track. Al Rashid looked at him sadly as he walked past. Paul's ears were ringing and he felt disjointed from his physical body as he approached the stones. The pain in his heart felt heavy and as if he was falling inside of himself. If he pushed the sword through his chest, would he even feel it? he wondered. He could not quite believe his family were now all dead. He knew in his mind that their spirits are eternal and were elsewhere like Arri's and his mother's, but that did not assuage the pain that ran through him, the sword only seeming to pulse harder with every beat of his heart. He needed to see Alisha and Ailia properly to make it real somehow, but he also reasoned Percival would not have pushed him away for no reason. Percival had seen the flesh burnt away from her face, her eyes appearing large and grey, boiled and split, the eyelids having being burnt clean away. Her teeth all showed in a fixed grin of death stare. It was something he knew would haunt him for the rest of his life and he did not want Paul seeing it. After a few moments stood in silence, the crackle from a fire nearby the only sound, Paul raised his sword and clasped it with both hands. The blade was too long to hold out away so its tip touched his chest, so he held it by the cross handle guard and placed the tip against his stomach. He knew the sword would easily slice through the chain mail. Suicide was considered a sin but at that moment he simply did not care. The words of his first ever poem to Alisha flooded his mind. 'Sword to my heart, sword through my soul.' He could see Alisha's face and the tears she had shed the day he first caught her reading it. He laughed emotionally to himself as he recalled her laughter. Then the deep collapsing realisation hit him like a bolt surging through his entire body, followed by a feeling like an explosion of energy leaving him as rage overwhelmed it.

"Paul, think of Father," Stewart said softly behind him. Paul had not even seen his brother arrive. He glanced over his shoulder to see Stewart stood with Brother Teric, both looking concerned. "This is not your time."

Paul looked back at the sword in his hands and thought of his father and the pain he would suffer if he were to take his own life. Paul stood shaking for several long minutes considering his next action. He nodded his head several times as he decided that somehow he would find Turansha and he would kill him regardless of all that Kratos had told him…but not with this sword. This sword that had promised so much yet had brought him nothing but bad luck. He raised the sword up, its tip now pointing downward toward the middle of the largest boulder in front of him. With all his might and rage, his face gnarled and snarling, he thrust the blade downwards into the stone. It sparked at first, and a great heat glowed from the blade as he pushed it further into the stone. Stewart went to stop him but Brother Teric pulled him back. A loud but deep groaning sound echoed throughout the entire valley which drew everyone's immediate attention. Taqi started to run toward him as they watched the sword being slowly pushed deeper into the stone, Paul's face turning red, the veins on his forehead and neck bulging as if about to explode under the pressure. A blue horizontal light suddenly pulsed outward in a radiating circle away from the sword until Paul could push it down no further. A loud bang echoed out as Paul let go of the sword, just its handle now visible. With his hands feeling hot, and shaking from head to toe, the picture of Ailia still held in his left palm, he stared at the sword. He stepped backwards, but his legs collapsed under him as if useless and he fell onto his side hard. Taqi went to pick him up but he pushed him away as he tried to catch his breath.

"This cannot stay here," Taqi remarked and went to pull the sword out but it would not move. He pulled harder but still it would not move.

Paul shook his head and started to sob…an empty sob of an utterly broken man. Nicholas approached him and knelt beside him placing his hand upon his back. He wiped his own face as tears fell silently from him onto Paul. When Al Rashid approached, Paul curled himself up and just cried. Stewart could do nothing but look down at him, helpless to offer any words of comfort. He closed his eyes as a tear ran down his cheek. Master Douglas stopped Al Rashid and indicated with his eyes to look at a pile of stones with a small bee emblem scratched into it. After many minutes Paul stopped sobbing, stood up and pulled his clothing straight. He could sense everyone was looking at him. He could see the hurt in Nicholas's eyes too as he stood up beside him.

"Let us bury them and when ready we shall fetch you," Upside said softly and clasped both Paul and Nicholas's arms. They looked at each other and nodded silently in agreement.

Paul turned to see Percival stood beside Abi. He walked toward them closely followed by Stewart and when they reached Percival he just nodded at them. Abi was sat on her knees rocking back and forth looking at the remains of Tenno. Paul knelt down beside her and sighed heavily.

"'Tis truly the end of all things…and my soul is annihilated," Paul whispered emotionally. He looked at Abi, tear streaks visible down her cheeks. She just nodded in agreement.

"Theodoric and Sister Lucy lay yonder amongst those scum," Percival explained and pointed toward a pile of black clad bodies. Blood was everywhere on the stone pavement and over the ruined walls. So much had been set on fire and was blackened and scorched. "They must have used a lot of naphtha grenades and they certainly took a lot with them."

Master Douglas approached slowly, surveying all the carnage as he stepped through it. Al Rashid noticed something was playing upon his mind and he beckoned him back over.

"What puzzles you?" Al Rashid asked in a whisper.

Master Douglas pointed to another small pile of stacked stones again with a bee symbol etched upon the top one.

"Can you get Paul back to Jerusalem safely?" he asked.

"I can do that," Al Rashid said as Attar and Ishmael arrived and dismounted, looking utterly shocked. "Why, what plans do you have?"

"I am not sure yet but something is very odd here," Master Douglas replied and looked around the scene. "Very odd. Notice the amount of valuables still left."

"Do you think this was deliberate to kill Alisha?" Al Rashid asked quietly.

"It is looking that way…so most likely and definitely the hand of Turansha. I shall find out from the prisoner."

"If he lives long enough," Al Rashid remarked and looked over at the man, his head cover now removed. He looked no more than a teenager.

11

"He will live for his injuries are minor. Whoever knocked him out saved his life," Master Douglas explained and rubbed his beard in deep thought, still looking around the area.

Paul rested his head against Abi's shoulder. After a minute she put her arm around him just as Count Henry and the other Templars arrived, Upside immediately informing them of what they had found. Paul and Abi remained as they were for several hours as the others respectfully and carefully dealt with the bodies, Al Rashid's forces keeping an ever watchful eye out. Stewart spent his time picking his way through the area looking for Paul's notes and pictures. Some were too badly burnt to even recognise but he found Paul's main leather folder in perfect condition wedged beneath the front legs of one the large caravan's horses. Stewart cried for several minutes out of sight of the others after he opened it and saw all the pictures inside...especially the one of Alisha. When the time came after Alisha, Ailia, Theodoric, Sister Lucy and Tenno had been buried within a small clearing set between several trees, Percival fetched Paul, Abi, Taqi and Nicholas to lead them to the graves. Al Rashid's men quietly but efficiently buried all the other bodies within a larger clearing and removed the Templars' severed heads. Looking around the valley, the old ruined Roman town looked beautiful, almost romantic in its idyllic setting, but the barbarity that had taken place had been extreme. Not even babies had been spared.

Count Henry and Attar stood by the fresh graves alongside Brother Teric and Stewart as Abi steadied herself using Paul for balance as they walked toward them. Paul felt numb as if in a dream but Abi was suffering and could hardly stand up let alone walk. She had seen and experienced a lot of death in her long life, but this incident and the death of so many she loved had utterly ripped her heart out. The loss of Tenno was a pain she had never experienced before, but she was also completely lost in the confusion of her own mind how they had all been killed. It went against everything she had believed in and fought for. Everything she had ever learnt from Kratos had all been for nothing. The last of the Crimson Thread was all but virtually extinguished...and there was no mistaking the facts for she had seen it with her own eyes. Taqi stared wide eyed unable to really accept or take in that his sister and niece were actually dead. Upside put a reassuring hand upon Nicholas's shoulder as he looked down at the graves. The sun started to vanish behind the steep side of the valley, casting a large shadow across the town that only added to the sense of death as it slowly crept its way toward the clearing.

Port of La Rochelle, France, Melissae Inn, spring 1191

Ayleth gulped hard cupping her mouth as she was nearly sick, Sarah immediately moving closer to her side. Miriam buried her face in the chest of the Templar, sobbing quietly. Gabirol stared at the old man and tapped his quill up and down gently. Simon sat back in his chair looking dazed as the wealthy tailor wiped away a tear. The Genoese sailor had his eyes shut, his hands clasped together with his head held low. Peter and the farrier looked at each other, shaking their heads in sadness. The Hospitaller looked across at Stephan and raised his empty cup. His throat was dry and he shuddered as he recalled the many images of burnt and dismembered bodies he had seen during his service so he was only too aware of the sight that must have greeted them. The Templar kissed Miriam softly on the side of her head and he held her close.

"'Tis sad that Alisha never got to ask Theodoric whom her real father was, then," Gabirol remarked quietly.

"No, she never did get the chance," the old man replied sadly.

"So after all of that...everything they had gone through and endured was all for nothing as they all, bar Paul, were killed. So the codes cannot be carried forward," Peter said and gulped as emotion finally caught up with him. He sat back in his chair hard and folded his arms, shaking his head as if in disapproval.

"No, not at all and that is why I tell you this tale now. For the codes are complete and they can and must be taken forwards. Remember at the start of this I told you that toward the end I would ask but one request of you all. Well, that time is soon to be upon us," the old man explained.

"What is so suspicious about the bee symbol being etched upon the stones?" Gabirol asked. "And how come Alisha's dagger did not burn?"

"Master Douglas could not understand why so many of Turansha's men were killed and why the bodies had not been removed as was their usual practice, but also the amount of fire grenades used and the damage caused to so many caravans... even the ancient walls had been blasted in places," the old man started to explain, when Simon leaned forward and put his hand up. The old man stopped talking and looked at him. "The dagger...I know not why".

"What of Thomas and his men. They were with Alisha so what happened to them?" he asked.

Sarah raised her eyebrows in surprise at Simon's question.

"That was another aspect Master Douglas was puzzled about. They checked all of the bodies but could only find what they thought may have been one of his men. But their swords were nowhere to be found...and the scratched bee emblems?"

"Ah...were they taken prisoner, then, their valuable swords looted and the symbols they left as a marker to alert others of their plight?" the Genoese sailor asked.

"That was the line of thought Master Douglas had...," the old man answered and paused.

"There is a 'but' coming though isn't there?" Gabirol asked.

"Yes, there is a but," the old man replied. "But to Master Douglas and even Percival the whole attack was wrong but they could not quite understand what, how or why."

"So what happened and what did they do?" Ayleth asked, sniffing and wiping away a tear.

"They vowed to establish exactly what had happened, both Master Douglas and Percival," the old man said and leaned forwards. "Paul refused to remove the sword and the symbolism of it being the sword in the stone was not lost on any of them, I believe."

"As in sword in the stone of the King Arthur tales?" the farrier asked.

"Yes, exactly. Al Rashid true to his word watched Paul, Taqi and Abi, and to a lesser degree Nicholas too, as Master Douglas and Percival scouted the area thoroughly. Ishmael tried to remove the sword for Paul to use later but even he could not remove it."

"Was it Queen Tamar's caravan that had been destroyed?" Simon suddenly asked. "Because she was supposed to meet up with Alisha and it could have been her who was dead...you did say she looked unbelievably like Alisha."

Ayleth looked up and smiled upon hearing Simon's reasoning, but it soon vanished when the old man shook his head no.

"You forget the necklace and her dagger were found upon her," he said softly.

"So Paul survived at least...for then. But what happened after they had buried them all?" Peter asked.

"Count Henry read out a short service, not that Paul or anyone else was really listening to his words. Paul just knelt at the feet of Alisha and Ailia's grave. Upside had made sure they were laid to rest together," the old man explained.

"So who were the people in the caravan that Alisha had joined with?" Gabirol asked, puzzled.

"'Twas another caravan heading from the Port of Tyre, mainly Lord Montferrat's

people. He had boasted his men were safe to travel as he had an arrangement with Saladin. They were taking supplies to Tiberias to sell at extortionate prices no less, I must add," the old man explained. "But as Master Douglas correctly deduced, Turansha had not attacked the caravan to steal their wealth."

"'Twas to kill Alisha and Ailia," Ayleth stated.

"Yes, yes it was," the old man acknowledged and nodded slightly.

"What did they find out from the prisoner?" the Templar asked.

"Master Douglas set him free once he had established in his own mind he was indeed one of Turansha's men."

"What?" Sarah asked, looking confused and angry.

"Something or someone had interceded in the killing frenzy of Turansha's men causing them to flee without taking their dead. They never leave their dead for fear they could be identified and where they came from. The massive amount of fire involved was far greater than any amount of naphtha grenades could cause, even if all the caravans had been placed together and then set on fire. No, something very odd indeed had occurred...and Master Douglas was determined to find out what. By letting the prisoner go free, having given his word to do so if he told him why he was there, he knew that it would get back to Turansha that Paul now knew his family were dead."

"I do not understand why though...for what reason?" the Hospitaller asked, bemused.

"If Turansha knew without doubt that Alisha and Ailia were now dead and Paul was broken, his sword forever stuck in stone, then perhaps it would afford him some safety that Turansha would no longer feel he had to kill him too," the old man explained. "Remember Turansha believed that the bloodline ran purely and only through the female line. Though in truth Turansha was obsessed with Paul's line too, so Master Douglas's reasoning was a little flawed."

"Seems mad to me. Should have killed him," the Hospitaller said as Stephan poured some syrup of Jule into his cup. He nodded at Stephan. "Thank you," he said quietly as Stephan looked around the table seeing if anyone else wanted a refill drink.

 2 – 4

"So Paul just left his sword very symbolically stuck in a stone and left after-wards did he...to where?" Simon asked.

"Paul did not care where he went or what would happen to him. He sat all that

night with Abi, Taqi and Nicholas at the graveside. Paul had no idea how he was supposed to get over his loss, but the words of Tenno kept echoing in his mind, almost as if he was beside him," the old man said and paused for a moment before recounting Tenno's words he had often said to Paul and Percival when he lost Nyla. "You never know how strong you are until being strong is the only choice you have."

"That is certainly the truth," the Templar said and pulled Miriam closer as she rested her head upon his chest.

"In the morning count Henry got Ishmael to physically put Paul upon Adrastos for he seemed to be in a daze, not even speaking properly. Abi saddled up beside him, took a deep breath and then looked at them all as if the previous day's events and pain had never happened. 'Twas her way of coping with her loss...for then at least," the old man said then sipped some of his drink. "True to his word, Al Rashid led Paul, Abi, Count Henry and the rest of the men to within sight of Jerusalem. He even gave Taqi the option of staying with Paul or coming back with him. Taqi wanted revenge upon Turansha and he knew he would not find it stuck within Jerusalem. Word had already got out, more than likely by Turansha himself eager to increase his infamy, that his men had utterly destroyed a massive caravan and its entire escort. Even Saladin was furious at the assault for he did indeed have an agreement still in force with Lord Montferrat and Count Raymond and the attack undermined his very authority."

"So Paul did return to Jerusalem again?" Ayleth asked softly.

"He did indeed. Though he did not eat on the journey back and only drank water when Count Henry insisted he drink. En route they met up with a Templar reconnaissance troop who had been sent to investigate. Count Henry sent two of their riders back to Jerusalem ahead of them to alert King Guy and Gerard of the developments."

"That means Princess Stephanie would have been made aware before Paul returned," Gabirol noted.

"Yes, she was made aware," the old man sighed.

"Well, Paul must have returned for the sword...for it sits right there," Simon stated and pointed to it.

The old man leaned across the table and pulled the sword toward him with both hands. He closed his eyes for a few brief seconds before looking at Simon.

"No, he did not return for the sword at all," he answered quietly.

"Stewart did then," the Genoese sailor said loudly, raising his hand. The old man just shook his head no in silence.

Simon looked puzzled and gestured with his hands toward the sword.

"Then how?" he asked and scratched his head.

"And this cutting of the elm...'tis a matter we heard much of, and plenty of rumour but we were never really informed much else about it other than it had something to do with an argument between Count Henry and Gerard. Is that so?" the Templar asked.

"You heard correct," the old man answered and sat back in his chair, letting go of the sword. "Paul hugged Taqi farewell where the main northern road opened onto the plain before Jerusalem. Al Rashid spoke to him but his words did not really register in Paul's mind. He was emotionally numb. Abi swore to Taqi she would look after him. Paul did not even look back as she led him away. Stewart and Upside had a similar situation with Nicholas, though he remained focused, his heart filled with anger and pain and he constantly clutched his chest, breathless. It was a truly sad and a very solemn column that rode into Jerusalem that day. News of the massacre had reached the population and many thronged the streets to look on as the column slowly made its way toward the Templar headquarters. Word had even reached Balian and he was already on his way to Jerusalem to see them. Paul was inconsolable at the deaths of Alisha, Ailia, Theodoric, Sister Lucy and Tenno. He kept shaking his head in disbelief."

"Dead...all dead," Miriam sighed and wiped her eyes. "All dead!"

City of Jerusalem, Kingdom of Jerusalem, March 16th 1187

Paul dismounted from Adrastos, oblivious to those around him. Nicholas pulled up and dismounted just as Gerard walked toward them fast. Nicholas helped steady Paul as he almost collapsed. Stewart pulled up in front of Gerard, blocking his path.

"Sorry, Master, they are not in a good state of mind right now. I pray you give them some time before questioning them...please," Stewart requested, looking down at him.

Gerard wiped his beard then put his hands upon his hips.

"'Tis the worst fate a man should ever suffer. I can give them a few hours to gather their emotions then I will need to speak with them. Time is not our friend and any information they can give us needs to be addressed," Gerard explained and strained to look past Stewart. Abi rode closer to Stewart and looked down at Gerard. "It would seem that everything you ever schemed and planned with that old man of yours has come to nought."

Abi leaned forwards resting her hands upon the saddle pommel. She stared hard at Gerard, which made him pull back his shoulders, feeling uncomfortable.

"If what you state is true then we are all in a whole world of unparalleled evil that is about to fall upon all of us…perhaps you will convey that to your masters," Abi said, her stare intense. She sat back up and pulled her horse around and nodded at Upside as she rode past him.

Stewart looked at Gerard, bemused. Upside stood behind Paul and Nicholas and gently ushered them toward the entrance of the headquarters. Gerard noticed Paul's sword sheath was empty and frowned.

"I need a full after-action report from you within the hour," Gerard ordered Stewart just as Princess Stephanie came over holding her beige and white dress up slightly so she could run. She stopped still when she saw Paul being led inside. The look of shock on her face was instant and obvious. "I would suggest you keep her away from him for now. Do not give Reynald any excuses…please."

Stewart looked at Gerard, surprised. It was the first time he had ever said 'please' in all the years he had known him. Brother Teric dismounted and walked slowly toward Princess Stephanie, the solemn look on his face confirming to her all that she had heard. She cupped her hands over her mouth.

⋘⋙

Paul sat slumped on the bed resting his elbows upon his knees just staring at the polished stone floor. Nicholas sat opposite in the same manner, both in silence. The small room was part of the Chapel area used for men to rest and contemplate in silence. A small stained glass window let through a single beam of sunlight that ended in a starburst upon the simple wooden door. Nicholas sighed and ran his fingers through his thick hair, his face pained with sorrow. Paul just ran the burnt leather and wire strap of Alisha's pendant through his fingers time after time. He now had her three pronged dagger fastened inside his leather purse on his belt…somehow its scabbard remaining undamaged from the fire. Images of the flesh just peeling off of Alisha's arm kept invading his thoughts no matter how hard he tried to push them out. He was grateful both Percival and Nicholas had stopped him seeing their faces. It was the right thing to have done. He looked up at Nicholas, his head resting in his hands as he looked down at the floor, his feet covered in darkened dried blood. Paul's mind drifted back to the time he had sat outside on the balcony with Theodoric watching a storm roll in. Paul felt convinced now that Theodoric had known all along what was coming for too many times he had said or hinted at events to come, and they had indeed come to pass. 'Understand that you own nothing, everything that is around you is temporary, only the love in your heart will last forever.' Theodoric's words echoed in his mind. All Paul had now were indeed just memories and the love in his heart for his family. He shook his head sadly and sighed. A light rap at the door drew their attention. Abi peered in and opened the door fully. Quickly she closed it behind her and knelt down between the two beds and just looked at Paul and Nicholas. Even kneeling down she was still the same height as both of them. Nicholas sighed.

"I have no right to be here or grieve as you are entitled…but I do not know what to do or where to go from here," Nicholas said emotionally and looked at Paul.

"My friend…you have as much right to grieve as I. You loved her as I did…still do," Paul replied quietly. Nicholas nodded silently in agreement. "We have lost so much…and you, Tenno," Paul remarked and looked at Abi.

"I never got to tell him he had a child…but I am sure he knows now," she replied sadly. She lowered her head, closed her eyes and put her hands together as if in prayer.

Nicholas started to sob quietly, fighting to control himself. Abi put her right arm around him. Paul watched as she pulled him close as he sobbed openly. He wanted to cry but he felt numb inside. Abi reached out with her left arm and put it around Paul and pulled him close. With their heads together they huddled as one. Paul closed his eyes and simply sighed, a deep sigh of resignation and the hope and wish for an early death. As he thought that Abi spoke as if she had read his mind.

"Do not seek an early death. You dishonour their memories and sacrifice if you do. Growing old is a blessing not afforded to many…and you will grow old."

Paul did not wish to draw a single breath more than he had to he told himself despite her words. An hour later Paul was led away to a more comfortable room by Count Henry. Paul followed him to the very same room he had stayed in the first night he had visited Jerusalem with Theodoric many years before. A single candle was still set in the same place. As Master Jakelin entered the room carrying a change of clean clothes for him, he silently placed them upon the nearest bed as Paul walked over to the small balcony. He glanced back at Master Jakelin briefly as he quickly left the room.

"Paul...we are all hurting for you. I hope you know and believe that," Count Henry said softly.

Paul placed his hands upon the balustrade that ran around the balcony and rested forwards looking out across the main courtyard. He watched as Nicholas was led to his quarters by Brothers Teric and Upside. He looked over toward the building he and Alisha had stayed in. In his mind he could not believe they were all dead. In denial he reminded himself as his father had told him about people's reaction to loss. He shook his head but stopped when his eye caught sight of Princess Stephanie stood back a pace inside the large open balcony on the building to his left. She was looking directly at him. She acknowledged him with a slight bow of her head before she stepped backwards and out of sight.

"What shall you do?" Count Henry asked.

"Honestly I do not know. My wife and daughter have been butchered and set on fire on purpose. How do I address that...do I seek vengeance which I have vowed to seek...become a hermit for I certainly now understand why people do that...or leave this land for ever. Return to my father?...I just do not know."

"This is not the time to ask, though I do not think there will ever be a good time to ask, but you have God given talents we could sorely do with. You need not seek out Turansha for I am certain he will in time come to you. But I am faced with a greater danger from him that threatens all that people like your father and I have fought for."

Paul stood up and faced Count Henry.

"But is it all worth it?"

"You know it is. Men like Turansha...they feed on the weaknesses and low intelligence of men who lack direction and purpose and he gives that to them. A sense of purpose. A belief in something bigger than they would ever amount to, or what they believed they could ever amount to for all have the potential for great deeds. But Turansha knows how to convince his followers that they are on some great holy adventure. We know he plans to inspire many thousands in the name of Islam to rise up and challenge all and any other religion and establish a caliphate that will spread across the entire world. Turansha truly believes he can achieve this and this belief is only reinforced as more and more young men throng to his side in answer to his call."

"But I can do nothing to change this or avert what is coming."

"But that is where you are so wrong. People like Turansha only become powerful because too many good people do nothing...until it is too late. Saladin himself knows this. Why do you think he is as keen as your father and I are to form a joint force? 'Tis a commission we all know only you can achieve for all sides admire and respect you."

"You are right...now is not the right time to be asking me about such matters."

"Actually, no...I was wrong...and you are wrong. Now is very much the right time. I knew Alisha well enough to know she would not be happy to see us watch you fall into a pit of despair...one few people can pull themselves out of. You know exactly what she would say right now to your face if she could," Count Henry said and paused, waiting for Paul to respond, but he stood still just staring at him. "She would want you to do all and anything to stop what happened to her from happening to others."

Paul thought on his words for a moment then turned away and rested against the balustrade again.

"I never wanted to be a knight...ever," he finally said.

"You think I chose this path too?"

"You were born into it?"

"You forget our previous conversation we had here in this very city when we first met. My father made the choice for me."

"And what would you choose right now if you could?" Paul asked and looked across to where Princess Stephanie had been standing.

"To be home in France in Gisors...with the love of my life," Count Henry answered and stepped onto the balcony beside Paul.

"And who is that?"

"Isabella, the sister of Queen Sibylla...she captured my heart the first time I ever laid eyes upon her. Do you not recall I told you this before?"

"But she is married."

"I am fully aware of that fact," Count Henry replied and looked at Paul. "But it does not diminish my love for her. 'Tis the only saving grace I find in being here...that I am sometimes able to steal a sight of her when she visits."

Paul stood up straight and pulled his filthy clothes. He looked at Count Henry.

"Love can be such a curse, eh?" Paul remarked. Count Henry half nodded but then shook his head no. "I still have some time to serve out as a Templar...according to Gerard, of course. Whilst I am here I shall serve you in whatever capacity or manner you best see fit."

"Turansha fears you for he knows what you can do."

"Not any more for my family is now gone...perhaps Stewart if he were to find a woman with the same bloodline Ali had, perhaps he could continue the Crimson Thread."

"You are still alive. Try not to forget that simple fact. Everything may seem wrong at the moment, but understand this...a great evil has been set in motion and Turansha's desire for an expanded Islamic caliphate is gaining momentum. He recruits young impressionable men, and women, by quoting the Qur'an, usually totally out of context, and he promises them martyrdom and paradise. But he also knows of great secrets. He stole a copper scroll from the Order once and very nearly revealed a sacred hidden chamber deep within a mountain in Transylvania (*Romania*). 'Twas Elek who succeeded in stopping him. I fear that you have been faced with and fought impossible odds. But the evil now growing threatens not just us...but all of mankind's future."

Paul looked at Count Henry.

"How so?" he asked.

"You must surely know by now. You know of the hidden chambers and all that they contain. Imagine someone like Turansha gaining access."

"But even if he did, he would not be able to enter or use what he found."

"No, but he is a resourceful man and he would soon figure out that all he needs is to find someone like you, your brother or even Percival to gain access. That is why I say you need not go looking for him, for he will come for you." A cold chill ran down Paul's back and he shuddered. He was not fearful of the potential encounter. Quite the opposite...he would welcome the opportunity. "Your family was sacrificed...don't let it be in vain and for nothing."

"I have had to unlearn most of all that I believed and thought was real these past few years...to protect my family, and I failed, so how am I supposed to begin to even start with the whole of mankind...and is that not what our Lord Jesus Christ did already?"

"Ask that of Master Douglas for I am the wrong man to answer. But we must face the reality that now faces all of us. To safeguard a greater treasure for future generations' benefit, to help them unshackle themselves from the grip of a self styled secret elite who manipulate religions, governments, queens and kings alike to stop us from reaching our full potential. We must overcome our fears and protect the legacy...one that the ancient Magi and Druids fully understood and protected but one we must now sacrifice all else to guarantee its continuation...whatever the cost."

"I do not think I can lose any more than I already have, can I?" Paul replied and lowered his head.

"'Tis why I fear you are perhaps the only person who can do this. 'Tis a terrible burden to carry and endure, but if I can help in any way, then I shall," Count Henry said and put his hand upon Paul's back. "And you will need to recover your sword for you are going to need it."

"No...I shall never wield it again. Please do not ask that of me," Paul replied and shook his head wearily, the reality of Alisha and Ailia being dead still not sinking in. He expected Theodoric to enter the room at any minute. His mind returned to the images of all of them lying dead, their bodies badly burnt. He sighed.

"Then I shall have Ishmael sign out another sword from our armoury. He waits outside, you know?" Count Henry said and pointed to the door.

Paul turned and looked toward the door. He now knew and understood only too well how Ishmael feels daily having lost his entire family.

"Then wherever I go, he goes too. I will even put on the mantle and robes of a Templar if I must...but do not expect me to do vespers seven times a day," Paul finally replied and stood up straight.

"Good. You will need a direction lest you lose your mind from your terrible loss. I shall meet you after last vespers at the great hall. But be warned, Guy and Reynald will both be in attendance."

∞CR

Count Henry nodded at Paul and Ishmael as they approached the main double doors to the main hall. The corridor was dimly lit by several lanthorns and several free standing candles. A turcopole guard moved quickly to open the right hand door. As he swung it open, the corridor was immediately filled with the muffled sounds of men speaking from within the hall. Count Henry indicated for Paul and Ishmael to enter and then followed them inside, the door being closed after them. Gerard looked up from leaning over the main table set in the centre of the hall and then quickly walked over to Paul.

"This is not how I wished to meet you again. My utmost and genuine condolences on your loss. I know it is still very raw," Gerard said sincerely and placed both hands upon Paul's shoulders and looked at him intently. "I will do everything in my power to bring Turansha and his men to justice, that I swear."

King Guy looked up from his seat at the head of the table, maps, food and a large goblet of wine in his hand. He was dressed in a full length golden silk robe replete with gold edging and inlaid designs. He stood out compared with the sparse whitewashed walls of the hall. Queen Sibylla sat by his left side wearing a pale purple full length dress and matching head dress held in place by white lace. She acknowledged Paul with a slight nod. Paul was taken aback by Gerard's apparent sincerity and looked at everyone around the table as he ushered him over. Brother Teric sat next to Master Jakelin whilst Reynald sat to the right of King Guy.

"Ah, the Bull's Head Slayer himself no less. Come to impart your great insights have you?" King Guy said loudly, clearly a little drunk, Queen Sibylla frowning hard at his remarks.

"He is a Muslim lover so I would not fully trust him, My Lord," Reynald said as he stood up from the table. Master Roger entered the room carrying several parchments and maps. He smiled when he saw Paul, but his face soon dropped when he remembered exactly how and why he was there.

"I know of many Muslims who would join with you and fight against Turansha...and live in peace if only you gave them the opportunity," Paul replied.

"Are you serious?" King Guy called out loudly and laughed.

"Deadly," Paul retorted instantly.

"Ha!" Reynald called out and sat back in his chair. "After what has happened to you I would have thought you would want to send as many Muslims to their graves as you could. For heaven's sake, man, you have read their book...the Qur'an. How many times does it speak of subjugating all non-believers...I can quote you chapter and verse all night long if you want until you get the message. You cannot reason with them. They will not stop unless we are all dead or converted to Islam."

"I can quote the same back selectively from our Holy Bible and clearly you have not read the Qur'an fully...it is all subjective is it not?" Paul replied.

King Guy leaned closer to Reynald.

"What does subjective mean?" he whispered, but still loud enough to hear, Queen Sibylla shaking her head, embarrassed.

 2 – 6

Paul looked at Gerard as he shook his head and proffered a chair for him to sit in. He moved the chair slightly out and sat down. Paul knew from Princess Stephanie that the queen was a quiet woman but highly intelligent and often distanced from King Guy. She understood unrequited love and the loneliness of a cold loveless marriage only too well just like Princess Stephanie.

"You need not pain yourself with recounting the ordeal at Pella for your brother has already availed himself eloquently enough all the facts. But I summoned you here for I will need you to go with Balian," King Guy said loudly and waved his finger at Paul, then laughed. "You will have to go with him and speak to Raymond. Make sure he understands just who is king. Will you accept this charge?"

Paul looked back at Count Henry as he walked past him and pulled up a chair.

"I am happy to visit Count Raymond if you wish," Paul answered as Count Henry nodded yes silently.

"Good, then when he arrives you shall be off again," King Guy said and laughed again and started to pull at a piece of chicken. "You do know my good friend here is on a mission from God himself," King Guy smirked and pointed a piece of chicken at Reynald. "His mission is to wipe them all out for he has vowed to eradicate them from history. He has seen visions, you know?"

Reynald leaned forwards and rested upon his elbows on the table and grinned at Paul.

"Unless of course you would rather stay here and see to my wife's needs now you are no longer married and I...soon to be divorced...speaking of which how are we progressing with those papers?" Reynald mocked and looked at Master Roger.

"'Tis out of our hands, Lord Reynald," Master Roger replied and laid the parchments and maps down on the table beside Count Henry. "Paul...my sincerest sympathies."

Paul nodded at Master Roger in acceptance of his words.

"Horse shit! He will be fucking my wife within the month," Reynald laughed and started to rapidly eat a piece of pork.

Paul stood up slowly.

"Whatever it is you plan here this eve, my presence is not required. I bid you all a good evening," Paul said politely, bowed his head to Queen Sibylla and turned away. Ishmael followed him to the door.

"Erm, excuse us, we did not excuse you," King Guy called out but Paul feigned deafness and kept walking to the door. A Hospitaller sergeant opened the door quickly and winked at Paul but he had to stand back a pace as several other knights of King Guy's court entered.

"Sire, apologies for our lateness but we were informed to meet you at your residence...not here," one of them exclaimed and bowed.

Ishmael looked at Paul and frowned. Paul shook his head and looked back at King Guy. If they could not even arrange to meet properly, then what hope of organising a campaign to repel Saladin if he attacks? Paul thought. His eyes met King Guy's, who was sneering at him. Paul turned his back on him and left the hall.

"He is exhausted, My Lord, and does not yet know the ways of the court," Count Henry explained.

"Well, I have never trusted him...I want him out of my city as soon as Balian arrives. Master Gerard, make sure he is stationed at Tiberias once we have taken it from Raymond if he has not fallen into order by then," King Guy ordered.

"If who has not fallen into order, My Lord...Paul or Count Raymond?" Gerard asked for clarification.

"Sometimes I fear you mock me, Master Gerard, for did I not make myself clear?" King Guy shot back, irritated.

"No, My Lord, no you did not," Gerard replied politely but firmly and sat down beside Master Roger. "Now if there is nothing else to discus, then I suggest we start planning our next move."

King Guy threw his chicken down on the plate and folded his arms, shaking his head at Gerard. Reynald patted him hard on the back and laughed.

"Come on, Sire…'tis your best interests we have at heart. Now drink up for we are slack with our wine this eve," Reynald said and laughed again as two maids entered the room carrying more food.

Master Roger looked at Count Henry and raised his eyebrows disapprovingly just as Queen Sibylla nodded in agreement with him.

℘℺

Paul turned with Ishmael into the corridor that led to his room and immediately saw Princess Stephanie stood outside his door waiting patiently, her hands across her stomach, looking nervous.

"Paul…I am so sorry. Forgive me but I just had to see you," she said emotionally and stood awkwardly in front of him. She quickly looked at Ishmael and her face flushed red. "Words of condolence fail to express my sadness at your loss…and…and," she started to explain but could not finish. She sighed heavily and looked down, a tear falling from her cheek.

Paul looked at her as she stood vulnerable and alone. She had lost weight as her usually tight fitting dress hung looser than he recalled. The small headband sparkled in the light of the corridor oil lamp set in the wall just feet from her. It made her hair appear more golden than normal. Nervously she pulled the silk and lace shawl around her shoulders and shivered.

"You are cold," Ishmael stated, breaking the silence. She simply shook her head no still looking downward.

"We cannot be seen together, you know that don't you?" Paul asked.

"I know," she replied but did not look up at him. "My heart breaks in so many ways for you and your loss…and I shall miss them more than I can say," she said quietly, almost whispering her words. When she finally looked up, her blue eyes were wet and full of tears ready to fall. She started to shake and her bottom lip quivered as emotions overwhelmed her. The look of pain and desperation in her eyes called out to Paul to say or do something. Ishmael suddenly poked Paul hard in the back forcing him toward her. Instinctively Paul clasped her delicate hands in his as Ishmael turned away and kept an eye on the corridor. "I am so alone," she said and started to cry.

"No you are not…we have each other whatever comes next," Paul heard himself say as he put his arms around her. As he held her, she rested her face against the side of his chest and slowly, hesitantly at first, put her arms around him and hugged him tightly as she sobbed. Her perfume filled Paul's nostrils with a pleasant smell and just for a moment, with his eyes closed he imagined he was holding Alisha. His throat swelled tightly and his heart physically ached. As Princess Stephanie sobbed he just held her tightly. He thought of Taqi as his own words 'whatever comes next' went through his mind. He wondered how he was doing having lost not only his father but now his sister. Paul kissed the side of Princess Stephanie's head and she responded by holding him tighter. Tenno's words that he had given Percival when Nyla had been killed echoed in his mind. 'If you can't find something to live for, you best find something worth dying for.' It felt as if Tenno was constantly with him. Perhaps he was, he told himself, but either way, Paul felt that his entire heart and soul was forever annihilated and it would never recover. Never!

Chapter 74
Fortress of Solitude

Port of La Rochelle, France, Melissae Inn, spring 1191

"So what did happen to Queen Tamar's caravan?"

"Her caravan was still secure...the caravan that was attacked came from the Port of Tyre as I previously explained. Lord Montferrat had sent it with the mistaken belief that as he was dealing with Saladin directly and Count Raymond, his people would be safe. Alisha's group had joined them just hours before the attack by Turansha's men," the old man explained quietly. He hesitated for a few moments in silence before looking up.

"So there was no way the burnt woman was her mistaken as Alisha?" Simon sighed and shook his head sadly.

"No...Queen Tamar was quite safe and very much alive," the old man replied. "Messages could not be transmitted by heliograph either as it had been discovered that Turansha had gained access to both the codes and decryption of them. As soon as they were changed, somehow he was always able to get the next set of coding sequence."

"How?" Peter asked, frowning hard.

"I shall come to that shortly, suffice it to know for now that a highly placed lord was passing over that information...and with the sole intention of making certain Alisha and Ailia were killed," the old man explained and clasped his hands together.

"That is beyond evil," Ayleth remarked.

"The man in question did not see it as evil...but purely expedient and a necessary measure to secure his claim to the throne of Jerusalem," the old man replied.

"How did Paul cope?" Gabirol asked.

"At first he appeared to be coping...but then he started training harder and longer every day despite being warned against vowing any kind of vengeance against Turansha. He hoped that the tiredness would exhaust him and allow him to dream as he had done previously. He hoped above all hope that in his dreams he would be able to see his family just as he had seen his mother and Elek, but it was not meant

to be. He simply exhausted himself more. Stewart sent word to their father and both Nicholas and Upside kept an ever watchful eye upon him and Ishmael never left his side."

"And Princess Stephanie?" Sarah asked.

"Oh she tried to see him as often as she could. She even had the help of Queen Sibylla deliberately orchestrate reasons and excuses so they could be in each other's company...but that only served to push Paul away further. He felt utterly abandoned by all," the old man sighed and shook his head.

"So he was angry?" the farrier remarked.

"No...he was beyond anger. Brother Teric tried to channel Paul's emotions to leading one of the Templar squadrons, which Gerard whole heartedly endorsed."

"Gerard did?" Simon said, perplexed.

"Of course," the old man replied. "Gerard knew Paul would make a formidable knight, which he was desperately short of. He used the death of Alisha and Ailia to pull Paul into his ranks despite many protestations from Reynald."

"But how did his sword come to be here now?" Ayleth asked.

"I will come to that. But all came to a head when Paul was given a new sword made by the same blacksmith whose daughter, Tara, had been killed saving Paul. When the blacksmith handed over the sword, there was no word of thanks or appreciation from Paul. Brother Teric apologised for Paul's lack of manners, but the Blacksmith told Paul he had a hard cold look in his eyes now. He was not the same noble man he once knew. Paul just checked the balance of the sword, sheathed it in the old leather cover Arri had made him and simply walked out of the building. Even Master Jakelin told Paul he looked different. It was after receiving his new sword that Nicholas, under orders from Master Jakelin, was given leave to take Paul out for some rest and recuperation. Despite hurting himself at the loss of Alisha, Nicholas reluctantly agreed despite feeling it awkward, but as Master Jakelin pointed out, if anyone knew best how Paul was feeling, it was him."

Jerusalem, Malquissinat Quarter, Kingdom of Jerusalem, April 22nd 1187

"So Master Jakelin ordered us here?" Paul asked as he looked into the wooden cup filled with mead beer. "And he wishes us to get drunk...bit against the Order's rules is it not?"

Nicholas, wearing just a simple beige robe and cotton shirt, adjusted his sword belt as he made himself comfortable on the wooden bench opposite Paul, who was dressed the same. The tavern was filled with all manner of people but it was open and airy with several large awnings stretched across the roof area to shield them from the fierce afternoon sun. In the distance Paul could see Muslim and Christian workers still preparing food and bread together just as they had been doing the first day he had entered the city years previously.

"It was more a recommendation…besides you know how many frequent here when they can," Nicholas replied and smiled. "He also felt that I was perhaps best placed to speak with you." Paul looked up at him intently. "If this is wrong or awkward, we can leave."

"I think our Master Jakelin knows us only too well," Paul answered and held his cup with both hands. "I am proud and honoured to call you a friend as well as a brother."

"And I you. You forgave me for what I did when I know many would have killed me on the spot," Nicholas said, the emotion and sincerity in his eyes clear.

"I knew you meant it when you said you were ashamed and sorry… besides, I would be mad to believe that other men would not love Alisha as I did," Paul replied and sighed, shaking his head sadly. "I know how much you loved her too."

Both looked up as loud laughter roared from a group of merchants challenging several new pilgrims to a drinking match. Several soldiers eagerly set up a line of drinks and just for a moment Paul thought one of the men was Thomas, from the side, until he looked directly at him and paused for a moment. It was not Thomas and Paul's heart sank. He wished he could close his eyes and never wake up again and then be with his family. He quickly drained his drink and placed the mug down hard, wiped his mouth and looked again at the other men starting their drinking competition.

෯෬

Paul opened his eyes, his head spinning and feeling sick. His knees felt wet and as he focused he realised he had spilt a long glass of wine over himself. Confused, he tried to look around the room. He was no longer in the tavern but in a large richly decorated room surrounded by marble columns with a large bathing pool set in the middle. Large fans were gently swaying back and forth above him. Nicholas flinched, half asleep, resting beside him. Incense filled his nostrils as he saw two partially dressed females approach them. They smiled beautifully at him, one outstretching her hand for him to take. He shook his head as he tried to recall how he got there. Vague images of drinking and laughing as he challenged the soldiers began to enter his mind. The man who looked like Thomas had bought him and Nicholas a drink, the rest he could hardly recall. Nicholas started to laugh even though he was still half asleep resting against Paul's shoulder. He looked across toward the pool as a naked female stepped out leading a naked man by the hand. Slowly he began to realise that he was in a brothel, one frequented by the more affluent of the city. The naked man following the naked woman was the one who looked like Thomas. He smiled as they walked past and indicated with his head nodding toward the girl offering her hand to go with her. Paul looked at the woman stood before him. She wore just a small lace and silk slip that barely covered her hips. He could see she wore nothing else beneath it. Her breasts were covered in a thin band of silk only. Her hair was pulled back and plaited. Her tummy was flat and her olive skin appeared smooth and flawless. He was surprised to see she had hazel eyes. She beckoned him to stand as the other woman knelt down to look at Nicholas. Paul stood up but could hardly stand he was so drunk. He laughed at himself as the woman helped steady him. Her strength took him by surprise. His ears were ringing and his heart pounding loudly as he looked down at Nicholas, who was now trying to focus his eyes upon the woman knelt before him. Without thinking Paul followed the woman as she led him up some stairs to a room and onto the first floor. No sooner had he entered her large room when she shut the heavy wooden door and smiled at him. Several candles lit the ornately decorated room. It reminded him of the first house he had ever stayed in when in Jerusalem. A large oval bed was positioned in the middle of the room with silk sheets and pillows. Paul shook his head trying to clear his mind when the woman approached him. She was undoubtedly beautiful and moved in a very sensuous and provocative manner. She put her hands upon his chest, her perfume immediately filling his nostrils. Without speaking she started to untie his robe lacing at his chest. 'Have I paid for this?' he asked himself. As the woman moved gently against him he could not stop the sensations of arousal he was beginning to feel. He felt dizzy and swayed but the woman gently ushered him to the side of the bed and sat him down. Quickly she straddled his legs sitting herself upon his thighs. She rolled his robe top down over his shoulders and then pushed herself forwards so she was resting upon his hips. Gently she pushed him backwards so he fell flat on the bed. She pulled off the silk band around her chest to reveal her pert breasts and started to gyrate herself against him, her eyes firmly fixed on his. He closed his eyes and felt her as she moved against him. He put his hands upon her hips and shuddered as the sensation of her soft warm skin coursed through his body. He felt dizzy as the room appeared to spin around him when he opened his eyes. His vision kept blurring as he looked up at the woman and for a moment he thought it was Alisha. He smiled and put his hands up higher just as she lowered her right hand to arouse him further. Confused and his head spinning more he looked toward the door as shouting from downstairs echoed throughout the building. The woman immediately stopped moving and looked in alarm toward the door. As more shouting and a woman's scream filled the air, she jumped off of Paul and grabbed her nightgown. Quickly she tied it around herself and rushed out of the room. Wearily Paul stood up, staggered momentarily, then went after her.

Paul stumbled down the wide stairway pulling a wall rug off as he tried to steady himself. It sounded like Nicholas shouting. With his head spinning and now full of pain, he walked around the last column of the pool chamber to see Nicholas pushing and being shoved by two large men, clearly security for the brothel. Nicholas was shouting and flailing his arms around as they were trying to eject him. Another man behind him was trying to pull him outside. Paul instantly recognised the man as being the blacksmith, Tara's father, who had recently made him his new sword. 'What is he doing here?' Paul thought, bemused, and staggered toward the group as several women looked on, one crying, being comforted.

"Nicholas?" Paul called out in a dry voice.

All in the hallway turned to look at him. Nicholas, seeing him, tears in his eyes, pushed the man holding him hard.

"I thought they had done you harm," he exclaimed emotionally and clearly still very drunk.

Quickly Paul moved to grab him to hold him upright as the blacksmith looked at him almost in horror at seeing him there.

"It is you," he said shocked and cupped his mouth. He shook his head in disapproval as Paul held Nicholas up, who was now sobbing with relief. "I thought it was you I saw enter but I could not believe it."

"What are you doing here?" Paul asked, pained, as his head pounded.

33

"I wish to ask you the same," the blacksmith replied, still shaking his head. "So this is how you live your life and honour the memory of my daughter."

Nicholas stood up straight and turned to face the blacksmith as other men appeared from the various rooms curious as to the noise and unfolding fracas.

"'Twas I and my friends who dragged him here...he...he lost his entire family...did you know that?" Nicholas blurted out and quickly put his head in a large vase as he threw up.

"We know that," the Blacksmith stated just as his wife stepped up to the front door and looked on. "But why is he here?"

As the blacksmith's question echoed through Paul's mind, the hallway and the people stood in it appearing to stretch and shrink, his head pounding even more, he tried to help Nicholas stand back up but he fell to the floor pulling Paul down with him.

"Out! Out of my reputable establishment now," a deep loud voice shouted out from behind them as the owner accompanied by two armed escorts rapidly approached along the main corridor. "You get out of my establishment now or I will have you in chains," the short but stocky man yelled angrily.

One of the armed men went to pull Paul but he pushed him away. The man quickly drew his sword, looking at Paul threateningly. The blacksmith quickly stood between the armed man and Paul.

"That will not be necessary," Princess Stephanie said calmly from behind the blacksmith's wife as she stepped into view accompanied by both Brother Teric and Stewart, one on either side. "We were told you had been brought here." She smiled reassuringly and stepped closer toward Paul and Nicholas. The owner bowed his head in acknowledgement and surprise at her presence. "We shall take them away and pay whatever is due."

Nicholas looked up at her half laughing and crying.

"I did not know where we were...but when I realised...I could not find Paul," he explained.

Princess Stephanie looked at him then up at Paul. She shook her head slightly and sighed, but then smiled.

"Well it looks as though we found you just in time," she said as Brother Teric helped pull Nicholas to his feet. Paul looked at Stewart, puzzled, as he beckoned him to follow him out. Paul managed to stand then took a few steps but nearly fell over, Princess Stephanie quickly holding onto him to steady his balance. She looked into his eyes. "You come to a place like this to seek comfort when you could have come to me," she whispered.

"I do not even know where here is or how I got here," Paul replied, his breath making Princess Stephanie pull away a little. Paul looked over at the blacksmith holding his wife's arm, both looking sad and disappointed. He stood himself up as straight as he could and approached them. "I am sorry if I have insulted your daughter's memory. Tonight is the first time I have ever drunk so much," he explained.

"I am sorry that Alisha and your children are all gone…but I did not expect this from you," the blacksmith replied hesitantly.

Paul swayed as he looked at them both. He sensed Princess Stephanie touch his arm reassuringly.

"'Tis alas sadly true they are gone…and I am lost," Paul finally answered and just stared down at the marble floor. The blacksmith's wife burst into tears and put her head against her husband's chest as he comforted her. He shook his head several times, unable to speak, lost for words. "All gone… Alisha, Arri, Ailia, Theo, Lucy, Tenno…all gone," he finally blurted out.

"Come on, brother. Let us take you back," Stewart said as he gently put his hand upon Paul's shoulder and began to usher him down the steps. Ishmael stepped into view looking at him, concerned. "He will be fine," Stewart told him as Ishmael took his other arm.

Brother Teric lifted Nicholas up and glared at the two armed escorts. Princess Stephanie winked at him as he helped Nicholas. She turned to the blacksmith.

"Thank you for letting us know of his whereabouts so quickly. You were right to do so for I think his mind is not his own this night. I know he will thank you for it in the morning as I do now," she said softly and put her hands upon his. "Thank you."

ഇ ന

Stewart and Ishmael sat Paul down on the single bed in the dimly lit chamber. Paul's room was small as he had requested despite being offered a larger chamber. His Templar robe and armour were all hung and laid out immaculately Stewart noted. With the position commissioned to him by Gerard, Paul was allowed a room on his own. Paul looked up wearily as he heard Nicholas being sick again outside.

"You never could handle your drink could you?" Upside said loudly. "Come on, I will look after the drunken fool from here."

As Upside led Nicholas away, Brother Teric stood in the doorway to check in on Paul.

"I do not envy you two in the morning," he said half jokingly. "Will you be all right left alone?"

"I can sit with him," Ishmael said instantly as Paul rested his head in his hands.

Stewart stood up and nodded in agreement with him.

 1 – 19

"May I have a few words alone with him, please?" Princess Stephanie asked, causing Brother Teric to jump, surprised at her presence. "I know I should not be here but Reynald is otherwise occupied with company so my presence is not missed."

"Do not be too certain of that," Brother Teric replied and stood aside to let her step down into the room. "We shall keep watch no one else comes by."

"Thank you," she said, smiling, and placed her hand upon his forearm briefly. Stewart and Ishmael quickly left the room followed by Brother Teric as he rubbed his arm where she had touched him. Quietly he closed the door behind them as she sat down beside Paul. They sat in silence for several minutes before Paul even realised she was beside him and then only after she took his hand from the side of his face. "Paul...take one of these." He looked at her, his face tired and etched with emotion. He looked at her other hand holding out a small sweet similar to one Master Jakelin had offered him on his first visit to Jerusalem. "It is strong tasting but it will freshen you and help with the pain in your head," she explained and put the sweet to his mouth. She smiled and nodded at him it was okay.

"You cannot be here...for if Reynald knows, he will use it as an excuse," Paul said, his voice low and dry, his head throbbing.

"He is already passed out by now I should imagine...in his bed with whatever maid he has chosen," she replied and put the sweet into his mouth. He momentarily shuddered at the sweet minty taste. "Besides, outside we are guarded," she remarked then held his hands in hers and looked at his tired eyes. She sighed with a look of sadness.

"I do not even know how I ended up in that brothel," Paul said as the sweet made his cheeks tingle and he pursed his lips. Princess Stephanie smiled seeing the look on his face. He clasped her hands tightly in his own. Her words she had whispered to him suddenly came back to him and he looked at her intently. "You said…that if I wished for comfort I only need come to you?" Princess Stephanie let out a nervous laugh and shook her head yes but did not speak. She pulled him close and held him tightly.

"I know now is not the time, but when the time is right, know that I am yours…and have been since the first day I ever met you," she whispered to him and kissed the side of his neck softly. "We must in time both move on and forward…and when that time comes I pray you consider me."

Paul gently pushed her back so he could look at her. She looked beautiful as she studied him intently, looking for any sign of his thoughts in his eyes and face. The longer he looked at her, the sadder she looked back. He placed his hand upon her face gently and she quickly held it with both of her hands. Her eyes looked deeper into his. She licked her dry lips immediately moistening them and she gulped nervously. Her perfume filled his nostrils and he knew in time he could easily fall in love with her. But now was not that time. There was a genuine warmth from her and there was no denying it felt comforting. She pulled his hand away from her face and pulled it against her tightly, just staring at him.

"It feels like my god has abandoned me…all that I knew and believed in is dead. We do not know where Master Douglas and Percival have gone for we have had no word from them…and no word of Thomas and his men. They may be dead, or prisoners yet no ransom has been forthcoming. And rumours spread that they set Alisha to be ambushed as they were but mercenaries…taken payment and fled!" Paul sighed heavily.

"And do you believe that…of Thomas and his men?"

"Therein lays the problem, for I do not know what to believe any more. Even Abi has no answer." He sighed again then looked up at her. "Yet you remain," Paul whispered. She let out a laugh, more of relief, and kissed his hand. "I cannot show you the appreciation or love that dwells within me for you…," he remarked and paused. Princess Stephanie sighed and lowered her head in sadness hearing his words. She took a deep breath and sat up straight looking embarrassed. Paul gently raised her chin to look at him. "But I pray you give me time and have patience for you are all that I have left worth living for."

"And you are all I live for," Princess Stephanie replied as a tear ran down her cheek.

Paul pulled her closer, her lips quivering in anticipation and emotion as she felt the strength in his hand against the small of her back. He cupped her face in his left hand and looked intently into her searching blue eyes. Slowly and gently he pressed his lips against hers, both with their eyes still open. She blinked fast several times and broke away from the kiss, surprised, her heart beating so fast she could hardly catch her breath. Paul pulled her close again and pressed his lips more firmly against hers. She felt herself close her eyes and lose herself in his embrace as he did in her sweet and tender kiss. He lowered her down until she lay on the bed beside him as he kissed her more intensely. Suddenly she pushed him up and away gasping for air as her body was overwhelmed with pleasure and a sensation she had never experienced or felt before. Surprised she drew in breath quickly as she looked into Paul's eyes.

"I...I...we cannot do this here for I know I will not be able to control nor contain myself," she explained, half laughing as tears rolled down her cheeks and she tried to catch her breath.

Paul ran his finger down her cheek wiping away her tears and smiled. His head was full of pain still and thoughts of Alisha flooded his mind but he sensed that she would approve. Gently he pulled her up so she sat facing him. He kissed her once more on the lips and savoured the taste of her and the feel of her body held against his. She was right of course and it would be wrong, especially with Ishmael and Brother Teric just outside the door for they would easily hear. "Go...you must leave now...and perhaps we can arrange to go somewhere isolated...when it is safe to do so."

Princess Stephanie looked at him and smiled. They had much in common and the intimacy just exchanged between them had felt so right. She stood up and walked over to the door and opened it, Ishmael and Brother Teric immediately looking in.

"I thinks he is going to be alright, for now," she told them and stepped up out of the room.

When Ishmael and Brother Teric looked at Paul he nodded in agreement and gave a slight wave with his right hand as Princess Stephanie moved out of sight.

೪ ೧೫

Paul walked toward the blacksmith's workshop with Ishmael by his side. His head still throbbed and he vowed he would never drink again. Having slept in until late afternoon, he felt it only fair and proper to visit the blacksmith and apologise as well as thank him for his actions. Paul would never get over losing Alisha and his children, and it hurt deeply every waking moment, but the prospect of not being totally alone and potentially a future with Princess Stephanie gave him some small measure of comfort. Maybe he was being emotionally weak, he thought, but at the moment in time, it is what kept him going and he did not feel so alone as he had. Ishmael nodded toward the brothel as they walked past it. It was not that far from the blacksmith's. No wonder he had seen Paul and Nicholas enter. Ishmael opened the front covers to the blacksmith's to be greeted by the man's wife. Immediately she saw Paul, she stood up alarmed. Paul entered the large open lobby surprised at its spacious and welcoming style. Last time he had entered to collect his new sword, he had taken no notice...just took the sword and left. Several shields, swords, helmets and various sets of chain mail were all displayed on the walls and stands. Two large chairs were set in front of a wooden table. The blacksmith's wife stood behind a small raised work bench where she had been stitching a leather scabbard together. Nervously she looked at Paul, which concerned him.

"Please...why do you look so worried?" Paul asked her, trying to reassure her.

"For getting you into trouble last eve," she replied hesitantly and fumbled with her fingers nervously.

"Have I changed that much I now solicit fear?" Paul asked and sighed as he stood before her. She silently nodded yes. "I came to thank you and to apologise...for I seemed to have lost my way momentarily."

"And are you still lost?" the blacksmith asked as he stepped into view from behind the room divider, holding a large axe in one hand and a sword in the other. Ishmael immediately stood between him and Paul.

"No...no I am not," Paul replied quietly and bowed his head slightly. "I have come to apologise. I did not even thank you properly for the new sword you made for me. As for last night...I do not even recall how I got there. Your intervention was therefore both timely and appreciated."

"We understand your loss...," the blacksmith's wife said and moved to stand beside her husband.

"I see you have done well here in Jerusalem," Paul remarked, looking around the room.

"Aye that we have...thanks to your Templar and Hospitaller friends awarding us lucrative contracts...but we would exchange it all in a heartbeat for the return of Tara," the blacksmith replied instantly.

Paul looked at them intently and stepped closer toward them.

"If I have shamed the memory of your daughter then I pray you will forgive me. I shall not do so again that I swear."

"You have," a gravelly old female voice interrupted from behind him. Both Paul and Ishmael spun around to see the old woman who often hung about stood staring at Paul. "For you have forgotten who you are...and who you are meant to be," she continued and rested her hands upon her walking stick. The room filled with the stench coming from her just as the young girl who always accompanied her appeared at the doorway. She was now a young woman and not the frail little girl Paul had first met with Taqi years previously in La Rochelle. She smiled and bowed her head politely at him. The old woman gave an exaggerated smile then nodded at the blacksmith and his wife. "You did well to seek help for him when he needed it most. He will remember, and he will honour your daughter's memory, I promise you that," she said to them before looking back at Paul intently. She smiled then nodded at him, turned her back and walked toward the young woman. Gently she touched Ishmael's arm as she passed him and he shuddered briefly. "And Paul...you of such little faith...you of all people should know the path you must now follow until once again you are reunited with your loved ones...and shame upon you if you doubt the motives and intentions of Thomas and his men...so start trusting what your heart tells you," she said, then stepped out of sight.

Paul watched her leave, bemused, before finally turning to the blacksmith and his wife. As her words echoed in his mind he did not know whether to chase after her or just let her go. 'If I chase her, would she take me away again to meet Kratos as before?' he thought. He shook his head, puzzled.

"Do you know her too?" he asked the blacksmith.

"Yes of course we do...ever since we lost Tara. She was the one who somehow secured our first commission from the brothers here also," the Blacksmith explained. "Without her, we would most certainly have floundered."

"She even promised that one day we would have another daughter, but that has not happened yet," the blacksmith's wife explained and shook her head sadly. "She refuses any payment from us other than our company sometimes."

Paul looked at Ishmael, more confused.

"What name did she call herself?" Paul asked.

"She calls herself Cerridwen," the blacksmith's wife replied, looking alarmed. "Do we have cause for concern?"

"No, none at all…she simply goes by different names, that is all," Paul answered and shrugged his shoulders.

Port of La Rochelle, France, Melissae Inn, spring 1191

"Why is her name relevant?" Gabirol interrupted.

"As Paul explained, he knew her under various names. But Cerridwen was new to his ears. But the Cerridwen of Welsh and Irish myth is regarded as a woman of incredible power and magic and recognised as an emblem of wisdom and rebirth. She is renowned as a woman of fierce magical talent, yet her story is often less about herself and more about the children she bore," the old man explained.

"What did she mean about Thomas and his men?" Ayleth asked, sheepishly quiet.

"That he should listen to what his heart was telling him," the old man replied and paused for a moment. "Reynald had mocked Paul asking in front of the court where was his army of kings now...and look what good they did."

"Did Gerard share this sentiment?" Peter asked.

"No not at all. Gerard had changed quite a lot since his first encounters with Paul and Alisha...plus he had seen the madness that appeared to be growing in Reynald and it concerned him."

"Why did Gerard change?" Sarah asked, still puzzled.

"Gerard could not understand it himself, to be honest. I personally do not think it was so much he had changed as a case of himself remembering who he actually was again. All of us are influenced by the people we spend the most time with...and his almost constant contact with Reynald certainly wore off on him. But it was both Paul and Stewart's behaviour that slowly and surely got under Gerard's skin. This became obvious to Paul when he ran into him just prior to taking Queen Sibylla and Princess Stephanie out as part of their escort."

"But where was Thomas and his men then...and Master Douglas and Percival?" the Templar asked.

"*Master Douglas and Percival continued in their quest to discover just what exactly had happened to them. Some claimed they had been taken as slaves, others as hostages yet no ransoms ever came, as I said before...,*" the old man explained and sighed. "*And on the morning before Paul was to leave on escort duties, Stewart entered his chambers and handed him his old folder with many of the drawings and poems he had managed to recover. Some were, as you have seen, slightly burnt, but the rest were still perfect. But Paul could not bring himself to open the folder and look at them...instead he placed them in a travel trunk beneath his bed.*"

"*Where was he escorting them too?*" Simon asked.

"*Queen Sibylla had deliberately orchestrated a visit to a nearby shrine and beautiful location beside a river...purely as a distraction and day out so Paul and Princess Stephanie could be together,*" the old man started to explain.

"*But surely that was too risky?*" Ayleth asked.

"*'Twas indeed...but Queen Sibylla could be trusted for she was a good and close friend of Princess Stephanie's...and she knew only too well the loneliness and heartache of a loveless marriage. Near the river was an old ruined chapel that once belonged to a former knight and hermit. The queen knew they could have privacy there without the prying eyes of all of Reynald's men and King Guy's courtiers watching their every move.*"

"*But what of Saladin's forces in the region?*" the Hospitaller asked.

"*That helped serve their purposes even more for Reynald hoped that perhaps they would indeed encounter his men...and not return.*"

"*And King Guy was all right with this?*" Gabirol asked, bemused.

"*Of course. It was just a short distance from Jerusalem...,*" the old man said quietly and nodded his head. "*King Guy had secured his position through the queen so if she was sadly killed in an ambush, or taken hostage and held for ransom, then it would serve his position well.*"

"*That is disgusting and immoral,*" Ayleth protested, shaking her head.

"*This being a princess or queen certainly is not the fairytale rubbish we are fed is it?*" Sarah remarked and folded her arms.

The old man shook his head no.

"*Like Paul, both the queen and Princess Stephanie had to become a refuge within themselves...a fortress of solitude just to endure and survive,*" he said softly.

Templars' stables, Jerusalem, Kingdom of Jerusalem, April 26th 1187

Long shadows slowly shrank back from the outer walls as the sun began its early morning climb into the clear blue sky. Paul checked Adrastos's hind leg that had still not fully healed. Some of the deep lacerations he had suffered when Paul had ridden him hard through dense underbrush trying to reach Alisha had almost cost him his life. The Templar farriers had done a remarkable job at stitching his wounds, but Paul would not be riding him today. He patted him gently as he approached his face and looked into his eyes. Many images flooded his mind recalling Tenno teaching Arri to ride upon his back. He smiled as he recalled his laughter. Several weary Templars appeared, some coughing having just woken up. Paul was already fully dressed in his chain mail and surcoat. As he patted Adrastos, he checked his sword. The blacksmith, after insisting he wished to do so, had kindly etched in the same designs he had put upon Paul's original sword. It only then occurred to Paul that his original sword must have somehow sensed and let the blacksmith etch the designs up itself, for no pain or ill effect affected him as he did so. 'Maybe the blacksmith is connected to the sword somehow too,' he thought. But despite having left his original sword firmly stuck in the stone, he would not change his scabbard as made by Theodoric and Arri. He rested his head against Adrastos and sighed.

"Paul," Gerard suddenly said quietly behind him and put his hand upon his right shoulder. "We have another horse for you."

Paul turned around to face him.

"Thank you," Paul replied, looking surprised to see him.

"You look amazed I am stood here, but worry not, I am not coming with you. Your brother will take the vanguard if you can take the rear. These little jollies the women take does them good, which in turn makes life more bearable within the court."

"I shall do whatever is requested."

"Aye…," Gerard replied and paused as he looked at Paul. "We have certainly come a long way you and I since our first encounter, no?"

"Yes, that we have…and you have changed much…for the better."

"Huh….changed yes, but I am not so sure if for the better."

"I think you have."

"That is then in no small measure down to you and your brother," Gerard remarked and looked across toward Stewart as he approached with Brother Teric, Upside and Nicholas. "Your brother has become like a son to me. His wise counsel has been invaluable…and he has reminded me who I once was and am again. But if you ever tell him that, I will personally murder you in your sleep," Gerard joked and smiled with a quick wink. "And…and I was very wrong where Alisha was concerned. All I saw in her was a threat…for I know the true bloodline that flowed within her and what that could do here, even back in France. The legitimacy of all the lords and the position of the king…it would have led to chaos and all out conflict amongst ourselves. I was blinded by my own zeal, greed and desire to be the Grand Master." Paul could see the genuine look in Gerard's eyes and the sentiment in his words. "It surprises you to hear me speak like this?"

"Yes, in all honesty it does."

"The day you saved Reynald and I…that was the day I started to wake up to myself. I am now the Grand Master…and yet it does not live up to what I expected it to be. 'Tis but in reality a poisonous chalice to pick up."

"But it gives you access to the higher initiate secrets. Does that not help?"

"Alas, nowhere near so. Besides, I am a realist and pragmatist. I know I do not have the wherewithal to even begin to understand what the secrets mean. I leave that to men like Count Henry and you," Gerard replied and nodded at him. "But I made my bed with Reynald…for a man must always choose a side or lose himself. I have and will continue to try and steer him on a straight path, for all of our sakes, but ultimately, as God is my witness, I have put my colours to his banners. In an ideal world I would follow a man like you, over Reynald, any day. You have genuine legitimacy, true courage and real natural skill."

Paul hesitated for a moment, caught off guard at his remark.

"It is never too late to change one's mind or position."

"Not in my case…I will have some serious answering to do when I walk through the gates of Heaven…if I am given the key that is." He laughed and shook his head. "You know, Alisha kicked me once in the groin… heaven help me but I certainly cussed and took the Lord's name in vain that moment," Gerard laughed more, then paused as he looked at Paul. "I wronged you both, for that I am truly sorry and hope one day you will forgive me. I was also wrong where her father was concerned. If I could change that, I would in a heartbeat. 'Twas a mad period I went through, though that does not excuse my behaviour."

"Ah here are my scheming men at arms," Reynald suddenly interrupted as he appeared accompanying King Guy beside him. "So we have found a job for you at last, looking after the women, eh," Reynald mocked as Gerard stood back a pace and part bowed his head toward King Guy, who nodded back.

Dressed in a golden silk gown, King Guy looked at Paul and raised his eyebrows as if waiting for him to bow or speak. Paul just shrugged his shoulders and looked over at Gerard.

"So where, as my friend said before, is your army of kings now?" King Guy asked in a drawn out manner. "I hear they sold you out and have left, like the mercenaries they always were."

Reynald laughed but Gerard shook his head slightly at Paul not to bite.

"My Lord, you are indeed correct and now you are the second person to ask that exact same question...but only the good Lord in Heaven himself can answer it...and yes, I am honoured to have the task of escorting the women for the day. After all if it were not for women, what would any of us be?" Paul replied politely, more out of respect for Gerard.

King Guy looked at Reynald hard and frowned.

"Does he make fools of us?" he asked.

"Aye probably, my King...'tis hard to tell with this one," Reynald replied and stared at Paul.

"My Lords, he is one of my knights now, and one of the best may I remind you. He is not the same man he once was," Gerard interrupted.

"Horse shit...men never change," Reynald shot back and looked at Paul dismissively. "I bet the first chance you get you would fuck the arse of my wife."

"Reynald," Paul replied and stood up straight. "I can assure you that as she is truly a real lady, she would not accept, even if I was to offer...and I bet half the men in this city would die for the chance to hold her in their arms and look at her...face to face, not from behind to hide her face by f..."

"That's enough," Gerard interjected rapidly and pulled Paul toward him. "Here, take him to his horse," he said as Brother Teric stopped walking just before them.

1 – 55

"How dare you insult me or my wife," Reynald snapped, Brothers Upside and Nicholas immediately moving to stand beside Paul. "You are a fine one to preach about such matters, especially when you even share your wife like she as a common whore!" he snarled louder and pointed at Nicholas.

Gerard screwed his face up and winced at Reynald's words. He pulled a pained look of discomfort as he faced Paul, looking to see what his reaction was going to be. Nicholas looked at Paul as both of them shook their heads no. Paul took a deep breath, and though his heart was now pounding and he felt both embarrassed but also angry, he knew he had to temper his rising fury. He smiled and let out a light laugh. King Guy put his hands to his chest and stood back worried. Nicholas grasped his sword handle.

"No, Brother Nicholas…," Paul said immediately and put his hand up for him to stop. "My Lords…you may see much, hear much, experience much…but you know so very little, especially about women. Perhaps that is why you seek constant reassurances by indulging yourselves with countless maids, of which I am most certain you have both shared on more than one occasion."

Reynald's eyes widened in anger, his face reddening fast. He took in several sharp breaths, lost for words. King Guy took another step backwards fearing trouble as Paul looked hard at Reynald, then slowly turned his gaze to the king. Gerard could not help but let out a laugh.

"By the heavens 'tis a good job Lord Balian is soon to arrive for then you can accompany him to Tiberius," Gerard stated and moved between Paul and Reynald and started to usher Paul backwards. Reynald fumed and looked as though he was about to explode as King Guy just shook his head looking at him then Paul rapidly. "Ah look, 'tis the queen," Gerard said louder and pushed Paul further backwards, Paul still staring at Reynald. "Just help me here and move," Gerard whispered in Paul's ear.

Nicholas kicked his heels in the dirt and looked at Reynald as Upside took his right arm to follow him. Nicholas flounced his arm away from Upside and continued to stare at Reynald until he realised he was looking at him.

"My Lord, I think it best when Paul leaves with Lord Balian, you let me accompany them also…for I fear I no longer have your best interests at heart," Nicholas explained in a low and deliberate tone. Brother Upside grabbed his arm harder and physically pulled him away quickly before he could say any more.

"Does he speak treason?" King Guy whispered to Reynald, leaning near to him.

Reynald watched as Brother Upside led Nicholas away, Paul walking with Gerard toward Queen Sibylla and Princess Stephanie. King Guy put his hand upon Reynald and was about to speak again when he pushed his hand off aggressively, flounced around and walked away slapping his hands against his side, still furious. Brother Teric laughed to himself as King Guy blushed with embarrassment standing alone awkwardly pointing his finger one direction then the other, unsure what he should do next.

Valley of Hinnom, Kingdom of Jerusalem, April 26th 1187

The day had been long but enjoyable and Queen Sibylla ensured that the main party of the group pulled up to rest before continuing back to Jerusalem near to an old donjon they had deliberately been discussing. This was the opportunity Princess Stephanie had been anxiously waiting for all day and whilst the party arranged an early evening meal, she led Paul and Ishmael away and down toward the old donjon, the excuse being they would not be long. When they could see the donjon, Ishmael pulled up his horse and stopped and indicated they go on alone. He would remain where he could keep an eye out for any approaching trouble or in case anyone came after them from the party. Paul raised his hand to thank Ishmael for accompanying them, adjusted his sitting position upon the unfamiliar horse, tightened the long leather guige strap slung around his neck and shoulder holding the targe kite shaped shield across his back. It constantly caught the base of his neck with every step taken. He hoped Adrastos would be well again soon.

"We shall not be long I assure you," he said, Ishmael simply nodding in acknowledgment.

Paul opened the front of his surcoat feeling increasingly hot under his heavy chain mail hauberk. He looked ahead at Stephanie as she began to manoeuvre her horse through the thickets that partially blocked the old path they were to follow. It was only now when they were alone that he noticed she was wearing a purple and light blue silk dress similar to those Alisha and Nyla had made back in Alexandria. His heart jumped just remembering her. He shook his head then noticed that she was also using an Arabic saddle of the High Islamic Riding School style set on a thick woven blanket. It had been a gift from Saladin years previously. The bronze harness pendant, bridle attachment and trefoil strap linkage kept catching the sun's rays reflecting off it brightly. He half wished he had such a comfortable saddle rather than the simple wooden framed one he now had, the rear cantle creaking having been made too high. He placed his Phrygian shaped helmet upon the saddle pommel as he released and dropped the chain mail head over coif to his shoulders letting the air get to his face. All day he had been apart from her as she and the queen had talked, laughed and enjoyed dangling their feet in the small stream they had visited. Stewart and Nicholas had made sure none of Reynald's own men or those of King Guy had followed. Paul felt guilty that he was following Princess Stephanie whilst his own brother and friends believed he was doing so in all innocence. In truth both Stewart and Nicholas knew full well her intentions but did not discourage it for they both knew the pain and heartache they were suffering. Nicholas was silently pleased and whispered under his breath 'up yours Reynald' when Paul and Princess Stephanie rode off.

The cool evening breeze began its nightly course across the open sandy plain that stretched ahead of them filled with various sweet scents. The whole area looked beautiful Paul thought with many hues of yellow and light brown grasses interspersed with tufts of greenery for as far as the eye could see. Princess Stephanie sat fully in the saddle as she always did, like a man, her feet firmly set within the stirrups, and not side saddle like other women of her position. This made him smile. As she led them down a slight incline from the high plateau, his eyes fixed upon her slender figure, momentarily silhouetted, when the setting sun shone through the layers of thin silk that hung elegantly from her white shoulders and tied at her waist. She turned her head and looked at him and smiled back, the usual tension in her eyes not present. Her golden hair fell across her face and she laughed mischievously before looking forwards again. Leaving the safety of the full escort was at best risky, but to go as night was falling was foolhardy. He knew she had ulterior motives and his heart paced faster as he knew she wanted him…whatever the risks. He looked over his shoulder momentarily to double check they were not being followed but Ishmael was still visible keeping guard on the approach. Knowing what they were setting out to do was wrong made the trip exhilarating, almost intoxicating in its intensity, but he also felt very guilty; certainly not toward Reynald, but for Alisha. Should he accept what Princess Stephanie had advised and offered him and move on and give into temptation and the obvious attraction between them now? Everything he had ever loved or thought he understood and knew about the rules of his faith had been turned upon its head over the past few years. As he ran through these thoughts and feelings, Princess Stephanie constantly motioned him to follow but something was beginning to make both their horses nervous; perhaps a snake nearby or a Muslim reconnaissance party was hiding in ambush. Either way Paul was taking no chances and pulled up alongside her.

"Listen," he whispered, holding her horse steady.

Princess Stephanie smiled broadly and just looked at him intently as he surveyed the surrounding area, the land opening into a clearing a short distance from the old Eglise-donjon (*fortified church*) abandoned years earlier.

"What is the matter...can you not wait any longer?" she asked with a mischievous smile, her eyes almost glazed in anticipation, but in truth she was very nervous and unsure if Paul felt as she did. She thought of Alisha and sighed sadly knowing he would forever love her more. But at that exact moment in time, she could at least hope and dream.

Outside of the city now alone with Paul, she acted and looked so different compared with the almost austere facade she put on in court. Paul surveyed the old Eglise-donjon with suspicion. Princess Stephanie laughed as he frowned and squinted against the setting sun. The old church had once belonged to a famous Norman knight who had converted to Judaism. He had been condemned to hell upon his death by the Pope. In AD 1102 he had taken the name of Obadyah the proselyte and toured the Middle East looking for a new messiah. All of his lands and possessions were confiscated, or like the old church where he had lived, destroyed. Paul's interest in the man and the earlier deliberate discussions had now placed him at the old church and proved a perfect excuse for Princess Stephanie to arrange the visit. Her horse suddenly reared up in alarm nearly throwing her off, Paul just managing to grab its reins and calm it. Quickly he dismounted and helped her down, placing his hands firmly upon her waist as he took her weight and lowered her to the ground. She stood still, her hands resting upon his chest and momentarily looked up into his eyes. Paul stared back; the overwhelming desire to just pull her close and kiss her was something he could no longer resist and he leaned forward. Just as his lips were about to touch hers, both their horses' reared up violently alarmed and kicked frantically. Paul tried to grab their reins but they both bolted racing back up the narrow overgrown path. Immediately drawing his sword he pulled Princess Stephanie behind him as he frantically looked about them for what had frightened them off. When the dust began to settle and nothing untoward could be seen or heard, Princess Stephanie put her arms around Paul and tucked her face hard against his back.

"My man, and you are my man, you smell so good...like a man should," she remarked warmly and hugged him tighter.

"Really, My Lady...but I am afraid that is not going to help us out here right now. I need to get our horses back before it is too dark," Paul replied, still holding his sword at the ready with both hands.

"I am sure Ishmael will stop them. They only have one way to go...and have I not told you to stop calling me Lady when we are alone...and besides, if Ishmael does not have them, then we shall have to wait here awhile until he comes looking for us," she said softly, paused for a minute then smiled. "Which means we will just have to stay here alone until he does, which could be at least a couple of hours?"

"It is inappropriate that we are like this. Something is obviously trying to warn us that this is wrong."

Princess Stephanie let go and moved in front of Paul. She gently grasped the end of his sword and placed it against her chest. Holding it still she stared at him.

"What are you doing?" he asked and pulled the sword away.

As Paul tried to look at her and also the surrounding area, his instincts told him something was wrong but he could not see from what or where.

"Are you just making excuses not to be with me...now we are finally truly alone, for if so you may as well pierce my heart with your sword for that is how you have affected me. You have come into my life and pierced straight through my very soul as cleanly as a sword would have," she explained, her voice soft and yet tinged with sadness.

Immediately Paul recalled his own poem he had written to Alisha, 'Sword to my heart, sword through my soul'. He knew Alisha had let her read it years previously.

"I don't think it would be as clean as you say," Paul answered, still looking about them.

"I am in love with you can you not see that?" she retorted, her voice now clipped, her eyes glistening as they searched his.

"But...you are still married to Reynald and he seeks any excuse to accuse you and I...we cannot be...not now and not like this," Paul pointed out as he looked upon her face, her eyes wide and full of emotion. He knew he could easily love this woman now stood before him. Perhaps he could make a new life with her as she had offered.

"You and I both know, as does the entire court, I am married but in name only. My life is empty and meaningless. Reynald is almost twice my age and has no idea how to love a woman," she replied and paused, her lips moist and inviting so close to his. "But you do."

"It is a sin that I even covet you with the feelings I have," Paul confessed as they both stood motionless looking at each other as the sun dropped further behind the horizon setting off red hues across the sky.

"A sin you say. Now I know you are making excuses for how can warmth and love be a sin? Is that not the very essence of what our Lord was trying to tell us all along...that love is the key? What Reynald feels for me is not love, and I have no love for him that I know. It is not loneliness or desperation that sets my heart on fire for you...it is love. Not a sin!" she responded and placed her hand against his face, looking at him longingly, raw emotion etched upon her face and tearful. When Paul looked deeper into her clear blue eyes, the tears welling in them only adding to their beauty, he recalled the words of Alisha as if echoing in his head when she had said to him their love could not be a sin either but that it was beautiful and God sent. "I offer you my heart, soul and body and all that I am. I do not offer it lightly but in full knowledge of the risk that doing so could cost us both our lives," Stephanie said emotionally and stood back momentarily as he looked at her, her dress hanging loosely and gently blowing in the wind revealing the sensuous curves of her figure. Slowly she outstretched her hand for him. He looked around once more before sheathing his sword and gently clasped her hand in his. Her very touch as her soft skin met his rough hand sent a shiver through him as he accepted that no matter what, he did want her. He knew Alisha would not want him to waste away his remaining years in solitude and misery all alone and so he began to follow her as she led him toward the old church, passed through the crumbled outer perimeter wall and stopped at the entrance of what was once a beautiful chapel. Paul looked inside briefly. "Unlike our Templar friends and my husband, you wash and bathe. You can't remain one of them for that reason alone…and you most definitely must not, I forbid it, have a ridiculous hair cut, shaved at the sides and long hair at the back as some Templars still wear theirs," she joked, trying to ease Paul's apprehension clearly showing across his face. His eyes stared intensely at her as she stroked his arm.

"I do not know where we go after this or what is to become of us, but know this that I too do not enter into this lightly or seek simple gratification," he told her.

"Give me a minute to prepare myself," Princess Stephanie said in a soft whisper and started to untie the fastenings of her dress; she turned gracefully and walked through the building toward the far side where another more secluded room led off. An open hole where a window once was let the last beams of sunlight stream into the room bathing her in an aura of light as she passed through it.

Paul's heart raced and he felt it pound. He had only ever known Alisha and he tried to push her image from his mind feeling guilty that he was about to make love to another woman; guilty toward Alisha for betraying her in his mind so soon, but also guilty towards Princess Stephanie for he should only be thinking of her at that moment. Paul suddenly heard horses, their sound carried upon the wind. He spun around but saw nothing. Suddenly Princess Stephanie let out a shrill scream of terror. Without hesitation he drew his sword and rushed into the old church, across the chapel towards the room she was in and literally smashed through what was left of the door, nearly falling over as he did. As he rapidly stood upright, his sword held out clutched with both hands, his eyes darting from corner to corner of the darkened room, he saw Princess Stephanie cowering terrified to his right, her hands up against her face in protection. With just a single beam of sunlight streaming through an open window space, dust particles diffusing it further, he suddenly heard the roar of a mountain lion to his left. His heart missed a beat; his head exploded with instant adrenalin as he instinctively brought his sword up in front of him just as a large male mountain lion jumped ferociously at him. As one paw lashed out and its claws dug deep into his left shoulder, shards of broken chain mail flying off, the lion's huge open mouth was just inches from his face. He rolled backwards and thrust the sword upwards as hard as he could into its chest, blood instantly pouring down the blade over him. Princess Stephanie screamed in terror, shaking uncontrollably as Paul fell to the ground with the lion on top of him. She froze with her hands across her mouth, eyes wide as both Paul and the lion lay motionless. In the gloomy darkness with dust swirling she could not see what had happened. She started to sob and stood perfectly still for what seemed an age.

"A little help here would be appreciated," Paul coughed and tried to move the dead lion off. Without hesitation she rushed over and helped push the lion away and then threw her arms tightly around him. They just sat on the floor hugging for several minutes. Blood began seeping from Paul's torn shoulder wound but she would not let him pull away as she clung ever tighter. Paul tried to push his shield aside from behind him, part of it broken from his fall and splinters from it stuck in his side causing him added pain. His sword and Templar mantle were soaked in the lion's blood as well as his own.

"I have seen and experienced many things in this land, but never have I felt so terrified in all my life as then," she whispered quietly, half sobbing and shaking.

"Well, at least we know what scared the horses off...for that is one big lion," Paul replied, his voice shaking as he tried to stand but Princess Stephanie held him too tightly.

"The lion scared me," she replied but paused as she tried to compose herself, her voice broken with emotion, "but not half as much as when I thought it had killed you," she continued and looked Paul in the eyes clasping his face within her cupped hands. "Those Knights Hospitaller may have developed a whole mystique around dying as a martyr in battle but I need you to stay very much alive. You are all that I live for do you know that?" she explained quietly.

Paul touched her bottom lip gently with his finger, her lip was dry and bleeding slightly where she had bitten it in terror. He wiped the blood away then stroked her face. She had always been so calm and collected and utterly fearless but this one episode had truly terrified her. For a few moments he just looked at her.

"There is nothing that I can give you. What sort of a life can I offer you? You come from an opulent and luxurious background surrounded by wealth."

"Yes, true but it is all meaningless and worthless. It holds nothing for me now...'tis why I am happy to hand it all to Reynald," she replied, sighing deeply.

"What of Reynald's intention though?" Paul asked, holding her tightly.

"What of him! Huh, he knows only war and hate. He is bigoted in religion, insensitive to diplomacy, land hungry and brutal," she replied and hesitated for a moment. "He was once big and strong, as well as a brave knight, but his heart still belongs to his first wife, Constance of Antioch. His sixteen years as a prisoner in Aleppo only served to harden his heart further. He is responsible for much of the present troubles in this land… always tormenting Saladin and Muslims. He has learnt nothing," she explained, then looked at him again. Blood was still oozing from the wound on his shoulder. Gently she untied the fixings of his chain mail coif around his neck, and pulled the opening of his hauberk aside. Gently she moved Paul into the beam of sunlight to see blood seeping across his jupeau d'armer (*padded jerkin*). Suddenly they heard horses approaching; their eyes fixed upon each other. Quickly Paul moved to stand and winced in pain when he moved to get up. Princess Stephanie stood up fast behind him as he leant towards the window opening. Gently he eased his way over and very slowly, at the base of the window, looked out so as not to reveal his position. He saw the ever darkening landscape as the almost blood red sphere of the sun sank slowly on the horizon, casting long dark shadows that seemed to reach out as if wanting to grab him. He heard horse steps again to their far left but could not see anything, his view obscured by a large bush and thickets.

"Is it Ishmael with our horses or Reynald's men?" Princess Stephanie asked in a whisper.

Paul strained to see, holding his sword tightly in his left hand upright whilst holding Stephanie away from the window with his right arm across her protectively.

"I cannot see, but whoever it is, we are surely in trouble either way if they are not our horses," Paul whispered turning to look at the dead lion. Anyone coming up close would see it, immediately giving away their presence. Hurriedly he passed his blood covered sword to Princess Stephanie and started to pull the lion's body across the room into the darker corner furthest from the window. A horse snorted loudly outside bringing Paul's attention back to the window. The lion was just out of the light cast by the weak sunrays but not where he wanted it to be when he had to rush silently over to Princess Stephanie just as she was about to look out and inadvertently reveal herself. He managed to grab her with his left arm and held her back from peering around. He pulled her tightly against his side, her head pressed back hard against the stone wall, his head close to hers as they both looked to their left at the window opening. They were only just out of the line of sight and held their breath in anticipation as a horse approached. Princess Stephanie momentarily flinched letting out a gasp when she heard Arabic being spoken to another rider nearby. Paul cupped his hand across her mouth and pulled her ever tighter against him, pain reeling through his body as she inadvertently pushed a large splinter from his broken shield deeper into his side, but he could not make a sound and sweat began to rivulet down his face and back. As the Arabic horseman drew ever nearer, the sun's rays of fading light caused the shadows cast upon Princess Stephanie to move across her features in ever longer bands as if enveloping her in darkness. She strained to hold her breath and stared at the opening, Paul's hand still across her mouth, so he gently released his grip so she could breathe easier. When his hand moved away, she remained still and focused towards the window. Paul watched her as the sunlight passed through her hair, highlighting the sweat forming on her brow from nervous tension. Her eyes were wide and fixed and she did not blink, her chest heaved up and down as she tried to catch her breath, panic beginning to take its ugly grip upon her mind. Paul moved his right arm, sword in hand, slowly and gently across her chest protectively, but still she stared fixated at the window. Paul's arm pressed against her chest and he felt her breasts push against it as she breathed deeply. He could not help but look as his gaze followed from her open mouth, down across her chin, to her white slender neck and then her collar bone and on to her bosom as a bead of sweat rolled down her chest. Her dress pulled tightly against her figure every time she breathed in and hung loose when she breathed out. Paul looked back to her face. She was terrified and only he stood as her protector against whoever waited outside. As he studied her face his heart beat harder and he knew that should they survive this night, he would make love to her whatever the risk without any further guilt or hesitation. She placed her right hand upon his and together they gripped his sword. She slowly turned her head to face him and they stared at each other as one of the Arabic horsemen edged his way alongside the window opening and crouched slightly to peer in, a long lance prodding through the opening first. Princess Stephanie froze, not daring to move, just looking into Paul's eyes as he slowly placed in her left hand his arming dagger.

The lance pierced deeper into the room as the horseman moved ever nearer to get a better look inside. Princess Stephanie's eyes were wide and she visibly shook unable to control the fear that was overwhelming her. Paul then realised that as the horseman had a lance, a weapon most Muslim cavalry were loath to use, that they were most likely out hunting the lion, not them. That is why the lion had been hiding in the old church in the first place. Any moment, however, the Muslim would peer in and see them in the dim fading light. Princess Stephanie's legs swayed as she started to hyperventilate with the tension but Paul steadied her balance. He mentally prepared himself rushing through his mind a plan of attack should the Muslim see them. He would jump into view and instantly knock aside the lance and thrust his sword directly into the horseman as he leaned in. Paul began to stand away from the wall, ready to attack, when the lance was suddenly withdrawn, the horse rearing up momentarily, its rider struggling to control it. For a few seconds Paul and Princess Stephanie awaited the attack that would surely now enter the room; but it didn't come. From the safety of the shadows within the room, Paul moved just enough to see four well armed Muslim cavalrymen, their horses snorting and excitable, no doubt having caught wind of the smell of the lion still in the area. As Paul studied the men, he noted their clothing and weapons. Two were armed with long lances and wore heavy jawshan lamellar armour; their horses were also covered in lamellar plated blankets. Their helmets were of a Qipchaq design made by a mixed people, mainly of Muslim, Christian and Shamanist origin, who were amongst the finest armourers known. They had detachable visors and they had round shields brightly painted with yellow circles in the middle and red arrow fletched type patterns upon them that affixed to their left forearms. These were professional cavalry and in all their splendour and bright colours Paul had to admit they looked impressive. When they checked the ground looking in the dusty soil for footprints of the lion, they rode carefully back and forth as the two other horsemen, Muslim horse archers, kept their composite bows aimed keeping an ever vigilant look out for the lion. Large bright blue horse blankets covered the archers' horses, their unsheathed swords drawn and hanging from their right forearms by a leather strap ready for instant use. They too were professional horse archers, and their aim was deadly accurate with their arrows easily able to pierce Paul's chain mail at such close range. They could aim accurately up to a distance of 180 feet and could repeatedly shoot five arrows, held in the left hand with the bow, in two and a half seconds and quickly snatch another five arrows from a quiver. Despite the horses' natural fear from the scent of the lion, they were well controlled and if the men discovered Paul and Princess Stephanie, they had no chance of fleeing. One horseman suddenly looked in Paul's direction. Paul froze knowing it was movement that would give him away. If he remained still, in the shadows, chances were he would not be spotted. Princess Stephanie could not catch her breath and began to keel over towards the opening. Paul had no choice but to move swiftly and catch her before she passed the window. Just in time he pulled her up straight again, both with their backs against the wall. Paul's mind raced; what were these professional men doing so far inland hunting a lion so close to Jerusalem? It could only mean that there must be far more troops somewhere nearby as this was clearly not just a reconnaissance party for they were mixed heavy cavalry and light horse archers. Should he take them on by surprise or pray they would leave, he pondered momentarily, and what if Ishmael showed up? As he pulled Princess Stephanie tighter against him he was just able to see one of the horse archers load a nawak high velocity dart and aim it towards the window opening. Paul looked at her eyes burning into his with fear and anticipation, sweat running from her temples, her mouth open as she fought to control her breathing quietly. Her eyes moved to look upon Paul's sword as he held it next to her face.

 1 – 15

"Do not let them take me alive," she whispered nervously and gently shook her head as she pulled the arming dagger towards her chest, her fingers fumbling around the twin edged quillions.

A flash and instant buzz sound zipped passed their ears dangerously close as the high velocity dart flew into the room and embedded into the opposite wall causing Princess Stephanie to flinch again, her body beginning to tremble more. The horse archer shouted at his colleagues as he approached the window, but the others turned away and started to move off in the opposite direction. The horse archer, however, still drew nearer, his suspicions aroused. He pulled out a naphtha fire hand grenade, lit it and threw it through the window. Paul grabbed Princess Stephanie and bodily threw her sideways towards the other door into what was once the chapel hall and dived upon her, shielding her just as the grenade exploded throwing out a large gout of orange flame, the force of which flashed over Paul's broken shield still attached to his back as it instantly illuminated the room before collapsing in on itself into just a small smouldering fire. Paul lay perfectly still upon her both trying not to cough as smoke wafted about them and they listened as the horse archer's colleagues called for him. With Princess Stephanie on her back and Paul lying on top of her, both looked up towards the openings where several windows once lined the chapel. Only as the sound of the horses faded into the distance did Paul look down into her tear filled eyes as she started to sob uncontrollably. She tried to wipe her tears away, embarrassed almost, Paul's dagger still waving about in her hand a little too close to marking his face and he grasped her wrist, stopping her movements. As a tear rolled down her face barely visible in the gloom of the room, the very last shafts of sunlight were cast in great horizontal beams through the openings in the wall to finish in square bursts of light on the far wall. Paul hesitated as he became aware that he was actually lying on top of her, her dress torn and pushed up high, her legs showing wrapped almost around his thighs. She did not push him away. After a few moments, she stopped sobbing, and then hesitantly leaned up and kissed him gently, then harder as passion began to take over. As Paul kissed her back, his lips tingled at the sensation of her lips pressing on his and his body was flooded with an overwhelming sense of desire; his hand moved her dress up higher revealing her thigh and she started to undo his chausses chain mail stockings, but then he stopped her, hesitating as he looked at her, her chest heaving and her lips pouted and she looked at him quizzically wondering why he had stopped. Paul caressed her exposed forearm then held her hand up to his face and kissed it. His heart pounded so vigorously she could feel it beat against her chest as she breathed in and out, her eyes fixed on Paul's as they lay still, neither moving, the tension and desire between them coursing through their veins. Paul, his mouth turning dry, tried to speak but she placed her finger upon his lips in silence. He wanted her, longed to kiss her again, to taste her and hear her as she made love with him, yet he could not; his main priority had to be to get her to safety and also warn the others about the Muslim force's presence.

"I dare not beg but I will if I must. Can I not just have this one time, this one moment alone with you?" she pleaded almost.

Paul clasped her hair and smelt the fragrance of the perfume she had in it and closed his eyes as he remembered Alisha and the smell of her hair. He knew in his heart that despite the promise he had made just some moments earlier that if he survived he would take Princess Stephanie without hesitation; but now as he lay cradled between her thighs, the physical act he could not commit to. Besides, Ishmael could appear at any moment. He wanted to make love to her but not in these circumstances.

"In my heart I have made love to you already, but...," Paul started to whisper.

"You are too honourable for I know it is in you to take me and that you want me. I know of no other man who would act as you. I envy her... Alisha," she interrupted quietly, looking at him sadly, her lips quivering as she fought to control the mix of emotions flooding her senses. A single tear fell from her eye. "But this night is mine and I shall forever remember it; for never have I been so terrified and at the same time so exhilarated as now." She looked at him in silence for several minutes intently before pulling him close and embracing him with a single gentle kiss and then hugged him, her face pressed against his as she started to cry softly. Paul took his weight upon his elbows as she wrapped her arms tightly around him not wanting or wishing to let him go. "There will come a time that is right... and know that I will be ready for you," she whispered.

Paul looked up as Ishmael silently but quickly entered the room with both swords drawn. He acknowledged their presence and seeing they were okay stood up straight and backed away.

Chapter 75
Cresson – Clash of the Wolves

Hospitallers' quarter, Jerusalem, Kingdom of Jerusalem, April 27th 1187

Paul moved on the edge of the wooden bench as Master Roger tied off the last stitch in his lower back. Gently he placed a gauze bandage against it and pushed himself away slightly upon the small wooden stool he was sitting upon. Paul looked at Ishmael stood with his arms folded in the corner of the room waiting patiently. The sun shone brightly off the whitewashed wall of the treatment room.

"There…you were very lucky the splinters did not penetrate deeper, though I am still concerned for the larger one…it may have punctured the lower part of your lung," Master Roger explained as Paul turned to face him. "So if you start to cough any blood, you must inform me immediately."

"Thank you…I am fortunate to have you on hand again," Paul replied.

"Let us not make a habit of this…and it is fortunate that Ishmael verified and confirmed your account. It matters not to me if you were alone with the Princess if accompanied by Ishmael as he states," Master Roger said and looked up at Ishmael and raised his eyebrows. Ishmael said nothing and showed no signs to give away the fact he had lied. "But you cannot take such risks again…for you will give Reynald exactly the excuse he wants. 'Tis why I am declaring you fit enough to travel with me and Lord Balian to Tiberias. That way I may keep an eye on you and hopefully out of trouble."

"'Tis not your responsibility to watch over me," Paul replied.

"Perhaps not, but I promised your father I would always keep an eye on you. Fear not, you shall accompany us," Master Roger stated, nodding at Ishmael, who simply nodded his head slightly in acknowledgment. Master Roger stood up and walked to the large wooden door which could be unhinged and doubled up as a makeshift operating table if required. "Now then, you have some guests requesting a brief audience with you. You must get some rest so keep it brief," Master Roger said and opened the door to reveal four Knights of Lazarus stood patiently waiting. He beckoned them to enter and once they had, he nodded at Paul and left the room, leaving the door open.

"Gentlemen…what can I do for you?" Paul asked and started to pull on a clean cotton robe, wincing as his lower back burned with pain when he moved.

One of the knights stepped forward offering a Knights of Lazarus white mantle emblazoned with its green cross for Paul to take. Puzzled, he looked at it unsure what he was supposed to do. He looked at Ishmael, who shook his head, just as perplexed.

"Sire…we understand that your commission will be served with the Templars soon…and," the knight started to explain before looking at his three colleagues briefly. "So…we were wondering if when that time comes, you would consider serving with us…for we are all agreed that we would be honoured to follow you."

Paul looked again at Ishmael, puzzled, and then back at the four knights stood before him. Outwardly looking they looked fit and healthy, save the bandaged hand on one and a small bandage wrapped around the head of another, but beneath their robes and mantles he knew they were in various stages of leprosy or other serious ailments. He stood up and looked at the mantle.

"But I am not afflicted with illness nor leprosy as you all endure… though it is a great honour to be asked…but why me?" Paul asked.

"You are as broken and as hurt as anyone of us here…if not more so," the knight at the rear of the group said quietly and stepped forwards. "We all share and feel the loss of your family for they touched us deeply…your wife, Alisha, especially. Truly an angel who walked amongst us. We know some wounds never heal…and your loss makes our suffering pale by comparison."

Paul felt instantly touched and emotional upon hearing his words. He gulped and went to speak but instead just stared at the white mantle being offered up to him. After a few minutes stood in silence he looked over at Ishmael.

"We also have a place for you too," the knight holding the mantle said directly to Ishmael. "Please, you need not make a decision now…but please consider our request."

Paul opened his hands palms up as the knight gently placed the mantle upon them. Alisha had looked after many of these men, including the far more seriously ill members as they lay dying. He shook his head lost for words as the image of Alisha filled his mind, of the time he saw her talking and laughing to a bed-ridden member of their order. He closed his eyes and held the mantle close and took a deep breath. The four knights slowly backed away toward the open doorway and part bowed as they each in turn left the room. Paul opened his eyes just as the last one was about to close the door.

"Thank you. 'Tis a great honour you bestow upon me and the memory of Alisha. She would approve," Paul said, his voice dry and full of emotion, tiredness from being up all night, the blood loss he had suffered beginning to finally catch up on him. His left shoulder hurt when he turned to look at Ishmael, making him wince in pain, the stitches pulling tightly. "Thank you," he whispered.

Ishmael stepped closer to Paul.

"I go wherever you go for as long as you need me," he said and placed his hand upon Paul's shoulder and looked him in the eye. "Now I must go and repair your shield."

₧₧

In his private quarters, Paul sat upon his bed just staring at the Knights of Lazarus mantle neatly folded and placed beside him. He recalled how Theodoric and his father had told him how the disciple Lazarus was the most favoured confidant of Jesus Christ for he was Mary's brother, hence why other disciples were envious of him and her. How he wished he could speak with them now. His own Templar mantle hung against the wall. It was torn and covered in both his and the lion's blood, his chain mail armour now at the blacksmith's being repaired. He shook his head wearily then reached below, pulled out his travelling trunk, opened it and removed both Alisha's three pronged dagger and his leather bound folder Stewart had rescued. Placing it upon his knees he ran his fingers over the folder whilst holding the dagger in his left hand. The scabbard was only very lightly fire damaged but when he flipped the small side panel, two acorns were still inside and untouched. He placed the dagger down and stared for some time at the folder, unable to open it. He recalled the night he stood with Theodoric on the balcony just prior to when Arri and Ailia had been kidnapped. 'Nothing physical lasts forever, only the love in your heart. If you never remember anything I have ever told you, always remember the most precious gift that ever comes to a man in this world is a woman's heart, and that what comes easy to us in life, won't last, but that which lasts won't come easy.' Paul shook his head, heavy with sadness...a sadness he felt would never leave him. How prophetic Theodoric's words had proved to be. He smiled briefly as he laughed to himself that he never would get the chance to ask about the connection between Sister Lucy and camels. If he had the chance he would return to their graves he told himself...but he would not recover the sword, he vowed. It can stay as a reminder like the sword of San Galgano and Durandal...perhaps that was always the intention for such swords he pondered. Memories of Sister Lucy flooded his tired mind. How stern she'd always looked yet had had a heart of pure gold. He remembered how she had told him he was artistic, insightful, gentle of spirit...but with a raw courage that would help him through even the toughest of times that would break the strongest of normal men. He certainly did not feel courageous, too fearful to even open his own folder of art and poems. He laughed momentarily as he recalled how she had slapped him hard across his face. A sudden rap at the door drew his attention and before he could respond, Stewart opened it and stepped down into his room.

"Forgive my intrusion, brother...but we have had confirmation of the lion you killed. Brothers Upside and Nicholas have just thrown it at King Guy's feet as a gift for Reynald to have mounted," Stewart explained and smiled. He could see the look of tiredness and sorrow etched deeply upon Paul's face. Quickly he knelt down on one knee in front of him. "My dear brother..."

Paul looked at him. No words could express how he was feeling. The deep emptiness that made him feel dead inside. But a flicker of light shone out from within him when he thought of Princess Stephanie. As he looked at his brother, he knew the dangers that were coming to all of them. He knew the battles that lay ahead if Reynald persisted in his actions. The Muslim men he had seen at the donjon in all their splendour and Saladin's wish to have a contingent of Muslim Templars. If that could be achieved, how many lives could be saved? Paul wondered…and his brother would be in good company if he was to become part of it. He ran his hand across the Knights of Lazarus mantle without realising it until Stewart looked down at it, puzzled.

"I cannot accept their offer…for I have another commission I must do first," Paul explained and with that stood up and placed his folder down upon the mantle. As he did, a small bible slipped out of the side. Paul froze as he stared at it. It was Sister Lucy's bible. Hesitantly he picked it up as Stewart stood up, even more puzzled. A marker was still inserted and Paul was surprised to see it was still set where she had left it all those years previously in La Rochelle when she had given it to him to read from 1 Corinthians 13: 'And now abide faith, hope, love, these three; but the greatest of these is love.' He gulped hard, reading the words again. "You know Stewart…I once swore I would protect Alisha…that I would always protect her…take three bolts through the heart as that would be preferable to living without her…and yet here I now stand having failed her," Paul said, turning to look at Stewart as tears welled in his eyes. "I can still feel her finger run down the scar on my face the day I swore that to her…so tell me, brother, how am I supposed to ever live with this pain?"

"Paul…I cannot answer that for I do not know," Stewart replied.

"You know she told me never to be ashamed of a scar…for it simply meant that I was stronger than whatever tried to hurt me…but this scar… in my heart and deep within my soul…it will never heal," Paul whispered emotionally.

"Then I pray you live long enough to see that pain heal…for I sorely have need of you in my life as do a great many others. I have been the worst of brothers to you, but I am also the proudest brother of you," Stewart said emotionally. He placed his hands upon Paul's shoulders and looked at him. "Honour me by staying alive, little brother…whatever it takes, for you are the best of all of us in every fashion. You shine like a beacon in the darkness showing all of us how we should be…or at least aspire to be, me included."

Paul gulped hard, surprised at his comments. Stewart's eyes were filled with tears as he spoke. Without hesitation Paul pulled him close and hugged him tightly thankful for both his presence and words. He thanked God he had him in his life still after all that had happened.

"Now that is truly a wondrous sight for old eyes," Philip suddenly interrupted as he stood in the doorway. Both Paul and Stewart pulled apart and stared in total surprise at seeing their father. He smiled broadly but his eyes could not hide the sorrow within. He stepped down into the room outstretching his arms. Both Paul and Stewart placed their arms around each other and Philip. In silence they just held each other, their heads together as they had done when young boys with him. Philip took a deep breath and sighed as he held his two sons in his arms once again. A tear ran down Paul's face as he held his father close and just for a moment he felt safe and as a child again. It was fleeting but comforting before the reality of their predicament flooded his thoughts again. Philip kissed the side of Stewart's head and then Paul's before pulling them close against him again. None of them sensed or saw Princess Stephanie look in on them before silently backing away.

Port of La Rochelle, France, Melissae Inn, spring 1191

"That is so incredibly sad. I assume Philip knew about the deaths of Alisha and all the others?" Gabirol asked.

"Aye that he did. He had also visited their graves prior to seeing Paul and Stewart. He had enlisted the help of Al Rashid to travel safely enough, plus signed warrants to pass unmolested by Saladin's forces as arranged via Ernoul and Count Raymond," the old man explained.

"Ah...so if he visited the graves, then he would have seen Paul's sword in the stone...and that's how it is now here," Simon interrupted.

"No he did not...for it was no longer there," the old man answered immediately.

"Gone! How?" the farrier asked.

"It had been taken already," the old man replied.

"Oh no...not by Turansha...or is that sword just the copy...the one the blacksmith did up as a replacement?" Peter asked, looking concerned.

"No...this sword is the original one and not the later one Paul used."

"Then who took the original from the stone?" Gabirol enquired, charging his quill again.

"Let me guess, you will come to that later," Simon remarked.

Sarah shot him one of her disapproving stares and scowled hard at him. The old man laughed lightly seeing her do this again.

"I shall indeed cover it later...but it was perhaps not whom you would think," the old man explained and looked at the sword.

"I wish to know how the acorns Alisha carried lasted so long and did not germinate or perish like acorns usually do?" the farrier asked, perplexed.

"All I can tell you is that they had been treated by Kratos years previously...that is all I know. It protected them and kept them viable until a time when eventually planted," the old man replied by way of a brief explanation, the farrier simply nodding his understanding.

Abbey de Notre Dame du Mont de Sion, Jerusalem, Kingdom of Jerusalem, April 28th 1187

Paul pulled up just behind his brother and father then dismounted Adrastos. It was early morning but the sun was already beating down fiercely. Paul held the reins tightly and patted Adrastos. It had been his first run out since injuring his legs. Philip dismounted and beckoned Paul over to look at the small abbey. Stewart remained upon his horse and looked back to see where the rest of his troop were. It was only a short ride from their headquarters, but after the visit to the abbey it was planned that they would continue on outside the city walls to meet Balian and escort him and his men in. Ishmael had volunteered to assist Abi in training up some female knights recently arrived. Paul looked up at the small abbey. He already knew its history from Niccolas, Theodoric, Firgany and his father. This was the abbey where the Templars were originally conceived of by the Prieure de Sion. Within minutes several Knights of Lazarus appeared alongside several monks from the abbey. Paul instantly recognised their robes as being identical to the long full length off white one worn by Theodoric for so many years. Stewart dismounted and as the monks took charge of their horses, Adrastos snorting, reluctant to be led away, Paul laughed to himself seeing how upset he appeared. Philip ushered Stewart inside the entrance lobby area and looked back ready to call Paul over. He stopped and just stared at Paul. Seeing him stood side on, tall and erect, he was suddenly overwhelmed with immense pride. Paul had suffered much yet still refused to be defeated in spirit. Having lost his own wife he knew exactly how he was feeling and the deep unending ache that went with that loss. But he also knew there was nothing anyone could do. He had heard the rumours of Princess Stephanie's affection toward Paul and perhaps in time he would find comfort and love again with her. He was thankful that many years previous he had not given into temptation when she had made advances to him. He laughed lightly to himself as he recalled those events. She was just a child of fifteen back then. He took a deep breath and stood himself up straight as he studied Paul watching Adrastos being led away to sheltered stables. Some dust blew up around Paul and he waved it from his face. In Philip's mind Paul was and always would remain his little boy. In that instant as he studied him he wished he could capture that moment and hold it in his mind forever. Before him stood not a boy, but a tall handsome and strong man, his Templar uniform and sword never looking more appropriate on an individual. Paul placed his hand upon his sword and turned to face him. He smiled and for that moment all Philip could see was his face and smile despite the pain in his eyes. He had many of Paul's drawings, but none of him. Somehow he would get Paul to draw himself. Paul was surprised to see his father just staring at him; his full length dark blue, almost black, robe stood out in stark contrast to the whitewashed walls of the abbey. Philip closed his eyes briefly and tried to burn the image of Paul into his memory and how proud he truly was of him, the emotion of that one simple look taking him by surprise.

"Master Fucking Philip," Master Douglas called out from the abbey as he appeared into the sunlight.

Philip turned around surprised to hear his voice.

"Master Douglas. I see and hear you have not lost any of your finer traits," Philip replied and faced him. Paul immediately ran over, keen to hear news of Percival and their search for Thomas and his men. "The years have been good to you."

"Not you, I see...what is with the outfit?" Master Douglas joked. "But My Lord...'tis good to see you, old friend."

"Aye and you," Philip replied and greeted him by placing their knuckles together in a clenched fist to form a square with their hands, then grasped each other's forearms tightly. "Truly great."

Paul looked at them as they smiled, clearly happy to see each other. They held their shake for some time before he stepped closer.

"Father...sorry to interrupt, but Master Douglas, where is Percival and have you found out anything...anything?" Paul asked.

"Paul, Percival is not with me. Fear not, he is not injured nor dead, but he refuses to return until he has learnt of the fate of Thomas and his men," Master Douglas replied and broke his shake with Philip. "He sends you a message. He will not return until he has found them…and he has your sword, which you must take back when he does."

"My sword…but how…how did he remove it?" Paul asked, puzzled.

Philip put his hand upon Paul's shoulder and looked at him.

"Percival is your cousin…the same blood of the Crimson Thread flows through his veins as yours…that is how."

"I…I did not think…I," Paul half blurted out, taken by surprise. It was obvious of course but it had never occurred to him that Percival would even try to remove the sword. He shook his head. "I do not want it back. Perhaps he is better suited to it."

"Horse shit, my friend…I think we all need to go inside and talk," Master Douglas remarked and beckoned with his outstretched hand for Paul to lead the way inside.

ഇരു

Stewart sat himself down hard against the whitewashed wall so Philip could sit upon the bench beside him. Master Douglas moved to sit opposite Stewart as Paul sat down opposite Philip. The room was small but cool. The single window set high in the wall streamed sunlight in. Incense burned away in a small ceramic tub filling the room with its pleasant aroma. One of the abbey's monks entered carrying a pitcher of previously boiled water now cooled. Quietly he placed it down upon the table along with four small blue glasses. Wearing the long off white robe the monk reminded Paul of Theodoric. He shook his head and sighed, remembering him.

   7 – 33

"So where exactly is Percival?" Philip asked Master Douglas, bringing Paul's mind instantly back.

"As of this moment I have no idea…but he travels alone and mainly at night. He is adamant that a mystery remains about the attack which took your family and friends…and the disappearance of Thomas and his men. I would have continued with him but I am afraid to admit it, but my age was slowing him down. 'Tis a young man's quest he follows…and he wanted me to pass on his message to you."

"I have never stopped thinking of that day and I have oft wondered if Thomas and his men were taken by God himself for having vanished so completely," Paul remarked.

"He also vowed that if ever there was a way that he could find a means to bring back your family, he would find it," Master Douglas explained quietly.

"Knowing Percival he would," Paul sighed. "But that is not a reality likely to happen in this life time. His quest I fear will be a long if not impossible one," Paul replied as Stewart nodded in agreement with him.

"No such thing as impossible," Abi suddenly said, stood at the doorway, her size blocking out the light. "Percival knows the saying...'impossible' when split becomes 'I'm possible'. If anyone can do it, he can," she explained with a broad smile as she entered fully into the room. "Ishmael is outside with a troop of female knights. I think he has found his calling," she joked and pulled up a single wooden stool and sat down at the head of the table. "Have I missed much?"

"No, I was about to speak of this place and its importance," Philip answered. "Plus what is required of both Stewart and Paul if they choose to."

"Ah, you mean the codes and such matters. Surely 'tis ended when Alisha and Ailia were slain," Abi stated and looked at Paul quickly. "Sorry, Paul, forgive my bluntness."

"No, not ended...changed yes but not ended," Philip replied. "But if you are willing to listen, I have much to tell you of this place."

"We have time so please tell us," Stewart replied and leaned forward, putting his elbows upon the table.

"My sons, then let me explain that the Prieure du Notre Dame du Sion, or Priory of Zion, or Priory of Sion, based here in this very abbey had its earliest roots formed within a Hermetic and Gnostic society led by a man named Ormus. He reconciled paganism and Christianity. 'Twas in 1070 that a group of monks from Calabria, Italy, led by one Prince Ursus, founded the Abbey of Orval in France near Stenay, in the Ardennes. I have mentioned this to you both before. Well, these monks formed the basis for the Priory of Sion, into which they were incorporated in 1099 by Godfrei de Bouillon. That is when the Order of the Temple, our Knights Templar and Sion were unified under one leadership, which is presently Count Henry of Champagne."

"And he has the official name of John, much like you once had...yes?" Paul asked.

"Aye that I once did. But I resigned from that position as you are aware."

"Why did you resign, Father?" Stewart asked.

"Because I had you two to look after…but also because I needed time to concentrate upon my works and ideas. Ideas that I hope will outlast any military or religious orders. I wished to construct in stone, across the whole of France just as those before me had started, and hide in plain view, the codes of antiquity that we must guarantee reach across time for the generation that will need it the most, when the fifth flight of the Phoenix begins," Philip explained.

"But how will future generations know or recognise what is hidden in plain sight?" Stewart asked, perplexed.

"Because our souls are eternal and many will remember and recognise the esoteric symbolism encoded within our cathedrals and churches we shall lay out across the lands. But as I now agree with you, Paul," Philip continued to explain and looked at him. "We need a new order that is open to all good men and women and not reserved exclusively for just men at arms and military orders. As you once told me, it must be made up from ordinary people where we can take good people and make them better. With enquiring open minds not restricted or hindered by religious fear and dogma. Made up from all walks of life. 'Tis something Count Henry also now agrees with."

"But men like Gerard will never agree to that," Stewart remarked.

"I think you will find he just might now," Paul replied.

"That is true," Philip said as he looked at Stewart. "He does not have the passion and ambition he once had. He is also wise enough to know that he does not have the mind for such esoteric knowledge and understanding. For that he must be given credit. But if he should refuse any such moves or continues to very publicly disobey the rule of the Priory of Sion and Count Henry's instruction, then the time rapidly approaches when Henry will have no choice but to sever the connection and cut the elm."

"I have heard of this cutting the elm during arguments between Gerard, Reynald and Count Henry but I know not what it means," Stewart said, looking more puzzled.

"My son, at the Prior's headquarters at Gisors in France, an elm tree was planted. It was written down within both Orders' statutes that should a day ever come when the military arm became too big, arrogant or uncontrollable, then the Priory of Sion would physically cut down that elm tree. It would mean that both physically and symbolically they were severing their ties with the Templars for good. It would mean that all the major secrets, documents and items held by the Order would be hidden away and no more would the upper initiates be granted access to or understanding of what it is the Order is charged with safe guarding."

"So it would only be in the hands of the members of the Priory of Sion?" Paul asked.

"To start with yes. But that is why much has been moved to Alba already in anticipation of such an event. From Alba many items will be moved to an island situated across the western seas in the New World as Tenno confirmed exists. Our Norse friends and several of our Order have already established the route and we have two islands named Oak Island. But only the island with the oak trees yet to be planted will mark the true one."

"Oak trees!" Paul remarked.

"Yes. Oak trees not indigenous to the lands in the west. Grown from acorns taken from the original Oak of Abraham. Once fully grown they will stand out as unique and a clear signal to those who know what they seek. Later generations will be able to confirm that the oaks grew from sacred acorns taken from here," Philip explained then looked at Paul intently. "So tell me, Paul, do you still have Alisha's dagger?"

"Of course I do," Paul answered and gently removed if from beneath his robe. Carefully he placed it upon the table as Stewart looked on. Philip smiled, but it was a smile masking the sadness he felt as he looked at it. "And it still contains two of the acorns placed within its sheath."

"Good, for that means we can at least still complete that task," Abi interrupted.

"Aye perhaps," Philip replied and looked up at her. "I can inform you more of the purpose of the acorns if you wish?"

Abi nodded yes he should just as Ishmael appeared at the doorway. Abi looked at Paul and he could see the deep pain that still registered in her eyes. All this time he had not even considered her feelings or how she was coping after the loss of Tenno. Her entire reasons for being in the region had all but been destroyed around her. She nodded at him.

"'Tis fine, Paul. You need not say anything," she said quietly as if she had read his very mind again. She squeezed his hand reassuringly. "The acorns at least give me some purpose again."

"What do you mean?" Stewart asked, shaking his head, becoming more confused.

Philip beckoned Ishmael to enter then faced Stewart.

"I was tasked by Kratos to remove bodies laid in La Rochelle, in Cougnes to be precise, and to take them to Balantrodach, to lay until a greater more sacred chapel can be constructed not too far away. This commission I have completed, as well as designs for that new chapel. It will take some time before it is completed, but many of the secrets we hold dear shall be incorporated within its design and construction as well as the harmonic codes. I shall also include clues that will lead to the Oak Island in the new world. But someone must travel there to plant the acorn seeds of Abraham's Oak," Philip explained.

"'Tis a charge I am happy to undertake," Abi said instantly.

"Where are your plans for all of this?" Paul asked.

"The plans for the new chapel are safe within La Rochelle. They also contain most of the details of how to relocate the sacred Chambers of Creation...of which you already know the location, but that I am afraid I cannot complete for only you have those final details."

"Yes and that is why I lost my family for I was warned not to commit the details to paper," Paul sighed.

"But you can commit it so long as it can only be understood by those worthy enough and learned enough to understand and break the codes... so long as you encode correctly in the first place. That was where I was supposed to help. And the final plans for Oak Island also reside within you...not me," Philip explained, looking at him intently.

"Me?...I think not, Father."

"Then you think wrong," Abi smiled and clenched his hand reassuringly. "Elek knew this too."

"You, my young son, are the Nautonnier, the navigator. 'Twas always meant to be you. 'Tis written upon your parchment no less," Philip explained.

"Father, no disrespect but they have been proven to be wrong...have they not?" Paul replied.

"Not wrong...perhaps confused. I do not know for certain but they have never been wrong before," Philip answered sincerely. "Every aspect as detailed within them has so far been accurate..."

"Even down to losing my family...for I did not see that written upon them," Paul replied. "They showed me with my family at the end of my days, yet first I lost Arri, then Alisha and Ailia...I no longer have faith or hold any confidence in what they claim."

Paul looked at Abi but she looked away. She could not confirm Philip's belief.

"Paul, 'tis how you read them that is in error perhaps," Master Douglas said looking at him. "Perhaps you will have another family. You are young and I know of one person already whose heart you hold in your hands."

"Stephanie," Stewart said bluntly.

"Is it that obvious to all?" Paul asked and looked at them all in turn. Ishmael was the only one to nod yes. "Well I am not the navigator for that is the designation for Count Henry as the Grand Master of the Priory of Sion...so not I."

"For now," Philip said and placed both of his hands over Paul's. "But whatever is meant to be is still down to you and your free will. You do still have a choice, just as mankind will be faced with a choice. 'Tis why the Phoenix we draw is done with two heads looking in two different directions. But when that time comes, that is when man must know the truth of his past, so that it can make an informed decision."

Abi turned to face Paul and nodded silently in agreement.

"And how do we make sure they receive that knowledge?" Paul asked.

"It has always been in clear view within the myths, legends and ancient religions as you know full well. But we have started a new beginning with clues left within and around the small village of Rennes-le-Château. 'Twas Theodoric's idea as it sat next to an extinct volcano that has many peculiar aspects about it," Philip answered.

"The Mountain of God," Master Douglas stated matter of factly. Paul looked at him quizzically as Stewart leaned closer trying to hear him better. "You can explain that one," he laughed, looking at Philip.

"Not heard it called that in a very long time," Philip said and sat up. "'Tis named Mount Bugarach, or Mountain of God. 'Tis a place shrouded in mystery, myth and legend with its peak majestically dominating the whole area around Rennes-le-Château. Some claim that looking upwards to the sky, the face of this dormant volcano was given the facial features of Christ by God himself when his only son was taken to the area. 'Tis no ordinary mountain and some myths state that it was placed there, upside down, after a great upheaval to hide a gateway to other realms within the earth. One day man will be able to prove this fact, but for us, I can tell you there is much hidden around the area. Some claim its name was Bourg-de-l'Arche or Buc-de-l'Arche in Occitan and referred to the legend that the

Ark of the Covenant lies buried inside the mountain where it still serves as some sort of beacon. When Theo and I climbed it, we heard many strange noises, even apparitions..."

"Such as?" Stewart asked, intrigued.

"Oh, such as bright white lights and even tall white people stood staring at us. I am sure Paul can relate to that," Philip replied and looked at Paul directly. "More than a few people have simply vanished upon the mountain."

"Therein lies a hidden lake," Abi interjected, drawing a look from all of them. "'Tis true. There is also a great underground network of caves with other lakes. I know for I once had reason to enter beneath it. There is even still a hidden chapel that awaits the time of the fifth flight of the Phoenix. Theodoric claimed he was informed by the people he knew in the Emerald Isle that it was one of many entrances into the fabled city of Agartha."

"What is Agartha?" Stewart asked.

"'Tis the legendary city inside the earth's core," Paul said without really thinking. Philip and Master Douglas looked at him, surprised. "What?"

"I have never spoken of this before. I am just surprised you know of it," Philip remarked.

"You must have for I know of it somehow. I also know the whole region is connected with many of the black Virgin sites. Niccolas taught me that, I am certain."

"That is a subject we will have to cover another time then, but yes, 'tis indeed connected to the black Virgin. But I can tell you that even the name Prieure de Notre Dame du Sion, and its headquarters site in Orval is connected to the worship of the bear-goddess Arduina, venerated by the Sicambrian Franks of that area and their Merovingian kings, it is all interlinked. Notre Dame is not, however, reference to the mother of Jesus, but to Mary of Bethany who as you know is Mary Magdalene, a princess of the tribe of Benjamin, which was itself notorious for an outbreak of goddess-idolatry in the period of the Judges in the Old Testament. That Mary is also known to the Gypsies of the south of France as one of the three *Maries-de-la-Mer*, whom they call Sarah the Egyptian, the sun-burnt one."

"The one who travelled to France sailing in the rudderless and sail-less Stella Maris," Paul stated. Stewart shook his head.

"I know so little of any of this," Stewart said and shook his head again. "Yet the very road our home is built upon is named so. Hidden in plain sight!"

"But all of this aside, Father…even if Abi or I go to the New World, how will we find it?" Paul asked.

"I have maps already drawn. Remember when Tenno first arrived? Well, he brought with him new maps which included detailed outlines of the coastlines. We now know both Reynald and Uma Turansha wanted those very maps too. We have already written upon them and marked them as Nova Scotia. A simple image of a knight stands upon the area but not the island itself, though Kratos informed us the very shape of the island is identical to the outline of the ancient city walls of Jerusalem itself. 'Tis one of those islands as named Oak Island that the acorns must be delivered to. Men work upon the island even now as we sit here…but there is also an even older legacy that awaits hidden there."

Paul immediately recalled images and conversations he had had with Kratos on the matter. He realised in that instant that Kratos had been planting the seeds of knowledge he knew he would eventually piece together. He shook his head slightly and sighed. He recalled how Kratos had hinted at a staff used by the ancients similar to his own, that if Paul chose one particular path, as he always had a choice, he may be given the staff, though it was more like a small wand in reality. It was a wand used by Jesus as documented and known by the popes, but its authenticity deliberately suppressed by them.

"Where is this staff or wand now then?" Ishmael asked.

"Perhaps nearer than you all think," Abi answered then shook her head and looked at Philip. "But 'tis not allowed for us so do not even try to locate it…just concentrate on the new chapel and the island site."

"But if that site can be found, then surely men will dig up whatever is hidden there," Stewart remarked.

"No…that will not be possible," Abi stated bluntly and leaned forward. "Paul has the final key to the structures that are being made ready. Any future generations who discover the site before its time will all fail…just as they would with the secret Chambers of Creation in Egypt. They would flood and other dangerous matters would unfold. Only when the earth moves, and the island itself is raised will it become accessible."

"How do you know this?" Stewart asked.

"Kratos…wherever he is," she replied and lowered her head momentarily. "That is why despite the life within me wishing to depart this world, I cannot until these tasks are completed, for if not, then if the crimson stream is not continued, it will mean nothing in the end."

Philip placed his hand upon hers and smiled reassuringly, sensing her deep pain.

"Then what of the new chapel you speak of in Alba?" Paul asked.

"That will fall to the hereditary lords of what will be known as Rosslyn Chapel, the very name revealing its origins, as Theodoric knew and explained. The new chapel will hold all the keys, save for two final symbols hidden elsewhere, to unlocking many mysteries and will point to a fortress presently being constructed within the New World. It will in time confirm the connection between Rennes-le-Château, Rosslyn and Oak Island," Philip explained.

"And it all started here?" Stewart asked as Master Douglas smiled and nodded yes.

"Re-started would be a better way to explain it," Philip replied. "You are both aware of the myth, or theory depending upon what you believe, that *Christ* had descendants who moved to the south of France. I am certain Theodoric explained this on more than one occasion."

"He certainly did that...and where they originally landed at Roussillon, before moving on," Paul remarked.

"Some argue it was Marseilles but we know different. Well 'twas then that they intermarried with the royal Franks to found the mystical Merovingian Dynasty. The long haired Fisher Kings no less, and you are already aware of all the esoteric symbolism behind the Fisher King aspects so I need not repeat it now, suffice it to say that one of the real missions of the Templars and Priory of Sion was and is to safeguard genuine hidden secrets from antiquity, but also that very bloodline...the Crimson Thread or Crimson River, or stream that still flows. It has oft been written as 'Sangraal' or 'Sangreal', which translated as 'sang real' becomes and means 'royal blood'. In other words: the dynastic legacy of Christ, literally. That is why the Merovingians were considered in their day to be mystical warrior-kings vested with supernatural powers."

"'Tis why only their blood allows them to wield such items like Kratos's staff...but also the sword you had," Abi interrupted.

"That Percival now holds," Paul commented.

"For now, yes he does. But it belongs to you whether you wish it or not," Philip explained and then looked at Stewart."

"No...'tis not a burden I could carry. I am hopefully wise enough to know that," Stewart quickly replied and raised his hands.

"The Merovingians trace their ancestry all the way back to the Benjamites who, according to legend, fled from Israel to Arcadia in Greece, which eventually led to King Dagobert the Second and the Merovingian dynasty," Philip explained further.

"The Order of Sion was founded in the 1090s by Godfrei de Bouillon himself, who was one of the leaders of the First Crusade that recaptured Jerusalem. 'Twas this Order that lay behind Hugues of Champagne and the founding of the Templars."

"But why if that is so were you once the navigator if it was a hereditary role?" Paul asked, puzzled.

"Because originally it was not exclusively a direct lineage hereditary role...it was one that had to be afforded to the best suited so long as the crimson line flowed within their veins, as it does within ours," Philip answered as Abi agreed.

"But is the purpose of protecting this line purely for power later or something else?" Stewart asked.

"Good question," Philip said and smiled at him. "'Tis not for power. But for the recovery of man's true past and to reveal his true potential and inheritance for all to share. Officially to the lower initiates the objective of the Priory of Sion is the eventual restoration of the Merovingian dynasty and bloodline to the throne of not only France, but to the thrones of other European nations as well. By machinations of dynastic alliances and intermarriages, this line includes Godfrei de Bouillon, and various other noble and royal families, past and present."

"That includes Reynald's believe it or not," Master Douglas interjected and started to pour himself some water. He looked up at the others indicating if they wanted any. Paul nodded he did. "'Tis why the man feels he is destined to do as he does."

"Please," Philip said to Master Douglas and pushed his glass toward him. "Godfrei was, by legend, a member of the so-called Grail family, and by lineage a Merovingian and, apparently, rightful King of Jerusalem by his descent from David. He was aware of this and had in his possession ancient maps and directions written upon bronze and silver plates that gave directions to a greater treasure once hidden beneath Jerusalem. When he left for the First Crusade, he sold all of his property for he intended to stay in Jerusalem. Godfrei was close to de Payen and the count of Champagne, and Baudoin, his brother, was integral to the founding of the Templars."

"So you could say Godfrei de Bouillon was a sort of 'king of kings', or at least a maker of kings, since he founded the Order of Sion that could crown Kings of Jerusalem," Master Douglas stated.

"'Twas at the express command of Godfrei that here, to the south of Jerusalem on this high hill of Mount Sion, that this abbey was built upon the ruins of an old Byzantine basilica. As you will see later this abbey is well fortified with its own walls, towers and battlements. And this structure is called the Abbey of Notre Dame du Mont de Sion," Philip detailed and sat back against the white wall.

"There is more I can tell," Paul said quietly.

"I best sit," Ishmael said and pulled up one of the other single stools nearby. He folded his arms once he had sat down. Philip looked back at Paul then Stewart.

"Yes there is and so much of it. I can but scratch the surface this day and tell you the very basics," he remarked and clasped his hands together. "All across France we have set out a whole set of new chapels, fortifications and cathedrals. Cathedrals you already know of and others planned. As an example the castles planned for Bezu, the Château of Blanchefort and Rennes-le-Château are each located on mountain tops. Together, with the high spots of two other peaks, the locations form a perfect pentagon, of five equal sides, some fifteen miles in circumference. Rennes-le-Château and many of the churches across the land are and will be dedicated to Saint Mary Magdalene. Now let me explain that early astronomers saw the earth as the centre of the universe, around which the sun, the stars and the planets revolved. Each planet forms its own pattern of movement around the sun as seen from the earth. For the ancient watchers of the heavens, those differing patterns of movement allowed them to draw geometric shapes based on the positions of each planet when it was aligned with the sun. Only one planet describes a precise and regular geometric pattern in the sky and that planet is Venus, the heavenly counterpart of the earthly Mary Magdalene...and the pattern that she draws as regular as clockwork every eight years is a pentacle. We have thus aligned all churches, calvarias and castles to form an intricate web of alignments which intersect with perfect regularity on the zero Paris meridian. The distance covered by three of those divisions is the circle radius measure. Each point is separated from the next by exactly one third of 933.586 poles!"

"What is a pole?" Stewart asked.

"A pole is a unit of measure, also known as the rod or perch, of 5.5 yards. All of the measurements and placements of the buildings follow the patterns of the sacred geometry. This all leads back to the esoteric theories of Hermes, who was Thoth, the ancient Egyptian of writing, knowledge and wisdom and all connected with alchemy, the Ark of the Covenant, Tree of Life and the Qabalah," Philip explained.

 3 – 17

"No wonder Gerard has chosen not to follow these details," Stewart joked and rubbed his head.

"'Tis also all related to the sacred boat of Isis, that stellar barge that was positioned in the constellation of Argo. Jason and the Argonauts is but a later updated version of the very same story with identical codes contained within it. But in Egypt this constellation was named Sothis or Soth-Isis, the Star of Isis. The Egyptian legends also have this vessel representing the female organ of generation. The Ark of the Covenant of the ancient Israelites is believed to have been modelled after the ceremonial ark of Isis but also the dimensions of the sarcophagus within the Great Pyramid. Understand that Hugues de Payens, our first Grand Master of the Knights Templar, had been inducted into the Johannites, a sect which chose John the Baptist as their prophet. 'Tis why all Grand Masters of the Order take the name of Jean, as in John, out of veneration and respect," Philip explained, Abi again nodding in agreement with him. [113]

"It was explained to me before about the symbol for the constellation of Virgo being laid out across the whole of France," Paul remarked quietly as he thought back upon that earlier time.

"Ah…only now does it start to make sense. The reference to remembering 'O most gracious Virgin Mary' within in our initiation ceremony," Stewart remarked.

"Then remember that it was Firgany who all along was ultimately responsible in helping us understand the codes and geometry required to set the cathedrals and churches out across France," Philip said and smiled at Master Douglas.

"I do recall most clearly that even the great Notre Dame cathedral has been designed and laid out all based upon Virgo, the rose and other sacred measures," Paul said and paused briefly before continuing. "'Tis why the

French Royal house adopted the 'fleur de lys' as their personal symbol and insignia though the actual symbol of Osiris was the 'fleur de lys', of which I now know was certainly instigated by you and Theo," Paul remarked, looking directly at Philip.

"We helped point out the value and symbolism of the fleur de lys, that is all," Philip answered and paused briefly. "You see, Theo and I once tried to form a new order, not unlike that which you now propose to safeguard such secrets. 'Twas also another reason why Master Douglas and I parted our ways but also why Theo eventually took himself away," Philip said and looked at Master Douglas.

"Well 'tis all behind us now. Perhaps now it is time to restart the 'Brothers of the Ross Cross' as once hoped," Master Douglas replied. "We drew the five petal rose surmounted by a further eight if I recall, symbolising the value of fifty-eight."

Stewart looked at Master Douglas bemused for he was aware of the value fifty-eight being used within his initiation ceremony but had never bothered to look into the matter further. Only now as he listened to them all speak did he begin to realise just how much he did not know and had missed out on.

"We shall have to continue this conversation after we have met Lord Balian I am afraid to say," Stewart remarked and moved to stand up.

Paul thought back to Theodoric's dream of starting a new Order but said he would not live long enough to see it happen. Perhaps now, and with the request to form a new Order complete with Muslims his dream would come to pass. He also recalled all the other connections with 8 and 58 and how he had told him one day he would understand the meanings behind all the values he had taught him. Now he knew all about the value for 64, the 8 x 8 grid and 5 to 8 ratio grid set around the Giza pyramids, the head 58 connection as carried over into the Templars' initiation ceremonies. The 26 degree angle from the Great Pyramid and how it all pointed and led to the location of the area where Sirius was projected upon the ground, directly over the sacred chambers of creation. He put his hand upon his sword as he recalled details he had learnt about the 'Sword of Orion' and Excalibur and its mathematical value being the same as the side length of the Great Pyramid. He took a deep breath as the enormity of what that actually all meant registered in his mind with a clarity of thought and knowing that he had not felt before.

"'Tis time, for Lord Balian will be here soon," Ishmael said quietly and gestured for Paul to stand.

Port of La Rochelle, France, Melissae Inn, spring 1191

"We know Lord Balian set out from Jerusalem for Tiberias, but he never reached us," the Templar remarked and clenched Miriam's hand.

"Paul as ordered went with Stewart and his squadron to greet Balian, who was both surprised but also very pleased to see him," the old man explained. "He was very saddened to hear the news confirmed about the deaths of Alisha and the others. He was glad to hear that Paul would be accompanying him onward later to Tiberias to help in negotiations with Count Raymond. He knew his friendship would help greatly."

"What of Philip. Did he accompany them too?" Gabirol asked.

"No for he would only be in the way he told them, though in truth he stayed behind to speak with both Reynald and Gerard about unfolding events. He wished to convince Reynald to cease his hostile actions but it was to no avail," the old man replied.

"Why?" Ayleth asked.

"Because Reynald simply did his usual rants of quoting selected passages from the Qur'an where it states true believers and followers of Islam must expand their religion, subjugate all non-believers and convert or put them to death."

"Oh, just like us then," Simon half joked, the Templar actually nodding in agreement with him.

"In many ways yes indeed. But before Paul left for Tiberias he entrusted the safe keeping of his journal and artwork to Princess Stephanie as well as Alisha's dagger. Abi stayed with Philip," the old man explained then smiled. "And he got his wish for Paul agreed to draw himself for his father. He used Princess Stephanie's finest mirror to do it." The old man paused and looked at Gabirol and Paul's folder in front of him. "If you look, you will find his self portrait. 'Tis simply signed 'Paul'."

Quickly Sarah pulled the folder toward her and opened it. She pulled out most of the drawings and parchments in one handful and started to splay them out across the table as she eagerly looked for his drawing. She froze when she found it and stared open mouthed at the image. The old man smiled at her appearance.

"May I see?" Ayleth asked and moved to stand beside her. "He is truly handsome. Just look at those eyelashes. More than any woman would be proud of." She smiled as she studied the image. "So that is Paul."

Fig. 69: Paul's Self Portrait.

"Aye 'tis indeed," the old man replied and nodded. *"You looked so surprised, Sarah."*

"'Tis exactly as I had pictured him. Uncanny...unnerving in fact," she answered and sat herself down still holding up the picture.

"'Tis him for sure," the Templar said leaning across to see the drawing. *"No mistaking him. When Lord Balian was due I was split from my brother and sent to Belvoir castle. Last minute orders sent ahead by Master Roger. 'Twas a strange set of orders I must confess,"* he explained and sat back down.

"'Twas a deliberate order arranged between Philip and Master Roger to ensure your safety. By separating you and your brother, your family line stood a greater chance of surviving the impending calamity they all knew was to come," the old man explained and looked at him then the Hospitaller. The Templar let out a small laugh and shook his head.

"So even back then our fates were being set?" he stated and looked up at the old man.

"Well I for one am very glad they looked after you and kept you safe," Miriam said with a broad smile, raised his hand and kissed it.

"Why did Balian and Paul never reach Tiberias then?" Gabirol asked.

"Due to the actions of Reynald yet again. Though there is much debate even to this day to the exact circumstances that unfolded at the springs of Cresson. 'Twas a water crossing point that both sides would oft use to rest, let their horses graze on the fresh fields of grass and water themselves," the old man explained and paused as he thought to himself for several long minutes until Simon coughed. *"Lord Raymond still had a truce in place with Saladin at the time, and Reynald's actions have been seen as a constant independent provocation towards Islam, which is true of*

course, yet in Reynald's mind and as he argued to Gerard and King Guy often, his actions were to try to prevent Saladin from moving his forces north to take control of Aleppo, which would have strengthened Saladin's position. Any excuse to undermine Saladin's prestige, reputation and position and Reynald would take it. Some will of course even to this day argue that his actions were purely selfish, self serving and ultimately fatal for Jerusalem, but others will counter that argument that it was actually shrewd strategy shown by Reynald...but I can tell you exactly what happened," the old man explained then looked toward the folder and nodded. "Look further and you will find a drawing Paul did of him. I know not when or where he drew it but it is there...it has his name upon it," the old man answered and smiled.

Fig. 70.

Jerusalem, Kingdom of Jerusalem, April 29th 1187

Balian held his horse's reins tightly preparing to mount when Paul walked past leading Adrastos to the rear of the column. Stewart was already in position with Brother Upside and Nicholas positioned on either side of him. Stewart unfurled the Order's Beauseant standard as Nicholas secured a second rolled up one. It was a practice Gerard had introduced – should the first standard ever fall, the second one could be immediately unfurled. The column comprised Templars, Master Roger and a squadron of his Hospitallers, who made up the vanguard, a contingent of Knights of

Lazarus and most of Balian's knights and sergeants. In total they numbered just over fifty knights and a further two hundred men at arms on foot. Gerard approached already riding his mount. Despite the rising morning temperature, all knights were in full fighting order, including their horses with covers. Paul caught sight of Princess Stephanie looking on from across the courtyard accompanied by her maids, her son Humphrey and Brother Teric. He could clearly see the concern in her eyes as she stood and watched the column prepare. King Guy had made it very clear he did not wish for Paul to return to Jerusalem but to stay in Tiberias. He had not had the chance to even say goodbye to her properly but he knew he would see her again. One of her trusted maids had passed on a verbal message to him that when he passes the Sea of Galilee he should remember that it is heart shaped and to know that her heart is his. He nodded toward her and she took a deep breath. Balian looked across at her then back at Paul.

"Paul…Reynald watches you," Balian said quietly.

Paul looked at Balian as he nodded toward Reynald approaching on horseback.

"Oh Lord…is he coming too?" Paul asked.

"Yes. Reynald insisted and the king has agreed, so that he may convince Raymond to side with him. I urge you great caution, my friend. So please join Master Roger and his men if you will," Balian said and mounted his horse.

Reynald rode close to Paul and looked down at him staring hard but saying nothing. Gerard pulled up beside Paul and winked at him and indicated he move into position. Quickly Paul mounted Adrastos. Adrastos being a larger horse than Reynald's horse, Paul looked down at Reynard as he turned around and rode alongside him briefly. Reynald scowled at him hard, which made Nicholas laugh from behind. As horses snorted and men made ready, King Guy approached on foot surrounded by several Templars and Confrere Knights, some very brightly dressed. Gerard gestured for Paul to fall into position. Stewart smiled at Paul and motioned for him to move. Just as King Guy was almost at the front of the column, Paul turned Adrastos around and began to trot him toward the end of the column. Princess Stephanie took a deep breath, the sadness of seeing him about to leave tightening a knot in her stomach. She grasped at her stomach and followed him with her eyes, Reynald staring hard at her then toward Paul.

"Do not let anything stupid happen to my sons," Philip suddenly interrupted as he stood in front of Reynald and Gerard. "My King," he then bowed slightly as King Guy stopped beside him. Reynald and Gerard steadied their horses and looked down at Philip. "You have but one simple task... to secure agreement with Lord Raymond. Nothing more and nothing less. Once completed Saladin will be made aware and he will not prosecute his actions further. I am sure the king agrees with this as discussed last eve."

"You do not give me orders," Reynald replied, looked back quickly to check the column was formed and ready to leave.

"'Tis what was agreed, Lord Reynald," King Guy confirmed, which surprised Reynald and he frowned even harder. "We must have Count Raymond on our side."

Master Douglas approached on foot walking fast and stopped beside Philip. He looked at King Guy then down the column in time to see Paul pull up at the rear.

"You got your wish then, Sire," Master Douglas said and pointed toward Paul. "You would be as wise to have kept him here for you will need men like him to defend this city."

"He turns his back upon me when I approach and shows me no respect, much like you, Master Douglas, for neither do you show me the courtesy of bowing when you see me," King Guy replied.

Master Douglas stepped toward King Guy, who immediately took a step backwards.

"My King. I thought you more a man who knew the mannerisms and behaviour of men at arms. Fighting men need not bow to show their loyalty and respect to their lords and kings for that respect is already earned and acknowledged...but if it pleases you," Master Douglas explained as King Guy took another step backwards feeling intimidated, his eyes looking back and forth at Reynald and Gerard in turn.

"Douglas," Philip said.

"Of course...my great and noble Lord King," Master Douglas said and bowed forwards in an exaggerated fashion and held his head very low, his right arm up high to show he held no weapon and stayed in that position.

Gerard found it hard to hide his amusement and King Guy looked up at him. Reynald shook his head disapprovingly but likewise smiled at Gerard before looking back at the king.

"Master Douglas, you may stand away from the king now," he ordered.

Master Douglas stood up straight and stared at King Guy. He raised a single eyebrow.

"Then go…I bid you all the Lord's protection," King Guy said awkwardly.

Reynald bowed his head, raised his right hand and ordered the column to move. Philip smiled and nodded at Stewart as he rode past him, Reynald and Gerard leading the way out of the city. As dust began to kick up and men and horses filed past, Master Douglas stood beside the king closely. He winked down at him and folded his arms. Princess Stephanie walked over and stood beside Philip. Together they watched on as the column rode by, Paul riding beside Master Roger. Princess Stephanie's eyes met Paul's and they looked at each other momentarily.

"I shall take very good care of your sons," Master Roger called out to Philip. "As I always do," he then smiled.

Princess Stephanie instinctively clasped Philip's right hand for reassurance as Paul rode out of sight. Master Douglas nudged King Guy in the arm with his elbow hard.

"Impressive aren't they?" he remarked and smiled almost menacingly. King Guy stepped away from him rubbing his arm. "Oh I am sorry, I forgot my place. Not allowed to touch the king's personage are we? Just make sure you remind us of that fact should the time arise in battle when I need to haul your arse out of the shit."

"Master Douglas, if you would be so kind as to escort Lady Stephanie," Philip interjected.

"Of course. Much more preferable," Master Douglas replied with a large grin and ushered Princess Stephanie away, turning his back on the king.

King Guy stamped his foot down and clenched his fists hard. He pursed his lips in anger lost for words and action.

"My Lord, my sons serve you and despite what you may think, they will serve you well," Philip began to explain. "And Lord Balian will I am sure negotiate Raymond back to us."

King Guy shook his head then turned around and pushed his way through his entourage angrily. Brother Teric winked at Philip as he walked toward him.

"Paul would do as well to remain in Tiberias as the king commands. Too many have whispered in Guy's ear that Paul is rightful heir to the thrones of all the kingdoms and you know what rumours are like out here," Brother Teric remarked.

"'Tis why I must have both my sons returned to France. Back home where they belong," Philip answered and turned to see Master Douglas leading Princess Stephanie away, his arm around her shoulders. He laughed to himself for no other knight would even dare such a move. He would pray both Stewart and Paul would remain safe and that Lord Raymond would rejoin with them and recognise King Guy if only for the safety of the kingdom and to avert war.

"They will be fine," Abi suddenly said off to his right as she stood behind him. He had not even seen or heard her approach. "All else may seem wrong, but that much I do know," she reassured. She looked down at Philip and placed her hand upon his shoulder. "I have done a lot of meditation and consulting of the stones and though I am unable to sense Kratos, I do know the plans that Paul has started, those to which you now subscribe too, will come to pass."

"Abi, I am glad to see you have regained your sense of purpose and direction. Your words give me strength for I fear I too have almost reached the end of my understanding and faith of all that we have tried to achieve," Philip answered solemnly.

"The Crimson Thread will carry on. There are other ways and others who can and will help to achieve this. Both Paul and Stewart have other offspring to come...I know this for I have seen it," she smiled reassuringly.

Philip took a deep breath and looked toward the main entrance gates as they were shut, just the rising dust remaining from the column's passage.

ℰℭ

Paul looked back as they rode away. Ishmael had asked to stay with Philip and Abi. He gave no reason why and Paul did not push him to explain. Master Jakelin pulled up alongside him and smiled as he moved to ride with him. Adrastos snorted as if to greet him. Paul patted the side of his neck. Apart from his father and brother, Adrastos was the only remaining constant he still had from his life in La Rochelle. Both Alisha and Arri had ridden him and now all he had were memories of them. He closed his eyes briefly and tried to picture them both and Ailia. He had failed to protect them as he had promised Alisha. He could never undo what had happened but perhaps, just perhaps, he could initiate the new Order and new church he had seen with Alisha. If such an order could be made then it would surely stop so much of the violence and misunderstanding between all religions. He shrugged his shoulders and shook his head immediately dismissing his own idea as naive and deluded. An impossible ideal he pondered, but then perhaps not so impossible. He recalled how great and noble Firgany was, Tenno and Theodoric as well as the many others he knew and admired, both Christian and Muslim alike. When he looked forward he could not see Stewart as the front half of the column was already shrouded in dust and dirt being kicked up. Master Jakelin started to tie his headdress around his head to cover his mouth. Paul did likewise and looked upward at the clear blue sky above them.

"Lord spare me this unending pain within my soul and I shall find a way of continuing the codes…and give you your new Order," he whispered.

"Count me in on that," Master Jakelin said, overhearing him, and reached across to pat him on the shoulder. "We have dire need of such, trust me," he smiled and then covered his mouth with his head cover.

"You would have many join you," Master Roger suddenly said as he pulled up alongside his right side. "You whisper too loudly, my friend. But talk we must before we part."

"Yes, Master Roger, we must. We can do so at Tiberias undisturbed I am sure," Paul replied.

"That I doubt for I am to leave you before we reach Tiberias. Balian must also attend a gathering so you will head on a day before he arrives. Just make sure Reynald does not lose sight of his mission and orders when he sees Lord Raymond."

Paul looked at him, puzzled, having assumed they were all travelling together to see Count Raymond.

Port of La Rochelle, France, Melissae Inn, spring 1191

"Why did Ishmael not go with Paul then?" the Templar asked.

"Why…well you all seem to have forgotten that it had been Reynald's men who years previously had slaughtered all within Ishmael's village and thrown his son from the cliffs. Reynald had not recognised him due to his disfigurement but the desire for revenge within Ishmael had slowly burned deeper within him with every sighting of Reynald. He had vowed to protect Paul always, but to follow and serve

Reynald alongside Paul was something he did not trust himself to do. He knew that given the opportunity he would have his revenge and try to kill Reynald, which would only endanger Paul directly. Abi had sensed the growing ill ease within Ishmael and so it was that he stayed behind with Philip and her," the old man explained.

"So the group split up and that is why Lord Balian did not reach Tiberias in time to speak with Raymond," the Hospitaller remarked and shook his head, bemused.

"What meeting did Balian have to attend first that split the column up?" Peter asked.

"Let me explain then, for it matters as history unfortunately tends to forget the actual facts and believes all too often the later fabrication of events," the old man replied and shuffled briefly in his chair to get comfortable. "'Twas a simple fact that Lord Raymond, due to the heliograph network and communications network still being compromised, was not made aware that the full delegation of Gerard, Reynald, Grand Master Roger and Balian was en route from King Guy to talk peace with him...but as soon as Count Raymond found out, he immediately sent word to warn them that he had already approved for Saladin to send a reconnaissance party through his lands as per his truce still in force with him at that time. 'Twas more out of concern for Balian, Master Roger and Paul though, and not for Reynald of that I can assure you. 'Twas on the eve of the thirtieth of April that the column split so Master Roger could check on his other knights in the area and Balian could honour a previous arrangement where he had vowed to attend a celebration. If he did not, he risked offending many of his own knights under his command. By this time Saladin had indeed ordered his son al-Adfal to send an envoy to Count Raymond of Tripoli requesting safe passage through his fiefdom of Galilee and Tiberias. Raymond was obliged to grant the request under the terms of his treaty with Saladin as I have said. And so Saladin's force left Caesarea Philippi to engage the fighting force of the Knights Templar they knew was en route to seek peace with Raymond for their network of spies and communication was still very much in operation. King Guy had done the one thing Saladin had not expected him to do."

 8 – 1

"What was that?" Sarah asked, puzzled and listening intently.

"He had split his forces and sent Reynald out to speak with Raymond direct. This left Jerusalem in a very perilous position for defence," the old man answered.

"We knew that up until that time, Raymond had allied with Saladin against King Guy and allowed a Muslim garrison to occupy his fief in Tiberias. There was rumour that Saladin was going to help him overthrow Guy. We knew Saladin could now do this for he had pacified his Mesopotamian territories, and was now eager to attack the crusader kingdom to sort Reynald out once and for all. We all already knew he would not renew the truce when it expired," the Templar explained and sat up looking uncomfortable. "'Twas something none of us had any control over."

"And Reynald knew this due to his constant actions and breaking of the truce. He knew full well it meant Saladin would have no choice, having forced his hand, so when Saladin started massing his troops, this just served to justify even further in Reynald's mind, to attack even more Muslim caravans claiming he was actively disrupting Saladin's forces," the old man explained and took a sip of rose water before continuing. "King Guy at least had the sense to realise that by then the whole kingdom would need to be united in the face of the threat from Saladin, and that is why he ordered Balian to go and effect reconciliation between the two."

"But we were told the king only agreed to that after many of the leading barons, dismayed at Saladin's troop movements supposedly in support of protecting Muslim pilgrims, persuaded King Guy to seek the reconciliation with Count Raymond. That is what I was told whilst we held out in Tiberias," the Hospitaller remarked.

"Indeed that is in part correct. Balian, Grand Master Roger, the Archbishop of Tyre, Reynald and Gerard, however, took a leisurely pace towards Tiberias. The envoy from Al Adfal arrived at Tiberias with the message from Saladin politely asking his friend, Raymond, to allow a Muslim reconnaissance party to cross his land. It stated Saladin wished no harm to Raymond but wanted to reach King Guy's Royal Domain around Acre. Not aware of the approaching delegation of Balian, Raymond of course agreed on condition that they return the same day. But the Muslim party passed beneath the walls of Tiberias and headed west. Gokbori commanded them along with other Turkish emirs including Qaymaz al Najmi with his squadron from Damascus and Dildrim al Yaruqi with men from Aleppo. When Raymond finally learnt that a delegation from King Guy was actually en route to him, he sent a warning party to them but by then Balian and Gerard had separated from the delegation having stopped and agreed to catch them later at La Feve (Al Fulah). Once Gerard learnt about the large Muslim reconnaissance force, he immediately summoned all Templar troops in the region just as Master Roger did bringing together an extra ninety knights from the castle at Caco (Al Qaqun). Gokbori and many of his troops by then were already camped at the Spring of Cresson and had been since April the twenty-eighth. It was Brother Upside and

Nicholas who scouted ahead and confirmed Gokbori's forces were already camped there," the old man detailed as Gabirol charged his quill and Simon leaned further across the table eager to hear.

"But where was Paul all this time? Was he with Balian or Reynald's men?" the Templar asked.

"He was with Reynald and Gerard's men. They also had Princess Stephanie's son, Humphrey of Toron, join them. On the thirty-first of April Paul accompanied Gerard to fetch more secular knights from Nazareth whilst Reynald kept an eye upon Gokbori's men. Any excuse that the Muslim force was a simple trading pilgrim one was immediately dismissed as it was too well defended," the old man said and paused for a minute, licked his dry lips and continued. "As night fell at Reynald's encampment not far from Ayn Juzah, that is the Springs of Cresson, they readied themselves, Paul arrived back with Gerard and many more knights almost at the same time as Master Roger arrived strengthened by his other knights. Paul was not impressed to learn that Humphrey of Toron would be mentored by him personally. 'Probably Reynald's sense of humour,' he thought. As you can imagine Reynald was in a great mood and eager to engage with Gokbori...and Paul could not help but wonder if the attack Reynald was planning for the morning was the one he had dreamt of so many times, when the Red Wolf, Reynald would fight with the Blue Wolf, Gokbori. The only thing missing from his dream being the twin hill tops that looked liked horns."

Springs of Cresson (Ain Gozeh, near Nazareth), County of Tripoli, May 1st 1187

Paul checked the straps around Adrastos just as the sun was breaking over the horizon and trees but shrouded behind a dewy haze. Horses snorted and men coughed as they woke themselves up. A cold mist hung around their feet from the wet grasses. The valley was green and fertile and one of the main reasons so many used the area for resting. Just a few short miles away Gokbori's forces were doing just the same. Stewart put his hand upon Paul's shoulder and leaned in close. No fires had been lit during the night so as not to compromise their position and Paul had already eaten his dry breakfast biscuits. Humphrey looked totally lost as he stood alone shivering. Paul felt quite sorry for him and hoped for Princess Stephanie's sake he would be all right and survive whatever lay ahead, especially as Reynald had charged Paul with his protection. Maybe Reynald hoped Humphrey would get killed just to hit back and hurt her further.

"Brother…if we engage Gokbori this day, promise me you will stay alongside Master Roger and Master Jakelin within the rearguard. If all goes horribly wrong you will see quickly enough, and you will have time to save your charge," Stewart whispered and looked at Humphrey, who out here in the field was clearly out of his depth.

"Fear not for we shall be right beside them at all times," Nicholas said as he stepped into view leading his own horse already prepared for the day. "We shall need to move soon if we are to catch Gokbori whilst the sun is still low or he will see us coming a mile away."

"If Reynald decides to attack that is," Stewart replied.

"Reynald knows we are outnumbered heavily, but he will still choose to attack. Trust me for I know him well enough by now," Nicholas remarked.

Raised voices echoed out from Reynald's tent as sergeants and turcopoles were already packing away the camp. Paul looked over in time to see Master Roger throw the tent opening cover aside and rapidly walk out, clearly angered despite the low light. Reynald came rushing out after him and pulled him around.

"Unhand me or so help me I shall leave and take all of my men with me," Master Roger said, uncharacteristically angered. Reynald released his grip just as Gerard stepped out from the tent. "'Tis madness. Even you must see that? Their numbers are far greater than ours and I can guarantee we do not have the element of surprise for I wager they already have men with their eyes upon us this very minute."

"Master Roger…this is exactly why I loathed working alongside your knights all these years," Reynald sneered. "With or without you and your men, I intend to engage and stop Saladin's plans…and you can leave us, to save your pretty blonde hair to comb another day."

Paul looked at Nicholas, bemused, as Stewart moved to see and hear better. Gerard looked at the men nearby all listening as Reynald was clearly goading Master Roger.

"Gentleman…the men hear you. It will not bode well if they see that we are not united as one. But if we are to attack, then I insist we do so immediately without delay or hesitation whilst we have the initiative and element of surprise. Even if he knows we are here, he is not certain of our numbers for many arrived under cover of darkness. Nor would he expect us before the sun is fully up," Gerard explained quietly and looked at Master Roger directly. "My knights will charge first. My remaining knights will follow up in the rearguard with your knights...and if we do not break their lines, then by all means do not engage but report back to the king immediately."

Nicholas grabbed hold of Paul's arm.

"Paul...if I die this day, promise me you will bury my remains within Castle Blanc under the lemon trees," he whispered.

"What...you will not die this day," Paul replied, surprised.

"Paul...'tis ten years since I sat in that lemon grove with Alisha...when she carved your initials upon the tree no less. Ten very long years ago. I can think of no finer resting place...and after what I saw last eve, the numbers we face are greater than seven to one. It will take a miracle for us to defeat Gokbori for you know what kind of a man he is. No, Paul, I fear this day could see the end of many of us."

'Ten years,' Paul thought to himself and looked at Nicholas knowing he was thinking of Alisha at that moment. Recalling the events in the brothel Paul laughed briefly to himself, how upset and frantic Nicholas had become when he thought he had lost him. He was drunk but it showed and proved his genuine concern for Paul. Master Jakelin approached adjusting his chain mail and tightening his sword belt. Gerard looked at him and proffered his hand to look at Master Roger.

"Tell him...tell the Grand Master we must attack now," Gerard spoke.

Master Jakelin stopped and looked at him, puzzled, then to Master Roger.

"If we are to attack, then yes it must be now," he explained but then took a step closer to both of them. "However, I agree with Master Roger...'tis a great folly and unacceptable risk My Lords."

"Horse shit!" Reynald scoffed and wiped his arm across his face. "Gerard, your men cannot surrender or withdraw unless outnumbered three to one...so by the time we have completed our first charge that will be about the right balance. Saladin's forces must be stopped and now. If we do not they will, surely as that sun is rising, be in Jerusalem within the month."

"'Tis your call, Sire, but I wish it to be noted that I do not agree with this assault," Master Jakelin replied and stood up straight.

"Then it is decided...call your men to arms...all of them," Reynald ordered, looked hard at Master Roger then turned to walk back into his tent.

"Damn...I still haven't learnt the words Thomas challenged me to learn from his language of the forests," Nicholas remarked.

"Then do not die this day, my friend," Paul replied.

"Nor you, little brother," Stewart said as he walked by leading his horse. "And Nicholas, I pray you do not need that," he stated and pointed to the furled up spare Beauseant standard flag rolled up and fastened to the side of his horse.

Brother upside looked at it then at Paul and Nicholas.

"Well if he does, then we know we are in deep shit balls deep, my friend," he joked.

೫〇〇೩

Slowly Paul steered Adrastos into position behind the main squadron with Humphrey pulling alongside him but slightly to his rear. Tree tops were visible above the thin layer of mist that was clearing fast. The open plain before them was flat open grassland leading to the edge of the shallow river crossing point but no one could see where the stream started because of the mist. As the turcopoles and infantry moved quietly into position on either side of the mounted knights, the Templars making up the front spearhead of the fighting formation, Master Jakelin pulled Paul backwards to move further to the rear and beside Master Roger. Humphrey followed without a word. In silence the knights put on their full face helmets, whilst Reynald's knights wore a mixture of full face and nasal protective open helmets. Paul was worried for Stewart as well as Nicholas and Upside at the centre of the front of the squadron now practically indistinguishable with their helmets on. He prayed the assault would be swift and decisive. They readied their lances and shields. They looked an impressive and frightening sight.

"If that mist does not lift fast we will have no idea how Reynald's assault will go," Master Jakelin whispered.

"Then be ready to follow immediately," Master Roger replied and looked around himself at his knights forming up. He lifted his full helmet up and positioned it upon his head. As he adjusted the straps, his knights began to put on their helmets. Paul checked his black and yellow head bad, momentarily recalling the day he had received it from his father back in Cairo, and was just about to lift his full face helmet to put on, but before he could even lift his chain mail coif into position a shout went up.

"Stand fast together, trusting in Christ and in the victory of the Holy Cross!" Reynald shouted out as loud and as aggressively as he could, raised his sword high, then pointed forward only just visible to Paul. A large cry went up as the whole squadron of Knights Templar lowered their lances forwards and began to charge screaming out the same battle cry. Caught by surprise, Master Jakelin threw his helmet down and drew his sword quickly as Master Roger pulled his shield into position across his left arm, drew his sword and raised it.

"Charge!" he shouted.

Before Paul could put on his helmet or even drawn his sword, Adrastos was already being pushed along by all the other horses around him with Humphrey almost riding into him. As Paul struggled to gain control of Adrastos, his helmet fell away to the ground and it immediately became clear the knights and sergeants on horseback were already leaving the foot soldiers behind as they vanished into the mist going further than Reynald had anticipated. The noise of the horses and men yelling was met by battle horns being blown by Gokbori's men. Paul looked ahead at the shadowy figures of men on horseback as they engaged men on the ground but the majority of the spearhead squadron just vanished off towards Gokbori's men.

"We need to wait for the infantry," Paul called out and slowed Adrastos as the entire rearguard of Hospitallers rushed past him, only Humphrey stopping with him still fumbling with his own helmet. Quickly Paul looked back at the infantry desperately trying to catch up, the sodden river bank and wet grasses slowing their progress further. Paul's attention was immediately drawn back toward the river crossing as the clash of metal on metal and wooden shields filled the morning air. Men and horses started to scream out as Reynald's knights and the spearhead of Templars ran directly into Gokbori's main force of men who were waiting ready for them.

Gokbori had seen Reynald's men approaching via scouts positioned in the tops of the trees. He had deployed Dildirim al Yaruqi's troops from Aleppo to take the brunt of the initial charge and to hold their ground. As soon as Reynald and Gerard's knights engaged Dildirim's troops, most parted to let the lead element pass straight through them but then closed back in rapidly to stop the main group dead in its path by large pole spears and scythes cutting into the horses' front legs. Many were immediately pulled from their horses. As the mist appeared to lift fast, Paul saw Master Roger lead his troop directly into the fight just adding to the number of knights now being surrounded. Paul was now the only knight amongst the infantry who were desperately trying to catch up. Humphrey looked at him the fear in his eyes evident. Paul saw Stewart thrust his lance into the chest of one of the opposing mounted Muslim cavalry as they entered the assault, then lift the Order's Beauseant banner higher and start waving it around whilst hitting out with his rapidly drawn sword at attacking infantry. Without hesitation Paul rode Adrastos toward him as fast as he could, Humphrey trying to follow him. Paul drew his sword and pointed it forwards, his heart beating so fast, desperate to reach Stewart in time as more men surrounded him. Nicholas turned his horse around and rode back toward Stewart as Upside rushed to follow. Most of Dildirim's men had simply parted when Reynald had led the charge through their lines, forcing most of the spearhead knights to simply run straight through. It was a simple tactic and Reynald knew of it but in his eagerness and over confidence he had completely ruled out the possibility that Gokbori would use it here at the stream crossing. As they regrouped and turned ready to re-engage back into the main assault, Gokbori and Qaymaz were already bearing down upon the melee leading a counter charge with sword and spear. Reynald was clearly visible with his white headdress tied around his head and not wearing a helmet fighting alongside Gerard slashing and hacking everything that was moving around them, the Muslim infantry, in a carefully practised manoeuvre all quickly ran away from the knights after a single loud horn had been blown. Master Roger pulled up his horse beside Gerard, puzzled, just as a hail of arrows was loosed in their direction followed by many crossbow bolts being fired into the area horizontally turning the area they were in into a killing zone. The sky momentarily turned grey with the number of arrows in flight. Quickly Reynald, Gerard and Master Roger raised their shields above their heads as they tried to dismount at the same time. But for many of the mounted knights it was too late as the arrows and bolts rained down upon them, screams of agony filling the morning air. As Paul charged forwards he could see the unfolding carnage and that they were being totally surrounded. Humphrey focused upon Paul too afraid to look elsewhere. He did not even draw his sword.

Several Muslim crossbow men with their backs toward him moved to form a line and knelt ready to take aim. Paul turned Adrastos toward them fearful they were aiming at Stewart still waiving the Beauseant banner. Luckily for Stewart, Upside and Nicholas, they had not been in the centre of the killing zone. Master Jakelin quickly remounted his horse and struck two Muslim cavalry men with a single blow as they charged past him. Master Roger saw Paul and immediately jumped back upon his horse. Many of the knights caught in the main fusillade of arrows and bolts lay motionless, dead with multiple hits, others crawled on the floor injured amongst the many dead and dying horses only to be seized and jumped upon by Muslim infantry who immediately stabbed them with their sabre swords. Paul looked behind him in time to see many of Gokbori's cavalry charge directly into the Latin force's infantry whilst more Muslim horse archers rode around them firing arrows into the infantry from all sides. Several Hospitallers rode up beside Master Roger and started to defend him, hacking and thrusting their swords wildly at Muslim foot soldiers and Cavalry alike. Paul had to look away and concentrate back on Stewart. Master Roger saw where Paul was riding toward and quickly turned his mount to follow him. Reynald pointed to Stewart surrounded by infantry and cavalry, still waving the Beauseant banner. Gerard followed his gaze and the moment he saw Stewart's predicament, he remounted his own horse, threw off his helmet and sped toward him knocking Muslim infantry aside with his horse and sword, Reynald immediately following him. Just as Paul and Humphrey reached Stewart one of the Muslim infantry men thrust a lance upwards towards Stewart's back but Paul just managed to swing his sword down upon it hard, breaking the lance. As it shattered he pulled Adrastos up hard and swung his sword back down across the man, taking off his arm at the shoulder, his blood spurting out in a large red gout of colour that splashed across Humphrey's face and chest. Another Muslim infantry man went to throw his lance at Paul but he used his shield to knock it aside and thrust his sword down straight into the man's throat. Stewart spun around to look at him just as he was hit around the side of the head by a Muslim cavalry man wielding a large mace; the loud clang of metal hitting his helmet echoed out loudly. Stunned, his eyes wide, Stewart looked at Paul through the slits of his helmet and he seemed to freeze in that position before finally falling forwards off of his mount onto the ground. Instantly two Muslim infantry stood over him and raised their swords about to thrust them into Stewart's back. Without thinking Paul barged Adrastos into them and struck the one nearest to him with his sword across his neck, the man's head flipping up into the air followed by a grotesque trail of blood. Humphrey gagged and nearly threw up. The other infantry man went to stand but before he could get to his knees Paul jumped from Adrastos, punched the man backwards with his shield then thrust his sword into the man's chest. Despite wearing chain mail, Paul's sword passed straight through the man, the look of surprise more than pain stared back at him. Paul used his foot to push the man away and free his sword. The air was filled with screams and calls for help. Paul knelt down and rolled Stewart over and quickly removed his helmet. He was covered in blood and it was impossible to see where he was injured or whose blood it was. Quickly he checked to see if he was breathing. He could not see or hear if he was. Nicholas suddenly jumped down beside him as Upside stood the other side of them protectively and held back other infantry as they pressed home their attack. Quickly Paul lifted Stewart and tried to get him to stand. Humphrey suddenly rode off fast toward Reynald some distance away on higher ground.

"You will never lift him with all that weight he's wearing," Upside shouted through his helmet as he struck down another infantry man.

Paul grabbed Adrastos's reins tightly and pulled him nearer. Master Roger appeared with a few of his remaining knights. Quickly Paul lifted up the banner and passed it to Nicholas. Paul looked at his eyes through his helmet slits and he winked acknowledgment. Without hesitation he raised it just as Reynald and Gerard rode up close now with Humphrey between them. A Muslim horse archer rapidly approached and aimed his arrow directly at Paul. Master Roger saw this and threw his shield at the approaching archer causing him to let his arrow loose high. But he still kept coming. Master Roger dismounted and stood beside Paul as he struggled to lift Stewart. Paul looked up in time to see Master Jakelin on horseback striking several Muslim infantry approaching them. But as he turned to head toward them, a Muslim cavalryman ran at him, lowered his lance and, despite Master Jakelin taking evasive action and turning his horse violently, and using his shield to deflect the lance, he only succeeded in forcing the lance downwards straight through his thigh and into his horse. The horse reared up in pain and let out a loud shrill scream of pain, but Master Jakelin remained upon his horse as he was now firmly pinned to it. Reynald hesitated as he looked around the fields on either side of the shallow stream now running red with blood. More Muslim cavalry were heading directly for them whilst many more infantry rushed in amongst the Latin infantry men. Greatly outnumbered it was immediately clear they were being mercilessly slaughtered.

"'Tis hopeless. You must escape now whilst you can," Master Roger shouted, looking up at Reynald, who saw Gokbori slowly moving toward him and their group.

Paul looked up and saw him approaching too. He gritted his teeth and with all his might lifted Stewart up and bodily threw him across Adrastos.

"Go! Get him out of here now!" he shouted at Reynald.

Master Roger grabbed Paul's arm.

"You too must leave for I promised your father I would look after you," he explained, his face suddenly going pale, his eyes widening. He gulped hard and slowly turned to reveal a large crossbow bolt in his back. He turned to look at Paul again. "'Tis my time but this day is not yours," he said, clearly in great pain. Before Paul could reply Master Roger turned around and waved his sword defiantly. "They are going to charge so you had better leave now!"

"We must go...to fight another day," Gerard shouted and grabbed the reins of Adrastos. "Get on Master Roger's horse and follow us!"

Reynald looked once more toward Gokbori as he started to ride faster towards them, his sword now drawn.

"There are at least three hundred on horse...now leave and I will follow," Paul shouted and patted Adrastos hard but he would not move. "Adrastos... GO!" he shouted and slapped him harder.

Immediately Adrastos started to move, being led by Gerard. Reynald looked down at Paul. They were all covered in blood.

"I will buy you some precious time," Master Jakelin said as he steadied his pained horse. "For we are truly undone this hour. Paul, go with Brothers Upside and Nicholas now," he ordered and without giving them the chance to respond, the lance still protruding from his leg, he started to charge toward the oncoming Muslim cavalry.

"Quickly, you must follow Reynald and make sure he gets Stewart away. I will follow," Paul shouted as Upside mounted his own horse as Humphrey immediately raced off after Reynald and Gerard.

Upside nodded at Paul and quickly set off after them but then stopped to look back realising that Nicholas was not following. Nicholas tried to manoeuvre his horse to mount it but it was hit by several crossbow bolts. As he tried to steady it Master Roger readied himself for the onslaught that was about to overwhelm them. Nicholas's horse made a gurgling noise then dropped to the ground dead catching Nicholas and twisting his leg beneath its belly. Paul instantly stood over him protectively. Upside started to ride back when he noticed an entire line of horse archers make ready and aim high. The arrows would blanket the entire area where Paul, Nicholas and Master Roger were positioned. He removed his helmet and watched in horror knowing there was nothing he could do. Paul waved him to leave. Upside could see Nicholas struggling to free himself from beneath his horse. Master Roger picked up his shield and threw it at Paul. Quickly he laid it across Nicholas just as the arrows were loosed off. Upside watched on wide mouthed in shock as his eyes followed the flight of the hundreds of arrows. Paul threw himself over Nicholas and pulled up his own shield upon his back to protect his head. Just as the arrows thudded into the ground all around them, hitting the dead of both sides and the horses with a sickening sound, one arrow hit Paul's shield and burst through just missing the side of his face. Paul looked into Nicholas's eyes as they just froze.

"Today we shall see Alisha and your family again," Nicholas remarked.

"Aye that we shall, my friend. I am honoured and proud that I shall pass from this world side by side with you," Paul replied.

"Despite what I did?"

"'Tis all in the past. I know the good Lord will not punish you for loving her."

 1 – 17

Nicholas grabbed Paul's hand tightly and gripped it. When the arrows stopped falling, Paul was amazed to sense he had not been hit anywhere. He turned to look back at the approaching cavalry charge just in time to see Master Jakelin make contact with the group at full speed. He wielded his sword ferociously, causing Gokbori to move aside, just as Master Jakelin cut the forearm off of one of the Muslim knights then thrust his sword into the chest of another, but as the rider continued forwards, he lost his grip on his sword. He went to turn around but a lance pierced straight through his stomach and out of his back. He grabbed it, pulled it out and started to thrust and wave it about. Several more blows rained down upon him, one slicing across his chest with such force it cut straight through his surcoat and chain mail. A single crossbow bolt suddenly struck him beneath his chin just under his helmet strap stopping him instantly. He looked forward to see Paul kneel up, Master Roger slowly staggering back toward him with several arrows sticking out of him. Master Jakelin forced a smile defiantly, closed his eyes and fell backwards, dead but still pinned to his horse by the lance through his thigh.

One of the Muslim knights yelled out 'Allah Akbar' and the mounted cavalry led by Gokbori started to charge at full speed toward Paul, Nicholas and Master Roger.

"Well, boys…it has been an interesting journey. It shall be even more so on the next journey," Master Roger said looking down at them.

Paul was amazed he could still be alive with the amount of arrows stuck in him. His blonde hair was covered in blood and he was unrecognisable as the kind gentle man who had first attended to him back in La Rochelle. Master Roger staggered on his feet to turn and face the oncoming charge. He steadied himself and gripped his sword with both hands. 'Such a waste,' Paul thought with sadness heavy in his heart. Paul lay down over Nicholas and pulled Master Roger's shield over himself. He briefly looked at the black eight-pointed cross with an inverted yellow seashell in its centre before looking up in time to see the first horse reach Master Roger. He swung his sword sideways cutting into the horse's leg causing it to fall immediately throwing the Muslim knight off forwards. Quickly Master Roger swung his sword to his left catching the leg of the knight of that horse. He then quickly fell to his knees as a third horse reared up in front of him. He thrust his sword upwards into the horse's chest. Paul watched on as the horse fell dead upon Master Roger and he vanished from sight. Paul looked behind to see Upside still looking on, but at least Reynald and Gerard were nowhere in sight with Stewart and Humphrey. Paul lay down flat and covered his head again with his own shield. He prayed that Stewart was alive for the sake of their father. At least if Stewart survived then perhaps the Crimson Thread would continue through him, he told himself.

"My friend…this is truly it this time," Paul said. "If you see Alisha first and lay a finger upon her I will cut your balls off." He then laughed. Nicholas laughed back and held Paul's hand tighter.

"Never thought I would die trapped beneath a horse," he replied and started to laugh more.

They both laughed louder as the noise of the rapidly approaching cavalry charge bore down upon them. Paul briefly heard the thud of horse's hooves striking Master Roger's shield but he did not even hear the final crushing hoof as it struck his own shield covering his head and everything went black.

℠)Ↄ

Gokbori stepped carefully through the dead and dying strewn across the stream and field. The mist had cleared revealing the full extent of the carnage. Women and children were busy picking their way through the dead looking for loved ones or items they could recover and take. A Muslim woman sat cradling her dead son and wept over him almost silently. She looked up at Gokbori through her tear filled eyes. He sighed and shrugged his shoulders looking sad. He shook his head as he looked around in dismay at the sheer number of dead from both sides. The battle had been a close one indeed and but for Reynald's infantry being so far back from the knights, and despite the overwhelming numbers against them, they had fought so fiercely and aggressively taking many of his men with them that they could have won the day. It had been the archers who had been the deciding winning factor, though that meant nothing to the mother holding her dead son now. Gokbori had ordered that his men look and check to see if Reynald and Gerard were amongst the dead but clearly they weren't. He turned and looked back toward the small clump of dead horses where Paul and Nicholas had been overwhelmed. Master Jakelin still lay back upon his horse pinned by the lance holding him there. His horse stood beside Nicholas's dead horse. Two civilians went to pull Master Jakelin down.

"No!" Gokbori shouted and immediately started to walk toward them. He had known Master Jakelin personally and admired and respected him greatly. He was saddened to see him dead in this fashion but also smiled knowing that Jakelin was still being defiant, even in death holding his position. "He attacked us with just 130 knights and around 370 infantry and turcopoles. What was he thinking?" he asked aloud as his secretary followed close behind him checking numbers off a parchment sheet. The smell of the dead and iron from all the spilled blood, and bodies, many with their bowels exposed from deep wounds, filled the air with a heavy stench. "Well, Red Wolf of Kerak, it appears your claws were clipped this day."

Chapter 76
The Candle is Lit

King Guy's palace, Jerusalem, Kingdom of Jerusalem, May 2nd 1187

King Guy paced up and down, agitated, his long golden silk robe flowing back and forth wildly with every turn. He constantly bit his thumb nail as Queen Sibylla sat in silence, her hands placed across her lap. It was now early evening and long white lace curtains that hung between the tall vaulted columns of the room were being drawn across them. A trail of dripped blood led across a large detailed and colourful blue carpet directly to the feet of Gerard, who was sat upon a reclining chair. He winced in pain as a Hospitaller surgeon struggled to cut away sections of his chain mail chausses, the end of a broken off crossbow bolt still protruding from his thigh. His beige mantle and surcoat were covered in blood but not his own. In the assault Gerard had not even realised he had been shot until he was half way back to Jerusalem. Reynald entered the room also covered in blood but uninjured carefully carrying a bowl full of hot water. Two maids were trying to help him but he was insistent on bringing it to his friend himself. The hall was full of other Confrere Knights and court officials stood in silence eager to hear news of what had happened at Cresson.

"'Tis but a scratch, my friend," he said loudly as he approached and placed the bowl beside Gerard on a small wooden table, knocking aside a bowl of dates.

"My army, 'tis all but gone! How could you do this to me?" King Guy snapped angrily.

Philip entered the room looking fierce and rapidly walked across the room toward Reynald ignoring both the king and queen.

"Where are my sons?" he demanded, his fists clenched. Queen Sibylla stood up and rushed over to him. "WHERE!" he shouted. Reynald took a step backwards surprised at the anger in Philip's eyes. "Answer me now or so help me I swear this day you will leave this world," he fumed and immediately drew his sword, the tip of his blade instantly thrust up beneath Reynald's chin.

Reynald looked at Gerard for support but he simply raised his eyebrows. When he then looked at the king, he just turned his back on them all and shook his head.

"Your elder lives," Reynald finally answered and raised his hands slightly in a submissive gesture. "We managed to rescue him from the battle. He is hurt but we know not how badly and he is within the hospital being treated right this moment."

Queen Sibylla placed a reassuring hand upon Philip's forearm and looked at him intently. She feigned a brave smile but Philip did not look at her, remaining focused on Reynald.

"And Paul...what of him?" Philip demanded, his voice laced with menace that unsettled Reynald.

"I fear he is dead...for we saw his position totally overrun as he shielded Brother Nicholas. I am sorry," Gerard interrupted. Philip looked at him hard.

"No....no, dear Lord, no," Princess Stephanie suddenly said aloud as she walked in from behind one of the lace curtains. She cupped her mouth feeling sick, a knot tightening like a vice in her stomach. Tears immediately welled in her eyes.

"At least I saved your useless son Humphrey as well as yours," Reynald remarked bombastically and sneered still staring at the tip of Philip's sword.

"Stewart is far from useless," Gerard stated and went to stand but grimaced in pain, the Hospitaller forcing him to sit back down.

"I did not mean he was...just Humphrey," Reynald replied and sneered even more at Princess Stephanie. Philip held his sword close to Reynald for several long minutes as he pondered his next move. Princess Stephanie slumped into one of the chairs and buried her face in her hands and started to sob, unable to hide her pain. "Who do you weep for, wife...your son's safe return or the loss of Paul?"

Philip pushed his sword closer to Reynald and as he went to move backwards the stone arch column behind blocked him from doing so. Philip's eyes narrowed.

"Philip...come. Let us check on Stewart," Queen Sibylla said quietly and placed her hand upon his sword and tried to lower the blade. "Please," she pleaded quietly. Eventually Philip stepped back in silence and quickly re-sheathed his sword. Princess Stephanie looked up at him, her face covered in tears. When Philip turned around to leave, she quickly jumped up to follow him. Reynald went to grab her arm but Queen Sibylla stepped in front of him. "I think not. You need to stay here for you have a lot of explaining to do."

"How many knights do we still have at Qaqun and al-Fulah?" King Guy demanded to know as Philip left the room followed by Princess Stephanie. "And tell me again, why did Balian stop at his fief of Nablus?"

"None, My Lord…for we already took them with us," Gerard answered as Reynald scowled at him, shaking his head. "And Balian had to attend a feast celebration he had vowed to attend previously."

King Guy raised his hands in despair and shook his head.

"Balian…probably warned off by his friend Saladin in advance I suspect…but we still have our Royal Knights stationed at Nazareth, don't we?" he asked.

Gerard looked at Reynald for a moment in silence.

"I am afraid, My Lord, we also had them with us…the only full contingent we still have is the female squadron of knights," he finally explained and shook his head, still looking at Reynald.

"Then the kingdom is surely lost…I must speak with the Patriarch Heraclius immediately," King Guy bellowed. "Lost…all is lost!"

"My Lord, do not underestimate the abilities of the female squadron," Gerard remarked.

King Guy just looked at him, utterly bemused. He shook his head several times, unable to think of a response. Queen Sibylla quietly left the room to follow after Philip and Princess Stephanie.

℘☙

The door to the treatment room opened with a loud bang, thumping into the wall as Philip flung it open. His face fired with anger and concern he looked around the four bed room. Humphrey sat on the nearest bed being looked over by a Hospitaller sergeant. Princess Stephanie pushed past Philip as soon as she saw her son and knelt at his feet grasping his hands tightly. He was still wearing his full uniform and covered in blood, but like the others it was not his. The remaining beds were empty except one in the right hand corner curtained off. Quickly Philip approached and flung back the curtains and gasped when he saw Stewart sat up, awake and having a head wound stitched closed. He was stripped of his uniform and wore just a white cotton night robe. Stewart's eyes opened wide full of emotion as Philip moved fast and sat on the bed beside him putting his arms around him tightly, the Hospitaller having to stand away quickly leaving a stitch half completed.

"By the Lord's mercy you are alive," Philip said emotionally and hugged him even tighter.

"Father...Paul," Stewart coughed as tears welled in his eyes both at the loss of Paul but also the display of outward emotion from his father. "I saw him go down, Father, alongside Nicholas...they were utterly over-whelmed."

Princess Stephanie pulled the curtain back further upon hearing Stewart's words. She fought to control the sickening feeling that was building up inside of her. Stewart just looked at her as more tears filled her eyes. She shook her head no in silence as Philip refused to let Stewart sit back. She stepped closer, her eyes pleading with Stewart to say differently but he shook his head again no. She gulped hard just as Queen Sibylla came in and stood beside her. Princess Stephanie coughed and gagged almost being sick. Quickly she rushed over to a wooden pan and threw up in it. Philip started to sob quietly as he continued to hug Stewart. Suddenly the entire curtain around the bed was flung open by Abi with Ishmael by her side. Princess Stephanie coughed as she tried to clear her throat, sick and tears smeared across her face but she did not care. She fell to her knees and buried her face in her arms resting across the bench seat the pan was positioned upon. She began to cry uncontrollably as Humphrey stepped closer and looked on awkwardly unsure what he should do. Abi placed her right hand upon Philip's shoulder.

"We have only just heard...is it true we have lost Master Roger and Master Jakelin too?" she asked, looking at Stewart. He could not reply, his throat dry and full of emotion but simply nodded yes to confirm. "And definitely Paul?"

Princess Stephanie looked up when she heard her ask this. Again Stewart just nodded yes silently. As Princess Stephanie lowered her head, sobbing, Ishmael closed his eyes briefly and took a deep breath. Philip just held onto Stewart. Brother Teric entered the room and looked at them. He shook his head with sadness but stepped back out of the room in silence. If Paul and Nicholas were also dead, he needed it confirmed, he told himself. He would seek permission to ride under a white flag to visit Gokbori and request the release of their bodies.

Port of La Rochelle, France, Melissae Inn, spring 1191

"Paul...dead!" Ayleth said quietly and held her hand to her mouth.

Sarah pulled the drawing of Paul closer and studied it.

"Did Brother Teric seek and get permission then?" the Templar asked.

"Oh yes he did ask and Gerard granted him that permission. Brother Upside and a small contingent of the Knights of Lazarus went with them," the old man replied.

"I wish to know why Balian was not in attendance. Was it because he had been forewarned by Saladin?" Peter asked.

"In truth Balian did have a previous engagement. He had vowed to attend at his fief of Nablus as I explained previously. Though when news did reach him he was still a day's travel behind having stopped at Sebastea to celebrate a feast day there. When he reached the castle of La Fève, where the Templars and Hospitallers had camped the day before, he found the place deserted. He sent his squire Ernoul ahead to learn what had happened, and news of the disastrous battle soon arrived with the very few survivors from the infantry. Balian was a man of his word...and besides they had not expected any trouble at that stage of developing hostilities. He would have reached Tiberias at the same time as Reynald if they had not attacked Gokbori at Cresson."

"I know Balian sent his scribe Ernoul to investigate immediately and he confirmed the scene at Cresson...of the many thousands of arrows that were evident everywhere," the Templar remarked.

"'Twas a massacre. But after Balian had heard of the full extent of the disaster at Cresson, he immediately went on to Tiberias along with the Archbishop of Tyre and explained what had happened to Count Raymond," the old man began to explain. "Nearly five hundred Christians were killed in the battle, the field strewn with thousands of arrows fired by both sides as Ernoul had confirmed. Raymond was shocked to hear that Reynald, Gerard and just a handful of knights and infantry had escaped. His immediate fear being that Saladin could now just as easily be forced by his own lords to turn on him despite the friendship and truce between them. There was much debate and confusion just exactly how many men Gokbori

had that day for he had entered the region with over seven thousand men, but there was no way of confirming that many were actually at Cresson. Either way, Reynald still lost over 130 knights and 370 infantry and turcopoles," the old man detailed.

"We were all informed it was indeed in excess of seven thousand men they faced that day," the Hospitaller stated, his brother agreeing with him.

"Gerard certainly argued at the court that there had been seven thousand Muslims and passed many scathing comments about how, previously, Count Raymond and King Baldwin had fouled up in battle that led to the death of Master Odo de saint-Amand in 1179. He argued this in defence of their own actions I suspect. But the debacle at Cresson galvanised Raymond into action and he immediately set off with Balian for Jerusalem despite Saladin having sent troops to support Raymond against King Guy as they were friends...and many in the court kept repeating this fact. When Raymond arrived at the king's court Gerard suggested that he should go and live in the Nizzari Ashashin state and castles for he was known to be friends with Al Rashid too. But it was during these arguments that Reynald yelled at Count Raymond often and loudly trying to shout him down. Raymond responded that if people like him were not so arrogant many lives could have previously been saved. 'Twas at that very moment the court fell silent when two Ashashin entered accompanied by Brother Teric."

"But I still do not understand how Raymond was so against King Guy," Sarah stated, looking puzzled.

"Because, as I explained earlier, the whole political situation in Jerusalem was tense because of the factional rivalries between the two branches of the Royal House, and Raymond himself, who as you know had previously been regent for the kingdom, and still refused to accept Guy as king even up until he entered the court that day. It had been that way since the death of the child king Baldwin the Fifth, Guy's stepson, the previous year," the old man explained patiently.

"But King Guy obviously accepted Raymond back then?" Simon asked.

"Yes...with open arms when Raymond finally acknowledged him as king, for the safety of the kingdom, but only because Balian had pleaded with him...however, the damage to the kingdom was severe and both Gerard and Reynald still considered Raymond a traitor. Guy, knowing that Saladin's army was already forming for a renewed assault, could not afford to let this internal quarrel continue. The entire kingdom was at stake and Raymond had many much needed knights and men at arms," the old man said and paused. "As soon as word reached Saladin that Raymond had recognised King Guy, he immediately tore up their truce agreement and *besieged Tiberias, which fell just six days later...though Princess Eschiva withdrew to the main citadel and held out, though in reality she became a prisoner in her own castle."*

"I know for I was there, and endured all that followed," the Hospitaller interrupted.

The old man looked at him and nodded before continuing.

"Of a more pressing concern however was the knowledge that Saladin had gathered a much larger army of twenty thousand men and planned on invading the kingdom by June," the old man explained and looked at the Templar now. "When Raymond discovered that the main force entering their lands, who made up the bulk of Gokbori's forces at Cresson, was actually commanded by Saladin's son, he was wracked with guilt and felt betrayed by Saladin and their once close friendship... but once reconciled with Guy, they began the process of assembling the entire army of the kingdom, a levée en masse, and planned to march north to meet Saladin. They would meet at Acre with the bulk of the remaining Crusader army, which then stood at some twelve hundred knights, and as many as twenty thousand foot soldiers, plus a large number of mercenaries, including turcopoles and other Muslims hired with money donated to the kingdom by Henry the Second of England. Gerard, who had been charged with its safe keeping, had no real option other than to use it. Also with the army was the relic of the True Cross, carried by the Bishop of Acre, who was there in place of the suddenly ailing Patriarch Heraclius," the old man explained and clasped his hands together and took a deep breath. "But before this, Saladin planned to lure King Guy and his entire army out into the open...so he planned to seize Princess Eschiva from her citadel to force Raymond at least to come to his wife's aid and split King Guy's forces further."

"You mentioned that Brother Teric entered the court accompanied by two Ashashin. What was that all about then?" Gabirol asked.

"Ah that," the old man said and smiled briefly and pulled his hood back slightly. "As you know, Brother Teric approached Gokbori under a white flag. On his return journey he met up with the new Grand Master of the Knights Hospitaller Armengaud d'Asp, who was on his way to Jerusalem to take up his new position. 'Twas not how he had wished to gain the position, by the loss of his friend Grand Master Roger. Well, he followed Brother Teric into the king's court that day."

Court of King Guy, Jerusalem, Kingdom of Jerusalem, May 3rd 1187

The late afternoon sun shone through the large western vaulted windows, the lace curtains blowing gently. King Guy sat forward upon his throne biting his thumb nails in pensive mood. Queen Sibylla sat beside him quietly as Gerard and Reynald paced around the open reception area of the hall. Several other knights and lords stood in silence waiting for the king to speak. Princess Stephanie sat in a smaller chair set back from the queen, her head held low. Count Raymond stood still with his two stepsons behind him whilst Balian shook his head having tried to calm Reynald down. The Patriarch Heraclius sat with his hands resting upon a golden topped staff constantly tutting and shaking his head dismissively at every word spoken. When Brother Teric entered the hall accompanied by two Ashashin on either side, Reynald immediately drew his sword, alarmed at their unchallenged presence. King Guy sat up immediately then stood up and backed away to the side of his throne chair. Heraclius moved to stand and knocked over an incense burner. A squire quickly started to clear it up as everyone else just stared at Brother Teric and the two Ashashin.

"What is the meaning of this?" Reynald demanded.

"Silence!" King Guy called out and hesitantly stepped forwards. "This is my court and I will ask the damn questions…is that understood?" he asked angrily, looking at Reynald. "IS IT?" he shouted. Queen Sibylla looked at King Guy, surprised, for he had never shown such a demonstration of anger in the court before.

Princess Stephanie looked up nervously fearful of the confirmatory news she knew Brother Teric was about to announce. She didn't want to hear the facts that would finally crush all hope despite the impossibility of what she prayed for. It was crueller to have hope and prolong the agony, she knew, but for it to be taken away completely and all her worst fears confirmed took her breath away and she struggled to sit up. Queen Sibylla outstretched her hand back to hold hers.

"My Lords and Ladies…I hope you will excuse my unannounced entrance but I am afraid time is not on our side this hour for the niceties of court protocol," Brother Teric started to say and stepped forwards. "I have this very moment returned from Cresson where I was afforded counsel with Gokbori himself. I have negotiated an agreement to recover our men to give them a proper burial. We have just two days to complete this and only a small escort for protection."

"What?" Reynald asked, confused, as Philip entered the hall, along with Stewart, his head still bandaged, having learnt of Brother Teric's arrival. "We cannot let Gokbori dictate to us."

"My Lord, we are well past that stage," Philip said and approached the king, nodding at Brother Teric as he passed him. "I am happy to organise the burial detail and escort myself...for as you know my son lies amongst them," he explained and looked at Princess Stephanie as tears silently ran down her cheeks unchecked. Reynald looked at her quickly.

"Master Philip...you are mistaken for my two travelling companions here bring word that both your son and Brother Nicholas are very much alive and well. Al Rashid was given charge of them by Gokbori to return them to the king."

Philips eyes instantly welled with tears and he took a step back. Instinctively he grasped his chest unable to catch his breath. Stewart put his hands upon him to steady him as the room fell silent. But in that silence Princess Stephanie could not hide her emotions and buried her face in her hands and cried openly with relief. Reynald scowled at her hard.

 1 – 2

"See...see how she cries for him...my claims against her are proved!" Reynald shouted and pointed to her, waving his finger frantically.

Queen Sibylla stood up slowly and raised Princess Stephanie's hands to get her to stand.

"Are you also accusing me of adultery or improper thoughts for Paul, for I too am shedding tears at this news," she stated proudly as a tear ran down her cheek. "Well...are you?" she demanded and began to lead Princess Stephanie away.

Philip was left speechless.

"Brother Teric...where is Paul now then?" Stewart asked.

"He was taken to Belvoir castle...," Armengaud d'Asp interrupted loudly as he entered the hall, brushing himself down, covered in dust. "I came as fast as I was able. He will be escorted here by a squadron of my best 'remaining' men and some of Al Rashid's finest. Or if it is easier we can take you to him at Belvoir when you go to recover and bury those at Cresson?"

"We do not deal with assassins," King Guy blurted out and sat himself down hard in his chair.

"If you wish to save this kingdom, My Lord, and keep your head as well as your crown then you had better hear what these two have to say. If not then you risk them all joining with Saladin against you...so think wisely upon your next remark," Master Armengaud said, his tone clipped.

"He must have been a spy for how else would he have survived and been set free? So no...over my dead body!" Reynald shouted.

"Yes...most likely...over your dead body," Balian replied and stepped forwards. "Are you all right?" he asked Philip, the colour in his face having drained. Philip could say nothing, still overwhelmed at the news of Paul.

"'Tis not up to you, Lord Reynald," King Guy said and looked at him through narrowing eyes.

"At last the king grows a pair of balls," Brother Teric whispered.

"I must go to Belvoir...now." Philip finally spoke and turned to leave. When he reached the door Ishmael and Abi appeared about to enter but he put his hand up for them to stop. "I need you to come with me," he said to them then looked back at King Guy. "My Lord, please excuse us...and my son Stewart is coming with me."

King Guy nodded his agreement silently.

"Make sure you return to us before things get interesting, Brother Stewart," Gerard called out. Stewart bowed his head toward him then immediately followed his father. "See what happens when families are involved," he said, approaching Reynald. "So Brother Teric, let us hear what these men have to say from Al Rashid."

Reynald re-sheathed his sword and flounced around angrily, shaking his head.

Belvoir Castle, Kingdom of Jerusalem, May 4th 1187

Paul and Nicholas lay upon their beds, the clean white cotton sheets smelling fresh. Both had been bathed and their minor scratches and head wounds treated by the main surgeon within the Hospitaller fortress they now found themselves temporary guests in. The morning air was cool as it blew in through the single window but neither spoke, lost in their own thoughts still not quite believing they were still alive. Paul's mind went over how he had pulled his shield up over his head and that was the last thing he remembered before being knocked out. When he came too he was looking up at Gokbori himself, who simply smiled down recognising him. The only Templar with a personalised shield made by Ishmael had caught Gokbori's attention and he knew immediately it was Paul. Al Rashid had arranged to meet Gokbori and Al Adfal to discuss a mutual truce and potential for working together, especially in hunting down Turansha and his men. Al Rashid knew that his men would need to work across both Saladin's lands and those of the Crusader barons if he was to succeed in eliminating Turansha, who was now proving to be an ever increasing threat to his own Order. He had sent two of his best men to negotiate with King Guy and in return Al Rashid and his men would cease all actions against the kingdom and remain neutral in any coming conflict with Saladin. He also wished to further the negotiations of forming a joint Order as proposed by Saladin, Philip and Count Henry. Knowing Paul personally, both Al Rashid and Gokbori protected him and Nicholas amidst the carnage that was left on the field of battle. Having deliberately offered them both fresh water and food Gokbori knew he was then obliged to keep them safe as was their custom, which appeased most of his men. Many already knew Paul but some had wanted Nicholas's head on a pole regardless. Gokbori knew the high regard Saladin held Paul in so it was not difficult to convince Al Adfal of his intentions to spare them. Consequently Gokbori ordered that Paul and Nicholas be taken under escort to Belvoir Castle to be handed over to the Hospitallers and to pass on the message to King Guy that Reynald must be stripped of his position and banished. If agreed, Saladin would enter into full and open negotiations to secure a new lasting truce. Paul was also asked to point out that Saladin had been gracious enough not to ask for Reynald's head.

But as Paul lay still, the images of the battle field would not leave his mind and he felt appalled at himself for his own actions. The whole field of battle had been turned into a mass of dead and dying men and horses which lay like a thick heaving and writhing mass of bright colours, like some great multi-coloured beast complete with foul smelling odours from the many ripped out guts of both men and horses. The image of Master Roger's last moments sent a shiver down his spine and a sense of great loss and sadness. 'Such an utter waste of a good man,' he thought and recalled the first time he had met him back in La Rochelle. Paul went over in his mind his own actions as he had slashed and hacked at men, men he would have otherwise called friends, yet had killed them without any consideration or thought. The image of the man whose throat he thrust his sword through without hesitation seemed to hang in his mind. He had decapitated another and the actual act of doing so had not even affected him...or so he thought. He closed his eyes, exhausted, and shook his head, shocked at how much he had changed. He was turning into a monster himself, he thought. For all that had happened to him he had changed and he knew it. He had been so ready for death and to see his family again yet forces beyond his control had conspired to keep him alive yet again. Nicholas had escaped with severe bruising to his left leg from his horse falling and trapping him, plus minor scratches all over. Paul had scratches too and a large swelling upon his head where his own shield had knocked him out when the Muslim cavalry horse had ridden over him. He also had a large bruise on his back and the scar from the stitches Master Roger had put in previously to his side had partly reopened and was weeping. It had been cleaned and bandaged but Paul ached from head to toe. Eventually he drifted off to sleep.

80C3

"You still do not remember fully do you?" Kratos said in a whisper Paul could barely hear. He opened his eyes, sensing him beside him, but as his vision came into focus he instantly realised he was no longer lying upon his bed. Quickly he sat up, his head immediately throbbing. He put his hand to the lump on his head and rubbed it. "Mebakker...does that help?" Kratos said again, but unseen.

Paul looked around but all he could see was whiteness tinged with a yellow and golden silkiness. He looked at his hands, bemused. It had been a very long time since he had experienced one of his vivid dreams.

"Father," Arri whispered and Paul's heart jumped.

"Arri...is that you...where are you?" Paul asked frantically.

Suddenly a soft image of Arri appeared, of his smiling face just in front of him. His eyes were full of life and looked at him, looked through him, he felt. Paul gulped hard.

"Father...I have missed you," Arri said softly and smiled again.

"Oh Arri, my little boy, I have missed you so. Are you well...are your mother and Ailia here too?" Paul blurted out emotionally, half laughing and crying together. He reached out and his whole body shook with a massive wave of emotion as he actually felt Arri's little fingers touch his then hold his hand. Open mouthed and speechless Paul just stared at him. Was this a dream or was it real, he asked himself as the intensity of the emotions and the fact that he could physically feel Arri took him by surprise.

Arri looked around then back at Paul and simply shook his head no.

"Father...I have to go now...I love you and I will be here waiting for you when it is your time. You are no monster and I love you...," Arri said and began to fade from view rapidly.

"No...no, no, no, no, Arri...please, stay a while longer...please," Paul cried out and reached out to touch him again but he vanished.

૪૦૦૧

"Arri!" Paul called out loudly as tears streamed down his face.

"Paul...Paul, wake up...'tis just a dream, Paul," Nicholas said gently, shaking him and holding his arm down as he thrashed out. "Paul!"

Paul opened his eyes wide then sat up fast, panting and emotional. He looked at Nicholas, momentarily confused before realising his surroundings. He rubbed his head, the lump throbbing hard. Before he could speak the door swung open and Master Douglas stepped down, placed his hands upon his hips and looked at them both on the same bed. He shook his head.

"Good job I entered when I did, eh boys?" he joked.

Paul and Nicholas looked at him as he stood smiling broadly. He then stepped aside as a black clad Ashashin stepped down beside him and started to unwind his face cover. Puzzled, Paul looked at Nicholas, who shook his head just as confused.

"Always getting into trouble," Taqi said as he revealed himself. Paul stood up quickly to greet him but nearly fell back down feeling dizzy. He took a deep breath and looked up at Taqi. "I have come to make sure you deliver your message to King Guy in case he does not listen to our other two envoys already sent," Taqi smiled and outstretched his hand as Paul grasped his forearm and helped pull him to his feet. Taqi winked at Nicholas as he stood up slowly. "'Tis great to see you, my friends."

Paul hugged Taqi unashamedly tightly, Arri's voice still echoing through his mind.

"These are strange and dangerous times we find ourselves in. 'Tis fortunate you were brought to this castle," Master Douglas said. "You would be wise to stay here as long as possible."

"But we have a message for the king we must pass on," Nicholas explained.

"I know of the message you must pass on but I fear the king will pay no heed to it. You will be wasting your time. I have already explained this to your friend here," Master Douglas replied and nodded at Taqi.

"'Tis still worth a try, and besides, I am under orders to ensure you deliver the message," Taqi replied and smiled at Paul as he pushed him back to arm's length and looked at him.

Port of La Rochelle, France, Melissae Inn, spring 1191

"He is no monster," Sarah stated and held the drawing of Paul closer.

"No but he thought he was becoming one," the old man said quietly.

"Master Douglas was correct though in saying they should stay within Belvoir for it is a truly impregnable fortress," the Hospitaller remarked.

"Aye 'tis that. But Paul knew he could not stay there long. He also felt honour bound to deliver Gokbori's message as well as Al Rashid's offer. But at least that night gave Master Douglas time to speak with Paul at length about being a warrior," the old man started to explain but then paused.

"What do you mean?" the wealthy tailor asked puzzled.

"Paul spoke of his fears about turning into a monster and losing all sense of who he was...and so Master Douglas spoke wise words with him. Words Paul would later write down so he would never forget them."

"Do we have those words here?" Gabirol asked and immediately started looking through Paul's leather folder.

"No they are not...but I know of what they spoke if you wish me to detail them... for his words will apply to you I am sure," the old man said looking at the Templar and Hospitaller in turn. They nodded in agreement silently. "Then let me start by saying that Master Douglas in his own fashion made it clear no one need attend any church or lay down making public protestations and prayers in front of others, as if that would make any difference to what is in a person's soul, for God can see what we do daily...so he knows what each of us deserves."

"I know where Paul is coming from in believing himself to be turning into a monster. 'Tis something we all must go through...and not let the horrors we see

totally destroy us from within," the Templar remarked as Miriam held his hand tightly. *"Those of us who fight monsters can also at times become monsters. 'Tis a matter some cannot handle."*

"Those who fight monsters do inevitably change, I agree," the old man replied. *"Because of all that you see and do in combat, you lose your innocence, and a piece of your humanity with it. If you want to survive, you begin to adopt some of the same characteristics of the monsters you fight. It is necessary. Gentle kind men must by necessity become capable of rage and extreme violence in order to survive. But,"* the old man paused. *"There is a fundamental difference between those who kill because they wish to for fun and sick pleasure and those who do so because they have to. Both types face or confront the monsters within each and every one of us... however, those of us who do so in order to protect those we love and cherish keep those monster tendencies locked away in a cage, deep inside us. That monster is only allowed out to protect others, to accomplish the mission, to get the job done... not for the perverse pleasure that the monsters feel when they harm others. Alas and sadly those same monster tendencies cause damage...of guilt, isolation, deep inconsolable sadness and the repeated images of horrific events that flash across the mind as if real again."*

"You speak as one who clearly knows and understands this," the Hospitaller commented.

"There is a cost for visiting violence on others when you are not a monster," the old man continued. *"Those who do so know one thing...the cost inflicted upon society as a whole is far greater without those who fight monsters. That is why they are willing to make that horrible sacrifice so that others may live peaceably."* The old man stopped and sighed as he looked at Ayleth and Simon shaking their heads, uncomfortable. *"Before you judge any one of us, remember this...we have witnessed things that normal people aren't meant to see...and we see them repeatedly. We perform the duties that you feel are beneath you. We solve your problems... often by visiting extreme violence upon others. We run towards the things that you run away from. We go out to fight what you fear. We stand between you and the monsters that want to kill or harm you. You want to pretend that they don't exist, but we know better. We do the things that the vast majority are too soft, too weak or too cowardly to do. We do not condemn nor judge a person who has been dealt a coward's heart for it becomes our responsibility to care and protect them with equal measure of obligation and duty for they are the very people who need the help and support the most. Your life is more peaceful...because of us. There are too many self serving religious bigots who preach peace and hold that there is nothing*

worth fighting for in this physical world...but to die submissively in the name of our Lord...and here within the safety of these lands far removed from Outremer's realities many returning men at arms are decried, denigrated, and cast as morally inferior despite the promises they went to war for in the first place. We know how childish, how asinine, and how morally and emotionally bankrupt that mindset is," the old man explained with a determined sense and presence to his words and tone. He paused as he looked at each of them in turn around the table. *"We know this... that there are things worth fighting, and dying for. We know that not every problem can be solved through rational discourse...that some problems can only be solved through the application of force and violence. And, while we do prefer the former... we are perfectly capable of the latter. This was most evident with Reynald for no amount of reasoning would subdue his passion for violence. He had succumbed totally to his own monsters within him. But we believe that fighting what others fear is honourable, noble, and just...and we are willing to pay the price for that deeply held belief."* He paused. *"And why? Because for us, it isn't a choice...it is what we are. We are simply built that way."*

"My friend, your words reveal you totally to have been a man of war yourself," the Templar stated respectfully and raised his tankard. *"I, Sir, know not who you really are, but your words speak truth...and I salute you."*

"Aye likewise," the Hospitaller said and raised his tankard.

"Can you repeat all of that so I may copy it?" Gabirol asked.

The old man smiled at him and laughed lightly.

"I am not sure I can," he replied.

"Powerful words of wisdom...but please explain why Master Douglas thought it prudent to stay at that castle?" Peter asked.

"Master Douglas had been stationed at Belvoir Castle during his time as a Hospitaller and he knew it well. It was a strongly built castle with two curtain walls. Of all the castles in the region, he felt it was the best protected and most easily defended. With the coming all out war fast approaching he knew they would all be best served by staying there."

"'Tis indeed formidable as a war castle," the Hospitaller interjected.

"That it is," the old man smiled. *"'Tis still known as the 'Star Castle' to some of us. 'Tis just twelve miles south of the Sea of Galilee. 'Twas Gilbert of Assailly, a Grand Master of the Knights Hospitaller, who began construction of the castle in 1168 so it is less than twenty years old. It stands at least sixteen hundred feet above the Jordan River Valley and the plateau. It commands the routes from Gilead into the Kingdom of Jerusalem and the nearby river crossing. The castle dominates the*

surrounding area, and at night it is set amidst the stars like an eagle's nest and abode of the moon...very fitting actually."

"I know the castle is considered our Order's most important one...," the Hospitaller remarked.

"'Twas that indeed. It certainly proved to be a major obstacle to Saladin's main goal of invading the Kingdom of Jerusalem from the east. It had previously withstood attacks by Muslim forces in 1180 and again in 1182...that battle being fought between King Baldwin the Fourth of Jerusalem and Saladin," the old man explained.

"How long did Paul and Nicholas stay then?" the Genoese sailor asked, his voice more gravelly than usual. "Sorry...'tis very late and my throat is sorely dry."

"Then may I suggest we take a short break. Refresh ourselves before I finish this tale," the old man suggested.

"I can sort some further refreshments," Stephan said as he stood up. "At this rate it will be breakfast," he joked.

"We have time to conclude this tale...but in answer, they stayed but a week before orders came through they were to report to Acre and meet the King there. But Philip, accompanied by Stewart, Abi and Ishmael, arrived the same evening Master Douglas had spoken to Paul and Nicholas. 'Twas certainly emotional...," the old man sighed.

Belvoir Castle, Kingdom of Jerusalem, May 4ᵗʰ 1187

Master Douglas was leading Paul and Nicholas across the main courtyard to secure a horse each for their journey onward back to Jerusalem. Taqi and his fellow Ashashin walked closely behind them. The sky was already turning a pale yellow with red hues as the sun set beyond the walls. Many Hospitallers busied themselves maintaining their weapons, uniforms and horses in preparation for whatever was about to unfold. There was an organised chaos to the calmness but a real sense of apprehension in the air. Horses entered the courtyard, their hooves echoing out drawing Paul's attention toward them. Instantly he recognised his father's long dark blue robe as he rode at the front immediately followed by Stewart and a mixed escort of Templars, Hospitallers and Knights of Lazarus. Several more riders followed behind but were obscured by the dust being kicked up as the horses pulled up. Philip saw Paul and dismounted quickly. Without tying up his horse he rushed toward him. Master Douglas stopped and held Paul back with his arm to stop him.

"Unexpected, as is typical of your father. I shall sort your horses for I think you will be otherwise distracted this eve," he said quietly and lowered his arm just as Philip reached them.

"My son...," Philip said emotionally and without hesitation grabbed hold of Paul and hugged him.

"Always stealing the attention as usual," Stewart joked as he approached taking off his riding gloves. "You had us worried for a while," he remarked as Philip then held Paul at arm's length and looked at him carefully. He shook his head unable to speak for fear of embarrassing them all by bursting into tears. "I heard what you did for me...you saved my life, little brother. Thank you," Stewart said sincerely and put his hand upon Paul's shoulder.

Stewart's thanks touched Paul instantly and deeply. Their bond of friendship and brotherly love had come a very long way since their fall out in La Rochelle. Nicholas looked toward the other riders and saw Upside sat upon his horse just smiling at them all. He gave a slight wave of his hand and indicated towards two horses leashed to his right side. One was Adrastos.

"No need for me to sort you horses then...so I guess we can all retire to the dining hall before evening vespers," Master Douglas said and started to usher Nicholas around.

Philip nodded in agreement and began to walk with Paul, when he stopped.

"I almost forgot." Philip finally managed to speak, his voice wavering as he fought to control his emotions. "We have brought someone else along. She refused to stay in Jerusalem...and I think you will discover that just about everyone within the court is now fully aware of her feelings for you," he explained with a smile and nodded his head as he turned Paul around to face the riders again. Abi and Ishmael were already walking toward him with someone following behind. "'Tis Stephanie."

Paul stood up straight, his heart quickening. What trouble would she have started by coming here, he wondered, concerned for her safety. Abi and Ishmael both looked imposing and serious as they approached. Paul could just make out Princess Stephanie walking behind them, her face down and head covered as if to hide who she was. Abi bowed slightly to acknowledge him. Ishmael shrugged his shoulders and leaned close to Paul.

"My friend...you cause my heart to fail again like that and I will have to kill you myself," he joked then stepped aside and gestured toward Princess Stephanie. "But this lady insists on seeing you first."

Paul stepped forward oblivious to the others all looking on, including the other knights and sergeants who had all stopped what they had been doing. Silently she stepped forward, looked up at him, her face full of emotion, and gently lowered her hood to her shoulders. Her golden hair was not tied up and fell loose. Her eyes darted to look at Taqi in surprise at his presence. He stepped forward.

"I know Ali would approve of this...and be happy for you," he said quietly but loud enough for them both to hear. "And you have my blessing, brother."

Paul gulped hard at Taqi's response. It was unexpected but heartfelt. He shook his head, momentarily confused, until Taqi nodded toward Princess Stephanie and nudged him. Philip mouthed a silent thank you to Taqi. Paul looked back at Princess Stephanie, her eyes searching his for any hint of what he was thinking. Her heart beat so fast she began to feel dizzy. Paul looked at her white skin in stark contrast to the dark green and blue dress and cloak she wore, her hair gently blowing in the evening breeze. She stepped forward and grasped his hands and without hesitation leaned up and pressed her lips gently upon his. Taken by surprise, Paul hesitated. She pulled back and looked at him just inches away, her blue eyes wet and filled with love he sensed he could almost touch. Lost in that one moment he took her in his arms and returned the kiss and pulled her as tightly as he dare against him. As she kissed him back, her hands now cupping his face a loud cheer went up from amongst all those looking on. Paul did not even hear them at first. When he did, he gently pulled away and looked at everyone. Stewart laughed as Philip nodded his approval.

 1 – 38

"Well that's the fucking cat well and truly out of the bag," Master Douglas said aloud.

Paul and Princess Stephanie both laughed, embarrassed. Paul looked into her eyes then rested his forehead against hers and just held her. As the cheering died down, she wrapped her arms around his waist and hugged him tightly resting her head upon his chest, her eyes closed. Abi winked at Paul.

"This is a war fighting castle. You will not find privacy within these walls but if you need some time alone to talk, I suggest you visit the outer western upper battlements. You will be afforded some privacy there to talk and discuss your futures together," Philip suggested as Master Douglas agreed and pointed to the wide stone stairway that led to it.

ುಾ ಲ

Paul looked at Princess Stephanie as she leant forwards against the battlement looking out across the plain beyond. The wind blew her hair gently, revealing her neck. He laughed when he noticed she was also carrying a sword that had been concealed beneath her outer robe. She smiled and looked at him, flicking her hair aside from her eyes. Paul took a deep breath. Maybe it was his final acceptance that Alisha was forever gone from him, at least in this lifetime, that he now wanted her fully and her love and that she now somehow appeared more beautiful than before. Perhaps he had been given a second chance after all. Reynald would certainly get to hear of their very public display of affection but that was a matter he could deal with later, he thought.

"You are armed," Paul remarked.

"'Tis a dangerous time we live in. A woman has to know how to look after herself," she replied, stood up straight and unsheathed the sword. "And I do know how to use it for since our lion encounter I have had lessons." She smiled and held the sword out. "Try me...," she laughed.

"Most weapons are designed to injure and maim only...not actually kill. Did you know that?"

"Of course...but try me," she teased and laughed again, waving the tip of her sword. "But I do know this is a deadly piece of weaponry to be respected," she explained further and quickly withdrew the sword away from him.

Paul unsheathed his own sword and moved to stand beside her. He placed his arm along the length of hers, both their swords resting together. He tucked his left arm around her waist and pulled her close into him. The scent of her perfumed hair filled his nostrils and he breathed in her fragrance as if a gift from God himself, the sun's last rays flickering through her hair. She laughed softly as she moved against him. If he was not already in love with this woman, then he certainly knew at that moment he could fall totally in love with her effortlessly. Alisha was gone and Stephanie would never replace her...he knew that as did she. He placed his face against the side of hers, kissed her cheek softly and held her in that position. She smiled then slowly lowered her sword until it rested upon the stone battlement, Paul's still resting upon hers. For the first time in a very long time she felt wanted, needed, loved and protected. It was a moment she wished would last forever.

"Sorry to interrupt...but dinner will be served in the upper mess hall within the hour," Master Douglas said as he approached them walking slowly along the battlement. Paul and Stephanie looked at him with their faces still held close together. "'Tis not my place to make any suggestions, but life is too damn short to wait around. Your father said you will find no privacy here within these walls. As always with him, I beg to differ. Yonder door you will find a night watch's room. It is lockable from the inside for security when under assault. 'Tis presently empty." Paul frowned at him, puzzled, as Princess Stephanie held his arm tightly and looked up into his eyes. "'Tis only manned when under siege...I do not foresee that occurring within the next hour," Master Douglas smiled, winked and turned around. "An hour!"

"Master Douglas," Princess Stephanie called out. He stopped and turned to face her. "You are a rare individual...I know...and I am more than aware that you hold no store in religion...so what you propose Paul and I do probably is not looked upon by you as a sin...so I thank you."

Master Douglas laughed lightly and walked back toward them.

"I know religion carries deeply held beliefs treasured by the faithful. It gives guidance and comfort to many as well as carry the codes from antiquity...but it is also filled with hypercritical and contradictory statements that make religion a platform and excuse to murder, maim and rape in God's name...'tis why I say religion, not God, but his so-called followers' interpretations that should be either banned or viewed as outdated and no longer required lessons and put firmly where they belong...in the past," Master Douglas explained and looked at Princess Stephanie as she shook her head, looking puzzled. "Let me explain briefly. Exodus 20:13...Thou Shalt Not Kill. It isn't even the first commandment yet the Bible goes on in many places to then contradict that very order...Deuteronomy 17:12... Kill those who do not listen to the priests. Exodus 22:18...Kill those of a different religion...Deuteronomy 13:13...Wipe out their entire villages. Leviticus 20:13...Kill all homosexuals...Deuteronomy 22:20...Kill your wife if she is not a virgin, and there are so many more...so yes, what I propose you two do is far from being a sin in my eyes. Life is too short so you must accept and take whatever blessings you are handed." He paused and pointed with his outstretched hand toward the heavy door. "So I hand you that."

Paul and Stephanie both looked toward the reinforced door that led into the watch room.

ဆာ ભૈ

Princess Stephanie stood up straight shaking from both nerves and from the coolness of the darkened room. A long thin strip of a window fronted by a long viewing bench let in the last warm rays of the sun as it set. Two single beds were positioned on either side of the room each with several blankets stacked neatly at their ends ready for use. Princess Stephanie laughed nervously and bit her bottom lip as Paul locked the heavy door bolt, sealing them in. He lowered a thick anti breaching blocking plank which meant no one would now be able to disturb them. He used the flint on the small table beside the bench to set the gauze kindling tray alight then immediately lit the night candle before the gauze burnt itself out. Paul's heart was already beating fast when he took Princess Stephanie's hand in his and kissed it gently.

"You shiver," he said quietly.

"Then come...join with me and make me warm again," she replied softly and led him to one of the beds. It was hard wood and only had a rough cover upon it. "At least I do not have to fight my way through chain mail to touch you this time," she laughed nervously as she sat down. She unfastened her outer cloak and let it fall to the floor. Paul held her hands and looked at her. "If you want me, of course?"

Paul knelt in front of her and rubbed his right hand along the top of her left thigh, her silk dress soft and smooth to the touch. He took her right hand in his left and held it to his face as he interlaced his fingers in hers. She was older than him yet she did not look it he thought as he studied every aspect of her face. She opened her legs slightly, her dress restricting her movement further. Quickly she half stood up, pulled up the sides of her dress over her knees and sat down again, her eyes never leaving his. Now as Paul rubbed his hand along her partly exposed thigh, it pushed her dress further up toward her waist. Her skin felt cool to touch and he could feel her muscle tense slightly in anticipation. She took a deep breath as he moved on his knees closer, her knees now on either side of his hips.

"'Tis not the best of places to make love to you...and certainly not a bed fit for a princess," Paul whispered and cupped her face in his left hand. She clasped his hand with hers and kissed his wrist.

"'Tis the best place regardless of where we are for I only see and feel you," she replied. She started to breathe faster, her chest heaving up and down with every breath. She saw Paul looking at her cleavage and she laughed softly then quickly started to untie the lacings that held the top of her dress together. "I have been yours since the very first day we met," she revealed. Paul leaned closer and softly, almost hesitantly and barely touching her, kissed the side of her neck. She closed her eyes and moaned with delight as the sensation of an almost whispered kiss sent shivers throughout her body. He kissed her again but slightly lower and harder and she wrapped her hands around his head, his hair running through her fingers as she pulled him closer to her chest. She moved slightly reaching down under her dress with her right hand and unfastened her under garment. She opened her legs further and pulled Paul closer still. "Take me...," she whispered emotionally as he moved up against her between her thighs. She put her hand under his robe and gently took hold of him feeling him through his undergarments. She smiled as he laughed nervously. "You are more man than I thought," she joked trying to ease his apparent awkwardness as he just looked at her. She pulled at his undergarment lowering it then taking hold of him, his eyes widening as he smiled, she gently guided him towards her. Paul shuddered as his body was washed over with a powerful sense of pleasure and the urge to take her as she held him. He was surprised with himself at just how natural and right it felt being with her. "I need you," she whispered and leaned forward to kiss him.

Paul placed his hand at the base of her back and pulled her gently toward him. As he did he felt himself up against her moist open and inviting body, her hand still holding him to guide him. He held his position as she pressed her kiss against his lips and with his other hand now placed around the base of her back too, he pulled her closer and entered her slowly, the wet warmth of her opening around him as he moved deeper inside sending shivers of delight through both of them as they joined as one. She closed her eyes and wrapped her arms around his neck and pushed herself against him harder, then lifted her feet off of the floor and wrapped her legs around him tightly. She moaned softly then opened her eyes to look into his. They held that position not moving for several long minutes not daring to move, the physical sensations engulfing them shutting everything else off around them. Paul could sense every pulse of her beating heart around him. He had never known any other woman except Alisha and though he thought of her at that moment, he could not help but feel the love and warmth from Princess Stephanie as she looked into his eyes intently, taking in short sharp breaths, her body tingling all over. She put her arms around his shoulders and pulled him closer and kissed him again, at first gently, her hips beginning to move involuntarily just as Paul started to move within her. She pressed her lips harder against his and Paul responded, tasting her as he returned the kiss. He eased her onto the bed fully and laid her down on her back, her legs still firmly wrapped around his waist. As she kissed him, her passion rising, she started to thrust herself upwards against him. With every push Paul made, she moaned and tucked her face into her arm unable to control the emotions and senses flooding throughout her body. Paul started to kiss her neck and chest pulling down her dress from off of her shoulders. As he moved lower and started to caress her breasts he became aware of her hand as she used her fingers to pleasure herself more with every move they made. He rested upon his left elbow and moved his right hand to cover hers. Gently he moved hers aside and with his fingers began to stroke her in rhythm as he moved. She closed her eyes tightly and panted as the tension built up within her until she could no longer control herself. For half an hour Paul moved inside her, slowed down then started again, each time the rising tension grew in intensity within both of them. This was not rushed, dirty or aggressive as Reynald always was, Princess Stephanie thought as she struggled to control her urge to scream out with pleasure. Eventually unable to contain the tension further, she started to orgasm in a full body convulsive wave that made her entire body shake, her legs jerking uncontrollably. Quickly she used them to pull him deeper inside, her arms now wrapped around his shoulders tightly. She let out a cry of ecstasy, unable to contain herself. She ran her fingers through his hair frantically as Paul kept on pleasuring her with every push of his body and fingers. Just when she thought she was coming down from the orgasm, Paul continued and her body responded again as an ever more intense wave of sensations overwhelmed her to the point she could not catch her breath. She sank her teeth into Paul's neck fearing she would scream, her finger nails digging into his bare shoulders beneath his robe. Paul could not hold himself any longer and as she moaned in delight, the added sensation of her thrusting faster and tightening her inner muscles as she did with every push he made, he felt himself start to come. With every push, she cried out and pulled him tightly and he gave in totally to the moment feeling as if his entire soul was flowing into her and becoming as one. She had never felt so desired and loved like this and it only added to the intense intoxicating sensations coursing through her mind and body. Paul's head started to spin and he felt dizzy as he started to come within her in deep pulsating waves that convulsed his entire body in spasms for what seemed an age until she started to slow her movements. Sweat beaded across her forehead, her mouth open as she gasped lightly, out of breath. Paul held his position and looked at her, her face framed by her golden hair splayed out around her. She laughed lightly when she became aware he had stopped and was now looking at her in the dim twilight of the evening. Paul leaned down and kissed her softly but as he did, she started to sob. He pushed himself up and away to look at her. Embarrassed she covered her face with her forearm, tears falling as she sobbed more.

"Stephanie...what is wrong. Have I hurt you...do you regret this act?" Paul whispered, concerned.

She shook her head no beneath her arm but could not speak. Paul slowly eased himself off of her as she lowered her legs from around his waist. He lay down beside her and went to move her arm but she pushed his hand away. Quickly she turned onto her side and tucked her back up against him and pulled his arm around her tightly. Still sobbing she kissed his hand and held it against her chest with both hands. Paul pushed her dress down to cover her exposed legs from the cold.

"Never have I been loved like that. Never," she whispered back, softly crying.

Paul held her closer and kissed her exposed shoulders. Gently he pulled up her dress and held her in silence. He missed Alisha with a pain that still cut deep within him every time he thought of her. He felt guilty toward

Princess Stephanie for even thinking of Alisha as he held her in his arms. Making love to Alisha had been different in a way he could not rationalise in his mind. He recalled Theodoric's claim that real intimacy is not the physical act itself, but the deeper connection two people can feel and achieve even just by holding each other when their minds and hearts link in a manner he had no words to explain properly. Each gives and receives a part of the very life force that makes us when two people share themselves totally and honestly. Both enrich and empower the other. Paul ran his hand along Stephanie's thigh and he began to feel aroused again, which surprised him. She sensed his arousal and pushed herself back against him. She raised up her right leg, her silk dress sliding to her thigh. She reached over and helped guide him back into her. She turned her head and kissed him softly. When she broke the kiss Paul supported her head with his hand, cupping her face. She closed her eyes and tucked herself up against him. Paul moved back and forth inside her slowly as he held her leg up slightly, his hand beneath her knee. When she lowered her leg, Paul felt her become tighter, the sensation almost too much for him. He used his fingers to touch her, and the moment he did, she jerked in delight. She felt incredibly sensitive as he pleasured her again. After a few minutes she buried her face down into her arm, screwing up her eyes as the tension became almost unbearable and she let out a deep low moan of ecstasy as an orgasm overwhelmed her again. Paul stopped moving as every time he did, she jerked uncontrollably she was so sensitive. He smiled and kissed her again, remaining inside her.

"I love you, Paul," she whispered softly and held his arms tightly across her chest.

"I love you too, Stephanie," he whispered back.

Whilst they lay there in silence, Paul thought back on Sister Lucy's words she had told him after Arri had been killed. At his lowest when he thought he would surely break, she had not been gentle in her advice to him. She had been blunt. Her words filled his mind as if she was with him now. 'The reality, my dear boy, is that you will grieve forever. Do not listen to those who say you will get over it for you will never truly get over the loss of a loved one…especially a child…ever! But you will learn to live with it. You will heal…painfully slowly. Then in time you will rebuild yourself and your life around the loss you have suffered and endured. In time, you will become whole again…but never the same. More importantly, neither should you want to be the same. Following a spiritual path will not prevent you from facing great pain, loss and darkness…but it does teach you how to use them as a tool to grow…and go on.' As her words echoed off he looked at Princess Stephanie. He did love her. It was a different kind of love but nonetheless a deep respectful and tender love. He pulled her closer and wondered if Sister Lucy would approve of his union with her. In his heart he knew she would just as Taqi had said Alisha would. He looked at the small candle burning away casting its light further as darkness fell outside. Any thought of going for dinner was now far from his mind as he carefully reached down for the blankets and pulled them up over them. He looked at Stephanie as she lay peacefully beside him. Suddenly the image of his previous dreams showing the candle burning down over Jerusalem entered his thoughts like an unwelcome intruder. When he looked up at the night candle burning down he knew in his heart the candle for Jerusalem had already been lit, its days surely now numbered. He held Stephanie even tighter. He had failed to protect Alisha and lost her, but he would not lose Stephanie, he vowed, as she now slept soundly in his arms. He brushed her hair aside so he could look at her. He softly kissed the side of her face and lay down as close to her as he could get. Closing his eyes, he fell asleep almost instantly…the candle still burning down.

ℬ ℭ

Philip stood with Master Douglas and Abi at the end of the battlement looking toward the watch house. The stars of the Milky Way sparkled brilliantly above them drawing a line from the horizon behind them and appearing to arch over and touch the top of the watch house as it vanished behind.

"The Crimson Thread flows within her veins too, does it not?" Abi asked, whispering.

"Aye it does…but distantly through her lineage," Philip replied quietly.

"Then perhaps all is not lost if they become as one. Perhaps the line will continue through her?" Abi replied as Master Douglas rubbed his chin.

"Or Stewart…even Percival for he now wields the sword," he remarked. Philip looked at him.

"There are two others perhaps more suited to carry it forward," he said and paused as Master Douglas looked at him quizzically. "As for Percival, we do not know if he even still lives. If he cannot wield the sword and Paul refuses to, then we shall have to return it to its place of origin if there are none who will accept it."

"You have to get it back first," Master Douglas stated.

"Why can they not simply return and stop all this madness? I will never understand why they cannot," Abi said, looking up at the stars. She shook her head in sadness.

"You know why. Man has forgotten his true past and origins. He is a species with amnesia…and until he remembers and chooses love, then he shall remain isolated," Master Douglas said.

"Love," Abi sighed and thought of Tenno. "Kratos always speaks of love as the most powerful tool any of us possesses," she sighed.

Philip could see the sadness upon her face as she still clearly questioned everything she had ever known.

"Abi…you know how the saying goes. Only when the power of love overcomes the love of power, will the world will know peace," he said softly.

"So never then," Master Douglas remarked sarcastically and feigned a large smile.

"Master Douglas, my old friend," Philip said and put his hands on Master Douglas's shoulders. "There will come a day when mankind remembers. Slowly at first, but as more proofs come to light and more lands are rediscovered with irrefutable proofs of a great former united worldwide civilisation, then, then my friend, they will remember."

Abi looked at the stars again and then pointed to a constellation.

"The Pleiades…," she said and shook her head. "'Tis only hope that keeps us going."

"But it is love that keeps us alive," Philip said.

"Perhaps…but a single thread of hope is still a very powerful thing," Master Douglas commented and looked up at the stars.

Chapter 77
The Sacredness of Tears

Paul heard horses screaming wildly accompanied by the distant thud of constant drum beats. He moved his head from side to side trying to breathe as smoke filled his nostrils. His mouth was so dry even his tongue was. Men shouted loudly and the clash of metal upon metal and shields echoed through his head. He opened his eyes and instantly gasped in shock realising he was in the middle of a pitched battle. King Guy's red tent was near to him but falling down as flames engulfed one side of it. Female knights had formed a defensive line to his front supported by the Knights of Lazarus as Muslim cavalry rode past thrusting their lances whilst horse archers fired into the ranks hitting most of them at least once each. All around him many men, both Muslim and Christian, lay either dead or dying. A large shadow fell across the ground and he looked up. A dark cloud shaped like an eagle, its wings outstretched swooped high above them all. Two large images of what looked like horns stretched up and over the whole battlefield, a blue wolf's head merged with one, a red wolf's head upon the other. Immediately Paul knew he was dreaming; the same dream as before. He spun around when he heard Nicholas scream out his name in agony. Four Muslim infantry had tried to attack Paul but Nicholas had run into them, killing one whilst holding another against him whose lance had pierced right through Nicholas's side. As he hacked at the third man with his sword, the fourth thrust his sword right through the middle of Nicholas's back. His eyes opened wide as blood spurted out of his mouth.

಄ ಐ

"No!" Paul cried out, his arms outstretched.

"Paul...ssh. You are safe. 'Tis just a dream," Stephanie whispered softly and ran her fingers through his hair gently. "Just a dream."

Paul rolled over and looked at her. The sun was already shining through the long slit window. His heart was pounding from the dream and Stephanie could feel it beating as she placed her hand upon his chest. Her dress was still open to her waist revealing her cleavage and tummy. Paul noticed a slight scarring from stretch marks just above her belly button. When she noticed him looking, she quickly pulled her dress together, embarrassed, as he looked up at her and smiled. Gently he removed her hand clutching her dress and leaned closer. Pushing the top of her dress further apart, he softly kissed the skin between her breasts. He pulled the rough thick blanket down and she shook her head no and went to pull him back up but he held her hands tightly and kissed lower. He kept kissing until he reached the silvered scar of a stretch mark. Softly he kissed the mark then rested his face upon her tummy and gently rubbed his hands over her beneath her dress. He pushed the images of the dream from his mind as they seemed to flash across his vision even when awake. He closed his eyes and tried to think of something else. He recalled Alisha's words when she had told him to never hide a scar for it was proof he had survived something that had tried to harm him.

 6 – 21

"These are but the marks that prove you are a real woman. You should be proud of them…not embarrassed," Paul said quietly and kissed her tummy again. Stephanie ran her fingers through his hair, surprised at his words but also deeply touched. She could feel herself becoming emotional and felt silly and embarrassed. A single tear fell down the side of her face. Paul sat up and looked at her. Noticing the tears welling in her eyes, he slipped the dress from her shoulders. He pulled her up slightly and lowered her dress down over her hips leaving just her upper under garment. Embarrassed she folded her arms across her chest, lying back down upon her back but Paul smiled again at her and removed the dress completely. She raised her legs and Paul parted them and moved between her thighs. Quickly he pulled off his shirt the unfastened the last loop link in her upper undergarment, letting it fall away leaving them both completely naked. "You look more beautiful than ever," he whispered. She laughed lightly as she looked into his eyes, her pupils wide as she became aroused feeling Paul was already. "You fire a passion and desire in me I thought I would never possess again."

"And you I," she replied and put her arms around his shoulders and drew him down towards her. She ran her fingers across the scars upon his chest and shoulder recalling how he got them. She moved her right hand down to his lower back and felt the bandage still attached to his side wound. "So many injuries you carry because of me," she sighed.

"And every one of them worth it," he replied as he slowly entered her and kissed her softly.

Port of La Rochelle, France, Melissae Inn, spring 1191

"And?" the Genoese sailor asked, eager to hear more as the old man paused for several minutes.

"I think you know what happened next," he answered and smiled. "And afterwards when they had finished they helped each other get dressed. They both had no idea how long it would be until they could be together again so made the most of it."

"First thing in the morning...with bad breath and all that...," Sarah grimaced and then laughed. Stephan shook his head mockingly disapproving.

"What did Brother Teric do when he found out they had been together for he loved her too did he not?" Ayleth asked.

"Why do you think he went and saw Gokbori? He had loved Stephanie from afar for as long as he could remember, but he knew how much she felt for Paul. I think by that time half of Jerusalem also knew. Brother Teric would do whatever he could to ensure Princess Stephanie was protected and happy...and he respected and admired Paul well enough to know that he would be able to offer her both. Brother Teric's love for her was unrequited but he could show her his love by putting her best interests first. When Reynald threatened he would have Paul's head, it was Brother Teric who said he would have to fight through all of his Templars first."

"Didn't Gerard say anything?" Peter asked.

"Yes. He told Reynald he was a fool and had long ago lost her heart and he should just accept it and concentrate upon the bigger threat from Saladin," the old man explained.

"I like this Brother Teric," Sarah said with a smile.

"He was a genuine and godly man. A very rare one of a kind," the old man said, looking at her.

"So Paul obviously had visions of what was to come at Hattin then?" the Templar asked.

"Yes he did. And because of it he insisted that his father leave for France as soon

as possible. He pleaded with him and even Stewart agreed he should go. The argument Paul used was that he should take all of the parchments and details of their new Order and ideas back to safety as well as those of Oak Island and the locations of the Halls of Records Paul had written within a code. Master Douglas agreed with Paul's request but Philip insisted he would remain until the dead at Cresson had been properly dealt with."

"But surely Paul's time was almost up and he could have returned to France with his father?" Simon asked.

"Perhaps. He could have gone on to Acre and served his remaining weeks there, but because of his dreams, he refused to leave his brother Stewart, Nicholas and Upside," the old man explained. "All the knights at Belvoir were informed not to return to Jerusalem but to wait until they were summoned on to Acre. They also received word that under no circumstances would the king enter into any deals or truces with Al Rashid and so Taqi and his companion were ordered to return to their lands immediately upon completion of another matter with Count Henry."

"Which was?" Gabirol asked.

Belvoir Castle, Kingdom of Jerusalem, May 5th 1187

It was mid morning when Paul and Princess Stephanie were escorted to the castle's main planning room led by Master Douglas. When he opened the main door, both Paul and Princess Stephanie were blushing, unable to hide their embarrassment, and entered the room hesitantly. Paul was immediately surprised to see Count Henry sat beside his father, Brother Teric standing behind them. Taqi and his colleague sat opposite with their backs to Paul as he approached. Stood beside the exit door Ishmael bowed his head slightly to acknowledge them as Abi stood up from a bench near the windows. Brothers Upside and Nicholas were already sat on a bench to his right. The room was full of light from the main windows, the sun shining directly onto the large table that had many parchments and maps opened across it. A small reinforced wooden chest was placed in front of Taqi, opened. It was full of gold coins. Taqi turned around to look up at Paul. He smiled and stood up quickly to greet him. Master Douglas shut the door behind him with a loud bang. Princess Stephanie moved to stand close to Paul, nervous and worried they were in trouble. Brother Teric bowed his head to her then to Paul.

"We trust you are well rested," Count Henry said as he stood to greet them and offered Paul to sit beside Taqi. "We have much to cover and not long."

Philip smiled at Paul.

"Yes thank you...we are well rested," Paul replied awkwardly and saw Brother Teric close his eyes briefly trying to hide his obvious pain knowing what they had done.

"My friend...I must leave this day but I have asked that I am able to entrust the safe keeping of this," Taqi said and gestured with his open hand toward the chest of gold. "'Tis funding and a gift from Al Rashid."

Paul looked at him, puzzled, then to Count Henry as Nicholas offered Princess Stephanie a chair. It screeched as he pulled it across the stone floor toward her. She thanked him and sat trying to compose herself.

"'Tis to help set up the new joint Order. 'Tis three thousand pieces of gold," Count Henry explained and proffered for Paul to sit. "But we must secure it before Reynald or the King knows of it."

"Why?" Paul asked as he sat down, looking back briefly at Princess Stephanie.

"Because they have already made Gerard use the coinage and gold sent from King Henry of England to pay for mercenaries. They run low of gold and will not hesitate in taking this," Philip explained. "Your brother this very minute rides for Acre. They received orders this morning to report there. Reynald and Gerard are also en route to Acre this day."

Paul looked back at Princess Stephanie again.

"I would strongly advise you return to Jerusalem before the week is out, My Lady," Count Henry said, looking at her. "And it may be as wise to move on back to Kerak from there."

She shook her head no in alarm and looked at Paul, panic written across her face.

"I understand you do not wish to be parted from each other, but for your safety I strongly advise you to return to Jerusalem. Reynald cannot do anything to you there," Philip explained reassuringly.

"Can she not accompany you back to France?" Paul asked, seeing the anxiety in her face.

"She can if I can arrange it first. But communication is broken across the land. We do not even know if Queen Tamar is still en route or stuck in her last location. Her treaty with Saladin may still be in force or torn up. But she has many knights we could certainly do with," Philip replied.

"And I have written orders from Gerard," Brother Teric interrupted and placed a sealed envelope on the table and pushed it across to Paul. "We must all head for Acre to arrive by the ninth of May."

Paul picked up the order and began to open it as Princess Stephanie looked on. He read the order, which confirmed what had been explained. He looked at Princess Stephanie and nodded confirming its content. She took a deep breath but remained composed.

"Then what must I do with this?" Paul asked and pointed to the gold.

"We can leave it here secured within the vaults. By taking this we are accepting to form the Order as agreed. Or we can return it with Taqi this hour," Count Henry explained. "It already has volunteers," he then said and looked at Upside and Nicholas then back to Taqi. They all nodded in agreement, Taqi smiling.

"You too?" Paul asked, surprised.

"Of course. You will need someone to teach you all diplomacy…and how to fight if that fails," Taqi replied.

"'Tis not my decision to make," Paul remarked.

"I am afraid it is, my son. Al Rashid made that very clear as did Saladin's secretary," Philip replied.

"But we are soon to be in all out war," Paul said, shaking his head, confused.

"More the reason to get this started. They all respect and trust you. 'Tis not treasonous what is being asked for in truth you are seeking to restore peace. That we can all argue should the likes of Reynald or Gerard raise protestations and accusations later," Count Henry explained.

Paul looked up at Abi. She nodded her head in agreement with what was being said. Ishmael stepped forwards.

"I go wherever you go and with whatever you decide," he said and bowed his head respectfully.

"But before I act upon any of that, we have to decide how best to return these documents to France," Philip said and indicated with open hands all the parchments and maps.

Paul looked at Princess Stephanie sat bolt upright on her chair trying to remain composed. She had his folder secured safely in Jerusalem already. She sat quietly and listened for the next hour as they discussed the best way to get the assorted parchments and maps to France safely, Philip finally though reluctantly agreeing to do so. The maps especially were considered too valuable to leave in Outremer with the approaching and seemingly unavoidable war coming. The maps showed the world as a globe, of a great landmass at the south, of another continent sized island in the southern seas, of the new lands to the west.

"Man will again crawl out of his amnesia of his true past, and when he does, he will again learn of these lands," Philip said as they were sealed away within reinforced travelling tubes. "And it will fall to the new Order to safeguard them as well as the secrets and codes to help recover the wisdom of our ancient forefathers."

Princess Stephanie took another deep breath, the sadness of knowing that Paul would have to leave her soon overwhelming her with a sense of dread and panic. She could feel the tears welling in her eyes and struggled to keep her composure. She stood up slowly.

"Gentleman...you must excuse me for I must leave you momentarily. I would like to freshen up if I may and have some food if possible?"

"Aye I can sort that," Master Douglas said and immediately opened the door. "If you would follow me."

Princess Stephanie looked at Paul, her eyes almost pleading with him to follow. She sighed knowing of course he could not. Without being too obvious she smiled at him and then turned to follow Master Douglas in silence. Taqi looked at Paul as he watched her leave. He placed his hand upon his forearm to reassure him.

"Brother, you have been blessed with love from two women in this life-time...do not be afraid or ashamed to tell the world."

Paul looked at him, both surprised and grateful. He had thought Taqi of all people would not have approved of his union with Princess Stephanie, or any woman for that matter, especially so soon after losing Alisha. Taqi's words of encouragement lifted his spirits more than he could express.

80 03

Master Douglas escorted Princess Stephanie to an empty room complete with its own garderobe room beside the inner chapel. As they walked past it Princess Stephanie stopped and looked inside at the brilliant colours shining through the small stained glass windows. Fascinated she opened the richly decorated oak door and stepped down inside. The walls were covered in brightly painted frescos depicting trees and scenes from the

Bible. It was an oasis of colour hidden within a fortress of pale hues. The vaulted columns drew her gaze upwards to the ceiling painted with an image of the heavens and stars. It was beautiful she thought as she slowly walked the length of the small aisle. Master Douglas followed her at a distance in silence. At the altar she knelt down and crossed her chest before closing her eyes and started to pray quietly. Master Douglas took a seat in a pew and watched her as she prayed. A Hospitaller squire entered the chapel, saw them and quietly backed out nodding at Master Douglas. After several minutes Princess Stephanie stood up, crossed her chest again and stepped back. When Master Douglas stood up she kept walking straight at him. Without hesitation she buried her face in her hands and rested against his chest and started to cry softly. Without hesitation he put his arms around her to comfort her. After a few minutes she stopped crying and pulled herself away.

"Forgive me, Master Douglas…I forget my place," she said, sniffing as she wiped her eyes. "I seem to do nothing but cry these days. 'Tis pathetic of me."

"No, My Lady…'tis far from pathetic. There is a sacredness in tears. You know that already so you of all people should not forget it." Princess Stephanie let out a light laugh, surprised at his words. "Come, sit with me for there is not much I am tasked with this day," he said and proffered her to sit upon the front pew. When they sat down, she looked up to her right to a small window that looked out across the plateau beyond. She smiled and then laughed to herself.

"I have heard so much of you, Master Douglas…and I shall be forever indebted to you for giving me last night with Paul."

"'Twas my pleasure; well more so your pleasure," he replied and smiled.

"You should smile more often for it suits you."

"Naturally miserable face, My Lady…that is all," he joked and she laughed again.

"I fear what Reynald will do to Paul, not to me, but him."

"Fear not for I strongly suspect Reynald would never get near to Paul to harm him. He knows his days with you are done and over and it has been made very clear to him not to cause harm to either of you. 'Twas your position and castles he was always after."

"Well he can have those with my blessings for they truly mean nothing to me."

"My Lady, Reynald was and is truly a fool of epic proportions for not seeing what he had in you."

"From you that is high praise indeed."

"I always speak as I find and see."

"I know...you are quite legendary for that," she laughed. "You really do not care what others think, or of religion do you?"

"Oh I do...I just don't show it," he replied and winked. "But as for caring. Look, look through that window to yonder fields afar in the distance. Well, do you see that?" he asked, looking serious. Princess Stephanie wiped her eyes and nodded yes. "Well then behold the fields in which I grow my fucks...lay thine eyes upon it and thou shalt see clearly that it is barren, for I do not give any," he said, straight faced. Princess Stephanie burst out laughing. For several minutes she laughed. When she looked at Master Douglas his face was still straight and serious, which made her laugh even more. "'Tis good to see you laugh. 'Tis good for the soul. You should do so more often for it suits you."

Princess Stephanie wiped her eyes dry but they were tears of laughter.

"It has been a long time since I laughed. I close my eyes and I pray daily for Paul and my children and I try to shut out all that is wrong and bad in my world. I even tried to banish all the feelings that I hold for Paul...out of fear for his safety...out of respect and love for Alisha."

"Paul can look after himself well enough...and Alisha, she is gone."

"She is gone...but not from his heart. I am not so stupid or naive to think otherwise. She was and always shall be his true soul partner...but I am thankful to the Lord just to be able to have a part of him."

"My Lady, as I have learnt in this life, you can close your eyes to what you see but you cannot close your heart to what you feel. And as for religion and politics...I think you know my views on that already. 'Tis a mechanism for the codes granted as I stated last eve, but it is used now by our so-called ruling masters to keep the masses distracted and fighting amongst themselves for if they ever came together in unity as Paul this hour plans with his new Order, they would wake up to the great deception that has been played upon them. Religion is regarded by the common people as true, by the wise as false, and by rulers as useful. They were the words of Seneca the Younger in the first century BC, not me, but still an accurate understanding. But what I know of the real God...is that it is love. We all know what the opposite is...so I always caution chose wisely."

"That is why I thank you for last eve. And you are clearly more learned than you let on," she smiled and paused. "But what of soul partners for why cannot I put aside nor bury this connection I have for him...I have prayed and wished it was not so strong," she sighed.

"'Tis a difficult one to know and accept. As I understand it, and I could be wrong, for look at me, I am still single," Master Douglas said and laughed at himself. "But I am sure soul partners differ from life partners. Some people will never encounter a soul partner or soul connection and so they settle with a life partner, which can be very satisfying of course. They are often built on mutual trust, respect and friendship. Perhaps to learn certain lessons in this lifetime for in reality we have no control over timing and less control of circumstance. Some cannot wait forever in the hope of meeting their soul partner, so accept any form of relationship...or like me remain alone ever hopeful. For others it is about survival, security or simple companionship, and the words soul partner do not even touch them or they find the whole concept wrong, dreamy or an unrealistic fantasy. Life circumstance, timing, availability, security and many other factors all influence our relationship choices."

"You are far wiser than I gave you credit for. Please accept my apology for thinking otherwise. You give wise counsel."

 1 – 37

"But," Master Douglas smiled. "But if a person is open, ready and blessed enough to meet a soul partner in this life time it will happen unanticipated and unexpected. It can feel unsettling and destabilising because it is a different connection unlike any other you have ever had."

"I know that believe me for I knew and felt it the very first time I ever saw Paul. But I was able to keep my emotions and feelings guarded and in check back then...but not any more."

"There are no words or explanations to articulate such a connection. It is an intuitive knowing that it just seems right. 'Tis not a matter of distance or time until you find your way to one another. There is a flow and a rhythm that seems to be guided by something much higher. You have to step back to catch your breath because deep down you know this is special...this is different...this is genuine. It is raw and it is so damn real you want to run away just to soak it up and take it in. Your soul partner, the one you can still sense and feel even if a thousand miles away, is the one you hear whisper when they think about you. The one who lets you move freely yet embraces your shadow from afar. That one, the one you feel like you have known for ever..." Princess Stephanie looked at Master Douglas, puzzled. "What? You are truly a man of two natures. One you show the world outwardly...a great warrior, the other a great insightful and soft giant of a man."

Master Douglas leaned closer.

"Then I pray you keep my secret about the softer side," he joked and winked.

She laughed lightly and looked at him.

"Thank you. Thank you," she whispered then looked up at the stained glass window.

„‘›

Paul sat with just Taqi looking at the chest of gold in the operations command room, the others having left to attend vespers or other matters. Upside and Nicholas had taken Taqi's companion to get some food.

"Who could have imagined we would ever end up here like this," Paul commented and looked at Taqi.

"Never in my wildest dreams."

"'Tis a long way from La Rochelle for sure...how I wish we could return to that time. To see Ali just one more time."

"'Tis a pain I cannot help ease, my friend...though I wish I could. 'Tis why I am heartened that you at least have the comfort of the princess."

Paul looked at Taqi directly in the eyes.

"I thought you would not approve. It being so soon after Ali being...," Paul paused, unable to say it.

"Murdered!" Taqi stated bluntly. "She leaves a massive hole within all our hearts. 'Tis a hole that will never be filled...but having many surround you that support you is one thing...'tis but another matter for someone to comfort you. I always foresaw a time when you and the princess would be as one. It did concern me that you would be unfaithful to Ali, but you never were. 'Tis why now...now that you need comfort the most, I give my blessing, not that it should matter what I think."

"Taqi...my dearest and most noble of friends. It matters...more than you can possibly know," Paul replied and quickly opened his leather side purse. "Here look....I kept this for I will never forget you."

"What is it?" Taqi asked as he took the small tied up piece of cloth handed to him. He looked at Paul quizzically before untying it. As he unfolded it and laid it flat he shook his head emotionally and gulped hard. "'Tis the embroidered sigils I made for Ali."

"'Tis indeed," Paul replied and then sighed heavily, lowering his head.

"How do you cope, my friend?" Taqi asked, looking sad.

"When you are walking through Hell...you just have to keep walking as I was once told."

"Will you seek vengeance against Turansha?"

"I was advised I should not...but it is whoever is the lord that commissioned Turansha to kidnap Arri and Ailia that I still struggle with...not knowing which one of them it was for he still walks freely. That eats away at me daily. 'Tis something I find almost impossible to bury."

"Well, when you find out, for you surely will, you let me know who he is and I will guarantee a swift and deadly end to their miserable existence."

"I have tried to find out but whoever he is, he is incredibly clever. Not even within my dreams can I get any information."

"What if it is a woman and not a lord?" Taqi asked, looking serious. Paul's heart skipped a beat as Taqi's words hit him. Momentarily he thought that Princess Stephanie could be that person. Her way of getting him. He felt sick and his stomach knotted. Seeing his sudden change of face and the colour drain from him, Taqi took his arm. "What is it?"

"Stephanie...," he said in a dry voice.

"No...in that you are mistaken, my friend, for I have seen how she has loved you and Alisha. You dishonour her for even thinking such. 'Tis not her, my friend. She is a good woman."

Paul rested his head in his hands.

"See how my mind plays tricks upon me...of course you are correct. What was I thinking?" Paul asked, shaking his head, annoyed at himself and feeling guilty. He looked at Taqi as he gently pushed the cloth with sigils upon back toward him. "I hope you find a good woman too, my friend."

"How do you know I have not already?" Taqi replied and smiled. Paul raised his eyebrows as if to question him. "I too have a woman of my own... you met her briefly before. She would have accompanied me here but for a slight matter."

"Such as?" Paul asked as he picked up the cloth.

"She is with child...my child," Taqi answered and smiled broadly.

"My Lord, that is wonderful news...truly wonderful news, my friend. Wonderful," Paul said excitedly and grasped Taqi's arms.

"And he will need a wise uncle by his side so do not be going off and getting yourself killed." Paul laughed then pulled Taqi close to hug him. "But first my Order needs Reynald removed so that we may indeed further our plans to form a united Order...He must go."

"How do you know it is a boy?" Paul asked, practically ignoring his comments about Reynald.

"We just know," Taqi replied and smiled again.

Port of La Rochelle, France, Melissae Inn, spring 1191

"What were the other parchments spread out if they were not the same as Paul had?" Gabirol asked.

"They were mainly copies of ancient maps Philip had taken for safe keeping from the main Templar headquarters in Jerusalem," the old man answered. "Count Henry added several others from the mother church...plus images of sounds," the old man replied.

"Images of sounds...and what did the maps show?" Peter asked.

"Yes sounds. You can create images using salt, sugar or water from various sounds. 'Tis part of a code but one we cannot yet fully understand. As for the maps...as I said before, they showed new lands to the west as Tenno had crossed, but also a great land mass made up from two large sections at the very south of our world plus a large continent sized island in the South Seas. As writings held by Count Henry claimed, it was the mythical land of Punt as detailed within the Bible and Egyptian history. Many ancient Egyptian writings gave details upon it as a land where they travelled to and mined for gold. They also spoke of a land to the very southernmost tip covered in snow and ice. But we will not confirm these details within our lives I strongly suspect."

"Are they not the same Gerard was after all that time when he killed Niccolas?" Simon asked.

"Somewhere, but in the main, no...and besides Gerard had by this time accepted he was not able to understand the codes from antiquity as he admitted to Paul. And you may recall it was Turansha's men who murdered Niccolas...not Gerard," the old man explained patiently.

"Of course...forgive me. You have spoken of so much 'tis hard to keep up," Simon stated just as Stephan entered carrying two trays with some light refreshments.

"The parchments also had details of the locations where great crescents had been formed into the earth set with great stones, like the largest uprights at Stonehenge. Two in particular...one here in Outremer and one not far from Stonehenge itself. Both are buried and shall remain so until man again works out their position and confirms their existence."

"Crescent...does that mean Islam has the correct symbol as they intend to use it?" the wealthy tailor asked, looking alarmed.

"No, no it does not mean that, my friend. But when they are again found it will be the start of the beginning...an awakening," the old man explained and paused briefly as Stephan placed a small bowl in front of him. *"The awakening...for the re-awakening has already begun."*

"And this Al Rashid...he was serious then about this new Order?" the Templar asked.

"Yes...deadly serious. Taqi and Paul decided to entrust the gold to Princess Stephanie to return to Jerusalem with her for safe keeping. Count Henry and Master Douglas finally managed to convince Philip to leave to both seek out Queen Tamar's caravan but also take with him the parchments and maps before it was too late. Taqi and his colleague arranged to travel with him as escort and managed to have a larger group of their own Order meet them outside the castle walls."

Belvoir Castle, Kingdom of Jerusalem, May 9ᵗʰ 1187

Paul stood beside Princess Stephanie with his arm around her waist looking down from the northeastern battlement of the outer curtain wall. Philip turned his horse around and looked up and with a quick farewell wave set off alongside Taqi and a full escort of black clad Ashashin. Paul's heart felt heavy as he watched his father and best friend ride away and disappear over the small brow of the hill as the path headed down steeply toward the plateau beyond. He took comfort in that he had a highly trained escort to keep him safe. The final farewell to his father and Taqi had been difficult and painful, his father only going reluctantly. Paul had made him promise that if he was able to get back to Alba, that he must go and revisit the Glen of Lyon, where his mother was laid to rest. Philip promised him in time he would. At least he had the parchments and codes for Oak Island as well as the drawn up statutes of what he hoped would be a new Order. How they would ever get Saladin and Al Rashid all to sign up to it Paul could not fathom as they all stood on the very precipice of all out war. Princess Stephanie rested her head against his chest as the riders vanished completely from view, saddened knowing that it would be her turn to leave next.

"This has been the happiest week of my life," she said quietly and hugged him tightly. Paul kissed the side of her head. He wished he could say the same to her but in truth it was not the happiest of his life. She had been more than a great comfort to him and given him a renewed sense of purpose and reason to carry on. He had not realised just how broken he was inside and how close to losing all faith and hope he had been until she put the pieces inside him back together. He laughed lightly to himself thinking if they should marry, as he planned to do in time, Humphrey would become his stepson. "Whatever happens, Paul, you must promise you will do all you can to survive whatever comes next."

"Whatever comes next?" Paul repeated and laughed knowing it was Taqi's favourite quote.

"Do not laugh at me...I am serious. You have a great responsibility to pass on all that you have been taught and learnt. Your father has more than done his part. He grows tired and weary...and it now falls to you to continue what he started," she explained and turned to face him. "I will miss you like you cannot even begin to imagine...but the memories of this week will help me endure that separation until you return to my arms."

"And I shall miss you."

"You know the Sea of Galilee is heart shaped?" she asked, searching his eyes. Paul nodded yes. "My father often told me that he always missed me so much that he would shed a single tear into it and that if I was to ever find that tear, only then would he stop missing me. 'Tis the same for me to you."

"So never then?"

"Never," she replied, leaned up and kissed him softly upon the lips. "Never."

Paul held her tightly in his arms and looked to the plateau beyond as his father's group appeared like tiny specks in the distance, just the dust being kicked up behind them revealing their position as they sped across the open plateau toward the mountain range beyond. He gulped hard with emotion as he recalled the many nights his father had sat with him and

Stewart reading them stories. He felt guilty and saddened that he had not been a better father himself to Arri and Ailia, always too busy drawing and working. He closed his eyes and sighed. If he could travel backwards in time he would do so much differently. He thought back on the many lessons he had had with both Niccolas and Theodoric. 'If we all live in peace and harmony, the world grows, thrives, remains in balance and can deal with anything that comes our way from out there in the Lord's eternal expanse of the cosmos. Mother Earth herself blooms and protects us all just like a mother does her own born children. But if we, all of us, become twisted, full of spite, greed, hate and violence, then Mother Earth loses her peace and harmony...she suffers, she begins to fail and she cannot then protect and defend us from what comes every so many thousands of years for she becomes weakened' Paul recalled Theodoric telling him. Images of the dark sun mural at the Templars' headquarters in Jerusalem flashed across his mind. Princess Stephanie could sense his sadness and hugged him tightly her own heart breaking thinking of her imminent departure. All too soon Brother Teric approached holding a sealed envelope. She looked at him as he offered it to Paul.

"Final orders sending you to Acre. Reynald and Gerard are already en route," he explained as Paul opened the orders.

"And you?" Paul asked.

"As was agreed with your father and Count Henry I shall escort My Lady back to Jerusalem along with the gold from Al Rashid. If you take it to Acre we know Reynald will seize it and use it to pay for more mercenaries," Brother Teric explained as his eyes fell upon Princess Stephanie's hands resting upon Paul's chest. Aware, she stepped away from Paul. "We leave first light tomorrow morn, My Lady," he said, bowed his head toward Princess Stephanie, turned and walked away.

"Just one more night alone," she said quietly. "Please draw this place for me so I may keep it to remind myself always of our time here."

"What if you fall with child?" Paul asked.

"'Tis a little too late to worry about that," she smiled but saw the concern in his eyes. "Then we shall love it and protect it the best way we know how. By the time Reynald returns to Jerusalem I will have secured my divorce from him...and he is welcome to my titles and lands. My love for you alone is enough no matter how selfish that sounds. All I need... is your love."

Paul looked deeply into her eyes. Here was a woman who had seen a lot and survived so much yet she stood with him looking so vulnerable. He did not want to leave her but when he looked at Brother Teric walking away he knew she would be in safe hands with him.

"Morning!" Master Douglas called out loudly as he approached from the opposite end accompanied by several Hospitallers and sergeants carrying a wide variety of weapons ranging from poleaxes, lances, maces, heavy horse scythes to spiked balls and chains. "I will cover your sorry arse with preparations so make the most of these remaining hours," he said and winked as he walked past.

Paul and Princess Stephanie looked on as the men filled past, all nodding and smiling.

True to his word Master Douglas had organised all the stores and equipment that Paul and his men would require for their onward journey to Acre. Brothers Upside and Nicholas helped make ready a lot of the new Hospitallers who had only recently arrived in the Holy Land. Paul and Stephanie spent the day almost in total silence just holding each other, except when Paul drew an image of the castle as she had requested. After dinner, as the evening sun set, they made love again in what had effectively become their own little private quarters within the watchtower. Princess Stephanie prayed she would indeed fall with his child. Naked and wrapped in each other's arms they fell asleep.

&)CR

"Paul," a female voice whispered. "Paul," it repeated.

Paul opened his eyes thinking it was Stephanie. But when his eyes focused he could see he was lying beside an ancient standing stone. He sat up, alarmed. He recognised it as Glen Lyon. Having recently spoken of it with his father he knew he was dreaming. He spun around on his knees when he sensed someone behind him. He looked up as a large man stood in silhouette before him, a bright light shining behind him.

"I can see I need to spell it out for you," Kratos said and offered his hand to help Paul up.

"'Tis a dream, I know," Paul remarked and looked around. "Where is the woman I heard calling my name?"

"Oh, your mother," Kratos smiled and rested upon his staff. "She is not here…she was, but not at this moment. You see I have to remind you what it is you are supposed to do."

"I have not forgotten…and I am trying."

"You distract yourself all too easily," Kratos said and moved his hand to his side as an image of Stephanie lying asleep appeared.

"She is no distraction I assure you," Paul replied defensively.

"Your union with her causes complications. Understandable but now you risk her safety and breaking her heart."

"How?" Paul asked, alarmed, as he studied the image of her asleep.

"If she falls with your child…it will kill them both for it is not written in her plan. It would go against that which was set."

"Then I beg of you change that plan," Paul pleaded. "Am I not to be afforded any comfort in this life?"

"Probably not," Kratos answered bluntly. "For you did volunteer for all of this…just as many more like you will do so again in the last days…when the great awakening duly begins."

 1 – 21

"Awakening?"

"Yes, Paul…now come on do not play the ignorant with me. You know it has already begun…for it starts with you and what you have already done."

"I do not know what I have done."

"Your father this very hour travels with the codes and statutes you have drawn up. 'Twas not he nor Count Henry but you. It sets the path that many men and women will in time follow. You have marked where the great Halls of Creation are located…and they shall be recovered just when mankind needs them again. Without you, those codes and locations would now be lost to humanity."

"But if that is the case then surely my work is done…and Stephanie and I can live the rest of our lives out together…surely?"

"That choice is yours freely to make as it has always been. But so there is no misunderstanding…a long time ago, that which is your soul chose this path. To help others. You and I knew each other…and you knew me as Mebakker and Alisha as your wife and soul partner." Paul shivered as the hairs on his arms stood up, his words hitting him like an invisible slap. He stepped back away from Kratos.

"I have oft heard and learnt much about soul partners, yet I cannot sense Alisha. I have tried so hard to reach her across the realms as both Theodoric and Attar claimed we could do...yet their teachings and methods have resulted in nothing for I cannot reach them as I do you now."

"Then that should tell you something...but you are not listening."

Paul frowned and looked at him hard, puzzled at his remark. "You have spoken with Arri have you not?"

"What are you saying? Please do not play with me. Does this mean Alisha and Ailia are upon higher plains of Heaven, however you explain it?" Paul asked, confused and hurting.

"I have already told you too much which you should have worked out yourself. I cannot tell you the rest."

"Then tell me what a soul partner truly is...for I loved Alisha with all my heart...yet I find I love Stephanie also.....so tell me I pray before you vanish or I awake."

"Paul....you are more awake here than you could possibly imagine."

"Then try me for I have a great imagination so I keep being told."

"Sit down," Kratos ordered, looking serious, and pointed toward a large stone lying upon the ground. Kratos stood for several moments resting upon his staff and looking down at Paul. "There is rapidly approaching a time when you must decide between what you feel and what you know. Now do not interrupt me when I tell you these things...but you will have to make a choice between your mind and your heart...between love and the truth." Paul went to speak but Kratos put his hand up instantly to stop him. "Listen...sometimes the love you feel will hide the truth from your mind...but it cannot hide truth from your soul. The connection between your mind and your heart is powerful and strong and both are in constant battle to rule over the other in the physical world you exist in. But neither one, either alone or combined, can overpower your soul. Only your soul can guide you."

"Why do you tell me this now?"

"Because the time fast approaches when you will be forced to make a decision and only your soul can guide you to make it. You must be prepared for the worst of all inner conflicts a person can endure between your mind and your heart. It will be so painful that it can only be overcome by the strength of your soul. This is when you will realise that your heart and mind are but links to your soul...for the physical heart and mind are but temporary...the soul eternal. 'Tis your soul only that can make the heart and mind act as one...but only when you accept it and allow it too."

"But what has that to do with Stephanie?"

"Ask your soul...is she your soul partner?"

"I do not think I even understand soul partners any more as I said... not since," Paul started to say and looked at the image of Stephanie as she started to fade from view.

"Speak with Master Douglas about soul partners...he is far more versed in such matters than most. He still waits to find his. Now go...I have reminded you who I was...likewise remember who you are."

Port of La Rochelle, France, Melissae Inn, spring 1191

"I think I feel angry at Kratos for telling him that and feel sorry for Princess Stephanie," Ayleth commented.

"So she returned to Jerusalem?" Sarah asked.

"The very next morning as Master Douglas had said," the old man answered. "She put on a brave face for Paul's sake. He wanted her to take Adrastos to keep him safe but the way he kicked and stamped you would think the horse could under-stand our language." He laughed to himself.

"Did she fall with child?" Ayleth asked.

"They spent their last night alone together...becoming as one in union," the old man started to explain but then paused. "It made it all the more emotional and dif-ficult when it came for them to part. Paul felt wracked with a sense of guilt about Princess Stephanie and like you, Ayleth, he felt sad and uncomfortably angry at the remarks Kratos had made. Dream or otherwise it affected him deeply. He felt denied of any normal life or a second chance...and he felt incredibly sad for her. Along with Count Henry, Brother Teric swore to him he would protect her and get her to Jerusalem safely...and she did not hide her affection when she kissed Paul farewell. Abi agreed, though very reluctantly, that she would remain with Princess Stephanie until further notice from Paul."

"Bit late by then anyway," Simon laughed.

"Just a bit and yes, Ayleth, she did fall with child," the old man stated.

The room fell silent as they all looked at the old man, Ayleth open mouthed.

"So as Abi said, the line could continue...unless she did die as Kratos stated would

happen," Gabirol remarked as the wealthy tailor shook his head and sighed heavily. "But I am sure I hear she still lives."

"She still lives," the old man answered.

"Then where is their child?" Sarah asked, her tone impatient and demanding.

"I can explain, but first I must tell you how Paul left for Acre accompanied by a contingent of Hospitallers, Brothers Upside and Nicholas and of course Master Douglas."

"Is this the image of Belvoir Castle?" Gabirol asked as he pushed a drawing forwards.

"That is indeed," the Hospitaller answered before the old man could reply.

Fig. 71: Belvoir Castle.

"Does not bode well if the image is here and not with her," the Farrier remarked as he studied the image.

"And you said the sword is only here because of her," the Templar remarked.

"As I said, she is still alive this day and the sword is indeed only here because of her," the old man replied and took a sip of rose water before continuing. "As you now know, Al Rashid as well as Saladin wanted Reynald removed, not just because of the trouble he had caused but also because of their desire and efforts at a fusion and unification of the Templars, Hospitallers, Al Rashid's Ashashin and other assorted Muslim forces, like the Faris Knights. Remember how I explained that they have almost identical vows and codes of practice? Count Henry and Philip knew the most prudent and wisest thing to do would be to have the Ashashin on their side, as they were ripe for it should hostilities with Saladin escalate. By the time Paul arrived at Acre, the machinations for all out war were well underway, especially as King Guy extended his 'arriere ban', the emergency call to arms to include all free Christians. Yet Raymond, despite his new pledged allegiance to King Guy, still remained at loggerheads with Gerard and Reynald. Gerard himself was forced into a difficult position, his reputation and credibility being called into question after the losses at Cresson...Brother Teric being urged to take charge of the entire Order when he safely arrived in Jerusalem with Princess Stephanie. Count Henry was prepared and ready to relieve Gerard of his position there and then, but Brother Teric refused. Gerard chose that time, his reputation now further dangerously compromised, to hand King Guy the money given to him by King Henry the Second with which he then proceeded to recruit more mercenaries, mostly mounted sergeants, who then displayed the coat of arms of King Henry the Second. Paul was more than pleased and relieved to meet Stewart again. Of course whispers and rumours of Paul and Princess Stephanie reached Reynald's ears but Gerard, for whatever his reasons, did manage to placate him and keep them apart."

"Told you that Gerard was not all bad," Sarah remarked.

"He should have stood up to Reynald more...for if he had there would be a great many of my men still alive this day so do not expect me to think better of him," the Templar interjected and shook his head dismissively.

"Everything became a cat and mouse game as both sides strengthened their positions and forces. Word reached Acre that Queen Tamar's caravan was indeed safe but was refused permission to travel to Jerusalem when she likewise refused to renege on her treaty with Saladin so she had to in effect simply sit and wait out the time and see what unfolded."

"Why did she not simply return home...why wait all that time?" Peter asked.

"Because she had promised her people she would return with holy items her countrymen rightly believed belonged to them held in Jerusalem," the old man answered.

"What happened when Reynald finally met Paul face to face?" Ayleth asked.

"'Twas at the emergency war council meeting in Acre. It was a packed gathering in the command hall and all senior Templars, Hospitallers and mercenary commanders were summoned to attend after receiving intelligence that Saladin had crossed the River Jordan on the thirtieth of June with a huge army. Paul still being *officially under commission until the end of June was of course expected to be present. By this stage he had spent nearly seven weeks training alongside his own troop of Templars, Ishmael true to his word accompanying him everywhere."*

"We were still holed up in the citadel at Tiberias when Saladin arrived," the Hospitaller stated and ate a piece of cheese.

"Saladin knew exactly what he was doing in having Princess Eschiva holed up besieged. He would use that fact to lure Raymond away as he planned all along. It was Reynald who demanded that Paul lead an advance party to Sephorie and prepare a full camp ready for the arrival of all other Latin forces. Paul readily accepted the order though Reynald hoped he would be an easy target en route... but nothing untoward happened and he reached Sephorie in good time and safely. Count Henry arrived there the same evening along with the newly sworn in Hospitallers' Grand Master Armengaud d'Asp. Count Henry handed Paul a note from Princess Stephanie. 'Twas a simple embroidered drawing of the Sea of Galilee in a heart shape with a small tear above it. Paul knew what it meant."

"So Paul was now in charge of a full squadron of Templars at this point?" the Templar asked.

"Yes...and Reynald wanted to make sure that his men would be at the forefront spearhead alongside Count Raymond for any engagements that were to come," the old man replied.

"What is wrong with that?" Ayleth asked, puzzled, seeing the looks upon both their faces.

"The spearhead always charges first. The lands they would be travelling across were within Lord Raymond's fiefdom...and as is customary, the lord of the land always leads the vanguard whilst others take the flanks and rearguard," the Templar explained.

"So Reynald wanted him in harm's way?" Simon asked.

"Pretty much," the old man replied. "But Paul's squadron ended up absorbing into its ranks several female knights to make up their full strength. Two days later King Guy along with Reynald and all the other lords and barons, except Lord Montferrat, all mustered at the springs south of the castle of Sepphoris. By this point Saladin had 45,000 troops, whereas King Guy's forces had just 1,200 knights, 4,000 light cavalry sergeants and turcopoles along with 15,000 to 18,000 mixed infantry that ranged from professional crossbow men to locals. Saladin had numerical superiority of three to one almost but there were still far too many men to fit inside the castle so many set up camp outside its walls whilst the last war councils were held."

"Why didn't Lord Montferrat attend?" the Genoese sailor asked.

"Because he argued his forces were too far away, were already dealing with attacks by Saladin's forces from Egypt as well as naval engagements. He argued he needed to keep his port secure and open to guarantee a supply route to Jerusalem... which was in truth certainly the case," the old man explained.

"I have never heard of this Sepphoris before," Simon remarked.

"'Tis known as Saffuriya in Arabic. 'Tis located in the central Galilee region only 3.7 miles north-northwest of Nazareth and set upon a high level that overlooks the Beit Netofa Valley. 'Tis believed to be the birthplace of Mary, mother of Jesus, and the village where Saints Anna and Joachim are often said to have resided. At the time of Jesus, Sepphoris was a large, Roman-influenced city. And so it would be from there that King Guy would lead his forces out to meet Saladin," the old man sighed.

Castle at La Sepphoris, Principality of Galilee, Kingdom of Jerusalem, July 2nd 1187

Paul entered the main hall along with Ishmael and Brother Nicholas by his side with Brother Upside following. Reynald immediately turned to face him. Stewart acknowledged Paul with a smile and slight nod just as Balian greeted Paul. Also present was Gerard, plus Grand Master Armengaud, Lord Raymond, Reginald of Sidon and Walter Garnier the Lord of Caesarea as well as Count Henry, who sat at the head of the table in council beside King Guy as they prepared battle plans.

"Paul, we have word Saladin's forces are still crossing the River Jordan. 'Tis surely a vast army he is sending to us," Balian said as he ushered him forwards.

"Yes it is indeed and we shall need a reconnaissance party to volunteer to go and check upon its true numbers," Reynald bellowed and grinned, looking at Paul. "And guess what...you just volunteered."

Paul looked at Gerard, who shook his head very slightly indicating no. Count Henry shrugged his shoulders and sat back in his chair as King Guy looked at Paul.

"My Lords...whatever you wish of me I shall do," Paul politely replied looking at King Guy and bowing his head slightly.

"Perhaps you can confirm numbers, if you are not captured of course, and report back to us so we may inform Raymond here that we must act and march for Tiberias to rescue his own dearly beloved wife Eschiva," Reynald explained animatedly and loudly as he bit into a large piece of chicken leg. Paul looked at Raymond, puzzled, then back to Reynald. "Yes...his own wife is holed up besieged within her own citadel and yet our great Lord Raymond refuses to march to her rescue. Does not want to engage in hostilities against his good friend Saladin I suspect in truth," Reynald sneered and threw the chicken leg at Raymond. It hit his chest and fell to the floor. Raymond shook his head in disgust but would not be drawn into a fight. "See...he does not deny it...just as you I am sure will not deny fucking my wife." Count Henry lowered his head in despair at Reynald's outburst as Master Douglas walked in behind Paul and stood by his side staring hard at Reynald. Gerard put his hand to his brow and shook his head almost disbelievingly at Reynald's comments. Paul just stared at Reynald. "And he is just a coward...even Gerard agrees!" Reynald shouted and pointed to Raymond.

"Gentlemen...this will not help our cause," Balian interjected and stood between Reynald and Raymond seeing the anger rising in his face. "This is neither the time nor the place for this. We must be united if we are to stand any chance of defeating Saladin's forces."

"And that is precisely why we must not move to engage him at Tiberias, where he will have us out in the open," Raymond shot back through gritted teeth. "Do that and Saladin will slaughter us. My wife has holed up these past weeks...another one will not hurt her."

"I beg to differ, Sire," Master Douglas interrupted. "I am afraid Saladin's engineers have dug another mine beneath the citadel walls. They aim to light it once all the pigs have been set in place."

"What?" Raymond asked alarmed.

"We have two more days maximum before his mine is ready to be torched. It will bring the walls down," Master Douglas explained.

Reynald put his hands upon his waist and started to laugh loudly.

"Devine intervention no less. Now you have no choice. We must march," he bellowed, still laughing.

"No...no we do not. We must not. You may call me a coward...a traitor even...but I know Saladin and I know warfare. 'Tis but a ploy to entice us out into the open," Raymond explained and approached King Guy. "If you order the entire army out to meet Saladin in the field, when our best strategy should be a defensive one until more men arrive, then we will be slaughtered."

"Then I demand you ask her sons what they think and wish...for they are not your sons as you cannot even father any of your own," Reynald shouted offensively at Raymond. "Well...ask them!"

Paul looked on utterly bemused at what he was seeing and hearing unfold. He recalled Theodoric showing him one of his charts he made about a great battle that would prove to be a fork in the road for all of them in the region. He sensed this was the very fork he foresaw. Count Henry stood up and walked around the table toward Reynald.

"Gentlemen. We are not that far gone yet that we cannot enter into negotiations with Saladin. May I remind you, Lord Reynald, that it is your actions that have ultimately led us here...to this day and this conflict," he said confidently without taking his eyes off of Reynald. "Saladin has already sent terms that all hostilities will cease immediately upon your banishment."

"Horse shit and you know it," Reynald shouted. "I spent years in captivity with those bastards and I know them better than most. They will not cease or keep peace until we are all converted to Islam. I have read every page and word of their Qur'an and all I see is their commands to slaughter all and anyone who is not of their faith...to expand their belief by force upon the world. 'Tis what they are commanded to do and if they do not, they break their own religion. Our men are in high spirits and more than confident of the fight. If you cannot see that then you are already lost!"

"Perhaps that is so but they do not know the numbers they are up against yet. And I wager you have not read fully our own Bible, especially the Old Testament, for it speaks and tells of exactly the same things...," Count Henry stated and moved closer to Reynald. "We must negotiate a lasting truce with Saladin...and if you can promise under vow not to break it, I am confident we can even levy that you be banished to your castle at Kerak and lands there. If you cannot, I see no real reasonable excuse as to why we should not banish you from all these lands."

"Or just hand him to Saladin!" Raymond finally snapped.

Reynald stepped back and drew his sword, his face turning red with rage. Paul immediately stepped forward in front of him.

"No one will be banishing you or handing you over to Saladin," Paul said standing directly in front of him.

"Brother Paul…'tis not your place to pass comment within this council," King Guy said loudly and stood up, banging his fist upon the table.

 1 – 40

"My Lord…I mean no disrespect but I believe I have earned the right to speak within this council…and though Lord Reynald and I have our differences, I will stand by him to protect him and his right to stay as I would any other person within these walls." Reynald looked at Paul, surprised, and lowered his sword stunned at his words. "'Tis a two day, possibly three day march with infantry from here to Tiberias…and no watering holes along the route. So regardless of whatever the king decides to do with Lord Reynald, if you march to engage Saladin, then what Lord Raymond speaks of will happen for the army will arrive thirsty and exhausted."

"So you support Raymond's plans…and what of Princess Eschiva's two sons? What do they think?" King Guy demanded. Balian looked at the two sons and beckoned them forwards. Hesitantly they stepped past Raymond and approached the king. "Well, speak, for it is your mother's very life we speak of here."

The elder of the two young men both wearing Raymond's colours stepped forward slightly.

"My King…I do not know what the stratagem is or should be…but I know my mother…and she would not want to put the whole army at risk for her sake alone. If the citadel falls, 'tis the Lord's will and I pray Saladin will show her mercy."

"Which he will," Raymond interrupted.

All in the room waited in silence for King Guy to speak. Reynald slowly re-sheathed his sword still surprised at Paul's comments. Gerard nodded at Paul briefly in acknowledgment of his timely intervention for he was aware that several within the council would gladly see Reynald handed over to Saladin if it would stop an all out war.

"Saladin has been massing his troops since the twenty-sixth of June… and he has yet more to still arrive and now he crosses en masse," King Guy said aloud as he started to pace up and down biting his thumb nail. He stopped and looked at the group. "You are on friendly terms with Saladin for he holds you in high regard. You must ride under a white flag and seek an audience with him and enter negotiations immediately…

you must be ready to leave at first light." Paul looked over to Balian but he shook his head no back at him. In that instant Paul realised that all were now looking at him as King Guy walked toward him. "You of all here have perhaps the greatest axe to grind with Lord Reynald yet you choose to defend him still...that shows you have the best interests of my kingdom at heart."

"Me?" Paul blurted out, surprised. "I do not know Saladin as well as Lord Raymond or Balian. Surely they are better qualified?"

"'Tis men like you who are our future. Saladin knows that and will look upon you favourably as you know he already does," Balian remarked and smiled and patted his shoulder hard. "Fear not for I shall accompany you in case you get lost for words."

Paul looked at Stewart as he shrugged his shoulders.

"Well?" King Guy asked.

"I am honoured...and I shall do my best," Paul replied and a collective sigh of relief was tangible within the room.

"But we have stripped the kingdom, My Lord, in preparations for this war," Reynald stated loudly and outstretched his hands in protestation.

"Yes indeed...a war you want but one we may lose," King Guy replied.

"But we have the True Cross of Christ!" the Bishop of Acre spoke up as he stepped into view. Gerard lowered his head as if in despair then looked up and laughed.

"Yes we do...but it will not stop Saladin's archers and cavalry. I agree with the king...we send a delegation to seek peace terms." Gerard said aloud to all.

"And what of all the death and destruction Saladin has already rent upon our people?" the bishop asked. "And the Pope has decreed it that we must not deal with nor seek new treaties with Saladin and his ungodly heathens...therefore by holy command you must attack him."

"Ungodly he says...should take a closer look at themselves," Brother Upside remarked a little too loud, Reynald glaring at him briefly.

"Be thankful it ends there...for you have seen nothing yet...and if the Pope believes and feels that so strongly, then I suggest he comes here and deals with Saladin himself in person. He will soon change his position then I am sure," Gerard replied and ushered Reynald to take his seat. "No disrespect, my good friend, but on this occasion I must agree with Lord Raymond that our best strategy would be to hold up in well defended positions…at least until Saladin's forces become overstretched and supplies begin to run out. Remember he has to keep them paid and fed too."

"Thank God for common sense to prevail," Master Douglas said loudly as the bishop sat down looking shocked at Gerard's remarks.

"Aye, and I am with you on that," Grand Master Armengaud d'Asp said loudly as he stepped forwards.

"Are we agreed then…we send a delegation to seek terms for a truce and if no truce is agreed, we move to a defensive posture?" King Guy asked. All in the room looked at each other nodding in agreement. "So be it… so be it," he said and immediately walked toward the small side door. "We shall break camp and return to Jerusalem as soon as Lord Balian and Paul secure terms with Saladin…or not." He opened the door and looked back at the assembled men that filled the hall. He shook his head then left the hall slamming the side door behind him loudly.

"And what of Al Rashid…do we still negotiate with him to side with us, or at least not side with Saladin?" Paul asked, looking at Count Henry.

"If that fool offers us more gold then I do not see why not," Reynald laughed as he sat himself down hard. "You think I am not aware of the gold he passed on…'tis now under confiscation in Jerusalem."

"Lord Reynald…I left that gold in the safe keeping of Princess Stephanie," Count Henry said calmly but clearly unimpressed.

"Well I have a note here saying it now sits comfortably within the king's coffers," Reynald smirked and waved the note then looked at Paul. "And when this matter with Saladin is settled, I shall return to Kerak…with my wife, for I have changed my mind on a divorce. You see, I think she serves me better remaining as such," Reynald mocked and stood up fast to face Paul.

"Reynald…like a man I once knew, I fear you have lost your mind to disease…," Paul replied.

"But you said you would defend me but five minutes ago," Reynald laughed.

"No…I said I would defend your right to be protected. And I promise you this…you will return that gold."

Reynald stepped closer to Paul and leaned in to whisper in his ear, Paul already placing his hand over his arming dagger, Gerard ready to step in seeing the look in Reynald's eyes.

"So tell me, young Paul," he whispered, his breath stinking. "What was my wife's favourite position with you when you fucked her senseless night after night as my informants tell me? And what happened to the diseased man you liken me to?"

Paul stepped back slightly and looked at Reynald intently, whose eyes were now glazed and wide.

"The diseased man, I killed," Paul answered as everyone looked on. Paul leaned closer to Reynald to whisper back in his ear. "As for favourite position...we are still trying them all to find out."

"And what a lovely sunset that is!" Master Douglas said loudly and pulled Paul back by his surcoat as Reynald's face went redder with rising anger. "I hope your tact and diplomacy is far better than that when you see Saladin."

Gerard started to laugh quietly as Balian turned away trying not to laugh. Stewart had to turn around fearful he would laugh as Paul had not whispered his reply quite so low. Gerard immediately ushered Reynald away toward the small exit side door as he spat with fury at Paul's words.

ℰℭ

Paul stood with Balian along with Count Raymond, Stewart, Ishmael and Nicholas looking down from the main gate house at the many tents and soldiers camped outside, small fires burning away dotted the blackness like small stars, with laughter being carried upon the cool night breeze. Master Douglas approached carrying a tray with several tankards balanced upon it, the battlement lit up by several small burning torches. Paul looked up and saw the stars that formed the Pleiades and momentarily laughed as he recalled the many lessons from Theodoric he had endured about them.

"Morale is certainly high...for the men are in buoyant mood," Balian remarked.

"I know someone who isn't," Master Douglas laughed. "He is still spitting blood."

"Look on yonder horizon," Paul said as he caught site of a faint glow and pointed toward the distant direction of Tiberias. "See that glow reflecting from the clouds? That can mean only one thing...the citadel is burning and is about to fall, or has already."

"Best we inform the king," Stewart said as he focused on the distant glow. He then turned and left to find the king.

Raymond lowered his head in sadness.

"Paul," Master Douglas said and leant against the battlements beside him. "I have been asked by Count Henry to return to Jerusalem with him in the morning. To prepare what few men we have left there in case tomorrow goes badly so I am afraid I will not be joining you."

"I am heartened to hear this to be honest."

"I shall keep an eye upon Princess Stephanie for I fear Reynald may seek to have harm done to her. Your response to him today was unlike you."

"I know...but I am afraid my tolerance with his like has been exhausted."

"Watch him carefully tomorrow and on the field of battle if it comes to that, for he will not hesitate to see you dispatched."

"The battle will come for I have seen it already," Paul sighed and lowered his head, images of his dreams flashing through his mind.

"Then make sure you survive it," Master Douglas said and put his hand upon Paul's shoulder. "Or come back with us for Count Henry can arrange it."

"No...I must remain with my brother. Someone has to keep an eye on him."

"And we shall have your back at all times," Nicholas stated and leaned forwards to look at the encampment below. "They think we are invincible with the True Cross leading us..." Nicholas shook his head. "And I get a bad feeling about this venture."

Paul looked at Nicholas, the images of him being attacked in his dream flashing through his mind.

₧₧

After a sleepless night Paul found himself fastening his sword belt as he was being hurried along the corridor into the main hall. Knights, turcopoles and sergeants of many Orders were rushing everywhere. Nicholas was waiting by the main doors and beckoned Paul in. The glare from the early morning sun beamed through the main windows forcing Paul to shield his eyes. The atmosphere in the hall was filled with tangible tension, the air heavy with the smell of iron, leather and sweat.

"'Tis confirmed, the citadel at Tiberias is about to fall," Nicholas explained as they moved their way forwards through the bustle of knights.

King Guy looked ashen faced and was biting his thumb as he sat in the middle of the long table. Reynald stood just behind him, smiling, his eyes narrowing as he saw Paul. Count Henry paced in front of the table as two Hospitaller Knights, clearly exhausted and covered in blood and filth, stood in silence. Balian and Raymond pushed their way through the group of men to the front and stared at the two men.

"Is it true?" Raymond asked, concerned, as two of his stepsons moved to stand beside him.

One of the Hospitaller Knights nodded yes silently.

"And Saladin let you go to come and warn us?" Count Henry asked. Again the knight simply nodded yes in silence. King Guy looked up at Henry. "'Tis as I warned. Saladin is using Tiberias as bait to lure you and the army out into the field."

"Then we must go and engage him. Give him his wish," Gerard called out as he entered the hall from the side door. "Our men are in great spirits, we have the largest army ever assembled now...so what are we waiting for?"

"Master Gerard, you surprise me for you of all know the march alone will quickly temper the men's enthusiasm...'tis far too hot to march, let alone wearing full battle armour. Without water many will fall before we even reach Saladin's forces. No, we must stick with our agreed strategy," Count Henry explained.

"Hah...what does it matter to you for you are to leave for Jerusalem this hour are you not?" Reynald asked, sneering. "Our men have marched in such conditions countless times."

"Yes...your men have...but not those out there now waiting. Most of those men are either too young, too old and most have never even seen combat. They will not endure what your men can," Count Henry retorted. "My Lord, you cannot agree to this."

King Guy looked at Reynald and sat up.

"Saladin's forces ravage our lands as we speak. I know of not one knight here who would not risk his life this day to ride to Tiberias and rescue the very brave and beautiful Princess Eschiva and her knights before Saladin cuts all their heads off," Reynald said aloud. Many men in the room started to nod their heads in agreement and started talking amongst themselves.

"Do not be fooled by this. Saladin knows many of you will feel this way. He is hoping you will act out of passion and your hearts instead of your heads. You march to Tiberias and you will fail...and Jerusalem's fate will be sealed along with it," Count Henry argued.

Count Raymond stepped forwards, bowed to the king and turned to face the assembled men.

"Listen to what Count Henry says for he speaks wise counsel. Eschiva is my wife and I know Saladin will not harm her. At worst he will ransom her...but he will not harm her therefore I say we do not fall for the bait. The assembled army out there right this minute prepares to march, but we do not have enough food and especially water to even attempt it, let alone engage in battle at the end of it," he explained.

Princess Eschiva's two sons stepped forwards.

"Father, for that is what you have truly been to us these past years," the elder of the two said nervously. "We beg of you to allow this action so that we may be given the chance to at least attempt a rescue of our mother. We could accept and agree with the plan yesterday for she was still secure in the citadel...but now, well, we must at least try to rescue her...if God wills it," he pleaded then looked at his brother, who nodded in agreement.

"Boys, I love your mother dearly, but even she would agree with me on this matter," Raymond replied.

"Then you stay here or go to Jerusalem with Count Henry. Run away like the coward you are," Reynald sniped.

"Twice you have accused me of being a coward. Say so a third time and I shall personally deliver your head on a platter to Saladin myself," Raymond snapped back, his tone clipped through gritted teeth.

"Silence all of you!" King Guy shouted and stood up. "We could be waiting here for days, even weeks, waiting for Saladin to come to us whilst his forces overwhelm our lands," he paused then looked at Gerard. "Master Gerard, are your men capable of this march and still able to battle at the end of it?"

"My King...of course they are. As are Master Armengaud's. We can end the rule of Saladin once and for all at the same time," Gerard replied as Reynald, nodding in agreement, smiling broadly.

"Rubbish...'tis madness that you state," Count Henry interrupted angrily. "I forbid this action. The Order of the Templars shall not march this day."

"But if the king orders it, My Lord, then we must obey," Gerard replied and gestured to the king.

"You have changed your tack since last eve, Gerard...why? But with all due respect to the king, may I remind you that the Order answers only to me first and foremost as written down in our statutes. I am the Nauto-nnier, the navigator, or have you all forgotten that? We only serve at the king's request, of which we have the right to refuse. This day, with this action, I refuse for it will be suicide."

"And I overrule that order as is also allowable under our statutes…as I am sure Brother Paul will confirm having once tried to enforce such upon me," Gerard shot back and looked at Paul, raising his eyebrows.

Paul became aware of everyone in the room looking at him.

"'Tis painful for me to confirm it, but only when an order is wrong," Paul replied and looked at Count Henry.

"'Tis a fucking bad order," Master Douglas said loudly and stood beside Count Henry. "Marching to Tiberias that is," he then stated.

Reynald stepped forward and stopped just short of Paul.

"Your chance to speak with your friend Saladin has now passed, and your navigator has clearly lost his way," he said pointing to Count Henry then facing Paul directly. He paused, staring at him, his eyes wide, his pupils large, then looked across at the others. "Men…we have faced far worse challenges and we have won the day. Today we have the True Cross to lead us. Our confident and determined army sits outside waiting. This is our chance…we must take it so we can forever be rid of the scourge that infects this land and spreads daily. What say you all? Who is with us?" Paul turned to look at the men behind him as they started muttering amongst themselves. "All in favour say aye!"

"God wills it," the Archbishop called out and stepped forward to stand beside Reynald.

"Aye," Gerard shouted and raised his fist. "Aye."

Count Henry shook his head in disbelief. King Guy started to smile seeing the men start to raise their arms and say 'Aye'. Paul looked at Gerard in surprise and suspicion as he moved toward him. As the shouts of 'Aye' grew louder, added to by the words reaching the men outside who also started to shout, Gerard leaned close to Paul.

"I have grown weary of all this folly. 'Tis time to settle matters once and for all," he whispered. "So if we do not survive this, do not think too harshly of my actions. You can leave with Count Henry if you wish and I will discharge your obligation and commission this very hour. You can fetch your princess and return to France as I once hoped you would."

Paul looked at him, puzzled at his comments.

"I have a duty to my brother…all of my brothers," Paul replied.

"Then stay…and I shall make sure you are in the rearguard with Brother Teric…not spearhead as Reynald wishes," Gerard said and looked across at Reynald, who was in congratulatory form shaking hands with the other lords. Balian and Raymond shook their heads in disapproval, Balian catching Paul's eye. He shook his head no.

Count Henry walked over and pulled Gerard around hard to face him. Paul had never seen Count Henry angry before but his presence was menacing as he looked fiercely at Gerard.

"Have you lost your mind and all reasoning? You know this will end in disaster. If you march with the king and Reynald this day with the Order, then consider the elm to be cut with immediate effect."

"Lord Henry…with all respect, if we fail this day, then the Order will be lost and Jerusalem shall follow. So pray we prevail," Gerard replied calmly and backed away. "But sever the elm if you must for we march with the king," he finished, looked at Paul and winked.

"Silence," King Guy called out and banged a candle holder loudly upon the table. "'Tis decided. We march on Tiberias…and to Princess Eschiva's rescue!"

A great cheer went up in the hall that permeated its way outside. Nicholas looked at Paul and shook his head as Upside started to check Ishmael's two swords upon his back. As the cheers grew louder Paul took out the small embroidered piece of cloth Princess Stephanie had given him. He unfolded it and looked at the small tear over the heart shaped Sea of Galilee. 'There is sacredness within tears' he heard Princess Stephanie say in his mind. He took comfort knowing she was at least safe in Jerusalem… for now at least. He sighed and looked up to see Reynald staring at him, smiling menacingly. Reynald had got his way and finally the war he had striven so hard to orchestrate.

"Paul, I must leave. 'Tis your choice whether you come with me and Master Douglas or venture on with this madness," Count Henry said, interrupting his thoughts.

"No…I must go with my brothers," he replied, staring back at Reynald.

Chapter 78
Hattin – Lost unto Dust

Port of La Rochelle, France, Melissae Inn, spring 1191

"We tried to negotiate with Saladin, but he would not enter into dialogue...his delegation saying Saladin's patience had run out and he would not be tricked again into a false truce...and so his forces laid waste to the surrounding villages. Many were killed, raped or taken as slaves to be sold off," the Hospitaller remarked sadly, the look in his eyes revealing a deep pain recalling the images he had seen that day. "We could do nothing but watch helpless from the citadel. Nothing!"

"You did your duty, brother, and you protected Princess Eschiva," the Templar reassured.

"Not well enough," he sighed and shook his head. "When we saw wagons of dead pigs arriving, we knew the citadel would be breached."

 2 – 15

"Pigs...why?" Ayleth asked, puzzled, as Simon shook his head bemused also.

The Templar leaned forward to look at them both.

"Because once you have dug a mine supported with timbers, you need something that will burn fiercely with great rapidity of heat to burn away the supporting wooden beams and cause it to collapse. Pig fat accelerates that process many times. When the beams collapse, the whole tunnel caves in including the ground above... and any wall or fortress above it," he explained.

"So much we do not know of." Simon shrugged his shoulders.

"I note you mentioned the Pleiades more than once...is there a reason why?" Gabirol asked and wiped his quill as it dropped an ink splash on his new sheet.

"Why mention Pleiades? Old habits I suppose," the old man replied. "You see in every civilisation there are references to the seven visible stars of the Pleiades. In the Bible the Pleiades are called the Seven Stars. They are mentioned seven times in the Old and the New Testament. They are connected with the female

D N Carter

principle, the symbol of peace and love, the heart, the centre of the galaxy and
the precession of the equinox. The Pleiades are an important reference point in
calendars and many civilisations were highly interested in a very special con-
junction of the cross of the zodiac and the centre of our creation...the Pleiades.
They believed human souls originated from there. Also the Pleiades are related to
water and the start of the rainy season, a theme associated with them around the
world. Water is the essential element of Aquarius, the Water Bearer, as you all
now know and as I have explained its symbolic meaning. When the world again
enters the period of that constellation, then the awakening will begin across the
whole world."

Gabirol quickly wrote down some words.

"I think I have heard of this before. 'Tis why the Jews have the seven candled
menorah is it not?" he asked.

"What is a menorah?" the farrier asked.

"The menorah was originally a seven branched candelabra beaten from a solid
piece of gold. It stands for light, wisdom and divine inspiration," the old man
answered. "It was one of the sacred vessels that stood in the southern part of the
Holy Temple and was lit every day by the High Priest. Only pure, fresh olive oil of
the highest quality was suitable to light the menorah. It still endures as a symbol of
divine light spreading throughout the world."

"So what happened to you, how did you escape from Tiberias?" the wealthy tailor
asked the Hospitaller, bringing the conversation back to Hattin.

"I was captured along with Princess Eschiva when she surrendered. I was later
released...but I suspect our friend will be able to explain how that came about," the
Hospitaller replied and looked at the old man intently.

"Aye that I can," he said and shifted in his seat. "'Twas on the third of July that
Saladin succeeded in luring King Guy into moving his army out from Sephoria.
Saladin had personally led the siege against Raymond's fortress of Tiberias on
purpose while his main army remained at Kafr Sabt. The garrison at Tiberias had
tried to pay Saladin off, but, as explained, he refused. When the outer fortress fell
Saladin's troops stormed the breach killing the townspeople and taking prisoners as
also explained and it was then plundered and burnt. When the citadel was about
to fall, King Guy acted exactly as Saladin had hoped he would for he had taken the
bait and marched his army to meet his."

"Where was the queen during all of this?" Sarah asked.

"Queen Sibylla...she remained in Jerusalem. She spent her days with Princess
Stephanie guarded by Master Douglas, Brother Teric and Abi whilst Count Henry

167

made preparations to bolster defences within the city...and Saladin sent for his entire army."

"I sense that our two friends here are of the bloodlines you speak...and it is they who will continue this Crimson Thread you speak of," Peter suddenly interrupted, looking at the Templar and Hospitaller. "I see you both going to Alba...to continue what the old man asks."

"'Tis partly true...and they have a choice," the old man replied with a smile and simple gesture of his opened hands.

"I wish I could go with them," Peter stated and shrugged his shoulders.

"Well perhaps you can," the old man said and winked at him. "I need to commission a stonemason who will carve and dress a stone, many stones in fact, that will one day be used in the New Jerusalem chapel to be built there. You come from Lombardy do you not?" he asked. Peter nodded his head yes in surprise. "Good... then you are the mason I seek. 'Tis just a Straight Arch lintel to start with, inscribed with some Latin...and you shall be paid handsomely." The Templar looked at his brother then at Peter as he shrugged his shoulders, lost for words. "When I have finished this tale, come and see me afterwards."

Miriam looked at the Templar, her face etched deeply with concern. Quickly he took her hand and kissed it reassuringly.

"Fear not. If I am to travel to Alba then, my dear, your name shall have to be changed to Seincler...as my wife."

"Is that a proposal?" Sarah called out loudly, excited.

Miriam placed her hand to her mouth.

"But you have known me but a few days only?" she said emotionally.

"Did not our learned friend here tell us that when you know, you just know? Soul partner and all that?" the Templar asked, smiling at Miriam as tears welled in her eyes. "If you would have me of course?"

Miriam looked around the table at everyone, Sarah nodding her head yes, smiling broadly.

"You will have plenty more time to learn of each other before you go," the old man stated, smiling.

"You know in my heart I have already said yes," Miriam replied and started to cry with laughter wrapping her arms around his neck tightly.

"Yes...a wedding!" Sarah said loudly.

The Hospitaller leaned over and patted his brother on the back.

"Can we marry the same way Alisha and Paul did?" the Templar asked and held her in his arms whilst looking at the old man. He nodded yes silently.

After a few minutes Miriam composed herself as Stephan fetched some wine to celebrate. When he returned and offered each a goblet to make a toast, Ayleth looked saddened.

"What is it, Ayleth?" Simon asked her quietly.

"Just reminded me of what we were told about Alisha and Paul's wedding. But I know of the battle that happened at Hattin...and what happened to all the knights," she explained and shuddered visibly. "But I do not understand Paul's dreams of the wolf heads and horns. The wolves I do in part but not the horns."

"Ayleth...," the old man said, almost whispering, his throat dry. He quickly sipped some rose water. "The wolves represented both Reynald and Gokbori as you are aware, but the horns Paul saw were in fact the nearby hornlike features of the land where the battle of Hattin took place. 'Tis why it became known as the 'The Horns of Hattin'. 'Twas a Saturday, the fourth of July, where a pass cuts through the northern mountains between Tiberias and the road from Acre to the west. The Darb al-Hawarnah road, built by the Romans, served as the main east–west passage between the Jordan fords, the Sea of Galilee and the Mediterranean coast. But just getting there proved an ordeal for King Guy's army..."

"Why?" Peter asked.

"As the king had been informed...the march was two days with an army on foot. An army on foot can at best cover ten miles but more usually just eight. The mounted knights and sergeants could not ride ahead of them for they would be required for any full engagement. But as the water ran out many became thirsty and began to fall even before the midday sun was at its fullest...and that is when Saladin's forces started to send in horse mounted raiding parties to harass the column from all directions and pick off stragglers either by killing them or capturing them. 'Twas something Paul found very difficult to watch...knowing they would have been better staying in a strongly defensive position like Sephoria rather than out in the open and exposed. Many who started to fall behind in the march were elderly or weak...not professional men at arms at all...and the column could not stop or slow down for them. It was the heat and thirst that affected them the most. Saladin knew he could only defeat the Crusaders in a field battle rather than by besieging their fortifications and he played upon the internal dissention between King Guy and Raymond."

"This battle...'twas the one where we lost the True Cross of Christ was it not?" Ayleth asked.

"Paul would argue differently," the old man replied. "You see he had earlier seen and touched the so-called True Cross and told Princess Stephanie he had felt

nothing, which, she explained, was probably because it was fake. It had been conveniently found by Constantine's mother. Many in the king's army knew this or had heard of this rumour so all the rubbish you hear about it being a rallying point is somewhat exaggerated...though many of the volunteers fell for it."

"That is the first time I have detected cynicism in your tone," Gabirol remarked.

"Then I beg you ignore my cynicism...besides...other factors set the men's minds ill at ease," he replied.

"Such as?" Simon asked.

"Such as the horses refusing to drink before the men set off...but also because of an old woman who followed the army cursing them and waving incense and other items at them. Eventually some of the men who were by this stage totally unsettled by her curses and rumours that she was a witch, actually tied her up and set her on fire...and even then she laughed out loud as her clothes burnt away...eventually one of the soldiers cut off her head. 'Twas truly a bad omen, they believed."

"On fire!" Ayleth exclaimed, shocked.

"Fear and rumour is an awful and powerful thing," the Hospitaller stated.

"As they marched, Gerard and his Templars, along with Master Armengaud and his Hospitallers, commanded by Balian himself took the rearguard. Stewart was made the Templars' overall Gonfanier. Armengaud agreed that Gerard as the more experienced, should command his troops also. The entire force was split into three divisions consisting of cavalry protected on all sides by the infantry...but they were spread over nearly a mile in length. When Saladin, outside Tiberias, was made aware that King Guy had taken the bait, he immediately led his guards back to his main camp at Cafarsset and left just a small force to watch Tiberias whilst smaller detachments were sent to harass the Christian army. Saladin moved his main force to meet King Guy at the Springs at Touraan arriving around ten o'clock. Some Christians had drunk there but the bulk of King Guy's forces had pressed on. Saladin's harassment then intensified as Christian forces moved across his front closer to his base at Cafarsset with heat, thirst, dust, constant skirmishes, booming Muslim drums and a steady wastage of men and horses under repeated arrow attacks. By noon, King Guy's army had slowed to a crawl and Raymond's vanguard was forced to halt at the road junction of Manescalcia (Miskinah) as news reached them that the rearguard had halted. At this point, King Guy believing that his army could no longer fight its way across Saladin's front, Count Raymond convinced him they should swing left down a track towards the springs at Hattin just three miles away. From there they could reach Lake Tiberias the following day," the old man paused. "However with his army spread over a mile on a relatively level *plain, with the Jabal Tur'an stretched along its left flank in a series of wooded slopes ending in a small hill topped by the village of Nimrin, and on its right flank the villages of Sejera (Shajarah) and Lubia stood on other wooded hills, and ahead the Horns of Hattin with the waters of Lake Tiberias visible to their right, King Guy decided to change direction and head for the lake; but confusion split the Christian forces heading off in different directions. Saladin saw this from his vantage point and immediately sent Taqi al Din's forces to block his way to Hattin. Taqi al Din had been commanding Saladin's right wing skirmishing Raymond's troops and Raymond, knowing that Taqi al Din would try and stop his forces reaching Hattin, ordered speed but this proved impossible and Taqi al Din somehow managed to get ahead of him and to the left of the Christian force's vanguard, as Gokbori's troops continued determined attacks against the rearguard which had forced them to stop in the first place. The Templars under Gerard, along with Reynald, upon seeing what was unfolding charged in the hope of driving their attackers away but the charge failed. Raymond advised King Guy to have the exhausted army make camp around Manescalcia whilst others, but mainly Gerard himself, urged an attack on Saladin's own position as the only remaining chance of victory. This time King Guy actually took Raymond's advice and prayed his army could strike out for Hattin afresh in the morning."*

"We heard that during the evening men from opposing sides actually exchanged friendly chat. Was that true?" Peter asked.

"'Twas indeed true," the old man acknowledged. "Throughout that night both sides' sentry pickets could hear each other and did as you say exchange chat. Taqi al Din's division held the open plateau between Nimrin and the Horns of Hattin while Saladin's held the hills around Lubia. Gokbori's division moved into positions within the valley through which the Christians had marched earlier and Muslims banged drums all night, chanted prayers and even sang."

Spring at the village of Turan, Hattin, Principality of Galilee, July 3rd 1187

Paul squinted as he tried to focus forward at the main army being led by King Guy. With all the dust and smoke from fires being lit on their route he could not see Count Raymond out at the head with the main vanguard. Nicholas and Upside rode beside him as he leaned forward to see where Stewart had been positioned ahead of him. Ishmael rode immediately behind him. A loud shout went up from the rear of the column and he quickly looked around in time to see another harassing assault by several Muslim horse archers. They approached fast out of the white smoke created by the fires, loosed off several arrows before anyone had the chance to engage them and vanished again. Several men on foot fell instantly when they were struck and two of Balian's men fell from their horses, also struck.

The sun beat down fiercely and many of the men on foot were struggling to even walk let alone hold their weapons and shields ready. Many men and knights had removed their helmets and replaced them with head covers only or peaked caps, Reynald looking more like a Muslim Faris Knight wearing his. Many banners and standards now hung low, the men carrying them growing weaker by the hour. Paul was dehydrating fast and he knew it, as was Adrastos. Ishmael seemed to be in some self induced state of meditation to cope with the heat. It seemed to be working for he looked in better condition than most. A mounted knight beside Stewart up ahead had his horse suddenly rear up backwards, snort loudly then collapse dead throwing its rider. Many more men collapsed from heat exhaustion before King Guy finally halted the army completely. Stewart steadied his own horse holding the Templars' Beauseant standard high and looked back at Paul just as Gerard did too and as their eyes met, Gerard shook his head slightly no for he knew things were rapidly turning from bad to worse. Reynald trotted forwards into the dust and smoke toward King Guy. Many of the horses were close to collapse having not drunk any water and Paul checked his water in his leather carrier. He was almost out but at least they had now reached the spring. Paul shuddered as a cold shiver ran down his back. He was hot and had sweated so much he could no longer sweat properly. He knew they were in trouble.

"We need to take out those men setting the fires or we are done," Upside remarked as Balian rode up and stopped beside them.

He rapidly surveyed the open area they were halted upon.

"Saladin sends too many of his skirmishers against us...he knows exactly what he is doing in smoking us and harassing our every step. 'Tis a miracle we have reached this far to the spring," Balian said as he steadied his horse. "We are but six miles from Sephoria and I cannot believe Saladin has not engaged us fully yet."

Count Raymond appeared trotting towards them through the ranks.

Paul could see immediately the serious look upon his face as he drew up. Gerard rode over to hear what he had to say.

"'Tis dry...the spring. Saladin has sealed it and blocked it off...we have no water to resupply ourselves," he explained, looking exhausted and half slumped in his saddle.

"'Tis dry...'tis dry. We are all slain!" one of the foot soldiers shouted as a turcopoler sergeant grabbed him and tried to silence him. The man pushed him away hard and began to run toward the rear of the column pushing men out of his way. Several others began to panic, including a mounted sergeant, and bolted away. One of the crossbow men aimed to shoot at them.

"No!" Gerard shouted. "Do not waste your bolts on them for we are going to need every one ourselves." Several more men on foot threw down their weapons and shields and began to run after the others as the rear elements of the Hospitallers moved their horses to deter others from abandoning their positions. All looked on as the men running away grew smaller as they distanced themselves from the column. Muslim horse archers appeared and all the men that had run were cut down immediately either by arrows or the sword. "Anyone else wish to desert us?"

As the thirsty and exhausted men looked at each other they all began to shake their heads no. An elderly knight pulled up beside Paul having moved from King Guy's main army group.

"Brave knights of the Temple. I request I may ride within your illustrious ranks," he asked politely. "My opinions differ considerably from that of the king's I am afraid for he wishes to make camp here. I cannot support his decision...but if my days are to end this day, then I would rather it be with men of honour, courage and with dignity."

"Paul...will you have Lord Montferrat join your troop?" Gerard asked.

"I see no reason why not...but I thought Lord Montferrat was younger... Conrad?" Paul replied, bemused, and looked at Ishmael, who shrugged his shoulders just as bemused.

"'Tis my second son you refer to. I as you can see am somewhat older. But I can still fight, young man," Lord Montferrat replied.

"Good because you are going to need to, Sire," Nicholas stated as he looked around as more of Saladin's men appeared on both sides of their ranks in large numbers.

"Can we not make for Tiberias?" one of the foot soldiers, his face ashen white, asked Paul directly.

"My friend…'tis over six miles, if not more, to Tiberias. We have less than three hours' marching light left…and this army will be lucky to make two miles in this heat without water," Paul replied as many of the men listened intently. "But I fear we may have no other option…and men…we shall be harassed every step of the way."

Reynald came riding back into view sat high and proud on his horse. He saw Paul speaking with the men and Gerard nearby. He pulled up between them.

"'Tis the king's order we march onward," he bellowed so all could hear him at the rear. A great moan and talking went up from among the men. "And…any man falling behind will be left to fend for themselves. We cannot slow for stragglers. Is that understood?"

Paul looked toward the horizon through the swirling smoke that drifted in all directions, men coughing, their throats already dry and parched with thirst. Paul could just make out two raised mounds on either side of the forward vanguard up ahead.

"Saladin is driving us between those…those horns almost," he said and paused as he realised the very words he had used referred to them as horns. He shook his head as images of his dreams momentarily filled his head then looked back at Ishmael. Stewart rode over toward them, the look of concern upon Paul's face obvious. Quickly he pushed himself up and stood in his stirrups to look backwards. He could see large numbers of Saladin's infantry running into position to cut off their rear. "There will be no chance of retreating or escape that way," he said and sat back down looking at Gerard as Reynald just smiled menacingly.

"Any line of retreat is now blocked…we must move forward as the king orders!" Reynald called out and turned his horse around to face forwards.

Many of the men looked at each other fearfully. As the column began to move off slowly following the main army ahead, Paul looked back again at Saladin's forces moving into position behind them with at least two entire wings of men manoeuvring into position.

"I have your back, Paul," Nicholas said and patted his shoulder to draw his attention back.

"And I both of you," Ishmael said and winked.

This was a fatal mistake and Paul knew it. He looked at his brother as he raised the Beauseant standard higher just as the Hospitallers formed up at the very rear. Stewart would be a primary objective along with the True

Cross to Saladin's forces and he prayed he would be safe and protected. The Hospitallers had not even finished forming up when a squadron of Muslim horse archers rapidly approached and fired into them, several knights falling instantly hit, horses screaming out in pain as they were also hit. The Muslim horse archers sped off before the foot archers even had time to aim properly and they loosed their arrows off blindly.

After nearly four more hours of forced marching, many men and horses collapsing and being left behind and with constant harassment and continuous attacks by Saladin's forces, King Guy was forced to call a halt on the small plateau set between the two mounds Paul had seen. Known as the Horns of Hattin, the whole Christian force was now caught between them. Even Gerard was surprised when the order came down the line to make camp for the night with the Sea of Galilee in sight. With no water and no hope of reinforcements or supplies, many men were close to full panic. Lord Montferrat approached Paul, his white beard framing his exhausted face.

"At least we have stopped this march to our deaths this day...but I fear many of us here, if not all, shall be visiting our graves by this time tomorrow," he said quietly looking around at the scene that surrounded them. "But at least I shall die in good company for I have heard much of you, young sire." Paul dismounted Adrastos and looked up at Lord Montferrat, puzzled. "My son has spoken much of you. 'Tis a great tragedy that befell your family. My son met you and your wife and he told me of her beauty."

"Thank you...but I think now is not the time for discussing such," Paul replied politely but bemused at the lord's comments. "I did not know your son that well."

"No...but he made it his business to know you," he replied and dismounted beside Paul and looked at him intently just as Ishmael dismounted. "Please, if you survive this action that is sure to follow...do not condemn me for whatever actions my son has or intends to take for I am not party to it. He is of my loins but he is not of my liking. I do not nor have ever endorsed his actions." Paul patted Adrastos and tried to reassure him as more smoke drifted in on the air. He was puzzled at Lord Montferrat's words and looked at him more bemused, Ishmael shaking his head also puzzled. "You, my son, are not like the rest of us and he knows that. Never trust him...ever...and may the Lord protect you and your line."

Paul was taken aback by his remarks. His throat was dry and he went to speak but his voice just whispered a word as Lord Montferrat turned himself away and led his horse towards Reynald and Gerard, who were positioning their men and tents for the night. Nicholas came and stood beside Paul and Ishmael and saw the look of confusion upon Paul's tired face.

"'Tis going to be a long night, my friend. I suggest you get some sleep first whilst I help with first watch," Nicholas coughed, his throat dry and his lips already beginning to split.

 3 – 13

"Sleep...I think not for we must convince the king to fight on to the sea. If we stay here we will all surely be slaughtered," Paul replied and looked toward the king's red tent being set up in the distance.

"Paul," Upside said and grabbed his arm. "Look around you. Look at the men. Most are not trained and many are unfit. 'Tis a bad choice the king is forced to make but a choice he has no other option than to follow. This lot can only just about stand, let alone fight on."

"Take cover!" Grand Master Armengaud shouted as a huge volley of arrows streaked up through the air toward them in such numbers it turned the sky dark.

Gerard dived beneath his own horse as Reynald just sat upon his and looked up refusing to move in total defiance. Nicholas pushed Paul against Adrastos as one arrow struck his saddle vertically as the remainder of arrows fell further into the main group of the Royal Battalions of King Guy's men. Many were hit in the volley, some killed instantly and many others wounded screaming in agony on the ground.

"That, my friends...'tis just the start," Upside said as he knelt down beside Nicholas and Ishmael whilst Paul frantically tried to check Adrastos.

Paul strained to hear above the noise thinking he could hear his name being shouted out. He looked at Nicholas, puzzled, just as he heard it too. Quickly Paul stood up and looked east across the plateau as hundreds of Saladin's men could be seen taking up positions all along their flanks and rear. As men lit fires, more smoke blew across toward the Christian army. Reynald rode up and stopped next to Paul trying to see what was happening. Paul saw a black clad figure in the distance waving his arms frantically with two small white flags and calling out his name. He realised it was Taqi and looked at Nicholas and Upside shocked. Ishmael frowned hard seeing him.

"Ah I see your friends summon you," Reynald sneered as he looked down at Paul.

Paul moved so he could see better and waved back to acknowledge him just as a squadron of Saladin's men rode up beside Taqi. He could see it was in fact Gokbori himself. Paul looked up at Reynald as he sat upon his horse staring out toward Gokbori, his eyes glazed, the wrapped head band blowing behind him gently as a breeze blew in bringing more smoke, but Reynald did not move or cough, his vision fixed upon Gokbori. Everything Paul had seen in his dreams was now unfolding for real. He looked at Nicholas in alarm.

"I must speak with them. See if we can stop this madness," Paul said, his throat dry.

"Good luck with that...you walk to them they will not let you return," Reynald said and looked at Paul then smiled.

"Paul...I forbid you to venture yonder," Gerard said as he approached him.

"Then you had better stop me...sorry, I cannot hear what you said!" Paul replied defiantly and quickly started to walk through the tall grass towards Taqi and Gokbori, Ishmael immediately rushing after him.

Nicholas shook his head and quickly followed them as Reynald started to laugh. Gerard shook his head disapprovingly at Paul and placed his hands upon his hips.

"Master...let me go so we know what unfolds," Upside asked. Gerard simply waved his hand at him to go, still shaking his head.

Upside ran to catch them up only just reaching them as they were only feet away from Taqi. Paul stopped, out of breath, his face dirtied with smoke. Gokbori looked at him from his position upon his horse behind and quickly raised his hands for his men to lower their crossbows and arrows aimed at them. Upside and Ishmael stood immediately behind Paul and looked at cart loads of arrows being moved into position all along the length of their entire flank. Several other wagons openly poured water into bladders positioned in shallow ditches hastily dug out as water reservoirs.

"Taqi...what are you doing?" Paul asked, breathless.

"King Guy and Reynald refused to work with Al Rashid...but also insulted him and sent word he intended to wipe out his entire Order... so now we are here aligned with Saladin this day...," Taqi explained and looked back at Gokbori briefly before looking at Paul again. "But we have orders to offer you the opportunity to convince King Guy once and for all to withdraw and hand over Reynald. Do so, brother, I urge you…or join us. I beg of you…one or the other," Taqi pleaded and threw the two small white flags to the ground.

Paul looked at Taqi, his eyes full of desperate emotion as he gestured to look at all the men Saladin was lining up. Gokbori rode forward nearer.

"Paul. Yet again we meet upon the field of battle. I so much, how do you say, preferred it when you were building ships for us," he said, smiling, and bowed his head slightly. "I had hoped we would meet again in better circumstances," he remarked and looked at Nicholas, Ishmael and Upside beside Paul. "And with good friends again." Gokbori paused for several moments looking toward the Christian lines and noting Reynald staring back. "'Tis that man who we seek to put an end to all this…the Red Wolf of Kerak. I pray you can convince your young king to see the wisdom in handing him to us…if not, many good men will die needlessly." Paul's mind raced as he recalled the first time he had met Gokbori when Elek had been beheaded. Nicholas had joined at his side even then and it was where he had first met Ishmael. "And my condolences on the loss of your beautiful wife. She was truly a remarkable woman. Was sad news hearing such."

"If you persist this day then I fear Paul will be joining his wife," Nicholas said and stood forward.

"'Tis why this very moment I proffer a way out. You have too many good and great men to throw their lives away for the actions of that man," Gokbori said and pointed at Reynald in the distance. "You know who we are and what we are like. We have both good and bad on each side, but that is even more reason we should work together…not in opposition. We have much need of men like you and we could offer you far more…and respect that his like cannot." Upside looked at him and then back toward Reynald as Count Raymond rode into view. Nicholas could see and sense that Upside was seriously questioning his own position. "I will get Saladin to give your king until the sun sets to make his decision."

"Paul, Nicholas…I beg of you see sense and stay with us. Ishmael…tell them please, they need not engage against your own but do not return… please," Taqi pleaded and grabbed Paul's arm tightly.

"You know I am honour bound and cannot do that," Paul replied.

"Yes you have honour, my brother, but your leaders do not have any so why waste yours upon them?" Taqi again pleaded as Upside again looked back at Reynald.

"Paul," Gokbori said and rode closer to him. "I was once in your position...the very same...and I had to make a decision. I chose the right choice to serve a greater and nobler man. I have been able to do far more good since that day. I beg of you please choose wisely if your king does not...that applies to all of you."

"Paul," Upside interrupted. "Do you not recall the words of Attar...his whisper of prophecy about this very day...between the horns and the two wolves?" he asked as Gokbori listened intently. "What say you we heed his caution...or do we just throw our lives away so that Reynald may die in all his splendour for nought?"

"I cannot protect you this time, my friend?" Gokbori said, looking at Paul as Taqi shook his head, his eyes still pleading with Paul.

Shouting went up further along the line of Saladin's men as several men appeared running from the Christian lines towards Paul, a Templar on horseback following close behind them as if in pursuit. But as he reached the men running, he continued past them heading directly for Paul's group. Several of Gokbori's men moved to a defensive position in front of them all. When the knight pulled up, he withdrew his sword and threw it to the floor. Nicholas looked at him, puzzled.

"My Lord...we beg your mercy and that we may seek your indulgence to allow us to join with you...for we are led by mad men who defile and defame all that was good within our Order and religion," the knight said, out of breath, as the other men on foot reached him looking up anxiously. "Brothers...we have discussed this many times have we not?" he asked looking at Nicholas and Upside.

"Come join us then for you are welcome," Gokbori said and waved his hand for his men to part allowing them to pass. "Paul...you have until sunset. You have my word for Saladin only seeks Reynald. But many within his court want you all wiped off the face of this world. Please do not let them get their wish."

Nicholas looked up at his fellow Templar as he rode by. He shook his head, bemused, as Upside simply acknowledged him with a slight nod.

"Taqi...if this ends badly, pray to our Lord we do not meet upon the field of battle," Paul said and gripped Taqi's arms tightly.

"My friend...if I see either of you, I shall turn away...for my main objective is Reynald. That is my task," Taqi replied emotionally and struggling not to show it.

"To capture him for we want to take him to Damascus," Gokbori interrupted. "Now go whilst you still have time."

Paul slowly backed away and hesitantly started to walk toward his own lines closely followed by Nicholas and Ishmael. It was only when they were some distance away that they realised Upside was still stood near Gokbori. Nicholas grabbed Paul's arm to stop him and they turned and looked back in surprise. After what seemed an age Upside finally began to walk back towards them.

"By the Lord he had me worried there for a moment," Nicholas said and sighed with relief.

℘ CR

Gerard pulled open the entrance cover of the king's red tent to be met with a grinning Reynald stood with his arms folded next to a collapsible table set up with the king sat behind it looking exhausted and strained. Set upon the table was the relic of the True Cross with the Bishop of Acre sat beside it. Grand Master Armengaud stood to the side with several other nobles, Lord Raymond, Balian and the elderly Lord Montferrat, whilst Paul, Nicholas, Ishmael and Upside stood just outside the tent.

"'Tis agreed, My Lord, that if Paul does not return with your answer before the sun sets, Saladin will take it as understood you will not hand over Reynald nor enter into negotiations for a new truce," Gerard explained as he held the cover open, Paul nodding to confirm his words.

"Then I suggest we reinforce the tents with catch nets and prepare for a long night," King Guy said as he stood up slowly. He looked at Reynald and shook his head slightly.

The Bishop of Acre stood up.

"Fear not...for we have the True Cross of Christ to lead and inspire the men," he exclaimed loudly. "We must set it up in full view for all to see."

Gerard shook his head and shrugged his shoulders at Paul before looking back at Reynald. King Guy waved his fingers as he thought for a moment before looking at them all.

"You do not make note of this in your diaries...nor repeat it outside to any others least they take it upon themselves to decide upon actions to hand Reynald over. 'Tis not our way," he said and looked at Reynald, who just smiled back and bowed his head slightly.

When Gerard stepped away from the tent, closing the cover behind him, he looked at Paul and Nicholas as Upside frowned hard whilst Ishmael checked his two swords just as Stewart approached with a spare rolled up Beauseant banner.

"Brother Nicholas...I would ask that you carry this tomorrow in case Brother Stewart falls," Gerard said and looked momentarily back at the tent. "I fear our fates are now sealed."

Paul looked at Stewart, concerned, but he simply shrugged his shoulders.

"If it is the Lord's wish and my fate...then so be it," Stewart remarked and handed Nicholas the rolled up spare banner.

"'Tis not all down to Reynald. We have all played a part in this campaign and God will decide the outcome," Gerard stated as he turned and walked away.

Paul recalled how Attar had spoken of his and Alisha's fate. As he recalled his words he shook his head at just how wrong Attar's prophecy had been and all of Niccolas and Theodoric's parchments too. Nothing had turned out as they had said it would. Attar had assured Thomas that his men had a duty and destiny to fulfil but where were they now? And as for the great secret he was to learn, it had amounted to nothing and most of what he had learned was about to be snuffed out save the scant few details he had managed to pass on to his father. A secret so powerful that it is a destroyer of worlds, he heard Attar echo in his mind.

"I hear Taqi is among them?" Stewart remarked and strained to look across the field towards Saladin's position through the small fires and rising smoke.

"Yes he is...I just pray we do not meet on the field," Paul replied, saddened, his mind drifting back to the time in La Rochelle when they had vowed never to fight each other and the scar he got that night. He ran his finger down the side of his face, the image of Alisha flooding his mind as she had cleaned the wound.

"I pray he meets Reynald...very quickly," Upside stated bluntly and loudly, Nicholas hitting his arm hard to stop him speaking further.

Port of La Rochelle, France, Melissae Inn, spring 1191

"What are catch nets?" Peter asked, interrupting.

"My friend," the Templar said, looking over at him. "They are a fine but strong wire mesh, like a net we set up upon spikes surrounding a tent of importance. Any arrows that fall get stopped when caught in the net. 'Tis just protection."

"Whilst the rest of the men and horses remain exposed," the Hospitaller remarked.

"Please do not tell me that after all of that, and their promises, Paul and Taqi did end up facing each other on the field of battle?" Ayleth asked.

"Oh they did indeed come face to face with each other," the old man replied. "For that night as all the knights dressed in full armour and splendour had to endure volley after volley of arrows as drums beat out, first slowly...then increasing in tempo then stopping just as the arrows were loosed. But then other times not firing. It had the same effect of causing terror within the Christian lines. Many looked on longingly as Saladin's men brought up cart loads of goatskin blister water carriers and poured them into the dug pits. Many men were tempted out and ran toward the Muslim lines," he explained.

"Were they killed?" Sarah asked.

"No, those that ran to them were greeted and given water in clear view of the others watching on desperately thirsty...whilst the dead and dying lay all around them just waiting for the next volley of arrows. During the hours of darkness, when the Christians thought they could not possibly have more arrows, Saladin brought up four hundred more loads of them," the old man explained and shook his head sadly. "Saladin also brought up the remainder of his troops from Cafarsset including more infantry and seventy camels were made ready with bundles of arrows to be sent wherever required during the forthcoming battles. They also set up a caravan of camels carrying more goatskins of water up from Lake Tiberias to fill the makeshift reservoirs with fresh water whilst the Christians' thirst increased."

"I heard that some men picked up and fired the arrows back at the Muslims," Gabirol remarked.

"Oh they did indeed try, but they did not have the range for Saladin's horse archers would rush up close, loose off and run out again. When one knight tried the same he was instantly cut down by crossbow men hiding in the grasses unseen."

"So all our men could do was watch and wait as they were smoked out and fired upon constantly?" the farrier exclaimed and folded his arms, shaking his head.

"Yes...with the added cruelty of having no water and being already of great thirst," the old man sighed.

"I oft wondered how our great military Orders failed that day and lost. Now I am beginning to understand," Simon commented.

"'Twas on the following morning after an exhausting night and many more now injured and dead, plus being almost blinded to what Saladin's forces were doing by smoke from the fires, when they were again pelted with a tremendous volley of arrows from the Muslim horse archers and cavalry together which turned the morning sky dark."

"Surely there would have been nothing left to burn of the grasses?" Simon asked.

"No...you see Gokbori had ditches dug and filled with straws, grasses and oils so he was able to control the fires within them. If the wind changed he could have them covered instantly so he did not smoke his own troops...plus Saladin used volunteers from his numerous untrained but brave Mutatawi'ah to set the fires and they proceeded to constantly set more along the line of the Christians," the old man explained.

"Clever bastard wasn't he?" Sarah stated, looking angered.

"Yes indeed...and still is," the old man replied and feigned a smile toward her. "Even as battle lines were being drawn up by King Guy, his men were already falling, and not just from the arrows but also from fatigue, the rapidly rising heat and lack of water. Morale was extremely low."

Hattin, Principality of Galilee, July 4th 1187

Nicholas coughed and found it difficult to catch his breath amid the swirling smoke bellowing across the encampment. Paul helped him to stand as Hospitallers, including several female Hospitallers, tried to tend to the many injured men being brought up the side of the hill. Upside held the reins of their horses steady as the increasing and decreasing noise of Saladin's drums continued to bang away. The sun appeared as a hazy circle through the smoke on the horizon as it began its daily course higher. Gerard approached with Stewart, both of them wiping their eyes as they ran with tears from the smoke just as several female mounted knights drew up alongside and looked to Paul for orders. No sooner had Paul looked up at them when the entire contingent of all the Knights of Lazarus approached him through the smoke, Ishmael pointing toward them as Gerard cleared his throat to speak.

"Brother Paul...the king's brother Amalric prepares our forces this minute. I have tasked you to remain here with the female knights and the Knights of Lazarus to defend the king and the Holy Cross," Gerard explained as he stopped just short of Paul and looked at the assembled knights. Paul frowned hard, puzzled.

"Master Gerard...," Upside said, wiping his brow. "Surely the king knows our best form of defence is to attack Saladin directly...and now. We know how his army operates for many of us have served alongside them."

"Do you think we haven't tried to argue that already?...but his other lords all argue differently except Raymond. 'Tis perhaps the only time we have agreed upon something," Gerard replied and coughed as smoke drifted past him.

"But what of my squadron? I have trained hard these past months with them."

"Fear not. They shall protect the rear with the remaining Hospitallers," Gerard answered. "If things go badly this day, it will fall to you lot to hold your ground."

Nicholas started to cough badly and leaned forwards trying to catch his breath, Ishmael trying to support him.

"'Tis, I fear, old injuries. This smoke does not help," he coughed again and spat out some mucus and nearly gagged as he tried to clear his throat.

"Then Brothers Nicholas I order you likewise remain with Paul. You just gained yourself a place amongst the Knights of Lazarus," Gerard said seeing the state of Nicholas as he looked up at him alarmed. "You are a liability to me and all your brother knights if you ride in that state. Just make sure you raise the spare standard if ours falls."

"He speaks fact, brother," Upside remarked and smiled at Nicholas.

The image of Nicholas in his dream ran through Paul's mind as he looked about him at the female knights, Nicholas now about to join him, and the red tent of King Guy nearby. The female knights were filthy, some covered in blood from earlier actions but they all looked confident and composed. They reminded him of Abi and he was pleased as well as proud to be standing alongside them. He shuddered. Forewarned is forearmed he told himself. He would make sure he stayed close to Nicholas to protect him. All looked down the slight incline of the hill as a great roar went up as another huge volley of arrows soared into the air. They all looked up and followed the path of the hundreds of arrows and then watched helplessly as they fell amongst the foot soldiers and forming up cavalry below. Yells and screams of pain filled the air as men were hit, arrows piercing straight through their shields held high but cutting into their forearms. Several horses fell dead and injured leaving their knights on foot. Gerard shook his head.

"We had better make a move soon or we shall have no knights left to take the fight to him," Gerard stated as he wiped his brow, sweat beginning to rivulet down his cheeks. "Brother Baldwin...I know of your love for these three so I order you to pull all knights dismounted back here as they fall...is that understood?"

"Aye Master...if that is your command," Upside replied.

"If I do not see you at the end of this day on this field, then I shall see you all on the other side no doubt," Gerard said and nodded at them. "Unless I am in Hell of course...May the Lord protect and have mercy upon you all this day."

"This is Hell," Upside smiled wryly.

Paul looked at Stewart as he held the Beauseant standard.

"Father would be mightily proud of you," Paul remarked and walked up to Stewart.

"If you see the standard fall, make sure Nicholas raises the spare immediately," Stewart replied, clearly emotional. He shook his head to compose himself. "If Father knew how terrified I felt this very minute, he would not be so proud."

"Brother...with that fear and still doing this he would be even more proud. Just make sure you do not fall," Paul said and pulled Stewart close and hugged him. "I love you, brother."

"And I you," Stewart replied and gulped hard.

"Come on, Amalric is forming battle lines now," Gerard said and patted Stewart and began to walk towards his horse held by a sergeant. Quickly Gerard mounted and beckoned for Stewart to follow quickly. "We need to convince him to charge Saladin directly."

Without further words Stewart backed away, nodded just the once and then mounted his horse. He looked back at Paul then turned to follow Gerard down toward the main line of knights preparing themselves behind the outer line of foot soldiers. A commotion went up toward the front of the formation as five knights from Raymond's men broke ranks and sped away towards the Muslim lines. At first Paul thought they had started to charge early but it soon became obvious they were running away from Raymond's forces to join Saladin as they waved their arms frantically displaying they had no weapons.

"Great...'tis bad enough they defect but they will inform Saladin how dire our situation is now," Upside remarked and shook his head. "Prepare yourselves for the king will have to move now."

"Sire...your orders?" a female knight asked as she looked down from her horse. "Where do you want us seeing as Reynald does not think us strong enough to charge?"

 1 – 46

"You are probably stronger and why he sets you here to defend the king," Ishmael remarked.

Paul looked at the tired, thirsty and dirty female knights and Knights of Lazarus as they surged closer to hear him. The female knights all looked remarkably calm considering all the death and chaos unfolding around them but he could sense the tension and fear within all around him.

"Just remember this, if we are full of fear this hour...then I tell you to remember another version of fear I was once told by a very noble man. Fear means 'Face Everything And Rise'," Paul said aloud as the Knights of Lazarus moved even closer, their Master stepping forward and smiling at Paul.

"'Fuck Everything And Run', I heard," one of the Knights of Lazarus joked loudly, making everyone laugh.

"And that is my second option and advice," Paul replied, laughing.

"Brother Paul...do you still have the mantel we gave you?" the Master knight asked.

"Of course. Why?"

"'Tis clear morale is low within the ranks of the other soldiers of foot. We have but a few horses left...not enough to form a conroise even...but our morale is high and we are honoured to be standing with you. We shall defend this line and charge given us this day unto death," the Master knight stated.

"Most of us are already knocking on Heaven's door anyway," the other Knight of Lazarus joked, making them all laugh again.

Paul did not know what to say as he looked at them, their green crosses clearly visible despite most of them already being covered in bandages to hide or protect their ailments.

"Likewise," the female knight said and dismounted. "Brother Baldwin...I suggest you give our horses to those knights without," she said and offered her reins to him.

"What was that you said about fear meaning?" Nicholas asked quietly as he stood up.

Paul tried to follow where Stewart was. Finally he saw him forming up with Gerard and moving to the rear of the main formation. Puzzled, Paul wondered what they were doing as Count Raymond formed his entire group into a wedge formation preparing to charge forward as soon as the footmen moved aside. Gerard led his full strength squadron of Templars back up the side of the hill and rode past Paul.

"Raymond has ordered us to reinforce the rear with the Hospitallers for Gokbori's men are moving into position there to cut us off and surround us," Stewart called out as he approached then rode past fast.

A loud moan went up again as men ducked for cover and raised their shields as another volley of arrows was loosed off. The arrows fell just short of Count Raymond's men, hitting many of the infantry. The moment the arrows stopped falling, Count Raymond stood up in his stirrups, raised his sword high as his knights lowered their lances in preparation. He then shouted but his voice did not carry to Paul and he watched as the mass of men and horses started to gallop forwards in formation. As soon as the knights had passed through the gap opened up to them, the infantry immediately formed up again and started to march forward in an extended line directly toward the Muslim lines following the knights' charge. Paul and Nicholas looked all around them just as the Bishop of Acre ran across their path carrying the Cross of Christ, Reynald following slowly behind him on foot. He glared at Paul, his eyes narrowing. As he approached Paul, Upside and Ishmael immediately stood closer to him, sensing trouble.

"Hah...so this is how we are likely to meet our end is it?" Reynald asked, sneering as several other lords filed past him on foot.

"A lot of us will die this day to serve your ego. You may wish to die a martyr but most here did not choose this," Nicholas stated.

"Oh do not hold back, Brother Nicholas, why not?" Reynald replied, smiling at him. "You should have joined your Muslim friends yonder before this hour when you had the chance."

"Perhaps we still may," Upside said and stood forward, looking at Reynald hard.

Reynald recoiled momentarily surprised at the intensity and posture of Upside.

"I suggest we all fully shield up for what is coming next," Upside said threateningly.

"Then I suggest you do so fast for if Raymond's charge falters, Saladin's men will be upon us within hours at most...," Reynald replied, trying look composed. "Those Muslims fear nothing more than being killed by a woman...so 'tis befitting that if they get this far, many will be dispatched by them," he said and pointed to the female knights forming up in a defensive position.

The leader of the female knights came over shaking her head with disgust at Reynald. Paul nodded at her in acknowledgment recognising her from their time in Jerusalem.

"We do not fight in defence of you...so if you should survive this day know that your time as a lord and master are done," she stated loudly. "All of us here know whose fault all of this is ultimately...and you will have to answer to that before the Lord. Let us see if your secretaries record the truth of this day shall we?" she remarked and looked across to Ernoul and several other secretaries and scribes hurriedly walking past.

"At least my presence will be recorded this day unlike you and your cohort of women abominations...more like nuns of the devil," Reynald snapped back.

Paul quickly stood forwards seeing the fury rise in the woman's eyes.

"We are proud and honoured to stand with you...," Paul said to the female leader. "Reynald does not have the capacity to understand or handle real women...and history will not forget you this day, but now we must hurry to fully shield up," he said and put his hand upon her forearm gauntlet. She looked at Paul hard for a moment then back at Reynald, spat at his feet then quickly turned her back on him. He drew his sword in anger, spit drooling from his mouth. "Lord Reynald...you need save your energy and anger," Paul remarked and put his arm up. Reynald swung his sword about himself several times and then raised it toward Paul. Paul frowned and looked at him directly in the eyes but held his ground as Ishmael drew both of his swords. "You really want to do this now, My Lord?" Paul asked, staring at him intensely.

"Finally you call me Lord properly," Reynald laughed in an exaggerated and deliberate fashion before lowering his sword.

A loud roar of men shouting went up from the direction of the infantry as they swarmed forwards following Raymond's charge. Paul turned to look just as everyone else did through the smoke transfixed as Count Raymond's charge gathered full speed. Paul watched as the point of the wedge formation made contact with the front ranks of Muslim infantry. For a second it seemed as if they stopped and all went silent, then the noise of the fully armoured horses and knights exploded with sound as they collided with the infantry and their shields in an almighty clash of iron and wood, horses screeching loudly as they were struck down, their lower front legs cut off by large scythe weapons and stakes impaling several throwing their knights off. All around Paul they stared at the unfolding carnage as knights fanned out on horseback into the Muslim infantry hacking and slashing with their swords, bright red gouts of blood being splashed into the air, some forming pockets of what looked like pink mist. Another loud cry of men went up to Paul's left flank. He turned as did Reynald in time to see Gokbori's troops starting to advance toward the rear flank defended by the Templars and Hospitallers. More smoke began to drift across the field obscuring the view further. Paul went to speak but Reynald spun around on his heels and rushed toward the king's red tent.

"All shields and arm guards!" Upside shouted.

Paul rushed over to Adrastos and quickly unfastened his travel satchel and removed his shoulder and arm shields. As he pulled them out, a small wooden box fell at his feet. He picked it up. It was the small wooden cedar box Theo had given him years previously when they had first met. Paul clenched it hard in his hand as a thousand memories flooded his mind of Theodoric and all that he had taught him. He looked upwards at the clear blue sky and took a deep breath.

"Ali, if it is God's will...then today we shall be reunited," Paul whispered to himself.

"Not this day, brother...not this day," Nicholas shouted and took Paul's arm shields and started to rapidly affix one to his left arm just as Ishmael started to affix his right arm.

Paul turned and looked at Raymond's knights as they started to break up the Muslim formation and the Christian infantry started to run toward them to engage in pitch battle.

"Oh dear Lord no!" Upside said loudly and pointed toward another full rank several deep of Muslim infantry appearing from just over the brow encircling the men fighting Raymond's knights. "Pull them back...pull them back," Upside said frantically, seeing what was unfolding.

"Okay...so maybe it will be this day," Nicholas joked, his voice dry as he tied off the arm shield. "But if I go first, I shall see Alisha first," he then said and winked. The image from Paul's dream flashed through Paul's mind and he blinked hard. "I was joking, my friend."

"Nicholas...make sure you keep beside me whatever happens...do you understand me?"

"Just try keeping me away, brother. I owe you everything and I will not fail or let you down. If I do go before you, I shall be waiting alongside Alisha for you...but take your time of course," he replied and tried to joke, his eyes quickly looking towards Raymond's men.

Raymond swung his sword wildly at Muslim infantry men but they kept their distance from him. Muslim crossbow men started to take up aiming positions. He knew if he stayed he and his men would be brought down. Quickly he rallied his knights to follow him up away from the crossbow-men and toward the closing gap of Muslim infantry blocking their way. Christian infantry started fighting the Muslim infantry but men on both sides fell under the horses of Raymond's knights and mounted sergeants when they started to charge their way back through the mixed ranks. Seeing this, more Christian infantry turned back and began running toward their own lines. Raymond and his remaining men, just twenty out of the original sixty that had charged in, burst through the closing ranks of Muslim infantry and galloped full speed back to their own lines. The remainder of the Christian forces on the slight incline of the hill looked on in horror as those men caught within the encirclement were first fired upon by a volley of crossbow bolts followed by horse archers loosing off into their ranks...then the infantry closed in with scimitar swords to finish them off. Paul looked back towards the rearguard and Stewart's position. He could still see the Beauseant flag being held upright but he also knew many would be seeking to bring it down. Out of the smoke he saw Balian and Joscelin III riding towards him fast their swords held outward covered in blood. He pulled up just short of Paul and Nicholas as Upside finished strapping on his arm shields.

"The rearguard will not hold. We must make a break for it through the pass and on to water if we can!" Balian shouted. He looked forward and towards Raymond's forces returning up the hill. "I will have word with

Raymond. We must repeat the assault and drive a gap between them. If we can do that, we can hold a line long enough for the remainder and the king to pass through...is that understood?" Paul nodded in agreement but before he could reply verbally, Balian immediately rode off toward Raymond.

"Prepare to break camp," the quartermaster of stores shouted and immediately started to delegate men to start pulling the other tents down.

"He tries that and fails, then we are fucked, brothers, alone on this hill... this fucking horn of death," Upside stated, several of the female knights looking back at him.

"Master of stores...I would not tire yourselves with such," Paul called out. "We shall not have the time and if we move, we must move fast and light."

Stewart suddenly rode into view and handed Nicholas the Beauseant banner to take. Puzzled, he took it just as several other Templars rode past heading to join Balian as Stewart removed his helmet.

"Brothers...Master Armengaud sends us to bolster Raymond's assault. 'Tis agreed we must punch through the pass and on to water for many will not survive this heat without it much longer and many already refuse to enter into the fight," Stewart explained. Paul noticed his horse was injured with several crossbow bolts stuck in it.

"Stewart...your horse. You need a fresh one for you cannot charge upon yours," Paul said and gestured for him to follow toward the other horses tied up. Quickly Paul checked the other horses but the only powerful one that stood out was Adrastos. If the charge worked at least he would get to water sooner Paul told himself and patted him. Adrastos snorted and shook his head as if he understood.

"No, brother, I cannot take your horse. No way," Stewart protested as he dismounted quickly. "Ishmael tell him...," Ishmael just shrugged his shoulders.

"Yes you can...and technically as fate would have it I actually out rank you...so I order you to take him...and on to water and safety. Not negotiable, brother. We shall follow."

"How much water do you have left?" Stewart asked, shaking his head no still.

"None except the piss pots," Upside called over. "It will keep us alive long enough."

Paul looked at Stewart as sweat ran down his face, his coif and down around his neck. His eyes widened at the sight unfolding before him. Quickly Paul turned to see what he was staring at. Below them a massed rank of Muslim infantry appeared a short distance away, their figures shimmering like watery ghosts as they walked up the slight incline and became more visible. They were carrying a vast array of weapons from spiked clubs, hammers, lances and swords with as many horse archers following behind them adding to the shimmering image caused by the heat haze and smoke. As they marched in formation down into a slight ridge, they momentarily appeared to vanish before reappearing a few moments later but even closer. Paul could hear the sergeants shouting formation orders as some of the Christian ranks broke away in panic.

"On me!" Count Raymond shouted, ordering his knights and mounted troops to form up behind him. "We must break this formation and punch a route though...now on me!" he shouted louder and waved his sword in a circular motion above his head.

Stewart placed his helmet upon the saddle's pommel then immediately mounted Adrastos. He looked down at Paul briefly, nodded, then quickly rode off toward Count Raymond. Paul looked back toward the massive formation of Muslim troops as they appeared to move like one giant dark wave. Then suddenly it broke just like a wave on the shore hitting the front ranks of Christian infantry positioned three ranks deep, screams and yells filling the air mixed with the staccato thump and clank as swords met shields and bodies.

ಬಿ ⊃ ೮ತ

Saladin stood perfectly still as he watched the battle. Stood dressed in his full battle armour, a crimson quilted gambeson covering chain mail, gold embroidered gauntlets and a full length robe, he looked every inch the regal commander he wished to portray. The golden arm shields had verses written upon them in Arabic. His gold helmet was topped with a white and beige cloth cover to help shield against the sun.

"Silence," he said and clicked his fingers. "Raymond's charge was far too close. Do not let that happen again," he continued and looked at his son Al Adfal whilst his own men behind rapidly erected a large and lavish pavilion tent to shade them and his staff from the increasing heat of the sun.

"Twice they have charged and nearly broken through toward me...but I note Reynald and Gerard did not ride this time."

"They will soon be beaten...and we must crush and kill them all once and for all," Al Adfal exclaimed excitedly.

"Keep still your tongue for I will not believe that until I see Guy's red tent fall. Do not underestimate the tenacity of the Orders you are up against. If you truly knew the truth of their Templar Order, you would not be so quick to see them eradicated," Saladin replied as he ran his fingers across his bearded chin in anticipation.

"My Lord...Count Raymond is forming another charge," Taqi Al Din said, pointing towards Raymond's mounted knights forming up. "They have Templars amongst them."

"Look...look, the king's tent...it falls!" Al Adfal shouted and pointed excitedly.

Saladin stepped forward and clicked his fingers. He was passed a small telescopic looking glass and quickly held it to his eyes to see closer.

"'Tis not falling, my son. 'Tis being moved to higher ground," Saladin replied and thrust the looking glass toward Al Adfal. "See for yourself."

"But it shall fall for we have almost surrounded them all," Taqi Al Din said as he looked to his left flank as more of their forces moved into position. "Look, My Lord...Raymond."

Saladin looked to where Count Raymond was now charging his men downward toward the Muslim forces, dust and dirt being kicked up everywhere almost obscuring his view. Even from the distance he was, he could hear the clash of horses and men as the tightly packed conroise smashed into the Muslim infantry, men running and diving out of the way as Raymond led the charge like a knife cutting through butter this time. Saladin's eyes widened in alarm and his face turned an ashen white seeing Raymond's men pushing their way through the infantry and heading straight for him. He grasped his beard but then Gokbori rode into view from his right flank followed by mounted archers and Faris Knights. Raymond saw them approaching and slowed his charged to turn to engage them. Both forces collided into a massive moving sea of men and horses as they rapidly mixed, the sun glinting off of swords and helmets. Saladin held his breath as he looked on as even more of Gokbori's men entered into the melee.

"My Lord...I know he is your friend but it is Allah's will," Taqi Al Din said seeing Saladin's look of concern.

"They are both my friends," he snapped back and continued to stare at the fight.

Count Raymond rode past Gokbori, both raising their swords high as they charged each other but at the last moment both pulled aside missing each other. Count Raymond pulled his horse up high. Gokbori turned his horse to face Raymond, their eyes locking. Gokbori lowered his sword and indicated Raymond should pass as several infantry crossbow men partially surrounded Raymond just as Stewart rode up fast beside him. He grabbed Raymond's arm and pulled him forcing him to move with his horse, Gokbori ordering his crossbow men to lower their aim. Stewart led Raymond back toward their own men closely followed by the remainder of their charge. Over half of the Christian knights that had charged were now dead, some being brutally clubbed on the ground after their horses had been shot out from beneath them or now being dragged off the field as prisoners.

Saladin sighed heavily, visibly relieved to see both Gokbori's decision and order for his men not to fire allowing his friend Raymond to leave the field of battle.

"My Lord...the five knights who want to join us wish to speak with you," Al Adfal said quietly and ushered in the five knights who had crossed over earlier. "They say morale is broken within the Franks' lines. They thirst and many are not in the fight."

Saladin turned slowly to face the knights as they were brought before him. They all bowed their heads submissively. All were filthy, tired and thirsty. The tallest of the five stepped forward hesitantly, his outer tabard covered in blood and ripped, almost hanging off.

"My Lord, 'tis an honour to meet with you and what we say is true. There are many who do not wish for this fight. Many were forced to attend...and many are aware of your more chivalrous character than those they presently follow. We beseech you to have mercy upon them...and us this day."

Saladin looked at the knight unsure whether to trust his actions and words as genuine or just self serving to save his own life. He looked back across the field towards the ongoing assault by his own troops as they appeared to be edging their way up the side of the northern hill.

"Despite their fatigue, thirst and dire position, I note many are still prepared to die for what they believe...in spite of the leadership that brought them here this day. Look yonder, the hundreds already slain...look!"

Saladin ordered and pointed toward the carnage before them. "We shall not have defeated them until that tent falls."

"My Lord…we understand," the Christian knight replied and bowed his head again.

Saladin could see the look on the knight's face.

"Fear not. You came over to us and as promised we shall honour that fact. You are safe for as long as we prevail," Saladin remarked, one of the other knights breaking down in tears, relieved. Saladin shook his head and then turned back toward the ongoing battle in time to see Raymond reach the safety of his own lines.

"My Lord…grave news I am afraid," one of Saladin's Faris Knights said as he entered and bowed his head. "Young Manguras has been slain. Whilst fighting on the right wing he charged forward alone and challenged the Christian champion to fight him man to man to decide the battle and save many lives…but he was thrown from his horse and dragged into enemy lines."

"What of his fate?" Saladin asked, clipped.

"They beheaded him, My Lord."

Saladin paused for a moment and pulled his beard. Manguras had been one of his youngest, brightest and bravest knights and a favourite of his.

"Taqi al Din, you must move all of your men and hold the ground, blocking the path to the Hattin Springs at the foot of the Horns to Nimrin Hill. We must move our main army between the foot of the Horns and Lubia hill to block the main road to Tiberias. I want Gokbori's division stood between Lubia and the massif of Jabal Tur'an so he effectively blocks any retreat west towards the spring of Touraan village. We shall shepherd the Christian forces eastwards, and push them onto the Horns of Hattin. Make it happen," he ordered coldly.

೫෮ೠ

Paul dived upon the ground with Nicholas, both pulling their main shields over their heads and backs for cover as another full volley or arrows arched through the air. Ishmael and Upside doing exactly the same.

"They draw ever closer, my friend!" Nicholas shouted out above the noise just as a chain mail piercing arrow burst through his shield, the arrow head stopping just inches from his face and missing his forearm by even

195

less. He laughed nervously as the thuds of more arrows ricocheted off their shields, one piercing Paul's tabard pinning it to the blood soaked ground.

As soon as the arrows stopped falling they all jumped back up to their feet and raised their swords in time to see Count Raymond and Stewart ride back into view followed by the remainder of the squadron. Adrastos snorted wildly but was unscathed as one of the female knights fell backwards dead, killed instantly by an arrow protruding from her forehead. Two of her friends quickly laid her flat, one taking her sword so she had two to wield. She nodded at Paul before quickly resuming her position.

"We must make another, and hopefully final, attempt immediately!" Raymond shouted loudly. "Have the infantry prepare to follow us the moment we have punched a path through. If not we shall all perish upon this damn accursed horn."

Stewart, out of breath, removed his helmet, patted Adrastos to calm him down and looked at Paul.

"We will need every mounted knight and sergeant. Fetch every lance left!" Amalric shouted as he rode up and down the rear lines, the forward lines still fighting off the Muslim infantry. "I shall fetch all the remaining Hospitallers and Templars still with horse from the rearguard."

Paul looked toward King Guy's red tent being speedily erected further up the incline as Reynald just stood with his sword by his side looking on, bewildered almost. His eyes were wide and his pupils large. He looked like he was transfixed in a daze until Gerard nudged him hard to get his attention. The Bishop of Acre cradled the True Cross in his arms as he rapidly sought safety from the arrows within the tent as King Guy stepped inside, the ropes and catch nets being pulled taut. The elderly Lord Montferrat stood beside a Hospitaller named Nicasius, who Paul had heard much about from Master Roger regarding his exemplary conduct and behaviour. But this was the first time he had actually seen him in person. His father had been a Muslim who converted to Christianity, his mother Frankish. When Paul turned to look at Stewart again, he had already pulled away reforming up ready for another charge. He heard Raymond calling out for all four of Princess Eschiva's sons.

 4 – 13

"Four?" Nicholas said, puzzled.

"I thought she only had two also," Paul remarked, his throat even more dry, his tongue beginning to swell.

As Raymond formed up, sergeants readied the majority of the remaining infantry into formation behind them to follow and force a way out. Most knew this would be their final and last attempt at breaking out and securing passage to water. The sense of desperation was everywhere as Paul, Ishmael, Nicholas and Upside made their way higher to get a better look as Master Armengaud pulled his remaining Hospitallers back towards the king's tent, their position being almost overwhelmed. Saladin could see what was being planned and moved his son Al Adfal to take his men further out and form a blocking group in support of the main forces. Stewart placed his full helm upon his head, glanced back at Paul just visible through the smoke. The outer metal of his helmet was too scorching to even touch let alone wear. He checked his sword was secure then couched the lance he had been given close to his right side then pulled his helmet down firmly and looked forward. This would be an all out full charge to the death, their shields slung across their backs. He tried to lick his lips but his mouth was too dry. He felt sticky and sore beneath his tunic, the chain mail feeling like it was rubbing raw his skin on every point of contact. To his left he saw two men collapse from heat exhaustion, one having a fit. The smell of smoke and blood hung heavy in the air as he looked through the thin eye slits of his helmet. It felt like he had put his head inside an oven the helmet was so hot and he felt like he was almost suffocating. He patted Adrastos to calm him as other horses neighed wildly some proving difficult to control. The horses of other knights were covered in many different colours and banners as they mixed in with the Templars and Hospitallers black and white covered horses, Adrastos being the only uncovered horse. Other infantry started to push from behind eager to move forwards whilst many of the sergeants and turcopoles strengthened the flanks trying to hold back the Muslim infantry. Most on both sides were now exhausted as the heat seemed to climb ever higher, shields being thrust against each other more than swords and lances. It was the arrows and crossbow bolts that were causing the most casualties. Stewart could see Al Adfal's men rushing to fill the gap across the pass to block their way.

"You ready to meet our maker?" the Templar beside Stewart asked as he pulled in close formation and lowered his lance ready. "If so then let's make this bloody memorable."

Stewart glanced either side as the other mounted knights and sergeants took up their positions. He had no idea who was beside him as they were formed up from both Orders and Raymond's knights. All other Templars and Hospitallers without horse were now on foot, their heavy full armour adding to their exhaustion. Stewart took a deep breath. Within minutes they would be either victorious…or dead. He looked back once more in time to see Nicholas hold up and wave the Templars' Beauseant banner. He laughed nervously to himself thinking he now had two banners.

"CHARGE!" Raymond shouted and sped forward leading the tightly packed conroise of men. Several knights had not had time to pull their helmets down when their horses were thrust forward by the momentum of the other horses around them. Stewart patted Adrastos once more, gripped his lance tighter and wrapped his reins around his wrist and sped forward. Men started shouting all around him, the noise of the horses and Saladin's drummers all mixing into one loud noise until all seemed to go quiet and all he could hear was his own heart beat in rhythm with Adrastos as his hooves hit the ground. Stewart opened his eyes wider as the charge drew nearer the Muslim line now four ranks deep and behind that Al Adfal's men. Adrastos jumped to miss many of the dead bodies of both Christian and Muslims from the earlier engagements but he still landed upon more bodies, some still alive, wounded. Several knights fell as their horses lost their footing. Stewart focused upon the back of Raymond as he charged, his hair flowing behind him wildly without his helmet. Stewart saw several crossbow bolts head toward him as if in slow motion and he ducked, one of the bolts slamming into the chest of the knight behind him. The multitude of colours of the banners and tunics of Raymond's knights seemed surreal and for a moment Stewart had to check he was not already dead for he could not hear anything. He couched his lance tighter and aimed it at the fast approaching mass of men knelt ahead of him, his heart pounding faster and louder in his ears as he saw some men were ready with their large horse scythes. When Raymond was almost upon them, the Muslim infantry jumped up and rapidly moved aside in a well rehearsed manoeuvre. They ran apart leaving a large gap in the pass and Raymond swiped his sword down into thin air, the momentum of all the knights behind him pushing him onwards within the tightly packed conroise. Stewart looked to his side, his eyes meeting those of the Muslim infantry as they just stood aside watching them rush by, the incline downward getting steeper as they moved. In the confusion Raymond tried to shout halt but with the force and speed of all the others, the charge could not be stopped. Balian stood up high in his stirrups from his position back on the hill to see how the charge was going in time to see the Muslim forces running back into position to close the gap. Al Adfal quickly moved his men and crossbow men to line up and face the rear of Raymond's column. Raymond managed to slow the charge and struggled to turn about. Stewart turned Adrastos around as the others tried to do likewise and reform for another charge but he looked on in horror when he saw all the Christian infantry that had tried to follow them were now caught out in the open and being rapidly surrounded by overwhelming Muslim forces.

"Make ready...make ready!" Raymond shouted as he pushed his horse through the column, trying to get to the rear of the squadron. One of Raymond's knights grabbed his arm.

"My Lord Raymond...'tis an impossible charge. We cannot gallop up this gradient with enough speed. We shall all be slaughtered without quarter," he explained, holding Raymond's arm tighter. "'Tis suicide and you have Eschiva's sons to think of too. There is nothing more we can do here this day."

Hearing this, Stewart pulled up alongside Raymond.

"We must attempt it. If not, all is lost and...and," Stewart started to speak when Al Adfal's men moved into position to block off the pass completely.

Raymond stood up in his stirrups trying to get a better view and kept shaking his head no as the knight held on to him, their horses bustling close.

"It leaves the king with no mounted men," Raymond said, alarmed, and sat back down and looked at Stewart hard then his other knights. They looked an exhausted pitiful sight, he thought.

"My Lord, we must retire from this field of battle...perhaps to fight another day for we are done this day...and Lord Balian still commands mounted men...look yonder," the knight holding his arm stated and pointed to Balian stood up high upon his horse.

"Then alas, Lord God, the battle is over! We have been betrayed unto death. The kingdom is finished...all is lost unto dust," Raymond sighed.

Stewart removed his helmet and looked back toward the Christian lines mostly obscured by the smoke. He shook his head sadly and contemplated riding back but as his gaze fell upon the massed ranks of Saladin's men, he knew it would be guaranteed death. He prayed Paul would survive.

80 03

Paul let out a sigh of relief seeing the conroise forming up down the hill and beginning to move away. Many others looking on started to jeer and shout calling them traitors. Paul could see the white of Adrastos so he knew Stewart was okay and still alive. They would be able to move on to water and safety he told himself. A sergeant started shouting orders and telling the men the charge had no other option.

"If you wish to live this day then you better form up!" Reynald shouted as he started to walk amongst the men and pushing them hard to get them motivated.

"What are we going to do?" Humphrey suddenly asked as he walked toward them awkwardly from King Guy's tent. His uniform was spotless and several men looked at him contemptuously.

Upside stood up straight and took a deep breath as he looked around at all the desperate faces staring at him whilst off to his right the remaining Templars and Hospitallers were still engaging more Muslim forces with Balian as they were slowly but surely being pushed up the hill by Gokbori's men.

"Well...I came into this world kicking and screaming and covered in blood...so I have no worries about leaving it in the same fashion," he said boldly and looked out toward the massed ranks of Muslim forces.

Paul looked at Humphrey, his face tired and ashen white, his sword held heavy in his hands. Clearly scared he was nevertheless trying to look composed which was more than could be said for the king, who was out of sight protected within the tent. Ishmael beckoned him over. As he approached, Paul thought of Princess Stephanie. She would be utterly devastated at losing her son, he thought, not even considering how she would feel about his own death.

"Humphrey...come, stand with us," Paul called out to him as Reynald and Amalric rapidly approached Gerard.

Reynald, seeing Paul, immediately headed for him instead.

"Well, well...your little assassin friend has not made an appearance yet has he?" he asked, grinning wildly. "I think I shall have to stand with you... see if you will indeed protect me from him and his coward friends," he remarked and then looked at Humphrey. "And what hope do you have for you cannot even hold a sword properly. Your mother will be mourning the loss of both of you before this day is done," he mocked.

"He need not fear or have use of it for we will protect his back," Upside stated and moved to stand beside Humphrey. "But I suggest you concern yourself more with your own back."

"At least they will have someone to mourn for them," Nicholas stated bluntly, Gerard shaking his head and rolling his eyes. "Master," Nicholas said, nodding at him.

Suddenly a large cacophony of trumpets and horns echoed across the dry and dusty plateau causing everyone to look down towards Saladin's forces massed below them. The drums they had all but gotten used to, but the horns sent a cold chill down the backs of all present. A foot soldier stood close by wet himself, shaking from head to toe upon hearing the sound.

Port of La Rochelle, France, Melissae Inn, spring 1191

"What are piss pots?" Simon asked, bemused, and grinned awkwardly.

"I can explain," the Hospitaller said and sat forward. "They are but small ceramic pots we carry should the need arise and we run out of water, you urinate in them and drink it later."

"Oh that is disgusting," Ayleth grimaced.

"Makes the difference between life and death. Sealed in the pots it can stay fresh for a couple of hours...'tis in fact cleaner than most water you will drink at that stage and if you have no water, you will not last long...especially in the heat," the Hospitaller replied and smiled seeing the face Ayleth was pulling. The Templar nodded in agreement.

"So Count Raymond and his men did not desert the battle, nor were they allowed to escape deliberately by Saladin, as we oft hear rumour claim," Gabirol stated.

The old man nodded his head.

"Too many rumours, my friends. 'Tis what caused the Pope to drop dead upon hearing the news of the losses from the Holy Land. But no...'twas a standard military practice to open a gap then close it once the knights had charged through when in open ground and if you have enough support troops...as Saladin most certainly had that day. 'Twas impossible for Count Raymond to remount a charge, especially uphill. If they had, they would all be dead too."

"So why did they run away and not hang around to see if they could help the king?" the wealthy tailor asked.

"*Because they were all exhausted and if they hung around, once Saladin had finished the main army off, he still had fresh troops he could commit to hunting Raymond's group down. So no, they headed straight for safety and water at Tyre. Raymond, but more so Balian, recognised that they would need as many knights and men as possible to reach Jerusalem to help defend the Holy City,*" the old man explained. "*So do not believe any such nonsense, writings and rumours you hear that they simply trampled their way over both Christian and Muslim men alike to flee the battlefield. 'Tis mainly vicious rumours to use as a convenient scapegoat and blame the Poleins.*"

"*What's a Polein?*" Peter asked.

"*'Tis a term used to describe Crusaders born in the Levant...Outremer. There was, and still is unfortunately, strife and quarrelsome tensions between those who come from Europe and those that are born out in that region. 'Tis insane but true,*" the old man explained.

"*I have read accounts claiming Raymond fled the field such as the anonymous text De Expugnatione Terrae Sanctae per Saladinum Libellus claims,*" Gabirol remarked, looking up.

"*Anonymous...exactly,*" the old man replied.

"*How do you remember such a name and title?*" Simon asked, facing Gabirol as he just shrugged his shoulders in response.

"*And who was the other Taqi in Saladin's tent for that was not Taqi...the one we know?*" Sarah asked.

"*Taqi Al Din...he was one of Saladin's most favoured officers and nephews even though he argued a lot with Saladin himself. Deeply religious and very generous he was an outstanding commander but he was never the less impetuous and obstinate. He has political ambitions himself and he quarrelled frequently with Saladin's son Al Adfal,*" the old man answered.

"*But as I understand it, that despite Raymond escaping it still did not leave them enough men to defend Jerusalem for here we are with King Richard about to launch another crusade to recover it,*" the farrier spoke up.

"*That, my friend, is indeed true...,*" the old man stated and sighed before continuing. "*For lying dead upon the field between the Horns of Hattin were the best from both sides in their many thousands as Paul and the remaining knights retreated further up the hill were clearly able to see. Gerard ordered that as many tents as they still possessed be erected as barricades to slow the Muslim onslaught... which to a point did deter a full Muslim cavalry assault at least...but you are correct for not a man fit for war remained in the cities, towns or castles having already*" been drawn to the king's Order. Now all of those who gloried in their multitude of men, the trappings of their horses, in their breastplates, helmets, lances and golden shields lay amongst the dead and dying like some great rainbow had been laid across the land the colours were so many...'tis a sight almost impossible to describe as the land seemed to heave a breath with all the bodies mixed with dead horses too. The small town of Marescallia was visible and Tiberias just but a tantalisingly few close miles away."

"Why didn't Raymond go to Tiberias and rescue his wife?" Sarah asked.

"Because he knew Saladin would follow and they would simply become his prisoners there...or dead," the old man answered. "Plus he had no idea or way of knowing how many of Saladin's men remained there. But things became worse when the remnants of what was left of the Christian army grouped themselves into a large wedge shaped formation, clambered at full speed to the very summit of the hill they were upon leaving the Orders and other remaining knights, sergeants and turcopoles to try and keep the Muslims at length. The Muslim light cavalry seemed to be everywhere, and they moved to contain the rampaging Templars. Confusion ran riot in the Christian ranks and the majority of the infantry streamed towards the northern Horn of Hattin, where they took up positions. The few remaining mounted knights were still fighting around the three tents erected at the foot of the horns as morale totally collapsed amongst the infantry, who refused to come down and fight. King Guy ordered them as the Bishops begged them to come and fight. Arrows struck down the majority of the knights' horses so many were left fighting on foot. With no alternative, King Guy ordered the remainder of his forces on to the Horns of Hattin, where they all took position on the larger flat topped southern horn, the army effectively now split in two. The King, the Bishop and others sent word again, begging the infantry to return to defend the Lord's cross, the heritage of the Crucified, the Lord's army and themselves of course. But they replied they were not coming because too many were dying of thirst and could no longer fight. Again the command was given, and again they persisted in their refusal whilst the Templars, Hospitallers and turcopoles continued to engage in a fierce rearguard action. They could not win, however, because Muslim archers constantly sprang up on every side, shooting arrows. When they started to be backed up the hill they shouted to King Guy, asking for some help, but the infantry were not going to return. That is when Gerard ordered the sergeants to erect all the remaining tents as obstacles. By this stage Paul, Nicholas and Upside had fought side by side constantly in the extreme heat to the point of almost total exhaustion but surrounded by both the female knights and the Knights of Lazarus, many taking fatal blows in defence of the three of them. At times they actually fought back to back with Gerard fighting close by, but Reynald always moving back nearer to the king's red tent. Eventually as the sun started to sink upon the horizon, all the organised battle formations were utterly broken up and all remaining units now gathered around the Holy Cross set outside King Guy's red tent as a rallying point. Raymond and Stewart were able to see this from their position as they made their way off to safety. Many Muslim foot soldiers that had previously dispersed behind the hill for safety then came over the summit effectively totally surrounding the entire remnants of what was left of the Christian army..."

"But where exactly did the final act of the battle take place for we heard it was on the southern horn, then the northern horn and then the saddle between?" the Hospitaller asked.

The old man sat up and looked at him intently.

"'Twas upon all three areas, my friends. Before Guy could issue further commands, Balian and Reynald, having decided all was almost lost anyway, mounted horses and made one more last valiant attack against the overwhelming Muslim troops of Gokbori's divisions. As explained, King Guy's bright red royal tent was moved and rapidly set up on the southern horn and visible for miles. After Raymond's charge and escape, Taqi al Din's division made a fierce charge which is when the Bishop of Acre, who by now was carrying the Holy Relic Cross, had to run towards King Guy's repositioned red tent. The Muslims attacked the Horns of Hattin from all sides. The northern and eastern slopes were too precipitous for cavalry, though a steep path climbed the northern side of the northern horn. Muslim infantry had engaged the Christian foot soldiers since early that afternoon and after bitter hand-to-hand combat, many surrendered. Saladin ordered Taqi al Din to charge the Christian knights as they made their last stand on the southern horn and he rode up the gentle western slope that led between the horns as Muslim infantry still fought on the northern horn. Several Christian knights who still had horses regrouped and made two vigorous charges in desperation. One came dangerously close to Saladin as his command group moved nearer the area. The Latin knight leading that charge shouted, 'Away with the Devil's lie', urging his men on...but by then the centre of Saladin's army was upon the Horns of Hattin and the charge, if it had killed Saladin would have won the day for the Christians. Muslim cavalry had to twice charge up to the southwestern foot of the horns before finally winning control of the saddle between the horns. Muslim horsemen fought their way onto the southern horn...and that is when the royal red tent finally fell. That marked the end as exhausted Christians threw themselves to the ground and were captured.

When Balian saw this, his troops were still fighting a rearguard action against Gokbori's forces, and he knew then the battle was lost. He managed to call some of his knights, including Reginald of Sidon, to escape with him along with several Knights Templar who wanted to rush back and help, but were forced back. Gokbori knew the special friendship Saladin had for Balian and stopped his troops from pursuing him further. Reynald returned to the red tent and dismounted, his horse severely injured."

Hattin, Principality of Galilee, July 4ᵗʰ 1187

Paul turned to check where Reynald was seeing his injured horse stagger past him. He was stood wielding his sword in both hands preparing himself to face the onslaught of Muslim infantry now charging down towards them. Gerard moved to stand beside him just as Nicholas knocked a lance aside being thrust toward him and slashed down his sword hard against the man's face cutting it off in one move. Men with lances on foot instantly registered in Paul's mind as being like those in his dream. Several crossbow bolts zipped through the air just missing Paul and one struck the Bishop of Acre in the side of his neck as he ran into view carrying the Holy Relic Cross. As he grappled at the bolt stuck through his neck, he fell to his knees. With his tongue sticking out and swelling up fast, he motioned with his eyes to the Bishop of Lydda to take the cross. Just as the Bishop of Lydda grabbed the cross, the Bishop of Acre fell forwards dead.

"You bastards….you fucking heathen barbaric devils will never take me alive!" Reynald bellowed loudly as he swung his sword around his head.

Paul pushed Humphrey backwards behind him closer toward Gerard and Reynald. Ishmael stood ready with both of his swords. They all knew it was now hopeless. They were totally surrounded and being overwhelmed. Paul gripped his sword tightly, blood squelching through his gauntlet covered fingers. Even if he had his own original sword he knew it would have made very little difference now, the sheer numbers being too overwhelming. He caught sight of Al Adfal and his men rushing up fast to join in the last throws of the battle. Paul turned to look at Nicholas, who was swinging his sword wildly keeping men away just as Ishmael jumped beside him, his two swords being wielded around in such fury and speed you could hardly see them except for when the blood of severed limbs momentarily slowed them. Suddenly Paul saw Taqi appear to his left running through the shielded Muslim infantry. He was heading for Reynald, who was still yelling he would not be taken alive. Taqi had a set of weighted iron balls connected to ropes that he was swinging. Paul recognised them instantly as throwing snares that would wrap around either your legs or arms. All the tents that Gerard had ordered erected started to be lit by fire arrows to bring them down. One zipped past Gerard making him duck as it careered on and imbedded within the catch net of King Guy's tent harmlessly. But then more fire arrows fell upon it, the burning oil of the soaked heads beginning to drip through the wire mesh and onto the red silken tent. Within moments the flames started to grow. Paul, his eyes now wide seeing his dream becoming reality, pushed Humphrey to the floor and threw his shield over him, then turned to face Nicholas, Ishmael and Upside stood just feet from him. Three female knights backed up fast against them and Nicholas had to pull one up and out of his way. As she fell backwards a Muslim thrust his lance at Nicholas, but Ishmael knocked the lance aside then slashed down hard into the shoulder of the Muslim soldier splitting him to his chest. 'This is where Nicholas gets stabbed,' Paul thought, alarmed, and jumped forwards standing on the female and launching himself bodily at a second lancer, his feet smashing into the Muslim's chest knocking him backwards as Ishmael pulled his sword from the other Muslim. Quickly Paul tried to scurry backwards away from the mass of Muslim infantry, Upside lowering his shield in front of him just in time to deflect several sword blows and a lance strike. Upside pulled him to his feet as the other two female knights slashed and hacked out aggressively with their hand and a half broadswords, one swipe taking the head clean off of one of the Muslim archers who was just drawing his bow to fire. Several Knights of Lazarus jumped into view forming a protective defensive line between them and Nicholas, Ishmael, Upside and Humphrey as Paul pushed him down again. Paul glanced back briefly at Taqi as he flashed past him running toward Reynald. Gerard saw him and raised his sword to stop him but he was too far away.

"Reynald!" Gerard shouted in warning, raised his sword with both hands over his head and was about to throw it at Taqi.

"NO!" Paul yelled and instinctively lunged out towards Gerard and dived at him wrapping his arms around his waist and knocking him to the ground, his sword flying off aimlessly away from Taqi. As they hit the blood sodden ground landing upon several dead knights of Lazarus, Reynald looked over at them just as Taqi's weighted ropes flew through the air and wrapped themselves around his legs just below the knees. One of King Guy's knights swung out his sword at Taqi but he dived into the air, somersaulted over the blade and landed upon his feet and threw a bladed sharpened star at the knight hitting him in the throat just above his chain mail coif. Reynald went to step back away from Taqi as he stood up in front of him but with his legs tightly wrapped together he stumbled and fell backwards, the king's red tent now fully ablaze. Taqi pulled out his sword strapped across his back.

"PAUL!" Upside screamed out loudly immediately drawing his attention back to the main fight.

Paul's eyes widened and his jaw dropped as he saw Nicholas holding the middle of a lance that had gone right through him, the Muslim soldier holding the grip end firmly, the Templar Beauseant banner still being propped up by Nicholas's body between his chest and arm. Frozen to the spot Paul could not move in shock as Upside smashed his shield into the Muslims pushing in from their left, Ishmael trying to fend off more to his right. Suddenly Gerard pushed Paul up off of him and jumped to his feet shaking him out of his frozen stare. Nicholas, his face twisted in agony, swung his sword up high and thrust it down upon the man's left arm severing it instantly, blood spurting all over Nicholas. Paul jumped to his feet, picked up the nearest sword and started to run toward them just as another Muslim soldier raised a large battle axe and swung it down hard into Nicholas's back, Ishmael instantly swinging his swords horizontally and cutting into the axe man. Nicholas stopped still, his eyes widening just as another lance was thrust through his left side, Upside swinging his sword down upon the man holding it so hard it almost cut him in half. Paul threw his sword at the axe man as he was still holding the axe despite Ishmael's assault. As it hit him sticking into his side, chain mail links splintering into the air, Upside smacked away another Muslim soldier with his shield and then grabbed hold of Nicholas as he slowly started to fall forwards to his knees. Paul jumped over two dead Knights of Lazarus and one of the wounded female knights and grabbed hold of Nicholas's left arm. Nicholas blinked at Upside then slowly turned to face Paul, his eyes wide but then he smiled. Blood started to seep from the corner of his mouth. Knights of Lazarus kept wielding their swords frantically trying to keep the Muslims from raining sword thrusts and lances down upon them as Ishmael struck out wildly in an almost frenzied and wild attack. One of the few remaining female knights came and stood next to Paul protectively.

"I shall taste the sweet waters of heaven this hour," Nicholas blurted out, his eyes staring at Paul's as he helped lower him down gently.

"And we shall be joining you," Paul blurted out emotionally, his mind rushing thinking how he had stopped what he had seen in his dream yet still Nicholas was mortally wounded.

Upside stood up, angered, and swung his shield about him violently smacking anyone who came near as the last two remaining Knights of Lazarus were brought down by sword, lance and crossbow bolts.

"Hold your arms...cease action!" Al Adfal shouted as he ran into view. He rushed over toward the True Cross being held by Bishop Lydda and kicked him away hard grabbing the cross as he did. He smiled broadly and raised the cross as King Guy's tent finally collapsed in on itself just a smouldering mess. Gerard was already being held captive by two Faris Knights, several of them lying dead at his feet having killed them in his last stand. "'Tis won...the day is won!" Suddenly his eyes widened in shock as a crossbow bolt shot into his back between his shoulder blades. Stunned he tried to turn around in time to see several of his own men rushing toward him through the smoke. One had shot him in error.

Paul looked across at him briefly in time to see him crumple to his knees, then fall forwards dead. Bishop Lydda rolled over and grabbed the Holy Relic Cross but as he went to stand up, a Faris Knight thrust his sword between his shoulder blades killing him instantly. He kicked the bishop aside and pulled out of his hands the relic and raised it high for all to see. Upside stood upright, his shield still held in a threatening manner as he stared at all the men stood against them. As ordered though they all held their arms and ceased fighting. Taqi was stood over Reynald, his right foot forced against his chest, his sword up close to his throat, as two other Ashashin rapidly tied his hands together.

"Kill me, kill me, you abomination...you fucking inbreeds...kill me!" Reynald shouted and snarled angrily defiant until one of the men shoved a blindfold into his mouth.

Once silenced Taqi rushed over to Paul as he knelt over Nicholas, Humphrey still lying perfectly still beneath shields, pretending to be dead.

"Stand down, my friends...you will not be harmed I swear it," Taqi said and motioned for the other men to back away. The female knight beside Paul stood up next to Upside and they positioned themselves back to back watching everyone closely as Ishmael cowered protectively over Paul and Nicholas. "Paul...'tis over..."

"'Tis for me," Nicholas said in pain screwing his eyes up. He took several sharp breaths trying to control himself and the pain as it overwhelmed his senses. He opened his eyes again and focused on Paul's as a tear ran down his blood covered and dirty face. "I pray the Lord has forgiven me the great transgression I did against you," he whispered as Upside listened and quickly wiped a tear away from his own eyes. "I am afraid I cannot survive this one, my friends..." Nicholas coughed and spat some blood as his chest gurgled and he started to shake uncontrollably. "I have been honoured to know you...and privileged to call you brothers...please...do what you must and survive this day and whatever follows for your days are not done...I have followed my Christ, for he alone whatever he proves to be was worth following...as were you,." He coughed as a hushed silence seemed to fall across the battlefield, everyone aware of the great enormity of what had just taken place. An event they all knew would be recorded in history and told for years to come. Nicholas coughed up more blood, some of it looking black. He grasped Paul's arm tighter and looked into his eyes intently. "I shall stand with Alisha and your children and wait for you...so take your time," he tried to joke, coughed once more, his eyes widening. He gripped Paul's forearm tightly again, though his fingers slipped across the sticky blood soaked chainmail. He went to speak once more but he could not get the words out. Slowly he relaxed back, his body going limp. He very slightly nodded at Paul, winked, causing another tear to fall from his right eye. Paul felt him go completely limp as he then died in his arms, the pupils of his eyes widening as they blew and his hand fell to his chest lifeless. Upside looked up and clenched his eyes shut in anguish as they became totally surrounded by many hundreds of Muslim soldiers and knights arriving upon the hill on horseback. Ishmael leaned closer and shut Nicholas's eyes as Paul lowered his head and clenched their blood drenched hands together. He wanted to cry but he was utterly stunned, exhausted and overwhelmed to the point of being numb. Humphrey moved from beneath the mass of broken shields and dead Knights of Lazarus. He sat up looking bewildered as King Guy was led into view by several Faris Knights and Mamluk guards. Paul looked up at them briefly, King Guy standing without so much as a drop of blood upon himself. He looked back down at Nicholas, his blonde hair stained with blood and dirt. Taqi rubbed his hand reassuringly across Paul's shoulders and only then did the enormity of what had just happened hit him. He lowered his head and rested it upon Nicholas's chest and quietly cried, his soul feeling as if it was pouring out and half wishing he had been killed too, the pain of all his losses feeling like they were all coming up at once. Upside collapsed with exhaustion, his legs finally giving way to cramp but he forced himself up to his knees and wrapped his arms around Paul protectively. A lot of the Muslim men stared at the female knight, her blonde hair blowing in the breeze as she stood defiantly. Her blue mantle was covered in blood completely. Taqi stood up beside her just as Gokbori rode up accompanied by Saladin himself, his men parting and bowing as he drew near. His gaze fell immediately upon his son's lifeless body being moved by two of his knights. He closed his eyes briefly, took a deep breath and looked up again, his eyes falling upon Reynald stood with his hands tied behind his back. His eyes were wide and his face still full of defiance. He grinned despite the blindfold tied around his mouth. Two Mamluks manhandled Humphrey towards Saladin and Gokbori as King Guy, his brother Amalric, Lord Montferrat, Hugh of Jabala, Plivain of Botron, Hugh of Gibelet and many others were pushed and pulled across dead bodies and brought before them. Saladin, his eyes narrowing, stared down from his horse at the men stood before him, the battlefield now eerily silent except for the moans of the wounded. Smoke still hung in the air and blew past like whisper thin images of men it seemed. A Faris Knight went to grab the only remaining female knight still standing but she deflected his arm and pushed him away hard. The Faris Knight immediately went to grab her again.

"Stand down!" Saladin commanded and looked over to her, the determination and fierce look upon her face clearly defiant. "You will not touch nor harm any of the prisoners. Not one," he said and turned his horse about and rode over to where Paul was still kneeling over Nicholas. "Enough killing has been done this day surely," he remarked as Gokbori moved beside him. Both looked out across the battlefield as more Christian soldiers and knights were being brought forwards captive. He shook his head in bewilderment at the sheer number of dead on both sides all around them.

"'Tis a truly remarkable victory," Gokbori said quietly.

Hearing Gokbori, Paul sat up and looked behind him, both Saladin and Gokbori recognising him immediately despite being covered in blood.

Slowly Paul stood up as Upside helped steady him and putting the female knight between them.

"Chivalrous to the end," Saladin remarked and shook his head wearily. He looked at Reynald, who was still grinning. Saladin looked away sickened by the sight of him. "Look after all the prisoners until I return for I must check on my men first," he said and pulled his horse around. "Take these prisoners to my tent...but hold the rest outside...under shade. Offer what assistance we can give their wounded...but give nothing yet to Guy and Reynald. Nothing."

"'Tis a great victory we have won this day," Taqi Al Din remarked as he drew up and bowed at Saladin. "A great victory, My Lord."

 1 – 35

Saladin looked around at all the exhausted men and the sheer number of dead again.

"No...this was no great victory. This was a great failure...If it was such a great victory, many would not now be dead...including my son. Today will be marked down as one of the defining moments in history. One day, a long way off in the future, the effects of this day will echo out across time... for today a path has been set that will only ultimately lead to even greater horrors," Saladin remarked and shook his head, saddened. He looked at Gokbori. "Now do as I request."

Gokbori nodded he understood and watched as Saladin slowly edged his way back down the hill through the dead and dying. Paul shuddered and looked at Reynald then at Gokbori, the Blue Wolf who had beaten the Red Wolf of Kerak. Upside threw his shield down hard and looked at Paul.

"I cannot do this again, my friend. We have I fear fought for the wrong side this day for there is no honour in their actions and behaviour...," he remarked and pointed at Reynald. "And Lord forgive me and thankful am I that Nicholas is not alive to see me choose this but I cannot follow men like them any more," he stated as tears welled in his eyes.

"My friend...then you are free to be on your way. Join us if you wish or just go. There are no restrictions," Gokbori said. "We have all lost much this day."

Upside fought to control his emotions as he turned to look at Gokbori in disbelief almost.

"I cannot just walk away from this...and my friends," he replied, his voice dry and broken.

"Do not die a martyr's death for the foolishness of men like those," Gokbori said and looked at Reynald, Gerard and King Guy. "My word too is my bond. It applies to any one of you here present."

Paul felt dizzy and his head started to buzz as he looked at the bloodied carnage all around him. He stepped back upon his own shield, its colours obscured by blood. His ears started to ring inside loudly and he could not hear Gokbori as he ordered his men to start moving the prisoners down the hill. Paul fell to his knees quickly and held Nicholas's hands and looked up at Taqi and Ishmael, who still held onto his two swords.

"I shall prepare and mark his body, my friend," Taqi said and sighed. "After this, we shall bury him together."

"I doubt that, Taqi, for I am now captive," Paul replied weakly.

"Paul...look at me," Gokbori ordered as he pulled up near to him. "You should never have been here in the first place. Remember once I said something to you about that man," he continued and pointed at Reynald. When Paul looked at him, Gokbori dismounted and knelt beside Paul placing his hand upon his shoulder. "You are my enemy yes...but also my friend. You always have been. That does not make you a traitor to your own faith for you were betrayed by your foolish leaders. We have and always will have a place for men like you...," he said and looked up at Upside and nodded at him before turning to Paul again. "I spoke with Hussam once about you...about a dilemma he had. But I swore secrecy with him...but recall he once said to you, if Reynald causes more death, it would be upon your conscience for saving him." He paused as Paul looked at him intently, his eyes bloodshot from exhaustion and smoke. "He was wrong for saying such and I know he takes back those words. He hoped you would forgive him for saying such for it was Allah's will, not yours." Paul let out a gasp of surprise and almost laughed. All these years Gokbori had also known how he had saved Reynald yet never acted upon it. He gulped hard as his eyes met Upside's. Together they looked at Nicholas. "You wish to bury your friend...it shall be so for as I said, you are free to leave this field of battle. I shall even arrange safe escort to be taken wherever you wish to go." Paul looked at Gokbori both confused and tired not sure if he was actually hearing him properly. "And I would suggest you take the surviving female with you otherwise she will not last an hour with the men," he said as he stood up and looked at her. Taqi tried to help Paul stand but he gently pushed him away and remained next to Nicholas. "Any others of you who wish to join us may do so now."

Several knights stood behind King Guy pushed themselves forwards, looked at him, shaking their heads dismissively, and walked toward Gokbori and his men, their hands still tied. Paul recognised two of the knights as being friends of Nicholas's. As soon as their bounds were cut loose they came and stood beside Upside. A Knight of Lazarus rolled over and outstretched his hand toward Paul. Mortally wounded he had lain unconscious. Taqi helped to lift him upright slightly. He beckoned Paul to come closer.

"You...you are the last Knight of Lazarus...honour us please...by wearing our mantle once more," the knight whispered, his throat dry. "Please..." He tried to lick his dry and cracked lips but his tongue was too dry. Quickly Taqi removed his water bottle strapped on his belt, opened it and gently wet the knight's lips. Taqi poured a small amount in causing him to cough momentarily. "Thank you," he said quietly, smiled, closed his eyes and then died. Taqi looked up just as Paul started to shake with shock, exhaustion and lack of water. Quickly Taqi passed him the water bottle and he took it, his hands covered in blood and shaking more.

"No!" Upside yelled. "The knight suffers leprosy," he explained, concerned.

"Not any more he doesn't," Paul replied and took a small sip of water, then took a full mouthful. It tasted like the most luxurious and softest water he had ever drunk in his life. He let out a nervous laugh and handed the bottle to Upside. He took it, hesitated for a moment, wiped it clean and then handed it to the female knight. She frowned surprised at first but then took it, looked at Gokbori, who nodded yes. She then took a mouthful, closed her eyes and sighed. Paul slowly forced himself up to his feet, picked up his damaged shield with several crossbow bolts still stuck in it, then stood still when he looked up again realising all the men around him were staring at him. All were exhausted. It had been a massive and bloody battle and as far as the eye could see lay the dead and dying. Gokbori turned his head indicating for Paul, Ishmael and Upside to follow him. Upside grabbed the female knight and ushered her to follow too.

ജ ര

Gokbori approached Saladin's pavilion made up from silks and outer awnings that spanned outwards offering shade from the fierce sun. Paul, Ishmael, Upside and the female knight followed close behind him whilst Taqi led Reynald by a length of rope attached around his bound wrists. Gerard followed alongside King Guy and the other surviving knights and men. They were not chained or tied but were heavily guarded on both sides. After Gokbori dismounted he entered the tented pavilion as Saladin stood with his back to them, sipping on some iced sherbet. Taqi led Reynald in and made him stop beside Gokbori, who removed the gag from Reynald's mouth. Defiantly Reynald coughed and spat upon the richly decorated rugs laid out. He took a deep breath and stood up straight, his eyes blazing as he stared at the back of Saladin. Saladin paused for a moment as he took another sip before picking up another goblet of freshly filled ice cooled sherbet and slowly turned to face Reynald and King Guy as they were pushed forwards.

PART XIV

Chapter 79
The Deepest Wound Unseen
that does not Heal

Just inside Saladin's main pavilion tent, Ishmael held onto Paul's arm to steady him as Saladin stepped closer to King Guy, who was visibly shaking, Reynald meanwhile standing up straight still defiant, the rope tied to his wrists still firmly held in Taqi's other hand. Upside and the female knight were moved closer inside the tent separated from Gerard, Master Armengaud, Lord Montferrat, Gerard, Amalric, Humphrey and the others. All around the tent more Muslim soldiers and knights edged forward trying to get a better look as all the Christian prisoners and surviving knights were led up and made to kneel in a long line so the Muslim soldiers could look over them. Amalric coughed loudly as Master Armengaud shook his head, the tension in the air heavy. The Muslim forces were not shouting nor cheering but in a sombre mood. It had been a hard won battle and all were exhausted. Saladin beckoned King Guy to sit upon a high backed wooden chair next to his own and very nervously he sat in it, biting his thumb nail anxiously. Saladin approached him and offered the goblet filled with the iced sherbet drink. Shaking and barely able, he took the goblet with both hands, looked at the cold drink and hesitantly took a sip. He shuddered briefly, Saladin smiling at him.

"It is a sweet and refreshing taste no?" he asked politely. King Guy nodded and took a larger mouthful, then gulped almost half of the goblet quenching his parched thirst. He closed his eyes savouring the sensation before remembering exactly where he was. Saladin turned around and looked at Reynald, his eyes narrowing in disgust at the very sight of him. Saladin motioned with his right hand for Reynald to sit at the third, smaller, chair beside King Guy. Taqi released the rope quickly from around his forearms and pushed him forwards. When Reynald went to sit, King Guy offered up the goblet of remaining sherbet drink. Quickly Reynald grabbed it and gulped it down fast, wiped his mouth with his hands still bound then threw the empty goblet to the floor and stared at Saladin, defiance burning in his eyes. He slumped himself down into the chair heavily and half laughed at Saladin. "I gave King Guy the goblet of iced water and sherbet as a sign of my generosity. 'Twas not offered by me to you...Lord Reynald, the truce and oath breaker, therefore I am not bound by our Muslim rules of hospitality," Saladin remarked calmly and stepped closer to them. The whole tent falling deathly silent.

Reynald wiped his forearm across his face again and laughed before sitting forwards resting his elbows upon his knees. Gerard shook his head no at him silently.

"ME!" Reynald shouted and raised his hands together. "Kings have always acted thus have they not?"

"But you, Lord Reynald...you are no king. This day my son, as well a thousand other sons, lies dead because of your oath breaking," Saladin remarked calmly.

"Your son is dead. Oh how sad but at least that will stop your inbred seed from furthering itself," Reynald replied and sat back in the chair and laughed again as he stared at Saladin.

Saladin stepped closer as King Guy recoiled further back into his own chair.

"Trying to provoke me is beneath even you, Lord Reynald, surely. I had expected more from you," Saladin said quietly, still remaining calm. "So I will ask you just once...will you convert to Islam and atone for all the sins you have committed as an oath breaker?"

Reynald sat back and rubbed his chin several times whilst smiling as Gerard shook his head knowing he was playing a dangerous game. Slowly Reynald stood up and smiled again.

"You cannot!" Nicasius, the Knight Hospitaller, shouted from the rear of the prisoners looking on.

Reynald laughed out loud and stepped closer towards Saladin, their eyes fixed upon each other, neither looking away.

"Every Templar and every Hospitaller, save only the Grand Masters themselves, Gerard and Armengaud," Saladin said calmly and pointed toward them, "shall be executed unless they denounce their faith and follow the true light."

"True light my arse!" Reynald bellowed and laughed again, two Mamluks immediately drawing their swords and moving to grab Reynald.

"Stop!" Saladin ordered, raising his right hand, the guards stopping instantly just feet from Reynald.

"I demand to be executed with my own men rather than be a prisoner and held to ransom, which our codes forbid!" Gerard called out. Reynald pointed with both his hands at Gerard and laughed again.

Saladin took a step closer to Reynald as he stood up straight, his eyes wide expecting him to pull his sword or arming dagger upon him at any moment.

"I am not afraid to meet my Lord and stand in judgement before him," Reynald stated.

"I consider myself greatly honoured now that I have in my power such valuable prisoners as the King of Jerusalem, the Master of the Temple and the other barons...and to those I say drink deeply, they shall be spared and held for ransom," Saladin explained and looked around the tent at the many knights and barons held captive. He looked at Paul and Upside. "Save those I order set free," he said before turning back to look at Reynald. "Drink once more, for you will never drink again unless you renounce your faith."

"If it pleases my God, I would never drink or eat anything of yours again," Reynald replied defiantly and deliberately antagonistic.

"Reynald, you may consider yourself a prince...or even a king, but tell me, if you held me in your prison as I now hold you in mine, what, by your law, would you do to me?" Saladin asked.

"So help me God," he replied instantly and laughed. "I would cut off your head."

Saladin's eyes narrowed and his anger grew at Reynald's insolent reply. He looked across at his secretary and other scribes who were quickly writing down events as they were unfolding. Everyone in the tent froze holding their breath except Reynald, who was breathing fast and smiling like a man possessed as if daring Saladin to kill him.

"Pig! You are my prisoner, yet you answer me so arrogantly!" Saladin remarked and paused for a few moments that felt like an age to everyone else looking on. "I, I must go and attend to the rest of my men. When I return, I shall decide what must be done with you."

Reynald started to laugh as Saladin stepped away from him and turned around and approached Paul, placing his goblet of sherbet in his hand as he passed him and walked out to his horse. Paul looked at the goblet briefly.

"You have no choice, and I demand you hold your peace and not offer so disgraceful a choice to a man who has spent his whole life in the service of the Cross of Christ in defence of the only true God and not your abomination of a religion!" Reynald shouted loudly as Saladin walked out of the tent.

Saladin stopped, his hand squeezing the handle of his scimitar, and half turned and looked at Reynald directly.

"You have only ever served yourself...and you did not ask permission before taking the drink. I am therefore not obliged to grant you mercy," Saladin stated then turned away to supervise the return of his own troops. Outside the tent he took a deep breath and looked at the many prisoners before him; nearly two hundred Templars and Hospitallers stood or sat collapsed in their battle-worn, blood covered, broken armour, their surcoats, mantles and tabards all bearing the badges of their Orders, torn and rent by many a fierce blow, their helmets removed from their heads, their empty scabbards dangling uselessly at their belts, their hands bound behind them and their faces streaked and covered in dust. Many more sergeants, turcopoles and infantry knelt behind them. Very few of them were without some wound on their body, their voices just a mere croak when they tried to ask for water. Saladin shook his head as he mounted his horse and rode away. Reynald laughed out loud and sat himself down beside King Guy again, who was now almost overcome with exhaustion and sat with his head dangling as though drunk, his face betraying great fear.

It was a very long hour stood or sat in silence before Saladin returned to the pavilion tent, by which time piles of swords, maces, lances, bows and crossbows of the Christian army had been piled high. All eyes were upon Saladin as he dismounted slowly and made his way back into the tent. King Guy sat up, anxious, biting his thumb nail harder as Reynald grinned and stood up. Saladin walked towards Reynald, stopped and just stared at him for several long minutes. Humphrey started to cry quietly but not quietly enough as Reynald looked over at him and started to laugh loudly then turned his back on Saladin to face King Guy.

"No wonder we lost this day to these goat fucking tent dwellers when we are manned by cry babies!" Reynald roared.

Saladin in one move drew his curved scimitar sword, took just one pace forward as he raised it and thrust it directly between Reynald's shoulder blades, links of severed chain mail rings falling from beneath his mantle.

Several knights gasped in shock and surprise as the blade pierced through his tabard, chain mail and padded gambeson in one swift strike, the tip of the blade pushing out the chain mail on his chest. Reynald's eyes widened as he froze and then tried to look down as blood started to gurgle up through his mouth and out onto his beard. King Guy started to shake uncontrollably and slouched off of the chair onto the floor and then onto his stomach in terror, his mouth wide open as he looked up at Reynald. Saladin stepped back withdrawing the sword instantly. Reynald turned around slowly his eyes catching Gerard's as he shook his head. Taqi stared at him hard then smiled as their eyes met before Reynald looked back at Saladin. He coughed spitting blood forwards at him but it landed upon the carpet at his feet. Reynald collapsed to his knees but fought to remain upright looking at Saladin defiantly. Paul looked at Reynald, everyone in the tent knowing these were his last moments alive. Reynald tried to speak but the volume of blood now coming up his throat and out of his mouth stopped him as he continually gulped. He then smiled defiantly and mouthed silently 'Fuck you!' Saladin swung his scimitar high above his right shoulder and with both hands thrust it down sideways across Reynald's neck. A sickening squelch sounded out and for a moment Paul thought Saladin had swiped short as Reynald's head remained upon his shoulders. Saladin held his position, the scimitar sword held outstretched to his left side, blood dripping off the point. He had sliced so fast and hard, and the scimitar was so sharp it had cut through in one clean movement. Reynald's eyes rolled, then his head fell off sideways, his body slumping forwards. Saladin stood up straight slowly and handed his scimitar to the nearest Mamluk guard. King Guy was now lying flat on the floor shaking in terror looking up at him. Quickly Saladin grabbed Reynald's feet and pulled his body over toward King Guy and rolled it in front of him, the stench of his blood and bowels filling his nostrils as his body had defecated upon death. Saladin knelt down and offered his hand to help King Guy stand up. Hesitantly he took his hand and stood up shaking uncontrollably. Saladin then put his finger in Reynald's blood and dabbed a spot upon his own forehead.

"This man was killed only because of his malfeasance and perfidy…and my vengeance has been served," Saladin said aloud for all to hear. "It is not the wont of real kings, to kill kings…but that man had transgressed all bounds, and therefore did I treat him thus…for he was no king." Upside helped Ishmael steady Paul as they all looked on at Reynald's lifeless body and his severed head facing upwards with a fixed white eyed stare in the middle of the carpet. It seemed unreal that Reynald was actually dead. Taqi shook his head as Gerard looked across at Paul, Ishmael and Upside. When Paul's eyes met his, he simply shrugged his shoulders. "Vengeance has been seen to be done."

Ishmael stepped forwards and knelt near to Reynald's head, several Mamluks surrounding him fast. Saladin looked at him as Ishmael bowed at him, then stuck his finger in Reynald's blood and dabbed it upon his own forehead, closed his eyes and said a silent prayer before standing up and acknowledging Saladin. Ishmael looked back at Paul and simply nodded.

ജ രു

Paul was escorted by four Mamluk guards toward Saladin's private tent. The sun was now just a deep red sphere sat on the horizon almost like a reminder of the day's bloody events. Every muscle in his body ached and despite having been given water and some fruit, he felt unsteady on his feet. Taqi ran up and began to walk beside him.

"Fear not, my friend, I shall be with you," Taqi said just as they were led into the outer awning of the tent.

Paul and Taqi stood alone in silence for several minutes, just the crackle of several flickering candles and a large lanthorn burning away illuminating the richly decorated tent. It was only when a silk screen was pulled aside revealing Saladin leaning over his dead son Al Adfal's body did Paul stand up straight with a jolt. He watched as Saladin gently kissed his son's forehead then stepped away. Paul looked at Taqi, concerned, but he very gently shook his head not to worry. Saladin stepped back and as the silk screen curtain was drawn, he turned and approached them. He bowed his head as they did in return. Saladin looked at Paul for several long uncomfortable minutes before finally speaking.

"As you are aware, I knew your fathers well. They taught me much when I was young. I am glad you have both survived this day...for you may just prove to be all of our salvation in the years ahead," he explained. "But I caution you," he said looking directly at Paul and stepped closer. "You must know whose side you are on for it is neither wise nor healthy to be undecided for it will blind you with indecision and confusion. I know for I speak from personal experience."

"My Lord...I need no side nor religion for I have a conscience and that is enough for me...therefore I act and stand by those my conscience tells me to," Paul replied.

"But what if your conscience is wrong, for I heard the same words almost uttered from the mouth of Reynald once. A very long time ago. Will I have the same problem with you? I must therefore ask myself."

"My Lord...I strongly believe you already know the answer to that. But if you do not and I am being presumptuous, then put me back with the rest of the prisoners," Paul replied as Taqi looked concerned, frowning hard.

"Most people are not afforded the luxury of being able to make a choice... and my earlier promise and that given by Gokbori still remains firm...you are free to leave and I will arrange safe passage for wherever you wish to go. Though I would suggest Tortosa and a ship back to your home."

"My Lord, I know not where my home is any more. I have...I have another obligation now who I hope waits for me in Jerusalem," Paul replied.

Saladin stood in silence for several minutes.

"I,...like you, have lost much, especially those I have loved. That pain we share in common. Like you I too have lost the woman I loved most in this life and also a son," Saladin remarked briefly looking back toward the curtained off area. "Am I correct, the obligation you speak of is one Princess Stephanie?"

"Yes, My Lord," Paul replied, surprised that he knew.

"Do not look so surprised for I have known her a great many years, and I would like to consider her a friend. She once helped me and I do not forget those who have done so. Like you helped my brother once. 'Tis a great pity you cannot decide to stay with us like your friend Brother Baldwin."

"My Lord...I was not aware that he had decided to join with you," Paul replied, looking at Taqi, surprised.

"He will be sent to Damascus along with the other Templars who have joined us. He is a good diplomat and will be of great service in our eastern provinces. He is not alone in choosing us," Saladin remarked. "But if you do not choose us, I understand but I would ask that you consider my original charge of forming a joint Christian and Muslim contingent of Templars. 'Tis something your fathers tried to form. Before you answer, I understand you wish to take one of your friends to Castle Blanc to bury. I can arrange escort part of the way for I have several commanders who will also be leaving for Damascus in the morning. They will be taking all of the prisoners along with the head of Reynald. 'Tis a practice I am loath to agree with but I have those in my ranks who demand it. To show and demonstrate that vengeance has been served upon the great oath breaker. His head will be displayed around Damascus along with the Cross of Christ."

"My Lord, I can escort him the remainder of the journey if allowed?" Taqi asked.

"I am sure that can be agreed. But I would ask that somehow in this madness that possesses men to act as they do, you must find a way to form a union. Now that Reynald is out of the way perhaps you will meet with some success?"

"I can only but try. I am at this exact moment in time feeling somewhat isolated and alone. Apart from those I love and hold dear…though most of those I have also lost," Paul answered and looked at Taqi.

 2 – 3

"Then may I suggest you bury your friend, return to Jerusalem and take what you must from there and return to whatever lands or peoples your heart chooses," Saladin said quietly and looked across at his secretary, who was taking notes. He raised his hand and shook his head no to stop. "I was once told when I was travelling with your fathers, believe it or not, by a tall blued eye man…a strange man, but his words spoke a truth I have never forgotten," he explained and paused, Paul and Taqi both knowing he was referring to Kratos. "He said, be strong enough to stand alone, be yourself enough to stand apart, but…be wise enough to stand together when the time comes."

"What will happen to the others…and Gerard?" Paul asked.

"Personally I would let them all leave now…and show their people we wish to live in peace and share these lands. Raymond understands this as does Balian. Reynald never would," Saladin replied and shook his head. "I have ordered that all the knights be taken to Damascus to be paraded through the streets to show I have done what I promised. They will be given the chance of converting or, sadly, I am afraid they will be executed. 'Tis what my people demand, not what I wish."

"Including Gerard, for he will not convert?" Paul asked.

"No. As I said before, he, the king and the other barons will all be ransomed. I know Gerard was led too easily by Reynald but I also know he is not the same man I once knew…for the better now but perhaps too late."

"May I speak with him before we leave?" Paul asked.

"Yes, yes you may. I pray your god protects you and should we meet again it will be to sign in our new Order, for this world sorely needs it," Saladin replied and bowed his head. "Your conscience serves you well… both of you. 'Tis why I request you deliver a message to Jerusalem."

⬥⬥⬥

The guarded compound was dark when Paul and Taqi were led to a small tent. Many of the prisoners were shackled together and lay upon reed mats in the open. Two dead knights were being carried out of the compound having succumbed to their injuries. A Mamluk guard carrying a flaming torch pulled open the tent and gestured for Paul and Taqi to enter. When Paul lowered his head the tent stank of blood, urine and sweat. From the light cast by the flaming torch Paul saw Gerard sat against the middle upright pole, his hands now bound in chains and rope. Behind him were King Guy, Humphrey to his left and Armengaud to his right. They all tried to look at him as he entered. Paul knelt down in front of Gerard as he blinked through his filth covered eyelids.

"Master Gerard, are any of you injured?" Paul asked quietly.

"Only our pride and vanities," Gerard replied and coughed.

"So you have joined with them have you?" King Guy asked loudly, trying to look behind him at Paul.

"No he has not. He has remained loyal. 'Tis Saladin's order he be let loose…to return to Jerusalem as an embassy and offer terms to Queen Sibylla," Taqi stated bluntly.

"'Tis partly true…after I have buried Brother Nicholas. Saladin gives us time to consider his proposition. If not accepted then there are many within his court who wish to sack Jerusalem at the earliest chance…but Saladin has given his word he will give us time," Paul explained.

"You cannot trust that man," King Guy blurted out angrily. "I order you to instruct the queen not to negotiate away Jerusalem."

Paul did not reply but looked at Gerard, the light from the flaming torch exaggerating his features making him look far older than he was. He shrugged his shoulders and forced a pained smile.

"Since when have you ever obeyed any orders from anyone?" Gerard laughed lightly. "You do what you must for it seems you are indeed guided and wiser than us fools."

"Speak for yourself," Armengaud joked and laughed painfully.

"You must get Brother Teric to take the helm and office of Grand Master for I will not allow myself to be ransomed...do you hear?" Gerard asked Paul, looking at him intently. "You must make him accept the position for this will be the last time we shall see each other in this life time."

"I shall return to Jerusalem and pass on what you both say...and Humphrey, what would you have me tell your mother?" Paul asked, looking over toward Humphrey.

Humphrey strained to look around at Paul so Paul moved so he could look at him directly.

"Only...only that I was a fool. That I love her and if the Lord sees me ever again a free man, I shall listen to her wise counsel not ignore it," he replied and paused, lowering his head. "And I pray she forgives me for not standing up to Reynald for her." He started to sob. Paul put his hand upon his shoulder.

"I will tell her...and she could not be prouder of you." Humphrey looked up at him, his eyes wide and full of tears. "'Tis true for she told me many times of her love and pride for you. You are far stronger than you think."

Gerard coughed and shook his head for Paul to come near.

"'Tis a great shame that we did not have a man like you to follow as a king...for you are the best of all of us. You also bring out the best in all of us...to do better and go beyond what we think possible for the good of all. That, my friend, that is the mark of a true king," Gerard said with emotion in his eyes. "You have saved me in more ways than you can imagine already. I doubt I shall ever be able to repay that or thank you," he said and paused as Paul looked at him, surprised. "I would have followed you, my friend."

The word 'friend' struck Paul hard and he gulped.

"Please protect my mother...," Humphrey said aloud.

"My advice...get her and leave for France for Saladin has no choice but to take the city even if terms are agreed. I know what his court is like and will demand of him. The best you can hope for is that he takes his time getting there," Gerard explained as Armengaud nodded in agreement. "Now go and should you ever be sat in your home in La Rochelle again, please write a true account of these events…and, please, I pray, tell it as it was. History will not recall me favourably nor the king for losing the kingdom."

"If it is the Lord's will that I live to return home, then I shall indeed write it as it was," Paul replied, looking at Gerard intently. "I sense indeed we shall not meet again."

"'Tis a long way from the day I slapped down that young boy with so much insolence in his eyes," Gerard remarked and laughed. "Now go before we all become like women." Paul took hold of Gerard's bound hands and looked at him. "I pray also that you will forgive my part in your father's death. I now see all too clearly that was perhaps the second biggest mistake of my life," Gerard said, looking up at Taqi before looking back at Paul. "Do not feel guilty about being freed. Take the opportunity and make it count. And thank you for reminding me of what and who I am."

Paul partially stood up and looked at Gerard, their eyes fixed. He fought to find some suitable words to say but in truth he could not think of anything. Perhaps that was the whole point…words were not required. He stood up fully, bowed his head at him, nodded quickly at Humphrey and then stepped out of the tent closely followed by Taqi. Immediately they were led away out of the compound.

"I would advise you replace your Templar surcoat and mantle for the coming journey, my friend," Taqi advised and put his arm around Paul's shoulders.

Port of La Rochelle, France, Melissae Inn, spring 1191

Ayleth held her hands to her mouth holding her breath as she listened intently. Sarah could see the look of horror on her face and gently clasped her hands and lowered them.

"Ayleth…breathe, girl," Sarah said softly.

"Well I think we all know now why Paul's shield was so badly damaged," Simon stated.

"Why did Ishmael do what Saladin did as a mark of vengeance…with the blood?" Peter asked.

"Have you forgotten that it was Reynald and his knights who had destroyed his village and thrown his son off the cliff?" the old man replied.

"Of course," the Genoese sailor remarked and shook his head. "How could I forget that?"

"But how come he was allowed to keep his swords?" Gabirol asked.

"The same reason Upside and the female knight were also allowed...because they had made it known they would not take up arms against Saladin again and had already been freed to leave if they so chose," the old man explained.

"'Tis a strange way to fight wars," Peter exclaimed and rubbed his head, feeling confused.

"We were told that all the other knights demanded they be executed at once and refused to convert or to accept water...so all were beheaded," the farrier remarked.

"That is the simple version told the length and breadth of Christendom but in truth it was slightly different to that. You see, as ordered, Reynald's head was placed upon a pole and taken to Damascus to be paraded around its streets. All infantry, sergeants and turcopoles were sold off into slavery or, as some did, they converted to Islam. Several knights, mainly captured knights of Balian's court, converted to Islam as well as a few Templars and Hospitallers, Upside being one of them, the rest of the knights being held in captivity befitting their status within the citadel of Damascus," the old man explained.

"So how did you escape?...you said you would explain" Peter asked looking at the Hospitaller.

"Let him explain," the Hospitaller replied pointing to the old man.

"Saladin sent some of his commanders and troops back to Damascus, along with King Guy, Gerard, Armengaud, Humphrey and of course many other nobles including the elderly Lord Montferrat. Many ordinary men at arms claimed they were knights in order to be executed rather than be held as prisoners or be sold into slavery. Two days after the battle, the captured Templars and Hospitallers were given the opportunity to convert to Islam. Most refused so after reaching Damascus they were put in prison as was appropriate for them. 'Twas on Monday the sixth of July that those who refused to convert to Islam were finally executed; truly out of character for Saladin but his hands had been forced due to the impossible attitude of the Christian leaders. Some did convert but two hundred and thirty were beheaded. The True Cross was also hung upside down upon a lance beside Reynald's head. And so it was that Saladin had to approve the final order even though he was not present. The knights willingly lined up, knelt down and offered their necks to be the first to be executed...and so they were, all of them beheaded in total silence except for Brother Nicasius calling out for them to remain steadfast and brave. But in answer as to how our good friend here escaped. Well Saladin travelled the six miles *from Hattin to Tiberias on the Sunday...the fifth of July, and Countess Eschiva surrendered the citadel of the fortress. But for doing so without further bloodshed, she was allowed to leave for Tripoli with all her family, followers and possessions including her knights for escort...and that is how our good friend here was able to leave alive," the old man explained.*

"'Tis a guilt many of us cannot carry lightly," the Hospitaller remarked and lowered his head.

"Then suffer the guilt no more, my friend," the old man said reverentially. "You found yourself having to do extraordinary things in extraordinary circumstances... and you more than defended the citadel...for I read the after action reports on your conduct. 'Twas mainly down to your actions and guidance that the citadel held at all. Surviving to live another day should not make you feel guilty. You were not born to die a martyr's death."

"So that is how we lost the most sacred Holy Cross," Ayleth remarked, shaking her head sadly.

"Even though you say it was just a fake relic," Gabirol said and looked the old man directly in the eye.

"Yes it was just that. But symbolically it had just as much power for those who believed in it. It was very conveniently discovered in AD 326 by the mother of Constantine the Great as I said earlier. The true relics still lay secure and hidden within Jerusalem within the Templars' vaults...and that is what Queen Tamar was after!" the old man revealed.

"And what of Jerusalem and Queen Sibylla?" Gabirol asked.

"She remained alongside Princess Stephanie...and waited anxiously," the old man answered and sighed again.

City of Jerusalem, Kingdom of Jerusalem, July 6th 1187

Queen Sibylla ran as fast she could pulling Princess Stephanie along by her hand as she tried to gather up her long dress. They ran down the stairs into the main hall and stopped perfectly still in alarm seeing the state of two messengers from Balian's men, exhausted and covered in blood, their clothing and chain mail armour torn. The looks upon their faces told them everything they needed to know in an instant. Queen Sibylla put her hand to her mouth as she slowly stepped forwards, Brother Teric holding up a note from Balian. His eyes were wide as he read the details. He looked up at Princess Stephanie, his face turning white. She felt sick, her stomach instantly knotting. She had to force herself to breathe and took in several short sharp breaths.

"My Ladies...'tis word from Lord Balian...all is lost," Brother Teric said, his voice broken with emotion.

"What do you mean lost?" Queen Sibylla demanded.

"Our entire army has been routed...and utterly laid waste between the Horns of Hattin. Lord Raymond and Balian are amongst but a handful who managed to escape. They are now at Tyre safe...but Tiberias has fallen...and..."

"Eschiva!" Queen Sibylla said aloud and looked back at Princess Stephanie as she stepped backwards shaking her head no refusing to hear what she was being told.

One of the blood covered messengers stepped forwards.

"Princess Stephanie," Stewart said in a low dry voice.

Princess Stephanie looked at him only then recognising him. She covered her mouth shocked as tears welled in her eyes. As other members of the court rushed into the hall along with several Templars, Queen Sibylla held her hand up for them to all stop and be silent. Brother Teric looked at the note again and continued to read it.

"Lord Balian further explains that the king, all of his court, the Grand Masters of all the Orders, which includes the Knights of our Lady of Montjoie from Spain, were all either killed or captured. All the Knights of Lazarus have fallen to a man...and the entire female contingent utterly wiped out too. It states that he has received word from an embassy sent by Saladin that he is prepared to enter into ransom negotiations for the barons and Masters only."

"Then what of the others?" Princess Stephanie asked, alarmed.

"My Lady...it says that all knights of the Templars and Hospitallers who do not convert to Islam shall be put to death...no exceptions and not negotiable...and...and," Brother Teric hesitated.

"What?" Queen Sibylla demanded and clenched her fists.

"It further states that the embassy sent from Saladin wishes it to be known that Princess Stephanie's son Humphrey lives and that they will willingly ransom him for the castles and estates of Montreal and Kerak."

"He can have them willingly but Reynald will never agree to that," Princess Stephanie replied, walking nearer to Brother Teric.

"My Lady…perhaps you should sit down and read the last part," Brother Teric said and handed her the note.

She took it, her hands shaking uncontrollably. She blinked as she tried to focus through the welling tears. The words were plain enough. She looked up at Brother Teric then to Queen Sibylla.

"Lord Reynald is dead," she said in disbelief. Feeling sick she faced Stewart and approached him now barely able to speak. She tried to ask him a question but the words would not come. She screwed the letter up tight in her hands and raised it in her clenched fist. Stewart knew what she wanted to know.

"My Lady…the last I saw of Paul he was surrounded by a countless number of Muslims…fighting a last stand battle besides the king's tent… when it fell, that was the last I saw. Not even a cat could have squeezed its way out of that mess. I am sorry," Stewart explained as a hushed silence fell over the entire hall.

Princess Stephanie clenched her stomach and fought to control her tears.

"How many men at arms and knights do we have to defend Jerusalem?" Queen Sibylla asked, breaking the silence.

The Bishop of Jerusalem, Heraclius stepped forwards and looked around the room and then at Stewart.

"My Queen…I believe just those two and the knights already in this hall are the only knights we have," he explained looking at Stewart and Brother Teric.

"You forget there are more of us," Master Douglas called out as he entered the room accompanied by Abi walking into the hall quickly.

"But only elderly and infirm knights remain," Heraclius replied.

"Well open your eyes for I am neither old nor infirm…perhaps a little aged but not infirm," Master Douglas shot back and approached Princess Stephanie and gently took Balian's note from her hands. "May I?" he asked. She nodded in silence. Quickly he read it then looked at her. "Paul lives…I just know it."

Princess Stephanie let out an involuntary cry of relief just hearing his reassuring words. She looked at Stewart then Abi as she nodded in agreement. All looked as Count Henry entered the room accompanied by his squire.

"Just how many were killed?" he asked loudly.

"Master…I do not know exactly how many were killed, but I can tell you that less than three thousand of us escaped, most of whom are injured in some manner," Stewart answered.

"Just three thousand! Out of nearly forty thousand men?" he asked, exasperated, looking stunned.

"My husband…he lives?" a woman asked from the back of the hall as she entered through a small side door and stepped forwards.

Stewart looked at her and recognised her immediately as Balian's wife, Maria Comnena, and the queen's consort. She stood nervously as she held one of her children close by her side, both looking desperate.

"Yes my lady. He lives and is uninjured," Stewart answered.

Balian's young son turned his head into his mother's side and began to cry with relief as she stood still fighting to remain composed, tears welling in her eyes as she stared at Stewart. She gulped unable to speak and then nodded in acknowledgement to him, a tear rolling down her cheek as she blinked. Princess Stephanie wrapped her arms around herself and walked over to the main windows and looked out, people outside running everywhere as word of the disaster began to spread out across the city. Brother Teric moved to stand beside her. She took a deep breath and looked upwards at the clear blue sky above and shook her head questioningly asking herself why when loving someone so much it also brings so much pain too. She closed her eyes and prayed just as Abi touched her shoulder gently.

"I sense he does indeed live and we will find a way of getting him back," she said reassuringly.

"'Tis this deep pain within me I sense. How is it that loving someone causes so much pain?" she asked.

"You cannot protect yourself from sadness without protecting yourself from happiness. The happier and the deeper the love, the sadder and greater the pain when it is lost. But you have not lost his love of that I am certain," Abi said reassuringly.

"Right!" Count Henry shouted out. "We need to prepare our defences now."

Stewart just watched him as he walked away then at Abi stood with Princess Stephanie and Brother Teric. Suddenly Master Douglas patted him across the back hard.

"Come on, Templar. This is what you signed up for and where you get to earn your position," Master Douglas said smiling. "You think you've had it tough so far…you have not seen anything yet…and we must help your new Grand Master," he finished and nodded toward Brother Teric. "Whether he likes it or not."

Castle Blanc, County of Tripoli in the Levant, July 12th 1187

Paul now wearing the mantle of the Knights of Lazarus stood back from the edge of the freshly dug grave set between the lemon tree and wall over-looking the plateau beyond. Two Templar sergeants wearing just their black working robes climbed up looking hot and sweaty. One of them nodded confirming it was deep enough as Upside delicately prepared the final stitching on the heavy cloth wrapped around Nicholas's body. Upside was wearing his full Templar uniform still but with the red cross removed where he had torn it off. He had been given a red crescent emblem to sew on once he made his way east after the burial to show he was now a convert as instructed for his own safety as well as that of the female knight accompanying them. The body bag surrounding Nicholas was thickly lined with leather and protective sealing oils that had reduced the smell greatly whilst they had journeyed from Hattin. It was a fragrant smell Paul would never forget. Taqi approached carrying a water pitcher and some wooden tankards. The afternoon air blew a cool breeze across Paul's face as his eyes fell upon the carving Alisha had etched deep almost ten years previously. It was partially obscured now by the years of growth and was higher up the trunk but at least Paul knew Nicholas was being buried where he had requested. Upside stood up slowly and faced Paul and wiped his face sadly. He simply nodded Nicholas was ready. After a quick drink Taqi motioned for them to help ease Nicholas into the grave. The local Templar Marshal approached and greeted them all politely accompanied by one of the Hospitallers and an order of service to read out. Ishmael stood some distance away keeping careful watch.

"My friends. 'Tis more than a little dangerous you staying here. The news you bring of the disaster at Hattin will soon be upon all tongues. I and my brethren, our brethren together, will not be able to guarantee your safety," the local Templar Marshal explained, looking at Taqi and then at Upside. "And what of her?" he asked pointing to the female knight.

"Her has a name, Master," she replied, irritated by his tone.

"Master, she is tired and weary. She fought at Hattin and is the only survivor of her troop, so please she deserves our respect," Upside remarked and looked at her.

"I shall be gone before sunset. I have done what was asked of me," Taqi interrupted, seeing the look the female was getting.

 1 – 17

"Likewise so shall we be gone too," Upside said and motioned with his hand to the female knight to stand closer to him. "We have served our time and we leave as granted by our Grand Master," Upside explained.

Paul looked at them knowing Upside had no choice but to lie to cover his real reasons. He recalled Upside's conversation years previous when he had said he would never lie under any circumstances…but today, with the safety of all of them at stake, he had no choice. If they knew he had changed faiths and was heading on to Damascus afterwards, his chances of staying alive would not be good. The Templar Marshal looked at him briefly with suspicion.

"Brother Upside. I have known you many years. I know not what really occurs here, nor do I need to, for I know of all people here you have more than served loyally for many years…but I agree 'tis wise you leave as soon as you are able," the Templar Marshal said, knowing Upside was being less than truthful. "Brother Nicholas was highly valued and respected here, as you know, so it is befitting that you should bring him to be laid to rest. I am sure he will thank you for doing so. But you, Sire, you wear the mantle of the Knights of Lazarus yet you do not look possessed of disease, ailments or gross afflictions."

"I am the last Knight of Lazarus, but formerly of the thirteenth troop of the Jerusalem chapter of Templars in which I served out my appointed commission," Paul replied. "I wear this now out of respect and in memory of all the Knights of Lazarus who fought and died to protect the king to the last man…save myself who was made one of theirs by their kind honour months past now."

"So a Templar before. That explains your bearing and manner," the Hospitaller said and looked Paul up and down. "You have been here before for I recognise you now. Will you not stay and help defend this position for when the time comes?"

"I am sorry, that I cannot do for I have another commission I must complete first," Paul replied then looked down into the grave at Nicholas's wrapped body. He placed his hands across his stomach and closed his eyes as if in prayer.

Taqi did likewise and as soon as Upside stood beside Paul, the Templar Marshal lifted up his order of service, coughed to clear his throat and, taking the hint from Paul, began to read it out loud. Paul closed his eyes and looked upwards at the clear blue sky. The sweet scent of lemons was carried upon the breeze. He closed his eyes and tried to imagine Alisha stood at this very spot ten years previous. He wondered if Nicholas was now indeed with her, Arri and Ailia. Paul had been so ready and prepared for death at Hattin yet here he was, still alive. His mind drifted to Princess Stephanie. She must be worried beyond despair about Humphrey he thought and perhaps for himself too. He would have to leave first thing in the morning to return to Jerusalem to secure her safe passage out, as well as pass on Saladin's terms to the queen before his forces marched on the city. As the words of the Templar Marshal were spoken, Paul did not really hear them as he tried to think of Princess Stephanie and hoped that she could somehow sense him...to know that he was still alive. Upside nudged him hard in the side bringing his attention back to the funeral. He nodded at Paul and then looked into the grave.

"Do you wish to speak some words?" the Templar Marshal asked.

As Paul stared into the grave he had a million words he wished to say but had no way of expressing them adequately. Eventually he just shook his head no, the sadness written across his face saying all that needed to be said. Upside put his arm around Paul reassuringly.

"I knew him well enough to know he died doing exactly as he would have wished. Still young, vibrant and in defence of all that he believed in... not old, decrepit and having his arse wiped daily by someone else," Upside said. "But I shall miss him sorely until the day I die."

Paul looked at Upside.

"Aye so shall I...and you also for I fear this shall be our last time together, my old friend," Paul said and sighed.

"Less of the old...but I agree I think you are correct."

"And what of you?" Paul asked, facing the female knight.

"I am going wherever he goes for we have an understanding of mutual support," she replied and looked at Upside as he smiled briefly.

"Before you leave, will you let me draw an image of you…so that I may never forget you?" Paul asked.

"'Tis a strange request but aye…aye indeed," Upside replied. "And when we leave…no tears do you hear me, for I do not want him looking down and laughing his head off at us…but will you be safe enough to travel back alone to Jerusalem?"

"I have a few friends close at hand that will ensure he travels safely," Taqi interrupted.

"Thank you," Paul replied and looked at them for several moments as the two Hospitaller sergeants began to fill in the grave.

"Oh shit…I so very nearly forgot to give you this," Upside said quickly and pulled out a leather binding from his rear leather kindling pouch. "He said if he was to fall and you survived I must hand you this." Hesitantly Paul took the small leather binding. "I would suggest you take yourself away for Nicholas said he would have the last laugh over you…in a good way."

"I shall then…after I have drawn you, if we may?"

℘℃

Paul rolled up the drawing of Upside and the female knight once they had viewed it and approved it. Upside shed a tear despite trying his hardest not to. Taqi made sure Nicholas's grave was completed and helped the Hospitallers erect a cross upon it. Paul took himself away and walked through the lemon and orange grove until he reached the far end overlooking the plateau beyond. The evening air was cool and welcoming and he sat himself down on the other side of the orchard wall and stared out toward the distant horizon. He could understand why Alisha had fallen in love with the place. Hesitantly, almost reluctantly, he placed the small leather binder upon his knees and untied it. Slowly he unfolded it to reveal a sheet of parchment. As he studied the words upon it, he immediately saw a whole section written in Elfdalian, the language of the forest Thomas had challenged him to learn back in Alexandria. He lifted the parchment closer to read it. 'If you are reading this, then we know I got to see Alisha first. But worry yourself not, my friend, for her heart and soul always did and always will belong to you. You are two halves of one soul. Had me worried a couple of times for I loved you more than I thought it was possible for a man to love another, though not in a boy lover's way,' Paul laughed to himself reading that part. 'Some wounds run too deep and some never heal, and now you cannot lecture me, I can say that I pray the wound I struck within you heals for I am eternally sorry for inflicting such a deep scar upon the most godly, honourable and noblest man I have ever been granted the honour to not only serve alongside, but also proud beyond measure to have been able to call a true friend. We share a wound that runs deeper than the deepest cut and bleeds unending, especially in the still quiet of the night. 'Tis one battle we cannot fight and win, the wound unseen. I cannot express the love I had for Alisha nor the guilt I carry for what was done, a wrong that cannot be undone. But I have copied a poem that always reminded me of her. I hope it speaks to you as I hope it will. 'Tis what we do when unseen by others that counts and shows who you really are.' Paul looked at the Elfdalian section and then to the poem. 'If I'd met her in a cave, in the dark where no light ever lived, she would still be the brightest thing I'd ever seen. For it always was the way she was, never the way she looked that made her so beautiful to me, and beautiful she was, though I never let it blind me, for it was only when I closed my eyes and stood there in that darkest cave that she truly blinded me with her beauty. Poem by Atticus.' Paul lowered the parchment sheet and his head in sadness. He closed his eyes and sighed knowing and fully understanding the words of Nicholas about the wound unseen that does not heal. 'But how do I honour you, Nicholas, for I feel you were a greater man than I?' Paul asked himself. He took a deep breath, looked up and sat back resting against the small wall and stared out across the plateau beyond. After a while enjoying the sound of small birds singing, the beautiful mixed scents blowing in gently on the evening breeze and the sense of calmness that enveloped him, he closed his eyes wearily.

შ⊃ငຊ

Paul shook his head to clear his vision as he felt himself being pulled forwards, images of the battle at Hattin beginning to swirl all around him. He recalled the many times he had heard from his father, Thomas and Upside how the mind could play tricks upon the eyes showing past traumatic events as if seen happening again. Usually in greater clarity and detail than when they were experienced as the mind fights to analyse and make sense of the event. He shook his head again as even the smell of the battle filled his nostrils. Flash backs Upside had termed them. Now as he sat against the wall, his vision was transfixed upon the images being replayed in front of him. He could see the faces of the Knights of Lazarus in absolute fine detail as they swung their swords valiantly against overwhelming numbers of opponents. But they all moved so slowly, everything slowed to the point where he could see even a single drop of blood move through the air as a sword cut through the neck of one of the knights opening up his throat clearly, his eyes looking directly at Paul just before they closed for ever. Paul looked over to see Upside swinging his two handed sword down upon the Muslim infantryman who had thrust a lance at Nicholas, his sword smashing and cutting through the man's mantle, chain mail and gambeson then through his back, Paul's eyes focusing in on the man's flesh as it parted, his backbone being exposed as Upside's sword continued down through him, the severed end of his spine flailing outwards, his spinal cord springing up and then back as it retracted within the exposed vertebrae, the man falling paralysed, his face twisting and contorting in agony. Blood flew across Paul's vision as another Muslim infantryman had a sword thrust vertically downwards through his collarbone near to his neck and into his chest and heart by one of the female knights just as she was then likewise struck dead as an axe cut deep into the side of her face travelling as far as the bridge of her nose, her right eye being horizontally cut in two as the blade sank deeper. The man with the axe pulled it out fast and swung it up in the air just as Nicholas blocked his view from throwing the axe at Paul. In the confusion of battle and the speed of action, Paul's mind had not even registered this action at the time. Nicholas released his grip upon the lance he was holding back as he tried to defend himself, and swung his right arm up and backwards knocking the axe man hard enough to stop him from throwing it. Paul could see in total clarity the Muslim lancer pull back and then thrust the lance into Nicholas's left side as soon as Nicholas's grip had released. If he had not let go to deflect the axe, Paul would have been hit by it, but by knowingly doing so, Nicholas had deliberately exposed himself to the lancer. Nicholas looked across at Paul, his mouth snarling with aggression as he lowered his sword down upon the lancer, his sword cutting through the man's shoulder and severing his arm completely, a gout of brilliant red blood spurting out all across Nicholas and the axe man behind him, Nicholas then looking up to check Paul was okay as he held on to the end of the lance now stuck firmly in him. As he straightened up, Paul reached out his arms feeling as if they weighed too much to lift. Paralysed all he could do was look on in horror as the axe came down into Nicholas's back, knocking him forwards slightly, but he still held his ground, his eyes again meeting Paul's. He gave a slight nod, winked and looked like he even smiled. A horse reared up, the knight being pulled off backwards as the main girdle straps were cut, his saddle becoming unseated. The horse's side opened up as a scimitar blade cut along its length bursting its ribs as it went. The female knight beside Upside swung her sword sideways cutting through a Muslim lancer as he rapidly approached Paul to his left side, her blade cutting into his abdomen, his intestines immediately falling out as he ran. He dropped his lance as he tried to pull up and hold in his own stomach, but as he knelt to gather up his own intestines, he looked down and the female knight followed through with a downward thrust against the base of his neck, being immediately decapitated, blood shooting forwards. Paul stared wide eyed as the headless and disembowelled Muslim's body fell at his feet. Paul blinked to clear his eyes and focus as the images started to fade, his hands waving outwards blindly. He felt sick and shocked at both the images he had witnessed now being seen again in all its grotesque detail...but also the realisation that Nicholas had deliberately sacrificed himself in order to save him. He sighed heavily as tears welled in his eyes.

"'Tis a cruel trick how the mind can do that is it not?" Attar said suddenly, interrupting his thoughts.

Paul blinked hard and wiped his eyes as he looked up to see Attar sitting himself down beside him. He smiled at Paul and made himself comfortable and sat in silence for several minutes.

"How come you are here?" Paul finally asked, bemused.

"When Taqi sent word ahead to Al Rashid to ask for support to have you escorted to Jerusalem afterwards I simply had to come. I have spent a lot of time with Al Rashid of late and he is still very much of the opinion you may get the opportunity of forming the joint Order now that Reynald is no more."

"I shall return to Jerusalem to collect Stephanie...but I cannot form such an Order out here. There are just too many separate and vested parties to contend with."

"No one said it would be easy. Besides you have Count Henry to help you. As for the Princess...well, we shall see," Attar said and nodded his head as he looked out at the setting Sun.

"What do you mean we shall see?" Paul asked defensively, unsure why he felt so.

"My dear young man," Attar replied and turned his face to look at him. Paul recoiled slightly away from him sensing something different about him and his eyes. "When Alisha died, your heart and soul were ripped apart yes?" he asked, Paul nodding yes. "'Tis greater than all the wounds you have ever felt before or ever will suffer, 'tis the wound unseen that still bleeds yes?" he asked and Paul nodded yes again, more puzzled as his words almost echoed those of Nicholas. "The Princess can never stem that bleed. Do not look for a princess in need of saving but find a queen willing to fight by your side. 'Tis all I shall tell you," Attar stated bluntly and then looked away and out across the plateau.

"So I am to be condemned to walk the rest of my days alone with no comfort. Is that it?" Paul demanded, irritated and confused.

"No. No one has ever said that to you have they? And when you get the chance, do indeed write kindly of Gerard for history will not look kindly upon him, tarnished alongside Reynald and King Guy's failings. The king is but a product of these times...but the fourth of July will echo out across the coming centuries. One day it will be remembered for its true signif-icance but for now look, look and see." Paul looked forwards but all he could see was the setting sun. "Keep looking."

As Paul stared harder he started to see the shimmering image of a man walking towards him, a brilliant white light growing in brilliance behind him as he approached. The man grew bigger as he got closer but he was in silhouette until almost upon them. Paul shielded his eyes from the light flickering around the figure when the man knelt down and reached for-ward clasping Paul's hand. Paul shuddered instantly at the man's touch. Slowly Paul's gaze followed the man's hand, then up his arm until he could see his face, and he gasped seeing Nicholas smiling at him broadly. Clean shaven, his eyes crystal clear and clothed in a clean mantle. Paul's mouth dropped open wide.

"Surprised?" Nicholas asked, half laughing. "This is the only way I am allowed to reveal myself."

"Have I died too from some unseen wound? What is this?" Paul asked, utterly confused, as Attar leant forward and knelt up beside Nicholas.

"No you are not dead. Now listen to what he tells you," Attar stated and stood up fully. He smiled at Paul then at Nicholas before turning his back and walking away.

"I do not understand this!" Paul exclaimed, shaking his head.

"My friend…I have someone here who wishes desperately to speak with you again," Nicholas explained and moved aside.

Paul's heart beat so loud he could hear it. He gulped hard as another figure started to walk towards him silhouetted by light behind.

"Alisha!" Paul gasped and tried to focus his eyes on the approaching figure. But as it came nearer, Paul began to realise it was a smaller figure.

"Father," Arri suddenly said as he stepped fully into view and smiled. Paul let out a deep gasp and grabbed his chest. "I can call you Father now can't I?" he asked and stepped closer. Paul instinctively reached out and Arri stepped into his arms wrapping his little arms around his neck. Shaking uncontrollably with emotion Paul held him tightly as tears began to well in his eyes. He looked at Nicholas as he stood up smiling. "You need not cry," Arri said as Paul rubbed his hand through Arri's hair half laughing and crying. He moved Arri back so he could look into his big eyes. "I am real."

"So I am dead…surely I must be," Paul stated and put his hands upon Arri's face then kissed him on the forehead. "For I can feel you and smell you…and…and," he paused and looked up at Nicholas. "And where is Alisha and Ailia?"

"They are not here," Arri replied and pulled Paul's chin to make him look back at him. "You must go back to Jerusalem to find out why and where."

"I do not understand," Paul exclaimed.

"Paul, I do not know where, but they are not here," Nicholas explained and smiled as Arri stood away from Paul just holding his hand still. "But I can tell you this, they have not ascended to higher realms…and know this too…the secret is so simple. It is love and the world you inherit is the world you manifest," Nicholas explained and took hold of Arri's other hand.

"I must go now, Father. I have missed you so much and Mummy and Ailia," Arri said softly and let go of Paul's hand. He immediately tried to touch him again but he could not reach. "My physical remains rest here too if you visit where grandmother is laid to rest," he explained and smiled before looking up at Nicholas.

"No no, wait please do not go. Nicholas…I saw you killed saving me and

I did not even realise it...and Arri...please just a moment more please," Paul pleaded and tried to sit up but could not move.

"And I would do so again, my friend," Nicholas replied as he started to fade rapidly from view.

Paul looked at Arri as he smiled at him and gave a slight wave and tilted his head then also vanished from view, Paul squinting his eyes as he realised he was staring directly at the setting sun. He looked to his left to see where Attar was but he was nowhere to be seen. Taqi approached walking alongside the wall as Paul forced himself to his feet and shivered. He must have been dreaming vividly again overwhelmed with exhaustion finally catching up on him he told himself.

"What is wrong, brother, for you look as though you have seen a ghost?" he asked as Paul grabbed hold of his shoulders and stared at him for a minute and shook him. Taqi frowned puzzled.

"Just checking if you are really real," Paul blurted out then quickly pushed past him and hurried along the path that ran alongside the small wall. Taqi quickly turned to follow him as Upside saw him on the other side and indicated he and Ishmael would also follow.

Paul walked fast towards the old graveyard outside the main keep's walls. He knew where Raja was buried and made his way directly to it. He froze as he saw the line of graves ahead of him as Taqi, Upside and Ishmael rushed to catch up. Paul ran across the open pathway and up to the graves. He read the stone inscription marking Raja's grave then looked slowly toward the newer smaller grave set beside it and marked with a cross. He fell to his knees as he read the inscription engraved upon it. Kratos said he had moved Arri's body for safe keeping and now he knew where as he leaned over and ran his fingers across the letters. 'Arri Plantavalu de Bouillon'. Paul held his chest, barely able to breathe. Taqi almost tripped over Paul as he slid to a halt beside him. He read the wording and was just as shocked. Paul looked at him and shook his head, utterly surprised, and half laughed.

"I saw them...both Nicholas and Arri. They told me he was laid to rest here...and that Alisha and Ailia are not with them!"

"What does that mean?" Taqi asked as he knelt beside Paul.

"Obvious is it not?" Upside said, out of breath, his hands upon his hips.

"What then?" Paul asked, looking up at him.

"I do not profess to know what you saw or heard exactly, but if anyone was ever going to get a message to you from beyond the grave, then you can damn well guarantee it would have to be our Nicholas," he explained and leaned forward to catch his breath. "Christ, I am too old for this running lark."

"What message?" Taqi demanded, looking concerned.

"Well, if Alisha and your daughter are not with them up there...and I am pretty certain they would not be in Hell....then it means but one thing," Upside said and paused, looking at both of them. Ishmael listened intently behind them.

"What?" they both asked together.

"They ain't dead!" Upside answered and stood up straight. "Somehow... somewhere...they are alive."

Paul and Taqi looked at each other in disbelief and shock. Paul then looked up at Upside again before slowly looking back at Arri's grave. Quickly he jumped to his feet.

"I must go to Jerusalem immediately," Paul remarked, looking stunned and confused.

"Not now you cannot. 'Tis too late. You must go in the morning," Upside said and grabbed Paul's arm. "And do so with an escort."

"And Attar...where has he gone?" Paul asked, looking at Taqi.

"What do you mean for he is with Al Rashid?" he replied, shaking his head.

Paul looked over toward the lemon grove, the sun now almost gone from view. His heart pounding and his stomach knotted. Even the merest hint at the possibility Alisha and Ailia could still be alive, no matter how impossible the odds, filled him with both dread and a sense of renewed purpose at the same time. He shook his head as the image of pulling the flesh off of Alisha's arm entered his mind. He felt for her dagger still kept close. He shook his head again, totally confused. It must be just a lucid dream he told himself, but then he looked at Arri's grave again. He would not have known about it unless Arri had told him and would have only found out later when he would have visited to pay his respects to Raja the following day. He shook his head again as his ears began to ring. In the back of his mind he could hear the words of Theodoric echoing. 'The parchments never lie.' As his bottom lip quivered with emotion, the sudden impact of what was being told to him hitting him hard, he put his arms around his waist and had to fight to control his emotions. If they were still alive, by whatever miracle, then he would find them even if it took the rest of his life, he vowed.

Port of La Rochelle, France, Melissae Inn, spring 1191

"Oh my Lord sweet Jesus," Ayleth cried openly. "Alive...but how?" she asked emotionally as Simon coughed, trying to hide his emotions.

"Not so quickly, young Ayleth," the old man stated and sat himself upright and leaned forward, resting his hands upon the table. "For all is not what it seemed."

"Yes like how come Arri has the addition of de Bouillon after his name?" Gabirol asked as he charged his quill with more ink, "for that I must know."

"Kratos marked it as such for he knew the full lineage of Paul's ancestral tree," the old man answered.

"So you are saying that Paul's family is in fact directly linked to the main founding member of the Templars, Godfrei de Bouillon, all along?" Peter asked bluntly, stubbing his forefinger upon the table.

The old man simply nodded his head yes.

"Will you just tell us if Alisha lives or not?" Sarah asked impatiently and clenched her hands together tightly.

"I can tell you that Paul left for Jerusalem the very next morning to try and find out if she was and if so how she could possibly be so. He bade an emotional farewell to Upside, both knowing it would be the last time they would ever see each other, though Paul had his drawing of him and his female knight companion. You will find that image amongst the others," the old man explained and motioned with his head toward Paul's leather folder.

"What of Taqi then?" the wealthy tailor asked.

"He escorted Paul along with several of his colleagues and Ishmael to the outer limits of the city walls of Jerusalem to guarantee he arrived there safely. Taqi wished to enter with him to see if he could help in locating Alisha and Ailia if they were indeed somehow still alive, but it was now too risky for him to do so," the old man answered and paused. "So it was agreed Taqi would wait in the nearby hills with several of his Ashashin on the understanding that if Paul found out anything, he would make contact with him immediately."

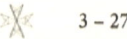 3 – 27

"*And what of Princess Stephanie?*" Sarah asked.

The old man looked at her in silence for a few moments, took a deep breath and began to explain.

Fig. 72: Upside and Female Knight.

Chapter 80
Jerusalem – The Candle Burns Down

City of Jerusalem, Kingdom of Jerusalem, July 1187

Princess Stephanie sat with her hands resting upon her lap staring out of the tall window of her private chambers. The sky was a bright blue outside but she felt like a dark cloud hung over everything. One of her maids was combing and plaiting her hair, weaving two side plaits to the rear and then down into long lengths in an intricate pattern. Abi stood with her arms folded staring out of the far window deep in thought. Two other maids sat quietly working on some lace covers whilst Queen Sibylla sat quietly just watching Princess Stephanie with concern who after a while became aware that she was being looked at and turned to face her.

"I am so sorry I am not good company," she said softly and turned in her chair to look at the queen properly, the maid standing back. She forced a brave smile and held her hands together. "The list of all the knights executed will be delivered soon enough...I just cannot stomach the waiting."

"These are testing times...we have been assured the list will arrive today...but at least I know my husband, for all his failings, is still alive and will be ransomed at some future time...Saladin has even offered me safe passage and conduct to see Guy now if I so wish it...but the longer the delay the better," Queen Sibylla remarked half joking and tilted her head and tried to solicit a smile from Princess Stephanie. "Come on...you are a princess so lift your head up or your crown will fall off," she joked.

Princess Stephanie sat up straight and ran her fingers through her hair. She had not had it tied up or plaited for days and it felt very tight now that it was being done adding to her sense of despair and sadness. Her face looked pale and she looked down at herself and her white and cream silk dress. She wore it knowing it was one Paul liked seeing her in the most. She sighed heavily before looking up the queen again.

"I do not feel like a princess and I certainly no longer possess a crown," she said sadly.

A sudden loud knock on the door made them all jump and drew their immediate attention, Abi immediately spinning around, her hand already covering her sword handle.

"Enter!" Queen Sibylla called out. "Sorry, 'tis your chambers," she apologised looking at Princess Stephanie but before she could reply, the door was opened wide by a Hospitaller sergeant allowing Master Douglas to enter looking his usual serious self, his spurs catching the wooden floor boards noisily. Princess Stephanie looked down assuming he was there again to speak with the queen and fearful he now had the list she was dreading. He bowed his head at the queen then nodded toward Princess Stephanie. "Stephanie…Master Douglas is here for you," she said quietly and stood up moving to stand by her side. Fearing bad news, she placed her hand upon Stephanie's shoulder reassuringly as they both looked at him anxiously. He stood silent for a moment. "Well…is his name upon the list?" Queen Sibylla asked impatiently as Princess Stephanie closed her eyes and waited to hear the dreadful news, a single tear already running down her cheek. Master Douglas coughed to get her attention but she kept her eyes closed as Abi moved to stand behind them and took a deep breath. He looked behind himself quickly as someone entered the room before looking back at the Queen. She frowned hard until he stood aside to reveal Paul stood there before them, looking tired, unshaven and dressed in the Knights of Lazarus mantle covered in dust. He part bowed his head in silence. "Stephanie…my dear, I really do think you should open your eyes now."

Abi smiled instantly at the same time as Ishmael stepped into room behind Paul.

Slowly and hesitantly she opened them. She saw Paul but her mind did not fully take in what she was looking at, confusing him for another knight, not recognising the Knights of Lazarus mantle. Paul took a deep breath, stood up straight then smiled at her raising his hands out to her, their eyes fixing upon each other's. Finally recognising him and without a word, her eyes wide, she stood up, outstretched her arms and walked to him. She looked down as her eyes filled with tears fearful to look at him in case he vanished and quickly placed her head against his chest, wrapping her arms around him tightly, then closed her eyes and started to cry softly as she felt he was indeed real. Paul put his arms around her, the maids sniffling and wiping tears away from their own faces, Master Douglas smiling. Paul held her close and closed his eyes and took in the sweet smell of her perfume and the sensation of her body pressed against his as she cried quietly and squeezed him tighter. The room fell silent for several minutes, Queen Sibylla turning away briefly to hide a tear. Abi gulped hard with emotion, her bottom lip quivering. Suddenly Brother Teric ran into the room closely followed by Stewart, their boots thudding upon the floor as they entered pushing past Ishmael. Both froze as they saw Paul and Princess Stephanie.

"'Tis true...you are alive," Brother Teric remarked and stepped closer. "Sorry and pardon us My Queen," he quickly added. Queen Sibylla just smiled and waved her hand. "How?"

Princess Stephanie opened her eyes but held on to Paul as he looked at them both, Stewart stood with his mouth open making her laugh briefly with both relief and joy.

"Brother, close your mouth or you will catch flies," Paul joked as he smiled at him.

Stewart rushed over and threw his arms around both him and Princess Stephanie together and pulled them close. After a minute Paul went to move but Stewart would not let go, his eyes screwed up tightly as he was barely able to contain his emotions. Eventually he broke his hold and stepped back still holding Paul's arm and laughed nervously, shaking his head, utterly confused but happy to see him alive and well. Abi could not stop smiling as she watched them.

"I shall explain all," Paul said, tiredness evident in his voice. "And Brother Teric...a message form Master Gerard...you are now in charge, like it or not."

Brother Teric shook his head no.

"No...'tis not a command I wish to accept...no! I have already told this one and Count Henry I will not do it," Brother Teric protested but looked puzzled when Paul laughed lightly.

"Words fail me, little brother...fail me," Stewart remarked and shook his head again. "Do not ever do that to us again."

Paul looked down at Princess Stephanie, the joy in her eyes evident as she held on to him tightly. He had so many questions and things he knew he would have to ask and tell her about what he had seen and experienced at Castle Blanc...and about Alisha, but as he looked into her loving eyes he knew now was not the time; perhaps later when alone...besides, what if all he had experienced had been just a vivid dream? Why cause her any more hurt than was necessary?

Port of La Rochelle, France, Melissae Inn, spring 1191

"Oh My Lord how much more of this tale can I take?" Sarah asked as she wiped away a tear.

"And me," Ayleth said as she wiped a tear away and laughed lightly.

"Did Paul immediately start to look for Alisha and Ailia then?" Gabirol asked.

"Not immediately for he had to help convince Brother Teric to take up the mantel and lead the few remaining Templars. Balian, who by then was at Tyre, which was being besieged by Saladin, sought and was granted permission by him to travel to Jerusalem to fetch his wife and children. News of his imminent arrival was delivered by messengers and Paul managed to convince Princess Stephanie that she should leave with them. She swore she would only leave if he went with her," the old man explained.

"I think it unfair on her if Paul still harboured hope for Alisha and Ailia," Sarah commented and looked around the table at the others, the wealthy tailor nodding in agreement with her.

"Paul did not hide what had been revealed at Castle Blanc. He felt it dishonest as well as disrespectful toward her if he did not...and so that very night he told her of the vision he had experienced. Much to his surprise and relief, she told him he must pursue it if there was but the slightest chance and miracle they were still alive. She knew if she did not, he would never really be hers. It just proved and showed the maturity and love she had for him, and Alisha," the old man said and paused before looking up and continuing. "She sensed something was different that very first night when she tried to make love to him and he feigned fatigue, which was partly true, but women have a way of knowing these things. She could put it down to the ordeal he had just endured and the possibility that Alisha and Ailia were still alive, but Paul did not see her tears fall that night as she held him, more from guilt hoping that Alisha was not alive for she knew she would not be able to keep him if she was. She hated herself for even thinking that and pushed those thoughts from her mind. Whatever was to happen, she loved him and she wanted what was ultimately best for him. She sensed the deep wound within him for Alisha and his children and so she vowed that night she would do all she could to not only support him in his search, but comfort him as best she could and for as long as she could."

"God but for that kind of love just once would be sufficient for me," Simon remarked. "I think I love her myself."

"She was...no, she is a truly noble, kind, wise and remarkable woman. A true queen who needs no crown. She was no defenceless princess that needed rescuing for she was indeed a queen prepared to fight for those she loved," the old man said and smiled.

"Aye and can you imagine the support she would have had as a queen with Paul as her king?" Peter remarked, thinking out aloud.

"Poor woman for she doesn't seem to have much luck with her men does she?" Sarah stated.

"You assume she had no luck with Paul?" the old man remarked, looking at her.

"Yes exactly for we do not know if Paul found Alisha or not do we?" the Genoese sailor commented and nodded at Sarah then folded his arms. "So let's just wait and see what happens eh."

"Then let me continue by explaining that news of the great disaster at Hattin finally reached Europe via Joscius, Archbishop of Tyre as well as many returning pilgrims. Lord Montferrat, that is Conrad, returned immediately to Tyre having previously left for Europe to garner support for his own future claims for the throne of Jerusalem, and he immediately refused to pay a ransom for his own father. Plans were immediately made for a new crusade and Pope Gregory the Eighth subsequently issued a Papal bull, the 'Audita Tremendi', and across England and France, the 'Saladin tithe' has been enacted to fund the crusade expenses."

"Huh yes tell us about it...as if we were not already paying enough taxes," Peter chipped in, shaking his head disapprovingly.

"Paul worked closely with Count Henry and Master Douglas alongside Queen Sibylla and the Patriarch Heraclius to prepare the city for Saladin's inevitable assault, which true to his word he did in fact delay by attacking other cities first, but in truth there was nothing Paul could do to even start to try and discover the whereabouts regarding Alisha and Ailia should they indeed be alive. He could not shake off the experience at Castle Blanc or the strange appearance of Attar, though he suspected it was not even him all along. He was mentally and emotionally confused on many levels and whatever lay ahead, he was more than thankful he had Princess Stephanie and his love for her did grow over the weeks," the old man explained. "Then Balian arrived."

"I remember news coming in daily of the fall of one city after another," Simon remarked and sipped some mead beer.

"His attacks were total...and uncompromising. Reynald had wanted total all out *war and now Saladin, having had his hand forced by him, was certainly carrying that out...further forced, or encouraged, depending upon how you look at it by his other emirs and nobles. By September Saladin had taken Acre, which fell on the ninth of July after a negotiated surrender set for the tenth of July, quickly followed by Nablus, Jaffa, Toron, Sidon, Beirut and Ascalon. Tyre still remained in Christian hands under Conrad, which is where Balian had travelled to. The defeat at Hattin heralded in the effective destruction of the Kingdom of Jerusalem. With the king in his hands, and the army destroyed, Saladin was able to capture city after city as you say."*

"How come Tyre did not fall?" Gabirol asked.

"Some say because the strong fortifications and fresh troops arriving just as they were about to surrender dissuaded Saladin from attacking fully while morale was low in his own ranks...but others say he withdrew for other reasons of which I shall come to later," the old man answered.

"You mean duplicitous agreements by Conrad with Saladin?" Gabirol asked knowingly, the old man just shrugging his shoulders.

City of Jerusalem, Kingdom of Jerusalem, September 19th 1187

Paul stood with Master Douglas looking out across the open plain beyond from the northern wall of the city. The sun was already setting on the western horizon in a dazzling display of colours. Torches were just being lit in the streets behind them as evening began to fall and shadows grew longer.

"When Balian arrives you must leave with him if you can," Master Douglas said quietly. "There are many here, including the queen herself, who say that you should marry Princess Stephanie and become king when Sibylla hands over the crown to this city."

"No, that I cannot do. Balian may leave with his family and I pray Stephanie goes with them, but I have promised both my brother and those I know well that I shall stay and help them. You of course are under no such pledge to stay," Paul replied.

"All due respect, Paul, but fuck off," Master Douglas replied and laughed. "I am going nowhere," he remarked as Ishmael and Count Henry approached accompanied by Stewart, Paul acknowledging them with a slight bow of his head.

"Evening," Count Henry said as he moved to stand beside Paul. "'Tis a wonderful eve is it not?" he asked. Paul nodded yes silently. "Has Master Douglas spoken with you of Queen Sibylla's proposition?"

"I was just getting to it," Master Douglas remarked as Paul looked at him quizzically.

"'Tis a genuine proposal…but I caution it," Count Henry said and leaned against the battlement and looked forwards, his dark blue cloak shimmering as the last rays of the sun shone through the hairs of the thick material. "You become king of this city and it falls, you know the consequences I am sure. 'Tis why I have instructed the chroniclers and scribes to make no mention of the offer…for your long term safety of course."

"Even if there was no threat from Saladin, I would not accept the title. Besides we do not know if Stephanie would take my hand in marriage," Paul replied.

"Of course we fucking don't…just like that sun will not shine tomorrow," Master Douglas stated and shook his head, looking at Paul. "Do not be a fool, Paul. 'Tis one thing I admire you most for…that you see things for what they are and speak as you see."

"'Tis what you think you learnt at Castle Blanc isn't it that holds you back?" Ishmael said seriously. Paul looked back at him. "Tell me I am wrong."

"No, you are not wrong for it does play heavy upon my heart," Paul replied and sighed.

"I am afraid we must all deal with the practicalities of our immediate predicament right here and now," Count Henry remarked bluntly.

"Really," Master Douglas said and frowned. "Of every hundred men they send me, ten should not even be here; eighty are nothing but targets; nine are real fighters, and we are lucky to have them, for they the battle make. Ahhh, but ONE, ONE of them is a WARRIOR, and he will bring the others back." All looked at Master Douglas bemused at his comment. "'Tis what the philosopher Heraclitus said…but very apt for this hour I think," he explained and smiled.

"You like quoting your philosophers, Master Douglas, however, many will die if we do not prepare fully," Count Henry said and paused, looking out across the city as darkness rapidly closed in. "For Jerusalem, the candle now burns down," he then stated, which immediately drew a look from Paul, recalling his own dreams and images of seeing the candle burning down over the image of the city.

"'Tis madness that men fight all claiming they see the light of the Lord only in their religion," Ishmael remarked looking up at the darkening sky, the first stars just beginning to appear.

"Aye…for humanity has grown so old that it has forgotten its infancy, and the origin of man is shrouded in mystery…but maybe one day all of mankind will awaken from his collective amnesia of his true past and learn that the same light shines brightly in all, but through different lamps… that is all," Count Henry remarked almost nonchalantly as he continued to look out across the city.

"One light, many lamps. I like that," Ishmael said aloud to himself.

"Well these walls are old and I fear they will not hold out for long against Saladin's siege engines," Master Douglas remarked and ran his hand along a dusty and crumbling wall section.

"My friends," Count Henry said as he stood up to look at them all. "The strongest walls are made by the bravest men, not brick and stone."

Queen Sibylla appeared with Princess Stephanie and an escort of mixed turcopoles and sergeants along with the queen's consort and Balian's wife, Maria Comnena, and Abi, who was still smiling.

"I heard what you spoke. I think we should have that read out to the entire city," she said as she looked at the state of the battlements then at Master Douglas as Princess Stephanie moved to stand with Paul, taking his hand. "Tell me, Master Douglas. If these walls catch fire, what steps will you take?" she asked in all seriousness.

"Well, My Queen…fucking big ones that way," he replied immediately pointing in the opposite direction.

Count Henry shook his head disapprovingly trying not to laugh but Queen Sibylla smiled and then laughed at his reply.

"'Tis that attitude that will serve us all well when Saladin arrives," she said then looked at Paul and Princess Stephanie. "The whole city speaks of you two. Rumours abound of a new Grail King and his Queen that will deliver us all, so have you considered my proposal for it will give many a reason to fight?"

 2 – 8

"I have only just been made aware of it," Paul answered and held Princess Stephanie's hand tighter as she looked at him intently. "I am no Grail King and besides, you would be giving up too much."

"No I would not be…but you two would. 'Tis a chalice I would not wish upon anyone unless I thought it absolutely necessary for the continuation of this holy city, and right now the people need hope. It matters not if you are a real Grail King, the fact is the people will believe it," Queen Sibylla replied. "The Lord tends to thrust upon us challenges and responsibilities we would not readily choose if not but forced upon us by circumstance."

Abi looked at Paul, intently searching his every reaction.

"You do not need to tell me about that one, Your Majesty," Brother Teric remarked, his tone laced with sarcasm.

"Does that mean you have accepted the position of Grand Master of the Order of the Temple?" Queen Sibylla asked, looking at him intently. Master Douglas folded his arms and looked at him too, smiling broadly. "Well?"

"It would seem I have but very little choice in the matter. But I shall only remain so until another, better suited, candidate can be found…or I am dead!" Brother Teric replied and bowed his head slightly.

All stood in an awkward silence for several minutes as Master Douglas simply kept on smiling at Brother Teric.

"My Queen," Paul said, breaking the silence. "I have to ask for I still do not know to this day…but what were the female knights who fought with us at Hattin called?"

"Your Queen," Queen Sibylla replied and looked at Princess Stephanie. "No, she is your queen. Never forget that. Count Henry, perhaps you will tell Paul his answer?"

"They were the knights known as the Daughters of Sion," Count Henry answered.

Paul nodded his head silently as he thought back upon the action that had seen them all killed save one as Abi continued to look at him intently. She could sense something in him.

"Why has Saladin not taken Tyre yet…that is what I wish to know?" Brother Teric asked out loud and looked west toward the coast."

"'Tis strategically vital to us for resupply…Saladin knows that so in theory at least he should take that first before moving on to us…but he still has not," Count Henry said in response.

"Whoever remains here, either as queen or king, will need to watch Lord Montferrat closely for he schemes and plots for his own ends," Brother Teric explained and looked at Queen Sibylla then Princess Stephanie. Maria stepped forward looking concerned.

"My husband comes tomorrow direct from Tyre, which as we speak is under siege. He has been granted leave from there by Saladin himself, to collect us and then depart from Jerusalem...not defend it," she explained calmly then looked at the queen. "He will not be able to help you."

"That we shall see...but right now we have more pressing immediate concerns to worry about. Such as the sheer number of Muslims we have in the city still, not counting the near three thousand Muslim prisoners held," Master Douglas interrupted. "Plus the daily growing number of refugees."

"We are aware of that. Those Muslims who have lived in the city and who wish to remain...in peace, then they may. Those that wished to leave have done so already ahead of Lord Balian's arrival tomorrow," Count Henry explained. "But fresh water will be our biggest problem. We have seen what the lack of it can lead to as evidenced at Hattin."

"'Tis getting cold and I tire. I must bid you all a good night," Queen Sibylla said as she stepped back and bowed her head, Princess Stephanie pulling away from Paul as she motioned for her to follow. "We must speak to the people on the morrow so if any of you can think of anything inspirational, please let us know of it."

"Please come see me later," Princess Stephanie whispered to Paul and kissed him on the side of his face. He simply nodded yes as she then followed after Queen Sibylla.

"Make sure we speak in private soonest," Abi said to Paul as she walked past him. "'Tis vital."

Paul nodded he would as she hurried after Princess Stephanie.

"So Master Teric...what's you plan?" Master Douglas asked and patted Brother Teric on the shoulders hard and laughed.

"Funny, Master Douglas, for you should be the one taking this chalice not I...or Stewart perhaps?" Brother Teric replied as he leant against the battlement and looked at Stewart.

"No way for I know my limitations," Stewart shot back instantly then looked at Paul and raised his eyebrows as if to ask him.

"Not me for I am done with being a knight...or a king," Paul replied.

"Ah but has life done with you being a knight...and possibly a king?" Master Douglas asked.

"He is already a king if he but stopped for once and realised just what he is," Count Henry stated, looked at Paul and sighed. "'Tis late...I speak out of turn. I too shall bid you all a good night," he said, his tone clipped, and quickly turned about and walked away fast clenching his fists as if regretting his very words.

"I think we should all retire for who knows what the Lord in all his infinite wisdom will throw at us tomorrow," Master Douglas remarked.

"Aye to that. And I shall pray for guidance and inspiration for the words the queen wishes us to compile," Paul said and began to walk away but Master Douglas grabbed his arm. "I hope the Lord hears all of our prayers."

"Paul...tell me in all seriousness. Do you really believe in all of that?" he asked and motioned with his other hand as he looked up at the ever increasing number of stars that were now shining. "That out there, there is something, a great being that hears you and answers. What do you really gain by praying to God?" he asked further in all seriousness.

Paul looked at him and the others now all staring waiting for his answer.

"You once said you did not believe in religion but you did believe in a higher consciousness or higher being. Well in truth what do I get by praying? Nothing!" Paul replied and paused before looking up at the stars. "But let me tell you what I lose instead. Anger, ego, greed, depression, insecurity and the fear of death. As a dear old friend once told me, sometimes the answers to our prayers are not in what we hope or think we should gain, but in that which we lose, which is ultimately the gain," Paul explained, bowed his head slightly, turned and walked away, Ishmael immediately following after him.

Master Douglas watched him as he began to walk down the end rampart's steps and out of view.

"Did tell you he was a smart bastard did I not?" Brother Teric laughed and nudged Master Douglas. "No disrespect intended," he said to Stewart.

"Let us hope he is smart enough to help us all out of the coming shit storm," Master Douglas remarked as he folded his arms and relaxed back against the battlement wall. "For this time we are most certainly in balls deep."

ഐരു

Paul and Ishmael walked along the main corridor of the Templar headquarters, the whole building eerily quiet, their footsteps echoing out loudly in contrast. When they turned into the main reception room, Count Henry was kneeling, his hands resting upon the pommel of his sword held in front of him as he prayed in front of the large wall mural. It still looked as fresh and as vibrant, despite the low light cast by three burning wall mounted torches, as it had the first time Paul had seen it. The Templar Beauseant banners were no longer at either side having been taken as spares for the field. Paul and Ishmael stood in silence and waited until Count Henry had finished. Slowly he stood up and turned to face them as Master Douglas entered looking at them as if asking if he was intruding with his hands held outwards.

"Come in Master Douglas and join with us," Count Henry said, beckoning him closer. "My dear friends…we live in strange days. Who would have believed such a calamity would befall us and all because of just one man?" he asked and walked up to them and sheathed his sword. "I am duty bound that sadly I must at some point return to France and sever the bonds that bind my Order of Sion with the Order of the Templars. Reynald's influence over Gerard proved one of the founding conditions could be broken…as in one person could bend the will of the Master of the Temple to his own whims and desires. It can never be allowed to happen again," he said then paused for several long minutes, finding it difficult to find the words he needed to continue. "'Tis regrettable but as I told Gerard if he rode with Reynald we would have to cut the elm and so it shall be. But alas Reynald will not be the last to lead many into wicked ways."

"What or who are you referring to?" Paul asked, puzzled.

"Oh…just things I have seen in my mind of things past and things to come. I have even seen the greatest symbol of peace become one that will be forever connected to evil. That is how the forces that work against us try to keep us bound in ignorance," Count Henry explained, looking sad. "You see, Paul, you are not alone in being able to see across the wheel of time. 'Tis a curse." Paul and Ishmael looked at each other, somewhat bemused at his remarks as Master Douglas stood impassive as ever. "You understand that mural and what it depicts now. But, my friends, that is so little a revelation compared with what is out there. Our ancestors left their wisdom for us to unlock yet we squander it. The symbol I speak of that will be corrupted, 'tis the four armed swastika. You know how it was formed, from the four stations of the position of the stars that form the plough. For winter, spring, summer and autumn. Ishmael, I saw you looking up at it this very eve," Count Henry explained. He sighed. "Oh but if we could only open our eyes truly. Let the people awaken and see through their eyes, including their third."

Ishmael looked at Paul quizzically.

"I have heard of this third eye, but how could we all open it?" Ishmael asked.

"'Tis a simple practice but one that is hidden lest people learn how to, and abuse it," Count Henry answered. "A simple raising of the tip of the tongue to run backwards and forwards along the roof of the mouth will help activate it as well as humming the sound of Aum..."

"Activate what exactly?" Ishmael asked, even more puzzled.

Count Henry opened a long drawer and removed several images drawn upon parchments and velum. He flicked through them quickly until he found what he was looking for and pushed two images toward Ishmael and Paul.

"These were recovered a very long time ago. 'Tis something your old tutor Niccolas studied at length. These are copies of his original drawings. But his were copied from even older sources supplied by your father...here look," Count Henry said as he turned the images around. One showed the stylised image of the Egyptian all seeing eye, the other a cutaway section of a medical illustration of the brain of a human."

"I have seen these before at his study library...but he never explained them to me," Paul remarked as he studied them closely.

"But I bet he said you would learn of them if you went to Alexandria yes?" Count Henry asked.

"Yes he did, but I ran out of time there before we moved to Cairo," Paul answered.

"What does it mean?" Ishmael asked.

"The eye is drawn up using precise mathematical ratios. You will see the values within if you look closely. And the side section drawing of the brain doth show the real internal part of the brain that sees but in a different way. The ancient writings tell us it is what forms early within the woman when she falls with child. 'Tis the seat of our conscious being so it states. Learn to awaken it fully and you will be able to access the higher realms of understanding and see people...I mean really see people. Imagine that, someone lies to you and you know exactly what they speak of as being false. You see someone and you feel and sense who they really are. 'Tis a greater power many would abuse I fear. The Church knows of this and suppresses it fully."

"No fucking surprises there then," Master Douglas interrupted and stood close. "'Tis why I say you need not have to pray within a church to speak with our higher selves or whatever greater intelligence is beyond us. 'Tis my view that if you have to have a leader or follow blindly the words of a religion, then you are not conscious yourself in the first place. Being truly awake and conscious means being able to think independently without being told what you must believe and think because your own logic and reason allows you to use your mind fully."

"But you, Paul, and Percival have both experienced its potential have you not?" Count Henry asked looking at Paul intently.

"I am not certain," Paul replied guardedly.

"You know of what I speak...beneath the Giza pyramids...what you saw and experienced, but also many things since that you have seen and felt as if real. The problem we all have is learning to know what is real and what is projected, from our wishes, or our fears, and what we want most...for then we can sometimes project that as something that appears real for our minds are truly powerful beyond measure. One day...one day, I know, man will again discover this. But in answer to you, Master Douglas, yes the majority of people have lost the use of this God given faculty and it is why so many are easily led."

"You mean misled?" Master Douglas replied.

"Yes...but that is why you put impossible expectations upon others to be open minded as you are, but in truth, most are simply not equipped mentally, emotionally nor physically to use such faculties yet," Count Henry explained further and sat down rubbing his hands through his hair, looking tired, his tone full of a deep sense of sadness Paul had never heard before. "You must forgive me this eve but my heart is heavy."

"Why?" Paul asked bluntly. "Is our position that truly impossible?"

"'Tis not the city I worry for. 'Tis a private and selfish matter that offends my heart this hour."

"Then share it so we may help carry the burden," Paul replied.

"I am afraid 'tis but a silly foolish matter of the heart, my friends," Count Henry explained and turned his face away embarrassed. He let out a light laugh as he shook his head and turned around to look at the mural. "I have this day learnt that Balian will urge the divorce of Humphrey of Toron, Princess Stephanie's son, from Isabella so that an alliance can be formed with the Ibelins," he began to explain and sighed. "I would never have thought it of Balian."

"How does that affect you?" Paul asked and stepped closer to him.

"Because once divorced they plan to marry her off to Conrad himself to gain legitimacy to the throne of Jerusalem," Count Henry answered and shook his head.

Ishmael looked at Paul and shrugged his shoulders, puzzled at his remark.

"Of course…I forget…you love her yourself," Paul said as sympathetically as he could.

Count Henry took a deep breath and faced upwards, closing his eyes.

"Always have and always shall," he sighed. "Oh what folly this cruel game of love."

୫୬ ୧୪

Paul leant forward resting his hands beside the wash bowl, Count Henry's words echoing through his mind endlessly. Wearing just his breeches, a single oil lamp illuminated the bowl as Princess Stephanie, wearing just a single silk nightshirt, quietly approached him, her heart aching for him, just the sight of him looking so tired and sad breaking it she felt. Softly she placed her hands upon his naked shoulders and rested her head against his back as he stood up straight. He stood still as she sensed his heart beat. Gently she moved her hands around his waist and held him, gently kissing his back just once.

"I fear this shall be one of our last few remaining nights together," she whispered, the sadness in her voice evident as she gulped. "If it is then I shall always cherish what little time we have shared. These past months have been the best of my entire life and I never thought I would be so lucky to have them with anyone…let alone you. If I were to die this very hour I would die satisfied and that I have known true love."

Paul turned around to face her and took her hands in his holding them tightly, her eyes searching his for any hint of his thoughts. As she looked up into his, he felt like he wanted to cry as emotions welled up inside of him for her. He felt a great respect and a growing love for her, but also for the feelings he could not shake from his mind about the smallest hint of a miracle that Alisha and Ailia could still be alive. He was beginning to resent the fact that he had seen Attar, or what he thought was him and Nicholas, but not Arri. If he had not had that experience, he would be able to love Princess Stephanie without the deep sense of guilt that kept entering his very soul as he recalled Alisha's laugh. How he missed her smile and every time he thought of her, his heart jumped and ached.

"I do love you," Paul said softly, looking into her eyes, wanting her to know it was true.

"I believe you…but not enough I fear," she replied sadly.

Paul raised her hands and kissed her fingers gently.

"I have only ever loved two women my whole life. Alisha and you. I felt the connection between us the very first time I ever saw you. But my whole life since coming here has been one of constant threat, always having to plan and be ever vigilant…that somewhere, somehow in that process I have actually forgotten how to live…do you understand that?"

"Of course I do for it has been exactly the same for me," she whispered emotionally. "Until you finally held me in your arms." Paul looked at the yellow and black wristband with the crimson thread through it wrapped around his wrist. "Please…tell me what it was like at Hattin and what we can expect to see here," she whispered as she ran her finger over the wristband, her eyes following his gaze.

"I cannot express Hattin in words…but I shall try and draw it if I can," Paul replied and pulled her close, his mind wondering if what he had seen at Castle Blanc was just some self induced images and feelings as Count Henry had explained because his desire and wish was so strong to see his family again. But then how did he know about Arri's grave beforehand? he pondered. "And I cannot say how it will be here other than it will be bad. 'Tis why I pray you leave with Balian and his family. My fear for your safety will be too great if you stay."

"No…absolutely not. You stay, I stay for I cannot bear the anguish of not knowing how you are. And if these last few nights prove to be our last…" She paused as she held him tightly. "Then it has been a blessing and enough." She shivered.

"Come, please," Paul said softly and led her to the large canopied bed with its richly embroidered hangings made out of warm velvets and taffetas. Curtains hung from the ceiling with the bed being slightly raised up on a platform. "This is far removed from the place we first made love," he smiled as he lifted her up onto the bed.

"Then please repeat what you did with me then…now," she said emotionally, leaned up and pressed her lips against his as she raised her legs and wrapped them around his thighs pulling him closer, her nightdress sliding down her thighs.

As Paul sensed her arousal, her kiss sending a sensuous warmth throughout his own body, he thought how fortunate he was to have her unlike the unrequited love Count Henry had to endure toward Princess Isabella. He lowered her down upon the bed and began to remove his own breeches, his arousal coursing through his veins as he touched her delicately, her body instantly shuddering with pleasure. She cried softly with both the physical pleasure of him entering her and sadness that it may be their last night together knowing Saladin's army was almost upon them. She held him tight against her and controlled his movements to make the moment last as long possible.

4 – 39

Port of La Rochelle, France, Melissae Inn, spring 1191

"I feel so sorry for that poor man Henry," the farrier remarked.

"Aye he had indeed loved her despite her youth compared with his," the old man said.

"But you said age of the physical body means nothing if our souls are eternal," Peter quickly interjected.

"Well yes, though in truth you would not show that love if the other person was still but a child would you? Well you should not...'tis wrong. But Count Henry had always felt a connection to her and a deep sense of knowing. It had been bad enough for him when she was made to marry Humphrey in the first place, but now to be made to marry the self serving Conrad who had shown no respect for women previously cut him to his very soul," the old man explained.

"What is this swastika thing you say he mentioned?" Gabirol asked. "'Tis a symbol I have heard of before. And what of the Egyptian Eye you mentioned?"

"Paul made drawings of it if you care to look," the old man said, indicating with his head at the leather folder. Quickly Simon pulled it across and looked inside. "Look for a four armed cross with arms coming off it." Simon quickly found a parchment sheet with several swastika images drawn upon it. "That is it. Paul drew up many versions taken from many cultures he had been able to learn of.

Fig. 73: Swastika.

| Hindu | Maltese | Greek | Jewish |
| Jain | Islamic | Japanese | Tibetan |

"If you look further you will find the very parchments Count Henry showed Paul, Master Douglas and Ishmael of the Eye of Horus and the brain section illustration."

Fig. 74: Eye of Horus.

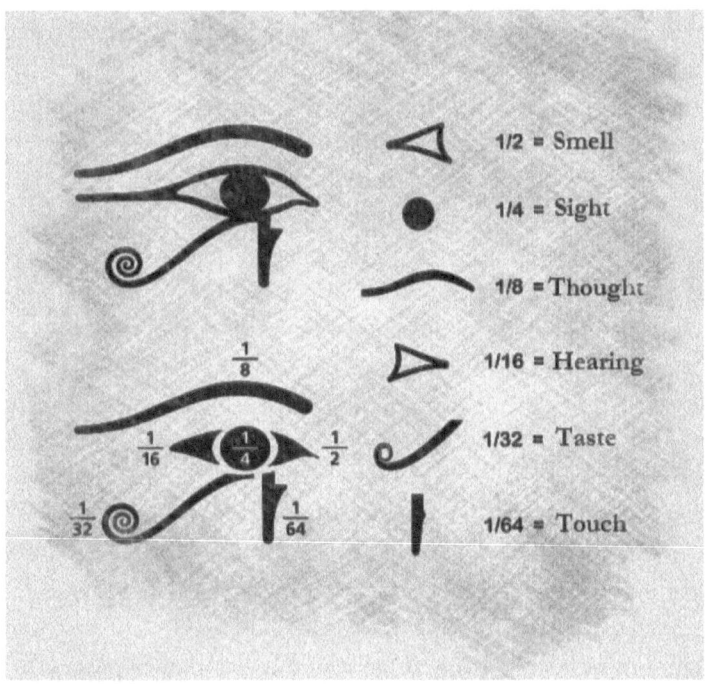

Fig. 75: Section Drawing of Brain.

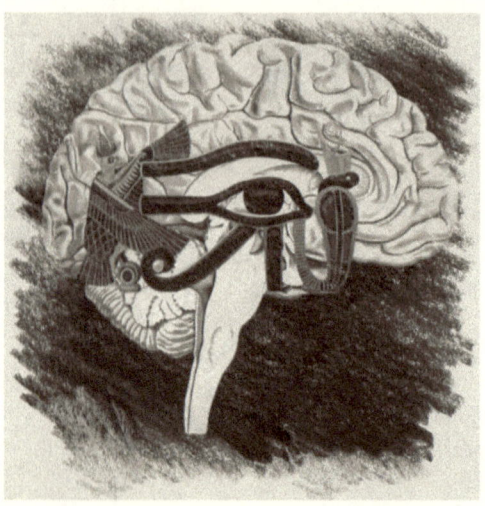

"And it is called a what?" Sarah asked.

"A swastika," the old man answered.

"And you say that Count Henry said he sees this one day being synonymous with evil...how so?" the Templar asked.

"After many sessions with Attar and other Sufi mystics who all claimed they had seen in dreams and visions a man, not dissimilar to Reynald in many ways, who would use the symbols of antiquity and rituals of magic to further a worldwide race...a master race based upon the technologies of our forefathers," the old man explained. "But his like must never be given guidance or access to such sites as Paul knows of. That is why it is so important his teachings and revelations are kept so secret except to those initiated so that only when man is again truly awakened can they be found. When man remembers his true past."

"A master race!" the Hospitaller repeated and shook his head. "Is that not what the Jews believe...that they are the master race, the chosen people of God, for what is the difference?"

"My friend, there is no difference," the old man answered.

"My Lord, so that means it will fall to the Jews who will bring such evil as you speak upon the world under this symbol," Sarah remarked and pulled the drawing from Simon's hand.

"No and you see there a clear reason why it is so vitally important to under-stand and interpret that which one may see within dreams and visions. This was *something Paul struggled with in regard to his visions and lucid dreams," the old man explained. "But the swastika, an ancient symbol of peace, will be used against the Jews specifically out of fear and fabricated stories to make many hate them...so no...like the Cathars shall discover to their cost, so too will the Jews discover an evil set against them on an unparalleled scale," the old man sighed.*

"If that is the case then why do we all bother with life at all?" the Genoese sailor asked.

"Why?" the old man said softly and looked at him directly. "Because in this life, death is the only certain thing we all share with absolute certainty. It is reliant purely upon the individual who holds it. Life is a gift, followed by the most beautiful, scary, painful thing any living thing will have to succumb to. 'Tis the one single commonality we will all partake of. Death is something we all fear. We know it is something that comes to all of us in time, but we never know when it will reach out and touch us. That is why life is such a beautiful and scary treasure, so do not waste it."

"And what of these?" Gabirol asked, holding up the drawings of the Eye of Horus and brain section image.

"That I fear we do not have the time to cover in any detail worthy of the subject; suffice it to say that as man carries memories within the very living matter of his being handed down from parents to child, so too are memories held within hair as I have explained previously. When man again remembers that which has been lost or hidden for so long, only then will he awaken and be able to use it fully," the old man explained.

"So knowing death was coming in Jerusalem, did Paul decide to stay or leave?" Simon asked and took the parchment of the swastika back from Sarah.

"He had vowed to stay and do whatever he could. He would not leave Stewart for a start or the other friends such as the blacksmith and his wife. Because he refused to leave you can imagine what Princess Stephanie likewise in turn decided to do," the old man answered.

"To stay also," Ayleth remarked.

"After Hattin, Balian, Raymond, Reginald and Payen of Haifa were among the few leading nobles who had managed to escape to Tyre but Raymond and Reginald soon left to attend to the defence of their own territories and Tyre came under the complete leadership of Conrad of Montferrat and Balian stayed with him up until Saladin arrived and began to lay siege to it, though in truth it was nothing more than a token gesture assault and one which afforded Jerusalem more time to prepares its defences. I guess we shall never know if Saladin did this on purpose

but during that time Balian was to become one of Conrad's closest allies. As I have already explained, leaving Tyre, Balian asked Saladin for permission to return through the lines to Jerusalem to escort his wife and their children to Tripoli. Saladin allowed this, provided that Balian leave the city and take an oath to never raise arms against him of which Balian duly swore and so it was he arrived in the city, a city now filled to capacity with refugees." The old man paused and nodded his head before continuing. "When Balian and his small group of knights arrived in the city, the inhabitants begged them to stay and called out his name as he rode slowly through the crowds. Then he entered the main court chamber...his wife Maria Comnena waiting for him with their children, Queen Sibylla sat upon her throne, Princess Stephanie standing beside her, Paul, Count Henry, Master Teric and Upside, Stewart and several other nobles and the Patriarch Heraclius."[114]

City of Jerusalem, Kingdom of Jerusalem, September 20th 1187

Abi knocked on Princess Stephanie's private chamber's door then stood back and waited. Princess Stephanie opened the chamber door and looked at her, surprised. Paul was sat at a small table drawing images of the battle of Hattin as he had promised trying to put down what he could not describe in words. Abi beckoned her to step into the corridor quietly leaving Paul in peace. Gently she closed the door and tied up her dressing robe. Looking alarmed she stared at Abi.

Fig. 76. Drawing of Hattin.

"Do not look so worried. I am here to inform you that Saladin has guaranteed Balian and his family safe conduct to Tripoli including you," Abi explained quietly and leaned in closer. "Listen to me...you must go for you cannot stay here."

"No. Paul and I discussed this and I am staying with him."

"Stephanie...if you do not listen to me on this matter, it will change another path that has been set in motion. You cannot think about yourself and your own selfish needs at this time."

"Wha...what?" Princess Stephanie asked and gasped in surprise at Abi's blunt statement.

"Are you so blind to your own body that you do not know you are with child now?"

Princess Stephanie gasped and raised her hand to cover her mouth in shock at Abi's revelation. Slowly she looked down to her stomach and placed both hands over it before looking back at Abi emotionally as tears instantly welled in her own eyes.

"I thought...I thought I had simply reached that age...where..." She tried to speak quietly. She laughed nervously as Abi shook her head to confirm what she had said. "Oh Abi...'tis the most wondrous news," she said and threw her arms around her.

"But Stephanie...you cannot tell him yet," Abi explained in a whisper. "I shall see you in the main hall as the queen wishes all to be present when Balian arrives."

Partly confused as well as overwhelmed Princess Stephanie nodded in agreement silently and bit her bottom lip to stop herself from becoming over emotional as she held her stomach and laughed nervously, a tear falling from her eye. As Abi walked away quietly, Princess Stephanie closed her eyes and smiled.

∞∞

Paul approached the large wooden doors with Princess Stephanie walking beside him holding his hand tightly, Ishmael following immediately behind them. One of the doors was wide open and they could see the room was already full as they moved to step inside. Queen Sibylla was sat in her throne chair, Abi stood off to her right side, the king's throne empty. The Patriarch Heraclius was standing in a small clearing of the room holding his staff of office and pointing it at Lord Balian as he stood perfectly still listening to him as his wife Maria and children stood behind him. Queen Sibylla shook her head just as Master Douglas moved to stand beside Paul along with Stewart.

"My Lord, I implore you, nay beg you if I must, and I absolve you of any oath to Saladin for our need is far greater...in fact the greater need of the whole of Christendom is stronger than the oath sworn to that non-Christian. We beseech thee to lead the defence of this holy city," Heraclius pleaded loudly in an animated and exaggerated fashion.

"As I have told you, I took an oath not to take up arms against him for allowing me to come here to fetch my wife and children only. I am a man of honour and I cannot go back upon this. Besides, Saladin offers terms as I have explained. Surrender the city and he will spare all here and allow Christians to stay and be protected. He is likewise a man of his word and your options are less than favourable for you do not have the men or the arsenal to defend this city any longer. It would be suicide to resist," Balian explained then stopped when he saw Paul. "By the Lord 'tis a miracle. I was told you had survived but I did not believe it," he said and walked over to Paul immediately grasping his forearms.

"Master Paul has already given Saladin's terms...terms the queen has already discussed amongst us, and turned down. So are you saying we now accept his terms and surrender? He will have us all convert to Islam at the point of the sword once his men are in charge," Heraclius shouted and looked around the room at everyone.

Abi moved and walked over to stand beside Princess Stephanie as Stewart and Master Douglas stepped further into view.

"We have men...and knight squires in training. There must be something we can do?" Master Douglas asked.

"My husband," Maria called out hesitantly. Balian let go of Paul and turned to face her as she stepped into the middle of the hall. Nervously she looked around at all the peering faces, many etched with obvious fear. "If Heraclius can absolve you of your oath, then you must accept this commission. 'Tis perhaps the greatest one the Lord has laid at your feet," she said and paused as she stepped closer to him. "But I cannot leave these walls and my friends... left abandoned. I would have a life time of regrets I would not be able to bear. I know you, my husband, so would you find the same in time. 'Tis better we stand and fight, whatever the outcome, than to run from this...for running is what we would be doing. I shall not leave my queen...and my friend," she said emotionally and looked over at Queen Sibylla.

Balian stood in stunned silence as everyone looked at him.

"There are better men here better suited to lead this than I," he protested.

"Then show us who," Heraclius called out as the queen rapidly walked over to Maria and clasped her hand gratefully.

"Him," Balian said aloud and pointed to Paul directly. "You have heard the rumours of his true lineage. 'Tis to him you should look for guidance and leadership this hour."

Princess Stephanie clasped Paul's hand tightly as everyone stared at him. Paul's mind raced as he fought to find some suitable words in response. The hall fell silent.

"My Lords, ladies and men of all," Paul started to say then stopped as he saw the look of confusion upon Abi's face, Count Henry stepping forward into view to hear what he was going to say. "I do not know how the story of my life shall be written down, if at all, but I will tell you this. That nowhere in it shall be written that I gave up. I have served as a knight of the Order of the Temple and as a Knight of Lazarus...but now I will serve as a knight of the people...for the people of this city, but not as a king, for I once served with an army of kings. You, you are all kings of your own kingdoms yet none of you have learnt that."

"Are you preaching to us?" Heraclius interrupted bluntly.

"No for I am aware that is most certainly your quarter not mine," Paul replied and stepped forward. "I suggest you put Saladin's proposal to the people of the city and see what they say in response. If they choose to defend the city and defy Saladin, then it will be down to all of us, and I mean every one of us to pick up arms and fight...as one. I have a sword that would suit you well," Paul remarked and looked at Heraclius hard. "As you seem eager to send others to fight on your behalf."

"Now let's not be too hasty on this matter. Perhaps we should negotiate...and...and if we are forced by the sword, then convert to Islam and repent later...what say you?" Heraclius asked nervously, his tone and manner awkward and embarrassing to observe.

Maria stepped closer to Balian and took his hand and looked at him intently.

"I would rather we live just a day as free people...with our honour intact for history will not record us well if we just surrender," she said as a hushed audience all listened. "Our place is here right now."

"I cannot organise the defence of this city with you here," Balian said and then looked around the hall at everyone. "But I know what you speak of has merit. I shall defend this city if it is the Lord's will."

"'Tis the Lord's will. God wills it," Heraclius called out loudly.

Balian looked at him and shook his head, unimpressed.

"If that is what the people choose," Balian spoke louder so all could hear. "However, I shall only do so if you leave with our children this very day for I have until sunset to leave myself. That is not negotiable," he concluded and looked back at Maria. "And we shall protect the queen!"

Maria stood shocked and struggled to maintain her composure. Eventually she stepped in front of Balian and took hold of both of his hands and held them up tightly.

"If the people of this city decide to fight, then you must stay," she said, her voice broken with emotion. "And I know the Lord's will is greater than mine so I shall reluctantly agree to your terms…for the sake of this city…not ours."

ഇൗരൂ

Paul stood beside Balian as they were flanked by Master Douglas, Stewart, Ishmael and several sergeants and turcopoles on the main balcony of the king's quarters overlooking the main square filled with desperate people close to panic. The sky was a clear blue and cloudless, the sun shining off of several walls making them appear almost white. Several squires from both the Templars and Hospitallers as well as several of King Guy's squires struggled to hold the gathering crowd back as many pushed up hard against the main stairs that led up to the open balcony trying to hear better. The main courtyard behind them was also crammed full of people desperate to know their fates. Abi moved back into the cool shadows of an alcove alongside Princess Stephanie and the queen.

"You have all now heard Saladin's terms and say you wish to defend this city," Balian said loudly but clear. "Pray that your fears may spur you into finding the strength and the courage and belief that there is something to live for, and great enough to die for. In solitude we must stand alone for no one is coming to rescue us or give us salvation, but in that solitude we must all lean upon each other here now present, each to support the other. I heard a man say not all walls are built of stone… some are built of brave and courageous men…and women. No…not the fearless types but those men who are terrified yet still stand their ground, who stand in the way of all that threatens all they love and hold dear the most. This day, that is all of you. Fear of the unknown makes you wear a mask but I say strip yourselves naked to that fear. Throw away that illusion that some great miracle that is heaven sent will save you all. Free yourself of that delusion and if you are going to fight, then fight for what is worth dying for. Your loved ones...not the bricks and stones of this city for it is not they that make a city, but those who dwell within it. I have heard many of you say that Saladin comes to fight us not because we are weak, but because we are strong and he knows it. Well I know him and he offers us terms to spare bloodshed and to seize these very bricks and stones. If you do not stand for something...then you are all doomed to fall for anything!"

"Great words, Lord Balian...but how many men at arms do you have and how many knights?" an elderly man shouted out, Paul recognising the man beside him as the blacksmith.

"I have but," Balian went to say and looked behind himself. "I have...I have," he said awkwardly.

Paul stepped down and walked up to Balian and stood by his side. Ishmael then stepped forwards accompanied by Stewart, Master Douglas, Master Teric and then Count Henry.

"All men who remain here standing when we are finished will be considered men at arms this day," Paul shouted just as a man in his mid fifties pushed his way past a squire and quickly rushed up to Paul. He stopped and stared at Paul for a few seconds. "I know you don't I?" Paul asked.

"Father, what are you doing?" a young woman called out and rushed forwards carrying a young child in her arms.

"I once did a cowardly deed...an act I never thought I would be forgiven for...but I was," the man started to say out loud and looked at his daughter. "And it was this man...this man who showed me how to stand and be the man I should have been. And if it is the Lord's will that he tests me again, then by all that is holy and precious to me, I shall not fail that test a second time. Just give me a weapon," he said emotionally.

Paul recognised the man as being the same man who had offered his daughter when they had been taken in error and nearly executed when Brother Elek had been beheaded.

"I have but a handful of Knights of Jerusalem mantles and robes left...

but any man who steps forwards will be given them and be made a knight this day," Count Henry called out.

A man shrouded in a dirty robe and hood pushed his way forwards through the crowd, his arms waving, the squires letting him through when Count Henry nodded for them to do so. Paul immediately saw he was wearing chain mail chausses as he approached up the stairs. The man was heavily bearded and looking down. Princess Stephanie looked on concerned but then the man looked up and pulled his hood down.

"You now have another to volunteer to take up the honour of finally becoming a genuine knight," Percival said, his voice dry. Paul's eyes widened in surprise. "I vowed I would not return unless I found out what had happened to Alisha and Ailia and Thomas and his men," he said quietly, his eyes full of emotion. "Well…here I am," Percival said and knelt down before Paul and Balian.

Paul's heart raced and his stomach knotted instantly upon hearing his words.

"Pray tell what you know, Percy, I beg of you," Paul asked and knelt in front of him, grabbing his arms and looking at him intently.

"I could not discover what has happened to Alisha," he started to explain and paused seeing the fierce frantic look in Paul's eyes. "But I finally tracked down Thomas and all of his men. They live….as does Tenno, Theodoric," he paused, "…and Ailia."

Paul let go of Percival and stood up quickly in shock. Princess Stephanie, seeing his reaction, rushed over to his side. His eyes were wide as he shook his head in disbelief. He took a step back stunned as Percival rose to his feet.

 3 – 10

"What?" Paul finally gasped as Abi ran over.

"I also recovered your sword. 'Tis presently held by Tenno," Percival said as he stood up.

"Tenno! Alive?" Abi asked disbelievingly. Percival smiled and nodded yes. Abi spun around and looked panic stricken as she looked at Princess Stephanie. She shook her head in utter confusion and raised her hands uncharacteristically flustered. She turned her head to look at Percival as she again nodded yes to confirm. "And Ailia?" she demanded to know, sounding angry.

"Yes, she is alive and very much well," Percival replied as Balian listened, bemused.

Abi grasped Princess Stephanie's arms and looked into her eyes. She went to speak but could say nothing still in shock at the news. Quickly she placed her hands to her ears and shook her head, confused, then walked away quickly up the steps and out of sight as Princess Stephanie looked at Paul, stunned. She clutched her stomach as she felt sick.

"I knew last eve would be our last together," she said quietly and fought to compose herself as she stood in front of the crowd.

"My Lords...if you will allow me, I would gladly take the honour of becoming a real knight. I shall stand and defend these people for as long as God wills it," Percival said aloud seeing how uncomfortable both Princess Stephanie and Paul looked as they stood staring at each other.

Paul quickly took hold of her hand and stood beside her.

"Nothing is set. If Ailia lives, we shall get her after we have dealt with the problem we have here first," Paul said to her and held her hand tightly as tears welled in her eyes. Paul's entire body tingled as the hairs on his back rose and a thousand questions filled his mind.

Count Henry moved closer to Percival and beckoned that he kneel down again. Balian approached them and withdrew his sword.

"You are recognised by all here as being the nearest thing to a king we have. Even Saladin acknowledges that...so please...knight this man once and for all...for Lord knows he deserves it," Count Henry said looking at Percival, then looked up at Paul and Princess Stephanie.

"'Tis long overdue and an honour," Balian replied and raised his sword. "You are more a knight than the best of all of us," Balian said out loud and gently dubbed the sword on either side of Percival's shoulders. "Now arise, Sir Percival, for no truer a knight of honour...and such perseverance has ever stood before us."

Percival looked up with emotion in his tired eyes revealing how deeply Balian's words touched him. He looked over at Paul as he nodded at him. Slowly he stood up and turned around to face the crowd. The other man with his daughter stepped forwards and knelt before Balian.

"Anyone else this day, step forward now and become a knight of Jerusalem," Balian called out.

Several men pushed their way through the crowd and walked up the steps toward Balian and Count Henry just as all the squires who had been knights in training themselves stepped forward. As they took up position kneeling, more men stepped forward including several women. As even more men stepped forward, the area in front of Balian became full. Heraclius walked to the front of the kneeling men and opened his Bible.

"Swear unto Lord Balian your allegiance and commit to carry out the Lord's mighty work this day and stand fast in the days ahead," he called out. "I shall read from the good book Ephesians 6:10 and by kneeling you are accepting under oath to serve as knights of Jerusalem unto death."

When he looked up his jaw dropped in surprise as nearly all of the men began to kneel. He looked at Balian.

"We have but sixty sets of armour and uniforms we can issue to the first who stepped forward...but the others...," Balian said as he looked out over the crowd.

"'Tis not the uniform that makes them knights, My Lord, but that fire which burns within them," Percival remarked, Balian immediately nodding.

"I want as many golden crosses as possible made up. Use yellow if that is all we have but I want every man kneeling who takes this vow to wear one," Balian ordered and nodded at Heraclius to continue.

Port of La Rochelle, France, Melissae Inn, spring 1191

"I heard they were all made knights," Peter remarked.

"Balian was able to swear in sixty full knights from amongst the squires and those first few men who came forward complete with all the equipment, weapons and armour they would need. The rest he made Confrere Knights. It certainly empowered them all," the old man explained.

"I feel so sorry for Princess Stephanie," Ayleth commented, looking sad.

"'Twas indeed a shock to both Paul and Princess Stephanie," the old man said and paused. "Paul took her inside and just held her in his arms as she cried. Words were useless and they remained like that for nearly an hour until Abi came and found them. It had taken her that long to get her own thoughts together. Everything was in turmoil for all of them. Just when Abi had thought she knew what she was doing and where they were going, everything changed again in an instant."

"And where were Alisha and Sister Lucy then?" Gabirol asked.

"Neither Paul nor Percival had any idea still. But Percival had used the small bee symbols upon the stones left at the site where they had been killed as his clue

to follow...and it had indeed led him to Tenno, Theodoric and Ailia being closely protected and guarded by Thomas and his men," the old man explained.

"So Thomas and his men are vindicated as the godly knights of honour we hoped they were. But where?" the Templar asked.

"Within the complex of the Cave de Sueth," the old man answered.

"And they had been there all of that time. Why had they not got a message to Paul sooner?" Peter asked.

"Because they wanted Turansha to believe that they were all indeed dead...to protect Ailia for the future. Percival getting through to Jerusalem was the earliest any of them was actually able to make their way from the cave complex. The disaster at Hattin had thrown everything into chaos and they could not rely upon the heliograph network nor carrier pigeons for fear of that information falling into Turansha's hands."

"'Tis the cruellest hand of fate to be dealt to anyone," the wealthy tailor remarked, shaking his head.

"I feel so sad for them both. And if Ailia was alive as Paul had already been told by Arri in his dreams...then what of Alisha and Sister Lucy?" Sarah asked. "And the princess now with child!"

"Indeed...indeed," the old man sighed then continued. "That morning after swearing in all the new knights, Balian sent word of his decision to Saladin at Ascalon via a deputation of burgesses, informing him that all within the city had rejected the sultan's proposals for a negotiated surrender of Jerusalem; however, and despite this, Saladin still arranged for an escort to accompany Maria, their children, and all their household to Tripoli. As the highest ranking lord remaining in Jerusalem, according to the chronicler Ibn al-Athir, Balian was seen by the Muslims as holding a rank more or less equal to that of a king so his decision was accepted."

"So Balian's wife did leave as he had demanded?" Simon asked.

The old man nodded yes.

"Balian found the situation in Jerusalem was indeed very dire. It was filled with refugees fleeing Saladin's conquests, with more arriving daily. So he was forced to rapidly prepare for the inevitable siege by storing food and money. Many of the women folk started to walk around the city walls singing prayers in repentance believing the Lord had abandoned them. Balian demanded they return to within the walls. When he stood upon the battlements to make this order, panic filled many when they saw the massed armies of Saladin approach the city that evening. Immediately after Saladin had Maria Comnena and her entourage escorted away safely, *negotiations were entered into between Saladin and Balian, through the mediation of Yusuf Batit, one of the Eastern Orthodox clergy, who had been largely suppressed under Latin Christian rule, mainly Heraclius, and knew that they would have more freedoms if the city were returned to the Muslims. Saladin preferred to take the city without bloodshed and still offered generous terms, but those inside still refused to leave the holy city, vowing to destroy it in a fight to the death rather than see it handed over peacefully. Saladin fully understood Balian's position and predicament...and thus the siege began."*[115]

"And Balian trusted Saladin to look after his own family even as they were about to enter into hostilities?" the Genoese sailor asked, bemused.

"Yes for that is the strength of the trust that Balian had in Saladin's word and honour," the old man answered.

"I think we all know the likes of Reynald would not have done so," the Hospitaller remarked.

"'Twas the sight of many siege engines being speedily erected that put the fear of God within all of them, quite a few suddenly having a change of heart, including the Patriarch Heraclius...," the old man explained.

"And Saladin forgave Balian for breaking his oath and word not to take up arms against him?" Peter asked, puzzled.

"Yes, yes he did. As I said, they were close friends," the old man replied.

"What a mad war," Ayleth remarked.

"Mad indeed...very mad," the old man said and smiled at her.

Chapter 81
Walls of Men and Shields

Paul and Abi entered the Master of Stores's room and looked for Percival amongst the men being sized up and kitted out with chain mail, mantles, helmets and swords. The arbalestery was already being emptied opposite of all its crossbows and bows. The room was heavy with sweat and smoke from several large burning torches. As soon as Paul saw Percival he pushed his way toward him, Percival standing up immediately upon seeing him approach.

"Percy, I must know everything. How are they still alive? How did you find them? Where is Alisha...is she still alive? My sword...how did you recover it when even Ishmael could not remove it?"

"Paul, slow down and I shall tell you all that I know. 'Twas Taqi who helped me get through to Jerusalem the last few miles. He has gone to seek Alisha within the caravan of her sister Queen Tamar for that is the last place they know of that she was heading for," Percival began to explain.

"And Tenno...he is truly alive?" Abi interrupted.

"Yes. 'Twas Theodoric's idea to stage their deaths to throw off Turansha for good."

"But we saw their bodies...and Tenno's armour. Everything!" Paul exclaimed. "The nights I have not slept seeing Alisha's flesh come away in my hands. Did they not think how we would react?"

"I have questioned them on this. Do you not think I have not asked the same?" Percival replied seeing the frustration register in Paul's eyes. "'Twas Tenno's old set of armour...and the bodies were taken from the caravans already destroyed. Theo said he knew you would recognise the signs he had left everywhere. But in your grief you missed them. We all did."

"You did not," Abi shot back looking at Percival intently.

"'Twas Master Douglas who made the connection not I," Percival replied.

"He did not mention it...but why not so much as a message to warn us? Have you any idea of what has happened since then? That I am with Princess Stephanie now...that I did not care if I should live or die?" Paul explained, his tone almost frantic.

"Paul, there was simply no other way of getting the message to you in time. It took me weeks to find them at the cave and that was more luck than judgement. If we risked getting a message out sooner then the whole point of staging their deaths would have been in vain and Turansha would still hunt you and your family forever!"

"Paul...'tis not Percival's fault. He has done you proud and a great service," Abi remarked and grasped his arm.

"I am sorry, Percy...truly I am," Paul said and sat himself down heavily upon the bench beside Percival. "I should be grateful but...'tis all such a shock," he explained and rested his head in his hands. "My daughter lives. It explains much." He sighed heavily as he thought back to Arri and Nicholas's comments in his dream.

"My friend...we shall defend this city, and when we are finished here, we shall go and fetch Ailia and the others," Percival said reassuringly. "And if Alisha lives, we shall eventually find her too."

"I did not mention anything so you were not filled with false hope," Master Douglas suddenly interrupted as he stepped into view. "I recognised Theodoric's old symbol posts but I could not be certain of their meaning...'tis why I agreed to let Percival follow them. I did not know it would take so long."

"Paul!" Balian called out looking for him as he entered the storeroom. As soon as he saw Abi he made his way over, concerned at the look of Paul when he saw him. "Paul. You must listen to me...all of you. I have had to make agreements with Lord Montferrat but they are not what you may hear them to be. I know he still works hand in glove with Turansha but I have to propose certain measures to ensure my own family's safety and future. But understand it does not extend to Conrad himself, only his family," Balian whispered close to Paul. "Now come, Saladin approaches this very hour. Meet me at the Tower of David as soon as you can."

Paul looked at Percival then Abi before turning to face Master Douglas. He stepped closer and offered his hand to pull him up to his feet.

"You need to get your head out of your fucking arse and back to the here and now if you wish to live and see your daughter again," he said to Paul bluntly.

A sudden commotion went up loudly as a sergeant started yelling and pushing one of the new volunteer knights. Quickly Balian walked towards them as the new knight, a tall but very thin and feminine looking man, pushed the sergeant backwards.

"My Lord…look at this man. He still wears make up from his iniquitous den of fornication. He is a boy lover so please pray tell how his sort can help us and take much needed weapons better suited for real men?" the sergeant asked, looking at the man with disgust.

Anger rose in the man's eyes clearly visible and, before Balian could answer, he lunged at the sergeant, tucked his head under his arm, his right arm going beneath the sergeant's groin and instantly stood up fully and started to spin around, the sergeant now held above his head. Then he threw the sergeant against a full rack of lances. With a crash of several lances breaking, the sergeant rolled down and onto the floor, the man immediately standing over him.

"I may love men but I am a dancer and an acrobat too. You should know whom you insult before you say such things for I wager I am far stronger than you," the man said, looking down at the sergeant. "Now do you still think I am not strong enough to fight?"

"I think he has made his point," Balian remarked as the sergeant rubbed his shoulder and looked up at him. "So give our acrobatic dancer here whatever he requires."

₱℞

The sun was only just beginning to settle on the far horizon when Paul made his way to join Balian, Master Douglas and Count Henry on the tower of David's Gate. Percival and Abi followed him in silence whilst Master Teric was busy placing men in positions all along the outer wall at intervals.

"Any words of wisdom or one of your philosophical quotes, Master Douglas?" Balian asked as he looked out towards the formations of Saladin's army.

"Yes, hurry up and get those praying idiots inside the gates," Master Douglas replied, pointing to many women who were still insistent upon walking around the walls in prayer. "We have dug out as much of a trench all around the walls as was possible given the time. Only sections left are at the entrances. It will make it more difficult for him to position his siege engines and limit what walls he can reach...which are the thickest sections only," Master Douglas explained.

"And I note you have left other sections within the ditch. Why?" Balian asked.

"In case they get one of their engines within the ditch. It will stop them from simply wheeling it along the length of the trench to a thinner walled section," Master Douglas explained.

"You know we cannot have this siege last too long for we do not have the supplies," Balian remarked.

"Nor does Saladin even if he starts to have them brought in," Paul commented. "We need to make every arrow and bolt we have count. Break them upon the walls so you cost him more men."

"I have ordered that all non combatants able enough, including children, are to collect all arrows after each volley lands so we can re-arm our archers and crossbow men and return them in kind," Count Henry explained.

"Good. I shall ride out this evening to try and negotiate once more with Saladin and see if we can resolve this utter madness," Balian said as he studied several siege engines being moved into position and set up. "Do not fear, he will allow me safe passage."

"And if he does not and keeps you hostage, then what?" Paul asked.

"Then you will find yourself as a king, my friend, like it or not," Balian answered and looked at him.

⚔ 2 – 13

"Then I pray you return," Paul replied and tried to focus upon Saladin's forces, their circular shields twinkling and reflecting the sun's rays. There were thousands of them like a moving wall of men and shields.

"Paul...you have someone to see you," Master Douglas said quietly and slightly nodded for him to look along the walkway.

Paul turned to see Princess Stephanie stood within the shade and protection of the tower's passageway that led through to the next section of wall. She fumbled nervously with her hands. Quickly Paul walked toward her immediately wrapping his arms around her when he reached her.

280

Port of La Rochelle, France, Melissae Inn, spring 1191

"I need a drink," the farrier exclaimed loudly and pulled his heavy woollen robe away from his neck, feeling hot. "I am seeing this conflict so differently from how we have been informed," he remarked, his face red.

"This tale is almost done," the old man spoke softly and looked at Stephan. "But if you require more drink, please do so."

"So if Taqi helped Percival get back to Jerusalem, why did he not stay around?" Simon asked.

"Were you not listening?" Sarah shot back. "He went away immediately to see if he could find Alisha within Queen Tamar's caravan."

"Yes...but why go there?" Simon asked.

"Ah...a good point," the old man said as Stephan got up to fetch some more drinks. "Let me explain. You see Percival had been told by Tenno and Theodoric that both Alisha and Sister Lucy had decided to go ahead to meet her sister Queen Tamar with some of her dress designs and simply meet again. They had been met at their campsite by several members of her advance reconnaissance riders. When the camp was later attacked, Tenno, Theodoric, Thomas and his men put up an incredible fight and beat off Turansha's men. Well, their first attack at least. It was then that Theodoric proposed the plan of faking their deaths knowing Turansha's men would return. And so they took the bodies of several of the dead and placed them just as they were later found. They dressed them in their own clothes before partially burning them again. 'Twas a disgusting thing to have to do but it was agreed for the long term protection of the family, it was the only way forward."

"So why didn't Alisha and Sister Lucy return?" Peter asked.

"That they did not know at the time...and as they could not wait, they had to make good their own escape, whilst several of the other knights volunteered to remain and engage any of Turansha's men should they return. As Tenno and Thomas led the others away to safety." The old man paused, shaking his head. "They travelled north and came across Queen Tamar's reconnaissance party and several others. All had been brutally mutilated and their bodies thrown into a deep crevasse, drawing the attention of vultures. There was so much blood and lumps of flesh everywhere. 'Twas impossible to know if Alisha and Sister Lucy were amongst them or not...but Thomas made them move onward to the Cave de Sueth before Turansha or any of his men returned."

"The knights who remained at the initial site...surely that was suicidal was it not?" Gabirol asked.

"'Twas indeed and they knew the probable outcome if Turansha's men returned. But they believed they were duty bound by their vowed pledge...to protect what they thought was the family of the True Holy Grail...Alisha and Ailia," the old man explained. "Most battles are lost or won in the minds of the combatants...and those brave knights believed they could deal with whatever came their way. Alas as we now know the numbers sent back against them were overwhelming."

"And they were the decapitated knights Paul and Percival saw, yes?" Ayleth asked hesitantly.

The old man nodded yes.

"And Balian returned after seeing Saladin as we know having learnt that his wife was safely under escort heading for Tripoli," the Templar remarked.

"Yes he returned...and so began the siege proper," the old man sighed.

City of Jerusalem, Kingdom of Jerusalem, September 20th 1187

Balian had only just returned through David's Gate when Saladin's army started to march slowly toward it and the Damascus Gate, their siege engines following close behind. The sun was almost gone and Saladin's massed forces seemed to stretch for as far as the eye could see, small flaming torches held along their ranks. As the gates were barricaded shut, Paul, Percival and Master Douglas looked down from the turret of David's Gate. Paul looked around thinking back to the first time he had passed through the gate all those years ago. Never in his wildest imagination would he have ever thought that one day he would find himself now defending it. Abi ran up to him accompanied by Ishmael as men ran to and fro carrying arrows ready for the bowmen taking up positions, shields by their sides ready.

"An entire fucking wall of men and shields and coming straight for us," Master Douglas said quietly and calmly as he studied the mass of men approaching, their drums beginning to sound out ominously. "'Tis perversely beautiful in its own way."

"Yes...but it will soon turn ugly," Abi remarked as she leaned forward to look down through the battlements. She looked at Paul. "We must do everything to survive what comes next. Whatever it takes."

"INCOMING!" a sergeant shouted loudly as a large flaming shot was fired toward the wall between David's Gate and the Damascus Gate.

Before the ball of flame had even reached over half way, many more were loosed off from large catapults set behind the advancing troops. When the first ball landed just short of the wall, it ran across the wide trench Master Douglas had supervised digging out and rolled at speed until it hit the wall and exploded in a bright gout of orange and yellow flame but no damage was done. The drums stopped beating and everyone looked knowing what was coming next. Ishmael pushed Paul hard against the battlement and pulled his shield up over them as Abi and Master Douglas raised a shield each as had been placed all along the walls.

"'Tis bloody fortuitous we have plenty of shields if nothing else," Paul said as a huge volley of arrows arched into the early evening sky.

"Whispering death," Master Douglas said as the whoosh sound of thousands of arrows sped toward them. "Okay, men, listen in. Those of you with the shits already, untie your breeches so you can drop them quick enough if needs be and use the pots to your left. Make sure you throw it toward the enemy afterwards...not this way!"

A turcopoler rang a hand bell frantically from within the safety of the tower passage to alert everyone to the incoming arrows. As men shielded themselves, others below on the ground ran for cover but even as they did, several flaming balls arched over the wall and crashed amongst them exploding into flames engulfing several at once, as another smashed into a two storey building passing straight through its roof. Paul looked at the scene as several men, women and children ran from the blazing building all screaming in agony, their clothes alight. A rush noise filled the air as the thousands of arrows started to fall like heavy rainfall thudding into walls, onto roofs, shields and men. Screams began to fill the air accompanied by the frantic bell ringing. Master Teric shouted out in the distance for the fire details to move to their predetermined sections as had been planned. Two arrows thudded into Ishmael's shield and one into Abi's. They were not the heavy armour piercing arrows. As soon as the thudding stopped from the arrow fall, Master Douglas jumped to his feet.

"Missed me again, you fuckers," he said then turned to look for Master Teric just as Stewart ran into view coming through the tower passageway. "Brother Stewart...you know what to do!" he shouted, Stewart simply raising his hand to confirm as he ran past not even seeing Paul against the wall. "Pick up, pick up, pick up!" Master Douglas shouted down to the men and children below. Instantly they started to collect as many arrows as they could.

"Stand by, stand by!" Stewart then shouted as he looked both ways along the line of the battlements, his sword held high. Immediately every knight, sergeant and turcopoler stood and drew their arrows back fully within their bows and aimed them high toward Saladin's forces. Stewart looked left and right again. "LOOSE!" he screamed and lowered his sword. A loud whoosh went up as the arrows flew. "RELOAD!" Stewart shouted again, Paul surprised at just how loud his voice was and carried. He felt unbelievably proud watching him as Balian appeared and ran up the steps towards them. "LOOSE!"

Paul looked over the wall to see the arrows arch towards Saladin's ever nearing army. He watched fascinated as the arrows met mid flight with a returning volley of arrows from their lines, many sparking like small fireflies in the sky as they collided. The thuds of the arrows hitting the lines of the Muslims' round shields thudded out almost drowning out the noise of the drum beats just as they started up again. The arrow bell ringer started to ring it again frantically and the bowmen quickly took cover behind the battlements and raised their shields again quickly, but some not quick enough as two were struck dead, the arrows piercing vertically down through the shoulder of one, the other straight into his head. Master Douglas had told them all not to bother with helmets as most had not trained to fight in them and, besides, they offered little protection against such arrows at speed and would hinder them more than help. Several of the new knights looked on in horror as the men fell dead.

"Stand fast and check your fear!" Paul shouted and stood up as the last arrows thudded into the ground below them.

"RELOAD!" Stewart shouted again, the men immediately forcing themselves back into action. He watched as they all reloaded, some of them visibly shaking with fear as the reality began to fully hit home. Their bow strings tensioned as they drew their arrows. "LOOSE!"

"Look. They intend to set the siege engine against the very gate's tower," Abi said and pointed at the large wooden tower being rolled toward them and the only section of land not dug away. She looked over quickly at the fixed wooden drawbridge that had been set firm many years previously. "Archers. We need flame archers," she said and quickly rushed off toward the stairs and disappeared below into the middle section of the tower.

Paul and Ishmael looked down quickly in time to see several flaming arrows being fired down onto the main wooden bridge itself. No sooner had they hit when several Muslim light archers sprinted forwards and tried to put the arrows out. They were immediately engaged at close range by other archers along the wall. As they fell dead or wounded, more Muslims sprinted forwards to try and stop the flaming arrows from setting the bridge alight, the siege tower drawing ever closer. Paul saw Abi's larger sized arrows zip out from the tower hitting the men one after another as they ran across the bridge. The Muslim drums stopped beating and Paul looked up in time to see the whole length of the approaching column kneeling down as the rear rank of archers aimed flaming arrows and loosed them all off one after the other from his right until the last one was fired to his left. It gave the visual impression of a wave of light as the arrows arched up into the darkening sky. The bell ringers along the walls all rang frantically. This time the men on the walls threw themselves hard against the battlements and pulled their shields together protectively. Stewart ran into the passageway alongside the bell ringer just in time as the arrows started to land. Paul knelt against the wall, his eyes looking into Ishmael's as he calmly watched him, their shields above their heads.

"'Tis amazing how small one can make oneself no?" Ishmael asked, half joking, as the arrows ricocheted off the walls whilst others thudded into woodwork and shields.

The moment the arrows stopped falling, Paul jumped to his feet and stamped upon a flaming arrow nearby to put it out. Stewart was already shouting to reload as Master Teric was yelling orders to the fire details. Paul listened out for the sounds of the wounded but he could hear none. As far as he could see no one had been hit with that last volley. No sooner had he thought that than several men started to shout 'incoming' as more large fireballs were launched against them. Some seemed to hang in the air motionless for a moment before continuing to flame their way across the sky. Some reached into the inner areas of the city, which concerned Paul thinking about Princess Stephanie. But he knew she would be below in the underground vaults. Balian yelled for the crossbow men to move and form up. As they all appeared and ran into positions between the bowmen, they immediately aimed toward the Muslim forces as they stopped at the very edges of the long ditches. Paul looked on as the men had to apply pressure with their front fingers to stop the bolts falling off as they aimed down slightly. A staccato of clicks filled the air as Balian shouted "Fire". His order was different from Stewart's to avoid any confusion. As the bolts hit, some piercing the Muslims' shields, whilst others bounced off harmlessly, many more still found their targets through the spaces between the shields, the crossbow men immediately reloading as Stewart ordered another salvo from the archers. As he shouted "Reload" followed by "Loose" again, children ran the length of the parapet dropping off more arrows they had gathered up. Ishmael pointed at a line of Muslim infantry running onto the bridge below supported by many light archers on foot firing up toward them rapidly. The infantry were fully covered with a long protective shield that also hung down the sides fixed upon a frame, just their feet barely visible. They were tasked with securing the bridge and extinguishing any flaming arrows. The siege tower was being pushed into position, its upper ramp being readied for lowering onto the top of the David's Gate wall.

"Oil!" Balian shouted down and grabbed Paul's arm for him to follow him.

Paul and Ishmael ran with Balian just as another volley of both ordinary and flaming arrows started to rain down upon the whole area. As they ran into the cover of the tower, a very young looking knight stood with his back against the wall, his eyes wide. He was shaking and had wet himself. Percival came running up the wide stone stairway that led up from the ground floor. He was carrying a small wooden fragmentation barrel with a large launching pole attached to it and closely followed by several sergeants all carrying identical barrels. Abi appeared with her bow part set with a large arrow.

"They are targeting the launchers' opening," she shouted. "The minute you open it to fire, you will receive many arrows. 'Tis suicide whoever aims it."

"Then let me," Balian shouted as horses screamed out after one of the paddocks was hit by a flaming ball.

"No, you are too important. You go down, they will all lose hope. I shall do it," Paul said as Percival looked at him hard.

"Like fuck you will," Percival said, swearing uncharacteristically, and pushed Paul aside and walked toward the large wooden ballista. You have never fired one of these before," he yelled back as he placed the small barrel onto the device and set the main pole into the launching groove. Quickly he started to wind in the tension pulling the ropes tight against the bow arms. "'Tis not just a large crossbow. Fire this wrong and you will destroy it. We only have but one shot at this, possibly two if we are lucky."

"You better make it fast as they are drawing near and they have men approaching with ladders now," Abi called out as she looked down through a small peep hole. She flinched as several arrows bounced off the wall and wooden cover a little too close to the hole.

As the ropes were pulled tighter by winding the winchbaliwide device, the ballista eventually clicked when it was fully tensioned and ready to fire. The ropes were made from a mixture of hair twisted with animal sinew but as soon as it was ready, Balian could see the threads beginning to unravel under the tension. He quickly stood behind Percival as they both pushed the ballista forwards to the opening. Two sergeants moved to stand on either side, one pushing Abi out of the way. Another two men knelt at their feet holding small ceramic pots that held burning candles inside. Paul looked on as they prepared to open the cover.

"Now!" Percival yelled.

A third knight rushed forwards and pulled the shutter cover locking pin away, the entire board swinging upwards and inwards on its counter weight. Instantly many arrows started entering, some hitting the ballista's main wooden bow arms, others the roof and several zipping too close to Percival as he ducked. His eyes widened as his vision focused upon the looming siege tower less than fifty feet away, its upper drawbridge having a reach of nearly fifteen feet once dropped. He could see the many Muslim soldiers peering back at him through the small slits and side slit where the drawbridge was already being lowered. Percival pulled the main trigger release, but nothing happened. They all looked at the ballista in horror, the knight nearest to Abi being hit in the neck by an arrow instantly falling on the floor in agony as blood spurted out in large bursts covering the wall and ballista. Abi pulled him away fast as he grasped his neck and fought to breathe. Balian looked at the trigger mechanism and thumped it sideways as hard as he could, the tension making the whole unit jump as it fired, two arrows hitting the small barrel as it flew forwards. Abi pulled Balian away from the ballista as more arrows zipped into the room. Percival rolled off and onto the floor just as an arrow hit the area he was standing in. The sergeant to his front quickly glimpsed out to see if the barrel had hit the siege tower. He was not certain but was just able to make out a slight shimmering from what he took to be the oil. He pulled himself back out of the line of fire, lowered his flame prepared arrow and the knight kneeling at his feet opened the top of the ceramic lantern and guided the arrow head onto the candle. All watched for what seemed an age before the arrow head caught light. The sergeant took a deep breath and stepped quickly in front of the opening, drew his arrow fully and aimed it at the siege tower. He loosed it off just as an arrow thudded into his left forearm. He dived out of the way grimacing in pain. Paul could hear Stewart outside repeatedly ordering the bowmen to reload and loose followed by Master Douglas shouting for the crossbow men to reload and fire. Abi squinted to see if the arrow had hit. It was stuck in the rampart section of the tower blazing away but it had not set any of the oil alight. The tower drew nearer. She knew if it made contact, the men inside were highly trained and would be across and inside within moments. She looked at Ishmael, his face registering her concern. Percival kicked the counter weight and the cover closed immediately, more arrows thudding into it. He rapidly tried to load another barrel shot but Ishmael grabbed his arm and shook his head no.

"I need you all to cover me. Come, follow me," he said and picked up the barrel shot and took another from the sergeant nearest him.

Quickly he ran to the wooden staircase that led to the top of the tower. Balian looked at Paul bemused as Percival ran up the stairs after him. Abi started to push Paul and Balian to follow snatching the ceramic candle holder from the sergeant nearest her and several flame prepared arrows. When they reached the top, they all had to crawl over to the battlements as so many arrows were coming over in what felt like a never ending stream. Before they even had time to speak, Ishmael stood up exposing himself completely, raised one of the barrel shots and threw it down upon the siege tower now almost level with him. It smashed into the side of the tower. Instantly he bent down and picked up the second barrel shot and threw that, several arrows zipping so close, one passed through his tunic beneath his armpit. Balian pulled him down hard. Ishmael looked at Abi and smiled.

"I have done my part. 'Tis now your turn," he said looking across to Abi.

Lying upon her side, she took three arrows and placed them side by side and charged them up against the bow string. Paul quickly opened the ceramic lantern and carefully held it beneath the arrow heads until all three were alight. She moved up on to her knees pressing herself hard against the wall as more arrows zipped overhead and ricocheted off the wall. She took a deep breath, winked at Paul then moved up and out into a firing position, aimed at the siege engine and drew back the arrows as far as she dared. A crossbow bolt hit her upper left arm imbedding deeply but she did not even flinch. Paul saw her fingers release the tension on the bow string, the three arrow shafts bending under the stress as they were launched forwards. As soon as the arrows' rear fletchings had cleared her bow, she ducked down fast. She looked at Paul, then Ishmael, before looking at Balian as he lay flat out before her. Neither of them dared look up as the number of arrows zipping overhead intensified. The darkening night sky suddenly lit up as the oil on the tower finally ignited engulfing the top and front side of the siege engine. As screams filled the air from men inside burning, cheers went up from along the length of the wall, Master Douglas immediately shouting for men to retake their positions, Stewart still calling out orders to reload and loose.

"You are hurt," Paul said to Abi as she looked at the bolt stuck in her arm.

"Not half as bad as it could have been," she half smiled, but her eyes revealing the pain she was really in. It was now almost dark.

Balian raised his head slightly to look at the siege engine as flames started to fully engulf it. Paul eased himself up in time to see the Muslim wall of shields backing away slowly. The covered shielding frame the other men had been using was now also alight and abandoned. Several men were running around on fire, one screaming so loud it sent a shiver down Paul's spine. Slowly he stood up and helped Abi to stand as Ishmael stood up the other side of her. Percival looked down at the many dead and dying beneath them, the siege engine now fully ablaze lighting up the whole area.

Balian immediately rushed to the side of the battlements and waved for Stewart and Master Douglas to cease fire.

"That was just the start. It will get far worse before this siege is done," Abi said, Balian turning to face them.

"We have lost so few, yet they have lost many. If we can keep doing this, we may just stand a chance after all," Balian said as he looked out towards Saladin's position in the distance. "I know he will be watching us. We have several ballistae and just as many mangonels and catapults. Whatever he throws at us, we shall send it straight back."

 3 – 9

"We best get you to the infirmary," Paul said and pointed to Abi's wound and started to usher her towards the stairs.

"You all did very well. This city already owes you a great deal. 'Twas raw courage you displayed. Thank you," Balian acknowledged and bowed his head at them. "Thank you."

Paul looked over the edge of the battlements toward the inner quarters of the city, several fires burning away dotted across the outer limits only, men busy passing water buckets along lines forming human chains to fight the fires. He turned to look north. Ailia was out there alive, and possibly even Alisha. Never had he wanted to live so much as he did at that moment. Abi saw the look in his eyes and gently squeezed his forearm and motioned with a slight nod that he should follow her. When he followed her down the stairs he stopped after seeing the young knight who had wet himself crying. He put his hand upon his shoulder and pulled him around to face him.

"Do not feel ashamed for I too did that the first time I experienced combat. It proves you have a mind," Paul said reassuringly. "Go and change and report back to Brother Teric and tell him I sent you. He will find you a position that will get the best out of you."

The young knight half smiled then sniffed, wiping his face. He nodded in silence, sheathed his sword and quietly walked away. Paul turned just as Stewart approached him.

"That was a little too close," he remarked, his voice dry and coarse from when he had been shouting so loudly. "Master Douglas's ditches were inspired." Paul just nodded and looked at Stewart, proud to call him his brother. "What?" he asked, realising Paul was looking at him.

಄ ಅ

Paul sat down opposite Count Henry whilst Percival poured out three drinks of water. A solitary lanthorn lit the room positioned in the middle of the table, several maps of the city laid out.

"Balian has inspired the city...but when our water starts to run out and casualties mount, that is when our real problems will begin," Count Henry said as he studied a detailed map of the city up close.

"We have wells Saladin cannot block off," Paul remarked.

"We do, but he can get his engineers to poison them. He has done it before," Count Henry replied and sighed. "I have made preparations to hide deep beneath the stables some of our more important items just in case the city does fall. But here, I wish you to take these and keep them upon your person."

Paul looked puzzled as Count Henry passed him two small vellum parchments. Gently he opened them to reveal images, one of which looked like a Celtic spiral design. He frowned as he studied them for the first time yet they seemed familiar.

"I know these," Paul remarked and held them closer to the lanthorn as Count Henry stood up.

"Good. 'Tis made up using mathematical values. When man understands that fully, then will the gates be opened," Count Henry said as he walked over to the door. "I must check upon the queen. I shall inform Princess Stephanie you are safe and well."

Percival placed two drinks upon the table as Paul studied the images closely. Count Henry smiled seeing the interest in Paul's eyes. Quickly and quietly he opened the door and left, Paul only realising as the door latch clicked shut. Percival sat down opposite Paul and folded his arms waiting for Paul to look up. Eventually he had to cough to draw his attention.

"I am sorry, my friend. I was just trying to remember where I have seen these before," Paul remarked and laid the vellum sheets down.

"You have still not asked me more about Ailia and the others fully. Why?"

"Why...simply because we have not had time, besides you have told me enough for now," Paul replied and sat up. "Also, what else could I ask? You have told me she is alive as are the others and that you could not establish if Alisha was. To be honest 'tis all I can cope with at this moment in time."

"'Tis much and painful I understand...but," Percival paused hesitant to ask his next question. "But you and the princess?"

"'Twas not planned nor intended. It just happened. Call me weak if you must, but after losing all my family...so I believed, I did not care for much else. She...she saved me from myself is all I can say," Paul explained quietly then turned over the vellum sheets and read the word 'Khemet' stencilled in ink. "She is a good woman and perhaps I was wrong to be with her. Too soon...maybe, but I needed her as much as she needed me just to survive this nightmare place."

"Do you still need her?"

Paul looked up at Percival as he sat with his arms still folded.

"Yes I do, but if Alisha also still lives," Paul said and choked emotionally gulping hard as the impact of his own words hit him deeply, "it changes everything." The words of Kratos warning him that one day he would be forced to make an impossible decision, the hardest of his life and one he could only make by trusting his soul, not his head nor his heart, came flooding back.

"Some will accuse you both of committing a great sin. Many know you became one whilst Reynald still lived and she was married…but more so if it turns out Alisha is still alive," Percival said and leaned forward resting his elbows upon the table. "I swore I would find out what happened to your family, Tenno, Theo, Thomas and his men. I have all but done that save finding out about Alisha and Sister Lucy. But I will if it is the last thing I ever do."

"And the sword…how did you recover it…and do you not think Alisha dead then?"

"The sword…'twas easy. I simply asked it to release itself…and it came straight out as I pulled it. But I left it with Tenno for he too is able to wield it and I thought he could use it to better serve and protect Ailia…if he chose to use it," Percival explained and paused briefly, looking at Paul intently. "As for Alisha…when I found the remains of the reconnaissance party, their bodies thrown into the crevasse along with others they were obviously escorting, I knew they were not amongst them. I do not know how I know…but I know as should you have known!"

"That is just it…I do not know and nor does Abi. If she does not know then just how am I supposed to know?" Paul replied, raising his voice in frustration and an inner anger toward himself rising. He shook his head. "I am sorry…you have done more than was ever asked or expected."

"She lives…this I know," Percival stated and placed his hand upon Paul's and looked at him. "Do you hear me? She lives."

Tears welled in Paul's eyes, his heart feeling like it would stop as his very words cut through him.

Footsteps outside the door walking away fast drew both of their attentions. Quickly Paul jumped to his feet and rushed over to the door and opened it looking both ways but in the darkened corridor he could see no one. Puzzled he slowly stepped back inside and closed the door. Further down the corridor Princess Stephanie had pressed herself back hard inside one of the alcoves to hide out of sight. She was shaking, tears rolling down her cheeks as she fought to remain silent having heard Paul and Percival's conversation. She placed her arms around herself in comfort but felt utterly devastated. If Alisha was alive she knew she would not be able to keep Paul. She felt guilty for wishing and hoping that she was not alive and closed her eyes ashamed at her own feelings. In silence she stood feeling more alone at that moment than she had ever felt, as if all hope for the future had left her.

Port of La Rochelle, France, Melissae Inn, spring 1191

"Good Lord, that poor woman," Ayleth remarked, shaking her head sadly.

"'Twas a terrible sense of guilt she felt. But like a true queen, as she should have been, she stopped crying, wiped her tears and stood up straight. She took a deep breath and vowed she would focus upon the child that was now growing within her at least grateful for that. Perhaps after her time with Paul, he would choose to remain with her even if Alisha was still alive. It was an impossible dream of hope but one she would cling too. Besides, they had to get through a siege first which many of them may not survive," the old man explained.

"For a minute I thought the footsteps were going to be one of Turansha's men. You know, overhearing that Ailia was still alive and now knew where she was," Simon said, the Genoese sailor nodding in agreement with him.

"What were the images Count Henry passed to Paul?" Gabirol asked.

"They are within the folder if you look. The two small vellum sheets," the old man answered as Simon started to look through the folder and splayed out all the parchments and sheets across the table. "There, those two," the old man said and tapped his finger down upon two vellum sheets tied together with a single piece of crimson coloured string. As he leaned over, his sleeve pulled up revealing a wrist band of yellow and black with a thin crimson thread woven throughout. Only Gabirol noticed it, the old man winking at him.

Fig. 77: Celtic Number Value Symbols.

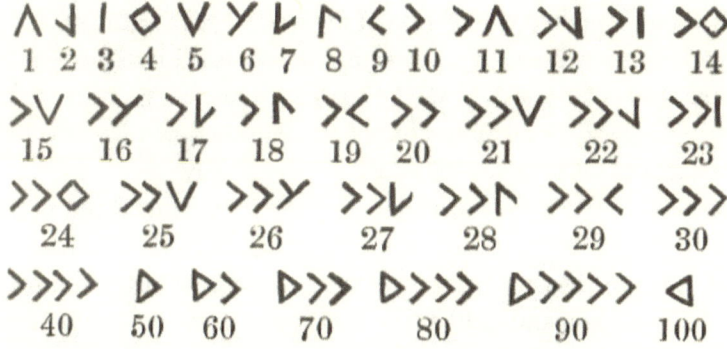

"We know the siege continued, but how did Paul get on? Did he survive?" the Templar asked as Miriam put her arm around him, looking tired.

"For six days, skirmishes were fought with little result. Balian using the ballistas and mangonels to great effect against the siege engines. More and more of Saladin's men died hourly in huge numbers. No matter what he did, Saladin's forces suffered heavy casualties after each assault, while the defenders lost only a few men. Master Douglas, Master Teric and Stewart kept on doing what they had started and it appeared to be working despite the physical exhaustion creeping up on everyone. Princess Stephanie kept herself busy by assisting with all the wounded as they came in. She did not let on to Paul that she had heard his conversation. But a change of tactic by Saladin on the twenty-sixth of September forced the stalemate to change rapidly," the old man explained.

"Why what did he do?" Peter asked.

"Saladin moved his camp to focus upon a different part of the city, on to the Mount of Olives where there was no major gate from which the Christian forces could counter-attack as they had done for each and every assault so far. The walls were constantly pounded by the siege engines, catapults, mangonels, petraries, Greek fire, crossbows and arrows and portions of the wall were even mined. Consequently his forces were able to knock down sections of the walls, but they were unable to gain entrance to the city as they were met with a devastating volley of arrows and crossbow bolts each and every time. The more Saladin threw against them, the more they were able to return. I believe that if Saladin had realised this one simple fact, the outcome would have been vastly different. But the twenty-ninth was a day that changed everything," the old man sighed.

City of Jerusalem, Kingdom of Jerusalem, September 29th 1187

Master Douglas pointed to a section of the wall where Saladin's engineers were working away beneath a protected roof wheeled into position fifty feet short of the outer curtain wall. Paul wiped his face as sweat rivulets ran down his neck. The sun was high and burning down fiercely. Balian looked tired and filthy as he studied the men carefully.

"And you are certain they have dug a mine?" Balian asked and stood up straight.

"Seen it before," Master Douglas answered. "I am telling you now, that wall will come down and unlike the other breaches we will not be able to contain his army from swarming through it. It is not overlooked. Saladin has chosen well this time."

"How long do you think we have?" Paul asked, the chain mail coif hung around his neck beginning to burn his skin as the sun heated it.

"Hours...perhaps less," Master Douglas answered.

"And we have no other men available...none at all," Balian asked and sighed. He looked to his left at the many women marching around the inner walled area chanting. "They still sing for penance and for a miracle?"

"Oh yes...how does your prayer system work now, Paul?" Master Douglas asked.

"Exactly the same as it has always worked," Paul replied and looked back at the Muslim engineers. "I think we should engage any of his forces that breach the wall only with archers for the briefest encounter then withdraw to the inner walls and engage them again...for then we will have the advantage of shooting down directly upon them. From here we cannot do that and we shall lose men needlessly in open combat for there are too many of them."

A fireball flamed directly over their heads and they looked up and followed its course as it came down within the inner city walls. Several boulders and stones followed closely behind it, one thudding into the inner wall smashing out a chunk of stone work with hardly any effect at all. Hand bells started to ring and the children and women collecting arrows quickly ran for cover, Paul, Balian and Master Douglas moving back inside the cover of the tower passageway just as a volley of mixed arrows arched their way across the sky and then fell mainly within the open area between the walls.

"What I said all along. Let the wall fall," Master Douglas stated bluntly as Balian faced him.

"Master Douglas...'tis true what they say about you, isn't it. People say you act as though you do not give a fuck."

"Who said I was acting?" Master Douglas replied and winked. "Now come, we must set up within the buildings that directly overlook the approach there," he said and pointed to the open ground that led from the wall to the inner wall and buildings above them.

"You do realise that is the whore house quarter?" Balian remarked.

"Yes. I suspect we shall suddenly find ourselves with plenty of volunteers wishing to beat the wool whilst they await the Lord's great calling,"

Master Douglas laughed and began to walk away and down the wide stone steps of the wall.

Balian looked at Paul and smiled, shaking his head.

⁊ ☙

Paul stood and listened in silence as Balian's squire Ernoul explained to him and Master Douglas how many of the civilians were in great despair. Many women were shaving their children's heads and immersing them chin deep in cold water as an act of penance praying for forgiveness upon Mount Calvary. Master Douglas just shook his head upon hearing this. The vaulted store room was dark and cramped but it afforded protection from the incessant barrage of fireballs and slung boulders. Master Teric entered the room stepping down the stone stairs and banging his head on the low ceiling.

"Do they honestly think their penances aimed at turning away God's wrath from the city will work?" Master Douglas asked incredulously.

"Well it won't hurt," Balian replied.

"Ask the children and see if they agree with that," Master Douglas shot back as Master Teric came forward rubbing his head.

"Smoke has been seen coming from the tunnel entrance. I have moved most of my men back within the inner walls and left just a few of my crossbow men to engage and delay any breach when it comes, as instructed," Master Teric explained.

Princess Stephanie stepped down into the room. She looked tired and her dress was covered in blood. Paul looked at her alarmed and quickly moved to take her hand.

"'Tis not my blood. I have been helping tend the sick and wounded," she quickly reassured. "The queen asked me to come and report back to her the latest news. She presently sits with Count Henry securing items away…as does Heraclius. He is too busy packing away much gold," she explained and shook her head disapprovingly.

Master Teric looked at her and sighed with a clear sign of relief that she was not injured in any fashion.

"I shall escort you back to them and explain as we walk," Paul said and ushered her back up the stone flight of stairs. "I will be back shortly," he stated looking back at Balian and climbed the stairs after Princess Stephanie.

"Ah but a thousand slow cuts bleed my heart unto the day my soul must surely die for my heart breaks daily," Master Teric said to himself out loud without realising the others could hear him.

Master Douglas coughed loudly to draw his attention.

ဆဝ

Paul escorted Princess Stephanie through the buildings and corridors back to the queen's main residence. Every place someone could sit, someone sat. The city was packed to capacity with many people, their tired and scared faces looking up at Paul and Princess Stephanie as they walked past them. Desperation lay heavy in all of their eyes. Actual physical casualties of fighting men had been mercifully low considering but many civilians had been injured by the constant bombardment of fireballs and rocks. Food was being rationed and water was being constantly drawn from the wells to store for both drinking and to put out the fires. Saladin's assault was unrelenting never stopping even during the hours of darkness. Paul took Princess Stephanie into the queen's private office, expecting her there but she was not.

"She said to meet her back here," Princess Stephanie said, alarmed.

"Do not concern yourself for I am sure she is safe wherever she and Count Henry are," Paul replied, trying to reassure her. He looked at her and took her hands. They were covered in dirt and he laughed lightly. She pulled her hands away embarrassed but he quickly took hold of them again and kissed them.

"Oh Paul," she sighed and looked at him, her hair falling in front of her eyes.

"Do you know you look more beautiful now like that than I have ever seen you?"

"Oh lovely. Filthy, unwashed and looking like I have been dragged behind a horse."

"No...alive and beautiful."

"Paul...you cannot say such to me any more," she said sadly and tried to pull away.

"Yes I can and I shall continue to do so. I know you have avoided me these past days on the pretext of letting me concentrate on the tasks at hand...but I know you. What has changed?"

297

"You know what has changed," she replied quietly, staring at him intently. "We both know Ali lives…and….and if so, then what we do, have done…is a sin."

Paul clasped her hands together in his tightly and pulled her toward him.

"I have prayed beyond all possible prayers for a miracle that she lives… but we do not know she does. If she lives she may not wish to have me anyway…"

Princess Stephanie looked at him and fought to hide the deep collapsing feeling inside as Paul's last words told her all she needed to know in an instant…that if Alisha was alive, he would seek to be with her. If she was alive but chose not to be with him, would Paul simply remain with her as second choice? She shuddered both from that thought and a deep tiredness of the last few days finally hitting her. All the dead and seriously wounded she had helped…the images of badly burnt people in agony as she tried to ease their suffering knowing they would soon die. Her own desires and wishes made her feel momentarily selfish. Paul looked into her eyes puzzled at her long silence without realising his last comment had made it very clear he would return to Alisha.

"You know that is not true for she loves you like no other woman's love for a man I have ever seen….save my own for you," Princess Stephanie finally spoke softly and placed her hand upon his cheek.

"We shall have to cross that bridge if…and only if, it comes upon us to cross," Paul said, took her hand, kissed it again then looked into her eyes as they welled with tears. "And what we have done is…I know with all my heart, not a sin…no sin at all and even Ali would tell you that herself," Paul said and pulled her closer and gently placed his lips upon hers, her lips pressing against his with no resistance. Slowly and reluctantly he broke the kiss. "For this man does love you."

   1 – 23

Princess Stephanie let out an emotional laugh, put her hands around his face and kissed him back filled with a sense that even if Alisha was still alive, it did not necessarily mean the end to her and Paul. Despite his earlier words, it was but a desperate small flame of hope, but it was one she would cling on to she told herself as she lost herself in his embrace.

෨ඏ

Paul ran through the many lace see through curtains that hung from the ceiling of the brothel as he made his way towards the large balcony fronting onto the building. His eye caught two men lying upon a big circular bed of cushions having sex with three women. Master Teric followed Paul as Ishmael ran across to the other side of the large room with Abi beside him. Another fully naked man was having sex with a woman taking her from behind; he just looked across at them as they rushed past and continued with his movements, the woman just turning her head briefly to look up. When Paul stepped out onto the large balcony, the Sergeant who had insulted the male dancer in the arbalester stores called Paul over and pointed at the outer wall where he had stood just hours earlier with Balian and Master Douglas. He could see Master Douglas on the ground forming up a troop of archers and several crossbow men in a long line of defence midway between the outer curtain wall and inner wall. A sound similar to a trumpet echoed out as stone and rock began to move under pressure beneath the outer wall. He saw Balian watching the wall from the top of one of the outer wall turrets further along. The tall male dancer appeared beside Paul, smiling, holding two swords.

"We meet again," he said confidently then half bowed and looked across at the sergeant, raised his swords and smiled at him before looking back at Paul. "Oh do not worry...we are best friends now aren't we, my handsome?" he joked and blew a kiss at the sergeant.

"Yeah that's right...best fucking friends," the sergeant replied, Paul not sure exactly of the inference in tone meant.

"Oh he is a dear really," the male dancer said. "Now don't you go worrying about us here for we will not let any of those barbarians pass," he explained and pointed one of his swords towards the wall. "Pity really as they pay well," he joked, the sergeant shaking his head and raising his eyebrows. "I promise you, this wall will not be breached whilst I am alive."

A loud noise of shouting echoed out below from Saladin's men as the wall between the square turrets started to crumble, slowly at first it appeared, but then in a thunderous rumble like a distant storm, the entire wall section started to sink and collapse in on itself, a huge cloud of dust being thrown upwards and outwards. The dust cloud immediately blew over the turrets, Balian vanishing instantly as it enveloped him, the cloud reaching out across the open area and engulfing Master Douglas and his men below. Paul looked down frantically wondering where Stewart was just as Master Douglas could be heard shouting above the noise for them to hold their positions. When the dust began to settle, many Muslim infantry and Turkish mercenaries ran and half stumbled into view as they scrambled across the collapsed wall. Covered in dust they looked more like ghostly apparitions than men as they approached.

"For fuck's sake fire," the sergeant said through gritted teeth.

"Don't worry, my darling, I will protect your lovely firm arse," the male dancer joked and pinched the sergeant's backside.

As the dust settled like a blanket being laid out, Master Douglas could be seen standing with his sword held high, his archers and crossbow men all standing or kneeling firm. Paul could not hear him shout the order to fire as many were now shouting and screaming but he watched as his arm lowered and they all loosed off, the front ranks immediately reloading as a second rank stood up, aimed and fired a second volley almost instantly. Many of the Muslim and Turkish troops were hit and fell but were simply pushed aside or trampled over by the overwhelming numbers of men following behind them. Paul took a deep breath as he watched Master Douglas run backwards to a marker and stop. He yelled and all the archers and crossbow men immediately ran backwards to the same new line. They repeated the same actions again and more Muslims and Turks fell. But in the distance, at the far end of the line, several Muslims emerged from the settling dust cloud and were upon the archers before they could draw their own swords. Some crossbow men switched their aim to help defend their friends but as they did more Muslim infantry ran through the dust. Master Douglas waved his sword around his head calling his men to follow him. As he began to run for the main reinforced door of the inner city wall, several of the archers following him were cut down as Muslim light archers came through the breach and started taking aimed shots.

"Stand by! Stand by!" Paul suddenly heard Stewart shout out loudly further along the inner wall on the battlements above his head. All along the wall and adjoining buildings, men with bows appeared and readied their aim down at the swarming Muslim forces below. Paul could see Balian and several others running to join Master Douglas just as Stewart yelled out his order. "LOOSE!"

With a sound like sails being unfurled, Paul thought, a mighty wave of arrows and bolts filled the air streaming their way down toward the Muslim forces below like a great scythe of death, many hitting their mark. Paul watched as the whole operation was repeated and more Muslims fell until the open ground between the outer curtain wall and inner wall was crawling with injured men and the dead.

"Now there you go. Did I not tell you it would be all right," the male dancer remarked and patted the sergeant on the back. "See," he smiled.

Quickly Paul turned around and moved to walk back through the brothel to get up top and see Stewart. As he rushed through the room, the man and woman on the bed were still having sex, the man just outstretching his hands as if to ask 'what?' The other two men and three women were likewise still engaged openly in sex as Paul walked past them as if he wasn't even there. Ishmael stopped and stared at them hard, the nearest woman opening her eyes as she sat on the naked man. She winked at him and beckoned him over with her finger as she started to thrust her thighs backwards and forwards on the man. Ishmael stepped forwards and pushed the woman off. She let out a short yelp as she fell sideways onto the large cushions, the man trying to look past the second woman, who was sat upon his face almost. Ishmael looked at the man's still erect penis and slapped it hard with the end of his gauntlet covered fingers, the man recoiled his legs up instantly in pain.

"Get yourself a sword and start putting your energies to better use this hour or by the Lord so help me I shall put my sword through you myself," Ishmael ordered, his voice low with controlled anger.

All looked up hesitantly as another fireball slammed into the building further along accompanied by screams. Quickly Paul rushed out of the room, Ishmael following closely.

As they ran along the battlement on top of the wall, they could see several buildings already ablaze. Balian appeared running into view from the side connecting battlement. He stopped as they looked down into a collapsed building, its roof having been destroyed by a boulder, but fire was now spreading into it from the adjoining building now fully alight. Master Teric was trying to organise the fire detail just as another building's roof caved in amid screams. Paul looked down into the remnants of the house built up against the inner wall itself. He could see a small girl looking up, crying, her arms outstretched. Flames were beginning to spread toward her fast. Without hesitation he jumped down onto a large wooden roof support beam and swung down beside the girl. Quickly he grabbed her around her waist and started to climb back up the beam. Half way up it started to move. Quickly Balian reached out and grabbed his hand tightly, but as Paul pulled, he nearly dragged Balian down, Ishmael just grabbing hold of Balian around his waist. As he pulled him back, Balian pulled Paul up just in time before the wooden beam cracked and then snapped in half crashing to the floor, flicking up the roof section as it went. Immediately the father of the little girl appeared at the bottom looking up and called out her name. She wriggled free from Paul's arm and rushed to the very edge of the wall and looked at her father below. He shouted at her to stand back as flames rapidly started to inflame the entire building below. The little girl, tears streaming down her face looked at Paul confused, then looked back at her father.

"Papa!" she cried.

Paul instantly realised that she was going to jump. He dived to grab her, just missing her foot as she leapt down to her father. Paul could only look on in horror as her father caught her in his arms and held her tight, placed his hand over her head and closed his eyes just as the remainder of the roof and outer wall fell directly onto them. There was no screaming. Nothing as Paul stared, his hand still outstretched toward them as he lay half hanging over the edge, the flames beginning to fan out across the destroyed house below. Ishmael grabbed Paul by the belt and pulled him away from the edge as flames started to rise. Paul swung around on his backside and looked up to see Balian staring into the burning house.

"We have bloodied Saladin's nose more than he has us…but perhaps it is time we sought terms with him to end this madness," Balian commented sadly.

Paul lay down onto his back exhausted and feeling sick, the little girl's face still in his mind.

"Come on you, we have not finished yet this day for they will be back within the hour," Master Douglas said as he reached down to pull Paul up. "You can deal with that emotional shit later if we survive the night," he said, pulling Paul up to his feet and faced Balian. "Unless you can indeed agree terms but you had better do it fast."

"You promise me you will hold this wall and this city, and I will negotiate favourable terms…of that I am certain," Balian answered.

"In that case why are you still here?" Master Douglas asked. "Master Teric, send a signal to Saladin."

ഔ ൠ

Paul walked closely beside Balian with Ishmael following watching their backs as they were escorted on foot into Saladin's main command tent. As an agreed mediator between Saladin and Balian, Yusuf Batit, one of the Eastern Orthodox clergy, accompanied them to record any agreements despite his obvious apprehension. The large awning above their heads flapped in the late afternoon breeze. It looked out across the plain toward Jerusalem giving Saladin commanding views of the city. Several of Saladin's senior officers looked at them in disgust, the atmosphere tense. Not surprising considering they had lost so many men over the past nine days, Paul thought. Paul could see the white marker stones Master Douglas had positioned outside the city walls so they could gauge the distances correctly to aim their weapons accurately. Surprisingly they were still in place, the Muslim forces having not realised what they were obviously set for. Saladin appeared as he stepped through from a curtained off area. If he harboured any ill will for Balian for breaking his oath, they would soon find out. Balian took a deep breath, his hand placed upon his sword handle.

"As salamu alaikum wa rahmatullah wa barakatuhu [may the mercy, peace and blessings of Allah be upon you]," Balian said politely and bowed his head.

Saladin stepped closer and looked at Balian in silence, then at Paul before looking back at Balian. Both Paul and Balian looked dishevelled and were covered in dirt and soot.

"Wa alaikum salam wa rahmatullah wa barakatuhu [and may the peace mercy and blessings of Allah be upon you]," Saladin finally spoke and proffered them each to take a seat positioned so they could look at the city. Ishmael pointed at himself, surprised he was being offered a seat too.

Whilst Paul and Ishmael sat down, Balian moved his chair slightly so he could see toward the city as Yusuf Batit was ushered to a smaller seat behind them much to his clear disgust. Saladin had some iced rose water brought in and immediately handed them a goblet each. Whilst they each sipped the cold drink, Saladin moved to stand in front of them, his back facing them as he looked forward. It was a clear sign and demonstration he was making that he clearly trusted them. Paul looked around at the thousands of men, horses, siege engines and catapults that surrounded them.

It was surreal, he thought to himself, to be sat in the very midst of their enemy drinking iced rose water.

"I had not expected to see either of you two in conflict against me," Saladin commented quietly, his hands behind his back. "I understand you now wish to negotiate my original terms. Is this so?"

"'Tis true enough," Balian answered.

"Then why could we not have done this sooner before the huge loss of life?"

"Must I explain that?" Balian asked.

"Yes you must," Saladin replied and turned to look at Balian directly. "I have many of my senior officers demanding we storm the city and finish this once and for all in the manner and fashion it was originally taken by your crusader forebears." Balian looked past Saladin as he noticed a huge number of well armed Muslim infantry and support archers moving through the breach of the wall. "As you can see, my forces this very minute are about to storm your inner walls...and this time I think they may breach them."

"I see that our flag still flies," Paul remarked.

"I cannot believe it is you two that I find myself negotiating with," Saladin replied and shook his head. "'Tis such a pity you are not Muslims...or at least on my side as Montferrat wishes to be."

Yusuf Batit raised his eyebrows upon hearing this. Ishmael looked at him hard with suspicion.

"Lord Montferrat?" Paul asked immediately.

"Yes, the one named Conrad. After our siege on Tyre he has agreed a new truce with me," Saladin replied. "However, I cannot trust a man who still deals with the likes of Turansha who this very moment sits in council with him."

Paul closed his eyes briefly upon hearing Turansha's name.

"Conrad is ambitious and has his mind set to wear the crown of Jerusalem himself one day," Balian said just as Al Rashid accompanied by Taqi entered the tent. Taqi smiled immediately upon seeing Paul, but surprised.

"'Tis why I have asked the Master of the Mountains to monitor him closely...for all of our sakes," Saladin explained and looked at Al Rashid as he bowed his head. Al Rashid then bowed his head slightly at Paul directly, Saladin acknowledging his action before continuing. "You here present and I are not enemies, this much I do understand...which is why this is all madness…but the likes of Reynald were, as will Conrad become if he insists upon maintaining his ambitions and dealings with Turansha." Saladin paused to look at Paul seeing that he was now looking past him toward the city.

"You know I have never considered you an enemy," Balian said and stood up.

✳✳   1 – 15

Paul stood up as he saw the Muslim infantry and archers vanish over the breach in the wall. Even from the safety of their position he could hear the cries of battle as they started to engage Master Douglas and his knights positioned along the inner walls. Large siege ladders could be seen going up against them.

"I do not think your flag of Jerusalem will be flying much longer. At least you will be afforded safety here," Saladin remarked.

"And what of the queen and Princess Stephanie?" Paul asked, alarmed.

Saladin looked at Paul.

"You should have taken her away whilst you had your chance," he replied quietly then looked back toward Jerusalem just as one of Saladin's banners was being raised. "But my men have orders not to harm any of the queen's court under pain of death." He paused as he watched his own banner being set against the inner wall. "You come now offering the surrender of the city as per my initial terms…yet after your refusal, I swore to my senior command that we would take the city by force and we would only accept the unconditional surrender of it. So you see my hand is forced yet again."

"Who is in command…you or your officers?" Paul asked, Taqi immediately walking over to him and shaking his head no. "I will ask as I see."

Saladin clicked his fingers and raised his hand. Immediately several of his leading officers walked over, Yusuf Batit looking up suddenly fearful. Taqi Al Din nodded at both Balian and Paul just as Al Isfahani, Saladin's secretary recognised Paul and acknowledged him as he walked past. He handed Yusuf Batit some writing material and utensils much to his surprise, and relief.

"Lord Balian…please tell me and my officers what you propose by way of negotiation this very hour as our forces take the city," Saladin asked.

305

Balian faced them, took a deep breath and thought hard for a few tense moments. When he saw that Yusuf Batit was ready to take notes he took a deep breath.

"I have known all of you for many years, some closer than others, but you will at least know me and my word. I therefore tell you, whatever happens right now, right there at this very moment within those stone walls, there is a greater wall made of men willing to die...who will fight you with a ferocity only known by God himself. They have vowed to kill every living thing within the city walls, including their own loved ones, one and all. They will kill every last prisoner and Muslim they hold, some five thousand in total. They will not cease until their actions cut so deep that even in a thousand years from now, men will remember this day," Balian said passionately. "Or they can remember this day forever as the day when Saladin and his emirs showed the way ahead and offered mercy over massacre."

Paul shuddered hearing his words and knew he meant them. Ishmael pointed toward Jerusalem. Paul recalled the story of Masada and the similarity made him shudder again.

"Look!" Ishmael said out loud as Saladin's banner was ripped from the wall and tossed to the ground, just as many Christian archers and crossbowmen fired down into the Muslim infantry whilst others poured boiling water upon them. The screams of many echoed across the whole land it sounded.

Saladin paused and gently pulled his beard as he watched in silence just as his men started to reappear climbing back over the breached wall in retreat.

"And if that does not convince you then know also that they will destroy Islam's holy shrines of the Dome of the Rock and the 'Al Aqsa' Mosque if no such quarter is provided for a suitable and acceptable negotiation," Balian said, his eyes narrowing and serious as he looked at Saladin and then the other officers. "You know they will do it!"

Saladin turned slowly and looked at Balian in silence.

"I never wanted this massacre in the first place," he sighed. "Please... return to your city whilst it is still yours and I shall have counsel with my officers to discuss the terms. I will send for you at sunrise tomorrow to let you know the outcome."

"With all due respect you need not summon me unless the original terms remain. If not accepted you need only fire your catapults for us to get your answer," Balian replied.

"'Tis no one's city. Neither of you seem to have learnt that," Paul stated and started to walk away, Ishmael close behind him. "I suggest you remain, Lord Balian, until you have an agreement."

Both Saladin and Balian looked at Paul in surprise. All of Saladin's officers moved to block Paul's path, Taqi quickly stepping to Paul's side.

"My brother, you never were any good at social etiquette were you," Taqi said and feigned a smile. He could see the tiredness and frustration within his eyes and he gently placed his hand upon Paul's shoulder. "All will be as it should be. Remember…whatever comes next?"

Paul looked into Taqi's eyes. There was a sincerity and kindness in them that somehow did not fit the figure stood before him. Paul turned his head to look back at Saladin, who bowed his head slightly. Paul bowed his head in return then looked at the immaculately dressed officers stood in his way. Saladin nodded yes for them to stand aside and Paul passed through them without any further words. Al Rashid looked at Taqi. Paul had changed and they could both see it in his eyes.

ഇ◌ആ

Paul, accompanied by Ishmael and Yusuf Batit, rushed past the many exhausted knights on the battlements that remained in their positions as children delivered more collected arrows and water. Paul saw Master Douglas and Master Teric supervising several of the new knights including the young one who had wet himself during the first engagement. He stood up fast seeing Paul approach, Master Douglas turning to face him.

"Paul, where is Balian?" he asked calmly.

"He remains with Saladin," Paul answered but looked around for Stewart. "Where is my brother?"

"So Balian deserts us to his Muslim friends," one of the sergeants said under his breath.

Paul lunged at the sergeant, furious, with a sudden outburst of rage and threw him against the ramparts hard pushing his forearm up under his chin forcing his head backwards.

"He negotiates this very hour for your miserable life so don't you dare ever insult his good name or intentions again…do you hear!" Paul said angrily. The sergeant nodded frantically struggling to breathe. Paul's eye caught the young knight staring at him, his eyes wide.

"Paul!" Princess Stephanie said softly and placed her hand upon his shoulder. "Paul...calm down."

Paul looked at the sergeant and quickly released him, shocked at his own outburst. He pulled the sergeant's mantle straight.

"I...I am sorry. I do not know what came over me," Paul apologised and shook his head. The sergeant stood up straight and wiped his mouth and looked at Paul and nodded quietly unsure what to say. Paul looked to his left at the young knight again. "I am glad to see you survived this too."

"Paul...what conditions has Balian negotiated?" Princess Stephanie asked, her loose hair blowing on the early evening breeze.

"I can explain for I have it written here," Yusuf Batit interrupted and unfurled a small parchment sheet and began to read from it. "As it stands presently, Lord Balian must surrender the city unconditionally but we can leave by paying a ransom of ten dinars per man, five per woman and two for a child. Those who cannot pay are to be enslaved," he explained as everyone listened intently, just the crackling of burning wood making any noise and a baby crying off in the distance. "Lord Balian stays to negotiate further for as we know, there are at least twenty thousand here within these walls who could never pay such a sum. So pray Lord Balian negotiates hard."

Paul took hold of Princess Stephanie's hand as everyone started to talk frantically among themselves.

"Now where is my brother?" Paul asked.

"He is seeing to the wounded within the brothel. We lost a lot of good men there during that last assault when they breeched the wall," Master Douglas explained, fresh blood covering his mantle and face.

Paul turned away and quickly headed for the brothel pulling Princess Stephanie with him.

೫ ೦೪

Paul stepped over several dead Muslim soldiers partially blocking the main double door entrance into the brothel. Princess Stephanie let go of his hand and covered her mouth from the stench of blood mixed with vomit and excrement from the bodies of men cut to pieces, parts of arms, legs and heads strewn everywhere. Several Christian soldiers and Muslim prisoners were being treated together for their wounds further along the wall. When Paul stepped inside fully, the room was dark, small fires were being put out by women as others checked through the dead, some piled several deep. He saw Stewart standing near the balcony doors, his hands placed upon his hips and looking upwards breathing in deeply. Paul stepped over more bodies to reach him and recognised one of the dead as one of the naked men who Ishmael had threatened. He was pinned to the wall by a lance, several arrows in his still naked body and a bolt in his forehead. He was holding a sword in his hand, the other end stuck fast in the body of a Muslim soldier slumped against him. Paul looked behind as Ishmael entered the room, keeping Princess Stephanie back. A hand suddenly grabbed Paul's foot. Quickly he pulled his leg away in time to see the man who had been present at Elek's execution and who had first stepped up to volunteer to be a knight looking up at him. The man's white hair was covered in blood, his eyes bloodshot. He half laughed revealing his blood covered teeth.

"Thank you," he whispered. Paul leant down to help him. "You saved my soul...thank you."

"What, for nearly getting you killed?" Paul asked him and motioned for Ishmael to help move him.

"My wounds I have been reliably informed will heal. I just need to rest. I ...I rather quite think I perhaps chose the wrong building to help defend," he half laughed again.

"I think the Lord chose you to be here in the right one where you were clearly needed the most," Paul remarked.

"'Tis all rather too easy to kill isn't it I have discovered," the man said and shrugged his shoulders and then started to cry with relief, Princess Stephanie stepping closer finding it hard to control her own emotions.

Stewart looked over toward him. Quickly Paul stood up and walked over to see Percival sat propped up against the balcony wall his eyes shut tightly and covered from head to foot in blood. Beside him the male dancer lay dead over several dead Muslims. The sergeant with him sat just staring at him clearly in a state of delayed shock. Alarmed Paul jumped over three bodies blocking his way and grabbed Percival and shook him. Percival blinked several times as he tried to open his exhausted eyes. He saw Paul's face and smiled wearily.

"You took your time," he coughed and smiled broadly.

"Brother...never in all my days have I seen a man fight like our Percival did this day," Stewart remarked and stepped down beside Paul. "And I pray I never see such a day again."

Paul stood up and pulled Stewart close seeing how close to tears he was.

"So do I brother, so do I," Paul replied and hugged him.

Percival forced himself to stand up. Shaking and barely able to hold his own sword he looked at Paul and Stewart.

"I hate this fucking city," he said aloud and forced a smile. "Fucking hate it."

"Percy, swearing does not suit you," Stewart laughed.

"I am learning fast from Master Douglas," Percival replied and offered his hand for the sergeant to take.

The sergeant took Percival's hand but nearly pulled him down so he quickly let go and knelt beside the dead male dancer, who had several bolts in his back and many sword wounds. The sergeant took the dead dancer's hand and held it. Gently he kissed it then looked up at Paul, Stewart, Percival and Ishmael.

"He...he saved my life...not just once...but several times. He...he stood in the way and took all of those...for me," he explained emotionally, lowered his head and started to cry uncontrollably.

"Do not forget what Master Douglas also did here," Percival said quietly and leaned himself against Paul as exhaustion overwhelmed him. "Have we negotiated terms with Saladin?"

"I...I believe we may have, by the grace of Balian and Saladin," Paul answered, not absolutely certain but trusting his own deep down instincts.

"I promised you we would defend this city and we have. And if this insanity is now finished, then now we just need to go and get you your daughter back," Percival said and stood up straight. "Then Alisha, my friend, then Alisha."

Paul gulped hard and he had to look away as his stomach knotted painfully. He looked out across the whole scene spread out before them like some grotesque nightmare image beyond description. The walls below were piled high with dead Muslim infantry, archers and Turkish mercenaries. He felt Princess Stephanie take his hand and stand behind him.

"The candle is indeed burned all down," Paul whispered then looked north, his mind already travelling to get Ailia. A tap on his shoulder drew his attention back to the present. He turned to see the blacksmith and his wife stood before him next to Princess Stephanie.

"Thank you," the blacksmith said emotionally and stepped forwards. "Thank you for being the man we knew you were. You have more than honoured Tara's memory," he explained and put his arms around Paul and hugged him. "Thank you," he cried.

Paul looked at Princess Stephanie as she smiled at him then at the blacksmith's wife, her face full of emotion. She simply nodded at him appreciatively.

"But I have done no more than the others," Paul replied, puzzled.

"We know you have done far more than you obviously realise. Whatever comes next, we just wanted you to know how proud we are of you," the blacksmith said as he looked at Paul, still holding his arms firmly. "Thank you."

Chapter 82
Everything to Live For, All to Die For

Port of La Rochelle, France, Melissae Inn, spring 1191

"Lord Balian did indeed stay the entire night negotiating further, mainly to compromise and appease Saladin's own senior officers," the old man explained and took a small sip of rose water.

"I thought Taqi, Paul's friend Taqi not the other one, went off to see if Alisha was with Queen Tamar's caravan," Simon mentioned and waved his finger.

"He did but then Al Rashid ordered all of his men within the region to join with Saladin and the coming assault upon Jerusalem...besides, Taqi had already been made aware that Saladin had granted safe passage for Queen Tamar to travel south for Jerusalem where she had requested an audience with him to submit her formal request...for the return of items held within the city as claimed by her," the old man explained.

"I remember you saying before that her people wanted to request some items," Simon replied and sat back in his chair.

"Why would Master Douglas tell the men to untie their breeches?" Sarah asked, bemused.

The old man smiled and looked at the Templar to respond.

"Some suffer loose bowels due to sickness...others down to fear. If it is sickness, then it comes upon you almost instantly. You do not have the time to untie your breeches and lower them quickly enough when that happens. Have you ever tried to untie a knot when you cannot hold it in?" the Templar answered and laughed lightly. *"Some involuntarily shit themselves through fear, which is not so funny."*

 3 –21

"Like the young knight in David's Gate tower who wet himself?" Ayleth asked.
The Templar nodded yes.
"That young knight you speak of conquered his fears and went on to fight side

by side with Master Douglas within the brothel. Master Douglas had been taking him there after Master Teric had sent him to help Percival. Little did he realise the strategic importance of that one building upon the wall," the old man revealed. "The young knight had a choice...fight or die. He fought...and well."

"Why did Balian not just agree to Saladin's terms from the very outset and why did he change his mind after seeing that poor little girl jump into her father's arms only to be killed?" Ayleth asked.

"Because history would have written that Balian simply gave up the city without a fight. His family name would have been condemned, though even now some already condemn him for his later actions with Conrad," the old man answered. "But what most of you do not appreciate, though our two friends here certainly do," the old man said gesturing his hand toward the Templar and Hospitaller, "is that seeing the little girl throw herself to her death in her father's arms was the last straw for Balian. I cannot express it enough, the sheer horror or the carnage of battle. The many sick and injured, faces half cleaved off, jaws missing condemning the individual to a slow death, limbs hacked off...a dead knight sat upright against a wall, his eyes open but the entire back of his head missing, burnt bodies and the volume of blood. These are impossible things to explain unless you have seen it."

The Templar and Hospitaller both nodded in agreement as the room fell silent for several long minutes.

"We know Saladin took the city, but what terms were negotiated?" Gabirol asked and charged his quill with ink ready to take more notes.

"Saladin wanted to accept a hundred thousand dinars to free all the twenty thousand Christians unable to pay the agreed ransom...however Balian told him they could never raise that amount so it was proposed that seven thousand of them would be freed for a sum of thirty thousand dinars to which Saladin did finally agree. It was then further agreed that Balian would hand Saladin the keys to David's Gate, in effect symbolically the whole city, peacefully, and that Saladin would free two women or ten children who would be permitted to take the place of one man for the same price," the old man explained and sighed heavily before continuing. "So it was that Balian returned to explain the negotiated terms on the morning of the first of October. No fighting took place that day and on the morning of the second of October Balian accordingly handed over the keys to the Tower of David, the citadel, and thus the whole city. There was a fifty-day period for the payment of ransoms to be met."

"What of those who could not afford to pay a ransom?" Ayleth asked, concerned.

"Those who could not pay were forced into slavery. They were mostly the very

poor sadly. However, Saladin freed some of them and allowed for an orderly march away from Jerusalem, unlike the massacre that had occurred when the Christians first captured the city in 1099. Balian and Patriarch Heraclius offered themselves as hostages for the ransoming of the remaining citizens, but Saladin refused and the final agreement was read out through the streets of Jerusalem so that everyone had forty days at least to raise their ransom and pay Saladin the agreed tribute for their freedom. 'Twas an unusually low ransom but even then many could not raise the money, but Saladin, against the wishes of his treasurers, allowed many families who could not afford the ransom to leave regardless. Patriarch Heraclius of Jerusalem organised and contributed to a collection that paid the ransoms for about eighteen thousand of the poorer citizens, leaving another fifteen thousand to be enslaved. Saladin's brother al-Adil asked Saladin for a thousand of them for his own use and then released them immediately on the spot whilst most of the foot soldiers were sold into slavery. Saladin summoned the Jews and permitted them to resettle in the city. The residents of Ashkelon, a large Jewish settlement, responded to his request immediately. Eventually three entire columns of ransomed inhabitants finally marched away, with Balian and the Patriarch leading the third and final one to leave on the twentieth of November. Balian went on to join his wife and children in Tripoli."[116]

"And Paul and Stephanie waited all that time? I would have been straight out of the city for the cave place," Peter said.

"I shall explain what they did shortly for they did leave earlier than that," the old man replied. "Of course some Christians were tricked by other Muslims, but on the whole, it was a highly organised affair. The large golden Christian cross upon the Dome of the Rock was pulled down and all Muslim prisoners were released. Saladin allowed many of the noble women of the city to leave without paying any ransom. Queen Sibylla was granted safe passage to visit her captive husband in Nablus and all native Christians were allowed to remain in the city."

"What do you mean, native Christians?" Simon asked.

"Those born there...not from other countries," the Hospitaller answered.

The old man nodded in agreement and continued to explain the takeover of the city.

"Heraclius left with treasure-laden wagons and relics from the Church of the Holy Sepulchre which Paul argued should be used for the remaining ransoms but he was totally ignored. This is when Al-Adil was so moved by the sight and asked Saladin for a thousand of them as reward for his services and promptly freed them as I explained. Heraclius upon seeing this act, and perhaps shamed into action, asked Saladin for some slaves to liberate. He was granted seven hundred while Balian was *granted five hundred and all of them were freed by them. All the aged who could not pay were freed on the orders of Saladin himself. He then freed another thousand upon the request of Muzaffar al-Din Ibn Ali Kuchuk, who claimed they were from his hometown of Urfa."*

"I don't understand how they could have monitored such numbers of people... as in who had and who had not paid their ransom," the wealthy tailor remarked, puzzled.

"Saladin had ordered the gates of the city to be closed and a commander was placed at each one, who checked the movement of the Christians making sure only those who paid the ransom left the city. Master Teric and the provisional Grand Master of the Hospitallers were approached to donate money for the release of the poor but refused, demanding the wealthier Lord and Heraclius should contribute more and a riot almost erupted after which they were forced to donate the money. Mercifully Saladin assigned some of his best officers to ensure the safe arrival of the Christians under their escort to other Christian lands."

"It does not sound like Saladin made much from the ransom payments then?" Gabirol stated.

"No he did not. According to Imad ad-Din al-Isfahani, he reported to Saladin that the value of the whole treasure was less than two hundred thousand dinars... but the psychological, political and religious gain was incalculable...beyond value."

"We have never been told these facts," the farrier remarked. "No wonder so many joined Saladin."

"Where did all the refugees go then?" Peter asked.

"I know a lot turned up in Alexandria because we had to ferry a lot back to Italy," the Genoese sailor remarked then shook his head. "'Twas quite a shameful affair in all honesty."

"Why?" Ayleth asked immediately.

"Because," the old man started to say but looked at the Genoese sailor first. When he nodded for him to carry on, he continued. "Many refugees reached Tyre but Conrad would only allow men who could fight to enter the city, which was few enough! The remaining refugees went to the County of Tripoli, but they were denied entrance and even robbed of their possessions by raiding parties who came out from within the city. Most of the poorer refugees went to Armenian and Antiochian territories and were later successful in gaining an entrance into Antioch. The remaining refugees fled from Ascalon to Alexandria where they were housed in makeshift stockades and received hospitable treatment from the city officials and elders." The old man looked at the Genoese sailor again.

"'Tis okay, you should tell them exactly how it was," he said, motioning with his hands for him to continue.

"Many refugees boarded Italian ships which arrived from Pisa, Genoa and Venice in March 1188...some four months after Jerusalem fell, but initially the captains of the ships refused to take them since they were not being paid, nor had supplies for them. But the governor of Alexandria had earlier taken the oars of the ships for payment of taxes...you may recall I explained this practice from Paul's time in the port city? Anyway he refused to grant sailing permits to the captains unless they agreed to take the refugees along with them and were made to swear decent treatment and safe arrival before they left."

"Which we did," the Genoese sailor remarked defensively. *"I was just a hand... not a captain."*

"So what happened within the city after the surrender, other than the cross being removed?" Peter asked.

"The Church of the Holy Sepulchre was closed by Saladin whilst he considered what to do with it. Some of his advisers demanded it be destroyed in order to end all Christian interest in Jerusalem. But the majority of his advisers recommended that he let the Church remain claiming Christian pilgrimages would continue regardless because of the sanctity of the place and also reminded him of the Caliph Umar who allowed the church to remain in Christian hands after conquering the city. Saladin consequently ordered it reopened after just three days and Christians were allowed to enter upon paying a fee. Many holy sites, including the Al-Aqsa Mosque, were ritually purified with rose water by the Muslims. Christian furnishings were removed from the mosque and it was fitted with oriental carpets, the huge mural Paul had studied so often being immediately painted over and its walls illuminated with text from the Qur'an and with candelabras. The Orthodox Christians and Jacobites were allowed to remain and to worship as they chose. The Copts, who had been barred from entering Jerusalem by the Patriarchs who considered them heretics and atheists, were allowed to enter the city without paying any fees as Saladin considered them his subjects. Also all the Coptic places of worship were returned to their Coptic priests and they were allowed to visit the Church of the Holy Sepulchre and other Christian sites. Even the Abyssinian Christians were allowed to visit the holy places of Jerusalem without paying any fees. Some of the few surviving Templars and other knights were so impressed with Saladin's chivalry and conduct that quite a few took a pledge of allegiance to him."

"But when did Paul leave?" Sarah asked, looking impatient.

"Saladin allowed him to leave the same day as Queen Tamar's caravan was

entering the city. As you know, Saladin was on friendly terms with her and she had sent envoys to request the return of confiscated possessions of the Georgian monasteries in Jerusalem. Despite being Christian herself, Saladin allowed her and her pilgrims and knights a free passage into the city with their banners unfurled. She even outbid the Byzantine emperor in her efforts to obtain the relics of the True Cross, offering two hundred thousand gold pieces to Saladin, who had taken the relic at the battle of Hattin, but that was to no avail as it had already been sent to Damascus along with Reynald's head remember?"

"So if Alisha had been alive and with the queen, Paul would have missed her?" Ayleth commented quietly.

"I can understand why Saladin's behaviour is recognised by both the Muslim and Christian chroniclers as an act of great generosity. I never realised why until now," Peter remarked.

"Let me backtrack then to detail how and when Paul left the city," the old man said.

City of Jerusalem, Kingdom of Jerusalem, October 2nd 1187

The main hall was virtually empty, its lace curtains having all been removed as a fire risk during the siege and used for bandages. Queen Sibylla sat upon her throne as Balian and Count Henry stood either side of her. Masters Douglas and Teric stood further to the right just as Paul and Stephanie moved to stand with Count Henry, Abi stood near the main windows looking out. All in the hall looked exhausted. The Patriarch Heraclius stood a short distance in front of the Queen nervously watching the two main doors set open awaiting the arrival of Saladin himself. Ishmael and Stewart stood holding several banners and flags in preparation to lay down as part of the symbolic surrender gesture, the temporary master of the few remaining Hospitallers was laying several more banners behind Heraclius. Ernoul prepared his quill to write down a description and account of what was about to unfold. They could all hear the footsteps of Saladin's escort running toward them along the stone corridor outside. Queen Sibylla gulped hard with tension, Princess Stephanie clasping her hand to reassure her.

"And you are certain this is all he wanted here...just us few?" Count Henry asked, Balian just nodding yes.

Queen Sibylla took in a sharp breath as a troop of Mamluk guards ran into the room in two lines, each forming up quickly on either side a protective path for Saladin to follow. Dust particles reflected the sun in small bursts of light as slowly Saladin stepped into view and stood still framed within the doorway, several of his senior officers moving to stand behind him. He looked directly at Heraclius hard, who, feeling uncomfortable, quickly stood aside so Saladin could look directly at Queen Sibylla. As he started to approach he removed his ornate helmet and held it under his left arm. He stopped when he reached the banners laid out before him. Nervously Queen Sibylla nodded quickly at Balian. Without hesitation he stepped forwards holding a small blue cushion with a cloth laid over it. He offered it up to Saladin.

"As agreed here is the key to David's Gate. Take this key and the city is yours," Balian said calmly, looking Saladin directly in the eye.

Saladin looked around the hall then at all of the people stood perfectly still within it. He nodded briefly at Paul then looked back at Balian. He removed the cloth and held it out at arm's length and dropped it. When it landed upon the floor, only then did he pick up the large iron and gold embellished key, mainly symbolic as it was not a functioning key. He clenched it in his hand and looked at it intently for several moments before looking up at Queen Sibylla.

"My word is my bond. You are all free to leave at your own choosing," he stated, his tone clipped. "My officers have their orders to escort you to wherever you wish to be taken," he then said and turned his back to them and walked away.

Queen Sibylla looked on open mouthed as he turned left out through the doorway and vanished.

"That is it? That is it?" she asked, exasperated, and clutched her hand at her chest, short of breath.

"My Queen," Master Douglas said as he stepped down and walked over to her. "Words are useless this hour from either side."

Suddenly Princess Stephanie ran off after Saladin, Paul immediately rushing after her. She pulled up the side of her dress so she could catch him up and pushed her way through Saladin's officers who parted quickly unsure of her actions.

"No!" she shouted after Saladin. "No you do not do this to me!" she called out loudly as he stopped. With his back to her she slowed down to walk. "You do not just walk away." Paul ran up to her and stopped her by grabbing her hand tightly. "You have my son and I was given assurances by your delegation he would be returned."

   4 – 9

Saladin remained still for several long minutes before finally turning about by which time all those from the hall were now in the corridor looking on, the line of Mamluk guards forming up either side watching them closely.

"My delegation made it clear that your son would be returned to you upon surrendering both Kerak and Montreal did it not?" he calmly replied.

"And I sent back my word and promise to honour that agreement did I not?" Princess Stephanie replied, looking furious, though in truth it was nervous tension that raised her voice.

Saladin put his hands behind his back and slowly approached her and Paul. He looked at both of them in silence.

"That, my dear princess…and friend, is why your son awaits you this very minute outside. I did not trust your husband's word…but I have always, always trusted yours," he explained and part bowed his head out of respect.

Princess Stephanie looked off down the corridor to the vaulted exit, the sun shining through it, brightly obscuring in a white haze the men stood outside. She gathered up her dress again and immediately ran for the exit. Both Saladin and Paul watched her. When she vanished from view, Saladin looked at Paul and raised his eyebrows.

"You still have a commission requested by me and Count Henry, I hope?" He paused as he looked into Paul's eyes. "I hope you will complete that commission so that in the future, unnecessary events such as this need not happen again. An impossible commission perhaps, but one only someone like you can make happen."

Paul knew immediately he was referring to the formation of the joint Order.

"I can do my best…but there will always be men like Reynald to contend with," Paul replied.

"That is why I have also commissioned Al Rashid to keep Lord Montferrat closely observed for I see another Reynald in the making," Saladin replied and looked at Paul in silence. "I pray the next time we meet it will be to sign agreements...so please do not let it again be upon the field of battle."

"I have somewhere I must go first after which I shall indeed complete the commission given unto me...and then, then shall we indeed meet again," Paul replied and part bowed his head in respect.

"I must go for I have another queen I must speak with. Queen Tamar. Shall I convey your best wishes?" he asked, Paul nodding yes silently. "And may I suggest that perhaps you meet with her at your earliest...after all she is still your sister-in-law. I am sure she would rather hear from you about her sister's sad and untimely death," he explained quietly, then paused. "I will have my best guards escort you to wherever you need to go...and until that day comes, may Allah protect and watch over you as he clearly does already." Saladin bowed his head again, stepped back a pace, smiled and turned away, Paul watching him as he walked down the corridor, his Mamluk guards running past Paul to catch him up.

Outside the building Princess Stephanie saw Humphrey stood beside several horses and their Mamluk guards amidst the many hundreds of people on the move. She ran toward him. Humphrey looking dishevelled and tired saw her and immediately tears welled in his eyes. He had been well looked after and was not bound, as was customary befitting his position. Princess Stephanie threw her arms around him hugging him tightly as he closed his eyes and held her in his arms unable to speak. Paul stepped out of the building, passing through the vaulted archway entrance into the sunlight making him shield his face with his hand. Many Christian men and woman saw Saladin walking along the raised stone pavement and bowed reverentially as he passed them, his Mamluk guards keeping a watchful eye for any hint of trouble or assault. Paul could not help but admire the man. He knew the almost impossible task he had in keeping his own officers in line with his policies, many having wanted to sack the city completely. Saladin had played a very delicate but masterful plan as had Balian. Paul's heart began to beat fast as the thought that Alisha, if she was by some miracle still alive, may be within her sister Queen Tamar's caravan. He looked back at Princess Stephanie still holding Humphrey, then back toward Saladin. He had to check if only for his own peace of mind and quickly decided to follow Saladin's route.

When Paul arrived at Queen Tamar's caravan, her knights all upon their horses in their full splendour, their banners held high, his heart nearly stopped as he saw Queen Tamar step down from her caravan. He had always thought how similar she looked to Alisha but as she stepped down, the sun shining upon her face, and wearing one of Alisha's actual designed silk dresses, he was nearly sick. He steadied himself against a marble column and watched her as she walked towards a building Saladin had taken as his headquarters. Queen Tamar did not even see Paul and even if she had, she would not have recognised him. Several women dressed all in black walked past him, one briefly looking up at him before continuing on her way.

"Here you are," Taqi suddenly said, invading Paul's thoughts loudly as he placed his hand upon his shoulder hard. "I wish you would stop vanishing," he remarked.

"I need to know if she is here or not," Paul replied and stood up straight.

"Paul, you are exhausted. Please go and rest before you collapse. I will check every last person in the Queen's Company. If she is with them, I will find her...I swear it," Taqi said and pulled Paul around to face him. "But if she is not then, my friend, you must once and for all confront your grief and move forwards as she would have wished."

Paul's stomach knotted tightly.

"I shall be waiting within the old church upon the mount. When you have news, find me there. Afterwards I must head for Ailia for I cannot wait yet another single day."

Taqi nodded in silence seeing the sheer turmoil in Paul's eyes just as Abi and Ishmael approached, both looking concerned.

"I shall have Abi assist me. Ishmael can go with you," Taqi said and motioned with his head for Ishmael to come closer and mouthed silently and indicated with his fingers to his eyes to keep an eye on Paul. Ishmael nodded in acknowledgment as Abi moved to stand beside Taqi. She nodded in agreement.

୨୦ ଓଃ

Paul remained silent as he held his hands in prayer kneeling within one of the pews at the rear of the chapel. Wide sunbeams shone down through the large stained glass of the arched windows. A larger shaft of sunlight shone down near to the altar through a large hole in the ceiling made during the assault, the final pieces of roof timbers and plaster being carried away by two monks. Two Turkish horse archers stepped inside, looked around briefly, saw Paul and then Ishmael stood two rows back, his arms folded. They bowed politely and stepped backwards out of sight. Three women silently entered the chapel dressed in black. Ishmael had seen them with Queen Tamar's caravan. Two of them sat down on the front pew the other stepping forward and clasping her hands together as she looked up at the stained glass. Ishmael gently prodded Paul to look up. They could not see the faces of the women. A tingling sensation ran through Paul's body and he felt overwhelmed with a sense of knowing Alisha was indeed alive as if an echo of her soul was reaching out and touching him. Feeling like his heart was in his mouth, he slowly stood up.

"Ali..." He coughed lightly, his throat dry. "Alisha!" he called out louder to the woman stood up.

The two women sitting down immediately turned to look at Paul and Ishmael. They wore the headbands of nuns. Paul could feel his heart beat faster and louder as the standing woman very slowly turned to face him, the sunlight flickering across her features...her eyes then meeting Paul's. It was not Alisha, he saw immediately, as she smiled lightly then faced forward again. Paul slumped to his knees clasping his hands in prayer, Ishmael placing a reassuring hand upon his shoulder just as Percival and Master Douglas came and stood beside them, Ishmael raising his finger for them to remain silent. Paul sighed heavily.

"'Twas just wishful thinking," Paul whispered and closed his eyes heavy with sadness.

The standing woman opened her clasped hands upwards as she began to sing. Her voice was echoed within the chapel as the acoustics of the domed ceiling enhanced her voice in an almost angelic manner sounding like a whole choir was singing in perfect harmony. The hairs on Paul's back stood on end and he looked up at her again. He recognised the song immediately as one of Alisha's favourites...'Lord have mercy'. It was one of the oldest recorded songs from Celician Armenia and the surrounding area. With a paraphrase of the Kyrie Eleison with deep choral melody, the song was very impressive and Alisha had often sung it. Perhaps that is why he had felt so strange just before she started to sing somehow sensing its importance to him. He shook his head the exhaustion of the past days seeping deep into his bones and very soul. He listened in silence as the woman sang the entire song in the most beautiful manner he had ever heard. Never had he heard a more beautiful voice sing so perfectly. He smiled to himself as if the song had been a gift from God himself. When she finished several minutes later, all three women bowed toward the altar, turned and walked towards Paul as they followed the path of the aisle. He stood up and they stopped.

"You must be Paul," the first nun leading them and who had sung suddenly stated. The nun closest to her slapped her side but not hard and shook her head no.

"You were sworn not to," she said looking at her harshly.

"We have all heard of you and your union with the princess," the first nun said and looked briefly at her two friends and then stepped closer to Paul. "So has your wife!" The word 'wife' cut through Paul like a blade piercing his chest and the punch felt so real, his eyes instantly filled with tears, his throat feeling like he would choke himself. Ishmael and Percival looked at each other puzzled as Master Douglas stepped forward looking at the nuns fiercely. Paul could not speak. "She learnt of your daughter's death and those of your friends whilst she visited with us to meet with Queen Tamar. She then learnt you were likewise dead...but then recorded as surviving when you returned."

"Nicholas...does she know of Nicholas?" was all Paul could ask, the nun's words not really registering in his mind.

"She does," the first nun answered.

"You vowed not to reveal her presence. You have broken a vow, Sister," the other nun said quietly.

"What vow?" Paul demanded and grabbed the first nun's forearm tightly. She frowned in pain, his grip hurting her. "I...I am sorry," he said and released her quickly.

"With all of your friends and daughter dead, and having thought you dead many weeks until word finally got through you had survived, by which time you had also joined with Princess Stephanie...she did not wish to cause you further pain than she has already brought upon you," the nun explained and hesitated, "and so prayed and believes it better you think her dead so you may start a fresh life happy with the princess."

"'Tis cruel what you speak, Sister," the third nun said, shaking her head disapprovingly.

"Alisha loves you that much she puts you before herself...but no...'tis far more cruel and wrong to deceive and tell such a great lie," the first nun replied instantly and looked into Paul's eyes intently. "I sat night after night alongside Queen Tamar trying to comfort Alisha's broken soul as she cried for your daughter, your friends and you. I have never seen such a depth to love as she has…and that is why I cannot tell this lie she is dead… for she is very much alive."

"Then in the name of the Lord pray tell me I beg of you where is she?" Paul pleaded, his voice broken as a tear ran down his cheek.

"She was with the one you call Sister Lucy but they were to leave the queen's caravan this day. They did not wish to be followed…but simply left alone to grieve and find a way to help others until their days are over. Alisha said many a night, as she cried, that she would see you again in the next life," the first nun explained and clasped her hands over Paul's.

"Why are you here in this chapel of all days and how did you know Paul?" Percival asked bluntly.

"Because a tall white haired old man, a monk we think, asked us to and donated a large sum of money to help pay for the ransom of the poorest if we did," the first nun answered.

"Besides, the whole city knows of the true Grail King who serves as the last Knight of Lazarus…a man also raised again from the dead," the second nun explained.

Instantly Paul looked at Percival knowing within his heart it must have been Kratos, the description fitting perfectly. He looked down at his filthy mantle and the green cross then looked up again. He pulled the nun close and kissed her upon the lips quickly and immediately turned and ran for the exit.

"His daughter still lives…as do his friends. Alisha should be told," Percival explained as the first nun gently wiped her lips then half laughed.

"See, Sisters…I knew all was not done as it should be done. Now it shall be," she said to her two fellow nuns as the third nun gasped and placed her hands over her mouth upon hearing Percival's words. "I told you the Lord's work was at hand this hour."

"And I note he did not deny being called a Grail King," Master Douglas remarked quietly and rubbed his chin.

ଞଔ

Paul ran as fast as he could pushing his way through the mass of people in the street as he rushed to Queen Tamar's parked caravan and men. He could see her knights' banners still held high. Percival rushed after Paul trying to catch him up. Paul saw Abi towering above the crowd near to the queen's caravan. Frantically he had to push his way against the mass of people walking in the opposite direction. Out of breath he finally reached Abi and pulled her around to face him, Taqi stood opposite holding a small vellum sheet staring at it.

 2 – 17

"She lives…she is alive," Paul revealed emotionally. Taqi looked up from the vellum sadly and then looked at Paul. "What?"

Taqi handed Paul the small vellum sheet just as Percival ran up to his side.

"Yes, yes she does…but read that. 'Twas found in the caravans the sisters used," Taqi said, shaking his head, and started to rub the back of his head as emotions that his sister was still alive began to sink in. "She is nowhere to be found here though."

Abi looked at Paul utterly puzzled as he rapidly began to read the words upon the vellum sheet through tear filled eyes, his only thought to find her.

'These words shall go unread by the love of my life. The man who cradles my soul and all that I have ever been or ever will be, lest some impossible miracle is granted. But if you should then you must know that I have lost you in this lifetime only, but should the Lord grant you another lifetime, wearing a new face that I have not seen, with a new name I have not heard, it matters not for I will still know you. If separation should last centuries, I would still sense you and feel you close for somewhere between the sands, the rocks, the trees, the sky and the heavens of this realm, there is a connection that links us, the echoes of your soul and mine as one eternally remembered. Love, love is the only thing any of us ever take with us as we always carry it from one life time to the next.'

It was signed simply 'Ali'. Paul looked at Taqi and Percival in panic then all around himself in all directions not knowing where to look or go.

"If she is still within the city walls, we can find her. No one can leave without paying for all the gates are sealed," Master Douglas explained, out of breath, as he stopped just short of them and looked around at the sheer number of people moving, both Christian and Muslims together, soldiers and mounted knights adding to the organised chaos surrounding them.

Paul closed his eyes and held the vellum sheet against his chest, Alisha's perfume on it filtering up to his nostrils. Opening his eyes, he placed the vellum sheet against his nose to smell it better. He took a deep breath and sighed closing his eyes again to quieten the noise within his mind. Kratos, Theodoric and Attar had shown him so many times and spent so many months teaching him how to meditate and clear his mind to learn how to listen to his own deep inner voice. Now as he stood within the street, the noise all around him, he prayed beyond all prayers he had ever offered up for some guidance; just the smallest piece of information, sense or slightest inkling where she was or heading. Where would she go? He concentrated harder as he tried to control his breathing and shut out all other thoughts and senses. Kratos was somewhere in the city and had most obviously made sure the nuns got the message to Paul. Why he could not have simply told him directly mattered not at that exact moment. Abi looked at Paul, concerned, as he stood perfectly still with his eyes closed for several long minutes, Taqi, Percival and Master Douglas having to push people away as they passed by close. Paul clutched his chest as it tightened painfully, his heart beating slowly but feeling as if it was throbbing loudly. Suddenly he collapsed, Abi just managing to catch him and lay him down, resting his head upon her lap as she knelt on her knees holding him.

"Oh fuck!" Master Douglas said and quickly started to pull open Paul's chain mail coif and mantle.

❧ ☙

"Oh you of such little faith in the parchments," Nicholas spoke, making Paul open his eyes. "You really should learn to trust those instincts, my friend," he said as he offered to pull Paul up, bright light making Paul shield his eyes.

Paul sat up and tried to look around but could only see white.

"Oh dear Lord no. Not now…please do not say I have myself died…my heart," Paul said alarmed and clutched at his chest.

"No, Paul…your heart is fine. 'Twas just the sun," Nicholas laughed. "Arri and I did tell you Ali and Ailia were not here with us did we not?"

"This…this is just another dream isn't it?" Paul asked.

"If that is what you wish to tell yourself. But I wish to ask you a question. Where, within this whole city would Ali now go...where she would make a difference and could help others? Think, Paul, think!" Paul shook his head, confused. "Where would a person go where they can help others yet no one would go unless they absolutely had to?" Nicholas asked and stepped away from Paul. "Now, my friend, look down yourself...use that so-called intelligence of yours and work it out. You will not be seeing me again, my friend...not in your lifetime."

"No wait!" Paul said as Nicholas vanished almost instantly.

℠ℂ

Paul gasped out loud for some air as he came around, Abi looking down at him, her large blue eyes looking into his deeply. She raised her eyebrows slightly then smiled. Quickly Paul moved to sit up but Master Douglas held him still. Paul looked at Taqi and Percival staring down at him. Slowly Abi raised Paul until he was sat up fully. He shook his head as Ishmael loomed into view and offered him his own ceramic water pot from his belt.

"'Tis water not piss, my friend," Ishmael remarked and smiled.

Paul drank a mouthful and cleared his head. As he passed the ceramic water pot back he looked down at his mantle and the green cross of Lazarus, then up at Taqi.

"I know where she is," Paul stated and forced himself to his feet and smiled emotionally. "I know where my Ali is." He patted Taqi on the shoulder and motioned with his head that he should follow him and quickly walked off half pulling Abi as he went.

Master Douglas looked at Ishmael and shrugged his shoulders just as Princess Stephanie approached them both, looking concerned.

"I could not find you. Where is Paul going?" she asked, leaning up trying to see where he was heading, Brother Teric approaching her fast.

"We have no idea but I suggest we follow," Master Douglas answered.

℠ℂ

Paul ran up the wide stone stairs and into the entrance corridor of the Hospitallers' infirmary, Taqi only just managing to keep up with him despite wearing half the amount of chain mail as him. Paul stopped to

327

catch his breath as he stood looking around the hospital entrance hall as several sergeants tried to organise many wounded, both Christian and Muslims alike, in an orderly fashion. A Muslim Faris Knight saw Paul and immediately walked over to him.

"Are you looking for someone in particular?" he politely asked. "I have been charged to bring some order to this chaos."

Paul stared at him as he looked familiar. Percival ran up behind Paul and Taqi and bent over forwards out of breath.

"I recognise you," Paul said. "You were the knight who defeated all of my friends...Thomas and his knights!"

The Faris Knight rubbed his immaculately cropped beard and looked at Paul.

"Ah...yes of course. You look different now...with the facial growth and...and dressed as a knight yourself," the Faris Knight replied, shook his head then smiled. "I as you can see now deal with the sick and wounded... so tell me who it is you seek."

"My wife...dark hair, beautiful eyes and smile," Paul explained. "She is to me anyway."

"We have many women here treating the wounded, my friend. Feel free to look where you choose," the Faris Knight said and stood aside, Paul immediately rushing to run down the main corridor. "If she is truly as beautiful as you say...there was one woman...but she went to the lepers' section...that way," he revealed and pointed to where the Knights of Lazarus were usually billeted.

"I know...and I know where!" Paul replied loudly and pulled at his Knights of Lazarus mantle, its green cross barely visible beneath the dirt and dried in blood. He wiped his hand across it to reveal the cross more.

Percival stood up straight still trying to catch his breath as Paul turned and ran toward the furthest end of the corridor. When he reached the end where the doors to the leper wards were located he stopped running and began to walk slowly. He took a deep breath trying to compose himself, his heart beating so fast he could hardly breathe. Hesitantly he looked in the first ward, his eyes scanning all the faces of men and women in there. Many were not lepers but wounded brought there as the rest of the hospital was overflowing with injured. With his ears now ringing, he could see Alisha was not in there. Quickly he moved on to the next ward and looked inside. A man yelled out in agony as his badly burnt lower leg, that was also smashed and open, was being dealt with, but he could not see Alisha in that room either. He felt sick fearing he was wrong. Percival and Taqi followed behind him as he went and stood in the next doorway. A little boy aged about seven at the most sat on the end of the nearest bed looking dazed holding up his left arm. His clothes were scorched and his left arm was badly burnt, so badly the bones across the top of his hand were exposed showing brilliantly white as were parts of his wrist. The boy's father sat behind him just holding him against himself, tears streaming down his cheeks. He looked up at Paul.

"Please, you are a Knight of Lazarus...you know medicine. Please help my son...please," the father pleaded. Paul looked down at his tunic and placed his hand upon the green cross now visible despite the dirt and blood smeared across it where he had just wiped it clear. "Please...his mother is dead as are his sisters," the man pleaded. "He is all I have left...please."

Quickly Paul knelt down in front of the little boy and looked into his eyes. He was clearly in shock. He looked at his hand. There was no way he could save it, the burns being too deep and the cooked flesh having been pulled clean away. The risk of infection was too high and without any skin that could be pulled over to cover it, he knew the boy's only chance was to have it removed. The father's eyes met Paul's and he knew the same. Paul looked around just in time to see Abi and Ishmael arrive behind Percival and Taqi. He motioned for Abi to come closer and check the boy's hand.

"I cannot save the hand, but Abi here can remove it safely if she is willing?" Paul explained to the father then looked at Abi for confirmation.

She nodded yes and without hesitation removed a length of leather strapping, wrapped it around the boy's upper arm and pulled it tightly. She looked at the father in silence but nodded at him. Still in a state of shock the little boy just stared at Paul. Several people entered the ward whilst others left carrying blood soaked sheets. The ward was mayhem with relatives trying to help and more injured being brought in. Abi sat beside the boy and held his arm out across her lap and blocked the view from the father. She took out her smallest knife. She nodded toward a candle burning away near the window and Taqi quickly brought it over. She held the sharp blade over the flame for several minutes to make sure it was clean then pulled part of the linen sheet over her knees and placed the boy's little hand upon it. The father lowered his head tearfully as he cradled the little boy as best he could. Percival and Ishmael stood so others did not have to witness what Abi was about to do. Paul held the boys other hand as he knelt in front of him maintaining eye contact. Paul was aware of other people coming and going but kept his eyes fixed upon the little boy. After a few minutes Abi prodded the exposed hand near to the wrist. Cutting off the blood supply with the tourniquet had numbed the area almost completely. Quickly Abi made an incision with her knife all the way around the wrist just short of the burnt skin. The boy instinctively pulled his arm as he felt a brief sensation when Abi started to cut deeper into the flesh and around the bones of the hand where it joined to the wrist. The little boy started to feel the pain, his eyes widening and filling with tears, the father holding him tighter with tears streaming down his own face. Several people passing stopped to see what was taking place as Paul held the little boys other hand and stared at him trying to keep him looking at him only. The boy's mouth opened wide as tears streamed down his cheeks but he did not make a sound. Abi managed to grasp the tendons and tie them off before finally removing the entire hand. She pulled the remaining skin she had managed to keep and motioned for Taqi to apply pressure as she put a small knot in the main artery. Once she removed the tourniquet the blood would rush back in force and she hoped she had tied it off strong enough. She reached for a small bottle of previously boiled water, Ishmael quickly passing it to her, and washed out the entire area of the wound.

"'Tis done, now all I need is to stitch and cover it. The other burn I can also cover," Abi remarked. "But it is going to hurt him when I release the tourniquet."

The father just nodded, Paul still looking at the little boy intently.

"You are unbelievably brave. Very brave," he said reassuringly to the little boy as Abi started to loosen the tourniquet. Abi looked at the wrist still open as blood flow returned to the limb. It did not spurt and she nodded with relief knowing she had tied it all off successfully. "Almost done now, little man, almost done," Paul said and wiped his finger down the little boy's face.

The little boy closed his mouth and rested his head sideways against his father's chest and closed his eyes still in a lot of pain and started to cry quietly. The father just sobbed and silently mouthed 'thank you'. Paul sat back upon his legs, kneeling, and looked up in time to see two women wearing shawls and hoods over their heads quickly walk behind Ishmael and Taqi, walk up the steps and out into the corridor. Paul was about to tell the father he needed to thank Abi when just for a minute he thought he heard Sister Lucy speak…but it was too muffled to hear properly. His mind replayed the image of one of the woman's feet as she stepped up the last step, the sandals she was wearing. Instantly Paul jumped up, Taqi looking at him, alarmed, as he pushed Percival aside hard and rushed over to the steps and jumped up all three into the corridor in time to see one of the women flounce her arm away from the other shorter woman trying to pull her back.

"You cannot…and you must not run from this. 'Tis stubborn and stupid beyond reason…'tis truly wrong. You are being a martyr and I will not be a part of it. He should know," Paul heard Sister Lucy say through gritted teeth and again she grasped the other woman's arm tightly.

Paul's heart stopped upon hearing Sister Lucy's voice but still unsure it was her as both wore their hoods up fully over their heads.

"Sister Lucy," Paul said emotionally, barely audible as several turcopolers rushed past carrying an injured Muslim on a stretcher board, the Faris Knight at the end of the corridor looking on.

 1 – 7

The two women froze where they stood. Paul took a few steps closer his stomach knotting so tightly he thought he was going to be sick, his throat swelling feeling tighter. He went to speak but could not. Slowly the smaller woman of the two stood up straight, released her grip from the other woman and turned to face Paul. As she turned she lowered her hood. Paul's eyes widened and he stood speechless as Sister Lucy looked back at him. His lips quivering almost uncontrollably and unable to speak, he sensed Percival rush up beside him followed by Taqi who both froze as if they were looking at a ghost. Paul went to take another step forwards, but his legs were trembling and he only took one pace. The other woman clenched her hands nervously and immediately Paul recognised them as Alisha's hands. Still unable to speak he forced himself to take another step forward. Sister Lucy gently hit the side of Alisha.

"Paul," Alisha spoke, the word hitting him like the most powerful sound and voice he had ever heard as it cut through him. He clutched his chest unable to breath. "'Tis best you consider me dead for as Sister Lucy said at the beginning…all along, that I would bring you nothing but pain and sorrow, so please, please if you ever loved me, please start a new, better and happier life with Stephanie where you can do some real good for a great many people." Sister Lucy raised her hands and rolled her eyes shaking her head no. "Do not come near me please I beg of you…in memory of our lost children I beg of you grant me this one wish…please for I cannot bear to look upon your face once more…for just hearing your voice is killing me," Alisha said, her voice heavy with emotion as she fought not to cry. Paul took a step forward. "Please, Paul, I beg of you…Taqi, I know you are there so please take him from here."

Taqi shook his head, utterly confused, but then his face turned to anger, his eyes narrowing.

"Madness, my woman, utter madness," Sister Lucy said aloud and pulled Alisha around to face Paul hard but she lowered her head immediately and looked down, her face covered and hidden by her hood, just her neck visible.

"Allah be praised," Taqi exclaimed emotionally as a tear ran down his cheek. "But…but you had no right to hide that you are still alive. 'Tis cruel!" he then said sternly, shaking his head.

"I felt you before I even saw you Ali…I have kept feeling you every minute of every hour of every day…so you cannot walk…away from me…again. You are the very essence of my soul," Paul finally blurted out, breathless, and outstretched his hand toward her. "Look at me, Ali…you walk away from me this day, then I am truly dead." Alisha stood perfectly still, the Faris Knight holding several people back at the end of the corridor as he looked on. Paul saw a single tear from Alisha fall and hit the stone floor. "You are and always shall be my one true love…in this life and the next… and beyond, so Ali…please look at me," Paul pleaded.

"Ali…," Taqi said and stepped forwards past Paul and stopped short of Sister Lucy. "You are clearly not aware that Theo and Tenno live also." Sister Lucy gasped loudly and grasped at her chest with both hands, shocked, Alisha quickly grasping her arm to steady her. "As is your daughter… Ailia," Taqi stated bluntly. "Now look up, my sister back from the dead."

"Ali…did you honestly think that once I knew you were still alive that I would ever stop searching for you?" Paul asked, his voice broken with emotion.

Sister Lucy stepped forwards looking intently at Taqi then Paul, her eyes searching for confirmation of what Taqi had just said. Paul nodded yes silently and she covered her mouth struggling to contain her emotions.

"Ali," is all she could say in a whisper.

Alisha remained perfectly still staring down at the floor, Paul feeling like he would collapse at any moment, the ringing in his ears sounding louder, his vision focusing in on just Alisha. So very painfully slowly she started to look up as the news of Ailia being alive started to sink in. All the weeks and months of total grief along with the belief that she had lost all she had ever loved and held dear, then learning that Paul was alive but now with Princess Stephanie was again now all being turned upside down within her. It was overwhelming her senses completely. Paul looked on utterly paralysed as he first saw her chin come into view, then her mouth, her lips quivering as she fought her emotions, then her nose and cheeks, Paul drawing in a deeper breath unable to exhale, then her wide open tear filled beautiful emotional eyes finally looked up at him as she opened them fully to see him.

"Oh Lord!" Paul cried out involuntarily loudly and fell sideways against the whitewashed walls just stopping himself with his left arm, his legs feeling like they were about to collapse beneath him having lost all strength and control in them. Alisha blinked as the tears rolled down her cheeks and put her hands together in front of her almost hunching forwards. Paul's eyes stayed fixed upon hers unable to believe the sight before him. It was really Alisha.

"Ailia...she lives?" she said tearfully, hardly able to ask the question, Sister Lucy now crying silently, desperately trying to wipe away her tears.

Paul went to step forwards but his legs gave way and he fell, Taqi just grabbing him in time to keep him upright on his knees as he kept his eyes firmly fixed upon Alisha's eyes. He simply nodded yes and mouthed 'alive' silently, unable to speak. Alisha stood motionless, just blinking, also unable to speak, her heart pounding harder than she had ever felt before. Paul raised his arms out to her and as a tear ran down his cheek, he tilted his head looking so sad and exhausted...then she rushed forwards, her hood falling to her shoulders as she threw herself to her knees in front of him and wrapped her arms around him tightly. Paul slowly placed his arms around her waist in disbelief that he was actually holding her, afraid in case she vanished and this would turn out to be just another vivid dream. He could smell her hair again and sense her start to sob as tears fell down his own cheeks. She squeezed him tightly several times unable to believe she was actually holding him. She knelt back to look into his eyes and just stared at him in disbelief. Paul moved his hand to the side of her tear streaked face. Gently he leaned close and kissed her cheek, immediately tasting her tears.

"She is alive, yes...but I need you to come with me to fetch our little girl...will you?" Paul asked emotionally as Percival covered his face as he started to cry quietly, Ishmael looking away as he tried to control himself. "Percy...tell her."

Percival wiped his face quickly, sniffed and then looked at Alisha, shaking his head finding it hard to believe that she was indeed alive. She looked up at him almost begging for him to speak her eyes so full of emotion. With tears in his own eyes, his lips closed tightly unable to speak he simply nodded yes. Alisha kept looking at him desperate to hear his confirmation and not just a nod. He coughed and cleared his throat.

"Ailia is very much alive and well for I have seen her...and she believes she is in charge of Tenno and Theodoric," he finally managed to speak and let out an emotional laugh.

Sister Lucy cupped her face as she cried openly as Alisha looked back at Paul, put her hands upon his face and smiled like it was the first time she had ever smiled, her eyes blazing with an inner beauty that shone from behind them and touching Paul's very soul, he felt. She ran her forefinger over his lips, then gently and tenderly pressed her lips upon them, the kiss sending a sensation through both of them unlike they had ever felt before and they both started to cry unashamedly and openly as they embraced each other.

Sister Lucy came and knelt beside them and put her hands upon Alisha's shoulders and looked at Paul.

"You try stopping us getting her...and you wait until I see that Theo," Sister Lucy said, smiling emotionally.

Alisha leaned back still cupping her hands around his face.

"But what of Stephanie?" she asked and took a deep breath.

"She has a part of my heart I cannot deny...but you have my whole soul... you always have and you always shall," Paul replied.

"And you I," Alisha said and pressed her lips against his, both of them feeling whole again only now knowing and realising just how broken they were when apart.

Overwhelmed Paul started to cry again uncontrollably as he pulled her against him still unable to believe she was real and in his arms again.

Alisha cried softly and they both knelt on the stone floor holding each other tightly gently rocking back and forth. Abi stepped up from the ward having finished stitching the little boy's stump and forearm. She saw Paul and Alisha on the floor together and blinked several times unsure of what she was actually seeing, unable to believe her own eyes. Stewart came running into view and froze next to the Faris Knight when he saw Paul and Alisha, the Faris Knight wiping away a tear quickly. Abi looked at Sister Lucy, who simply shrugged her shoulders at her. Abi looked at Stewart as he stood wide mouthed and she carefully walked past Paul and Alisha and over toward him. She shook her head lost for words and needed some fresh air utterly stunned at what she had just seen. Shaking her head she passed Stewart and walked down the steps where she saw Count Henry who acknowledged her silently as he stood beside one of the two side alcoves. He was actually blocking her from seeing Princess Stephanie hiding inside out of sight.

"'Tis safe, she has passed," Count Henry said and turned to look at Princess Stephanie after Abi had walked a short distance still shaking her head, confused.

Princess Stephanie held her left hand across her tummy, her right hand covering her mouth as she gulped trying not to be sick. Tears welled up in her eyes but she looked more terrified than hurt as panic filled her entire body having just seen Paul and Alisha. It was not like the fear she had felt when she was nearly attacked by the lion within the old donjon. This was a different all invading fear that shook her very soul. She started to pant finding it difficult to breathe. She stood up on her toes then down again unsure what she should do and started to shake uncontrollably. She wished the ground would open up and swallow her or that she could close her eyes and never open them again.

"'Tis truly unfair," she cried as tears began to flow down her cheeks.

"Come on, you, you need to come with me. Come on," Count Henry said softly and gently helped her stand away from the alcove. "Do not look back...for you must think of your unborn as your priority right now," he said gently as Princess Stephanie looked at him in shock. "What, you think I would not come to learn of such matters?"

Count Henry slowly led her away through the crowds, himself looking back just once in time to see Abi looking at them go. She nodded at him briefly before turning back to the infirmary.

Port of La Rochelle, France, Melissae Inn, spring 1191

"You hear about a city being besieged but unless you actually experience it...you cannot possibly imagine it, as you say," Gabirol remarked and dotted a full stop onto his parchment.

Peter was wiping his eyes as Ayleth shook her head, a tear rolling down her cheek.

"Oh please, Ayleth, do not start or you will have me in tears again too," Sarah said as she pulled Ayleth close and hugged her.

Miriam hid her face in her hands as she cried quietly, the Templar rubbing her back gently and kissed her shoulder.

"I apologise if I am perhaps too detailed in what I reveal," the old man said.

"I think everyone should be told just exactly how things are," Peter remarked and sniffed loudly. "And you, sirs...you and your kind should certainly be afforded more respect than you are all given. 'Tis a shame upon us that we are ignorant of what sacrifices you have made," he continued to say, looking directly at the Templar and Hospitaller.

"You may think ill of me but I feel sorrier for Princess Stephanie," Simon remarked sadly.

"There were no real winners in that siege...not for Paul, Alisha or Princess Stephanie," the old man said in response to Simon's comment.

"I cannot believe how one minute men are fighting and killing each other...and yet the next they are tending to each other's wounds," the wealthy tailor commented, utterly bemused.

"Fighting men have a common bond as I explained previously," the old man said. "'Tis truly a brotherhood of minds...of shared experiences and horrors that only those who have endured it know."

"What did Princess Stephanie do after witnessing the return of Alisha?" Ayleth asked.

"Sadly," the old man started to say but paused. He shook his head, took a deep breath and continued. "She took herself away to her chambers and Queen Sibylla came and sat with her as she cried like Mother Earth herself mourning for the whole world...'tis the only way I can explain the depth of her sadness and heartbreak...and the physical and emotional toll of the past weeks I am afraid to say levied a high price upon her."

"Oh Lord...how?" Sarah demanded to know and leaned forwards.

"Paul gave Alisha her three pronged dagger back and then escorted her to the

citadel to seek out Princess Stephanie. Count Henry intervened and informed them that she had witnessed their reunion and strongly advised that they should leave her alone and set out to get their daughter," the old man explained and paused again before looking at Sarah. "But Alisha refused to have things left that way."

"Oh my Lord, she didn't go to stab her did she in a jealous rage?" Simon asked.

"Don't revert back to being a total fool...I am only just beginning to tolerate you," Sarah said and slapped Simon's arm.

"No of course that is not what she was going to do," the old man replied and smiled at Sarah's actions. "Count Henry asked Paul to remain where he was and that he would check on Princess Stephanie first and if she was in agreement, for Alisha to come to her chambers in order that they both speak and resolve matters amicably and as befitting their positions."

City of Jerusalem, Kingdom of Jerusalem, October 2nd 1187

Princess Stephanie lay upon her bed crying, a single bed cover pulled up half way over her legs and tummy, Queen Sibylla sat beside her holding her hand. Count Henry stood looking out of the main window at all the people outside, smoke still hanging heavy over the city. A knock at the main chamber door drew all of their attention as a chamber maid entered the room through an adjoining door carrying a bowl of hot water and new towels. Quickly she placed the bowl down upon the trunk at the foot of the bed and hurried to open the main door. She opened it slightly.

 3 – 1

"I request permission to speak with Princess Stephanie," Alisha spoke politely, just out of view.

Princess Stephanie sat up, alarmed, Queen Sibylla standing up quickly. The maid looked around at Princess Stephanie as Count Henry nodded at her she should allow her in. As soon as Princess Stephanie nodded yes, the maid opened the door fully to reveal Alisha stood alone looking in hesitantly. Their eyes met and Alisha could instantly both see and sense the pain and turmoil in her. She knew how much she felt for Paul too and felt partly guilty at the pain she was clearly suffering now. It is not what she had ever wished upon her.

"Have you come to quarrel with the princess?" Queen Sibylla asked bluntly.

Alisha stepped down the step into the chamber shaking her head no just as Count Henry shook his head no.

"Of course not...as I am sure Count Henry should have explained," Alisha replied emotionally, not moving her eyes off of Princess Stephanie. "I came to offer my sincerest apologies...for returning to Paul...for...for," Alisha tried to explain and paused, lost for words seeing the tears fall down Princess Stephanie's cheek.

"You, you come here to apologise," Princess Stephanie said and gulped and tried to sit up higher. "You come to apologise to me," she repeated, Count Henry looking at her unsure what she would say next. "What...for living? For returning to your husband...and you come to apologise to me for that?" she asked.

Alisha looked at her not totally sure what she was meaning.

"I know you became as one," Alisha remarked emotionally and clasped her hands together just as Abi stood in the doorway and looked into her eyes looking through Alisha in wonderment that she was still so very much alive. "But you, too, thought me dead," she whispered, seeing the look on Abi's face.

"'Tis for that reason it should be I apologising and seeking your forgiveness....not you," Princess Stephanie said and wiped the tears from her face just as more fell. "'Tis I who beg your forgiveness. I...we...we thought you dead, and, and..."

"And nothing!" Abi stated and moved to stand beside Alisha. "What was done was done with love and in honour. Neither of you need apologise."

Alisha stood silently looking at Princess Stephanie for a few moments, her eyes then seeing the bowl of hot water at the end of the bed, then the sheet drawn up over Princess Stephanie as blood started to seep into it where it was lying flat beside her thigh. In alarm Alisha rushed forwards realising instantly what was happening.

"You are with child!" Alisha gasped and moved to stand beside Princess Stephanie as she looked up at her, her eyes full of sorrow.

"She was...but it has arrived too many months before time," Abi explained.

Alisha sat on the bed beside Princess Stephanie, clasped her hands with hers and held them tightly against her chest and looked intently into her eyes. It was not just the princess's baby but also Paul's.

"I am sorry…but you must not tell Paul for he does not know," Princess Stephanie cried.

"'Twas the shock of these past weeks, I fear," Count Henry remarked. "Abi will help Princess Stephanie and when well enough, we shall leave for Tripoli."

Alisha looked at Princess Stephanie, sensing the final shock was probably seeing her and Paul together. Princess Stephanie clasped Alisha's hands tighter and looked at her pleadingly.

"You cannot tell Paul for you have a daughter you must fetch…together," she said emotionally.

Alisha pulled Princess Stephanie close and hugged her tightly, kissing the top of her head softly. Queen Sibylla stepped away and winked at Count Henry and Abi in silence as Alisha and Princess Stephanie hugged each other both crying quietly.

Count Henry walked over to Abi and pulled her back toward the chamber door.

"I thought you said the parchments for Paul showed another daughter?" he asked in a whisper.

"They do…'tis why this did not make sense unless Alisha will fall later with another," Abi replied quietly and looked at Alisha and Princess Stephanie still hugging each other in comfort.

"Or already has," Count Henry replied.

ॐ

Count Henry entered the small room and immediately closed the door behind him. Paul looked up from the table where he sat alongside Percival with Ishmael stood behind them. Light streamed through the open window, its shutter slightly banging against the wall as a breeze began to blow outside.

"Fear not, Paul, they have not argued…quite the opposite," he said and pulled out the bench pushed up against the table and sat himself down opposite Paul and Percival. "Abi and the queen remain with them whilst they talk. There was a lot of tears."

"How is Stephanie?" Paul asked, concerned, just as Taqi entered the room and looked at them, a little puzzled. "Ali is fine with Princess Stephanie," Paul quickly explained as Taqi sat down beside Count Henry.

"They have a close bond those two," Count Henry explained, putting his hands together on the table. "They are both intelligent enough and mature enough to see matters for what they are. You, my friend, are exceptionally lucky."

"I do not wish to upset Stephanie...but with Ali being alive, I have no choice," Paul sighed.

"She will have other priorities to contend with...such as her other children still in Kerak. They have lost a father after all even if he was a reckless fool," Count Henry said and looked at Paul. "But you...you have a daughter to collect and your friends."

"'Tis all so absurd," Paul replied and shook his head. "I can still hardly believe it all."

"Well you better believe it and fast," Count Henry stated bluntly. "And the sooner you get on your way, the better. I shall liaise with Princess Stephanie to have her two children escorted here from Kerak. If you can go to the Cave de Sueth, recover Ailia and the others, we can meet you at the river crossing before heading on to Tripoli. Saladin has promised us safe conduct and it would be wise to travel north as one. Once you are safely on your way back to France...then I shall take Princess Stephanie wherever she wishes to go."

"You mean I shall not see her again?" Paul asked.

"Briefly...to travel, but after that, never again. It would be cruel upon all of you...trust me for I know how this works." Count Henry sighed as he replied.

"Kratos is somewhere within the city," Paul said and looked at Taqi. "Can we find him?"

"We can try," Taqi answered and looked at Count Henry.

"Unless he wants you to find him, you will not succeed so you would be wasting your time. Besides, we need you all to leave as soon as is practicable. Are we agreed?" Count Henry asked and looked at each of them in turn.

Paul nodded silently, his thoughts wandering back to Alisha and Princess Stephanie. He knew he had everything to live for...and all to die for.

Chapter 83
The Cave of Despair

Port of La Rochelle, France, Melissae Inn, spring 1191

"I cannot begin to imagine how they must have all felt. Such emotional turmoil," Ayleth remarked sadly.

"It was certainly that," the old man said and looked at the Templar, who had raised his hand slightly.

"We were told that Balian was refused an audience with Saladin twice and had to return in the morning to see him only after the assault to breach the walls failed. That is different to what you tell us," he said.

"Balian had become aware that certain sectors within Jerusalem were actively discussing opening up one of the gates to Saladin's forces. 'Tis but yet another reason why Balian decided it was time to negotiate. But remember, Saladin had sworn to take the city by force and he had to be seen to be a man of his word," the old man started to explain then leaned forward, resting his arms upon the table. *"But in truth, Balian did visit in the evening as I explained. Saladin's forces very nearly breached the city walls and Balian was forced to wait outside for most of the night after their initial meeting whilst Saladin discussed the negotiations further with his officers. Balian's threat to utterly destroy the city and its holy shrines was taken seriously. Balian pointed out the earlier eclipse of the sun that occurred, which many on both sides saw as a bad omen. But there was so much more to the siege of Jerusalem than I have covered thus far."*

"Then please tell more for I wish to learn of it all...the real facts and not the simple rubbish peddled on us by the Church," Gabirol said, expressing his desire for more facts as he readied his quill again.

"As I have explained already, when Saladin arrived on the twentieth of September, his engineers immediately studied the walls of Jerusalem whilst his forces made camp. As you know, the following morning Saladin's troops attacked the north-western wall between David's Gate (Bab Yafa) and the Damascus Gate...or as some call it St Stephen's Gate (Bab Dimashq). The battle cries that went up from

341

both sides could be heard with frightening clarity across the city...especially when accompanied by those drums. I neglected to mention all of the Christian mangonels positioned along the walls, especially those at Tancred's Tower. The many individual and group sorties that went out to engage the Muslim forces are too numerous to detail...a thousand acts of bravery for sure. In the morning the sun would be in Saladin's eyes, but by the afternoon it would be in the defenders' eyes. Saladin also made good use of the prevailing winds blowing up and across the city by firing bucket loads of dust into the air and consequently the eyes of the defenders. As I explained Muslim losses were high compared to Christian forces and after the death of one of Saladin's senior officers, Amir Izz al Din Isa, he decided to change his battle plans on the twenty-fifth of September."

"This is when he attacked the whore house yes?" the Genoese sailor interrupted.

"Not just the whore house. That just happened to be the main building upon that section of the wall. You may recall the blacksmith had his home and workshop near to the same section of the wall?" the old man replied. "When Saladin dismantled his siege engines and mangonels, along with his tents, many within the city believed he was leaving. It came as a bitter psychological blow when his entire army reappeared having travelled around the hills out of sight to the north of Jerusalem. This actually caught Balian off guard initially. Saladin cut down all the surrounding olive trees and used them to make zaribas."

"What are zaribas?" Simon asked immediately.

"They are a thorn fence with stakes to fortify a camp position. This in effect stopped any Christian raiding sorties whilst Saladin's men erected their siege engines again. Saladin also used a more powerful trebuchet to fire Greek fire into the city. It fired three massive balls of fire that day. It was the same weapon that destroyed the houses where the little girl jumped to her death. Saladin used over forty mangonels from his new position. As I detailed, Saladin sent in three battalions of his best armoured engineers protected beneath large shields and supported by archers. As you now know, one tunnel dug over ninety feet in just two days brought the outer wall down...on the twenty-ninth of September. Saladin had to keep in reserve a large unit of cavalry in case Balian sent out a sortie."

"You did explain, and as accounts we were told of, that the defenders endured covering fire so intense they were hardly able to shoot back at Saladin's engineers," the Hospitaller said and looked at Simon.

2 – 3

"It is argued that if Saladin had been given adequate intelligence he would have found a far easier way into the city. However, he did know but deliberately withheld the information in order to force a stalemate," the old man revealed.

"What do you mean?" Ayleth asked, puzzled.

"Because Saladin knew full well about the so-called Solomon's quarry beneath the northern wall. If his miners and engineers had reached those tunnels they could have worked beneath the city with virtual impunity," the old man answered.

"You say that Balian's forces mounted a sortie out of the city. What happened there as you did not mention it previously?" Gabirol asked.

"'Twas a reckless but bold attempt led by Master Douglas. He led a horse charge out of the Jehoshaphat Gate (Bab Ariha), which led directly down a steep slope into the Kidron valley below. Master Douglas had argued for an offensive attack to reach Saladin's headquarters now camped on the Mount of Olives opposite. His sortie came very close to achieving its objective, only just being repelled by Saladin's cavalry...but the action certainly reminded Saladin and his senior officers just how fanatical the Christian forces still were. It would have a direct impact upon their later decision to agree to terms...but not much is mentioned of that action."

"So you mean to tell us that Saladin had an opportunity to get into the city yet he chose not to?" Peter asked, bemused.

"That is correct. He was also made aware that many within the city wanted to do a suicidal night sortie against his position and die fighting rather than become prisoners or be killed by the coming assault that was sure to follow."

"How did Saladin know that and why didn't they do the sortie?" Sarah asked.

"Because Heraclius talked them out of it saying it was all well and noble them dying in battle and that they may win Paradise, but what of the women and children?"

"You see, we know none of this," the farrier exclaimed, perplexed, and shook his head.

"But in answer to your other question. Saladin was aware of their suicidal suggestion because he was already in direct contact with non Latin Christians of the city. Yusuf Batit, who was one of Saladin's closest and most trusted aides and born in Jerusalem as well as being an orthodox Christian himself, was openly negotiating with his fellow orthodox Christians to open a gate in the north-eastern quarter where most of them lived. This is where Saladin finally made the breach."

"The same Yusuf who met Saladin with Paul and Balian...and you mean they were prepared to surrender the city behind Balian's back?" Simon asked, shocked.

"Yes. The same Yusuf, or Joseph as his Christian friends called him. Hearing what Balian had threatened to do, he felt it was his duty to stop such a brutal response to Saladin. This is why people do not fully appreciate the delicate position that both Balian and Saladin found themselves in. Balian's threat to utterly destroy the city and all of its holy shrines was sheer genius and a gamble of huge proportions," the old man explained.

"You said that Paul went to a church after the city was handed over. You only said he went to a church upon the mount. Which mount, please?" Gabirol asked.

"'Twas the Church of Saint Mary of Mount Sion...just outside the main city walls."

"And Kratos, if it was him, knew he would be there and sent those nuns on purpose?" Ayleth asked.

"Yes he did...he did indeed," the old man answered and smiled at her whilst Gabirol wrote more notes.

"So when exactly did Alisha and Paul leave the city for the cave place and Ailia?" Peter asked.

"Paul wished to leave immediately but Alisha asked to remain another day to spend it with Princess Stephanie. To put things right between them, she explained, Paul still not knowing that Princess Stephanie had just lost their baby. Plus word came back from Kerak and Montreal that they had refused to yield and surrender as ordered by Princess Stephanie. Consequently and true to her word she immediately handed her son Humphrey back to Saladin as a captive."

"What?" Simon asked out loud.

"Yes. She made a promise to Saladin and her people had refused her orders. She knew Humphrey would be well looked after...and besides as most of you probably know by now, Saladin was so impressed with her integrity that he allowed Humphrey to go free without ransom just a few months later."

"She certainly demonstrates more chivalry than most knights and kings," Peter remarked as Gabirol nodded in agreement.

"She does that and more," the old man sighed and looked toward the shutters as the first dim rays of sunlight began to shine through around the edges. "My...'tis morning already. I must hurry to conclude this tale."

"Please do not hurry and miss anything for I doubt any of us shall leave however long you take," the Templar remarked and looked at the others as they all agreed.

"Then let me explain that Saladin commanded a whole troop of Taqi al Din's men to form an escort for Alisha and Paul to be taken to the Cave de Sueth and wherever beyond. He also gave him four of his best Askar guards along with Taqi and one of his fellow Ashashin," the old man explained.

"What are Askar?" Ayleth asked.

"They are an elite bodyguard unit formed from the best Mamluks...fiercely loyal and disciplined they would carry out Saladin's command to the death," the old man answered.

"And Kratos...did they find him?" Gabirol asked.

"Oh yes...they found him," the old man answered and looked up at them all.

City of Jerusalem, Kingdom of Jerusalem, October 3rd 1187

Paul waited nervously by the main hall stairway for Alisha. She had spent the night with Princess Stephanie in her chambers but still unbeknown to him she had been helping her through the delivery of the placenta and subsequent bleeding. Abi assisted having sent word to Paul that Alisha was simply over tired and had decided to remain with Princess Stephanie whilst they actually talked late into the night. Paul did not sleep well being concerned for both of them but he respected their decision even though all he wanted to do was hold Alisha. Taqi and Ishmael were in the stables sorting out their horses when Stewart approached still wearing his Templar uniform and he looked at the state of Paul's Lazarus mantle.

"Sure you do not want to revert back into our Order's dress?" he asked.

"No I am fine as I am thank you. Besides I am no longer of the Order... but I am of this," Paul replied, tired and concerned, as he looked up to the windows of Princess Stephanie's chamber.

"You look worried, brother. You should not be."

"The two women I love most in this world and I have to hurt one of them in such a cruel fashion 'tis impossible to forgive."

"You have been lucky enough to have two of the most remarkable women I know love you. I envy you that...but I do not envy the pain it causes you. I could not handle it as well as you are."

"Who said I was handling it well?"

"Because you always do, my brother. 'Tis why I am so proud of you," Stewart remarked and put his hand upon Paul's shoulder. "They are closer than sisters. Both understand the other's position here with no animosity. But now we must go and fetch Ailia and then get you all home to France," Stewart explained then rubbed his right forearm as if in pain.

"And what of you?"

"What of me? I have been tasked by Master Teric to accompany you back home. 'Twas an order...and one I am happy to follow."

"And what of all the others...will they be ransomed in time for we cannot leave whilst many of the soldiers remain prisoners?"

"That, my brother, is something Master Teric and Master Douglas are presently arguing with Heraclius about. It appears most of the money sent by King Henry for his penance was used by Gerard to pay for mercenaries at Hattin. Not much remains but Master Teric is doing his best as we speak. But you must concentrate on getting Ailia, Theo, Tenno and Thomas and his men," Stewart explained further and again rubbed his forearm.

"You are in pain. Are you injured?" Paul asked.

"Not injured no," Stewart replied and smiled. "'Tis a reminder I carry. Remember?" he asked and raised his arm and pulled down his chain mail sleeve and under shirt to reveal the scar from the wound Paul had inflicted upon him back in France. "'Tis a scar I carry with pride...and as a reminder of how foolish I once was."

Paul did not know what to say but when he was about to speak, Taqi al Din, his bright yellow twin flag style banner on full display, rode into the open courtyard accompanied by several Mamluk guards and four Askar guards. He pulled up just short of Paul and Stewart and dismounted. Both noticed he was carrying a hand and a half straight sword. Rapidly he walked toward them and saw the look of concern on their faces.

"Fear not, my friends, for I am here under orders to pass over command of this escort," Taqi al Din explained and stopped just short of them. "Plus I am to present this gift from Saladin himself," he explained and presented up the ornate sword, its scabbard richly decorated with gold and silver leaf patterns. Puzzled, Paul looked at him. "My Lord said you would know what it is for and your commission." Hesitantly Paul accepted the sword, Stewart smiling. "As soon as you are ready and whomever else you have within your party, these men will escort you to the Cave de Sueth as requested and beyond."

Alisha walked into view dressed in a dark blue dress and dark green shawl. Slowly she stepped down from the corridor onto the main steps accompanied by Abi and Sister Lucy. She stopped and stared at Taqi al Din as he turned and smiled at them. He bowed politely. Paul's heart raced at seeing her still hardly able to believe she was actually real and stood before him. Alisha bowed back and then walked up to Paul taking his hand and clutching it tightly. Her eyes searched his. He could sense the pain in her.

"Will either of you forgive me?" Paul asked, hesitantly fearful of her response sensing she was withholding something from him but she quickly shook her head no. He frowned, surprised.

"I mean yes, for there is nothing to forgive," she blurted out and clutched her hands around his tighter. "We have both agreed 'tis best you and I leave…without you seeing her this day, for she fears she could not bear it to say goodbye…she asks that you do not see her until she is ready and strong enough again…when we join her and Count Henry after we have Ailia. She asks for a little time that is all," Alisha explained emotionally, making excuses so Princess Stephanie had time to recover from her miscarriage. "Unless you have changed your mind?" she then asked sadly, instantly fearing his reply the moment she had asked it.

Paul looked into her eyes, the desperation and hurt clearly seen and felt within him just as Percival walked into view and looked at Stewart as they waited to hear Paul's response. Paul looked up at Princess Stephanie's window in time to see her step back out of sight quickly. Alisha took a deep breath, her heart beating fast, as he then looked back at her, passed the sword to Stewart quickly and then held her hands up and kissed them.

"Never," is all he could reply emotionally. He wanted to kiss her there and then but was conscious that Princess Stephanie may still be looking down upon them. He hurt for her and his heart ached knowing she was likewise hurting, but his love for Alisha meant more to him than his own life.

Count Henry approached with Master Douglas by his side.

"If you are ready to leave, then we have arranged to meet you at the Yarmouk valley crossing once you have Ailia," Count Henry explained as Taqi and Ishmael appeared leading their horses, Adrastos at the front. "We shall be there on the fifth, which gives you plenty of time to reach them, pack up and meet us. Princess Stephanie I am afraid will have to deal with whatever emotions she has and wishes she wants until we are all safely away."

"She is already dealing with those," Alisha remarked in her defence.

"And I am coming with you like it or not," Master Douglas interrupted and nodded at Alisha.

"Will you ride with me upon Adrastos?…for I do not want you out of my sight or arms," Paul asked. Alisha simply nodded yes and looked across at her brother Taqi as Taqi al Din mounted his own horse and looked at Alisha and Paul.

"From what I know of you it will be you protecting my men," he said and smiled. "As you know I do not agree with all that my Lord commands me to do…but this is one order I am honoured to carry out. May Allah bless and watch over you."

When Taqi al Din turned away Paul caught a glimpse of the old lady from La Rochelle stood some distance away watching them all. As soon as she knew Paul was looking at her, she smiled and quickly walked out of sight behind the main wall heading toward the north-eastern sector of the city. Without saying a word, Paul clasped Alisha's hand tightly and hurried her along to go with him as he set out to follow the old woman. Taqi and Percival immediately ran after them as Ishmael was left holding the horses' reins, Stewart taking two as they tried to pull away. Abi frowned and shrugged her shoulders before setting off after them. Ishmael quickly tied the reins to a nearby pole and likewise hurried after them. Master Douglas frowned hard and looked at Count Henry, who motioned with his head that he should follow them.

ℬℭ

"Paul, slow down you are scaring me," Alisha called out as he half dragged her through the crowds of people, trying to keep his eye upon the old woman as she walked fast through them with apparent ease.

 3 – 1

"I am sorry…but she is here for a reason…I know it," Paul explained and stopped to look where the old woman had gone. Immediately he recognised the blacksmith's workshop just as she stepped inside. "Come on."

After they had pushed their way through the moving crowd, Paul held Alisha's hand tightly as they stepped through the main entrance archway leading into the blacksmith's forge area. Both froze when they saw the old woman standing beside Kratos as he laughed and gently handed the blacksmith's wife a baby girl wrapped in swaddling. The blacksmith had his arm around his wife and both were crying with happiness. His face was covered in black dirt where he had been smelting. Slowly Alisha started to walk forwards and now pulled Paul to follow her. Kratos became aware they were approaching and stood up straight and turned to face them as the blacksmith and his wife cradled the new born baby girl.

"Well this is a sight for old eyes...the pair of you back together as it should be," Kratos remarked and leant forward slightly upon his staff as his deep blue eyes looked at them both. He smiled at them. "But this meeting will be brief."

"What are you doing here? Where have you been and why did you not come sooner?" Alisha asked shaking her head, puzzled.

"Oh I had much to sort before I could come," he answered and looked at the blacksmith and his wife. "New families for a start," he remarked and looked back at Alisha and Paul as Taqi and Percival ran into the forge area. "My time amongst you is coming to an end for another who sleeps will awaken to take my place."

"Why, I mean where are you going and who is taking your place?" Paul asked, alarmed, as Taqi came and stood beside him.

"I have I am afraid suffered far more than I was meant to...so another, named Jaromir, who sleeps in India will take up my mantle, and I shall rest until a time when my kind are welcomed back again openly and without fear," Kratos explained and smiled at Alisha as she became upset sensing this was the very last time she would see him. Kratos nodded knowing she knew. "Do not be saddened for I have done far more than I ever expected. But I caution you now...do not hesitate in getting Ailia back for even now as we speak, Turansha and his men seek her."

"How...how do they know she lives and her whereabouts?" Paul asked, alarmed.

"Sadly as is the way of this world, service to self types heard rumours and information when it was passed to the ears of Balian. For monetary gain a person within his company passed that information on to one of Turansha's spies. Also some amongst Saladin's camp heard you were going to the Cave de Sueth to collect your daughter."

"Surely...you can do something to help us?" Paul asked frantically.

"Paul, remember when you stayed with me in the desert?" Kratos asked and looked at him intently. "You know why I am not able to interfere directly in most cases. This I am afraid is one of them for it is tied to the destiny of many others' paths."

Alisha clasped Paul's hand tightly and looked up to him, alarmed, just as

Abi and Ishmael ran into the courtyard and stopped when they saw Kratos. Abi shook her head and then rapidly walked over to him immediately putting her arms around him.

"You were told you should not come here," she said emotionally and held him tightly until the baby made a cry and she stepped back a pace looking at it as it began to suck its fist. "But I see you have found good parents for this one."

"Yes indeed. So you see I had to come," Kratos replied and smiled at the blacksmith and his wife. "But now, Abi...I have but my last request of you."

"No...please do not say it...and what of my child?" she shot back instantly.

"Fine of course and very well looked after where we agreed. But you always knew this day would come...and it is upon us now. Jaromir stirs. Now you must reunite Ailia with Alisha and you must protect them no matter what else comes your way. 'Tis my final request of you."

"Who is Jaromir?" Percival asked bluntly and stepped forwards seeing how pained Abi looked.

"He is the brother of Kratos," Abi answered, her voice full of emotion.

Kratos stepped toward Alisha and Paul and gently lifted their hands in his large palms, then wrapped his hands around theirs.

"You two have caused me the greatest of troubles...and believe me I thought your parents were trouble enough," he laughed as he looked at them adoringly. "But I have so loved you both unlike any others...across time. We shall not see each other again in this world, nor other realms of this time," he began to explain and quickly raised his finger at Alisha as she went to speak. "But we most certainly shall in the next...that I promise you just as I once did a very long time ago."

Abi placed her hands over her mouth trying not to cry.

"But we still need you now," Paul finally spoke.

"No you do not...trust me on this matter. But please, you must hurry and reach Ailia...and Abi...do not forget the item I gave you in the desert. Pass it over if necessary, but only as a last resort."

Alisha went to speak but as soon as Kratos looked into her eyes, she knew that no words were needed. The old lady moved to walk around Kratos and as she did, smoke and water vapour seemed to momentarily blur her image, her black dirty clothes suddenly changing to white, her hair an almost silvery white with a pale blue sheen to it presenting herself just as Paul had seen her in the desert previously when she had kissed him.

Percival's mouth dropped in awe. The old lady was totally transformed before their very eyes, the blacksmith and his wife looking at the now beautiful woman standing beside Kratos in wonder.

"What magic trickery is this?" Ishmael asked as Taqi stepped forwards and gently touched the forearm of the woman. "Is this real?"

The woman smiled mesmerisingly at Ishmael.

"I am as real as you are. And you, Sir, are a greater soul than you believe yourself to be…and your son says he is very proud of his father," she said softly, her voice no longer the gravely harsh tone Paul was familiar with. She gently placed her hand upon the side of Ishmael's disfigured face as tears instantly welled in his eyes hearing her speak of his son. She looked back at Kratos and he nodded as if to agree to some unspoken question. Gently she placed both her hands on either side of Ishmael's face and stared at him intently as the others watched on utterly captivated. "You were spared death to live in order to help secure and carry forward a legacy. You have done this well…though more is still to pass…and though you thought at times your life was cursed, you are in fact truly blessed. Your son watches you always," she said and closed her eyes. She concentrated and her hands appeared to shine though it was difficult to tell if they did or if it was the sun, but Ishmael's face changed, the grotesque lumps upon his head reducing in size, the out of shape bones across the brow of his forehead reducing too. As Ishmael's eyes widened fully compared with the compressed almost closed way that they had been left after his cliff fall, tears began to fall silently down his cheeks. The woman let out a deep sigh and stepped backwards away from him. All looked at Ishmael as his features were now totally different, his disfigurements gone. He felt his own face in disbelief. Alisha laughed lightly and walked up to him and looked into his eyes. Smiling and happy for him she leant up and kissed him on the cheek.

"You are truly a handsome man," she said softly as Ishmael looked over at the woman just as she opened her eyes.

"Are you an angel of the Lord?" the blacksmith's wife asked, barely able to speak, full of emotion.

Kratos looked at the woman and smiled.

"She has been called that before," he replied and nodded with satisfaction at what she had just done. "Do you honestly believe that what appear to be miracles are confined exclusively to the distant past? 'Tis all but a leap of faith…remember that," Kratos said looking directly at Ishmael.

"Jesus Christ!" Master Douglas said, out of breath, as he staggered into the courtyard then froze when he saw Kratos and the woman stood before the others.

"Douglas, we meet again," Kratos said and bowed his head.

Master Douglas approached slowly, shaking his head and smiling. He looked at Ishmael and had to take a double look and motioned with his fingers around his own face. Ishmael simply smiled back speechless.

"Aye that we do…and I see you have been up to familiar practices," Master Douglas remarked nodding toward Ishmael."

"'Tis not my handiwork this time," Kratos replied and indicated with an open hand toward the woman beside him.

Master Douglas bowed his head toward her as Paul held Alisha close. Looking at her features, he still could not believe she was real and with him. He studied every facet of her face losing himself in her beauty, becoming oblivious to those around him. Her hair blew gently and time itself seemed to slow down. He knew he was tired but everything else around him just stopped. He felt so much for Princess Stephanie, loved her even, but what he was feeling for Alisha was something far more profound and deeper. In silence she gently turned to look at him, her eyes blinking slowly. Her beautiful eyes looked into his and all he wanted to do was hold her, become part of her and never let her go again. She asked him a question but he could not hear her, his eyes wide and fixed upon hers as if in a daze. Only when Kratos gently placed his large hand upon his shoulder did Paul's mind fill with noise again.

"Fear not, Alisha, for he is well enough. 'Tis this city…or what is buried here that affects him so," he explained as she sighed with relief.

"Then best we get him away from here and on our way. We can catch up as we travel," Master Douglas said, everyone else now becoming silent. "What?" he asked, bemused.

"Kratos will not be coming with us," Alisha replied then looked at Kratos sadly.

"Let me guess…after all these years…Jaromir awakens just like you said he would after Jerusalem is wrestled form Christianity?" Master Douglas said, shaking his head. "I never quite believed you all those years ago…but here we are…in the very city you stated and with the very people you said would be present."

Alisha and Paul looked at Master Douglas, puzzled.

"'Twas a story I once told Master Douglas and your fathers many years ago. That they would have a son and daughter accordingly...who would lose each other only to be reunited when the city fell, after which Jaromir will wake and take my place," Kratos explained.

"Yes...and about a disfigured man made anew by his actions," Master Douglas interrupted and looked at Ishmael.

"So if you have always known these things why could you not have fore-warned us so we could have avoided so much pain and turmoil?" Paul asked.

"That negates the whole purpose of life, and besides you did volunteer for this previously. Though in fairness I did assist Niccolas and your fathers in preparing your parchments to guide you," Kratos explained as the woman beside him moved to stand before Paul and Alisha.

"You must all leave, this very day, to fetch your daughter for she grows impatient," she said, her tone of voice gentle but commanding.

"How could you know all these things?" Alisha asked, looking at both of them.

"Paul knows the answer to that already for he was taught whilst he was with me in the deserts. He just has to remember," Kratos answered softly. "And he will."

Abi stepped closer to Kratos and held his arm.

"Tell me this is not the time?...I am not ready to let you go just yet," she asked, clearly sad.

"'Tis I am afraid. This will be our last time together in this world," Kratos answered, his own eyes welling with emotion unlike any of them had ever seen before.

"And you and Master Douglas have known each other all along?" Paul asked as Percival and Taqi looked on.

"We go back a long way," Kratos replied, Master Douglas simply smiling and nodding in agreement. "Now Abi...you know what follows and what must be done so hurry for things have had a nasty habit of late of not going quite as planned."

Abi placed her arms around Kratos, closed her eyes and silently hugged him. Alisha quickly pulled away from Paul and put her arms around them both as best she could, Kratos laughing emotionally as he put his arm around her and Abi. He looked directly at Paul, winked and nodded slightly. He kissed Alisha gently on her forehead then Abi. After a short while he broke away from them both and stood beside the woman who took his hand. Slowly they both stepped backwards a few paces. The blacksmith stared wide mouthed still in awe at what he had witnessed done to Ishmael. Master Douglas laughed lightly himself and rushed to stand behind Alisha and Paul as Percival, Taqi and Ishmael stood beside them. A sudden wind blew up rapidly kicking up a mini whirlwind of dust forcing them to all shield their eyes. Abi shielded hers trying to remain focused upon Kratos as he smiled at her. The wind intensified, Paul having to hold Alisha tightly as they struggled to remain upright. As suddenly as the wind had started it stopped. Percival coughed to clear his throat as Abi stepped forwards through the rapidly settling dust, the blacksmith holding his wife and new baby close. Abi wafted the dust away but both the woman and Kratos were nowhere to be seen. Sadly Abi turned and looked at Paul.

"I always did hate it when he did that," Master Douglas said, half joking, and took a deep breath. "Right you lazy amateurs…best we get organised, we have a right royal little princess to pick up!" he said aloud and smiled, his hands upon his hips as he looked at them all.

Port of La Rochelle, France, Melissae Inn, spring 1191

"What…and they just vanished like that…into thin air?" the Genoese sailor asked disbelievingly.

 1 – 26

"Apparently so," the old man answered and smiled. "But note, Paul had trouble remembering much of what he had learnt during his time in the desert with Kratos. But that was done to him on purpose so that he would recall it all later when he would need to remember."

"So Master Douglas knew him all along?" Peter asked.

"Yes. As you all know, Master Douglas is somewhat unique amongst men. Men like him step into the pages of history to help with the destiny of others," the old man said and smiled as he shook his head as if remembering past events.

"I take it they went straight to that cave place then…to get Ailia and the others," the Templar remarked.

"Yes, though the journey takes two days so they planned to stop over at Belvoir Castle en route for the night. Paul and Abi wasted no time in getting themselves on

the move," the old man replied. "They said an emotional farewell to the blacksmith and his wife and were already on their horses and leaving the city by midday."

"And they could just walk out...despite having just fought a war with Saladin who had beaten them?" the farrier asked.

"Yes as per all the agreements and assurances given. Plus do not forget they had a full Muslim escort so no one was going to stop them."

"What happened to the sword Saladin gave Paul?" Ayleth asked.

The old man looked at Stephan and he lowered his head partly toward him. In silence Stephan stood up, Sarah looking up at him, surprised. Quickly he left the room and they all sat in silence waiting for his return, the Templar and Hospitaller looking at each other in anticipation. After a few moments Stephan returned carrying a long and thin wooden box sealed at the ends and sides. Gently he placed it down upon the table and then stood back. Sarah ran her fingers over the box before looking up at him.

"This has been under our bed since we moved in. You said it was something from your past you would one day explain," she said, looking confused.

"Aye that I did, my woman, therefore you can open it," Stephan replied.

Sarah looked at the old man for permission. He nodded yes and smiled as he folded his arms and sat back in his chair and watched her as she tentatively fumbled with the seals. She kept looking up at Stephan confused as to why he would have such a sword in his possession and what his part in having it would prove to be.

"You told me this was given to you by a queen to safeguard...but I always thought you were jesting me...I mean you, meeting a queen and all," Sarah remarked and coughed, her face turning red with embarrassment as she realised what she had just said. "There is so much I do not know of you," she sighed and broke the last wax seal. She sat down and pulled the wooden box nearer as Simon leant closer to look. Gabirol looked at the old man quizzically as the Templar and Hospitaller stood up to get a better view. Peter and the farrier stood up and made their way around the table to watch as hesitantly Sarah raised the lid. It fell open backwards revealing a red silk inlaid container covered in a gold and yellow silk layer. She looked up at Stephan again and shook her head, puzzled. He simply smiled and motioned for her to continue. Carefully she lifted the end of the golden silk cover and pulled it up and along the length of the box to reveal the ornately decorated sword Saladin had presented Paul in Jerusalem. She shook her head, open mouthed and speechless. She covered her mouth unable to speak as she looked at the beautiful sword.

"Huh, finally something that shuts her up," Simon laughed. She looked at him but laughed back shaking her head.

"How...just how did you come to be in possession of this?" she asked, staring at Stephan.

"It's...it's a long story," Stephan answered and looked across at the old man. "But our friend here knows of it and how."

"Then pray tell how?" Sarah immediately responded and looked at the old man.

"My dear Sarah...I have personally known your husband a great many years," the old man answered, the Templar and Hospitaller looking at Stephan. "He once served alongside me...and when the time came to entrust this sword and Paul's documents, I could think of no other more trustworthy or honourable man than he."

"You served!" the Templar asked and turned fully in to look at him.

"Aye...that I did a while ago now...when I was not so portly," Stephan replied and shook his tummy with his hands.

"So you know who our esteemed guest really is!" the Templar remarked and looked over at the old man.

"Aye Stephan does indeed know me as you must have surely guessed prior to now?" the old man replied.

"'Twas obvious for Stephan held the documents and folder," Gabirol commented aloud as he finished off a sentence before looking up again. "But I am still confused as to who you actually are."

"As I promised at the start, I shall reveal that before this present day is over," the old man replied as Gabirol looked up. "If you have not already guessed!"

Gently Sarah lifted the sword out of the box with both hands and looked at it carefully. After a while she looked at the old man.

"This must be incredibly valuable...and the hands of Saladin himself touched this?" she asked emotionally.

"He did indeed, as did Paul and others I have mentioned. But it has not even begun to be used for what it was meant for," the old man explained and looked at Gabirol.

"You mean...as in the sword to knight those men...and women of the new Order Paul was commissioned to form?" Gabirol asked.

The old man nodded yes silently as all looked at him then back at the sword.

"I sense this story will not end well for why is this Paul not here and why do we now have this sword too?" the Templar asked and took hold of Miriam's hand.

"I want to know about this cave place and if they got their daughter back," Ayleth remarked and covered her mouth as she yawned.

"Then let me explain that Paul sat Alisha upon Adrastos with him and held her tight as they set off out of Jerusalem. Balian had wanted to say goodbye but Paul *could not find him in time so left word he was leaving...Alisha and Paul looking back toward Jerusalem both feeling for Princess Stephanie. But they would see her again soon enough when they were to link up with Count Henry at the bridge."*

"And was it true that Thomas and all his men, along with Tenno and Theodoric, were at the cave place with Ailia?" Peter asked and sat up eager to hear more.

"Aye that is true as I said."

"But what is this cave complex for we have not heard of such places?" the wealthy tailor asked.

"'Tis known as the Cave de Sueth, known in Arabic as Ain al-Habis or Spring of the Hermit's Retreat. It overlooks a gorge from the plateau into the Yarmouk valley where a seasonal stream forms a waterfall down an overhanging cliff known as Araq al-Habis. Sometimes the stream floods as it was doing that year due to all the unseasonal heavy rainfall that fell. The caves in this cliff were originally excavated as a hermitage and monastic retreat long before being used as a military outpost. When the Christian Crusaders first fortified the lower Yarmouk valley in 1105 they called it the Terre de Suethe, from the Arabic word sawad meaning 'cultivated zone', in contrast to the semi-desert further east. That same year a new Crusader outpost on the Golan Heights was destroyed by the ruler of Damascus. Instead of provoking further retaliation by building a castle on the Heights, the then Prince of Galilee garrisoned the naturally defensible site of the Cave de Sueth on the southern side of the river, primarily as an observation post and a peaceful arrangement lasted until 1111 when the cave fell to a force from Damascus. Two years later it reverted to Crusader control but in 1118 it again fell to the Muslims before being almost immediately retaken by King Baldwin of Jerusalem. Thereafter the entire Yarmouk valley was held by the Crusaders, to be used as a base for further raids. Wooden stairs, ladders and walkways link the three levels of caves, being partially removable in an emergency. There is a fourth higher level but the rooms were so low and small they were used for storage only. Now Theodoric chose the site to hide and wait as it was set within a vertical cliff, inaccessible from above or below and reached solely by a precipitous path across the mountainside. The caves have many rooms fully supplied with the necessities of life plus plenty of good water. It was even supplied with livestock stabled in the lower caves, the only drawback was its vulnerability to earthquakes. One section had already fallen away into the deep valley below. External galleries and timber hoardings are placed outside the most important caves in the complex upon the third level. There they have a large water-storage cistern and a series of neatly carved chambers that originally formed part of a monastic retreat."[117]

"It also had a church carved into it. I know this for I was once garrisoned there for a week. If you do not like heights, 'tis an uncomfortable sense to walk the wooden sections," the Templar explained.

"You say it was accessed by a single path...so Turansha would have to cross that first then?" Gabirol asked.

"Yes, the cave is accessed along a single path that runs across the sloping lower part of the cliff. There is a gatehouse and wall at each end of the path so Theodoric certainly chose well...if they had been facing a normal adversary," the old man explained.

"Oh no...Turansha's men were not exactly your normal adversary or typical knights and soldiers though were they?" Peter remarked, both the Templar and Hospitaller shaking their heads in agreement with him.

"Why?" Ayleth asked.

"Because all of Turansha's men were highly trained just like Taqi and the other Ashashin," the old man replied, looking at her directly. "A cliff was no obstacle to them...if anything it would only help." Ayleth looked at Sarah, alarmed. "Kratos's warning could not come soon enough for as Alisha and Paul set out for the Cave de Sueth via Belvoir Castle, Turansha and his men were already planning their assault from both above and below completely bypassing the single pathway."

Miriam covered her mouth, looking shocked, the Templar putting his arm around her as Sarah placed the sword presented by Saladin back into its box heavily.

"I do not wish to hear more bad news," she said aloud and sat back in her chair folding her arms.

Belvoir Castle, Kingdom of Jerusalem, October 3rd 1187

Alisha stepped inside the small lookout room, Paul following her as Master Douglas beckoned them in, the light from his single lanthorn shining brightly. Outside the night air was already cold and Alisha pulled her shawl tighter around her shoulders. Paul frowned at Master Douglas for his choice to rest for the night.

"'Tis as you know the only place I can give you privacy," he explained as Alisha looked around the small room. "Now I suggest rest whilst Stewart and I see that our Muslim escorts are provided for without incident with our other brothers."

"Stephanie was here with you wasn't she?" Alisha asked as she studied the two small beds then turned to face Paul, looking into his eyes. He could not lie to her and Master Douglas's suggestion they stay in the room was painfully inappropriate. "Does this not remind you of her?"

"Of course it does," Paul replied and sighed, looking pained. "We do not have to remain here."

"'Tis just a room," Master Douglas stated bluntly. "When all is said and done...the memories you both have are matters you will one day have time enough to open up about...but none of us presently have the luxury of time nor place other than to accept what we must."

"We thought you were dead, Ali," Paul remarked sadly, sighing heavily.

Master Douglas placed the lanthorn down on the small table and stepped out of the door.

"I suggest you both talk as much as you are able...then rest," he said as he pulled the door shut behind him.

Paul could see the pain in Alisha's eyes, standing in the very room he had made love to Princess Stephanie only adding to her pain. She looked at Paul emotionally. Paul did not know what to say or do. Had Master Douglas done this on purpose? he asked himself. Surely there must be another place they could have slept for the night together?

"Paul," Alisha spoke softly and looked at him as tears welled in her eyes. "You and Stephanie did no wrong. You thought me dead..." She paused as a tear ran down her cheek. "But I lay with Nicholas when you were still very much alive...and this, this pain I feel inside knowing you have been with her...it makes me know and understand more so that pain which I must have put you through...yet...yet you forgave us both. How?" she asked, her lip quivering with emotion as another tear rolled down her face.

"Nicholas was a great noble and honourable man whom I shall always hold dear and in great respect. I can understand what happened between you," he paused. "But in answer to your question fully...'twas easy... because I truly love you," Paul blurted out emotionally, sensing the sheer turmoil still within her even after all that had passed. He looked at her as she started to sob looking at him. "Ali?"

 6– 2

"Please...please just hold me," she cried.

Without hesitation Paul walked up to her and pulled her against himself wrapping his arms around her tightly. He kissed the top of her head as she sobbed in his arms, a tear rolling down his own cheek.

"I buried Nicholas where he requested…in the lemon grove beside the tree where you carved our initials…and our son Arri also lies beside Raja now," Paul explained, Alisha immediately pulling back and looking up at him. "'Twas Kratos." Alisha looked into his eyes, puzzled but also deeply touched. "But next we must fetch our daughter…and do you know that even after I saw with my own eyes that you were both dead, something very deep within me could never quite believe it. I could still feel the presence of you both. Does that make any sense to you?"

"Yes, yes of course it does for despite everything, the only one thing that stopped me ending my own life was I too also had that sense within me. I thought it was perhaps just hope and desperate wishful thinking…but it was more," she replied and then leaned up and pressed her lips against his before he could reply. She held the soft kiss and placed her hand upon his face. When she broke the kiss she looked at him in silence for several long minutes. "I shall never again doubt my instincts and my love…though my love for you I have never doubted," she said softly and rubbed her thumb gently down the barely visible scar on his cheek. 'What other hidden scars must he now carry?' she thought sadly and kissed him again.

৯০ ৫৩

Master Douglas stood away from the door as Sister Lucy came and stood silently beside him. He nodded at her and smiled, his features only just visible in the darkness. He ushered her away from the door and along the battlements passing several night watchmen on guard until they were far enough not to be heard.

"You took a bit of a gamble putting them in there," Sister Lucy whispered.

"Not really. Their situation is rather unique would you not say?"

"Yes most certainly…but still, what if she had stormed out?"

"I knew she would not," Master Douglas answered then looked east to the horizon.

"Is that the way of the cave?"

"Yes…'tis just under a day's ride from here…I just pray we get there before Turansha has had time to assault it."

360

"So do I for there is someone there who if he is not already dead, I am going to most certainly kill him myself."

"Your Theo," Master Douglas said and looked at her as she stared out toward the far horizon. He noticed the defined features of her determined face. "He is a lucky man too...if you were but just ten years younger," he smiled.

Sister Lucy looked at him and frowned hard then slapped him playfully.

"In your dreams, Master D...you could never handle me," she joked and walked away.

Master Douglas laughed to himself as she disappeared down the stairs and out of sight leaving him alone with his thoughts. No word had been received at the castle for over two weeks from the men at the Cave de Sueth so no one had any idea if in fact it had not already fallen.

Cave de Sueth, Kingdom of Jerusalem, October 4th 1187

Under cover of darkness Turansha approached the edge of the cliff with four of his best trained assassins. With just their eyes visible they lay down and crawled silently to the very edge itself so they would not skyline themselves against the backdrop of stars. Turansha had chosen this night knowing there would be no moonlight at all, his spies having watched the cave for three days and confirming Ailia was indeed within the complex. Impatient to finish his task and wipe out the crimson line unaware that Alisha still lived, his men had all studied the small drawing Paul had done just the previous year of her so they knew their target. Turansha had joked how Paul had helped deliver her into his very hands. He knew the entire strength of the vastly reduced garrison and that the very few knights and sergeants could easily be dealt with whilst they slept, Thomas and his men being his only concern as a potential problem. He wanted Ailia's head in a bag by the morning so he could ride back to his main accomplice and prove she was indeed dead. Turansha had fought Paul and Alisha's fathers over many years but now his perseverance would at long last pay off he thought and smirked, then lightly laughed to himself as he crawled back away from the edge. His men knew what they had to do and he had every confidence in their abilities.

A Templar sergeant, his black mantle merging it seemed against the dark wooden wall, leant against it looking out of the small viewing window. A Hospitaller leaned against the opposite side holding a crossbow, laughing lightly just as Thomas approached them trying to walk quietly across the thick wooden floorboards that creaked loudly despite his best efforts. A small candle glow could be seen flickering inside a room set back inside the cave complex. Tenno sat upon a small stool perfectly still almost hidden from sight up against the far end of the cave passageway part meditating and part asleep. Inside the small chamber room Ailia slept soundly, Theodoric asleep in a chair beside her small bunk bed. The night was eerily quiet apart from the sound of Luke snoring very lightly in the opposite chamber. No news had arrived from Jerusalem or any of the other posts but they all knew the city was under attack after two Hospitallers had arrived two days before detailing the full assault by Saladin's forces they had witnessed from the hills. No one knew if the assault had been successful or repelled but Tenno and Thomas were taking no chances and had ordered the main track entrance to be sealed, its doors barricaded and all entry ladders and drawbridge sections raised. Tenno had also been busy preparing naptha grenades mixed with his own explosive mixture he had learnt of whilst in China and several larger shaped pots filled with shards of iron.

"Anything?" Thomas asked the sergeant in a low whisper, who shook his head no silently.

Tenno opened his eyes wide immediately. Quickly he stood up and approached Thomas.

"Stand to!" Tenno said and pulled Thomas around to look at him directly. Thomas frowned puzzled. "Get your men to stand to now…trouble is upon us this hour."

The sergeant stood up straight and laughed at Tenno's suggestion as the Hospitaller pointed toward the pathway being clear below. Thomas shook his head, confused, but as he turned to look at the sergeant, the Hospitaller grabbed his neck with both hands as a black metal throwing knife embedded into his throat. At the same instant an arm swung in from the window and pulled the sergeant back against the wall, another hand flashing into view, the sound of flesh being ripped as a knife stabbed into his throat.

Neither man could speak nor scream out it was so sudden. Tenno grabbed Thomas with his left hand pulling him backwards toward him whilst reaching over his own shoulder and unsheathing his large two handed sword. As the sergeant fell to his knees, the horror evident in his eyes as blood glistened through his fingers, the assassin swung into the room, his feet landing silently upon the floorboards, but Tenno's sword was already coming down toward him. The assassin went to move but Tenno's blow was faster and the blade sliced straight down through the man's head, Tenno continuing the swing downwards and then backwards up and over his shoulder again just as another assassin jumped into view on the right side of the window kicking the Hospitaller aside as he entered. Thomas looked up as he heard many more assassins running along the wooden roof top of the awnings.

"STAND TO!" Thomas screamed loudly as he stepped back and drew his sword.

The assassin threw a knife at Tenno but his sword deflected it, the assassin immediately throwing another one, Tenno knocking that one aside too, the assassin then diving toward him drawing out two blackened short swords from over his shoulders. Tenno raised his sword high to his right and with both hands thrust it downwards to his left in a wide arch, the blade severing straight through the assassins first sword then slicing into his neck, the blade continuing downwards across the man's chest until it finally stopped just short of his right leg. Tenno had almost cut the man in half. Quickly he pulled his sword backwards and kicked the body away. Thomas just stared at the sight of the assassin's cleaved in half body drop to the floor but had to instantly look up as another two assassins swung in through the window and another three ran into view further along the internal walkway running silently toward them.

"Oh no you fucking don't!" Luke called out as he fired off a crossbow bolt from his chamber's doorway just as John knelt beside him and fired off a second bolt. The bolts zipped dangerously close to Thomas and struck the assassin nearest him in the chest and groin.

Tenno ducked as the second assassin swung his sword at him, Tenno then spinning on the floor in a circle swinging his sword around like a scythe cutting the assassin's feet off. No sooner had the man hit the floor landing on his back, than Tenno was already standing up over him and swinging the sword down across his chest instantly splitting wide open his rib cage and through his heart, blood spurting up and out in a large spray of red, most of it covering Tenno. Hand held alarm bells began to ring out within the various rooms and levels of the cave complex accompanied by others shouting 'stand to'. Thomas raised his sword and braced himself for the three assassins running directly at him. A side door opened and two Templars ran out directly into the path of the three running assassins. They collided and fell to the floor in a mass of entangled arms and legs. Thomas and Tenno ran toward them as one of the assassins rolled forwards and jumped to his feet brandishing a sword and naphtha grenade already lit. As the two Templars struggled with the other two assassins, the third ran directly at Tenno and Thomas. Tenno threw his sword to the side and ran at the assassin. As the assassin swung his sword down hard from his right at Tenno, Tenno ducked and dived to the right of the assassin and wrapped his arms around his waist as he passed beneath his sword. As Tenno rolled he flung the assassin to his side with all his might against the outer wooden wall between the main support beams. He threw him with such force he smashed through the lighter wooden panelling and plunged straight out, the grenade exploding just as he went throwing a blast of hot flame and metal shards into the corridor, the majority fortunately hitting the outside but one piece slicing across Thomas's left ear. Even before the flames from the blast had vanished Tenno was already rolling over onto his side and drawing his second short sword. Luke ran up beside Thomas checking the other direction of the walkway as Tenno instantly thrust his sword into the back of the assassin trying to stab the Templar beneath him. The other assassin looked up but the Templar he was fighting seized his lapse in concentration and bare handed pushed his head up and back violently instantly breaking his neck. He pushed him aside and stood up wiping his hands, Thomas and Tenno nodding at him.

Theodoric woke up with a jolt still half asleep as Ailia sat up in bed, her eyes wide having heard the explosion and the alarms being rung. She looked across at Theodoric, fearful. Quickly he stood up and grabbed her lifting her up into his arms. She looked at him, her young face lit up on one side from the single candle.

"Remember what I told you?" Theodoric said quietly. "That if bad men ever came, you must be brave and hide?" Ailia nodded nervously and gulped trying her hardest to indeed be brave but as the room filled with louder screams and explosions beneath them, she looked terrified.

"But my papa will come again…just as he did last time," Ailia whispered. "I know he will."

"My dear child…I cannot lie to you, this time I think not…but we have Tenno, Thomas and his men here to look after us," Theodoric whispered back and held her closer and kissed her on the forehead. He looked over to the small candle flickering away, Paul's sword placed on the side unit next to it. "It looks as though I may have to use something I have not used in a long time," he sighed and moved over to the sword. Ailia's eyes were wide and full of fear sensing the concern within Theodoric. She looked at him intently. "My dear child, fear not for I swear I shall let no harm come to you…upon my very life do you hear?" Silently she nodded yes.

 9 – 3

Two large explosions echoed out across the plateau above immediately followed by two more below. Luke rushed over to the small viewing platform and looked down through the window in time to see the lower ladders and walk ways falling away having been deliberately destroyed to stop anyone getting out.

"Well we ain't going anywhere now?" he called out before Tenno pulled him away from the window just as several arrows zipped through and embedded in the roof above them.

Screams of men being attacked on the two lower levels filtered up through the noise along with the clash of swords, axes and shields.

"Great, we do not know how many assault us and we have no way out and they are already within the complex," Thomas remarked and wiped his face. "But who in hell are these…these fuckers?" he asked and rolled one of the dead assassins over and immediately pulled off his black face mask.

"Language, please," Theodoric said as he stepped into view carrying Ailia as she held onto him tightly. She looked over at them all standing over the dead bodies, the two Templars checking themselves as the rest of Thomas's men ran into view, swords all drawn. They looked a fearsome and scary sight in the light of the two flickering wall mounted torches. "I think you will find they are Turansha's men for this is not the work of Al Rashid."

"'Tis Ailia they seek," Thomas remarked and looked at her. She buried her head into Theodoric's chest and covered her face with her little hands.

"I am sorry, little princess…I did not mean to scare you," he immediately said and rushed over putting his hand upon her little shoulder. "I promise you they will not pass us…they will not get to you."

Theodoric looked at him and both frowned at each other knowing it was a reassuring comment but one he could not really promise.

"There are two levels beneath us and one above. If they have taken out the ladders and bridges then the only way out is by rope. But I suspect they will be coming from inside already for us so our options are limited," Theodoric explained.

"We do not know how many of them there are, so I suggest we hold a defensive line at this level right here. Let them come to us…in whatever number they are," Tenno stated and looked at the men around him, who all nodded silently in agreement. "Thomas, divide your men at either end and I shall take the windows…and time to put to good use those special swords of yours," Tenno ordered, Thomas immediately agreeing and ushering his men along. "Theo, this is one time we cannot afford to argue. You must remain within the furthest chamber that leads to the cistern and stay inside with Ailia whatever happens. Is that understood?"

Theodoric looked down the narrowing corridor behind him cut into the rock that led to the store room with the main water cistern cut beneath it. Slowly he looked back at Tenno. It was a desperate measure as they would be sealed in with no exit.

"'Tis indeed our only option I fear," Theodoric remarked but nodded in agreement just as Thomas's men engaged several more black clad assassins trying to enter the corridor from the left. "Please, my friend…do not let this become a cave of despair."

Tenno leaned forwards and placed his large hand upon Theodoric's shoulder.

"My friend, indeed…we have an army of kings remember…and Paul's sword…they will not pass me…this cave will not become her grave," he said, winked and immediately turned and rushed into the room containing Paul's sword.

"That is the way, my friend…use the sword and use it well I pray," Theodoric whispered and kissed the side of Ailia's head as she held him tightly.

"My papa is coming, I promise you," she remarked seriously.

Theodoric looked into her wide eyes then at the door that led into the store room and water cistern. When he turned to look back, he was in time to see Tenno stepping back through the door holding in both hands Paul's sword before him. Tenno stopped and looked at Theodoric and Ailia. He simply part bowed his head, winked then smiled broadly before immediately turning towards the window platform area.

"After all these years, only now does he smile," Theodoric laughed to himself then quickly carried Ailia toward the end of the carved out corridor and store room.

Theodoric bolted the heavy wooden storeroom door as Ailia stood beside him holding a single ceramic oil lamp, her little hands shaking from both the cold and fear. Quickly Theodoric led her to the far end of the carved out room, just the odd wooden crate and stacked shields placed in the north-eastern corner of the room. A small raised stone built wall with a wooden cover was set just a few feet away from the end wall that led down into the main vaulted cistern beneath them. He brushed the dirt away from the floor and sat Ailia down and then sat beside her. Awkwardly in the restricted position he withdrew his sword and placed it on top of the small cistern access wall that was high enough to hide them behind if they lay down. Ailia tucked in close to him as he wrapped his arm around her for both warmth and comfort. She looked up at him as shouting and noise echoed down the carved corridor.

"Theo," Ailia whispered looking up at him, her eyes wide. "My papa will come I promise you."

Theodoric smiled and stroked her hair.

"My dear child. I told you I would never lie to you and we have already spoken that your father may not even still be alive after the big battle remember?"

"I do but I know he is alive, and he will come for us," she replied softly.

"Ailia, you are so like your mother…but," Theodoric said and paused as another naphtha grenade exploded somewhere in the distance followed by men screaming in agony. "Listen to me, Ailia. There sometimes comes a time when you have to become your own hero. Do you understand me?" he asked and held her little hands. She simply nodded yes in silence.

Outside in the corridor Tenno stood guarding the windows, hearing footsteps above him on the wooden roof. Quickly he looked to his left as Thomas, the two Knights Templar and Luke were slowly but surely being pushed backwards towards him as several black clad assassins engaged them with swords and by throwing small ceramic pots that went off with a small explosion and blinding white flashes. At least they had managed to get hold of the defensive siege shields and were using them to great effect frustrating many of the attempts by the assassin to get past them. To his right, the remainder of Thomas's men were doing the same, struggling against the overwhelming numbers and restricted within the confined spaces. One of the naphtha grenades had started a blaze all along the western awning cutting off any chance of reinforcements from the men below getting up to them. Simon, Mathew and John fell backwards heavily as a larger blast from a set of naphtha grenades exploded up hard against their shields. No sooner had they skidded across the wooden floor on their backs than the assassins vaulted forwards, swords raised ready to rain down their final killer blows upon them when Tenno ran at them letting out a loud scream of rage. He jumped and landed standing over the men on the ground and with one almighty side swipe with Paul's sword, he cut through the first assassin to his right, the blade continuing straight on to the second assassin, the third one trying to jump up against the wall, but the sword continued as Tenno roared with aggression, the blade cutting through the assassin's thighs severing his legs instantly, the sword then carrying on smashing a hole into the wooden wall before Tenno stopped. Blood sprayed everywhere, the assassin with his legs removed instantly rolling onto his back and withdrawing several throwing knives. Despite being in agony he readied a knife to throw at Tenno as he stood himself up with Paul's sword but Simon lunged forwards with his own arming dagger, kicked the assassin's arm away and instantly stabbed his dagger down into his forehead as hard as he could, the assassin's arms shaking in a convulsive spasm as he died. Tenno looked down at one of the other assassins he had cut in half who was still alive, his eyes staring up at him through the slit of his face mask. With one hand, Tenno flung the sword backwards, over and down upon the assassin's head splitting it in two instantly. Tenno quickly pulled the sword backwards as he stood up looking toward the approaching fire then to the roof as he heard more footsteps. Two more assassins jumped through the open window but Tenno dived at them thrusting the sword at the nearest one to him. The sword went straight through his stomach and pinned him to the wall. With his left hand, Tenno grabbed the other assassin by the top of his mask and smashed his head back against the window ledge, the man's skull fracturing with a sickening crack sound. Tenno withdrew the sword and as the assassin held his hands across himself, blood seeping through his black outfit, he looked at Tenno stunned. Tenno stepped directly in front of him and head butted him hard forcing him to topple backwards against the window ledge, the momentum and force of the hit sending him over and out. The assassin did not scream as he fell to his death below. Tenno looked to his left to see Thomas on his knees as sword hit after sword blow rained down upon his shield, one of the Templars already dead pushed up against the wall. Without hesitation Tenno ran toward him and Luke.

"Get down!" Tenno shouted as he ran directly at them.

The assassins looked up briefly in time to see Tenno swing the sword in a circular motion around his head and jump upon the shield covering Thomas. In one lightning fast move, Tenno swung the sword from behind his right shoulder all the way around to behind his left shoulder, the three assassins' heads being sliced off, one having half his shoulder and raised arm also taken off. As Tenno froze, the dead assassins' bodies fell, Thomas, Luke and the surviving Templar looked up at him, stunned. They were all covered in blood as were the floor, walls and parts of the roof.

"Jesus Holy Christ," the Templar remarked as he stood himself up.

"No...just Tenno," Tenno replied and part bowed his head at him and stepped off of Thomas and immediately offered him his hand to help him up.

"'Tis a pity we do not have more of those," Thomas said looking at the blood soaked sword in Tenno's hand. "We must douse that fire or the likes of this lot will count for nothing," he continued and pointed at the flames Simon was already trying to knock out.

"'Tis a wondrous weapon to wield for sure," Tenno stated. "But Thomas... the cistern...are you certain there is no other way into it or out?"

"Absolutely. The only way in or out is through that door," Thomas answered and pointed to the store room door. "There is a tiny inflow and overflow drain but 'tis far too small for any of us. So unless there are some dwarf assassins amongst them, then Theo and Ailia remain safe inside... for now at least."

"Keep away from the openings!" Tenno called out as Thomas then quickly ran across the walkway towards Simon and the others to help put out the fire. Thomas ducked and moved to the furthest side of the walkway as he passed the openings. Tenno stood up straight and looked at the blade of the sword carefully. It appeared to sparkle, he thought, with a shimmering sheen of silver and blue as the blood ran from it, not sticking like it usually did on other swords. He shook his head in amazement at the lightness and lethal effectiveness of it unlike any other sword he had ever seen or held and could feel the energy running though his entire body from the handle as it pulsed in rhythm to his own heartbeat.

The Templar started to use the dead bodies of the assassins and his dead friend as a barricade across the walkway as Luke moved the shields in preparation for the next assault as they could all hear movement below them. There were no more shouts or clashes of swords so they all knew the men below them had obviously been completely overwhelmed by the assassins. As Simon and Mathew began to win the fight with the fire, a voice called out from below asking for Theodoric to respond.

"I am below you on the opposite side of the ravine. My men will not open fire if you approach the window to negotiate," the assassin shouted up.

Tenno moved to stand beside the viewing window as Thomas moved into position on the other side.

"We can hear you well enough without having to see you. What do you want?" Thomas yelled back as Simon and Mathew put out the last of the flames behind him.

"My master will spare all of your lives if you simply hand us the little girl named Ailia," the assassin replied.

1 – 43

"And where is your master now?" Tenno shouted back.

"Not far is all you need to know. Hand us the girl and you have his word you will be spared. All of your other men, save these few prisoners, are now dead...Refuse and you will perish. Our numbers are too many. You cannot win this and we have more men arriving by the hour." Tenno looked down through a small arrow firing slot and could just make out the assassin stood upright whilst other assassins stood on either side of him with knights forced to kneel in front of them, knives being held to their throats made visible by other assassins holding flaming torches. Several assassin archers stood by with naphtha prepared arrows. "If you do not agree we shall burn you out first, then kill you all."

"You speak our language pretty good for an assassin of Turansha's," Thomas called down.

"That is because I was once a knight of Tyre before I saw the hopelessness of our Christian position," the assassin replied and paused. "I must have your answer now or this will be done to you."

Tenno and Thomas looked down as the captured knights had their heads pulled back, their throats immediately slashed and then kicked forwards so they fell headfirst into the ravine below. Thomas looked at Tenno as anger rose within him. All of Thomas's men and the Templar stood in silence shaking their heads no just as Theodoric stepped into view holding Tenno's bow and quiver of arrows with Ailia by his side.

"We heard him call my name and Ailia's and I am wasted in there...so here, they think they are out of our range...send them our answer," Theodoric said and handed Tenno the bow and arrows. "I will keep Ailia safe so long as you keep them delayed."

Ailia looked at the men all staring at her as Tenno took four arrows out and set one in the bow. Immediately he pulled it taught, the tension in the string creaking as he stepped up to the arrow shooting slot, lifted the cover completely and aimed it at the assassin stood smugly. Tenno steadied his aim as he breathed out, he loosed off the arrow, the second it had gone he was charging a second arrow and aimed it at the other assassin nearby holding the flaming torch. No sooner had that arrow loosed off than Tenno charged a third arrow and loosed it off aimed at the other assassin with the second torch.

"There is our answer," Tenno stated as he looked down in time to see his first arrow strike the standing assassin just above his chest, then his second arrow hit the first torch bearer in the forehead and his third arrow slam into the third assassin's arm causing him to spin, his torch lighting a pile of prepared naphtha arrows which instantly burst into flames catching his clothing as he went. As the flames began to engulf him he spun around frantically and slipped sideways screaming as he fell into the ravine. Tenno ducked back out of the way as a stream of ordinary arrows and crossbow bolts instantly zipped through the larger open viewing window and imbedded in the roof as others struck the wooden wall outside. "He should have stayed in Tyre!"

"Theo," Ailia said hesitantly and clenched his hand tighter.

"Here they come again...get her away," Tenno called out and readied himself grabbing one of the shields in his left hand as many assassins started to run towards him along the walkway.

Thomas and his men immediately picked up shields and positioned themselves in a semicircle in front of Theo and Ailia.

"Templar, I know not your name but I pray you lock yourself, Theo and Ailia in the store now and do not come out under any circumstances do you hear...protect them with your life," Thomas said as he started to push the Templar back towards the store door, Theodoric picking Ailia up and running with her down the cramped passageway. The Templar knight looked at Thomas, momentarily confused, until Thomas pushed him hard. "Anything that comes through the door, you kill it do you hear!"

Hesitantly the Templar nodded and backed his way toward the door as Theodoric beckoned him to hurry just as Tenno started to engage the assassins now jumping all around him, Thomas and his men moving forward as one, their shields linked together as they had done a hundred times before in close quarter combat.

As soon as the Templar had entered the store room, Theodoric slammed the door shut and pulled the wooden locking bolt down hard then edged his arming dagger into the latch as it was only meant to be locked from the other side. Ailia ran to the other side of the cistern opening and quickly sat down against the small stone wall pulling her knees up to her chest, her eyes wide with fear but trying her hardest to remain brave, the single ceramic oil lamp the only light visible. Yells outside the door mixed with the clash of swords upon swords and shields and the sounds of men grunting, heaving and the groans of men dying as metal met flesh.

"Papa," Ailia whispered and clasped her hands together in prayer and looked up as Theodoric jumped down beside her, his sword held at the ready.

Chapter 84
The Final Hour!

Paul lay propped up against the bed headrest while Alisha lay upon his chest asleep. Both were still dressed with just a single blanket pulled up over them having fallen asleep exhausted. Paul opened his eyes instantly alarmed.

"Ailia!" he said, waking Alisha. She rubbed her eyes as she pushed herself up, the blanket falling to her waist. "Ali...'tis Ailia...we must head for the cave now...we cannot wait until sunrise!" he said, alarmed, and sat up fully.

"What...how do you know?" she asked, confused, but her heart already beating fast with concern at his words. "Paul, you are scaring me. What do you know?"

"I heard her call for me."

"My darling, 'twas a dream I am sure," Alisha said softly and placed her hand upon his cheek and looked into his eyes. She suddenly shuddered as a cold chill ran all over her and the hairs on the back of her neck stood up on end as she felt a presence. Slowly she looked around but no one was there. She paused as she tried to make sense of the feeling she was experiencing then looked back at Paul. "I think you are right...I sense something too."

Quickly Paul swung his legs around to stand up but as Alisha went to stand, she stopped and held her hands across her belly and took a sharp intake of breath. Paul looked at her, concerned, as she looked up at him.

"What...what is it?" Paul asked as he knelt beside her. "You look very pale suddenly."

"Paul...'tis because I am with child again," she said emotionally and searched his eyes immediately in the low light of the room. "Before you ask, it is most certainly yours...from our time in Jerusalem before we left and became separated," she said nervously and sighed with sadness knowing Princess Stephanie had just lost her baby...Paul's baby! She wondered if she should tell him about that but she had sworn not to, at least not for now.

Paul let out a light gasp and shook his head with surprise. He took hold of her hands in his and pulled them to his chest. He could sense sadness in her voice and see it in her face.

"Do you not want this child for I see pain in your eyes?"

Alisha shook her head yes fast and pulled her hands free immediately wrapping her arms around him and pulling him close.

"More than ever, I want this child of ours. A sister for Ailia…my sadness is for Arri for I still miss him every single hour of every single day," she said softly and hugged him.

"Sister…it may be a brother," Paul replied and kissed the side of her head.

"'Tis a girl…I sense her already."

"Then let us waste no more time," Paul said and stood up and held her hand. "Come on…let us go and get our daughter back."

Cave de Sueth, Kingdom of Jerusalem, October 4th 1187

Thomas held the large defensive shield outward as he knelt and fired off the crossbow at point blank range into the assassin's groin that was kicking the shield just as Luke thrust his sword into the face of another. Tenno was to their left kicking assassins and wielding the sword slicing into them one after another as they pushed their way ever closer in greater seemingly endless numbers along the internal walkway. Tenno let out a loud roar as he screamed and started to chop downwards, swinging his sword back up over his shoulder then chopping it down again, each time pushing and stepping forwards and every time cutting through an assassin until he had to step over them. Luke noticed one was injured but still alive on the floor behind Tenno as he started to push the assassins backwards. Luke grabbed an axe beside him and swung it down hard between the assassin's shoulders hard killing him instantly. With unbelievable speed Tenno kept swinging the sword until he reached a turn in the walkway that led to a set of stairs. He cut two men almost in half where they stood just as another stepped up the ladder, looked up at Tenno and only had time to blink before Tenno sliced off his head and kicked his body back down the ladder hard onto the others trying to climb up. As several assassins fell upon each other, two more aimed their crossbows at Tenno as he swung the sword down shattering the ladder's top rungs. He then cut into the securing rig and pushed the remainder of the ladder away. He just stepped back when two bolts zipped through the air and struck him in the chest and shoulder but Tenno did not even flinch as he raised the sword again and roared down at them sounding like a wild bear. He snapped off the bolts and threw the ends down at the assassins looking up at him, his tall figure filling the entrance as flames from the wall mounted torches behind silhouetted him. Small black grappling hooks were thrown up, two locking behind the large wooden support beams and immediately the ropes were pulled taut. Tenno had to step into view to slice at the ropes but as soon as he did, more grappling hooks started to be thrown up at various sections and beams. Tenno stared down into the gloom below and tried to see how many more assassins there were just as another bolt struck him in the knee. He grimaced sensing it lock his knee. In pain he swung himself back against the wall and looked toward Thomas as more assassins were engaged with the rest of his men at the other end of the walkway. He staggered as he half walked and half hopped his way back to them. He sheathed the sword and started to pile the dead bodies across the carved out passageway that led to Theodoric and Ailia, Luke immediately helping him move them not even realising Tenno had been shot three times already. Once Tenno and Luke had formed a wall of bodies they rushed over to help Thomas and the others. In the confined space it was hard to swing a sword fully especially as they had all set up the defensive shields but it became clear to Tenno and Thomas that his men were slowly but surely each receiving injuries. Simon turned to face Thomas and just as he went to shout, a blackened straight sword blade flashed between the gap in his damaged shield and was thrust directly into his mouth instantly bursting out the back of his skull. His eyes widened without him making a sound, and just as quickly the blade withdrew, Simon falling backwards dead his eyes now fixed wide open staring upwards. His shield went down with him and instantly other assassins jumped through, Tenno immediately pulling his sword out and across sideways into the first assassin's right leg taking it off in one move. The assassin rolled over and Thomas thrust his sword directly down into his head, the assassin's body shaking in a convulsive fit of death. Tenno threw himself bodily into the space between the large defensive shields and started to swing his sword around in a frenzy with lightning speed that Thomas could hardly see where his arms and sword were in the semi darkness. Thomas looked on in awe as the large presence of Tenno just kept moving forwards cutting assassins down like a farmer cuts wheat, he thought. The scene was surreal as limbs were hacked off, chests and stomachs ripped open, and yet no screams from the well trained assassins. Never in all his years as a knight had Thomas seen anything like it as Tenno pushed or killed the assassins as they rushed toward him. Luke and the others looked up over their shields amazed, mouths wide open as they watched Tenno clear the entire walkway, the last assassin to step into view being sliced straight down the middle through his head and out of his groin. Only then did Tenno pause to catch his breath, Paul's sword sending out what sounded like a hum.

"Thank the Lord he is on our side," Thomas said, relieved, and laughed anxiously before his eyes fell to Simon dead at his feet.

Tenno turned around and started to drag dead bodies back with him for the defensive wall. Only as he dragged two past did Thomas see that Tenno was injured, Tenno simply shaking his head no slightly.

 1 – 48

"There are even more below us…and more above. They will be coming back," Tenno remarked and threw the bodies down. "The sun will be up soon so they will not wait around. I hope you are all ready to die this hour?"

Thomas looked at his men as they listened intently.

"We have all been ready to die for a very long time, my friend. This day… this very hour, this is our final hour, but it is the hour we have trained and waited our entire lives for. This…truly this final hour, my friend, is what the good Lord put us here for," Thomas said emotionally as his men all stood up and nodded in agreement.

"I die in exalted and honoured company," Tenno replied and bowed his head slightly toward them. "You hold this walkway for as long as you can… and I will not yield and I will not let them reach Ailia…this is my solemn vow to you all."

"Well, men, we have oft practised our final song of death…that hour is upon us. Let us show these bastards we will be taking a lot of them with us," Thomas said, took a deep breath and looked at each of them in turn, their faces bloodied, their uniforms ripped and covered in so much blood no one could tell their colour.

Luke stepped forwards.

"We always knew we had a purpose...we found it in Alisha and Paul and wherever they are, if even alive, the Grail lives. 'Tis real...she sits in there," he said emotionally and wiped his face quickly. "We will not fail her."

℘℘

Turansha looked to the horizon and saw the first glimmer of sunlight breaking.

"How much naphtha do we still have?" he asked as he peered down the cliff face. "Do we have enough to burn them out?"

"Yes, My Lord," his second in command answered.

"Then prepare to pour it if the next assault fails...even if our own men are still inside. We have to eradicate that line forever no matter the cost...is that understood?" Turansha asked and looked at his second in command.

"My Lord...can we not wait until the remainder of our forces arrive. There will be three times the number of men?"

"NO! No we cannot wait. There is no way they can hold out and they have no way of escaping neither," Turansha sneered. "Make sure all those about to attack know what will happen if they do not succeed this time."

℘℘

Tenno stood behind Thomas as he placed his men in a line across the entrance to the carved out passageway. They had piled as many of the dead as they could in front of them as a wall and readied their large defensive shields.

"Hold this line while I prepare some items...in case they do pass us," Tenno said and quickly ran into one of the small side rooms he had used to prepare his mixture with naphtha and other chemicals.

Thomas looked over his shoulder toward the small door of the cistern room and saw the Templar peering through the small peep hole square. He nodded silently. Inside, Theodoric pulled Ailia closer to him as they lay down lower upon the dusty floor and placed the ceramic oil candle nearer to his side. Tenno had placed several naphtha grenades ready for use but he would need the candle to light them if Turansha's men breached the door.

℘℘

Dust kicked up all around Abi as she rode her horse hard to catch Alisha and Paul riding Adrastos flat out. It was dangerous to ride at such a pace in the darkness, their escort falling behind them despite Master Douglas and his attempts to keep them all together. Eventually she managed to draw up alongside and had to lean across and physically slap Paul's shoulder to get his attention.

"Ease up!" she shouted as both Alisha and Paul looked over at her. Paul eased back the pace. "You are separating from the others...you must slow down," she explained, out of breath, as Percival and Stewart rode up behind her, Master Douglas, Ishmael and the remainder of the escort some several hundred feet behind them. "You cannot go ahead alone."

Paul slowed Adrastos to a trot as he held Alisha close with his left arm around her waist.

"We do not have the luxury of taking this route slowly," Paul replied and pointed ahead as the sun was already beginning to break across the horizon. "Surely you can sense it too?"

Suddenly Sister Lucy rode up alongside Abi riding as fast as she could manage her horse, Alisha letting out a nervous laugh seeing her in full flight.

"If she cannot...I certainly can...come on!" she shouted and galloped ahead, Abi shaking her head disapprovingly but immediately riding off after her.

Paul held Alisha tighter and pushed Adrastos onward faster.

೫ CನR

A large cacophony of noise went up as many assassins ran into view, this time all screaming, from both sides of the walkway just as more swung down on ropes and jumped through the main viewing platform opening. Thomas and his men all fired off a volley of crossbow bolts striking several of the assassins, but as they fell dead or injured, the other assassins behind jumped over them or pushed them aside as they rapidly approached launching throwing stars and knives whilst wielding their swords. Many thudded into the large defensive shields but a few hit their mark and embedded in Thomas's men, the tips piercing the chain mail on their arms or legs...and they were tipped with poisons. Tenno steadied his injured knee and readied himself raising Paul's sword. The Templar inside the cistern room slammed the viewing cover shut on the door and looked back at Theodoric, alarmed. As the assassins ran and jumped up upon the shields, Thomas, Luke and Mathew had to stand up in order to strike them down with their swords, Luke taking a knife in his shoulder as a poisoned star skimmed across his temple. He fell backwards dazed but immediately jumped back up on his feet as Thomas and the others were slowly pushed backwards toward the door. Tenno flexed his hands around Paul's sword sensing the energy and power surging through it and into him. Thomas looked back at him quickly as Tenno held the sword forward then roared loudly once again sounding like a bear, hardly human. As Tenno stepped forwards, Thomas pulled Mathew down and pushed Michael over forcing a gap in their line, Tenno instantly stepping into the breach swinging the sword violently around, the blade slicing through flesh and bone of the assassins unfortunate enough to be in its way. Tenno elbowed another assassin in the face hard to his left, then thrust his right elbow upwards into the side of the head of another with such force they all heard his skull crack. Swinging the sword down violently and up again then in a circular motion, assassins fell left and right mortally injured. Tenno pushed himself forwards directly into the middle of the group and despite taking wounds from knives and sword blows he continued to stand upright swinging the sword around with devastating effect. Thomas and his men looked on in awe again as he felled assassin after assassin until he eventually reached the far end of the walkway leaving a trail of dead and wounded assassins behind him in his path. He stopped and froze as he composed himself silhouetted against the rapidly rising sun light coming through the viewing opening. Mathew jumped forward thrusting his sword into the back of an injured assassin who was trying to move as Thomas thrust his arming dagger into the base of another assassin's neck killing him instantly. Tenno concentrated and tried to override the pain he was in from many injuries all over his body, his body armour pierced and shredded from the razor sharp blades used against him. Tenno sniffed, his nostrils being filled with the familiar scent of liquid naphtha. His eyes focused upon a trickle as it started to flow down from the roof above him on his right hand side. He turned and looked at Thomas.

"You must move all these dead across here...it will stem the flow from reaching us...for a while at least...and be ready to scream loudly to empty your lungs of air when the fire ball comes," Tenno stated through gritted teeth, trying to control his breathing, his head beginning to swim as dizziness from his injuries and the poison now in his veins started to take effect.

Thomas immediately stood up and started to drag bodies over to where he had pointed. Michael and Luke were also beginning to feel dizzy from the effects of the poisons now coursing through their veins. They all looked at each other knowing this was indeed their final hour but they would not yield. There was always hope. The Templar behind the door realising the silence behind the door and hearing only Tenno, opened the peep hole cover to see what was happening.

"Not unto us, O Lord, not unto us, but unto Thee give the glory," he whispered seeing the sight outside, a pool of blood seeping beneath the door into the room like a black oily puddle of death around his feet.

ಬಿ ೧೩

Paul could see smoke rising above the ravine at the location of the cave entrance, the sun rising rapidly now but the shadows of the cliff sides still covering the lower parts in semi darkness. As he pulled Adrastos up a short distance from the main entrance tower, he immediately saw that it was partially destroyed, little black dots just visible, the heads of assassins looking over toward him and Alisha. Abi pulled up hard beside him, her eyes searching the wooden structures above, smoke bellowing out of the far end. It was eerily silent. Paul's eyes were alerted to movement on the top of the cliff and saw the silhouettes of men pouring oil and naphtha down the cliff face onto the awnings below.

"Oh dear Lord no...Paul!" Alisha gasped in alarm, realising what was happening. She looked at Paul, her eyes filled with terror as he quickly dismounted.

"Dismount Ali," Paul said and physically half lifted her down from Adrastos.

"Paul...you cannot pass and get in there. Look, they have deliberately collapsed the entrance tower and it is manned and the single path yonder is likewise blocked," Abi explained as she rapidly studied the scene before them.

Taqi rode up fast and pulled up hard with Ishmael by his side.

"Master Douglas will be with us shortly with the others...do not do anything until they arrive," Taqi said as he steadied his horse.

"We do not have the time," Paul replied just as the sound of Thomas's men singing began to echo out into the ravine. Alisha looked at Paul, puzzled, and shook her head. Paul looked at Abi knowing she knew what they were singing.

Taqi looked at the cliff to see if there was another way he could get into the complex as the single path was blocked and all the bridge sections and ladders appeared to have been destroyed too. Taqi's colleague pulled up hard and dismounted behind them. Paul quickly unpacked several silk sheets from his travel roll. As he unfurled them they were all attached to flexible sticks.

"What are you doing?" Alisha asked, concerned, as he started to fasten them all over Adrastos until he was covered in many silk flags.

"That singing...'tis Thomas and his men," Paul answered and checked the straps upon Adrastos. "'Tis their much practised song of death. I must get to them and Ailia...across that if I must," he stated and pointed toward the blocked pathway.

"'Tis impossible," Abi exclaimed, alarmed, looking at him surprised.

 1 – 36

Paul pulled Alisha close, looked her in the eyes then kissed her.

"Our daughter awaits and needs me now," he explained and quickly mounted Adrastos before she had time to respond. He pulled up the reins into one hand then took out the sword Saladin had presented him with. He looked over at Abi as he raised the sword. "Impossible yes...but very necessary," he replied and instantly rode forward fast, Alisha swinging around to stop him too late.

Taqi shook his head as Abi went to ride after him but he grabbed her arm tightly.

"I can find another way in if you will follow me. 'Tis what I do best," he said as Alisha looked at both of them, her face etched with desperation just as Master Douglas and the others rode up the pathway toward them.

Paul pulled up fifty yards short of the partially collapsed first gate tower. He could see many assassins already aiming crossbows and arrows in his direction but he was out of their range. He looked up to see several more assassins at the top of the cliff starting to pour more oil. Suddenly one of the men was struck by one of Abi's large arrows throwing him backwards dead. Paul quickly looked over his shoulder to see Abi upon her horse charge another arrow as Master Douglas immediately rode past Alisha and toward Paul.

"Adrastos, my friend, I know you understand me as you always have… but right now, this minute I need you to get me across that ravine," Paul said as he rested his face against the side of Adrastos and patted him. "Ailia is in great danger and I must reach her do you understand?"

Adrastos snorted and shook his head as if to imply he did indeed know what Paul had asked. He snorted again as Paul sat up straight and readied himself. Taking the reins in his left hand and raising his sword in his right he took a deep breath.

"Paul…NO!" Alisha called out, her voice carrying across the ravine.

Paul did not look back but focused upon the collapsed tower section where it joined the wall. It was five stone courses high but if he could reach it, he knew Adrastos could jump it especially if he ran up the raised earthen ridge on the left of the approach.

"Dear Lord and by all the names of every sword of legend and myth, let me reach my daughter to protect her even if I should die afterwards…'tis all I pray," Paul said aloud to himself.

Turansha heard Alisha's call as it echoed out and he moved carefully to the edge to look down. He could see Paul upon Adrastos and Alisha some distance away already running towards him. He grinned menacingly as he rubbed his beard.

"Oh good…so they do still live, but not for much longer," he said as another arrow from Abi zipped past just missing him and striking one of his men behind him. "And Abi too. This I could not have asked for," he grinned and stood up straight and nodded to the two men holding flaming torches. "Do it."

The two men threw their torches forwards into two groves hastily dug and filled with oil. Instantly the flames ignited the path of the oil and it flashed across the ground, Turansha laughing.

Paul looked up to see two large gouts of orange flame ignite down the side of the cliff face in two paths of burning oil. His eyes widened when he saw the flames rapidly enter the top section of the western awnings, his heart stopping for a moment. The sound of Thomas and his men singing was drifting down toward him when suddenly all of the oil and naphtha that had been poured earlier ignited in a massive thunderous ball of rolling flame as it shot out through the window sections and viewing platforms throwing out large shards of splintered wood and bodies. The shock wave hit Paul a moment later causing Adrastos to rear up slightly. Alisha put her hands to her mouth and froze, shocked, as debris and flame rained down from the partially destroyed awning. Inside the carved out passage-way leading to the cistern room, Thomas and his men threw themselves upon their stomachs pulling the shields over themselves as a ball of flame filled their exit and came rolling toward them. They all screamed loudly so the fire would not suck out the air from their lungs hoping it would pass over them quickly, but Tenno, his left knee still locked only managed to bend half way down and pick up a shield. He looked up just in time to see the flames flash over the tops of Thomas and the others with such force it carried many of the dead assassins with it that had made up the wall. He braced himself and pushed his face hard against the shield as the flames hit him full force throwing him against the door, smashing it and hurling him backwards into the room, the Templar jumping aside and covering himself as he dived to the far corner. Theodoric rolled completely over Ailia and screamed as she let out a loud scream.

Paul heard her faint scream, his blood running cold as Alisha stood frozen to the spot as Master Douglas rode past her at full gallop.

"By the swords of Durandel, Gilgano and Excalibur I beg you all for your strength this day to run through this one," Paul said aloud, pointed his sword forward and started to ride, the silk sheets fluttering away as Adrastos picked up speed heading straight for the gate tower.

Alisha gulped hard nearly being sick as Stewart and the Muslim escort rode past her, Sister Lucy pulling up fast and jumping down beside her. Alisha waved her hand wanting Master Douglas to move as he was now obscuring her view of Paul as he gained speed. She held her breath as Paul drew nearer the gate house. He lowered himself behind Adrastos' head as crossbow bolts and arrows came straight at them, several hitting the silk sheets side on and deflecting them, some literally having the punch and power taken out of them as they hit into sheets. Paul half smiled seeing that Tenno's suggestion actually worked. Just as he thought that, a cross-bow bolt sliced straight through a sheet and clipped his shoulder chain mail. He gritted his teeth harder as he approached the gate tower and steered Adrastos up onto the raised earth section. All went quiet except for the beating of his heart echoing in his head and the muffled thuds of

Adrastos's hooves as they hit the grass. He held his sword forward as he galloped, more crossbow bolts zipping past, some deflecting off the sheets still. He steered Adrastos toward the lowest section of the collapsed wall, an assassin standing up aiming a crossbow at them. Paul gripped the reins tighter in his left hand and braced his legs ready for the jump. As Adrastos raised his front legs and launched himself into the air upwards, he struck the assassin knocking him down. Alisha gasped as she saw Paul stand high upon Adrastos raising his sword as they cleared the wall in full view. Quickly Alisha pulled away from Sister Lucy and ran over to her horse and mounted him. Sister Lucy put her hand up to stop her as she pulled the horse around to face the cave complex.

"We either get my family back this day or we die together for I cannot exist without them again…and I shall not!" Alisha shouted down and instantly set off after the others leaving Sister Lucy stood alone and utterly flabbergasted.

Turansha saw Alisha mount the horse below and laughed to himself.

"That is it…ride to your death at long last," he said smiling as nearly fifty of his men ran forward to the edge of the cliff face. "This time we will not fail. Go!" he ordered and immediately his men lifted ropes that had been secured in place and all along the edge of the cliff they started to descend rapidly.

Abi stopped Taqi as they ran toward the eastern section of the outcrop of rock before the ravine curved left toward the gate tower in time to see Paul and Adrastos land heavily on the pathway on the other side having just cleared it, but Abi pointed upwards at the many assassins now descending rapidly towards what was left of the awnings and enclosed wooden walkways. Immediately she pulled her bow over her shoulder and charged it with an arrow. Taqi watched as she pulled it back as far as it could go and loosed it off, then instantly charged another arrow. Taqi did not wait to see where her next shot went as he hurried off and started to climb up the sheer cliff face using the smallest of protrusions to grab hold of, quickly followed by his colleague who ran to join him.

Paul steadied Adrastos as he steered him toward the second gate tower, arrows and crossbow bolts now being fired at him from both ends of the narrow path. The far end gate tower had not been so badly damaged so the wall section was even higher to jump. An assassin jumped up just to their right side but Paul instantly swung his sword down hard catching the man across his shoulder and neck spinning him around as the blade cut into him and then out with a red splash of blood. Paul concentrated upon the wall ahead as they sped ever closer, the many crossbow bolts appearing to fly almost slowly toward them, only zipping past at the last minute or stopping and dropping as they hit the silk flags. Adrastos snorted and struggled as Paul pushed him harder and faster.

Master Douglas raced his horse and prepared to jump the first gate tower but just as he was about to, his horse screamed out in pain and reared up as several crossbow bolts thudded into its chest and front legs nearly throwing him off. The horse came to a rapid stop then collapsed forwards struggling to breathe, then it fell completely, Master Douglas rolling off and onto his side, his horse now dead. He glanced back in time to see the others coming but he realised immediately they too would all be cut down in the exact same manner. He dived behind the body of his dead horse and started waving frantically for them to turn back as a wall of arrows and bolts flashed over his head toward them just falling short, but a second volley would not miss if they kept advancing. Stewart pulled up his horse and raised his hand for the others to stop. As dust kicked up around them, Stewart looked up anxiously as he saw the assassins dropping onto the roof. Suddenly Alisha rode past at full gallop. Master Douglas stood up to try and stop her but she veered past him and continued just as the men at the gate tower aimed at her. She gritted her teeth and lowered herself as low as she could get, fired up with anger and desperation for both Paul and Ailia. She ducked and veered as bolts and arrows zipped past her, Sister Lucy now running across the open field toward Stewart and the escort as Ishmael and Percival moved to the front ready to follow Alisha. Abi saw Alisha out of the corner of her eye and quickly turned her aim to one of the crossbow assassins on the wall. Her bow creaked as she pulled the arrow back so fast and far then loosed off. Alisha could see the crossbow aimed directly at her as she was almost upon the wall but she was now committed. Abi's large arrow flashed across her vision slamming into the crossbow assassin just as he was about to fire cutting straight through his side knocking him down. Alisha reared up her horse, its hind hooves clipping the stone of the wall as she cleared it. Another assassin turned to aim at her as she past but was instantly hit by another large arrow from Abi.

The cistern room was full of smoke and dust as Theodoric looked up wiping his eyes still cowering over Ailia as she coughed beneath him.

Light shone through the small door entrance flickering as smoke wafted back and forth across it. He saw the outline of several assassins moving toward him down the corridor. He could not see who else had survived if any. He clasped his sword tightly and stood up. Ailia looked up at him her face covered in dirt and he put his finger to his mouth for her to be silent. 'Stay here' he mouthed silently and then quickly moved around the cistern wall preparing himself to fight the assassins. If he could reach the door it would be easier to hit them, he thought. As he stepped closer, a hand grabbed his foot. His heart almost stopping until he saw it was Tenno as he looked up at him. Theodoric grabbed his forearm and helped him to stand. His face was blackened and singed and he could see that he had many injuries. Tenno raised Paul's sword, which was making an audible hum both could hear. They both looked toward the door entrance as Thomas moaned and rolled into view, his tunic still smouldering and his hair also badly singed. Quickly Theodoric jumped over to him and pulled him further into the room just as more assassins appeared. Thomas coughed and struggled to stand up unable to breathe properly, his lungs full of dust and blood. Small fires lit up the carved out corridor, the smell of burning flesh hanging heavy in the air. Sections of floorboard were burning away as Thomas grasped his sword with both hands.

"The bastards have killed all my men…but worse…they have ruined my hair," he said half joking morbidly then coughed heavily and nearly fell backwards, Tenno just holding him up in time. "My men…all of them," he sighed shaking his head, his eyes wide in disbelief.

"My friend…Ailia. Watch over her whilst we deal with these. If we do not prevail, end it quickly for her," Tenno said in all seriousness, Thomas looking at him horrified then at Theodoric.

"You must…plus you will get in our way," Theodoric remarked and forced a smile then winked. "Come on, my friend."

   2–14

Paul held on tightly as Adrastos snorted loudly, then using all of his power, speed and strength, launched himself up and over the second gate tower wall. Two assassins stood up directly in their way but Adrastos smashed into them, one of them slicing his sword across him just as his front legs hit the wall hard not being high enough to clear it fully and with the two assassins slowing his jump, Adrastos fell on top of the wall itself, throwing Paul off forwards. As Adrastos rolled down the other side of the wall onto his back then side, Paul was thrown several feet managing to roll over on his shoulder before thumping into a section of the path wall and stopping. With his wrists badly grazed he looked up to see Adrastos struggling to get up but he had to look away as he heard men landing upon the wooden structures above him. Ailia had to be his priority and quickly he jumped to his feet just as an assassin ran in front of him. Paul instinctively kicked out into the man's knee cracking it loudly, then thrust his sword upwards with both hands forcing the blade up through the assassins chin and out the top of his head. Quickly he pulled the sword down and pushed the dead assassin aside and looked to see if he could find a way up to the first level as all the ladders had been destroyed.

Tenno stood on the left side of the door as Theodoric positioned himself on the right side. He looked briefly over in the corner at the Templar laying face down, his tunic smouldering and almost completely burnt away with his chain mail exposed beneath. His attention immediately returned to Ailia as he heard her cough lightly just as Thomas painfully lay down beside her in the near darkness, smoke still wafting across the room.

"'Tis good to finally see you smile after all these years," Theodoric remarked as he gripped his sword with both hands. "Now all I need to hear is you laugh."

"No you don't, my friend…trust me," Tenno smiled and placed Paul's sword in front of him upright. "I would like to see the day when you are never hungry," he joked.

No sooner had Tenno spoken when several assassins rushed the door. The first one jumped through so fast he nearly missed him but Theodoric swung his sword sideways across the assassin's shoulders severing his spinal cord as the blade cut through his back. The second assassin through was about to bring his sword down upon Theodoric as he pulled his sword out but Tenno swiped his sword sideways decapitating him instantly but as he raised his sword again, another assassin jumped forwards thrusting his sword straight into Theodoric's stomach as he turned to face them, the straight black blade coming out of his side. Theodoric's eyes widened, surprised but not in pain. The assassin's eyes met his as he then thrust his sword sideways slicing across Theodoric's stomach with a sickening squelch sound. Tenno brought Paul's sword down shattering the assassin's straight blade but then swung it all the way back and over his head and down with all his might hitting the assassin on the shoulder at an angle, his arm instantly falling to the floor. As the assassin fell backwards against the assassin directly behind him, Tenno thrust the sword right through the assassin's chest and straight into the one behind him. As Tenno kicked them both to the ground, he roared again, Theodoric looking at him as he fell to his knees, his hands across his stomach trying to hold in his own intestines. In a fit of total rage Tenno stepped out of the doorway directly into the path of the other assassins and swung Paul's sword around slicing into several of them, but one managed to thrust his sword into Tenno's side. He momentarily froze as he turned to look at the assassin still holding the sword. Tenno struck him on the head with the pommel of his sword hard then slashed across his neck half cutting off his head. Another assassin's blade entered Tenno's chest passing straight through his left lung and protruding out of his back. Theodoric looked on as Tenno cut the sword away then hacked the man holding the handle. Through the blur of smoke and his eyes failing, Theodoric could see Tenno still standing and swinging his sword but gradually the doorway filled with smoke and he could no longer see what was happening in the corridor though he could still hear moans and the sounds of metal upon metal and flesh.

Paul heard hooves hitting stone to his left and he looked in time to see Alisha land on horseback having cleared the wall of the second gate tower as arrows and bolts flashed past her. She saw Paul and steered directly for him as several bolts hit the hind quarters of the horse causing it to jolt nearly throwing her off. Paul saw an assassin stand and aim at Alisha but was brought down by one of Abi's arrows. Just as Alisha was about to pull up in front of Paul, the horse collapsed, its head dropping down as its front legs buckled beneath her. Instinctively Paul opened his arms as Alisha was thrown forwards and she crashed into him, both falling to the floor as the horse careered into the dirt and rubble beside them. Paul hauled Alisha over hard beside him as he used the dying horse for cover, several bolts thudding into its other side and saddle. Paul grabbed Alisha and looked at her, both angered but also surprised.

"Are you mad?" he asked.

"Me mad? Lord if we survive this I will be having words with you," Alisha replied and looked up over her shoulder at the other assassins running along the awnings and wooden roof sections as more roped themselves down. "I see a way up for us," she said and stood up pulling Paul's hand. "We stick together, we do this together, we get our daughter back together...or together we die trying," she said and looked back at Paul her eyes ablaze, her hair blowing around her face, full of determination and a resolve he was not going to argue with.

Theodoric crawled backwards towards the cistern access wall area keeping his eye on the doorway, his sword held in his right hand, his left trying to contain his intestines. Thomas rushed forwards and immediately helped pull him backwards to the wall and rested him up against it.

"Thomas...hide yourself...do not let Ailia see me...like this," Theodoric whispered.

Thomas looked down at the state of Theodoric's wound. Quickly he ripped off a large section of his own mantle and placed it over the exposed intestines and then placed Theodoric's hand over it to hold it in place.

"'Tis truly not survivable, my friend," Thomas whispered as smoke wafted past his face as a breeze blew more in through the door. Both looked toward the door as Tenno reappeared limping toward them. He approached walking backwards slowly holding Paul's sword upwards with one hand whilst carrying a large chest under his left arm. When he reached Thomas he looked at him briefly.

"Quickly, Thomas, we do not have much time...fetch me the oil burner... then hide," Tenno ordered and sat himself down painfully beside Theodoric and leaned into his right side for support breathing with difficulty as blood oozed from his mouth. "'Tis the poisons that slowed me...I am sorry I could not do better."

 1 – 1

"You did more than better...and there is nowhere to hide...but I shall stay with Ailia and do what is necessary," Thomas whispered.

"So what do you have planned?" Theodoric asked quietly, looking at Tenno through bloodshot eyes.

"To put us out of our pain quickly my friend and take them with us," Tenno coughed and lowered Paul's sword and placed it beside him. "I will not need that again," he said as he then opened the large chest. He pulled two shields over and placed one on top of Theodoric and one across himself before positioning the opened chest on his own shield facing the doorway then laughed lightly.

"Now I know we are dead for now you laugh," Theodoric remarked and smiled painfully as Thomas handed Tenno the oil burner. He patted them both on their shoulders.

"We shall all see each other in the next world," Thomas remarked quietly and crawled back behind the cistern cover to Ailia as she looked up, her eyes wide trying to look through the wafting smoke still hanging in the air.

"My friend...it has been my greatest honour to have fought alongside you...and soon to accompany you to the next world," Tenno whispered as he prepared himself holding the oil burner next to a strip of covered fuse rope he had made up. "I just pray this works."

"What will it do if it does?" Theodoric asked and winced in pain. "You know, you can't argue with me now about feeling hungry as this time my stomach really is empty."

Tenno looked at him, his face turning up a large grin, and then he started to laugh in an exaggerated bah ha ha fashion which took Theodoric by surprise. Tenno seeing the look in his eyes laughed even more in what was perhaps the most ridiculous laugh Theodoric had ever heard. Thomas looked over and had to laugh.

"No wonder you never laugh, my friend," Theodoric laughed back then grabbed the cover over his stomach with both hands. "Now you have made me spill my guts with laughter," he laughed more despite the pain.

"This...this...when it goes off," Tenno laughed as he struggled to hold the chest facing forwards and the oil burner at once, "this will blast anything forward of us with a thousand shards of metal and spoil from the blacksmith's floor."

"And if it doesn't?" Theodoric asked, trying not to laugh more.

"We...we won't know anything about it for it will blow us to pieces," Tenno replied and laughed again but when he stopped laughing he looked directly at Theodoric. "You know...I have seen so many things in this life and been blessed by meeting people like you. I buried a treasure of coins in the new world I walked across...I will never recover those," he said quietly and paused. "As a child I walked along the beach near my village with my parents. We would come and watch the beautiful and magical scene of a thousand sea squid come into the shallows to mate at night. They shone a bright light blue in the waters. With the stars above us, I always knew this world was a beautiful magical one…despite the madness of war."

"I am sure you will see such wonders in the next life, my friend…soon," Theodoric replied and laughed again. "But I agree, this world is full of far more beauty than badness…people forget that. You know I have seen the most beautiful multi coloured warrior women of Persia. Their beauty alone is enough to stop a man's heart. I have witnessed the colours of the rainbow in a desert, a waterfall through a cavern splashing wondrously into an emerald green cave full of turquoise waters…that is what I pray to see again in Heaven."

"I think we shall soon find out," Tenno said quietly, his eyes now heavily bloodshot. He sat himself further up and tried to breathe, his chest oozing blood and gurgling as air leaked through his pierced lung.

Alisha half dragged Paul up a section of the cliff face where a very narrow goat track wound its way partially up the side towards the original entrance but it ended in a large gap, the ladders to reach the cave complex completely destroyed below. Paul looked around in time to see Ishmael and Percival engaging other assassins on the second gate tower wall, Master Douglas climbing up behind them closely followed by Stewart and the rest of the escort. A crossbow bolt zipped past Paul's face causing him to flinch backwards just as Alisha pulled him against the cliff wall hard. Above, other assassins were trying to aim down at them but the slight overhang was blocking their direct line of sight. Paul flung his left arm across Alisha protectively and held her forcibly from moving.

"Please I beg of you stay here," Paul said through gritted teeth as he tried to judge how far the distance was to jump from the narrow goat ledge across to the wooden walkway.

"No…I just rode through all of that…and I will follow you wherever you are going," Alisha replied and pulled out her three pronged dagger.

On the cliff top above, Turansha rubbed his beard, scowling up his face as he strained to see what was happening below through all the rising black smoke. He looked around to see that he only had a few men remaining having committed the rest to the last assault. His second in command stepped away from the edge shaking his head.

"My Lord, all the remaining teams are in their positions now. Do you wish me to give the signal?" he asked just as the sun broke fully above the eastern horizon behind them.

Turansha stood up straight and nodded yes and another assassin nearby acknowledged the order and fired a flaming arrow horizontally across the wadi, the lead assassins below immediately seeing it just as Alisha and Paul saw it arch over. Percival saw it and quickly rushed forwards faster followed by Ishmael as Stewart struck down another assassin that had stood up to fire at Percival. Master Douglas half fell down the wall of the second gate tower as the Askar guards ran past him to help Stewart deal with more assassins. Paul sheathed his sword, pushed Alisha back again then ran for the edge of the gap and launched himself off flailing his arms to remain upright as he went, then started to drop rapidly under the weight of his armour only just managing to grab hold of the last protruding wooden beam, Alisha gasping in shock. Hanging on just by his finger tips he struggled to get a better grip as smoke billowed past him from the fires beneath him on the ground floor sections. Crossbows from above started to embed in the wood all around him then suddenly dead assassins started to fall past him. Alisha looked up to see Taqi and his colleague crouched within the cliff face itself. Quickly Taqi edged his way along a section of the cliff hanging by his finger tips, turned and dropped down onto the wooden awning above Paul then swung himself over and dropped onto the floor and instantly leaned down and grabbed Paul's other arm. Paul looked up at him never more happy to see him. An assassin ran up behind Taqi, his sword raised ready to strike him but just as he was about to lower his blade, a large arrow zipped past Taqi's head and struck the assassin in the chest killing him instantly. Taqi looked down to see Abi some distance away recharging another arrow. Quickly Taqi heaved Paul up resting him on his chest then grabbed his sword belt and pulled him up completely. Paul looked toward the section that led to the cistern room in time to see many assassins, swords drawn, running into the carved corridor section. Immediately Paul stood up, unsheathed his sword ready to run.

Tenno looked at Theodoric as he rested his head upon his shoulder, his eyes closed.

"You dead yet, my friend?" he asked.

"Not yet…but nearly," Theodoric replied and forced his eyes open in time to see the whole corridor filled with darkness as the many assassins rushing toward them blocked out all the light.

"You will be now, my friend," Tenno stated, his hand shaking from exhaustion and from his injuries as he tried to get the fuse rope to light.

Theodoric clasped his hand around the ceramic oil burner to steady his hand and the flame beneath the fuse. Both smiled at each other.

"See you, my ugly friend," Theodoric said quietly and in pain.

"And you, my fat friend," Tenno laughed as the fuse lit.

Paul and Taqi had only taken a few steps when a massive pressure wave pushed out from ahead of them immediately followed by a huge blast wave of flame and body parts mixed together in a huge cloud of rolling death as Tenno's explosive device detonated not only firing out a deadly salvo of hot metal shards that tore through flesh, but also ignited all the other barrels of his explosive mixture he had lined along the corridor. The force of the blast blew Paul and Taqi backwards nearly throwing them both over the edge of the wooden platform, Alisha looking on wide eyed in shock. Turansha was pushed backwards by the percussion of the explosion even though he was above it. Stunned he grabbed hold of his second in command as the ground beneath their feet shook, the sound of the explosion echoing out along the ravine and across the plateau behind. Everyone below froze where they stood at the sight of such an explosion, Sister Lucy clutching her chest as she was half way across the entrance pathway and able to see the extent of the explosion in full as bodies and wooden panels and shattered beams were thrown through the air a great distance. She shook her head and forced herself on running faster fearing for Theodoric. Alisha moved herself back on the small goat track, took a deep breath and ran for the gap. Without hesitation she threw herself forwards across the gap and in one jump she cleared it, her feet landing a clear two feet inside the walkway platform, the momentum and speed of her jump forcing her to roll over as she landed. Frantically she jumped back up and ran straight into the smoke almost immediately falling over Paul landing hard beside him, her face scuffing on the burnt wooden panels. Paul sat up and looked at her as they both feared the worst for Ailia. Taqi helped them both to their feet, but looking back momentarily at the large distance Alisha had just jumped and the sheer drop below. When he turned to look at her, she was already pulling Paul into the swirling smoke patches stepping over dead bodies, many grotesquely disfigured. She clasped her hand over her mouth as she saw several of Thomas's men, what was left of them anyway. She slowed her pace as she stepped cautiously over the bodies, Paul moving to stand in front of her. Taqi moved to stand the other side of her as they moved toward the cistern room, the bodies leaving a clear trail toward it.

Alisha took in a deep breath as fresh air blew away a patch of the smoke momentarily. She could hardly breathe with the anticipation of what they may find any minute now. No one was moving as anyone who had been alive would have had the air sucked from their lungs by the huge explosion. The walls were all pitted with shards of metal from Tenno's devices. Paul put his hand up for Alisha and Taqi to stand still as he slowly entered the darkened cistern room, the smell of burnt flesh and blood overpowering. A man coughed in the far corner of the room, Paul instantly raising his sword.

"What in the name of heaven happened?" the Templar asked as he tried to stand covered in blood, his mantle and cloak all burnt, his hair singed all over. He rubbed his eyes as he stepped forward trying to see in the dim twilight." Am I in hell?" he asked and coughed dryly nearly stumbling on dead assassins.

"You…took your time," Tenno suddenly said quietly in a low broken dry voice.

Paul sheathed his sword instantly as he rushed toward the voice of Tenno but then froze as he saw him lying beside Theodoric, the shields covering them shattered and burnt, Tenno's hands and forearms completely blown off, Theodoric with his stomach opened, his intestines hanging out and smouldering, the smell overpowering. Both of them were missing their lower legs too. Paul's eyes darted around in panic looking for Ailia.

⚜ 2 – 11

"War is brutal and disgusting…but I would not have wanted to go any other way," Tenno said, forcing his eyes open to look up at Paul. "She…she said you would come."

Paul hurriedly knelt beside Tenno and held him up slightly and looked into his bloodshot eyes as Alisha and Taqi slowly entered the room, Taqi maintaining a look out behind them.

"Where?" Paul asked, choking emotionally on his words as Tenno looked into his eyes.

"Thomas…he, he has her," Tenno answered in a lower voice, almost a whisper now.

Alisha rushed over and placed her hand upon his left shoulder and her right hand upon Theodoric's shoulder as he leaned against Tenno, his eyes shut, his face blackened from burns. With tears in her eyes she looked at them both.

"Where does he have her?" she asked emotionally, struggling not to cry at both the sight of them and her fear for Ailia's whereabouts. Tenno smiled as he looked at her and indicated with his head and slight nod behind him.

"In the cistern?" Paul asked. Tenno nodded slightly yes. Instantly Paul jumped up and moved around the small cistern wall with the cover on and rapidly felt around until he found the latch. Quickly he flipped it up and flung it open. As it thudded down on the other side, what little light there was filtered down the back side of the brickwork, Paul's heart stopping when he could see nothing except water. Alisha saw the alarm on his face and stared at him wide mouthed...but then a chain mail covered forearm and hand flashed forwards out of the darkened side grabbing the single metal step opposite. Painfully slowly, Thomas loomed into view as he looked up hesitantly, his eyes wide but widening even more as he recognised Paul. Thomas moved and ripples of water reflected light around his waist just visible, but then as he moved around the cistern access hole, Paul saw he was holding Ailia tightly against his chest trying to keep her out of the cold water. Thomas coughed to clear his throat.

"Ailia," he said and coughed again. "'Tis all right, my child...'tis your papa."

Immediately Ailia turned her head and looked up, her big eyes opening to look directly into Paul's eyes. The recognition was instant.

"Papa!" she called out and reached out her arms towards him, her little fingers moving back and forwards frantically.

Paul leaned down and with both hands took her from Thomas, the moment he touched her he took a sharp intake of breath barely able to comprehend she was actually alive. He pulled her up out of the cistern and wrapped his arms around her, closed his eyes and kissed her as she wrapped her arms tightly around his neck in silence unable to speak. She started to pant as emotions overwhelmed her little body. Paul opened his eyes to see Alisha stood motionless just staring at them. After all the months of believing them both dead, to now be standing looking at them was almost too much. She went to speak but her throat was too dry. She gulped and licked her lips and raised her hands towards them.

"Ailia...your mama is here too for you," Paul whispered as he stroked her hair and kissed her again. "Look."

Ailia let go of her tight grip and moved to look into Paul's eyes. Her wide eyes just stared into his as if in disbelief unsure how to handle the many emotions running through her. She was shivering from the cold water. Slowly she turned her head to look at Alisha, who sighed and smiled emotionally as a tear ran down her filthy and scuffed face. Alisha still could not speak as she stepped forwards reaching out for her.

"Mama!" Ailia finally spoke and threw herself toward her, Paul only just managing to keep hold of her until Alisha took her. "Mama...where have you been for so long?" she asked and then started to cry as Alisha took her in her arms and kissed the side of her face several times holding her tightly, half laughing and half crying. She looked at Paul, his clothing all scorched and covered in blood and dirt just as Thomas pulled himself out of the cistern, soaking wet and shivering. "Theo," Ailia whispered as she looked down over Alisha's shoulder.

Quickly Paul rushed around and knelt down beside Theodoric as Tenno turned his head slowly to look at him as he moved Theodoric's head to check him over. Tenno motioned with his eyes towards his stomach. Paul pulled up what was left of the shield so Ailia would not see the mess, though the smell was intense. Alisha hugged Ailia and kept kissing her as she clung to her. Paul gently moved Theodoric's face toward the light, his eye lids momentarily blinking.

"He still lives," Paul remarked and looked up at Taqi as Ishmael and Stewart entered the room looking shocked at the scene before them. They were closely followed by several Askar guards. Paul looked at them all, puzzled how they had all managed to get up so quickly.

"'Twas the other injured Templar...," Stewart said as he rapidly walked over nearly tripping upon the many dead and dismembered bodies. "He threw down the emergency roped ladders...but Abi is bringing Lucy up now," he explained and looked at the state of Tenno and Theodoric, Tenno forcing a smile and raising his arms revealing his missing hands and bloodied mangled stumps.

"Stewart...please, Turansha is still above us," Paul remarked and moved to stand but Tenno raised his knee and nudged him hard. Paul looked at him, puzzled, until Tenno nodded towards Paul's sword lying just beneath his partially destroyed shield. Tenno blinked unable to speak as he grew weaker, his lungs wheezing with every breath he took.

"Oh my Lord have mercy no!" Sister Lucy said aloud putting her hands to her mouth in shock as she entered the room supported by Abi staring at Theodoric whose eyes fell immediately upon Tenno.

Ishmael and Taqi stood aside as Stewart helped Sister Lucy move toward Theodoric, Abi stepping around them and immediately kneeling down beside Tenno, looking at him in despair. Gently she pulled his face to look at her. His eyes narrowed as he tried to focus upon her in the dim light, but immediately opening wider again as he recognised her. He went to speak but coughed as dark, almost black blood oozed from the side of his mouth. Quickly Abi wiped the blood away and then kissed him gently upon the lips as tears welled in her eyes. Sister Lucy stared at Theodoric as she knelt in front of him and went to move the shield, Paul instantly shaking his head no. Tears immediately welled in her eyes as she lifted Theodoric's hands and held them tightly looking into his blackened burnt face.

"Only you of all men could have a woman mourn you three times you... you bastard...my love," she said emotionally and kissed his bloodied hands and held them against her chest. Alisha looked at Paul as Stewart started to usher the Askar guards back out of the room to safeguard their position from any further assaults. "Oh look what they have done to you," she sighed as a tear ran down her cheek just as Abi pulled Tenno up slightly and put her arms around him.

Sister Lucy looked at them as Abi held him close. Abi kissed Tenno again and rested her head against the side of his face as she started to cry softly.

"I mourned you so hard...hard because I thought you dead before I had time to tell you something," Abi whispered as she held him tightly. Tenno coughed and tried to move but could only manage to place what was left of his arm against her side. "We...we have a son. 'Tis your son and he is very well," she revealed then moved to look him in the eyes. He blinked and smiled as he slightly nodded his approval. "A son," she repeated and kissed him on the lips once more, softly. As she kissed him, she sensed his body go limp, his arms lowering to his sides as he breathed out his last, his eyes closing slowly. Abi started to shake as she began to sob and pulled him against her chest and cradled him.

"Always...always has to be first doesn't he?" Theodoric whispered, his eyes still closed, having sensed Tenno had died beside him. "Paul....Paul."

"No Theo...'tis I. I am here, my love, I am here," Sister Lucy said and ran her fingers through his singed hair whilst she held on to his other hand, the blood on them sticking them together.

"Paul," Theo called out again and coughed. "I swore an oath to your mother...so hear me, Paul. After you have finished with the sword...it's time to be wielded by man is done...and you must hide it...you must for I cannot fulfil my promise," he explained and coughed as he tried to look up at Paul but too exhausted to open his eyes fully. "Protect the crimson line, hide the line and then hide the sword when it is done..."

Alisha quickly wiped away a tear as they all looked at the sad heart breaking scene unfolding before them. Ailia blinked hard not really sure what was happening but knowing it was sad as tears ran down her cheeks as she looked at Abi cradling Tenno and Sister Lucy holding Theodoric.

"Aye, my friend," Paul replied sadly. "That I promise I shall do."

"My Luce," Theodoric coughed lightly and forced open his exhausted eyes to look at her one final time. He smiled. "You...you, my Luce...you are the best thing I ever did in this world...the best thing."

"Sssh, my love...you must conserve your energy, you must," she replied as tears began to stream down her cheeks as he shook his head slightly indicating no.

"Luce...this one I cannot beat...but promise me....just one thing," he asked quietly as she moved closer to him and sat beside him resting his head against her bosom, putting her arm around him. He closed his eyes unable to keep them open. "Tell Paul about the camels," he said and let out a little laugh but then coughed, his chest making a gurgling sound. Sister Lucy held him closer and closed her eyes, resting her chin on his head and rocked him gently as tears continued to fall down her cheeks. "Luce...I always knew I would leave this world in your arms...and so," he whispered and paused as he smiled. "And so!"

Theodoric said no more as his body went limp, his face looking serene, Sister Lucy just sobbing. Paul stood beside Alisha and put his arm around her and Ailia as tears welled in his eyes at the sight of Abi and Sister Lucy both cradling the men they loved dead in their arms. Taqi wiped away a tear as Ishmael turned, alarmed, just as Master Douglas entered the room out of breath and leaned up against the door jamb shaking his head at the scene before him. He sighed heavily his face instantly turning to one of sadness realising what had happened. Paul placed both his arms around Alisha and Ailia, lost for words, his heart heavy with sadness at the loss of Tenno and Theodoric, for the second time, and an eternal gratitude for their sacrifice. He opened his eyes to see Thomas standing wide eyed and exhausted before him holding out his original sword, clearly able to hold it with ease.

"My men and I failed you once before...when we lost Arri. 'Twas a stain upon all of us. A stain we can never remove," Thomas started to say emotionally and paused as he fought to control his emotions. "But we vowed we would never fail you again. At the Roman town of Pela we all suffered many injuries fighting off Turansha's men...and we knew then our days as fighting men were numbered having used grenades so close. I have asked myself why the Lord in all his infinite wisdom has seen fit to spare my life many times when I should be dead...I now know why...for he had a far greater task and work for me and my men to do...clearly. And this day they have fulfilled that task, with their lives," Thomas said passionately, his voice shaking, a tear rolling down his cheek. "So I ask you now...as they now stand guard at the gates of heaven," he paused, the sword shaking as he held it out and looked directly at Alisha. "Do you forgive my men for failing you before?"

Alisha cupped her mouth, shocked. She outstretched her hand and placed it upon his forearm.

"'Tis we who ask your forgiveness...for thinking you should even ask it of us. You have never failed us," Alisha replied emotionally as Thomas shook, trying to hold in the emotion overwhelming him. "You have more than honoured us...and 'tis us who should honour you..."

Thomas turned to look at Paul. "Then honour them...by taking this back," he blurted out emotionally. "And never give it up again...for this day I have witnessed the power of it when wielded by a great man," Thomas demanded and flipped the sword over to hold it just below the hand guard and offered up the handle. "But for this...we would not now be standing here having this conversation...take it!"

Alisha moved so she could see him as Ailia lifted her face to look at Thomas offering the sword. Thomas, having lost all of his men, and his friends Tenno and Theodoric, Paul sensed his deep pain immediately and quickly looked down at Abi as she looked up at him. Hesitantly he looked back at the sword gleaming in the dim light of the room as if almost glowing. His eyes met Thomas's with the look of pain in them, his mouth contorted as he fought to maintain his composure. Paul had vowed he would never again wield the sword, yet Percival had recovered it and it had clearly played a massive part in the defence and survival of his daughter.

>⚔<   1 – 2

"Papa," Ailia said softly and sniffed.

Paul looked at her as she clung to Alisha. They both looked at him intently and then both nodded yes. Slowly Paul placed his hand around the handle instantly feeling the familiar sensation from it as his fingers wrapped themselves fully around it. Thomas let out an involuntary gasp, releasing his grip instantly as Paul took the sword. With his left arm around Alisha and Ailia he inverted the sword so the tip pointed upwards and he pulled the sword up close seeing the etched patterns and symbols clearly, a pulse entering his hand and body causing both Alisha and Ailia to feel it. Alisha pulled Paul close and together they hugged Ailia, their eyes shut, Sister Lucy and Abi remaining where they were sat in total silence beside their dead men.

Port of La Rochelle, France, Melissae Inn, spring 1191

All sat around the table simply staring at Paul's sword positioned in the middle of it in total silence, apart from Ayleth sniffing and Miriam wiping a tear from her eye. The old man looked at them all in turn, their faces appearing drained, perhaps from tiredness but also shocked maybe he thought as they remained totally silent. After a few minutes Sarah finally leaned forwards and gently pulled the sword toward her careful not to fully hold it.

"So...Theodoric and Tenno really did get killed that time," she stated and paused as she looked closely at the gleaming blade and etchings upon it. "Yet you say this sword is only now here because of Princess Stephanie, along with journals and drawings...how so?" she asked and looked at the old man.

"What about Turansha...what happened to him?" Gabirol asked.

"I shall explain both I assure you," the old man replied softly. "Turansha was not aware that Tenno had Paul's sword and was the reason why he was so over confident. Nor could he have known of Tenno's expertise that caused such an explosion. Mark my words, 'tis such knowledge and power that will shortly come to change the very face of warfare," he explained further but paused again. "But Turansha had expended some of his best men in the final assault, so assured of his victory, and so he left with the few men he still had to go and meet up with his other forces that were en route."

"I still find it hard to believe that for all those previous months, word could not have been sent to Paul or Alisha that Ailia was alive, or that Alisha was alive to Paul," the farrier remarked, shaking his head.

"My friend," the Templar said and looked at him. "I can promise you that communications were severely hampered or restricted if not at times deliberately stopped. Saladin knew how to disrupt our communications systems and he did it very well. But from what you tell us, this Percival certainly made a difference to have been able to locate Ailia and the others as he did."

"Yes but as I said, he had some inspirational help," the old man replied.

"Did Turansha come back with his other men?" Ayleth asked hesitantly.

"Let me say that after Stewart and Master Douglas had secured the cave area, they had to bury the dead. Abi and Sister Lucy as you can imagine were heartbroken...again. 'Twas such a cruel set of circumstances."

"Were there no great words of wisdom or some last deep and meaningful statement given by either Tenno or Theodoric then...or was that it, they just died?" Peter asked rather bluntly.

"Peter...that was a little insensitive was it not?" Sarah asked him.

"'Tis a valid question and observation," the old man said and looked at them both in turn. "'Tis no fairy tale or romantic fiction story I speak of so I am afraid I can only tell you of what happened. Death is not always some great noble act where words and platitudes are spoken that poems can be written about. In most cases it is messy and very unromantic."

"I think they died a very brave and noble death whilst saving Ailia," Simon said looking sad. "Thomas's men guarding the very gates of Heaven...for I bet they do."

"'Tis the way both would have wanted to die I am sure," the old man sighed. "After Master Douglas had secured the area and checked the surrounding countryside, only then did they remove their bodies and lay them to rest that afternoon. Their bodies still lie there to this day. Thomas...well he insisted on burying every single one of his own men alone as he had always vowed he would for each and every one of them...all with their yellow and black headbands set upon their chests clasped within their hands. Paul moved Alisha and Ailia out of the complex to open ground and set up the Muslim escort and Askar guards to watch over them, Abi refusing to allow Paul to help with the burials but to remain with them. As the sun set Ishmael came for them to come and stand at the graves of Theodoric and Tenno whilst Thomas continued to bury his men. Sister Lucy managed to remain composed supported by Abi right up until Paul arrived and stood by her side with Alisha and Ailia. She had asked the sole surviving Templar to read prayers but *he stood silent and shook his head and said he did not know them well enough to honour them and asked Paul to say something instead," the old man explained and paused deep in thought for several long minutes before looking up again. "I am sorry...when Paul went to speak, Sister Lucy looked at him and before he had even said a word, she collapsed to the floor onto her knees and sobbed openly, Abi and Alisha immediately comforting her. The only solace Abi had was knowing that at least Tenno knew he had a son before passing over. Even as she knelt beside Sister Lucy, she sensed his presence and even smiled as she felt it so strong. She said that neither of them needed any words spoken for they knew already what they felt. But this time, this time Sister Lucy knew her Theo would not be seeing her again in this world."*

"Did they go on to meet Count Henry and Princess Stephanie at that bridge you mentioned...or did Turansha stop that...and why do we have the sword now?" Ayleth asked hesitantly and lightly bit her thumb nail.

Cave de Sueth, Kingdom of Jerusalem, October 5th 1187

Paul followed Master Douglas and Percival whilst Ishmael followed closely behind with Alisha and Ailia being guarded by Taqi at their rear. Smoke still hung heavy in the air and Alisha tried to avert Ailia's view of all the dead, some horribly disfigured and burnt! Abi helped Sister Lucy stand up but she refused to move from the side of Theodoric's fresh grave. Thomas was still laying to rest the last of his men and politely refusing help from several Mamluk guards. Master Douglas stopped when he reached the lifeless body of Adrastos and put his hands upon his hips as he looked down at him. Paul knelt down and ran his hand along Adrastos's neck. It was only now in the full light of day that he could see the large sword injury and many crossbow bolts and arrows all over his body. Paul sighed heavily, closed his eyes and rested his head upon Adrastos. Despite being severely and mortally wounded, Adrastos had got him across the path and into the complex before succumbing to them. He had died alone and Paul felt guilty for that.

"Mama...does everything have to die?" Ailia asked quietly.

Alisha simply nodded yes silently unable to speak, her heart breaking for Paul knowing the sadness that was running through him. Paul put his arms around Adrastos's neck and kissed him softly and hugged him. A million memories of Adrastos ran through his mind from that very first day he had ridden him in panic after Alisha back in France to the thousand and one other journeys since. The night when he and Taqi rode him without his saddle after being attacked in the woods by Stewart. Paul laughed lightly to himself recalling that night, now such a distant memory. He opened his eyes as he rested his head on his side running his hand over his white hairs. He could see and hear Arri riding upon his back in Alexandria when Tenno taught him to ride. His chest felt tight and he sighed heavily as his mind suddenly registered Ailia's question. He kissed Adrastos once more and slowly stood up and turned to look at Ailia and Alisha. So many people had died over the years because of them and for them. He placed his hand upon his sword, his other sword and the one given by Saladin now strapped across his back. Alisha held Ailia closely, putting their heads together. As he looked at them he knew that every drop of blood that had been spilt was, in his mind, worth it. He walked up to them as they looked at him intently and he wrapped his arms around them hugging them tightly.

"Ailia…nothing ever really dies…but everything changes. That is all," he whispered and kissed her on the side of her face, Alisha welling up with tears again. She took a deep breath, closed her eyes and rested against Paul's chest as he held them.

PART XV

Chapter 85
The Long Shadow of Rome!

**Yarmoch bridge, Yarmoch plateau, Kingdom of Jerusalem,
October 5ᵗʰ 1187**

The sun, a perfect blood red sphere, was sinking over the horizon as Ishmael led the Mamluk escort toward the large stone and wooden Yarmoch bridge closely followed by Stewart, Taqi and Master Douglas. The bridge spanned a great distance, the tall stone built supports outlined by a red hue from the sun, the high escarpment to the west of the river also reflecting the redness of the sun along its length for as far as the eye could see. Paul had Ailia sat in front of him as they rode alongside Alisha closely watched over by Percival and the Askar guards at the rear, whilst just in front of them, Abi rode alongside Sister Lucy likewise keeping an eye on her with Thomas, all visibly exhausted. Count Henry had already pitched his tent for the night alongside Princess Stephanie's caravan. Someone in the camp called out alerting that they were approaching, Count Henry immediately rushing from his tent as Princess Stephanie opened her caravan door and tried to see who it was whilst many of Count Henry's men stood too, weapons at the ready alongside other Mamluk guards. She took a deep breath preparing herself to see Paul if it was indeed him, her stomach immediately knotting. She looked briefly at the blood red sun as it sat lower on the horizon. The last time she had been in the desert and seen it like that was when she had been alone with Paul in the old donjon chapel. She stepped down from the caravan checking her hair and composing herself and then walked through the temporary encampment to join Count Henry as he strained to see who the approaching column was. He recognised the two yellow flag configuration of Taqi al Din's Mamluk escort as they drew nearer.

"'Tis Paul as arranged," he remarked but looked puzzled.

Ishmael part bowed his head at Princess Stephanie and Count Henry as he pulled up just past them and turned in his saddle to look back as the escort stopped. Both Princess Stephanie and Count Henry looked at each other puzzled at how different Ishmael looked, not totally sure if it was in fact even him. Paul saw Princess Stephanie and his heart jumped. Alisha leaned across from her horse and touched his forearm gently as he held Ailia close. He looked at Alisha as she forced a tired smile and nodded at him.

 4 –12

"You must speak with her. I understand that so please do not be afraid to," she said softly and put her hands up to take Ailia, who was half asleep.

Paul looked around the camp site and was quietly surprised and relieved to see Count Henry had brought a lot of men with him and already had pickets out on guard. They were set up on the open plateau before the main bridge, which would afford them some protection against anyone approaching during the night. After handing Ailia to Alisha, he dismounted and approached Count Henry and Princess Stephanie. As he brushed himself down he could already see the tension and pain in her face just as a gentle breeze blew her dress against her figure, Alisha looking on with sadness in her heart for both of them.

"My Lady," Paul said respectfully and bowed his head slightly at Princess Stephanie then at Count Henry. "My Lord."

Princess Stephanie took a deep breath shocked at the bloodied sight of Paul now that he was stood close to her, his eyes searching hers as she struggled to keep her emotions under control but the tears were already welling in hers giving them away. The fact he called her 'My Lady' in an official manner cut like a knife which she felt as a physical pull in her chest and feared he had now placed a barrier between them. Alisha bit her bottom lip as she looked on with a mix of emotions.

"Why so few of you…and where are Tenno and Theo…and Thomas and his men?" Count Henry asked, making Paul look back at the party.

"I am afraid Turansha was already assaulting the cave fortress," Paul replied then turned back to face them. "Thomas is with us…at the rear with Sister Lucy and Abi," he explained but then lowered his head as the realisation finally hit him hard that Tenno and Theodoric were really dead this time. He took a deep breath and looked down, then pinched the bridge of his nose trying not to cry as his body was overwhelmed, in part with relief he had met up with Count Henry safely. "But Theo and Tenno…and all of Thomas's men I am afraid were killed defending Ailia," he finally managed to reveal and looked up directly at Princess Stephanie. "And Turansha still lives and is out there," he said emotionally.

"Paul," Princess Stephanie finally spoke as more tears welled in her eyes. She looked across at Alisha who nodded to her as if to say yes understanding what she was thinking, then stepped forwards and put her arms around Paul and hugged him tightly, Paul leaving his arms by his side aware that Alisha was watching though every part of him wanted to put his arms around her and take away her pain.

Alisha held Ailia tightly and moved her horse closer.

"Paul...'tis okay," she said and handed Ailia to Count Henry then dismounted. Princess Stephanie moved her head away from Paul, her arms still around him wanting to make every last moment of holding him just one more time last longer. Her heart felt as if it was being split in two within her and a tear ran down her cheek. Paul looked at her as Alisha came and stood beside them looking at them each in turn. Gently she placed her hand upon Princess Stephanie's shoulder and her other on Paul's. As tears filled her own eyes seeing and sensing the heartache between them as well as her own, she pulled them together. Princess Stephanie resting her head upon Paul's chest again and closing her eyes not even bothered that his mantle was burnt and covered in dried blood. Paul looked at Alisha as a single heavy tear ran down her cheek and she gave a pained smile. But it was pain for both of them. She lifted Paul's arm and placed it around Princess Stephanie to comfort her. He closed his eyes as Alisha wrapped her arms around both of them resting her forehead next to Princess Stephanie, who opened her eyes and mouthed 'thank you' silently. Paul moved his arm around Alisha and pulled her close so he was holding both of them against him, Alisha placing her arm tighter around Princess Stephanie. Together Alisha and Paul held Princess Stephanie as she sobbed quietly, the understanding, love and mutual respect between them was felt by each intensely. After a few minutes, Princess Stephanie stopped crying and stood back a pace and looked at Alisha and Paul then wiped her face and forced a brave smile as she straightened her arms down her front holding her hands together.

"You have Ailia back now...and all is as it should be," she said emotionally as Count Henry came and stood beside her holding Ailia, who was rubbing her eyes, tired.

Alisha looked at Paul as he stared at Princess Stephanie and gently squeezed his hand reassuringly. She knew this was not easy for either him or Princess Stephanie, but she also knew he would be staying with her out of his own free will and choice because of just how much he really loved her and Ailia. Paul finally broke a smile and nodded at Princess Stephanie. She nodded back, quickly turned around and walked back to her caravan. She stopped momentarily as if about to turn but then continued on her way, the red sphere of the sun now half vanished below the horizon. Paul placed his arm around Alisha and pulled her close just as Thomas rode up beside Ishmael.

"That, my friend…that is how true queens behave," he remarked.

೮೦

An hour later Paul found himself sat opposite Count Henry in his tent as he poured him some wine, a single Lanthorn lit the small collapsible wooden table. With two swords slung across his back and his original sword around his waist, Paul looked more than ready for any trouble.

"Thank you," Paul said as he accepted the goblet of wine and held it with both hands.

"You are exhausted, Paul. You should clean yourself up. I have fresh water being boiled as we speak. Ishmael, Percival and Thomas have taken watch with the Askar guards positioned all around the caravan. They shall be safe this night," Count Henry said as he sat himself down and looked at Paul. "You must tell me some time how Ishmael was changed," he asked as Paul nodded yes silently.

"Alisha and Ailia sleep with Sister Lucy and Princess Stephanie in her caravan," Paul remarked after a short pause, looking at his wine. His hair was matted with blood and his uniform torn, burnt and ripped as well as covered in black soot and more dried blood. "And I do stink so I shall accept your offer…and as for Ishmael. 'Twas Kratos and the old woman's doing."

"You need say no more about Ishmael then for I understand fully now."

"Do you…really?" Paul asked, looking up at him. "Many would never believe such a thing possible. 'Tis just too fantastic…the stuff we only hear about in myth and legends."

"You, my friend, are what legends are made from…'tis a power and one I trust you will be able to handle over the coming years."

410

"No I am not…men like Theo, Tenno and Thomas and his men…they are the true men of legends, not I."

"Paul…they gave their lives to protect the Crimson Thread that runs through you and your family. Do not cheapen their sacrifice by not accepting that which is true."

"But I have learnt that all of us, every single being upon our world, is part of that thread. Some can access such items like my sword simply because of their blood, but we are all from the same source…our eternal souls."

"Aye…that I can agree with. But you have a duty to fulfil and I am not talking about the Order we wish to form with Saladin…but the continuation of the codes from antiquity. Especially the one that shows the way back to our origins…to our very creation no less as encoded within all four major religions. To remember who we really are…but also to where we go next."

Paul's mind immediately recalled the first time his father and Firgany had told him and Taqi about the Apotheosis of man. Psalm 82:6 'Ye are gods; and all of you are children of the most High'.

"I worked it out our souls are created in the heavens…where we see Orion in the skies…but," Paul said and looked up at Count Henry. "But the symbols and images from all four…no one will believe they are all but a quarter each of the code…of a map no less."

"Why do you think I hold the title of Nautonier…as your father did before me…the Navigator? Not just of a boat or symbolic of some mystical esoteric reference to leading or guiding mankind…but a real navigator. One that will lead people back to where we belong. That, my friend, is the whole purpose of all this sacrifice. The navigator of a true celestial boat… Stella Maris for real."

As the words 'Stella Maris' echoed through his mind, he wondered how his father was doing as fond memories of La Rochelle flooded his thoughts and he lowered his head, tired. Count Henry stood up and walked across to a sectioned off area where a large bowl was being prepared with hot water and fresh towels upon a separate collapsible table.

 3 – 48

"I just feel so tired…yet I know there is still much I must do," Paul sighed.

"You must first look after yourself before you can hope to look after others. You cannot pour from an empty cup," Count Henry said as Taqi appeared at the entrance with his companion. He motioned with his head for them to enter. "I shall check on the others."

Taqi came and sat opposite Paul as his colleague remained at the entrance. Paul looked up at him then at Taqi.

"I must thank you both for all you have done of late. I had not even been made aware of your colleague's presence or what he did at the cave. Thank you," Paul said quietly.

"We do what we do in the shadows, without reward or glory for a greater reward...for our soul's growth...our spiritual advancement hopefully. We are not like Turansha and his assassins for they are in the main gullible, easily misled or simply not educated to the true ways," Taqi replied as Paul looked down, tired. "And I hear I am to become an uncle again as well as a father myself soon."

Paul looked up at him and nodded in silence and forced a tired smile.

"Taqi, forgive me if I look or appear uninterested...for I am truly happy Alisha is with child again, but I cannot rest until Turansha is dead...despite what I was told oft times that I should not seek revenge upon him...or who commands him from the shadows. Now I have no choice."

"My friend, let us get you home safely and I swear I and the Order I am part of will remove him and his poisoned influence once and for all. Al Rashid has given us that task...and to find out whom Turansha is working with and commands him." Paul looked wearily at Taqi, whose eyes sparkled in the light of the lanthorn. He exuded confidence and strength and he was more than glad he had his support. Taqi stood up, patted Paul on the shoulders and winked. "Now clean yourself up for you truly stink," he laughed as he made his way to the exit.

Port of La Rochelle, France, Melissae Inn, spring 1191

"What is this you speak of...about all four major religions having a quarter of a secret?" Gabirol asked, looking puzzled. "You have not mentioned it thus far but 'tis obviously very important."

"No I have not mentioned it for I wished to only impart it to those of you who would still be here as I conclude this tale," the old man answered and smiled. "It is difficult to explain and presently we do not have the means to confirm certain

details of it...but there will come a time when man will have the tools to be able to see and understand what has been obvious all along," he explained.

"Before you do, can you just explain who exactly that Jaromir is. I know you said he was Kratos's brother...but...," Simon asked.

"He is one of the nine, like Kratos," the old man replied. "Remember how I explained all about nine...nine circles, nine phases, nine spheres or realms of heaven, nine original knights who founded the Templars, nine levels within the Templar order, nine months for a child to grow and be born?" he asked and looked around the table at them as they all nodded yes. "Then know this...that there were originally nine like Kratos who volunteered to remain and help mankind evolve again. Most sleep within what can best be described as glass containers...sarcophagi even. I believe I mentioned before, inside they who sleep, half an hour of their time can pass, yet many thousands of years may pass in our world," the old man explained and paused to let what he had said sink in. "Jaromir...he sleeps, or did, in India."

"Why India?" the wealthy tailor asked immediately.

"Its history is far more ancient than you can imagine. Recall what I said about the three wise men...the Magi...and India, as well as their knowledge and connection to Egypt of course?" the old man answered as the wealthy tailor nodded yes he remembered. "Well, Kratos, Jaromir were just two of nine...simply known as the nine as I have previously explained."

"Is that why in English we have nine in feminine?" Ayleth asked quietly.

Simon laughed out loud but immediately checked himself as the logic of her question hit him. He looked over at the old man for his response.

"Perhaps," he replied and smiled.

"Can you tell us where the baby girl came from Kratos handed over to the blacksmith and his wife for it wasn't Tenno's child?" Gabirol asked.

"That I cannot answer for I do not know. Perhaps she was like Master Douglas?" the old man answered and raised his hands slightly.

"Or it was a child made from that old woman who changed into an angel," Sarah interrupted. "Well, she did change so I am calling her an angel. You did say Theodoric had a child or lay with her...or a similar being in the Emerald Isle did you not?"

The old man said nothing but raised his hands again and shrugged his shoulders.

"What about Theodoric's last comments about telling Paul...about camels?" Peter asked.

"Ah, the camels. I shall come to that in a moment but before I forget, I must *explain what I mentioned previously and how a nine looks like a reversed P. The P that runs through the Chi-Ro, that cross Constantine saw in his vision and painted upon his soldiers' shields. Well it is that cross which is part of the code that all four major religions each hold a part of. It includes the cross of Christianity, the Menorah of Jewish tradition, the Om symbol of Hinduism and the image that will one day become the accepted symbol of Islam."*

"What symbol of Islam?" Gabirol asked, puzzled.

"In time, for it is already written, Islam will adopt the symbol of the crescent based upon the ancient symbols. Many such crescents are made of stone and are buried across the world. I cannot divulge exactly how this will come to pass but as I hope you all know and understand, in the future, there will be those souls born who will understand. They will make the items that will allow them to see across to other suns, other worlds...and even other realms."

Yarmoch bridge, Yarmoch plateau, Kingdom of Jerusalem, October 5th 1187

Paul stripped off down to his waist leaving his chain mail, mantle and three swords on the floor beside his feet. He had already put his sword that Tenno had used so decisively back into the scabbard Arri had made him. His heart felt heavy as he remembered him and all the others. The hot water steamed lightly as he turned and lowered his face to look at his own reflection in the water. He sighed thinking back on all he had learnt from Theodoric, Count Henry, Master Jakelin, Attar, Kratos and so much he hoped he could still learn from his father. In the water he could hardly recognise the face that stared back at him, the steam only adding to the change in him. He pulled up the small collapsible wooden stool and sat on it resting his elbows on the table, his hands upon his head as he leant over the bowl and closed his eyes as the steam gently rose into his face. After a few minutes he scooped up some water and ran it through his hair. It took several more scoops to start cleaning away the dried blood, turning the bowl of water red. He sighed heavily again as he thought back on everything that had happened to him and all those he knew. He wanted to cry and he scowled as he tried to understand why Alisha would have wanted to remain dead to him, especially when she knew she was carrying his child. It was not so much a doubt but more a deep sadness he could not shake off. He sat up and shrugged his tired shoulders when suddenly Sister Lucy coughed lightly behind him. He looked up at her, startled.

"I can tell you are exhausted for you did not hear or sense me enter," she said as she looked at him with her arms folded. "I have been stood here some several minutes just watching you. Seeing how much you have grown," she explained and walked over to him. "Alisha and Ailia are cleaned, changed and asleep as is Stephanie…but I cannot sleep, so now then…as I am here, tell me…what troubles you?" she asked and placed her hand upon his fore-arm as she sat on the other stool beside him.

"'Tis hard to explain…but I find it hard to reconcile why Alisha would wish to have me believe her dead…knowing she was also carrying my child. I tell myself 'tis as she explained…but," Paul explained shaking his head, sadness evident in his eyes.

"Paul…grief can make us all do strange and confusing things, but trust me on this if you should never trust me again on anything," she said, star-ing at him intently and held his hands. "We received word from Queen Tamar's reconnaissance scouts that you were all dead. They stated clearly they had seen the graves marked with Theo's name…and Tenno's and several Templars. Yes we questioned who must have buried them…but I guess we both were not in a fit state of mind or nice place I can tell you. I thank the Lord we had the company of Queen Tamar and several nuns to help us through those very dark days. I am mightily glad they broke their vow to Alisha and told you she was still alive," she explained and looked at Paul more intently as he nodded silently in agreement. "'Twas many weeks later when we finally received word you were in actual fact still alive… and Alisha too became alive again. We were ready to leave immediately and risk the journey to reach you…me believing Theo was, however, still dead for his grave had been named and marked…and we assumed Ailia too, but then we received word of rumours that a real Grail King had made his presence known within Jerusalem…was now coupled with Stephanie and she was to be divorced from Reynald. You could have blown Alisha down with a feather…she was devastated all over again for we both knew immediately it was you. It was like having her heart put back in only to be ripped out again…and I will not tell you the number of nights she cried asking why you had not waited longer…questioned whether you had actu-ally fallen for Stephanie from the first moment you met her. All the mixed up emotional, logical and illogical questions a person in love and wounded asks," she explained softly and rubbed Paul's arm as guilt registered across his features. "Paul...Alisha went over all I had ever told you both... the parchments, the warnings...everything. Consequently she believed you would ultimately be better off without her...and your child she felt she could better protect from the likes of Turansha and others if they all believed her dead too...just as Theo and Tenno had thought and tried to do with Ailia...but her heart was truly broken and I could not make her see reason or sense...until you found us. Once you break, 'tis impossible to put it back to how it was."

"I...I shall never mistrust my instincts again...for even when I lay with Stephanie...I could always sense Alisha. But I did not believe in that instinct strongly enough and I should have."

 2 – 18

"What is done is done. We must get you all home...home where we belong and let others deal with Turansha as they have vowed."

"I am grateful you are in my life...have always been in my life. You are a much loved friend," Paul said and looked at her. "You have been a mother to me with much wise counsel and have always known what to do. Even now suffering your own heartache, you comfort me."

"And you are as a son to me," she replied as tears welled in her eyes. "You see...I am not such a hard bag after all," she smiled. "You called me that once as a child when I chastised you for making you take lessons."

"I do not recall ever calling you such, but if I did, know I retract it completely. You have taught me much...perhaps more than most over my life."

"Then pray tell me what you have learnt."

"Where do I begin?" Paul asked and paused for few moments before looking back up at her. "But first I must ask how you are?"

"Me," she replied and paused. "I...I feel broken too. I do not know many women who have had to mourn the same man three times...but then Theo always was different," she answered and smiled but the pain was obvious in her eyes. "At least I got to say farewell to him properly."

"I wish to know what the secret was about camels."

Sister Lucy laughed lightly and shook her head.

"'Twas when we first met. 'Tis no great secret but he actually exchanged me for a Turcoman horse...much like Adrastos, and thirty camels."

"Why?" Paul asked bemused.

"To save my life. He lied telling some Bedouin that I was a queen from France. They had ambushed us en route to Alexandria when we were travelling from Tunisia. He put on such a strong front and bluffed his way to freedom promising never to tell anyone of my whereabouts so the Bedouin leader could keep me as his pleasure thing. He was so convincing I even worried at one point that he meant it," she laughed and paused. "He managed to save himself and walk away with all the camels, promising to return with more women to sell on…he did return that evening under cover of darkness, scared the life out of me as he entered the tent looking like some evil spectre, killed the Bedouin leader, who already had his hands all over me, and then carried me out of the camp, the others all believing some evil beast had carried me off. He was a genius for doing things like that."

Paul immediately recalled how Theodoric had disguised himself as a flying angel when he helped rescue Alisha, Arri and himself from Turansha after the killing of Elek.

"I do not understand why he said we should never speak of it then?" Paul asked.

Sister Lucy picked up a soaked flannel and began to wipe blood off of Paul's upper arm and smiled as she recalled many memories.

"Whenever Theo and I argued, which was often, he would oft say he wished he had kept the camels and left me. It became so bad that after one argument I actually went for him with a sword whilst he was drunk and vowed if he ever said it again, I would kill him whilst he slept."

"My Lord…it must have been some row?"

"Neither of us can remember what we argued about…but Theo never did say it again, never became drunk and everything changed for us after that. And so we joke about never mentioning camels," she sighed and wiped more dried blood from his arm.

Both looked up as Count Henry coughed to make his presence known. He smiled as he entered, Stewart giving a quick wave behind him letting Paul know he was just outside.

"Is all well here?" Count Henry asked and pulled up a collapsed stool, opened it and sat down opposite them.

"We were just discussing what Paul has learnt over these past years," Sister Lucy replied and squeezed out the flannel.

"Ah I see. I hope I do not intrude then but I too would like to hear, if I may?" he asked. Both shook their heads they did not mind. "Then please pray tell us what you have learnt...though I am certain one night is far from enough to impart that which you have come to know."

"What have I learnt?" Paul sighed and wiped his face dry with a towel and placed it around his shoulders as he turned to face Count Henry and Sister Lucy. "I know that we as a species have forgotten who we are and where we come from. I know that we once reached great heights in knowledge and wisdom and constructed buildings and reminders on a worldwide scale, much of it still in evidence in their massive remains, such as Baalbek...and in the pyramids, yet most cannot see it, and those that do refuse to believe it. I know the pyramids and ancient standing stone sites are aligned with heavenly bodies...and that they constantly generate an energy that helps balance our world and keep it safe. They are all connected. I have learnt that our souls once created become immortal and grow...even through successive life times and realms. I know that our ancient forefathers encoded within the major religions great secrets that we shall again one day unlock...secrets that will show us the way back to remembering who we are and what we can become. I know that the four major religions all have a quarter of that secret that one day man will understand and will allow us to know and open a path back to what we all understand as God. I know where sacred ancient halls of wisdom and knowledge are hidden...and they still lie just waiting for when the time is right. They are a legacy left from a mighty and highly advanced worldwide civilisation that would appear magical to us."

"Like the one you entered in Cairo?" Count Henry asked.

"Yes. 'Tis just one of four also. The passageways beneath the pyramids are sealed so man cannot enter the sacred chambers of creation before the time is correct. But the chambers still remain northeast, on a heading of twenty-six degrees in a direction for Bethlehem. I know the codes and symbols that pinpoint exactly its position. I know the New Jerusalem dimensions and materials detailed within Revelation in the Bible are all identical but in scale to our planet we live upon. I know our ancient forefathers knew this world was a sphere before we forgot and believed it to be flat. I know that at thirty-three degrees in the heavens, a star that acts as a marker will reveal the location where our ancestors who advanced beyond our present state went to...and more importantly...that every one of us is equal and are all divine beings in the making."

"But do you fully understand the four elements...the symbols hidden within the four major religions?" Count Henry asked, looking at Paul intently. "And about the twin dark sun?

"Yes...though the symbol for Islam is not correct yet...but it will adopt the crescent in time. As for the twin star, yes I am aware of all of that. 'Tis also related to the Templar twin riders on a single horse as well as many more."

"Excellent...that proves you know and understand enough," Count Henry remarked and smiled. Sister Lucy looked at him, puzzled. "Islam will indeed adopt the symbol of the crescent...only then will it fit the codes that will give us a map of the heavens...a map by which we can one day navigate and set mankind on a new voyage of discovery. We have brothers and sisters already out there who await us...await us to mature."

"I know the symbol of the Chi-Ro is part of the greater secret to understanding the heavenly map, but I also know it is not meant for our times for we do not have the means to confirm aspects of it," Paul replied in response. "But there will come a time when the earth passes from this cycle of Pisces, the fish, to Aquarius, the water bearer, denoting the spiritual age. I know that period of time marks the end of the great year and the beginning of another...of some 25,900 years plus," Paul detailed and paused before looking at Sister Lucy only. "I also know that my father has taken nine bodies from La Rochelle and interned them temporarily in Balantrodach?" in Alba until a new chapel can be erected upon an ancient sacred marker that has properties that can open a portal...a doorway to other realms. I know that the acorns Alisha carries in her dagger are to be used to mark out an island in the New World where a greater secret is already buried. Kratos gave me details of a location in Alba, that should I live long enough, I should site and build a tower...a marker that would be exactly 2,160 miles from the island where the acorns will be planted. Incidentally, he instructed me that the City of David was built upon the original outline of this Oak Island...not the other way around as some people will one day argue, for they both share the same shape that replicates the bull's leg constellation of Taurus, identified in ancient Egypt as the place of 'those that came from above'," Paul explained, rubbing his fingers through his hair wearily.

"You mentioned you understood about the doorway to other realms. How so?" Count Henry asked.

"'Tis all part of the code surrounding the value of nine. The nine knights who lay in Balantrodach?", the Norse legends that speak of the nine inhabited worlds. The ancient Ennead, the group of nine gods that embodied the creative source and chief forces of the universe," Paul answered and saw the puzzled look on Sister Lucy's face. "The Ennead, being the Nine Principles through which the pharaohs ruled and ordered the forces of the universe, that dominated Egyptian thought," he quickly explained as Count Henry nodded in agreement.

"'Tis a great shame the Pope hides all the information on Egypt for they will keep it that way so we cannot understand the writings of their language," Count Henry remarked.

"But is that not why Theo and Philip both carved several Stella looking stones to guarantee they would be found so we could decipher their language if it was hidden by the Church?" Sister Lucy asked. "And what is this heavenly star map that you speak of all four faiths having?" Sister Lucy further asked as another bowl of hot water was brought in by one of Count Henry's men. He placed it upon the table and removed the now cold blood coloured bowl in front of Paul.

"Yes they did construct several Stella carved into stone…and it was to fall to the like of Kratos to ensure they would be found…but I understand that task will now fall to another," Count Henry replied as Paul nodded yes silently. "But I should let Paul explain about the secret each major religion holds a quarter of."

5 – 7

"I shall try," Paul replied and rubbed his hands through his hair again. "Hinduism, Judaism, Christianity and Islam all replaced their earlier belief systems that originally all shared sacred cow or bull veneration, even if they appeared to be very different systems. This was from a time when the earth was passing through the zodiac era of Taurus, the bull. Even in Egypt bull worship is found. In Hinduism we have the symbol for Om, but also its form traces the stellar figure of Taurus the Bull in the heavens. Remember the preceding cycle before Aries, symbolised by the Ram, was Taurus, symbolised by the Bull…'tis why when Moses in the Bible version, after being given the Ten Commandments, he returned late and his people had cast a golden calf to worship it again, fearing he had abandoned them…but 'tis just a time marker symbol. After Taurus the Bull came Aries the Ram, and is why the Hebrews used shepherd symbolism and goat sacrifice et cetera right up until the birth of the Jesus initiative, when came Pisces, symbolised by the fish. But all four major religions have within them an encoded reference to the bull."

"Why…this is not something Theo or your father ever covered before," Sister Lucy remarked, looking puzzled.

"That is because they were not made aware of it I think you will find," Count Henry remarked as Paul nodded in agreement.

"'Tis information Kratos imparted to me when I spent time alone with him in the desert," Paul explained. "'Tis esoteric and hidden, but will become obvious in the future. For now only a very few true initiates are privileged to know it. The secret is that all four religions share one piece of the same 'Map of Heaven'… the place in the cosmos where our true hidden history originates and where all of our human ancestors, or what some would term an Angelic bloodline, also originated from and returned. The true source of the Crimson Thread…but as I have learnt, our souls…we are all part of it. You I suspect already know much of what I speak," Paul said, looking at Count Henry.

"I know that many ancient Hindu records speak of the first lineage of Brahma and a heavenly Trinity that was not just coincidently the shortened word for Abraham which Judaism, Christianity and Islam all share. They do in fact detail the very same lineage of our original ancestors, that much I do know, including the creation of the universe, the Tree of Life, the source of all life, the light source all our souls originate from. But I also know…and this is what concerns me, that mankind once he understands this will have a choice. There will be two choices with the final outcome resulting from what mankind decides and how he acts," Count Henry explained.

"What do you mean?" Sister Lucy asked, looking even more puzzled.

"Everything in the universe is based upon choice and consequence," Paul answered as Count Henry agreed with him. "Even a thought sends out its own ripple effect like a pebble hitting water. One choice is for all of us to recognise and accept that we are all one. We are all beings of spirit. Together mankind must change to act as one in the light of love. The other is when we find ourselves in a world of greed, war, famine and set within the closed minded restrictive confines of religious dogmas that will ultimately lead to a backward slide in humanity as it wages mass killings in the name of holy wars based upon the ignorant blind faith and unquestioning obedience of words written within holy books."

"Then your task must surely be to educate people in a new way of thought?" Sister Lucy asked.

"One thing I have learnt and that is once we have a set of ideas, it is almost impossible to shake ourselves out of them no matter what other genuine evidence you can prove, especially our religious beliefs. Once instilled since birth, by the time we are old enough to consciously choose, it's too late. That is why it is an impossible task to change things now...in our time...for it will be a long and painfully slow process to awaken people's inner voice and souls."

"What do you see as an alternative then?" Count Henry asked.

"A completely new order, not religious per se, but spiritual, that does not impose its beliefs...but challenges you to seek for yourself answers. The true purpose of any religion should be to facilitate a direct connection with the Divine, and to support spiritual awakening. I have learnt that religion and spirituality are not the same. Granted religion acts as a vehicle and as a means of guaranteeing the codes from antiquity are carried across time complete...for they are held and continued with such zealous fanaticism, but that is why I wish to form a new Order...of masons, architects, builders...open to all members regardless of race, creed, religion or background. It is the only way a true spiritual awakening can begin."

"But religion helps answer many of those questions many feel a need to be answered," Count Henry stated, as if prompting Paul.

"Yes...but what if the contrived answers are wrong?" Paul asked back. "We have to start by asking why do we even seek answers to spiritual matters in the first place for that proves to me that we all have echoes within us of something long since lost...but our souls remember."

"You are talking about seeking answers to where do we really come from, why are we here, and especially, where do we go after death?" Sister Lucy said softly.

"Yes, but that is why religion is able to prey on the fears of people seeking those answers by giving them easy to follow and accept rules and laws, which leads to a false sense of security...which in some respects is not such a bad thing I guess. But that takes away our own responsibility and leaves it in the hands of priests, rabbis and those who would abuse their position within religion. That then stops us from ever being able to really find our true spiritual self. I used to tell myself that the Old Testament was for a time when man was young so had harsh rules...with a jealous God, yet the Bible says being jealous is a sin...so you can see the immediate contradiction in that one fact alone amongst many. The New Testament brought new laws and truths, but again that has all been abused and misinterpreted to suit the self serving purposes of those in control. Being taught that God is to be feared, and if you sin or break any commandments, you will be punished, and maybe even sent to a fiery hell to repent eternally is so far from what spirituality is about...'tis the dogma and fear that imprisons so many in the name of religion."

"How do you mean, Paul?" Sister Lucy asked.

"Because religions keep us away from that divine connection as we abdicate all responsibility to priests and Church elders. Too many believe they are not worthy and oppressed emotionally and spiritually and that they can only receive God's love and blessings through a third party...as I said, like a priest, rabbi or mystic guru, to be able to speak with God." [118]

"You mean like pushing upon them disempowering beliefs, a sense of unworthiness, powerlessness, judgment and exclusion, and guilt?" Count Henry asked.

"Yes, like believing your soul's salvation is dependent on your behaviour. That if you disobey, you will be judged and punished eternally. To question your religion immediately invokes feelings of shame, guilt, obligation or regret. These feelings, or the fear of these feelings, can be a more powerful deterrent than even the threat of physical torture. I know I used to be fearful when I started to question everything. I believed that all the bad that has befallen us...was down to my actions alone...but I know that is not the case."

"Theo oft spoke like that. You are so like him in many ways. It was his first lesson to me when I met him when he said I should not feel ashamed and guilty about making love," Sister Lucy explained and laughed lightly to herself. "Our religion says it is wrong and unholy to have sex outside of marriage, and if you do you will be condemned to Hell...but on a personal emotional level you also automatically punish yourself through feelings of deep shame, guilt, regret and unworthiness. The same applied if you were to think about going against the religious doctrines. Theo changed all of that for me."

"That is why I shall teach Ailia to question everything and keep her free will and to be inspired by her own inner spirituality and not that as forced upon her."

"But, Paul, that is exactly how the mechanism of religion works…to control the many by the few. Because control is coming from inside you, in the form of your own beliefs and emotions, people do not even realise they are being controlled. When we are threatened by an external force we can see, we can react with either fighting it or running from it, but when you cannot see that force as it is internal, then fear wins. Fear of the unknown is a powerful tool, which Theo certainly knew and why he was able to use people's own fears against them," Count Henry explained.

"Too many sacrifice their own God given power in exchange for what they believe is their eternal salvation by their religion, by handing their trust to their leaders rather than trust their own inner divinity and voice and that if you want a prayer answered or seek forgiveness, you must use a go-between because you are not worthy, or pure enough, for direct communion with the Divine," Paul responded back, his mind running fast. "Religions only work by mass consent to the unspoken decree of worthiness that all practitioners agree to, your worth being solely dependent on how well you follow the rules of your religion. If you do as you are told, according to your religion, or your religious leader, you are deemed worthy, and if you go against, or question, the rules or beliefs, you are deemed unworthy. Unworthiness induces deep feelings of shame, which leads to secrecy and fear of being judged, so everyone pretends to be a good follower, while secretly hiding any bad behaviour or desires and consequently making it impossible for you to speak your truth."

 3 – 2

"That is why the so called self righteous from any religion will always follow the belief and path that where they, the believer, is right, the non-believer will always be wrong, which then becomes another form of judgement and exclusion in the name of God," Count Henry remarked and sat up straight.

"That is why all that I have done and wish to do is not to make people leave or abandon their religion…but to see it for what it is and to reawaken the truth that is within all of us. To free themselves from disempowerment and taking back their power from everyone and everything...and that by necessity includes religious dogma. 'Tis easy to blame religion for keeping oneself powerless and controlled but in truth religions as we now have them only exist because we seek answers outside of ourselves rather looking inwardly."

"Theo said that religion as used now is set up to guarantee you fail spiritually so you will always be a slave to its leaders...unless you can break away from the enforced beliefs and look deeply to the only place you can find a true answer...within yourself," Sister Lucy said. "So I totally agree with what you say...but what you speak will be considered blasphemous and heretical by most. 'Tis dangerous for you."

"That is why all I hope to reveal will have to be hidden...in plain sight of those initiated though. It will all be allegorical and symbolic but complete with all the codes ready for when man will be able to see it without such conditions being imposed upon it."

"Paul, you must carry the codes forward in whatever inspired manner you find best. Odo de St Armand hid copies of his understanding about sound...we believe somewhere within the church he had commissioned on his family lands in France. 'Tis but a small scroll and deals with the harmonics of sound...alas he died before he told anyone exactly where he hid it other than to say it is the same as for the Chambers of Creation set twenty-six degrees northeast from the apex," Count Henry explained then handed Paul a small parchment roll. "But this I do have from him. Perhaps you will put it with the rest of your parchments and journals. The attached symbols your father also has but they must one day be incorporated within the chapel he wishes built...so in the future man will be able to use sound to open doorways, but also that secret that hides in the New World as well as the sealed chambers in Egypt."

Paul took the small parchment roll and opened it. He pulled the lanthorn closer and read the words upon it written by Master Odo. He ran his fingers over several patterned images.

'The harmony of sound holds everything in its place. Like waves in water so waves of sound are made. Understand the waves and the waters of creation will be revealed and the doors to Heaven and the stars beyond will be opened unto you. Understand the trident for it becomes the key.'

Fig. 78: Sound Patterns.

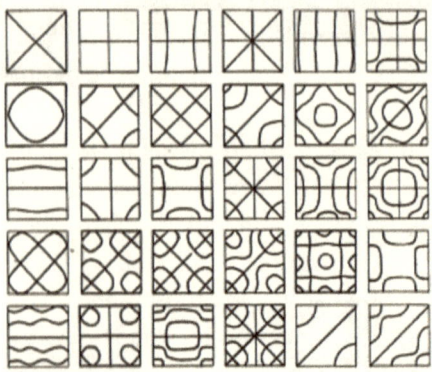

"But I do not have any of my work I am afraid," Paul remarked and looked up.

"Princess Stephanie holds all of your work as you entrusted it to her… for safe keeping remember?" Count Henry said and frowned at Paul. "And that is exactly what she has done. All of your work is within her caravan. I am surprised you did not know this."

"No…I did not know…Lord bless that woman. I shall put this with it all then…and the sword of Saladin," Paul replied and looked down at his swords. He felt deeply touched she had still kept his work safe. He knew that in amongst his papers and journals was the letter Princess Stephanie had given him years previously…one he had still not opened. If he got to France safely, then and only then would he open and read it, he told himself.

"I wish we had a name for the previous civilisation you oft speak of. Theo always said once something has a name, it becomes real," Sister Lucy sighed and placed her hands together, looking sad as she thought of Theodoric.

"But it did. It has many names but one is the 'Khemetians', where the root word Khem comes from, Khem being the original name for the land of Egypt in great antiquity. It was that civilisation who built the Sphinx, pyramids of the Giza Plateau, as well as other monuments to the north and south and many more across our entire world," Paul explained. "Judaism, Christianity and Islam all ultimately evolved out of Egypt…and via India before that. When man looks closely at the mighty works in stone they produced, then they will recognise just how truly advanced their skills once were before being lost within the sands of time. 'Twas Attar who explained much of this to me when we lived in Egypt. He said the Templars' highest initiates all know the duality of Christianity and Islam and that they share the same origin and ride the same horse symbolically...as in that form which carries them along."

"Aye that is true and is but another reason and meaning behind the two riders upon one horse," Count Henry explained. "As you know of the four hidden symbols, perhaps you can now understand the layout behind the design of the flag of Jerusalem. It originated from the coat of arms worn by Godfrei de Bouillon during the First Crusade, and it has remained in use as the arms of the King of Jerusalem ever since. The symbolism of the five-fold cross is variously given as the five wounds of Christ, Christ and the four quarters of the world, or Christ and the four evangelists. However, esoterically it represents the main Chi-Rho cross at its centre, literally meaning X marks the spot, heavenly speaking, whilst its four segments each represent one of the four major religions."

"And the holy books, the Bible and the Qur'an...you said they are just books," Sister Lucy remarked, perplexed. "I thought they carried many of the codes within...and real truths though not seen by the uninitiated, or have they...in fact all of us, wasted both our time and lives on falsehood and myth?"

"No...neither you nor the others have wasted your time for it is true they do contain many codes and genuine truths, even if veiled," Count Henry answered and paused as he looked back at Paul first. "But it is sadly how those truths are interpreted and how those very books are used to manipulate, deceive and as a means to wage wars, murder and oppress as well as remove freedom of thought to serve the benefits of just a few self proclaimed elites."

"Kratos explained to me that people have lost sight of how to read, interpret and use the books by means of the Holy Spirit we all have access to... our higher spiritual conscience no less and not held exclusively by priests, rabbis and imams alone," Paul explained, his eyes becoming heavy with tiredness. "We must again learn to rely upon that same real Holy Spirit to lead each of us individually to our own truths...not the actual books for they are just a tool all too often corrupted by the hands of men for good or evil depending on the spirit guiding its interpretation. Reading, using and interpreting the books without listening to that true higher self we all possess, the books simply become the dead letter of the laws in them... devoid of life."

"But what of the many thousands of books the Pope holds?" Sister Lucy asked.

"Oh he does indeed have many thousands of so-called original manuscripts sealed in vaults beneath Rome and elsewhere…but in reality there are no original manuscripts of the fashion they claim," Count Henry replied immediately and sat up straight before continuing. "Yes there are some eight thousand of them but they are all contradictory fourth century copies of documents the Church claims are first century letters. In time this fact will become clear. Even the four main gospels are by anonymous authors for they have no idea who really wrote them. Even all of the works attributed to Saint Paul were written by much later sixth century Catholics. The Papacy does, however, maintain other sealed vaults containing thousands upon thousands of truly original manuscripts, scrolls and books from the ancient world that were confiscated and hidden over a three hundred year period after Christ. The Holy Roman Church has so far successfully compiled a scripture taken from original ancient manuscripts then modified and rewritten it all prior to their first canonisation of accepted scripture that began at the Council of Nicaea in AD 325. The final canon of scripture, now accepted and recognised by all Christians as the Word of God these past eight hundred years, was settled on the 28th of August AD 397 by The Council of Carthage. That council met under the supervision of the Bishop of Carthage, North Africa, and the Western Roman Emperor, Flavius Honorius, the decrees being later approved by the Bishop of Rome, the Pope, who later also approved the definitive translation of Saint Jerome called the Vulgate. Since then, the Bible has been modified and rewritten countless times…and will most probably be rewritten again several more times, so you see, still the shadow of Rome is long." [119]

"Sister Lucy, Count Henry speaks the truth as I too understand it and have been instructed," Paul remarked and looked at her as she listened intently, her mind as sharp ever taking it all in. "Today, it makes no difference which scripture we choose or version because we are forced to believe they are the Word of God only, holy and infallible and we must not dare question any of it, because we are told so by the old Holy Roman Empire."

"The Roman Empire took control of all spiritual texts and records and they were either removed or destroyed… and those individuals or groups who had true spiritual knowledge and the true history of Creation were murdered, sometimes in their hundreds, even thousands," Count Henry explained further and looked back at Paul. "'Tis why the Cathars will soon see this horror visited upon them as Attar and others have foreseen. This has so far led to the almost utter total destruction of the very history of our world and has given the Roman Empire the power of authority to manipulate the ignorant and uneducated population to follow their own desired practices integrated into their canons of scripture. Confiscating or destroying the ancient records has allowed them to write an alternative invented 'history', which has disconnected humanity from its true origins. Controlling history through their written history and prophetic events is important because if one manipulates how people see what we call the past, this influences the present and the future."

"I have heard that many times...Who controls the past, controls the future," Paul remarked.

"Yes but there is also...who controls the present, controls the past," Count Henry replied and paused seeing Paul sigh and shake his head tired and weary. "That is why it is essential the present reach of the long shadow of Rome does not eradicate totally the past for sadly the Roman Catholic Church has been built upon murder, torture and lies and the only way a lie can survive is to create more lies and destroy the people who know the real truth. This is why you must remain hidden...your whole family line for as long as it takes. In time, then it shall be reawakened under the signs of the apple, bees and rose as an identifier marker. Until then, the Church will continue to use the very Bible itself to instil fear to make it believable. Countless hundreds of thousands of people suffer depression, hopelessness and confusion about life because Christianity as a whole has been placed under a powerful spell and indoctrinated not to question their Word of God. But it is the same within Judaism and Islam...or any form of religion that imposes impossible restrictions...and all of this has directly affected each and every one of us. Humanity has suffered unnecessarily because of the denial of this truth. People have been forced over the centuries by paying both financially and with their lives to keep these deceptions alive that continue to grow even stronger. The survival and prosperity of this deception on Christianity alone simply requires only one thing...total surrender to absolute obedience and of personal questioning and discernment...and any religion that forces that upon anyone is just as guilty, and sadly all religions are presently like this...through the use and abuse of fear...not love. But as was explained to you years ago in Jerusalem along with Theodoric, 'twas and sadly is at this time a necessity to guarantee the codes are carried forwards for when mankind will need to know the truth, recover and use that which was hidden for our eventual survival and growth as this very world starts to experience great changes and upheavals both physically and spiritually. That is why you must write those codes using the Atbash cipher and mathematical value codes used to express the very sayings and name for our Lord God...so it will be recognised, remembered and used again," Count Henry said, impassioned.

33 – 4 [120]

"That I intend to do, Lord willing...but if I am not able, then all is already prepared and written within the parchments and my journals Stephanie now holds," Paul remarked then raised his hand. "And to remind myself daily I still wear this," he said as he looked at the black and yellow wrist band with the thinner crimson thread running through it. "And this," he continued as he pulled the yellow and black cord hung loose around his neck. "I know of all the symbolism connected with bees, apples and roses... but I have seen so many times the image of a new cathedral being raised that has a single yellow rose...laid upon three red roses upon a white lily."

"I think we have spoken enough this eve," Count Henry said seeing the growing tiredness in Paul's eyes as he blinked heavily, trying to focus upon the wrist band. "You must rest for tomorrow we have a long journey ahead of us," he said quietly and stood to leave. "I will bid you both a good night each for I fear I shall talk you both to death this eve...'tis a passion I do not often get the chance to speak of."

Sister Lucy smiled up at him and nodded as he politely bowed his head slightly, looked at Paul, who was still deep in thought staring in exhausted silence at his wrist band. Just as Count Henry was about to leave Paul looked up at him.

"Before you leave us...I have something for you," he said and stood up slowly, reached inside his tunic and removed an old envelope. He looked at it for some while before looking back at Count Henry and offering it toward him.

"What is it?" he asked as he took the sealed envelope.

"'Tis a list of some people I wish you to seek out if I am not able to return to La Rochelle with you," Paul explained as Sister Lucy stood up quickly, looking alarmed.

"A list...why, and what nonsense do you speak of not returning?" she asked, shaking her head, puzzled.

"'Tis a list I compiled with the help of Kratos...when I stayed with him in the desert that time. As an insurance. Just in case," Paul answered then looked deep into Count Henry's eyes. "Please...you must swear to me you will seek these people out. Swear it and I can do what I must do and what comes next...for they must all know and believe, from proofs that will come forth, that it was actually Mary Magdalene who was the very real driving force behind Jesus...she had the power...she was the first true pope of the Church...and the Church will admit this very real fact one day. Then, and only then, will the veil start to be lifted."

Sister Lucy placed her hand upon his forearm, looking fearful hearing his words. Paul raised his eyebrows, prompting Count Henry.

"I shall take it as you request," he replied and took the letter and raised it. "I fear I know what you are telling me...but I pray I am wrong and that it shall be you who seeks these people out."

"Please...just swear to me you shall," Paul pressed as Sister Lucy sighed heavily and shook her head, sensing that Paul obviously knew what lay ahead.

"I pray Alisha does not have to suffer losing you a second time...it would kill her," she said sadly in a low whisper.

"I think we have all known all along how the story of my life would be written as per those damn parchments...but I must know you will seek out these people and continue that which I may not be able to...so please, swear it I beg of you," Paul pleaded, his eyes giving away the inner turmoil he was clearly struggling to control.

"Aye, aye, my friend, I swear it...by all that I am or ever hope to be, upon my oath I swear it," Count Henry said and placed his hand upon Paul's shoulder and looked at him intently. "But it is an oath I pray I need not have to honour."

Sister Lucy looked at the pair of them in silence for several long minutes. She instinctively knew that Paul clearly knew what was coming next as did Count Henry, she only prayed it did not mean losing Paul again. She looked down sadly at his feet.

"Come on you...your feet, they are soaked in blood so let us clean them and get you away to sleep," she said, looking down, trying to hide her sadness. "Come on don't be shy...remove your chausses and breeches," she tried to joke and forced a smile.

"Sister Lucy," Paul said quietly and looked at her sad face as she was still reeling from the loss of Theodoric. She shook her head emotionally as Count Henry stepped back a pace and folded the letter away inside his tunic. "Thank you...for everything," Paul said, seeing she was clearly trying to hide her feelings.

Sister Lucy looked at him briefly but quickly looked back to his feet, fearing she would burst into tears. Paul removed all of his remaining armour and stripped to his under garments only. When he sat down again, she lifted his foot and gently began to clean away all the dried blood that had soaked through his chain mail and garments. Count Henry looked back to see them and watched in silence as she began to clean his feet, Paul simply grateful for her loving and caring presence.

"Emotions take a heavy toll upon us...your mother knew this simple truth for she was far wiser and smarter than I for she would have seen what was coming and somehow avoided all of this...but I am beyond proud of you, Paul...beyond proud," she replied softly.

"No...she would have done exactly the same...and you have been more than a mother to me," Paul replied and watched silently as she bathed his feet. "Do you ever regret helping Alisha and I get together?" he asked softly.

Sister Lucy stopped wiping his foot for a moment and just sat in silence letting his words sink in. She shook her no lightly then continued to wash his feet.

"Never," she whispered.

Port of La Rochelle, France, Melissae Inn, spring 1191

"Sounds more like the image of Mary Magdalene washing the feet of Jesus, anointing him," Simon remarked.

"And the letter," Gabirol said and frowned quizzically at the old man. "I would wager the names Paul had written down are of those present here this day."

Everyone looked at the old man in silence waiting for his answer as he looked at the sword. Eventually he looked up at them all.

"Aye...yes indeed I believe you are correct," the old man answered and raised his hand quickly. "But if correct, do not ask me how Paul knew all of your names...for it is sufficient for you all to know he did and as a consequence you all sit here this

day as he made Count Henry swear he would seek out."

"But you did not know I would be here this day...or my name. I could have easily hit the taverns in the port," the Genoese sailor said, his voice slightly raised, and looking confused.

"But Paul knew, and I think I can prove it...for perhaps he had seen it during his time with Kratos," the old man answered softly.

"Are you Count Henry?" Ayleth asked.

"Me...no not I," the old man replied and put his hands together. "But I promise you in time, you will have an explanation for your paths in this life are all connected." They all sat in silence lost for words each pondering how Paul could have known their names. The old man gently removed a worn and battered envelope from inside his belt pouch and slowly placed it upon the table. He pushed it toward the Templar. With apprehension written across his face, the Templar lifted the envelop and started to open it. He broke the wax seal and unfolded the envelope. The old man nodded yes to take out the sheet within it. The Templar opened the single sheet and shook his head lightly as he read all the names one by one, looking up at each of them in turn nodding yes to confirm their names, Ayleth gasping when he confirmed her name was upon it. The old man smiled more broadly as each name was confirmed. "As I said before...'tis no coincidence you are all here."

"I shall have to accept your word upon that...even if I do not understand what unfolds fully," the Templar said as he placed the sheet back into the envelope. "Though I see other names written upon it who are not here."

"No...not yet, but those others named shall be a part of this story as we move forwards...that I can promise you," the old man explained softly and took the envelope back.

"Next you will tell us that we all likewise volunteered for this as Paul and Alisha did," Simon said loudly and laughed, but it was a nervous laugh.

"Actually Simon, yes you did," the old man replied and smiled at him.

"Are you telling me I actually volunteered to be a stinking fishmonger...I must have been drunk," Simon answered and folded his arms.

"You did...but only to lead you here," the old man replied and smiled again at him. "But your days of being a fishmonger are henceforth over, for a greater job awaits you, if you choose to follow that path of course?"

Simon shook his head, looking puzzled and emotional. Peter looked at everyone sat in silence. An almost awkward silence as they did not know how to respond to the revelation of their names having been written down in Paul's sealed letter.

"Well, I am still trying to understand how Kratos and that old woman who *became young just vanished in a cloud thing. I am not saying I do not believe you...I just cannot see it somehow. Things like that are not mentioned in the Bible as normal are they?" Peter asked, still struggling to understand and accept that part of what the old man had told them, but also to break the silence.*

"My friend, it does say such things in the Bible," the old man replied and smiled at him, grateful for his deliberate question. "'Tis in the Acts of the Apostles which detail for September the event which we have come to know as 'the Ascension'," he explained as Peter leaned nearer to hear clearer. "The one thing that the Acts do not do, however, is call the event 'the Ascension'. This is a name given to the ritual when the Roman Church doctrines were established over three centuries later at Nicaea as explained. What the text actually says is... 'And when he had spoken these things...he was taken up, and a cloud received him out of their sight.' It then continues that 'a man in white' said to the disciples...'Why stand ye gazing up into heaven? This same Jesus...shall so come in like manner as ye have seen him go.'"

"What you mean Jesus will return in the same fashion...and there was a man in white...like Kratos," the Genoese sailor said excitedly.

"I bet you any monies it was Kratos," Simon said aloud. "I bet you!"

"Sorry to change the topic as I backtrack a moment," Gabirol interrupted as he was checking through some earlier notes. "But before you continue I just want to confirm something you said earlier...is that acceptable?" he asked,. The old man nodded yes immediately it was. "'Tis the secret Niccolas mentioned at the start of this tale. He said there is a secret where the square meets the corner within La Rochelle and its churches. Was this his reference to the nine original Templars being buried here, as well as members of Christ's family?" he asked and looked intently at the old man.

Everyone around the table looked at the old man in anticipation.

"Gabirol...that is correct," the old man replied.

"But then," Gabirol said and checked his notes again quickly. "But then you say those bodies have been moved to Balantrodach?", to be moved later, but that there is also to be an Oak Island connection...yes?" he continued to quiz.

"Yes, my friend...that is all correct. 'Tis why the acorns Alisha carried within her dagger were so important, for they would likewise be planted upon that island in the New World so that in the future, it can be recognised by its non-native oaks that would be growing there. Plus quite a few other items such as rare Templar coins. But there is a greater mystery that already lies beneath that island," the old man explained and looked over toward the windows as sunlight started to shine brighter around the edges of the shutters.

"*Please, you must continue for I sense we are all now connected to this tale in some fashion,*" Sarah asked and clasped Stephan's hand tightly. "*And I think there is much you have to tell me...from your years away on the Crusades that you never speak of,*" she sighed, looking sad then kissed his hand lightly.

"*As I said earlier, I shall let him explain my past if he so chooses,*" Stephan replied and clasped his large hands around Sarah's.

"*I shall indeed,*" the old man smiled.

"*All the twin riders' symbolism you have covered so far. What else does it also symbolise for you said there are many?*" Gabirol asked.

"*What if I told you the twin riders upon a single horse also refers to landmarks... the horse being associated with the White Horse of Uffington in England, though in truth it was originally meant to symbolise a feline animal. It connects the Mountain of Pech Cardou where there is still buried remnants of an ancient temple, though now empty thanks to the likes of Paul's father, Firgany and Theodoric,*" the old man explained and paused as he watched the anticipation grow upon their faces. "*It held certain items taken from the so-called Solomon's temple in Jerusalem, though again that is misleading but that is another story for another time. Some members of the crimson line family were buried there, including Mary Magdalene and her daughter Sarah...though now also moved. There were many forbidden original gospels there too such as the second Gospel of John, and even, apparently,*" the old man said and winked, "*a book written by Jesus himself, The Book of Love.*"

"*What does that all have to do with twin symbolism of the Templars on horseback?*" Simon asked.

"*Because from there, items and remains were taken to a small village that is, both geographically and esoterically, the twin of Glastonbury in England. 'Tis the village of Rennes-le-Château...a little hilltop village located in the foothills of the French Pyrenees, about thirty miles south of Carcassonne. 'Tis a very old place, a magic place, a sacred place, and a place full of mysteries just like Glastonbury. Remember how I explained the monks there orchestrated the myth that King Arthur was buried there even though he is not?*" Gabirol nodded yes as the others sat in silence then the old man continued. "*Both areas act as a form of treasure map...but sacred geometry connected to the stars...in the main Virgo as I have previously explained. In Rennes there is a church dedicated to Mary Magdalene since AD 1059. The castle beside it now lies in ruins,*" he explained and laughed lightly to himself as he recalled a past event connected to it. "*'Twas Theodoric and Firgany who brought that down...to recover what was hidden beneath the sixth century chapel inside. If you ever perchance visit the church you will find no less than ninety-six anomalies* to what is normal in a small Roman Catholic church...but alas as the codes and secrets were all compromised, so a new place had to be sought...and that is where Balantrodach comes into our story again as I have already explained. Much was moved here before being moved on again by Paul's father. I have already explained about Jesus and Mary and the offspring they had so I need not repeat it again suffice it to say that members of his bloodline, his direct family in the Rennes-le-Château area, established the royal houses of Acqs and Anfortas, from which sprang the Merovingians, the counts of Toulouse and Narbonne, the kings of Septimania, a Jewish kingdom situated across southern France and the house of Burgundy. Also that the younger brother of Jesus went to England, to Cornwall and on to Glastonbury, where he married Princess Enygeusa. From that marriage sprang the royal Welsh houses of Powys, Gwynedd and Gwyr-y-Gogledd, the famous Fisher Kings, the emperor Constantine and the kings of Brittany, Cornwall and Alba. The most famous bloodlines of Europe were started in Glastonbury and Rennes-le-Château and where these two bloodlines met and intermarried, some of the most powerful rulers in Europe were born. Like King Clovis and the real King Arthur and the emperors Constantine and Charlemagne."

 7 - 2

"So we can read the two Templar Knights riding a single horse as referring to all of that can we?" Peter asked, puzzled.

"Yes...and both Glastonbury and Rennes-le-Château each have a strong claim to the Grail. Think of the two cruets that Joseph of Arimathea brought with him: one with the blood and one with the sweat of Jesus, so beautifully pictured in the stained glass window of St John's church at Glastonbury. And the cup used at the Last Supper, or as some believe to catch the blood of Jesus hanging at the cross. The same applies for Rennes-le-Château. There are numerous paintings, pictures, statues, stained glass windows showing Mary Magdalene holding the cup used at the Last Supper. Or the cup used by her to anoint Jesus. But the Holy Grail is as you should by now know and understand the bloodline of Jesus and Mary Magdalene as well as allegorical and symbolic codes that relate to stars and constellations."

"So what country should we associate Mary Magdalene with then...England or France?" the wealthy tailor asked.

"Both...and every other country in truth for she is of, and for, the entire world. But for now she is present in England and in France. In Glastonbury we find her in Magdalene Street, in chapels dedicated to her and in the many churches *throughout Somerset, Rennes-le-Château and in fact the whole of the south of France, especially the growing Cathar areas they are covered with images of Mary Magdalene. This fact is most obvious in the actual church in Rennes-le-Château. It was rumoured that Mary Magdalene, with a small group of followers, left there for the city of Avallon in France and then on to Avalon in England. Her aim was to reactivate all the sacred places of Isis, remember the symbolism if Isis and the Virgin as being identical? However, in the vicinity of Vezelay, so one version of the story claims, she was betrayed and brutally murdered. Her body was burned and her ashes dispersed. Strange this happened in Vezelay, a place that would later become one of the major cult centres of Mary Magdalene...but she was not murdered nor burnt as that story was corrupted from a connection to the Phoenix that followed her," the old man explained and paused for a moment taking a sip of rose water before continuing. "In England Joseph of Arimathea preached the teachings of Christ and Mary Magdalene, a religion the Roman Church vehemently still challenges even though it is a religion of love, of spiritual growth, of personal experiences with the divine spark in each person as described in the Apocrypha, the gospels that were suppressed and later declared to be heretic at the end of the fourth century by the Roman Catholic Church. These original teachings blended with the religion of the Druids in England, from which evolved the Celtic Church. Here in France, especially in the south, Mary Magdalene preached with so much love and such conviction, that people nowadays still remember and worship her. In this area the Visigoths were Arian Christians even though they did not believe in the divinity of Jesus. After them came the Merovingians, priest kings, descendants of the Holy Family, followed by the Carolingians, all powerful kings who held no great love for Rome. Then came the Jewish kingdom of Septimania followed by an early Renaissance in the southern regions where Jews, Muslims and Christians lived peacefully together, and women had equal rights. You may recall this is the actual Cathar religion I spoke of earlier? This beautiful, true religion will I fear eventually be savagely suppressed just as Attar has foretold."[121]*

"Where will all of this end then?" Ayleth asked, concerned.

"With the return of the sacred feminine," the old man answered. "For there will come a time in the future when we move from the age of Pisces into the Age of Aquarius...for that is when the demise of the present Church, with its dogmas, its rules and regulations and its doctrines based on guilt, fear, penitence, sexual suppression and the inferiority of women, will come to pass...especially if the codes have all been carried across time successfully. Codes, my friends, that this day I shall pass to you...so the last pope of the present Church will himself see

and acknowledge the past," the old man explained and leaned forward. He sighed briefly but checked his emotions fast and looked up. "As Paul always said...love is the answer, not power, not materialism, not money, nor guilt or fear, but love. And the last pope of the Roman Church...he will act upon a prophecy and will instigate the end of its present form and help usher in the new Church...that church of love built within a new cathedral as Alisha and Paul saw and experienced jointly. So in a bizarre strange twist, the very Church itself will be responsible for its own ending...and beginning of a new one."

"I pray he is correct. I only wish it were to happen now," Simon remarked.

"But why Rennes whatever you called it and Glastonbury...why not any other location?" Gabirol asked.

"Because both places are sacred and situated at the intersection of important lines of natural energy...the ancient paths of the dragon no less. But both also have doorways to other dimensions and huge zodiacs connected to them. Both are built according to the laws of sacred geometry. Places with a strong female energy and healing powers. Places where the earth, the trees, the stones speak to you. These are places of meditation where memories buried deep within our souls are triggered and where ancient knowledge and wisdom surfaces...where people discover who they really are...where people very often find their new destiny. Wonderful places set in a magical landscape, pure, unspoiled by human hands. With beautiful rivers, springs, trees and flowers. Places of wisdom and love. Places of joy and happiness. Both sites are truly sacred places. Rennes-le-Château was also once part of a far more ancient civilisation...some say as ancient as 46,000 years ago. Glastonbury and Rennes-le-Chateau both were outposts of this time where temples dedicated to Isis stood as seen in the frequent dreams of Paul."

"And these two new Orders Paul was charged with forming...are they also part of the twin symbolism?" the farrier asked.

"No for that is all a later addition. Paul has written down his ideas for a new Order...the one open to all people from all walks of life regardless of titles, position or wealth. The other Order, the joint one between Muslim and Christian Knights... that is one that I hope those among you here will help start. 'Tis why we have Saladin's sword with us," the old man explained.

"So what was Count Henry going to do in severing his Order from the Templars'? Was he doing that so he could align the Prior de Sion with whatever new Order Paul started?" Peter asked.

"No, Count Henry had seen at firsthand how so much damage was inflicted through the actions and influence of one man upon the Order...Reynald...and so

his decision to sever the link was in fact him simply following protocol and proce-
dure of such events having taken place."

"'Tis written in our rule, and we all have to learn it," the Templar interjected
and sat forward. "For we did not, and we do not wish the temple to be placed in any
servitude except that which is fitting," he recounted and paused briefly. "Reynald
certainly placed the Order in servitude to him alone...so yes, Count Henry has no
option but to sever the ties."

"And do you likewise wear a yellow and black bee cord?" Ayleth asked the Templar.

"Aye of course. Did you not see it earlier?" he replied and raised his arm to reveal
his yellow and black bracelet and then pulled up out of his tunic a larger yellow and
black cord hung around his neck.

   2 – 33

"My friend, if you accept that commission in your possession you will need a
new set," the old man remarked and smiled. "A black and yellow cord with the
crimson thread woven through it."

"I do not understand the black and yellow connection fully other than it is connected to bees," Ayleth commented and laughed, embarrassed at her own remark.

"Then let me briefly explain and repeat for your benefit," the old man said and
smiled at her before continuing. "The Egyptian goddess Neith is the Bee and Mother
Goddess and was also known as the Veiled Goddess. Her temple inscription reads
'lifting a veil'. Bees are often called hymenoptera, stemming from the word hymen,
meaning 'veil winged', representing that which concealed the holy parts of a temple,
as well as the veil or hymen of a woman's reproductive organ. Later the veiled wing
became associated with the goddess Isis. Neith was also called 'Net', which also meant
'bee' and was written with a hieroglyph depicting a bee. Her bee became the symbol
of Lower Egypt just as the reed-like sedge stood for Upper Egypt, and both make up
the pharaonic title 'He of the sedge and the bee', which represented the unity of the two
lands. The bee was an emblem of Potnia, the Athene-like Minoan-Mycenaean 'Mis-
tress' who was also called 'The Pure Mother Bee'. Her priestesses were called 'Melissa'
which means 'bee' in Greek. A few days' sail east from Crete, the name of Deborah, a
biblical prophetess and Judge of ancient Israel, meant 'Bee' in Hebrew and identified
her priestesses as well. Her 'bee' name came from a root 'dabar' that means 'Word'
or 'Pronouncement' and was used in the holy context to mean 'Word of God' or the
'Ten Words', which we all know now as the Ten Commandments. That same 'bee'

related root also designated the 'debir', the forever dark Holy of Holies in the Jerusalem Temple, and so highlights again the strong spiritual connections of this now often underestimated insect with divinity and darkness the yellow and black. The bee is also a symbol for wisdom on its own. The Egyptians sometimes gave Neith the title 'Opener of the Ways' because it was she that was the first conscious entity to begin the process of manifestation. It is said the statue of Neith in the House of the Bee was veiled, and that inscribed at its base were the words 'I am all that has been, that is, or shall ever be; no mortal man hath ever me unveiled.' The symbol of the veil is an important one throughout the Mysteries, whether they be Christian, Greek, Egyptian, Qabalistic, et cetera. The initiate in the House of the Bee was told by the goddess, 'Come look beneath my veil.' It is both an invitation, and a dare. When the veil is lifted to one by the grace of the goddess, the initiate perceives the inner workings and patterns of nature itself. The root word for bee in Egyptian was also used to describe persons of fine character or good quality. This is something Paul has written as a basic requirement for members of the new order...to take good people and make them better, but with the addition that even those fallen from grace may be given the opportunity to redeem themselves of past mistakes and actions if they are truly sincere and genuine in their desire to put right that which was wrong," the old man explained and shook his head briefly. "That way offers hope to all," he said quietly and paused for a few moments before looking up again and continuing. "The Melissae are always referred to as pure and virgin. They had to maintain a 'ritual purity' through a specific set of practices. The Pythian pre-Olympic Priestess of Delphi was named 'The Delphic Bee' and continued to be known as such long after the shrine was dedicated to the god Apollo. He acknowledged the gift of prophecy of the three bee-maidens or Melissae in a Homeric Hymn to Hermes. Neith never engaged in any kind of sexual union; that is, she was eternally a virgin. Yet, as the primordial Being, she was also generative. Thus, in Neith we have one of the earliest appearances of the archetype of the Virgin Mother, the Holy Parthenos, in her original, unadulterated form."[122]

"Is that why this inn is named such?" Simon asked, the old man simply nodding yes in reply. "Always did wonder why it had such a strange name."

"Plutarch...refers to an inscription on her statue in Sais where it states something very familiar as written in the Bible," the old man continued to explain. "It states 'I am everything that has been, and that is, and that shall be, and no one has ever lifted my garment'. The inscription is stating that symbolically Neith, as I repeat again to emphasise the fact, never engaged in any kind of sexual union; that is, she was eternally a virgin. Yet, as the primordial Being, she was also generative. It should be noted and understood that Neith is identified in antiquity with both the

Greek goddess Athena, who is likewise a parthenogenetic creatrix or virgin mother, as well as Isis. Isis is identified with the constellation of Virgo, the Virgin, likewise in antiquity. There are many such manifestations of the virgin mother, long before Christianity was ever conceived. And so where Orion is represented over the Giza pyramids, where Sirius that represents Isis is represented upon that ground, then hidden beneath the veil of the land, you will find the ancient Chambers of Creation laid out as twelve chambers surrounding a thirteenth larger chamber that at its centre holds the original capstone to the Great Pyramid. Gold sheathed but protected from early discovery until that time when man can again access it using sound. Within each chamber are those egg type devices as Paul and Percival witnessed with their own eyes. 'Tis because of the bee that Templars wear the yellow and black cords in remembrance and veneration as well as to protect themselves against deceit and envy...but know also that in time, the yellow rose will return as a symbol of remembrance, for yellow symbolises the divine."

"And did you not say the twin riders also represent the two Churches in Christianity...the exoteric obvious Church of St Peter and the esoteric hidden Church of St John that is one of love that you say will one day come to exist openly?" Gabirol asked as he checked his notes.

"That is correct I did," the old man replied. "It also represents the sun of light we see and its twin companion dark star we cannot see."

"I have one other question if I may quickly," Gabirol asked. "You did not say, but did Nicholas ever work out what the words were that Thomas gave him?"

"Yes he did," the old man replied. "It plainly and simply meant 'I have heard in the countryside told many a thing; but Alisha, the woman, is the bridge' but spoken in the Övdalian language. 'Twas meant to state that Alisha is a spiritual bridge."

"Does the twin rider emblem also mean and symbolise a woman at the front and man at the rear meaning they are equal and ride the same way together as one?" Ayleth asked.

"'Tis yet another meaning yes," the old man answered.

"Then where is the family now, Alisha, Ailia and Paul...and how brave was Ailia to put herself in that cistern? That must have taken so much courage," Sarah said.

2 -8

"Recall I informed you that Theodoric would oft tell her a story at bedtime... about a very young princess who would have to be brave and hide within a dark cave or hole? Well that is what Ailia recalled and used it to remind herself to be

brave. 'Twas as if Theodoric had known all along what was coming and going to happen to her...for it most certainly saved her life," the old man explained.

"But 'twas it all in vain...did they all subsequently perish anyway and why they are not here...yet Paul's sword and work all is?" Miriam asked hesitantly and sighed, instantly seeing the acknowledged pain register in the old man's eyes as he looked at her.

"Let me tell you what finally happened...and then this part of the tale will end... for you here now present to continue if you wish," the old man said and leaned forward clasping his hands together and taking a deep breath.

"If we are worthy and brave enough you mean?" Simon asked.

"Oh...I think you all worthy and brave enough," the old man replied.

"But how do we work out all the codes if they are all in Paul's work for there is so much you tell us. Do we head for Egypt, locate the Halls of Amenti, Chambers of Creation or whatever they are called, though you state we cannot open them anyway in this era...find the buried stone crescents or what? How do we marry up the stars to the ground locations and how do we calculate the codes you speak of done with numbers?" Simon asked, perplexed.

"How...by using the codes Paul inserted by way of markers, symbols and even crosses next to his own words. Use the Atbash cipher and the holy number he repeatedly emphasised, then use that whole number and take the first number for the first letter, then the second et cetera and then repeat as you work your way through the codes. It will spell out a sentence or more with a cryptic message to locate a treasure," the old man explained.

"Well that is me out of the running for I could not even work out the correct letters using the Atbash cipher you explained, let alone then solve a cryptic riddle too," the Genoese sailor remarked and folded his arms in mocking indignation, then laughed as Simon shook his head agreeing with him and smiled.

"But 'tis not for our time anyway so you need not waste your time...other than to safeguard and carry the secrets forward," the Templar remarked and looked at the old man. "For that is to be our commission I suspect?"

The old man smiled and partly nodded yes.

"But we do know the biggest and most obvious code is the Bethlehem line from the apex of the Great Pyramid at twenty-six degrees northeast...where Sirius is projected in relation to Orion on the land...that is where the Chambers of Creation lie waiting...yes?" Gabirol asked.

"Yes that is correct...and there will come a time when its exact position will be pin pointed...then years later, as the world passes into that band of light I spoke of, *then too will the harmonic sounds that govern everything increase and enable the halls to finally be accessed," the old man explained.*

"Why can't someone just put up a great building that stands proud celebrating all religions?...with what they have in common as people seem to believe it more when carved in stone," Simon asked, looking frustrated.

"They have, Simon," the old man replied. "'Tis the Minaret of Jam built just last year...in Afghanistan...It stands beside a mosque concealed from the world, due to its location within a distant valley. It has many scriptures carved and written upon its walls. One is a chapter, called Maryam, which tells of the Virgin Mary and Jesus, both venerated in Islam, and of prophets such as Abraham and Isaac. It's a text that emphasises what Judaism, Christianity and Islam have in common, rather than their differences. It was placed there to appeal for harmony and tolerance in the land, a message that is more relevant now than ever...but will be more so in the last days of this epoch as we are informed."

"You mentioned the shadow of Rome...is that the eagle shadow you mentioned before, or was that eagle shadow just symbolic of Saladin's eagle standard?" Gabirol asked.

"Both in truth...but the eagle symbol will have other meanings in the last stages of this epoch. It will mean the eagle of two whole new empires that will both use an eagle as part of their national symbolism. But either way, 'tis still the long shadow of Rome that casts itself across the world."

Chapter 86
The Impossible

Yarmoch bridge, Yarmoch plateau, Kingdom of Jerusalem, October 6th 1187

Thomas jerked his head up fast as he awoke from his broken sleep sat against Princess Stephanie's caravan steps. He shuddered in the cold morning air as Ishmael walked up to him, smiling. He proffered his arm to help him stand.

"I think they slept well enough," Ishmael remarked as he pulled Thomas to his feet.

"Where is Paul...for I thought he would return to be close to his family?"

"There...where he has stood all night on watch," Ishmael said and nodded toward a figure silhouetted by the rising early morning sun. "That man truly has the weight of history and the world upon his shoulders... and perhaps mankind's very future in his hands."

In the early hours of the night having cleaned himself and escorted Sister Lucy back to the caravan, Paul could not rest and so had stood at the end of the caravan, unsheathed his main sword and held it. As energy pulsed through it, he sensed imminent danger and knew Turansha was close at hand. If he was, and now trusting his instincts fully, he would be ready for him as he felt himself actually drawing strength from the sword itself keeping him both awake and alert. Whilst he stood, his mind had pondered much that had happened and despite knowing Reynald was dead, he sensed his presence. Perhaps it was the genuine family related connection that still linked them somehow as Kratos had explained so many years previously. How things would have been different if he had not saved Reynald's life back then...but Turansha would still be around regardless he thought as he scanned the horizon and bridge in the distance. It was going to be the bridge, he instinctively knew. Turansha would not sneak an attack upon the encampment as it was too exposed and even his best men would not be able to crawl in because of the bright starlight that had lit up the entire area. If he attacked, it would be during the day as they approached the bridge blinded by the rising sun in their eyes or more likely attempt to surround them and weaken them with volley after volley of arrows. Paul reasoned if they took another route to travel out and toward Tortosa, it would only delay matters and the inevitable confrontation with Turansha...at least here, Paul could force the matter once and for all. He would let Turansha believe he had the advantage of surprise, but he knew, without any doubt, an attack would come as they reached the bridge. He laughed lightly to himself as he recalled Theodoric's words when in such a situation: 'I have a plan'. Paul nodded to himself.

"Come on then, Turansha...but be warned...I am protected by gods you are not prepared to deal with...," he said aloud to himself just as Thomas and Ishmael walked up behind him.

 3 – 11

"Who be warned?" Thomas asked.

Paul remained staring at the bridge.

"Turansha...for he and his men await us," he replied and held his sword with both hands. "And I aim to see his days end...this day," he stated and turned to face them. He frowned when he saw the filthy and tired state of Thomas before him. "Thomas...have you not rested, and why have you not seen to yourself?"

"See all of this," he replied and gestured down himself with his hands. "This blood...'tis mainly that of all my men. If this day is to be my last...for I too sense what you say, then I shall take their spirit into battle with me once more."

"This day will not be your last," Paul said and glanced beyond him as Master Douglas appeared checking his own sword. Paul looked at the caravan door as Alisha appeared, her face fraught with concern. Suddenly her eyes widened as she looked toward the bridge, Paul seeing the alarm register in them. "Ali," he said and walked over to her fast as she raised her hand and pointed. Paul clasped her other hand and turned to look. Immediately he saw a black line of men appear all along the ridge line and blocking the bridge. Paul squinted as the sun was rising behind the bridge.

Master Douglas immediately rushed over to one of the Mamluk guards and got him to blow his alarm horn.

"In the name of the Lord will that man ever stop?" Alisha asked as she stepped down beside Paul. She looked at the two swords strapped across his back and quickly unsheathed the sword Saladin had given him. "I will need this," she stated as Paul turned to look at her, puzzled. "Tenno taught me enough…for this very hour," she said with defiance in her eyes.

Stewart and Count Henry ran into view both fastening their sword belts in a hurry. Paul simply pointed toward the bridge.

"I can see at least a hundred of Turansha's men," Paul said as they all scanned the horizon.

"Then I suggest we let them come to us for they outnumber us at least three to one," Count Henry remarked as he took a deep breath.

"Think again," Thomas stated bluntly and indicated with his thumb over his shoulder.

When Paul and Count Henry turned to look behind them, there were even more men forming up in a line in the distance.

"Shit!" Count Henry said through gritted teeth just as Princess Stephanie flung open the caravan door stepping down rapidly and alarmed.

"My God!" she gasped just as Sister Lucy pushed past her to see.

"Shit indeed," Master Douglas repeated. "They are all highly trained… so you better come up with something pretty bold…and fast," he continued and looked back at Paul.

Paul looked at the bridge and all the men stood in a line, their black swords all drawn. He could not see Turansha, though he could have been any one of them, their faces covered. He looked back behind him at the other line of men now approaching. He could feel his heart begin to beat within his chest, the surge of energy again pulsing through the handle of the sword. He clenched it tightly and closed his eyes to concentrate as Alisha clasped his left hand tighter. Where was Kratos now when he needed him the most? he asked himself and took in a slow deep breath. All of his papers, the sealed tubes Saladin's brother Turansha had given him and all of his drawings were secured inside Princess Stephanie's caravan, Ailia too. There were just thirty men Paul could count on within his ranks and although also highly trained, he had seen at firsthand how agile Turansha's men were. He took another deep breath as Alisha gripped his hand tighter. Half of Turansha's men had crossbows and bows and very soon they would be close enough to unleash death upon them if they remained where they were.

"Paul!" Master Douglas said and nudged him as everyone looked at him.

Paul opened his eyes meeting Alisha's immediately. Kratos had forewarned him during their time alone in the desert that such a time like this would happen if he and Alisha had followed a certain path, which they clearly had. 'You may not see me, but I will always be with you' he recalled his words. He smiled at Alisha, which surprised her. He looked over her shoulder at Princess Stephanie and Sister Lucy and smiled at them too. Count Henry wore a look of puzzlement at his expression.

"Put the women inside the caravan and all of you...prepare to mount up when I do," Paul ordered and ushered Alisha back toward the caravan steps. "You must trust me in what is about to unfold."

"Do you mean for us to try and run out...to escape, for either way we shall run into his men...look, they surround us," Stewart said and pointed to more black clad figures appearing on both flanks.

"He expects us to set up a circular defensive position. He will rain down volley after volley of arrows upon us...then he will move closer using crossbows and when our numbers are depleted sufficiently, only then will he send in his best men," Paul explained as his eyes then met Princess Stephanie's. "So we shall await their first volley to start and then ride for the bridge at full charge...all of us, for he will not expect that, and even if he does, he does not have enough men to stop a full cavalry charge. Ishmael, Master Douglas, Percival and Thomas...I would ask you stay with the caravan whilst I and my brother lead the conroise assault to clear the bridge."

"Paul no...you cannot!" Alisha pleaded and looked at him in alarm, Paul's eyes still looking at Princess Stephanie.

"Alisha...Paul speaks what needs to be done," Abi suddenly said as she appeared and placed her hand upon Alisha's forearm and acknowledged Paul with a slight nod as sadness registered across her face. "And Paul...I have something from Kratos I must pass on to you. He gave it to me in Jerusalem but said I must only give it to you should this happen," she explained and took out what appeared to be a short, dark coloured stick partially wrapped in cloth. "I pass charge of this staff to your charge and safe keeping."

Paul took hold of the small staff, puzzled.

"I know what this is…and it is a charge I cannot accept," Paul replied shaking his head no.

"You have no choice," Abi stated as she looked past Paul at more of Turansha's men forming up.

Ailia appeared at the caravan doorway, her hair all a mess and sticking up. She rubbed her tired eyes and looked around at the men…a mixture of Askar guards, Mamluks, Count Henry's men, a couple of Templars and Hospitallers rapidly preparing their horses. She looked across the open plateau and saw the approaching men in black. Her eyes then fell upon Paul and tears immediately welled in them when she saw the serious look upon his face and her mother stood holding the sword of Saladin. Paul walked over to her, quickly put the small staff inside his surcoat, then placed his sword up against the steps and took her little hands in his.

 3 – 5

"My little princess…today you must be brave again and act as a queen," Paul said softly and feigned a brave smile at her, her eyes wide in alarm. He kissed her hands. "You must stay inside the caravan no matter what until we have you safely across the bridge. Do you understand me? And Mama and Stephanie and Sister Lucy will be with you." Ailia silently nodded her head she understood. "Whatever happens…remember this…I shall always, always be by your side."

"And you will come back to us…you will not stay here will you?" she asked emotionally, her bottom lip quivering. She bit her bottom lip just like Alisha did, which made Paul smile.

"You know me, Ailia…so never ignore what is in here…what you feel," Paul replied and placed his hand upon his chest then to hers. "Listen to that quiet voice always."

Ailia flung her arms around his neck and hugged him tightly.

"I love you, Papa…love you," she said with her eyes closed tightly.

"Paul!" Master Douglas interrupted, drawing his attention back to the problem at hand.

Quickly Paul handed Ailia to Alisha, kissed her on the cheek and then ushered them to the steps of the caravan, Alisha still carrying the sword in her other hand. She turned to look at Paul and he simply picked up his sword, leaned in and pressed his lips against hers. Ailia buried her face into

Alisha's shoulder as they held the kiss. When Paul pulled away, tears were already welling in Alisha's eyes.

"I will not let any harm come to them," Princess Stephanie said and gulped emotionally trying to keep her fears under control.

Paul stepped away from Alisha and Ailia and took Princess Stephanie's hand. He raised it and kissed it before looking at her. He could sense every emotion in her wanting to reach out and hold him. He knew Alisha was more than capable of looking after herself better than Stephanie could but the comments were welcome. She blinked several times. Quickly Paul leaned closer and pressed a kiss against the side of her face.

"Perhaps in another life things would have been different…and I am truly sorry for the pain I have brought to your door…truly," he whispered then stood back and immediately turned away.

"Papa!" Ailia called out, reaching her hand toward him.

Sister Lucy quickly started to usher them all into the caravan only briefly looking back at Paul as he approached Taqi and his colleague, Stewart turning to follow him. Abi nodded at her.

"If all goes wrong this hour…do what you must," Abi whispered to her. Sister Lucy just nodded back slightly.

Within moments the caravan was ready to move minus a driver. Master Douglas and Count Henry had all the men stood by their horses ready to mount fast when the order was given.

"Taqi…I need you to drive the caravan for you are far better to defend it should it be stopped…please," Paul asked. "And Stewart…it will be my honour to have you lead the charge with me…if you will?"

"The honour is mine, little brother…mine," Stewart replied and held up his rolled up Templar Beauseant banner.

"May I ride alongside with you?" the Templar from the cave complex asked as he presented himself.

"Of course…for we shall need all those knights trained to form a conroise," Paul answered. "We shall need no rearguard this time, my friends."

"No…but I can do that…just in case," Abi stated, her armour and leather appearing red in the morning sunlight Paul thought.

"We shall not let them near the caravan," Thomas interjected as Ishmael nodded in agreement instantly.

"Once the caravan is over that bridge…keep going and do not stop whatever happens," Paul said as he looked at Taqi.

Inside the caravan, Alisha placed Ailia under several covers beneath a reinforced bench section and sat down beside her crouching low as Sister Lucy and Princess Stephanie did likewise on the opposite side. Princess Stephanie's two maids sat huddled together beneath the small table looking terrified.

"This caravan is solid. It will withstand many arrows and bolts," Princess Stephanie tried to reassure them, Ailia looking into Alisha's eyes more intently as she wrapped her arms around her protectively. "'Tis one of the strongest ever built so no matter how bumpy this ride may get, have faith it will hold."

"And should anyone dare try to enter, they shall be met by this," Alisha said and raised the sword of Saladin.

Sister Lucy feigned a brave smile at Ailia and winked.

"I am glad to be leaving this land…and never again will I see the long halls of Kerak…thank the Lord," Princess Stephanie remarked and smiled at Ailia. "After today, we shall all start a new life. A better life…I promise," she said reassuringly. Alisha smiled at her appreciative of her words for Ailia's benefit.

Quickly Alisha checked her three pronged dagger was still safely tucked away. She removed it and looked at it. Her heart skipped a beat as she saw through the netted curtains several Askar guards walk past before realising they were part of their own escort. Sister Lucy saw her reaction and immediately stood up to close all the internal shutters for added protection. She checked the two doors were both bolted shut before sitting herself down again. She felt inside her top and checked that a small note Paul had given her in the early hours was secure. She prayed she would not have to pass it on to Alisha as Paul had made her promise if he should not survive what he knew was coming. She checked herself emotionally and tried to remain calm. She looked up and shook her head. 'I may be joining you this day, my love' she told herself then pulled her knees up and folded her arms around them as she mentally prepared herself and looked at Alisha and Ailia. If they were to be taken, she was supposed to kill them both quickly rather than have them suffer at the hands of Turansha. She closed her eyes and began to pray silently.

Port of La Rochelle, France, Melissae Inn, spring 1191

Ayleth covered her face with her hands, feeling emotional. Sarah rubbed her shoulders reassuringly.

✠   1 – 6

"All Paul's work is here...so I am guessing the caravan at least made it or else we would not have them," Gabirol stated solemnly.

The old man simply shrugged his shoulders in silence, revealing nothing.

"And Princess Stephanie for you said the sword and all of Paul's work was here only because of her," Simon said looking at the swords upon the table.

"We know she lives remember?" the Hospitaller replied and raised his eyebrows at Simon.

"I do not think I can stand to hear what happens next...but I must listen," Ayleth remarked, still covering her face.

"Yes, and I wish to know just exactly how you, my darling, fit it into this tale... my love," Sarah said, looking at Stephan, who simply shrugged his shoulders and looked back at the old man.

"I shall explain his part in this tale," the old man said softly with a smile.

"And that Sister Lucy...she has a note from Paul?" the wealthy tailor asked. "Do you perchance have that too?"

"Yes...yes I have the very note," the old man answered.

"Oh no...that surely means he was killed then," Ayleth said aloud and looked up emotionally. "And what of his brother and the others? Please, you must tell us."

"That I am coming to as I wind up this tale," the old man replied.

"Just before you do," Gabirol interrupted and looked down at his own notes again. "Do Paul's journals cover the harmonic aspects you have mentioned before and the star connections to the land in France?"

"Yes...and you shall have ample time to study them, copy them if you wish," the old man answered. "Even copies of Master Odo's symbols of sounds which he had hidden in France within his own family church specially built to hide a sealed scroll. But those same codes need to be carried to a new place...in Alba...and it will require a very gifted stonemason who understands Catalan," the old man revealed and looked at John and smiled. "But look at the end of Paul's journal and you will see a drawing of the constellation of Virgo set over France. As I explained before, where the stars would project upon the land, there too in time will be great cathedrals and markers."

"You said that Paul tells us we all...or mankind...will have a choice to make in the end days as we pass from this age of Pisces into the age of Aquarius. What choice is that?" the Templar asked.

"To live together in peace and harmony with the world and nature...or reject the sacred feminine and let mother nature herself destroy us all," the old man replied matter of factly.

Gabirol flicked to the end of the pages in Paul's main journal and opened it to reveal a star map naming the stars but also places in France.

Fig. 79: Map of Stars and Churches over France.

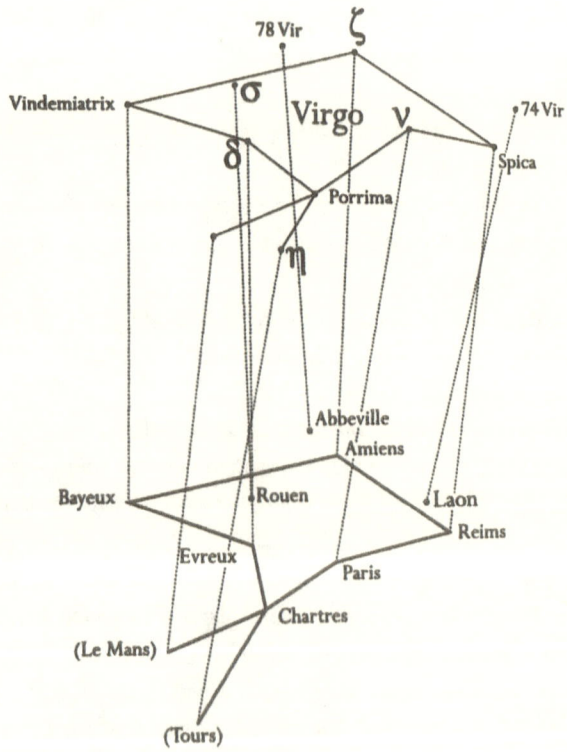

"What is so important about those symbols of sound then?" Peter asked.

"They hold a key...for it is sound that holds our realm, our reality, together as I explained before. 'Tis a combination of sounds that will help access the ancients' wisdom as well as help lead mankind to discover his true potential. A new field of study in the future when revealed from our times will show them we once knew

these secrets in great antiquity. And then in the final decades, great symbols of nature will appear across many lands. They will generate great interest and debate but those that recognise them will hear and sense the past calling out again across time," the old man explained then looked over at the windows as sunlight shone around the edges. *"For a greater secret is the fact that sound permeates throughout all of creation in our world. Every sound contains its echo from even before mankind came into being, even before the great forests. Sound spreads out from the source in great circles like those formed when a stone is dropped in a pool. We follow waves of sound from life to life and the dying man's ears will hear long after his eyes are blind. He hears the sound that leads him to his next life as the source of all beings plucks the harp of creation. The very structure of the rose stained glass windows designed for Chartres is identical to a certain sound when it is reproduced as a sound symbol, and recall if you can how I said that in Islam, and echoed in all Abrahamic and Hindu religions, sacred geometry provides the means to see the vestiges of God and its multiplicity in the universal order of things,"* the old man mused then looked at the windows more intently. *"I think it perhaps time we opened them."*

Stephan stood up and immediately began to unfasten the bolts and open the window shutters.

"My Lord, there is so much in here to understand, but you also said this world is not ready for certain harmonics to work...but would be in time," Gabirol said as he looked through more pages of Paul's journal, the old man simply nodding yes. Gabirol focused in upon images of large crescent drawings clearly made up of stone. He pointed to an illustration of what looked like Stonehenge and raised it to show the old man. *"This...is this the henge of stone in England for it looks different or is it another elsewhere?"*

"'Tis now part of Stonehenge in England...but what Paul drew there was what he saw of the original stones when they were first set before the world we live upon changed its position, which resulted in the original structure being re-sited," the old man explained.

   3 – 27

"How could Paul have seen this?" Simon asked, bemused.

"As I explained, by looking across the wheel of time. He did this when he spent time alone with Kratos in the desert."

"It seems he did and learnt a lot during that period," the Genoese sailor remarked and shielded his eyes from the bright sunlight beaming through the now opened shutters.

"Oh he did...that he did indeed," the old man replied and smiled broadly.

"But these drawings show Stonehenge with another massive crescent structure further out. Does that exist?" Gabirol asked.

"Oh yes...it all exists but simply hidden beneath the earth. 'Tis a great crescent and once it is discovered it will be as a marker to those who remember...within their souls of past times. It will act as a trigger for the first to begin to fully awaken," the old man explained and paused as his eyes adjusted to the light flooding the room. "All of you here in this room are not here by mere chance...as I shall explain."

"Briefly, so I may make note of it," Gabirol interrupted. "What happened to Queen Sibylla and King Guy? And what was the small staff Abi gave to Paul?"

"'Twas in 1188, at Tortosa, that Saladin released King Guy and returned him to his wife, Sibylla, though no longer the queen holding Jerusalem of course. They went first to Tripoli, then to Antioch but then in 1189, they sought to reclaim Tyre for their kingdom but were refused admission by Conrad himself, who did not recognise Guy as king any more. Guy then set about besieging Acre but it did not succeed," the old man answered and paused. He took a sip of rose water. "As for the small staff Abi gave Paul...'twas the staff, or wand, of Jesus himself."

Ayleth coughed loudly as Gabirol looked at the old man and frowned hard, the wealthy tailor shaking his head dismissively.

"The wand of Christ...never heard of it," the wealthy tailor remarked and folded his arms.

"Then let me explain something to you that you may check for yourselves," the old man replied softly. "Let me ask you, each of you, who from the Bible, as we have it nowadays, would you immediately associate with a rod, a staff or wand that he used to perform miracles?"

"Moses of course," Simon answered instantly, the others nodding in agreement.

"What about Aaron or Joseph...and indeed how about Jesus? For in truth, and the Church knows this full well, Jesus too had a staff. It isn't so well documented in the Bible as Moses's or his brother Aaron's, but he did have a magic staff. Not only that but his staff was much more powerful than that of any other prophet, prophetess or angel. Jesus was personified as the divine presence incarnate, as in God in the flesh. His powers are the powers associated directly with the Holy Trinity...they are the powers that allow life to even happen," the old man started to explain. "Read for yourselves, here," the old man said, opening the small bible on the table. He flicked through it until he found the verse he was looking for and began to read it out. "The Lord is my shepherd; I shall not want. He maketh me to lie down in green pastures: he leadeth me beside the still waters. He restoreth my soul: he leadeth me in the *paths of righteousness for his name's sake. Yea, though I walk through the valley of the shadow of death, I will fear no evil: for thou art with me; thy rod and thy staff they comfort me. Thou preparest a table before me in the presence of mine enemies: thou anointest my head with oil; my cup runneth over. Surely goodness and mercy shall follow me all the days of my life: and I will dwell in the house of the Lord forever."* He paused as he pushed the open bible toward the wealthy tailor to read. *"Notice the words 'rod' and 'staff' are mentioned. If you dig way down deep, you will also find that there are metaphors in this passage that tell the reader that the staff of Jesus Christ was packed with powers and mystical abilities. Further yet, the staff of Jesus holds the ability to grant these powers unto others...like Paul himself".*

"I said he was another Messiah all along," Simon remarked quietly.

"Let me explain a little more if I may," the old man said, the Templar nodding immediately. *"The original staff of Jesus, God the Son, was given to him by his paternal deification, God the Father. It was filled with the power, magic, call it what you will of the Holy Trinity, God the Holy Spirit. In this way, the trinity would be kept together at all times. When Jesus was very young, he was given the staff by his mother, who received the staff in a vision that she received from a host of Seraphim. However, Jesus was still kept in a mortal state of mind at this young age and had no idea of the power that was kept in his staff. Only after he was baptised by John as the recognised and anointed Messiah were the powers in his staff able to work fully. Prior to that moment, its powers protected him from both physical and spiritual harm. Only when he turned thirty-three did the power in his staff reach full capacity and he was able to use it to perform many miracles including healing the blind, making the deaf hear, curing lepers, walking on water, controlling the weather, feeding the masses, opening up the sky to peer into the heavens, and much more. In his staff were stones from Heaven. The same as mentioned in Revelation as set about the New Jerusalem..."*

"This does ring true with me," Gabirol interrupted. *"But I have heard that a staff used by Jesus, after his crucifixion, was sent to an island in the Etruscan Sea. Then nearly a thousand years later that same staff was presented to Saint Patrick by a hermit who had received the staff for safe keeping. Is that true?"*

"That is but part of the continuation," the old man answered. *"'Tis said that the hermit told Saint Patrick the staff shall be given to 'He that shall be called the Father of Ireland'. I am sure all of you here know that Saint Patrick was sainted and indeed became the patron saint of Ireland. You may also know that when Saint Patrick founded the Armagh Cathedral, he blessed and sanctified it with the staff of Jesus. He stored the staff, which he referred to as his sacred crozier, in his beloved*

cathedral upon its founding. The powers of his crozier have been emanated and used to make many religious relics including sacred crosses, grails, chalices and busts. It has been used to divine the gospels of Saint Patrick and many sepulchre alcoves. But according to certain accounts, after the death of Saint Patrick, the staff was burned on High Street in Dublin and given up as a sacrifice to the Lord by Archbishop George Brown. The staff was stripped of its gems, these same gems being the ones that have been venerated and continue to be venerated and that had travelled with Jesus all of his life." The old man sat in silence for several minutes before looking up. "But I can tell you the real staff of Jesus was not burnt as a sacrifice. It is still very much in one piece...somewhere." [123]

"Where?" Simon asked loudly.

"That I am afraid I no longer know," the old man answered sadly.

"Then if what you say is true and Abi gave Paul that very same staff, then he must have it still," Ayleth said hesitantly.

"If it was the real staff of course," the wealthy tailor remarked.

"'Twas the genuine item...of that I swear to you this day, my friends," the old man said, looking at everyone in turn. "The Church may deny such a staff existed... but you only need to simply visit Rome and the Pope's residency...for there, upon its very walls, you will see images of Jesus represented," he paused, "holding the staff. But know this, that there are in fact may such staffs, wands of power, such as Kratos likewise carried."

"And you know not where the one Paul was given is now?" the Hospitaller asked.

The old man shook his head no.

"Then I fear what you will be telling us next about Paul," Sarah said, looking sad.

"I shall come to that, I promise...but there is so much more on the staff of Jesus but time this hour does not permit such a lengthy discussion for I fear I will not conclude this tale otherwise," the old man explained.

"Then let us allow you to continue," the Templar said and looked over to Gabirol.

"I agree," Gabirol responded. "But please I have but one final, and I promise final, question I have written here to ask; why the name John to designate the Navigator status?...I heard once it was actually connected to a mythical beast called a Quinotaur or something like that and not just in respect of John the Baptist as you said earlier."

Sarah threw her arms up exasperated wanting to hear what happened to Alisha and Paul.

"'Tis an important matter, so I shall answer quickly, I too promise," the old man said, pausing briefly. "Quinotaur is a name synonymous with Poseidon, the Greek *god of the sea, and according to Plato one of the famous kings of Atlantis. Others see it purely as the fish symbol that Christ is associated with to indicate he was in fact the origin of the Merovingian bloodline. The Quinotaur myth is far more ancient than most suppose and the word can be broken into two parts. This reveals its true meaning. The last syllable, taur, means bull whilst the first syllable Quin, or Kin, comes from the root word for king, as well as the biblical name of Cain, who many claim is the original symbolic if not physical father of the Grail family. The idea of the 'King of the World' taking the form of a sea-bull has been a recurring theme in many ancient cultures, especially that of ancient Mesopotamia. In fact it origi-nated with that dynasty of kings who reigned over the antediluvian world and who were all associated with the sea, as well as this divine animal imagery. These kings included Sargon, Menes and Narmar. Their historical reality morphed into the legends we have in many cultures of gods said to have come out of the sea at various times who taught mankind the basic arts of civilisation and known as Enki, Dagon, Oannes or Marduk (Merodach). All were depicted as half-man and half-fish, half-goat and half-fish, or half-bull and half-fish. I believe I previously mentioned how Oannes was a man who came out of the sea wearing a fish's head but removed it to reveal his human head. This is but a simple description of a man removing some form of advanced suit...that is all. This same fish head is acknowledged as the origin of the mitre worn by the Pope but also as we all know, the Church has always been associated with fish and even Christ himself took on that imagery, as did John the Baptist, and the early Christians used the fish sign of the Ichthy to designate themselves as I have previously also explained," the old man detailed and paused again seeing Sarah getting agitated and impatient.* [124]

"But that does not explain how you get to the name John," Gabirol interrupted.

"Because from the name Oannes we get the words Uranus and Ouranos, but also by some accounts, Jonah, as in Jonah and the whale, to Janus, and ultimately John. Perhaps you will finally understand this as to why the Grand Masters of the Priory of Sion assume the symbolic name of John upon taking office," Philip explained as Gabirol rapidly wrote down more notes.

"And finally, I do swear it," Gabirol said and looked at Sarah quickly again almost pleadingly. "To confirm...the dark twin sun passes us every 3,600 years, the next time due when the whole set of planets and our sun also pass through what you called the band of light...yes?"

"Yes that is correct. Also it ties in when we enter the Age of Aquarius, the spiri-tual age...but also it marks the end of the great year and the beginning of whole new great year, which lasts for a period of 25,900 years." [125]

"Can we not just hear what happened to Alisha and Paul first?" Sarah asked pointedly, which made the old man smile. He nodded yes he would continue as Gabirol quickly finished off his notes before looking back up at Sarah then smiled.

Yarmoch bridge, Yarmoch plateau, Kingdom of Jerusalem, October 6th 1187

Paul studied the ranks of Turansha's men as they approached on all sides except those blocking the bridge. Ishmael leaned closer to him.

"They stop…which means they will soon charge their bows," he whispered.

Paul looked around at everyone to make sure they were all ready to mount their horses. Taqi took up the slack in the caravan horses' reins and nodded very slightly at him. Count Henry and Master Douglas looked at him clearly waiting for him to give the order. Stewart and Thomas moved up slowly with their horses either side of Paul's as Abi moved hers to the rear. Paul nodded at Stewart as he prepared to mount his horse and then looked at Percival as he climbed up upon the rear of the caravan to help guard it. Once in position he gave Paul a nod and thumbs-up. Paul turned to face his brother as he looked at him intently.

 2 – 7

"Paul, let us do Father proud," he said.

"On my move…," Paul said as he quickly looked again at the others as they anxiously waited. The Askar guard leader part bowed his head indicating he and his men were ready as did the Mamluk commander.

Paul took a deep breath and put his left foot in his stirrup. He wished he had Adrastos at this moment but at least the horse he now had was also a thoroughbred and well trained war horse. Quickly he checked the other three caravans and two carts and that their drivers were ready. The few infantry they had were all now either inside or clinging to them ready to move. Quickly Paul mounted his horse, the others all following suit instantly. The moment he was up upon his horse, Turansha's men immediately saw them and charged their bows with arrows. Paul thrust his reins and legs hard to get his horse moving, as Taqi instantly started to roll the caravan, his colleague by his side for protection. Arrows from Turansha's men from both flanks and the rear started to arch into the sky as Paul moved into position at full trot, Stewart pulling close by his right side, the Templar from the cave forming up to his left as the Askar guards, Mamluk knights, two Faris Knights and the rest of Count Henry's knights, Templars and few Hospitallers began to pack themselves in together to form a tight conroise. Several of the Mamluks had lances held up high as they all began to gallop faster directly toward the bridge, Taqi forcing the four horses pulling his caravan ever faster, those inside having to brace themselves as it bounced up and down, Alisha holding Ailia as tightly as she could. Count Henry manoeuvred his horse to the rear of the conroise so he would not hamper the charge. Abi looked behind her as the arrows began to fall short of them. Paul had timed the move perfectly. A few moments later and they would have been within range. Now all they had to do was punch a hole through the line of men ahead of them. Paul held his reins in his left hand and raised his sword pointing at the men ahead of him. He could see Stewart to his right lift the Templar Beauseant standard in his left hand whilst wielding his sword in his right. He was riding and controlling his horse purely by his legs, his reins wrapped around his left forearm. Paul's eyes narrowed as he tried to focus on the men blocking the bridge as they ran to form a three man deep human barricade. He hoped he had caught Turansha off guard having not expected them to attack instead of defend. All went quiet in his ears and all he could hear was his heart pounding, the surge of energy pulsing through the sword. The front rank of Turansha's men ahead of him raised small black shields but he knew they would be ineffectual against a full cavalry charge. Then the second rank raised and aimed bows directly at them as the distance between them closed fast. At this range they would hit them. Paul gritted his teeth and urged his horse on faster. All he had to do was smash a big enough hole through them to let Taqi pass he told himself. Taqi had to wipe his face frantically as the dust being kicked up by the cavalry charge was beginning to obscure his vision. At one point he could not even see the bridge but simply followed the cloud of dust ahead of him. As all of Turansha's other formations began to run toward the bridge from all sides, a volley of arrows was loosed from the bridge element toward the charging conroise. Paul steadied his horse as arrows flashed past him, one slicing through the Templar standard Stewart was still holding high. The Templar from the cave to Paul's left side disappeared forwards and down fast as his horse was hit by several arrows, the knight being thrown down hard and vanishing beneath the dust and other horses following. Just as Paul's horse was almost upon the three ranks of men, they looked up at him but did not move and held their positions. An Askar guard rode up beside him to take the place of the fallen knight and immediately thrust his lance down his left side and into the chest of one of Turansha's men in the second row just as Paul's horse smashed into them. Paul flung his sword in a wide arc and down upon the nearest man slicing through his right shoulder, but then Paul's horse veered to the left as its speed was stopped by the impact of the other two ranks of men behind the first, its front legs collapsing throwing Paul forwards over them. He landed heavily upon the first set of wooden planks of the bridge and rolled several times until he stopped, his horse landing heavily upon several of Turansha's men, Stewart smashing into and trampling more men to his right as he swung his sword violently. Instantly Paul jumped to his feet seeing the remainder of the knights on horse charge into view. They likewise smashed into the other men on foot knocking many down. As they slashed and stabbed with their swords and lances, some of Turansha's men cut the legs away of several horses forcing the knights to the ground. Quickly Paul ran back toward the melee to be confronted by four black clad men wielding large blackened straight swords. He did not hesitate and kept running directly at them, the bridge entrance now fully blocked by men fighting and Taqi drawing ever closer followed by the other caravans and carts. Paul swung his sword in a wide arch starting from his right toward the first man but he jumped incredibly high, Paul's sword flashing beneath his feet, but Paul pulled his sword back and upwards and spun himself around using its momentum, the other man landing back on his feet just as Paul swung his sword around again, this time slicing into the man's thighs and right through his legs completely severing them, Paul landing on his stomach face down. The man had not even hit the ground when Paul rolled over on the floor and thrust his sword upwards into the stomach of the man in front of him, the man to his left raising his sword to strike Paul, but then Stewart threw his standard the tip of which was sharp and it sailed through the air striking the man in the side of the neck. The fourth man now to Paul's right did a backward summersault to take him out of reach, then jumped again behind Paul. Instinctively Paul thrust his sword backwards and up at an angle, the sword feeling like it had a mind of its own, the blade piercing the man's chest and up into his heart. Paul held his sword with both hands taking the weight of the man as Stewart stared at him in utter surprise. Paul stood up and pulled the sword clear, the man falling dead at his feet.

"PAUL!" Taqi shouted loudly.

Paul spun around in time to see Taqi fighting to control the direction of the caravan as the two front horses trampled and pushed their way through the melee knocking aside both Turansha's men and their own. The caravan bounced up violently as it ran over several of the dead and then the larger dead body of the Templar's horse, Paul's horse neighing loudly as it jumped in panic trying to move. Paul looked on as the entire caravan dangerously leaned over to its right side as it came toward him at speed. The second line of horses pulling the caravan fell unable to get a proper grip on the bodies beneath them, but the two front horses kept on pulling hard. Suddenly the front left wheel shattered into splinters as it smashed into the side stone post of the bridge. It bounced the caravan with a violent jolt but then levelled itself out before digging the exposed axle into the wooden boards slowing it down rapidly almost to a stop, the two front horses still trying to pull it. Paul froze wondering if the caravan was about to fall over but it remained upright. He ran toward it as both Taqi and his colleague drew their swords as they were rapidly approached by several of Turansha's men. Paul caught a brief glimpse of Percival as he was thrown from the rear of the caravan and through the side supports and off the bridge. Percival waved his arms frantically as he tried to grab the wooden beams as he passed them, his eyes then meeting Paul's. Percival seemed to pause as he stared at Paul, resignation clear upon his face as he started to fall away from the bridge into the deep gorge below. Paul knew it was an un-survivable fall instantly and he watched helpless as Percival vanished from view. Stewart forced his way forwards on his horse toward the men, slashing his sword down violently on anyone who came near him. The entrance to the bridge was awash with bright colours from the knights, Mamluks and Askar guards as they fought close quarters with the many assassins. Paul could see several of the Askar guards being deliberately targeted and pulled down, their horses cut from beneath them. Stewart leaned half off of his horse as he swung his sword across the back of an assassin about to throw a naphtha grenade against the caravan, the assassin falling backwards and then being trampled by the two rear horses of the caravan as they fought to stand up. The grenade rolled away and exploded against the stone support, but the flames instantly licking up the side and across the main wooden spanning beam. Taqi took control of the reins again and tried to regain control of the caravan but more assassins were moving in around them. Abi was already dismounted and wielding her large sword in huge circles, a huge axe held high in her left hand. The second caravan came smashing through the line of men and horses and Stewart just managed to pull aside as they raced past through the tight confines of the bridge sides and Princess Stephanie's caravan as Taqi forced it onward. Once past, an assassin tried to fire a crossbow at Abi's head but Ishmael jumped into view swinging his two swords down upon the crossbow assassin's shoulders from behind him. The crossbow fell with the assassin's severed arms still attached to it. Thomas was by now standing in front of the left side door of the caravan blocking any entrance into it. Paul jumped over the dead assassins near him and made for the right hand doorway to protect that as Count Henry appeared through the dust and smoke thrusting his sword violently all around him, assassins having to dive aside. Several threw spiked stars at him, one bouncing off his shoulder shield. As the sound of clashing metal and screaming horses filled the air, Paul looked on as Turansha's men were now all funnelling into the bridge entrance, flames beginning to take hold on the wooden section set alight by the grenade. The third caravan came crashing through the melee but the driver lost control as it bounced over the dead horses and it tilted sideways smashing its way between two main support beams, the driver jumping off just as it began to roll off of the bridge. As it went it pulled its two tethered horses with it and the men still in the rear screaming as it fell at speed, exploding in a rumble of shattered wood when it hit the rough waters and rocks seventy feet below. Taqi finally managed to get his caravan moving again and slowly it bumped up and over the dead horses and men, but dragged along one of the rear tethered horses, its legs broken. The first cart suddenly sped through and across the bridge. Crossbow bolts started to flash through the air as Paul ran to the rear of the caravan and stood beside Abi and Thomas as he ran to the other side, the caravan now moving slowly across the bridge, its broken axle gouging a rut in the wooden planking as it went.

"You better start using that sword how it was meant to be used," Abi shouted as she thrust her sword forwards into the chest of an assassin and swung the axe down upon the head of the one following close behind him, his head splitting in two, his eyes bulging as his head fell apart in a grotesque pink spray of blood.

 4 – 7

The second cart could not pass through the melee and it suddenly exploded in a bright gout of flame as several naphtha grenades ignited inside, several infantry diving out engulfed in flames and screaming in agony. One ran to the edge of the bridge and threw himself off to kill himself quickly as his entire upper body burned.

Before Paul had time to reply to Abi, she was already swinging the axe back up and over her shoulder whilst thrusting her sword forwards again into another assassin, their numbers increasing. Paul tried to see where Turansha was amongst them but the majority were hidden within the dust cloud and smoke. Paul took a step back to follow the caravan as it slowly edged its way across the bridge. There was no way the caravan could now speed away he thought...but there was also no way they could kill all of Turansha's men save a miracle happening. He clasped his sword with both hands Abi's words echoing around his head. Thomas had told him what Tenno had been able to do wielding the sword and for a moment he wondered if he could do the same. If it would stall and hold Turansha's men up, the delay may be enough for Taqi to get Alisha and Ailia away on horseback once across the bridge. Kratos's voice suddenly rang out in his mind as he heard him call to him the same words he had dreamt of him saying so many times before. 'Would you die for her?' Paul clenched the sword even tighter in both hands, his hands becoming hot, the blade also changing colour from the bright silvered pearlescent colour it was to an almost shimmering crimson colour. He could sense the power within it as it surged through his entire body. He felt as though he was actually physically standing taller, his chainmail pulling tight across his thighs and arms. As he stared forward he could see two crossbow bolts heading mid flight toward Abi but everything had slowed down. He lunged forwards at what he perceived was normal speed to him and deflected the bolts with the sword. As they glanced off harmlessly, Abi turned slowly to look at him, as he quickly spun around in a full circle swinging the sword in a wide arc. As he spun, the assassins in its path were literally cut in half above their waists. Thomas had to duck backwards, Paul just seeing him in time and pulling the sword away. Without hesitation Paul threw up the sword behind him and then stepped forwards swinging the sword around a second time repeating the action. As the blade sliced through more assassins, those behind could see the unbelievable action and hesitated. That was all Abi, Ishmael and Thomas needed and started to step forward as one. Stewart steadied his horse and looked back in time to see Paul wading into the main group of assassins, limbs falling and men screaming, Abi stabbing those that fell injured as Thomas slashed and hacked his way forward beside Paul. Stewart could not believe the sight he was witnessing as his own brother wielded the sword which was now giving off a low pitched hum that everyone could hear above the noise of battle. Count Henry rode up to Stewart and looked on in awe but then a loud crack drew both of their attention above as a large wooden beam half snapped and sank downwards in the middle as the fire started to undermine the wooden structure's integrity.

"PAUL!" Stewart shouted, but Paul did not hear him.

Paul could hear nothing except his own heartbeat and the low hum. He could sense blows striking him and blood flashing across his vision but he could not tell if it was his own or the assassins'. His body was moving forwards as if on its own accord, his arms swinging the sword in great circles smashing and slicing through flesh, bone and armour as if it was not there. Again he heard the voice of Kratos echo in his mind: 'Would you die for her?'

"A hundred times!" Paul yelled out, his face snarling, his eyes wide and wild as he thought about Alisha and Ailia and the anger that still burned within him for the loss of Arri.

Everyone heard his shout, including those inside the caravan, Ailia immediately looking up at Alisha, her forehead bleeding from where she had banged it against the side when the caravan nearly rolled over. Sister Lucy looked at Princess Stephanie as she clasped her hands together in prayer. Alisha pulled the sword of Saladin closer and grasped it in her right hand whilst shielding Ailia with her other arm protectively. Taqi frantically forced the two front horses to drag the caravan. Over two thirds of the way across, they stopped exhausted unable to pull it any further, the shackled injured horses and broken wheel proving too great a task. Quickly Taqi jumped up and held his sword as his colleague followed. He looked back to see the ongoing melee in full progress at the far end of the bridge, the main cross spars now all burning and sections of the wooden panelling boards. Stewart glanced back at him and the caravan.

"Lord Henry, I beg of you move to get Alisha and Ailia out…and if necessary put them on a single horse and send them on their way with Taqi and his friend to protect them…the numbers are too many here," Stewart shouted just as another crossbow bolt flashed past him dangerously close. He glanced up to see the other surviving caravan and cart speeding away off in the distance.

"But this bridge will not hold," Count Henry replied as he studied the burning support beams.

"Good…then Turansha and his men will not cross," Stewart replied and immediately turned his horse to face the fight and rushed forwards, sword raised high.

Count Henry watched as Stewart galloped back across the burning bridge and directly into the melee then quickly turned his own horse and rode toward the caravan, his heart nearly failing when he saw a column of men riding toward the bridge some distance away. He could not make out who they were for they were too far away. He prayed it was not more of Turansha's men.

Paul thrust his elbow back hard into the face of an assassin who had jumped upon the shoulders of the men in front and vaulted behind Paul trying to get to him. With a sickening crack of bone, the man's face imploded with the extreme force of his elbow. Stewart could see Paul moving ever further forward into the assassins as Abi, Thomas and Ishmael fought to keep up with him. Several of the Askar guards and Hospitallers were still on horseback using their horses to ram the assassins on the ground, slowly but surely pushing them back and off of the end of the bridge, but most of Count Henry's men were now dead upon the ground. A single horn echoed out across the plateau beyond and immediately all the assassins began to run away from the bridge and re-form up some hundred feet away. Stewart looked on in horror as even more fresh assassins appeared.

"Dear Lord what evil do you throw at us?" he asked aloud and moved his horse forward.

Paul stopped swinging his sword and stood up straight trying to look through the dust and smoke bellowing across his vision. Abi rushed to stand beside him as Thomas stood the other side and Ishmael at his back. As Stewart picked his way forward, the surviving mounted knights and Mamluks all looked around them at the sheer number of dead, most in a line leading to Paul, who stood perfectly still. But he was covered in blood, his mantle totally torn and rent. His chain mail was slashed in many places from blows that had been so severe they had severed the linkages. He was clearly wounded but remained upright. Paul's gaze turned to look up at Stewart.

 5 – 5

"Stewart...the bridge will fall soon. You must all get across and protect the women...please, and I shall defend this end so they will not pass," Paul said in a deep and low voice.

"And I shall stay with you," Abi remarked and readied her sword and axe.

"No...I need you to protect them...always...and Abi, you knew this day would come, as did Kratos and I believe Theo," Paul replied and stared at her intently. "Please Abi...go now while you can I beg of you."

"I shall stay with you," Ishmael said and stepped closer to Paul. "Argue with me and I shall knock you out myself," he smiled and held both his swords up.

A loud crack echoed out again as two more wooden support beams gave way smashing through half the wooden planking and falling the seventy feet below into the river swelled by storm waters further up in the mountains.

"You must go...and Stewart, that includes you, my dear brother. My days are done this day for the power in this takes its toll regardless," Paul said as he looked at Stewart wearily.

"No...surely we can hold out," Stewart replied emotionally as the others listened in.

"No, he is right," Abi suddenly said and immediately grabbed the reins to Stewart's horse and forcibly started to lead it back across the remaining section of bridge, Stewart trying to wrestle back control of his horse. "Do as his dying wish asks...can you not see the injuries he carries. He does not have time to argue with you," Abi stated bluntly.

"NO!" Stewart called out and jumped down from his horse but as he turned his back on Abi, she hit him across the neck knocking him out instantly. Quickly she caught him and slung him across the saddle and began to walk the horse carefully past the fallen away section of the burning bridge.

"And nor do I have time to argue with you," she said and gestured to the other men to follow her.

The remaining Askar guards looked at Paul as he watched Abi lead Stewart away and he nodded in agreement they should go as more flames engulfed the wooden structure of the bridge in ever increasing larger sections.

"I cannot expect you to throw your lives away this day, my friends," Paul said, looking at Ishmael and Thomas.

"'Tis not throwing it away. We stand with you and together we shall stop them passing long enough for that bridge to fall. There is no other way past," Thomas replied and then looked toward all of Turansha's men forming up ready to advance upon them. "Just point out the bastard Turansha to me and I will get him."

Suddenly a loud roar went up as all of Turansha's men started to run toward them at speed screaming and yelling.

Quickly Paul gestured the others to leave and follow Abi. He then stepped forward and gripped his sword again with both hands, a surge of energy shooting through him and he shuddered. There was no blood upon the blade as it never seemed to stick to it and gently he kissed it as his eyes fell upon the symbols etched within the blade, the sun behind him reflecting upon it. Only now in his last moments did he realise just how truly powerful a weapon it was...and one he could not let fall into the hands of Turansha. He would throw it into the deep ravine and river below he vowed before he would succumb.

"For fuck's sake get off my fucking fingers," Master Douglas suddenly called out from beneath Paul's left leg. Master Douglas rolled over and pushed off two dead assassins that were lying on top of him. As he stood up rubbing his head and flicking his fingers he looked at Paul's face and frowned. Paul indicated with his eyes and a slight nod to look behind him. Slowly Master Douglas turned around to see the mass of assassins rushing toward them. "I knew I should have stayed where I was," he remarked and shrugged his shoulders. "Do you have a spare sword perchance?" he calmly asked and outstretched his hand. Paul unsheathed his normal sword slung across his back and handed it to him. "Well, the silly bastards are running blind with the sun in their eyes and smoke so let's make this interesting for them eh boys."

Stewart started to come around as Abi stopped the horse beside the caravan, Taqi looking on, concerned.

"He will be fine," she stated and immediately moved to open the door but it flung open as Alisha forced it. Alarmed she looked at Stewart across the saddle.

"Where is Paul?" she asked frantically, Saladin's sword in her hand.

"Ali…now listen to me and do not argue. You must get on a horse with Ailia and leave with me now," Abi started to say when the men approaching on horseback from the opposite end of the bridge all pulled up. Abi instantly saw it was Philip and a full contingent of Templars. "Miracles do happen," she sighed and smiled nervously. She turned to face Alisha but she was already off and running toward the burning side of the bridge and Paul.

Princess Stephanie stepped down holding Ailia close and both of them immediately saw Alisha running with sword in hand. As soon as Taqi saw what she was doing he set off after her, Abi's eyes turning to Ailia, her main priority now. Sister Lucy stepped into view and looked at her, deeply concerned.

"Grandpapa!" Ailia called out and broke away from Princess Stephanie and ran toward the men on horseback as Philip dismounted quickly, his large dark blue cape flung over his shoulders.

Abi turned to look at him just as he knelt down with open arms and scooped Ailia up and held her tightly as the Templars with him dismounted and rapidly formed a protective circle around them. Philip stood up with Ailia as she wrapped her arms tightly around his neck. He looked at the scene ahead of him in time to see Alisha running toward the other end of the bridge, which was now burning fiercely. His heart missed a beat when he saw Stewart lying across the horse near to Abi. Quickly he moved toward them, the Templars following his pace as they moved forward.

 6 – 12

Alisha jumped over a dead horse as smoke enveloped her. When she stood out into clear air she was met by two assassins who had swung down from their hiding positions up in the woodwork. She froze momentarily then held her sword up and raised it behind her right shoulder, her eyes meeting the eyes of the nearest assassin. Taqi ran out of the smoke and nearly tripped as he tried to stop himself, the second assassin swinging his sword up hard against Taqi's sword. Caught unawares, Taqi's sword was knocked out of his hand and it flew upwards and away from him just as the other assassin jumped forwards at Alisha. She did not move but focused upon the assassin's blade as it came towards her. At the very last minute, she twisted her body, the blade flashing past her right thigh but ripping through her dark dress. As she spun around, the assassin's own body momentum made him fall forwards. As he spun to bring his sword up and roll so he would land upon his back, Alisha swung her sword down in one movement slashing him across his chest, her sword then moving upwards again. She kept the momentum going and spun around using her body weight to swing her sword even faster as she returned the sword in a circle back down upon the assassin's stomach as he now lay on the bridge floor. Briefly Alisha looked to her right to see Taqi stretching out his right foot and catch his own sword. It momentarily balanced on the top of his foot before he flicked it up back towards himself and caught it, instantly grabbing the handle, the assassin looking surprised. He swung his sword in a rapid blur of movement at the approaching assassin now unable to stop his direction and he ran straight into Taqi's sword, the blade passing right through him and protruding out of his back. The injured assassin beside Alisha made a noise bringing her attention back to him. Rapidly she stepped over him, his eyes looking into hers. He blinked and appeared to nod in acceptance and closed his eyes just as she thrust the sword down with both hands into his chest killing him instantly. Taqi looked across at her. With anger written across her face, she pulled the sword out of the assassin and stood up straight and wiped her mouth, blood from the cut on her forehead running down her cheek. She looked back at Taqi then her eyes fell to the scene unfolding at the far end of the bridge. Several Templars appeared out of the smoke behind her, one looking at Taqi and raising his sword before seeing the dead assassin at his feet. A loud snapping and groan of breaking wood echoed out as a large section of the bridge in front of them collapsed falling away into the ravine below with a loud rumble. Quickly Alisha ran forward and onto the only clear part of the bridge still standing, just a thin section less than two feet wide now remaining connected to the end of the bridge on her left side attached to the stone supports. Taqi ran after her looking up at the remaining wooden beams checking for any other assassins.

"PAUL!" Alisha screamed loudly.

Paul heard her call and looked behind him to see her standing at the very edge of the gaping hole, sword in hand as Taqi ran up beside her.

"STAY THERE!" he yelled back, raising his hand for her to stop.

"Stand fast, brothers," Master Douglas said as he gripped his sword ready for the assault now about to fall upon them.

Paul turned to face them and held his sword in front of his face again. At least if the bridge was down, it was a two day ride to the next crossing he thought by which time Alisha would be far enough away and safe. He looked down at his long shadow cast in front of him, Ishmael standing just behind him to his right, Thomas beside him and Master Douglas to his left. As he stared at their shadows, he knew the moment the first assassin stepped upon them he would throw himself forwards with all his remaining strength. He drew energy from the sword but he knew these were his last moments. Out of the corner of his eye, he caught sight of the Templar from the cave whose horse had been shot away beneath him. He was dazed with a large cut across his forehead. He looked up at Paul, the sun silhouetting all around him, his sword appearing to glow as the sun lit up its edges. Paul immediately stepped forwards over him protectively and grabbed his main belt and pulled him upwards to his knees.

"Get across the bridge now while you can," Paul said calmly and looked into the knight's eyes. The knight coughed and tried to stand but his leg was injured. Paul pressed his sword against the knight's chest, who instantly felt a shock run through him which took his breath away. "Live and get my family to France."

Feeling overwhelmed with emotion as the energy from the sword pulsed through him, the Templar looked gratefully into Paul's eyes filled with a mix of emotions he had never experienced before. He felt as though Paul was taking every bad thought and emotion he had ever had or ever suffered from him. Tears welled in his eyes.

"What are you?" he asked emotionally.

"He is a real king of kings...now fuck off outta the way," Master Douglas interrupted and pulled the knight aside and pushed him behind.

The knight half staggered back toward the bridge trying to look at Paul as tears ran down his cheeks. He could see the assassins were almost upon

them and quickly he stepped onto the thin wooden ledge made from a supporting beam and began to edge his way across the wide gap, his fingers
gripping hold of any part of the stone supports he could grab, his eyes
closed tightly, fearful of heights. His foot slipped at one point as a burnt
plank of wood fell away. Taqi ran over and helped guide him back shouting
instructions to him, mainly so he could then run across to help Paul and
the others. The knight stepped away from the edge onto the main bridge
structure, Taqi pulling him in fast just as the stone support collapsed and
fell away completely cutting the bridge in half leaving just an upright section of stone arch in the gap between. Alisha rushed forwards, Taqi having
to hold her back as she stood dangerously close the edge. She looked at
Paul in alarm just as the other assassins fell upon them. Taqi saw a crossbow on the floor and picked it up but there was no bolt in it. Rapidly he
scanned the large gap between them. He backed up a few paces then ran
and jumped to the middle section of stone archway, and landing upon one
foot momentarily, leaped straight on to the other side only just landing on
the splintered remains of the bridge. As he rolled over, he came straight up
ready to fight.

The Templar from the cave stood beside Alisha as she contemplated
doing the same but seeing the look in her eyes, he grabbed hold of her
forearm and would not let go as he shook his head no silently, his face covered in his own blood and dust. Ailia struggled to free herself from Philip's
arms but he held her tightly as Abi moved to see through the smoke from
both the burning bridge and cart, having all heard the thunderous crash
of the collapsed section hit the ravine and river below. Flames began to
engulf sections of the bridge near to Alisha and the Templar forced her
to look at them concerned as the floor beneath them creaked and sank
several inches.

   2 – 28

An assassin jumped directly at Paul in a suicidal charge closely followed
by another just as others did the same toward Thomas, Ishmael and Master
Douglas. Paul lunged forwards at the assassin before his sword was even
coming down and thrust his own sword with both hands into the man's
chest, the blade bursting out of his back directly into the assassin's chest
behind. Paul used his leg to push them away and pulled his sword out,

swung it back and over his head already swinging in down toward the next assassin coming at him. Taqi jumped beside him and half crouching swung his sword sideways cutting the right leg clean off the man nearest him. As he raised his right arm holding his sword, he deflected the blow from another assassin whilst using his left hand he thrust his arming dagger down into the assassin's chest, who was now on his back trying to hold his severed stump of his leg high. Master Douglas and Ishmael moved to stand back to back and seemed to move in perfect unison as they both swung their swords, then thrust them into flesh…but Paul knew the numbers were overwhelming.

"Taqi…I beg of you return to Ali and Ailia and look after them," he called out as he swiped his sword violently down across the face of another assassin just as one of the assassins' blades slashed across his own upper thigh, links shattering and blood being thrown upwards. "Die needlessly now or save them!" Paul shouted and grabbed Taqi by the shoulder and physically hurled him backwards with such force it shocked Taqi as he landed heavily almost rolling over the edge of the fallen bridge. Quickly he stood up with his sword and could only stare at the sight of Paul wielding his sword with such ferocity smashing and cutting through flesh and bone, Ishmael, Master Douglas and Thomas pulling closer together so their backs were not exposed and following Paul deeper into the mass of black clad assassins, Paul desperately trying to locate Turansha. He kicked, punched and swung out in all directions nearly catching Thomas at one point again in a whirlwind of aggressive all consuming fury. Master Douglas let out a yell of pain as a sword pierced his left shoulder, but he grabbed the arm of the assassin and pulled him closer thrusting his sword straight up at an angle through the man's chest then pushed him away, all the while Alisha and the Templar looking on horrified. Taqi looked at them and noticed the fire beneath them eating away at the main wooden support beams. He looked quickly at Paul once more before moving back a few paces. He checked the ground for his run up, then ran for all he was worth, his right foot only just landing upon the remaining stone arch section as he jumped on it, and he continued his forward momentum only just landing on the bridge and rolling over hard. Alisha looked at him in shock as he jumped up and grabbed her and immediately began to drag her away. She flounced her arm away angrily and turned to run back to the edge so Taqi picked her up bodily from behind and held her over his shoulder as she struggled and wriggled to get off. He ran with her, the Templar by his side, toward the direction of the caravan when she bit the side of his neck hard to let her go. The shock of her bite made him hesitate and stumble and both fell to the floor hard. Taqi rolled onto his back as Alisha stood up rapidly, still holding Saladin's sword and gathered up her dress ready to run back. She had only taken a few strides when the entire section of bridge they had been standing upon dropped several feet, held its position for a moment then completely fell away, the remaining sections of the stone archways collapsing with it. She froze, her stomach knotting. She looked forward through the smoke and dust and could see nothing of what was happening on the other side. She shook in both anger and frustration but also the realisation Taqi had just saved their lives.

Paul powered his way forwards swinging his sword around with such speed and violence and force that anything in its way was simply sliced in half. The assassins seeing this began to hesitate long enough for Ishmael and Master Douglas to engage them as Thomas hopped backwards, his lower left leg severely cut but still managing to protect Paul's back. Paul could feel nothing nor hear anything as he stepped forwards and swung his sword with every step, men falling in agony, some beginning to turn away. All he could think of was Turansha. He knew once the sword was out of his hands, he would fall. He could sense the injuries he was taking but nothing else mattered. He quickly glanced back sensing something was wrong behind him in time to see a fleeting glimpse of Alisha, Taqi and the Templar standing on the opposite side of the gap. He felt the crushing smash of a blade come down upon his left shoulder and he instantly turned and swung his sword upwards against the blade slicing it in two, the assassin's eyes widening at the look in Paul's eyes as he then pulled the sword back ready to thrust into him. Just as Paul was about to kill him, the man jerked in pain and arched his shoulders backwards as an arrow shot through him, the arrow head bursting out of the front of his chest. Then the assassin beside him fell as an arrow hit him in the side, Master Douglas immediately taking his head off with one blow. Paul hesitated for a moment and stood up straight as more assassins began to fall hit by arrows and crossbow bolts. One zipped between the legs of one assassin and embedded in Paul's right upper thigh but he did not feel it. Ishmael went to strike an assassin as he raised his sword but he dropped it behind him as an arrow struck the middle of his back. Puzzled, Ishmael looked into the distance to see many men on horseback. Paul followed his gaze and saw many Muslim Tawashi cavalry horse archers riding closer and firing rapid aimed shots at the assassins. As the assassins began to run in all directions, Paul looked frantically for Turansha ripping the head covers off of many of the dead assassins. Within moments all the surviving assassins were surrounded by horse archers, some choosing to die and deliberately running at them only to be cut down by arrows instantly. Master Douglas rested his hands upon is knees bent over out of breath as Ishmael stood close to Paul. Al Rashid suddenly appeared on horseback and approached slowly, looking at the carnage before him. Several of his men rode up alongside as the last assassins knelt down with their hands upon their heads in submission. Several injured men moaned as another Mamluk was being sick with sheer relief. Paul staggered momentarily until Ishmael steadied him.

"I was sent word by Saladin you would need more help with your escort. He knew I was near so sent me his best Tawashi cavalry horse archers. Are we too late?" Al Rashid asked as he stopped his horse several feet from Paul.

Paul turned around to look across the wide open gap of the bridge still burning. Through the smoke he could just see Alisha and Taqi stood with the Templar from the cave and several other Templars. He wondered where they had come from. Master Douglas fell to his knees as blood loss from his shoulder weakened him and he felt dizzy.

 4 – 9

"Such irony," he said aloud and then sat himself down amongst the dead and dying as a horse lying on its back snorted. "We all kill each other basically arguing over what happens to us when we die," he half laughed and shook his head then looked across at Alisha. "But today…today was truly worth it."

Just as he said that, two assassins jumped down from the upper main beams of the bridge just beyond Alisha and Taqi. Philip saw them drop and handed Ailia to Sister Lucy quickly and drew his sword, Abi immediately moving to run toward them. Alisha turned around hearing the men drop down in time to see another two drop down from the main beams above them. Then Turansha stepped into view having been hidden within a recess in the main stone support tower section. He grinned menacingly at her as Taqi realised what was happening and instantly pulled Alisha behind him as two of the assassins aimed crossbows at them. Paul's heart almost exploded seeing them and he rapidly studied the distance of the gap. Several Tawashi horse archers dismounted and ran to the edge and charged their bows, but smoke from the fires kept obscuring their aim and they risked hitting Alisha and Taqi as well as the Templar. Paul squeezed the handle of the sword trying to pull as much energy as possible from it. As Philip and Abi ran toward the assassins, Turansha raised his hand still grinning.

"Come any closer and my men will cut her down instantly," he said coldly.

Abi pushed her way past the other Templars and stepped closer trying to see what she could do and shook her head angry at herself for her bow was on her horse at the caravan. Philip looked across the gap and saw Paul standing with his sword.

"Turansha...you cannot escape this. Let them go and I swear I shall guarantee you safe passage from here," Philip called out.

"You still do not understand do you...Navigator?" Turansha replied, smirking as he stared coldly at Alisha. "I do not fear death...but if I am to die this hour, I shall at least get my wish...for it has always been my intention to remove the crimson line for ever. That has always been my mission," he stated and lowered his hand fast, the two assassins immediately taking aim. As they fired at Alisha Taqi braced himself but the Templar from the cave pushed him aside and opened his arms wide. He was larger and wider than Taqi and both bolts slammed into his chest. Alisha gasped as the other two assassins aimed their crossbows at Philip and Abi whilst the other two recharged a bolt in theirs. Paul's eyes widened in fury. He took a few paces back checking the run up to the edge of the gap.

"You will never make it," Thomas said.

Paul looked up and across in time to see the Templar fall to his knees but smiling just as the two assassins aimed their crossbows again at Alisha. She spun her head around in time to see Paul start his run up. Taqi jumped to his feet and threw himself at Alisha knocking her to the floor. He pinned her down as she tried to look up. Abi filled with rage raised her sword as the other two assassins aimed and fired at Taqi and Alisha but he held his position over her. Abi rushed forwards closely followed by the other Templars to engage the assassins. As they turned to fight, Turansha ran over to Taqi and Alisha and pulled Taqi off of her and immediately thrust his sword up under her chin as she lay upon her back. Taqi coughed and blood gurgled up through his mouth, only then did Alisha realise he had four crossbow bolts in his back. He struggled to remain upright and outstretched his hand to Alisha but Turansha kicked him down hard.

"Mama!" Ailia suddenly called out as she ran into view closely followed by Sister Lucy and Princess Stephanie trying to catch her. Philip reached out to stop her as she ran past him and between the Templars and Abi as she cut one of the assassins down. "Mama!" she called out again and ran directly at Turansha and Alisha.

Quickly Turansha grabbed hold of Ailia and held her up tightly against his chest, throwing his sword down as she squealed and kicked out. He pulled out a razor sharp knife and placed it against her neck, her eyes widened in fear. Taqi coughed again barely able to move. A thud at the edge of the gap drew all of their attention as Paul slammed into the wooden panelling of the floor, just his hands gripping the edge. Turansha laughed as he noted his men were now all dead, the Templars, Abi and Philip now moving slowly toward him. Paul struggled to pull himself up and Alisha went to move to help him.

"Move and she dies this instant," Turansha said coldly and pulled Ailia's head back against his shoulder, the knife glinting in the sunlight. He smiled as he watched Alisha look at Paul in desperation then back at Ailia and then Taqi struggling to keep his eyes open and breathe. "This is perfect...you two do not fear death...but how do you feel about your daughter? Shall I send her on her way to meet her brother?"

Paul gritted his teeth, the anger in him at seeing Turansha fuelling his exhausted muscles. He managed to get his right elbow up on the woodwork, but the weight of his fully armoured body caused the wood to snap and he slipped only just grabbing hold with his fingers again.

"Papa!" Ailia called out and shook her head, her hair flicking in Turansha's face.

"Why do you so want us all dead?" Alisha pleaded, rapidly looking back and forth at Paul then Taqi, her sense of helplessness being total.

Turansha backed himself and Ailia away and near to one of the main wooden supports. He knelt down and forced Ailia to lay face down as he picked up a loaded crossbow and aimed it at Alisha but Ailia kept struggling. Paul managed to pull himself up in time to see him aim the crossbow at Alisha but the sight of Ailia being pushed face down filled him with rage. He swung his leg up and hauled himself over onto his side on the wooden floor. Quickly he stood up and unsheathed his sword as Turansha looked up at him. Instantly he fired off the crossbow, the bolt striking Paul in the chest. Paul took a deep breath, the pulse of his own heart coursing through him and the sword in his hand. 'Just a few minutes more I pray,' he said to himself as he moved to step forwards, Turansha reaching over and picking up a second crossbow and immediately firing it at Paul. Alisha gasped as the bolt struck him next to the first bolt.

"NO!" Princess Stephanie yelled out and ran across the open space between them.

Alisha knelt up as tears ran down her face seeing the bolts in his chest but he was still standing, the sword humming. Philip grabbed hold of Princess Stephanie as she tried to pass him. Paul's vision was beginning to fade and his ears were ringing loudly. He looked down at Alisha.

 1 – 24

"Ali…you must move aside," Paul said, his voice changed.

Philip pulled Princess Stephanie close as tears welled in his own eyes seeing all that he loved about to be killed and he could do nothing but stand helpless. Sister Lucy stepped forwards her eyes narrowing as she looked at Turansha charging a third bolt. Once charged he quickly knelt behind Ailia as he forced her down with his knee in her back. He placed the crossbow down and quickly held his knife against the base of Ailia's neck and then reached inside his tunic and pulled out a small parchment sheet. Quickly he unfurled it by shaking it then pulled Ailia up and stood up as she wriggled frantically, the knife pressed against her throat now. He waved the parchment in front of her face. She stopped wriggling when she saw the image of herself drawn upon it. Another assassin suddenly jumped down from one of the main beams above Turansha armed with a loaded crossbow and aimed it at Paul.

"See…your own father sealed your fate the day he drew this of you," Turansha said aloud and waved the picture of Ailia. Turansha's eyes focused upon Paul's sword as he raised it and stepped forward. "Stop or she dies this very moment," he called out and raised his knife closer to Ailia's throat.

Paul stepped in front of Alisha and grabbed Taqi and pulled him back toward her. She quickly cradled Taqi on her knees as Paul walked ever closer toward Turansha and the assassin, Turansha pushing his knife blade even closer to Ailia's throat as she tried to breathe, her eyes wide in fear. Turansha and the assassin moved slowly to their side moving toward the furthest edge of the collapsed section of the bridge. Paul looked behind him at Alisha and Taqi as Sister Lucy walked calmly across the bridge toward them. In her mind she wanted the assassin to shoot at her to give Paul a fighting chance of getting near to Ailia but Turansha knew this was her intention and raised his arm to stop the crossbow being fired.

"Ali...get Taqi away from here," Paul ordered then glimpsed his father looking on as Stewart moved to stand beside him rubbing his neck, Abi ready to launch herself the moment Turansha dropped his guard.

"You cannot live much longer...even less without the sword...so drop it over the side now or your precious Grail princess dies this very minute," Turansha demanded and pushed the very tip of the blade beneath Ailia's chin.

Paul's eyes locked with Ailia's as she stared at him fighting to breathe in short sharp breaths. With two bolts in his chest, he knew he could not last much longer and without the sword, even less time. Turansha grinned menacingly. Paul looked down at the Templar from the cave lying face down.

"I will do and give you what you want if you let her free," Paul stated as Sister Lucy helped Alisha to stand and drag Taqi toward Abi and the other Templars.

"I want to end your line here this day...and when I am killed, it matters not even with all your writings and codes for none shall remember them... you see you have always underestimated me. There is another lord who will reign as king in these lands...and when my soul returns to this realm, he that kills me this day I shall visit upon them such hell in the next life as it is written. You know these things to be true," Turansha said, grinning. "I know you well enough to have known you would come for the bridge and 'tis why I was hidden here. You are like your father," he said and looked across to Philip. "Predictable."

"Ailia...do not be afraid," Paul said and started to walk directly at Turansha.

"Paul NO!" Alisha cried out.

The assassin fired his bolt, which instantly hit Paul in the chest, the close range making it pass through him, the bolt head bursting out of his back just below his left shoulder blade. Alisha went to run back but Abi just managed to grab her and hold her as she screamed. Turansha started to move backwards against the wooden beams as more flames began to take hold along the collapsed edge of the bridge. Princess Stephanie placed her hands over her mouth unable to breathe as she watched Paul take another step forwards and kneel down to pick up the loaded crossbow Turansha had charged. As he stood up, his vision blurred, he could not breathe properly, the last bolt having pierced completely through his left lung. He staggered back and fell to his knees beside the Templar. Tears ran down Princess Stephanie's face and she started to walk toward him without thinking of anything else as Alisha kicked out and screamed trying to break free from Abi, Philip standing still unable to do anything but watch and pray. Paul thrust his sword into the woodwork floor and gripped the handle with his right hand. He tried to draw as much energy from it as he could but he knew he was too badly injured now. As blood came up from his chest, he coughed it out and nearly fell sideways off of the edge just managing to use the sword to pull himself upright again as the others watched on in horror. He focused his eyes upon Ailia and nodded at her. Master Douglas was going frantic on the other side trying to see what was happening as Thomas tried to find a way of getting across to help. Ishmael stood at the very edge and looked at Paul as he was on his knees. As Turansha moved along the bridge, the assassin moved with him. Ishmael took a bow from a dead horse archer near his feet and quickly charged an arrow. Before Master Douglas could stop him, he drew it back hard and loosed it off. Paul saw the arrow flash past his vision and strike the assassin through the neck killing him instantly, Turansha flinching briefly but forcing Ailia's head back as he placed the blade across her throat, Alisha gasping and collapsed, going limp in Abi's arms. Ailia looked at Paul then slightly turned her little face to look up at Turansha.

"I do not know what I have done to make you want to hurt me," she said softly and sniffed as a tear ran down her cheek, Turansha pressing the blade harder against her throat, drawing blood. "But...but you have hurt my papa," she said and gulped hard as everyone just looked on transfixed and helpless. Paul's vision was failing fast, his strength draining. "So I am giving you this," Ailia said and thrust up her little hand holding Alisha's three pronged dagger straight up into his neck below his jaw.

In utter shock Turansha dropped Ailia and she fell on the floor hard. Holding his throat as blood began to seep through his beard and fingers he stood on Ailia so she could not move and then pulled out the dagger, blood spurting out all over her as she wriggled. He pulled the dagger up high and thrust it down toward Ailia as Alisha fell to her knees, Princess Stephanie still walking toward Paul. A small black throwing knife flashed past Ailia into Turansha's wrist knocking his arm back and away from her. Paul had thrown it. It was the blade Brother Teric had given Paul years previously in Jerusalem to check out. Paul knew it had once belonged to Turansha's men…it was the only thing he had left he could chance using with Ailia so close. But as Paul fought to remain upright and focus his failing eyesight, Turansha simply grinned as he moved to stand over Ailia again. His eyes stared at Paul's as he was about to kill her, Princess Stephanie walking ever closer. She saw what he was about to do and reached out when a crossbow bolt flashed past narrowly missing her but enough to make her stand still. The bolt slammed into Turansha's chest knocking him backwards hard against the main wooden upright support beam that was burning. Paul looked to his right, as Alisha looked to her left to see the Templar from the cave leaning up having fired the crossbow, his eyes turning to look up at Paul, who nodded in appreciation and slumped back onto his calves and fell to his side. Princess Stephanie looked at him and moved toward him but he pointed at Ailia. Turansha reached out to grab Ailia as his own cloak caught fire, Ailia kicking him away, picked up Alisha's dagger again and stood up and pointed it at him. Turansha propped himself up and laughed as blood oozed from his mouth, his back beginning to burn, his left hand holding the bolt in his chest. Princess Stephanie ran over to Ailia and pulled her away as Paul fought to stand up holding the sword. The Templar beside him stood up and helped Paul to stand, Turansha looking on in disbelief. Paul grasped the handle of the sword with both hands and felt the energy from it pulse through him. He looked at the Templar in surprise with two bolts in his chest. Quickly the Templar pulled his tunic apart to reveal the broken halves of the bolts hanging loose as they had hit a metal plate secured in place to his chain mail. Paul forced a smile but coughed as blood streamed from his mouth. Alisha looked across at Paul in alarm and rising panic as he staggered backwards close to the edge.

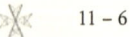 11 – 6

"Please…get them away from here before this bridge collapses," Paul said and swayed just as several large sections fell away blocking Alisha from getting to him. Philip started to move around the other side to get to Ailia and Princess Stephanie as Turansha rolled onto his back to extinguish the flames on his tunic.

"Kill me, little princess…," Turansha said, grinning, his eyes now bloodshot, the smell of burnt flesh filing their nostrils. Princess Stephanie pulled Ailia behind her and began to back away. Ailia stood up straight and looked at Paul as he stood by his sword. She started to run toward him but a section of the floor fell away and she stopped just in time.

"Ailia…!" Alisha shouted and beckoned her to move toward Philip as he made his way around toward them. Alisha shook her head frantically as the panic inside her started to overwhelm her with a sense of total helplessness.

"I will not let you stain her soul with your death and make any attachments for the next life," Princess Stephanie said and wiped her hand across her face as smoke and soot dirtied her cheeks mixed with her tears.

Ailia hesitated and looked at Paul. He smiled, his body now becoming numb and he indicated she go to her mother. The Templar beside Paul ran back and around then jumped across the new gap, landing heavily beside Ailia. He took hold of her and started to drag her toward Philip and Abi just in time as another section of the bridge collapsed. Philip ran and lifted Ailia up into his arms and looked over toward Paul as Abi moved to protect both of them. Thomas fell to his knees as he looked across the open gap, helpless, Ishmael trying to gauge the distance in preparation to jump across, Master Douglas grabbing hold of him. The section of bridge Paul was stood on suddenly dropped a foot as the main beam beneath him started to give way. Stewart tried to shout but his mouth was dry. Alisha just looked at Paul as he steadied himself with the sword. She had only just got him back and now she was to lose him again…but this time for ever, and she knew it with a total inner knowing that collapsed her very soul as she stared at him, utterly powerless…she wanted to rush to him…to die with him rather than suffer the unbearable crushing loss of him again, but then she looked at Ailia, then placed her hand upon her stomach and the child that grew within her. Taqi coughed weakly as more blood fell from his mouth. He knew he had very little time himself left but fought to see Paul. Princess Stephanie turned to look at Paul as he pulled the sword up and with his last remaining strength threw it toward her. Her eyes followed it as it flew through the air, hit the floor and spun across the wooden panels stopping just short of her feet. Philip ran back toward Alisha carrying Ailia as more flames took hold of the other side of the bridge. Ailia flung her arms around Alisha as she wrapped her arms around her tightly. Taqi coughed and raised his hand pointing to Paul as he fell to his knees. He smiled to himself knowing Turansha was finished and Alisha and Ailia now safe. Turansha strained to focus upon Paul. Princess Stephanie looked at Paul as he stared at her then the sword. Immediately she picked it up knowing what he was indicating. She stood up with the sword and felt its energy momentarily taking her breath away as it surged through her. A loud crack echoed out as the entire end section of the bridge with Paul on began to break away slowly. Princess Stephanie glanced back at Paul kneeling as he looked at her. He was now totally cut off from the others. 'I love you,' she mouthed and he nodded in acknowledgement.

"Ha! You kill me and I shall stain your soul for eternity," Turansha stated and coughed. "So go on," he goaded and smiled.

Princess Stephanie stepped forwards with the sword held in both hands.

"You forget…this sword serves out justice…the one who wields it cannot be touched nor stained for the sword itself takes it. Now die and spare this world your evil," she said through gritted teeth and thrust the sword down hard into his chest, his eyes widening in surprise having not expected her to do so. She leant into the sword to push it deeper into him until it struck the wood beneath him. "And we shall not hate you…for that is not our way. We shall forgive you, and we shall pray for you that you are forgiven…for that is the wisdom and love of the sacred feminine you have lived your life trying to wipe out. Love and forgive you!"

Turansha's eyes widened even more as her words echoed through his dying mind, just a slight cold stinging sensation pulsing through his chest, not pain. He could not comprehend how she could say such words. She must be saying them to add insult to injury, he thought. But as he looked into her tear filled eyes staring down at him, her hands wrapped around the handle of the sword, he knew she meant it. In that last instant he felt it, whether from the sword or through her, but he felt the power of real love and forgiveness. He suddenly felt warm as if wrapped up by some great unseen protective blanket of love. He blinked and shook his head lightly, confused by his own rush of emotions. What great error had he committed having just wasted his entire life on trying to eradicate Paul and Alisha's line, he momentarily pondered as the realisation struck deep within his very soul that he should have been protecting them all along, not blinded by his own greed…He shuddered as the full impact of his cruel actions and intentions only now became obvious as wrong. How could he have not known this before? He placed his hands upon the top section of the sword's blade and clasped it tightly as he stared into Princess Stephanie's eyes. His vision began to fail as sunlight shone around her head, her hair appearing to glow. 'Forgiven' he saw her speak as his eyes finally closed.

"'Twas Conrad…Lord Montferrat who commanded me," he whispered almost involuntarily with his last dying breath.

When his eyes shut and his body went limp as he died, Princess Stephanie stood up quickly and pulled out the sword and turned to face Paul, who had witnessed everything. He smiled and nodded. She let the sword hang loose, its tip resting on the floor, her shoulders slumped. Alisha held Ailia as they both looked on helpless. Taqi smiled and lowered his arm as his colleague tried to move him to support him better.

"Did you hear that? 'Twas Conrad all along," Taqi whispered and grabbed his colleague's arm tightly. "Make…make sure our Master learns of this," he said, his eyes closing slowly as he then died, Alisha not even aware he had as he lay beside her.

"Mama…Taqi is an angel, look," Ailia said, pointing to her side, but no one else could see anything. Quickly Abi checked Taqi as his colleague sat back. He was indeed dead but with a serene smile upon his face. She looked at Alisha and simply shook her head no sadly. Alisha put her hand to her mouth and looked over at Paul, Princess Stephanie stood several feet away from him but separated by the collapsed section. "Papa," Ailia whispered and looked toward him.

Paul looked over toward Alisha and Ailia and smiled seeing they were safe, Stewart wiping tears from his own eyes as Philip stood beside him. Paul looked at his father as he stood there. They all knew Paul's injuries were not survivable. Philip gulped hard and held onto Stewart. Paul's family were safe, his prayers had been answered and he was content with that and as his vision rapidly failed, he could see what he thought were people standing near to him. He could hear his own heartbeat slowing down but nothing else. He half laughed to himself as he realised he had three bolts in his chest and recalled his vow to Alisha all those years before that not even three arrows through his heart would ever stop his love for her. He shrugged his shoulders as he thought it mattered not they were bolts instead. Princess Stephanie moved to the very edge of the bridge and knelt down with the sword in front of her. Despite flames creeping ever nearer she remained there and just looked at him, her heart breaking seeing him out of reach and dying. She could hardly catch her breath and reached out her right hand toward him. Alisha jumped to her feet and ran toward Paul. She hesitated momentarily as she checked the bridge burning around her then gauged the distance of the open gap between her and Paul. Princess Stephanie looked at her alarmed and quickly stood to move toward her. Alisha looked at Paul as he shook his head no.

"I cannot...I will not lose you again!" Alisha called out emotionally as she frantically checked the space between them again. "I cannot live without you...and I cannot do what is asked of us alone," she called out as she took a few paces back and readied herself to rush forwards and jump.

The Templar from the cave could see the section of bridge she was on was about to fall and he ran around the far side of the burning bridge and up behind her. He reached her and grabbed her around the waist just as a sickening crack echoed out as the beam section Paul was kneeling on finally gave way. Princess Stephanie threw herself at Alisha and the Templar wrapping her arms around them from behind. Alisha gasped out loud and reached out her arms in desperation, the Templar struggling to hold her. Paul's eyes momentarily locked on Alisha's. He partly raised his right arm toward her.

"In you is where everything begins and where everything ends," he said softly then fell backwards, his vision looking upwards into the clear blue sky, the last image of Alisha still held in his mind. He smiled as a thousand images, emotions and memories flashed through his mind in an instant. He was about to die, but he was dying content knowing his family were at last finally safe. In his mind he could see Alisha smiling at him...As he closed his eyes he told himself 'I will find you in the temple, through the secret of the temple. Look for me there and you will find me'. He then recalled Theodoric's words spoken to Lucy. 'To love you more than you can understand is an honour. To love you unconditionally is the only way for any of us. To wrap one's heart around another person's soul is how we must love, and to give of the heart until it hurts, then give a little more again...for that is love being lived! When you find the strength inside, you can overcome anything. Even in death it does not end.'

Abi rushed up behind Princess Stephanie and dragged her to her feet then pulled the Templar up, Alisha coming up with him, his arms wrapped around her tightly, her arms still outstretched as Paul started to fall. Ailia ran up beside Abi. Alisha saw her out of the corner of her eye and quickly pulled Ailia's face into her side so she could not see as Paul fell away backwards and out of sight, Philip almost collapsing. Abi lowered her head in sadness as Alisha just stared in total bewilderment tears running down her cheeks as she sobbed. Princess Stephanie let out a gasp as Paul fell away and vanished out of view…the crash of the stone and wood smashing onto the rocks and raging river below echoing out down the ravine a moment later. She closed her eyes and lowered her head.

 9 – 4

"For this day I too am now dead to this world," she whispered to herself and bent forwards resting her forehead upon the sword's handle and began to sob, the Templar trying to urge Alisha and Ailia to follow him. Princess Stephanie opened her eyes and looked down to see the small drawing of Ailia looking up at her. Gently she picked it up just as she heard shouting from the other side. She looked up in time to see Ishmael pushing Master Douglas away, who fell on his side hard. Quickly he struggled to get to his feet again as Ishmael ran over to the very edge of the fallen bridge and looked down at the swirling angry river below trying to see where Paul had fallen, wooden beams being washed downriver fast, spinning and churning along in the white waves. He looked back at Master Douglas briefly and all the others stood looking on, then without any words looked across at Princess Stephanie and Alisha, bowed his head slightly and stepped off into the abyss. Master Douglas fell back upon his backside, stunned. Alisha saw Ishmael step off and fall out of sight and she just looked on open mouthed and in shock. She fell to her knees as Princess Stephanie stood holding the sword, the Templar beside her as other Templars rushed to her side. Stewart turned his back on everyone and broke down in tears, Philip gently placing his hand upon his shoulder reassuringly despite his own emotional pain, his heart broken. Ailia flicked her hair as she spun her head around and looked toward the collapsed bridge section.

"I do not wish to live in this world a moment longer without him," Alisha sobbed, her entire body shaking. Princess Stephanie knelt beside her and gently pulled her face to look at her.

Abi stepped beside them and looked down directly at Alisha.

"Today...was a turning point in history," she said and paused. "Today, a great evil has been stopped from spreading across this world, and none of you even realise it," Abi said, turning to look at everyone.

"Ali," Princess Stephanie said quietly, a tear rolling down her own cheek. "If you give up now...then all of this was for nothing and all the sacrifices in vain. You must," she gulped hard before continuing, " you must...and you will continue this."

"I cannot, for I do not know how to...and not alone," Alisha sobbed as Ailia put her arms around her neck.

"You do not have to do it alone," the Templar interrupted and stood up straight. "My sword is yours as is my life from this day onward," he said emotionally.

Abi knelt down in front of Alisha.

"Do not let the pain of this cause the loss of your unborn...for the crimson stream flows within you and your daughters," she said softly.

"I care not for such matters any more. 'Twas and is a curse," Alisha sobbed as Ailia hugged her tightly.

"Paul did not think so, my child," Abi said and wiped her finger down Alisha's cheek. "Now we must continue what he started...for you are indeed not alone," she explained then looked at Ailia. "And Ailia will soon have a sister to look after."

Ailia looked at Abi as she smiled and nodded.

"Papa," she said quietly and stared for a moment in silence. She sighed then looked at Alisha and placed her little hands upon her face. "Papa...we will see him again...he promised," she said softly, her big eyes filled with the look of innocent serenity and yet wisdom beyond her years. Alisha sobbed uncontrollably and exhausted. She kissed Ailia then hugged her tightly as Princess Stephanie placed her arms around them, Abi placing her hands upon each of their shoulders and lowered her head in sadness.

Chapter 87
An End, but the Voice Within Remains

Port of La Rochelle, France, Melissae Inn, spring 1191

"Oh my Lord," Ayleth remarked and wiped tears from her eyes, sobbing openly.

"So what happened to Percival...and Ishmael for that matter? Did he really just step off into the ravine?" Simon asked, looking half bewildered.

"Yes, yes he did," the old man answered and clasped his hands together. "And he was never seen again," he explained and paused. "As for Percival...we can only assume he was killed too as he was thrown from the caravan as it toppled. He must have fallen into the ravine and swollen river below or upon the many rocks. We never found out."

"So as you said, 'twas indeed down to Princess Stephanie that the sword is here this day," Gabirol stated. "But what of the staff of Jesus...did that not help...or why pass it to Paul at all?"

"Yes, the sword is indeed here this day because of Princess Stephanie, for the Templar guided her back to safety...and only just in time before the whole middle section of the bridge collapsed after them. But as for the staff...like Paul 'twas never recovered."

"He must have been a smart Templar to have attached metal plates to his chain mail," the Templar remarked.

"Clearly he saved Ailia and Alisha...for without his presence Alisha would have been shot as would Ailia have been killed," the Hospitaller said and looked at his brother then at the old man.

"He was indeed smart. An innovator too full of inventive ideas," the old man replied and looked at Sarah as she sniffed and wiped her eyes trying her hardest not to cry.

"He should meet this one then for he too is full of such ideas," she said and half slapped Stephan.

"Oh, I think it safe to say he has met him," the old man replied and smiled, looking at Stephan. "Stephan...will you or shall I?" Sarah looked at Stephan, puzzled.

She shrugged her shoulders impatiently when he said nothing. "Remember when I said the Templar in the cave received a bad cut across his forehead?"

Now everyone looked at Stephan puzzled as he frowned embarrassed. Sarah leaned closer to him and pushed her hand up against his forehead, pushing his head scarf up and back to reveal a thick but healed scar high upon his forehead. She sat back quickly and gasped. He shrugged his shoulders and smiled. Instantly she slapped him hard across his arms several times.

"You bastard...you never ever told me any of that...you said you fell down drunk and got that scar...why?" she demanded to know, full of emotions.

"Why do you think I know this man so well?" he replied and gestured his hand toward the old man. "Why do you think I hold most of Paul's work here and the sword of Saladin?"

"You were that Templar, brother?" the Templar asked.

 1 – 4

"Aye that I was...and I can tell you that all our friend has told us is all true. Very true and I was but a very small part of it," Stephan replied just as Sarah burst into tears and covered her face with her hands.

"You were in this tale only briefly, agreed...but it was a major part no less," the old man said and smiled at Stephan as he leaned over to hug Sarah as she sobbed.

"Aye perhaps...but it was Taqi who sacrificed himself. 'Twas his actions that inspired me to do as I did...but I knew I stood a chance of surviving being shot. Taqi knew he could not; he died saving them and for that I shall honour him always," Stephan explained. "Always."

"Then who...who exactly are you?" Gabirol asked, looking at the old man directly.

"Three days I have sat with you and you have still not worked it out?" the old man asked and smiled.

"It would help if you removed your hood and did not hide so much in the shadows," the Hospitaller remarked and grinned. "You clearly have wealth and connections that is for sure."

"Perhaps...but this tale is still not complete for you have both as yet to open your commissions...and Peter, a commission awaits you in Alba too if it is to your liking for a stonemason who knows Catalan is most certainly required there. You may even take whomever you wish to go with you," the old man said and sat up.

"Well you cannot be Paul's father because he visited that crypt of Niccolas's here in La Rochelle in his church. You said you had never been down there, but if you had I would have stated you were him," Gabirol commented and looked at his quill. "Plus the yellow, black and crimson wrist band you wear."

"Ah...well there you go for I knew you would think that so I told a bit of a white lie there," the old man said and smiled broadly at Gabirol as he lowered his quill. "For you are indeed correct," he explained and paused as he sat forwards into the full beams of sunlight now shining through the windows, then slowly pulled his dark blue hood back to fully reveal himself. "I am indeed Philip...Paul's father."

All sat in stunned silence for several long minutes, the only sound being Sarah sniffing as she sobbed still in Stephan's arms. Finally she looked up at Philip and sighed heavily before smiling yet still tearful.

"So for these past three, nearly three and a half years now, I have not only lived with a true Grail Knight and guardian of the Grail...but also one who saved a very real Grail family?" she asked emotionally as the Templar looked at his envelope, his hands shaking.

"If you believe all I have told you, then yes you have," Philip answered.

"I believe it all," Simon interrupted and sat forwards. "But please pray tell us, what happened to Alisha and Ailia for both you and Stephan sit here this day?"

"Went into hiding I suspect," the Hospitaller said quietly.

"No...that they would not do. And for that reason, I, and friends of mine, vowed to continue and complete the work and ideals Paul started," Philip explained.

"But was he not actually continuing what you started?" Gabirol asked, perplexed.

"Originally yes," Philip replied. "But Paul...he learnt, knew and understood so much more than we did. As for what happened to them? Well, at some point this morning I am expecting my other son, Stewart, to arrive with them. In three days' time we shall be travelling to England...along with some of you."

"What...but I have no commission from you. Am I supposed to go to England too?" Gabirol asked, half alarmed.

"No, my friend, for your path lays in Florence as I advised before. You shall have a good life if you choose that path. My property and all its contents await your arrival. 'Tis a gift, a gift I trust you will accept for you will start a new way of learning," Philip explained and smiled."

"A true Grail queen coming here," Sarah remarked emotionally.

"Some will call her that though she will not hear it of herself," Philip said.

"What of Princess Stephanie? What became of her?" Simon asked.

"Stephanie indeed. No truer queen ever walked the Holy Lands than her. I pray history will one day remember that. A gentle, kind and godly woman living in a *godless and cruel world,"* Philip said and sighed lightly. *"She remained with Alisha and I as we buried all of the dead, except Taqi, whom we took on to Castle Blanc and lay him to rest beside Raja and Arri, just a short distance from the grave of Nicholas. 'Twas indeed a strange day, Alisha still very much in a state of denial almost over Paul, the image of him falling away forever etched deeply in her mind. With every image flashing through her mind daily of that event, it felt as though a part of her was being pulled over the edge with him...every time a little more of her dying with him. Princess Stephanie was the only one who could offer comfort and support for she alone knew and sensed the pain Alisha felt. But Sister Lucy as always galvanised them both into action...to continue to live...to move forwards. Few words were spoken over Taqi as he was laid to rest for they were simply not needed. Afterwards, we sailed from the Port of Tortosa and home here to La Rochelle. Stephanie though..."* He paused again for a lengthy few minutes before continuing. *"As she said that day on the bridge, she died inside too. 'Tis a real matter that some people die from a broken heart as Alisha will tell you for she certainly felt it...as did Stephanie."*

"She really did love Paul didn't she, that Stephanie," the farrier commented.

"That she did. As of course did Alisha. But Stephanie, she accompanied Count Henry after they parted company with us after we landed in Marseille. 'Twas a very sad and tearful farewell but she wished to be present, as well as act as a witness for when Count Henry carried out the cutting of the elm ceremony at Gizors in 1188, and where and when Gerard himself was also listed for treason, rightly or wrongly, for having followed Reynald so blindly, though in truth not so blindly as you all now know. Again I hope history will remember well of him."

7 – 10

"How did Gerard commit treason?" the Templar asked.

"Because he went against the Prieure de Sion's plans for a fusion of Templar, Sufi, Islamic and Judaic reconciliation and working together. If he had not stopped that, our world would be a very different place now. Plus he deliberately disobeyed Count Henry's explicit order not to march to Hattin," Philip explained. *"In the future some will claim the cutting of the elm ceremony never happened...others that it was for other reasons and that the Prieure de Sion does not even exist, for we strive to hide its presence. A path we may ultimately achieve perhaps a little too successfully...maybe? But the truth is, the 'Cutting of the Elm' was performed at Gizors Castle in 1188, presided over by Duke Jean de Gisors,"* the old man explained then

looked directly at the Templar and Hospitaller. "This was the moment when the Prieure de Sion and the Templars separated into two distinct organisations. Jean de Gisors...you two will shortly meet him, for he is the new Grandmaster of a newly separated Prieure de Sion...and you are of the same bloodline and related."

The Templar and Hospitaller looked at the old man, both puzzled, then looked at each other. Confused they looked back at the old man in silence.

"What of Turansha's last words, it was Conrad de Montferrat who commanded him?" Peter asked.

"That, my friends, was passed over to Al Rashid by Taqi's colleague, who vowed to resolve the matter. For that we must await the outcome, but as Stephanie said to Turansha, she forgave him that day...as have Alisha and Ailia for they refused to let that man's evil hatred touch their souls." Philip paused. "For you see, love truly is the key...and I believe Turansha realised that at the very end for Stephanie said she sensed it so strongly through the sword."

"You mentioned Sister Lucy had some kind of note from Paul for Alisha should he not survive. What happened to that?" Gabirol asked.

"'Tis also kept within his folder if you look. Alisha entrusted all of his work to Stephan and I, all of which has since been copied," Philip explained as Gabirol immediately looked through all of the remaining items in the main folder.

Gabirol found the letter from Princess Stephanie written for Paul many years previously which he had never opened. He lifted it but Philip shook his head no it wasn't the one.

"That letter we shall leave sealed for it will serve no benefit now to anyone," Philip said softly. "No matter the curiosity it may arouse."

Gently Gabirol picked up an opened letter and studied its words. Philip nodded he had the correct letter.

"And Alisha does not mind that we all have access to all of her things from Paul?" Gabirol asked.

"Not at all for she feels like she knows all of you already. We had descriptions of you written by Paul, though not your exact names...for those he left sealed in the envelope. Like I said, we have planned it so we would have time enough to inform you of all that had happened in the hope you will agree to help us. But as I promised, none of you here are under any obligation at all, other than to promise to keep secret all that you have learnt...for now," Philip explained.

"Can you read what it says?" Sarah asked, holding Stephan's hands tightly.

The Templar leaned over and patted Stephan's shoulder and winked at him.

Gabirol began to read out the note.

"To my dearest and eternal love Alisha. If it is fate that you should read this, then 'tis only because I am gone from this realm to another. A realm from where I shall watch down upon you and our daughters until you cross that bridge which divides us. But we are two parts of the same and connected, so for now my love, go in the spring time and walk in our woods. Let the magic whispers of the trees carry my love into your heart. Remember me and lay the foundations of our feminine church! Make men be aware that women are the key...they always have been. Nothing is wanting save the key...the key is you...your blood...your love. Man will one day have to make a choice...when the love of power is no more, then the power of love will conquer. Trust the whispers within your soul that call out to you from me. Hold these words close until the day comes when once again I shall feel your hands' gentle touch upon my face. You my woman, my queen of such godly grace, never to be parted even in death's embrace."

Ayleth shook her head emotionally and turned her face away as more tears ran down her face.

"And you say she lives and will be here this very day?" she asked with her back to everyone.

The main front door was rapped loudly, drawing everyone's attention. Stephan broke away from Sarah and walked over to the door and unbolted it. As he swung the door open, the sun shining through brightly, a little girl of no more than three years of age jumped over the step and into the inn. Her black hair was tied up and held in place by side plaits. Her dark green and light blue sectioned dress appeared very smart as she looked in at everyone in embarrassed surprise and immediately started to bite her bottom lip. She looked at the many faces staring at her.

"Where is my grandpapa?" she whispered quietly to Stephan as he stepped aside so she could see past him better. Philip stood up slowly from his chair and walked around the table passing the Hospitaller, the Templar and Miriam. "Grandpapa!" she called out excitedly upon seeing him and rushed across the room immediately jumping up into his arms. She closed her eyes tight as she hugged him. Ayleth turned to look at them.

"I see no part I can play in this tale," she remarked just as a tall cloaked figure stood silhouetted in the doorway.

"Father, we are early...not too early I pray?" Stewart asked as he stepped forwards into the room. He paused as he looked at all the bemused faces staring back at him. "We have brought all you asked us to bring," he said as he walked across the room.

Ayleth looked up at Stewart wide eyed, her mouth open as she saw him. Wearing *a full Templar's mantle he looked tall and handsome and she felt herself begin to blush. Philip saw her reaction and smiled as he held the little girl in his arms.*

"Is...is that Ailia?" Ayleth asked awkwardly.

The Templar looked at Stewart and as soon as he saw his Templar surcoat and emblem of office, he quickly stood up, Stewart immediately placing his hand upon his shoulder.

"No please, there is no need to stand for as of this day my commission is at an end," Stewart said and smiled.

"Never the less, I would wish to shake your hand," the Templar replied and proffered his right hand. "This day I have met two brothers I knew not I had."

 2 – 6

"So my father has explained you are indeed connected by blood too," Stewart said as Philip nodded yes. The Templar grasped Stewart's hand in a simple normal hand shake, Stewart then looking to his left directly at Ayleth, their eyes locking instantly. She let out an involuntary sigh as his eyes met hers. "And my niece is named Mellissa," he finally answered Ayleth's question and smiled.

"Well, you know I, I, I..." Ayleth replied going redder in the face as Stewart looked at her.

"You asked what your part in this tale was. I think you just found it," Simon joked loudly, Sarah immediately slapping him hard.

"Where is your mother?" Philip asked Mellissa as she looked at everyone around the table.

"She is with Aunty Abi and Lucy outside chasing Ailia," Mellissa replied quietly.

"Has she run off to the light point again?" Philip asked and she nodded yes silently. "Ailia always rushes to the circle and the light we set each night. She hopes she will see Arri there as we set it in memory of him and Taqi."

"And my papa," Mellissa interjected quickly.

Sarah wiped her eyes quickly as tears welled in them again and she stood up.

"Well my blessed princess, I suspect you must be hungry," she said, Mellissa nodding her head yes. "Come with me and we shall see what we have," Sarah said and outstretched her hand. Philip put Mellissa down and she took Sarah's hand, Stephan looking at them smiling broadly as Sarah had to wipe another tear from her eye.

Stewart stepped closer to Ayleth, still looking at her. She smiled up at him.

"And you are?" he asked and part bowed his head.

"A woman," she blurted out, embarrassed, laughed and quickly put her hand across her eyes as she looked down shaking her head not quite believing what she had just said. Simon and Peter laughed as Gabirol chuckled, the Genoese sailor asking him to repeat what she had said.

"And I am Stewart...a man," Stewart replied as he knelt down in front of her and gently pulled her hand away from her face.

Sarah put her hand across her chest and smiled with a deep sigh as she watched them, Mellissa still holding her other hand. Ayleth finally looked up at Stewart.

"Ayleth...and I know who you are," she said and laughed lightly, still embarrassed. Stewart looked across at his father as he nodded and smiled.

"Grandpapa!" Ailia called out as she ran into the room closely followed by the tall presence of Abi playfully chasing her. Philip knelt down as she ran toward him. She had grown much in the past three years and he could no longer hold her up in his arms like Mellissa. She flung her arms around him as he hugged her back. "Grandpapa...is he coming today?" she asked excitedly and looked directly into his eyes then put her hands on either side of his face to stare at him. She raised her eyebrows as if to emphasise her question. "Is he?"

"Is who?" the Hospitaller asked, curious.

Philip stood up slowly and placed his hand upon her shoulder and looked down at her before turning to the Hospitaller.

"Her father, Paul. She always asks and she always tells us he will be back," Philip explained, his voice tinged with sadness, but he smiled as he looked back at Ailia just as her eyes fell upon all the open parchments, velum sheets and the two swords upon the table.

"Papa's sword," Ailia said and stepped closer to the table. Everyone looked at her as she stood beside the Templar, looked at him briefly, then at Paul's sword.

"I can sense the heavenly presence within you," he said quietly taken back by the strong feelings he felt coming from Ailia.

Miriam held his hand as he pushed his chair back so Ailia could reach onto the table just as Abi moved to stand behind her still as ever protective, Simon and Peter staring up at her sheer physical presence. Ailia gently placed her finger upon the sword blade and ran it along the fuller, a slight rhythmic hum coming off of it immediately, the blade beginning to shimmer a pearlescent blue and crimson. She stood perfectly still just holding her finger upon the blade as everyone watched her, fascinated. The wealthy tailor sniffed, deeply moved, and wiped his eye quickly. A tiny prick of bright white light seemed to appear between the tip of her finger and the blade where they met.

"Ailia!" Alisha called out sternly from the doorway, everyone turning to look at her, the Hospitaller's mouth dropping open. "Ailia come away from the sword please," she said as she gracefully walked across the room, her long pale green and cream dress flowing gently, her white shirt laced across her chest.

Ailia raised her finger and looked back at Alisha as she came nearer. Simon blinked several times as he looked at Alisha when she stopped nearest to him. He gulped hard taken back by her beauty, Stewart laughing lightly at the look upon his face. Gabirol lowered his quill and slowly stood up, Alisha looking across the table at him. He nodded a very slight bow of his head and she smiled beautifully at him.

"Mama...it tells me Papa will come," Ailia said softly and looked at her.

"You say that every time you touch the sword," Alisha replied and held out her hand for her to come to her.

"Is...is all that Philip has told us...all of this, is it all true?" Gabirol asked as he motioned his hands over the journals, folders and parchments spread out before him. "Is it truly? I ask."

 2 – 24

Alisha looked at Philip and tilted her head slightly and raised her eyebrows, but then smiled as Gabirol noticed the slight scar upon her forehead as Philip had explained she received upon the bridge.

"I cannot say for I have not heard what he has told you," Alisha began to say as she looked at the faces looking up at her in anticipation. "But I have never known him to exaggerate or lie ever."

"I have, and plenty of times," Sister Lucy bellowed out as she entered the inn and walked across the room. "So don't believe a word of it...none of it, I tell you," she laughed and leaned up to kiss Philip on the sides of his cheeks. She then stood with her hands upon her hips and looked at them all. "Bet you he told you I was a nun eh?" she smiled broadly. "Now ask yourselves, do I look like a nun?"

"Yes," the Templar replied. Sister Lucy playfully swiped her hand across his head. "Yes, definitely a nun," he remarked and laughed, pretending to duck away quickly.

"Then if this tale you have told us is true...what are we to do with what you have imparted to us?" the farrier asked as he stared at Alisha, captivated. He looked down embarrassed when she looked at him. Alisha looked to Philip to answer.

"Peter, you shall go to Alba with me to make some carvings after we have visited Tara in the Emerald Isle. It may take some time," Philip answered. "Gabirol, you *know where your destiny now lies in Florence. Simon...you shall remain here if you wish for there is much work that requires researching and documenting...and you have the mind for it. We shall also need a full time farrier here, for Stewart shall be retiring to this port to continue my trade in materials imports...but he shall also require a professional tailor to educate him to all the latest styles and fashions," Philip further explained and winked at the wealthy tailor. "Ayleth...you came here to find a new life and to learn. I believe you shall find far more than that if you choose to stay," he said and then looked across to Stewart as he stood up straight and smiled at Ayleth. "My good Genoese sailor. You wanted travel...come with me and you shall travel to lands beyond your dreams...for I have need of someone to plant some oak acorns upon an island...if you think you are up to the challenge?"*

The Genoese sailor let out a gasp of surprise. Philip walked across to Alisha as she raised her three pronged dagger, sheathed, with two acorns still inside and smiled at him.

"Oh I am most certainly up for the challenge...'tis a great honour I am not sure I am worthy to take. Are you sure you have not confused me with someone else?" the Genoese sailor asked.

"Believe me when I say we have not got the wrong man," Philip replied then looked at the Templar and Hospitaller sat staring up at Alisha as Ailia took her hand. "You two may now open your commissions...and when you do, you shall have three further days to ponder them."

"Mama...I am telling you, Papa lives. You know it too so why do you hide it?" Ailia asked quietly as she put her arms around her.

"My dear Ailia," Alisha said softly and knelt down to look at her in the eyes. "You grow so tall and so fast you will catch Abi up I am sure," she smiled and looked up at Abi briefly. "I know your father still lives...for he lives within us...in our hearts and in our souls and will do so forever," she explained and gulped hard, the emotion of losing Paul still as fresh in her heart as the day she lost him. "'Tis perhaps because his spirit is close to us and he watches over us as he promised."

"No, Mama...I have heard you talk at night. I have heard you speak to Aunt Lucy that you can sense him still...as you did when you thought him dead once before," Ailia replied and looked at Sister Lucy as she frowned as if in disapproval. "Mama...he will come back to us for he lives...the sword just told me so...very clearly."

Alisha looked at Sister Lucy then up at Abi, puzzled. Sister Lucy shrugged her shoulders and looked to Abi for an answer. Abi stepped forward and knelt beside Ailia but still towered over her, the Templar looking at her in awe.

"Ailia...did you say the sword spoke to you?" she asked. Ailia looked at Alisha, alarmed, fearing she may have done something wrong. "Do not worry, you have done no wrong but tell us what it said please."

   2 – 4

Everyone in the room listened intently as Ailia looked at them all in turn. Then she looked at Paul's sword laid across the table.

"It lets me see images with feelings in my mind...and it showed me Papa...alive and riding here...like I just said...very clearly," she said, beginning to get emotional. "Should it not do that...have I done wrong?"

"Oh Ailia of course you have not done wrong," Alisha said and pulled her close and hugged her. Philip looked at Alisha, puzzled, then to Abi and shrugged his shoulders. "Perhaps it just shows you your hopes and desires."

"The sword was once known to be able to do that...but that was a very long time ago," Abi remarked as she stood up. "It has not been done for thousands of years."

Simon sat staring at Alisha, everything about her looking perfect to him as she gently pulled back her hair that was partially plaited and tied in a knot and running down the middle of her back.

"You are a true vision of beauty seldom seen in this world," he said out loud without realising it, everyone looking at him. Alisha smiled and let out a light laugh and faced him. "Oh Lord...I said that out loud didn't I?"

Alisha nodded yes and laughed again as she stood up. She smiled at him as he just stared up at her.

"Thank you, Simon, isn't it?" she asked and he nodded opened mouthed and in silence. Alisha laughed lightly again. "There is not a day that passes when I do not miss Paul...and yes I sense him every day and every night when I lie down to sleep... but it has been three plus years now since we lost him at the bridge," she paused as she pulled Ailia closer. "Three very long years without him...but we always return here every spring, at Easter, to remember him, Arri and Taqi."

"And all of Thomas's men," Ailia quickly interrupted.

"And all of Thomas's men yes. 'Tis why Stephan keeps the lanthorn burning every eve."

"What happened to Thomas and Master Douglas for you did not say?" Gabirol asked and sat himself down. "And Princess Stephanie...please?"

Alisha looked over to Philip.

"I hope this does not upset you?" Philip asked Ailia. She shook her head no as

Alisha placed her hands upon her shoulders and nodded it was okay to continue. *"Master Douglas and Thomas spent days searching for Paul and Ishmael all the way to the sea, but they found no trace of them, nor Percival...in fact no bodies from all those that perished in the ravine that day for the waters were so violent. Most would have been washed away faster than Master Douglas would have been able to keep up with, and eventually taken out to sea...but they wished to try along with half of Al Rashid's men. They had to stop eventually when Thomas nearly lost his leg from his injuries and Master Douglas's injury started to get infected,"* Philip explained.

"And the reign of Turansha and his men was at last over?" Gabirol asked as Philip nodded yes silently.

"Thank the good Lord for that mercy," the Templar remarked with relief.

"And Stephanie?" Peter asked.

"Both Master Douglas and Thomas came back to France and linked up with Count Henry. After he had carried out the cutting of the elm ceremony, they escorted her back to Tortosa, for she felt she had nowhere else she could go...she was sorely broken in heart and spirit. Master Douglas and Brother Teric escort her still, whereas Thomas came back and as we sit this hour, he sits and writes his journal alongside others...of the tales of his men...of real knights...Paul's army of kings so their adventures and their memory shall live on in the stories and hearts of men for many years to come," Philip explained solemnly.

"We begged Stephanie to stay with us, but she would not," Alisha said softly and placed her hands upon Ailia's, shoulders tighter. *"After the birth of Mellissa, she left us."*

"'Tis why we named Paul's new daughter Mellissa Stephanie Tamara Amaya," Sister Lucy stated. *"Now come on...I want to see some happy smiling faces and none of this morbid miserable stuff."*

"You are exactly as you were described," the Hospitaller said and smiled.

"And from all that has happened to you and your family, what is the one main lesson it has taught you that you can tell us...if you can?" Gabirol asked, suddenly feeling awkward at his question and started to blush.

Philip looked at Alisha and Abi before returning his gaze to Gabirol.

"I can tell you quite simply...love. 'Tis love which is the greatest power that shall ever be known unto man and woman. Love...because as Alisha will testify, love conquers death!" Philip answered.

Alisha took a deep breath and nodded yes in agreement. Then she looked at the Templar holding his sealed envelope.

"*I think it time you opened them,*" *she said, smiling softly, Simon still staring up at her.*

The Templar turned in his chair to face his brother as both held up their envelopes. Together they broke the seals fully and unfolded them, the Hospitaller shaking with apprehension. The Templar read through his commission as the Hospitaller started to read through his. The Templar let out a gasp and visibly slumped in his chair before looking up at his brother, a single tear running down his cheek. When he looked up at Philip he shook his head.

"*Are these real?*" *he asked emotionally, his hand shaking even more. Miriam looked at the Templar, concerned as he looked so emotional.* "*Pray answer me yes.*"

"*They are as real as either you or I,*" *Alisha answered for Philip, who simply nodded yes, surprised at the emotion in their faces.*

"*Why...what are they?*" *the wealthy tailor asked and leaned up to try to see.*

"*They are deeds to lands in Alba...and titles to their family estates in their birth names of Sinclier. Copies of their true family heritages are also drawn and certified by the King of Alba himself,*" *Alisha continued to explain.*

 2 – 17

"*And you also have the designs and patterns that we hope one day shall be built within the chapel that shall sit upon your family lands...,*" *Philip said and looked at them, waiting for their reply.*

"*And you give us three days to decide upon this?*" *the Templar said, raising his opened documents.*

"*Is that not long enough?*" *Philip asked immediately.*

"'*Tis far too long for I can tell you this very instant, I accept this commission with all of my heart,*" *he replied then looked at Miriam.* "*On condition you marry us in the same fashion you married Alisha and Paul first,*" *he smiled, Miriam instantly throwing her arms around his neck.*

Philip looked at the Hospitaller as he simply nodded yes in silence, trying not to cry.

Alisha smiled at Philip. He looked so much like Paul in profile she thought to herself as she pulled Ailia close to her.

"*It looks as though Paul's work shall live on after all...thanks to you,*" *she said softly and reached out her hand for him to take. Emotionally he looked at her as tears welled in his eyes the realisation hitting him as Alisha's words touched him. All he could do was shrug his shoulders. Sister Lucy stood beside him and put her arm around him.*

"You did well...very well," she said reassuringly and looked across at Stewart pulling up a chair opposite Ayleth.

"There is hope...always hope," Philip said quietly and took Alisha's hand.

"Just promise us that Lord Montferrat will be dealt with, for if not we may need to sort that matter first," the Hospitaller said, looking at Philip. "For he would become a threat should he come to know of us...and that we cannot accept."

"That, my friend, I can assure you is being dealt with...that I do swear unto you this hour. He will have justice served upon him," Philip replied and part bowed his head to emphasise the fact.

"And pray tell, are you once again named John...and the Navigator?" the Templar asked as he continued to hold Miriam in his arms.

"For now...but only until another can take my place," Philip replied with a smile.

"Then we are indeed in good hands," the Templar smiled back.

Sarah entered the room carrying a large tray of bread and cheese as Mellissa tried to carry a small tray with a jug of rose water on biting her bottom lip in concentration just as Alisha often did.

Within minutes everyone had sat themselves down around the table to eat and drink, the room full of light after Stephan opened all of the shutters. Abi lifted Paul's sword off of the table and stood alone near the main door and watched over them all as they talked and ate, asking Alisha question after question. She leant against the wall and raised Paul's sword and looked closely at it. Had it spoken to Ailia? she wondered, Kratos having told her that once it could do such a thing, but only to those born of the purest love. She looked at Ailia and in her heart knew she would spend the rest of her days protecting her. Her own heart still ached for Tenno, but at least their son was safe, healthy and growing up. She would see him again soon enough too she also knew. She watched them all for ages as they continued to eat, drink and talk, Simon just gazing at Alisha mesmerised by her every move. Ailia sat beside Philip as he spoke answering many questions posed by Gabirol. Laughter echoed around the room as the Templar, the Hospitaller and Stephan recounted their adventures, Sarah holding his hand tighter than she had ever held it before. Abi laughed as she saw Mellissa pouring rose water into a bread bowl and stirring the remnants of bread into a mush. Stewart moved to a smaller table with Ayleth and Abi saw immediately the obvious and natural attraction between them already and she knew it would not be long before another wedding would be taking place out upon the circle. She folded her arms and sighed, then looked over her shoulder out of the main doorway toward the harbour beyond. She stood for some time breathing in the fresh sea air blowing in on a warm spring breeze. The horses would need seeing to she thought and so took another look back at them all talking away. This was not the end of things and she knew many more adventures lay ahead for all of them, but wherever those adventures led, she would be by their side. Silently she stepped out of the room, making her way to the stable area at the rear and started to prepare the horses for their stay.

છ૭ ૦૨

It was late afternoon, the sun beginning to set on the far horizon, the sky streaked with hues of golden yellows and crimson clouds. Alisha cradled a sleeping Mellissa in her arms, as Philip rested his shoulder against Alisha's, both looking out of the large windows at the sunset forming, the door framing a perfect scene before them out across the sea beyond. Stewart and Ayleth were still talking away now oblivious to everyone else and Philip nudged Alisha to look at them. Gabirol had gathered all of Paul's journals and parchments and placed them all back together in a neat and tidy bundle. Ailia sat drawing out small delicate symbols, making Gabirol laugh as she easily executed various intricate designs. Sarah came in carrying more food as Stephan followed with more drink. Simon, the wealthy tailor, Peter, the farrier, and the Genoese sailor were sat listening attentively to the Templar's and Hospitaller's tales of their time in the Holy Land with the added input of Stephan now he had revealed his true past as a Templar himself.

Alisha felt tired after the early morning start from their home north of La Rochelle where they had bought a house next to the woodlands Paul had loved so much, Alisha following Paul's instructions he had left within his last note to her. She often wondered if he knew what his fate was that day. Many times she had sensed him still being alive like Ailia had said, but this time she had seen him injured beyond what any man could survive and she had watched helplessly as he fell away, but his smile always remained in her mind as he went knowing they were now at last safe. She pulled Mellissa close and kissed the side of her face and sighed saddened to think that Paul had never met her. She quickly blinked as emotions welled up in her, Sister Lucy leaning over and checking she was okay and motioned she pass Mellissa over to her and so she gently eased her across her lap, Philip almost asleep as he watched the sun sink. Alisha went to stand, when Abi stepped into the doorway blocking out the sunset. She remained perfectly still not moving. Alisha stood up fully and nudged Philip, sensing something was wrong. Slowly Abi stepped down and approached Alisha, looking ashen white, her hand shaking as she clutched something in it. Everyone in the room stopped what they were doing and

501

looked at Abi as tears welled in her eyes. Philip sat up alarmed as Abi outstretched her hand and went to speak but she could not. Sister Lucy held Mellissa closer, concerned.

5 – 22

"Ali...I have a message to give you...," Abi finally managed to blurt out emotionally. "'Tis Percival."

"Percival!" Alisha said quietly but surprised, Stewart standing up immediately.

"He...he wishes to be allowed to come in, if you accept these first," Abi said and opened her hand to reveal the heads of three crossbow bolts. "Percival survived his fall into the river...and he later found Paul...and..." Abi started to sob unable to keep her usual calm composure.

Instantly Ailia ran around the table and up to Abi and stared at the bolts knowing immediately they were obviously the ones that had killed her father. She stared at them in silence before looking up at Alisha, who was beginning to shake with emotion but taking slow deliberate breaths to control herself.

"Percival is here?" Philip asked and stood up.

"Aye he is outside," Abi replied and wiped her face quickly with her other hand. "He apologises for taking so long but his own journey has been incredibly slow... and it took a long time for them to even reach Cyprus to fully recover in order to journey here," she explained as Alisha placed her hand across her chest hardly able to breathe, Abi's word 'them' echoing through her mind like a loud clang.

Stewart rushed across to the doorway but stopped as he saw Percival stood outside waiting hesitantly. Stewart could hardly believe it was him as their eyes met. Quickly he gestured for him to come in. Nervously Percival bowed his head slightly as he acknowledged Stewart and slowly entered the inn. With his hands clasped together across his stomach but still wearing his familiar green uniform and mantle, he stepped toward Alisha. A tear fell from her eye and she quickly tried to wipe it away as he drew near. She thought she must be dreaming and quickly looked around the room at the others before looking back at Percival.

"'Tis really you isn't it?" she asked quietly and bit her bottom lip. Percival simply nodded yes in silence. "Come here," she said and pulled him close and held him gently as she fought not to cry.

Percival gulped hard and blinked his eyes trying not to cry too as he looked down at the others looking up at them both.

"But there is someone else who wishes to see you," Percival said and stepped back *a pace and looked into her eyes, then moved aside as a large figure stepped through the doorway.*

"Ishmael!" Stewart said, shocked.

Ishmael wasted no time, winked at Stewart and then walked immediately across the room to Alisha, Percival stepping aside just as he stopped directly in front of her and clasped her shaking hands in his large hands. She looked into his eyes that were full of life and happiness, which puzzled her. Abi sniffed as she offered the three bolt heads to Alisha, Ailia looking up at Ishmael then toward the door.

"Alisha, hello," he said with a broad smile and bowed his head slightly, the handles on his two swords strapped across his back becoming visible. "Kratos once told me I would one day have to take a leap of faith, or at least have enough trust to take a leap...and so as you saw I did," he explained and smiled again as Alisha stepped back a pace shaking her head in shock. "Paul said, so he told me, that even three bolts through his heart would never kill his love for you," Ishmael then said calmly and smiled even broader. "We found Paul, and we took these from him to give to you."

Alisha recoiled away from Ishmael, momentarily confused at the macabre gesture.

"Papa...my papa is here isn't he?" Ailia said quietly almost afraid to ask then quickly ran to the doorway and looked out frantically but could not see anyone else. She turned and looked back at Ishmael, confused and hurt, disappointment etched across her little face.

"How did you know about that...and when did he tell you?" Alisha asked as Philip tried to stand up properly.

"After I had taken them out of him and when he eventually woke up," Ishmael replied and smiled then shook her hands. Alisha's legs went weak and she took in a sharp intake of breath and frowned at him hard, unsure if she heard him correctly. "He lives. He told me he once made you a promise after you made him swear that as Tenno had lived, that even after years of him being absent, if Paul was ever in a similar situation and alive...he must always come back to you no matter how long it took. Do you remember?"

Alisha snatched her hands away from him and covered her mouth in shock and looked at Abi as she tearfully nodded yes confirming his words. Philip fell back into his chair as Sister Lucy looked on, her eyes wide in disbelief. All in the room listened intently. Stewart strained to see where Paul could be as he looked out, Ailia beside him.

"I told you he was coming home," she said then turned to walk outside. "So where

is my papa?" she demanded, which made Alisha let out an emotional laugh as she began to shake uncontrollably.

"He awaits you in the stable out back...if you want to see him...for though he keeps his promise, to return, he will not hold you to it...but prays you will allow him to see his daughters," Ishmael explained, his tone suddenly more sombre now.

"He knows...knows I would," Alisha said emotionally, shaking her head in disbelief.

Instantly Ailia marched herself out of the main door. Alisha took the bolt heads from Abi's hand, Abi having to gently place them in her hand it was shaking so much. Stewart looked at Ishmael and shook his head in utter surprise.

"What in the heavens took you all so long?" Stewart asked.

"My friend...you have no idea how badly injured we were. 'Twas Percival who pulled us both out a considerable distance downstream. It took nearly two years just to get Paul walking again using a healing staff...the one Abi gave him the day of the bridge assault."

"'Tis impossible! What healing staff? I did not see such a thing. But...but why then did you not get word to us sooner?" Stewart asked, confused, Alisha shaking her head as if to ask the same question, still in total shock.

   3 – 4

Percival stepped closer to Alisha.

"We did not know if he would survive for a start...but the staff I found upon Paul when I came around took its time to work...but also when Paul awoke, he begged us not to until he knew he could make this journey himself...and it would be better the world think him dead for if not, your lives shall never be yours to live freely and in safety. Do you understand this?" he explained and asked, Alisha shaking her head yes but only very slightly.

"I knew that staff was given to him for a reason...I just knew it," Simon remarked, smiling.

Alisha slowly started to walk toward the main door clasping the three bolts against her chest still not believing what she was hearing. Outside Ailia was already stomping her way toward the main stable area around the back of the inn. When she reached the white washed wall with the gate leading into the stable courtyard, it was latched open. She put her arms down by her side and took a deep breath as she prepared to step through. She gulped as her heart began to beat faster at the sudden realisation she was possibly about to see her father again. Her mouth went dry and she could not even gulp again. She blinked as tears welled in her eyes but she shook her head determined not to cry. Alisha stepped down from the main step into the early evening air unable to breathe properly then slowly walked to the end of the inn and looked at Ailia as she hesitated. Very slowly Alisha walked closer toward her as Stewart followed, the others all jumping up out of their seats and rushing to the side window and door to look out, Sister Lucy the only one left seated with Mellissa asleep beside her, Philip just standing not daring to move...not daring to believe it was true. Percival and Ishmael gestured for him to follow them to the doorway.

Ailia drew a deep breath and took just two steps forward into the stable court-yard and froze sensing a man standing to her left beside a large horse patting it gently. Her bottom lip started to quiver as emotions began to overwhelm her, fearful to turn and look at the man in case, after all this, it was not her father. Paul stepped back from the horse as he saw Ailia standing side on to him perfectly still. He pulled the fur hood around his shoulders as he shivered, the cold now affecting him as he still recovered, but he was alive. He went to speak but the tightening emotional lump in his throat stopped him. He coughed lightly to clear his throat and he tried to keep himself calm as he looked at his daughter almost twice the height since he had last seen her.

"Ailia," he finally managed to say softly.

Ailia clenched her fists and sniffed as more tears welled in her eyes. Slowly she turned her head to face him, her eyes looking down toward his feet first. As the tears finally fell, she looked up slowly and into his neatly bearded but clean face, her eyes instantly locking on his, the recognition instant. She started to sob, her arms still held rigid down her sides. She half turned to face him fully then looked over her shoulder back at Alisha. As their eyes met, Ailia nodded yes slightly as tears ran down her cheeks. Alisha fell forward onto her knees, her eyes wide in shock and she struggled to catch her breath. Philip gently pushed himself past Gabirol and Simon in the doorway and quickly moved around to help Alisha as Stewart reached down to help her stand again but she pushed his arm away focusing upon Ailia as she slowly turned to look back at Paul.

 9 – 16

"Papa!" she cried out as the full weight of emotions overwhelmed her. She opened her arms and ran toward him. "Papa!" she cried again and disappeared from Alisha's sight behind the wall. Only then did she stand up fast helped by Stewart. Paul knelt down as Ailia threw herself into his arms and buried her head into his chest as he wrapped his arms around her and kissed the top of her head. *"Papa...'tis really you,"* she sobbed, squeezing him as hard as she could.

Paul closed his eyes and held her, taking in every sense of the moment, glad to be alive. He held her as she sobbed for several long minutes until he sensed someone approach. He opened his eyes and looked up to see Alisha standing before them. She was shaking her head in utter disbelief and shock, biting her bottom lip. Her eyes darted from left to right as she looked into his checking it was really him. He stood up slowly, Ailia still holding onto him tightly. Alisha held out her hand and opened it to reveal the three bolts. Gently Paul outstretched his right hand, held it just short of hers and paused as his eyes searched hers. Very slowly he moved his fingers closer and then touched hers. The touch was real and both felt the sensation like a mild shock spark between them. She rapidly stepped closer as he clasped his hand around hers. She shook her head still unable to believe she was looking at him. She raised her other hand, shaking uncontrollably, and almost reluctantly placed it against his face, tears instantly streaming from her eyes. Ailia looked up, her eyes filled with tears of joy. Alisha gulped hard and just looked into Paul's eyes, still finding it impossible to believe he was actually alive and standing before her.

 2 – 6

"Ailia always...always said you would return...but your injuries, they were mortal and impossible to survive...I do not understand," she finally managed to speak, Paul just shrugging his shoulders and then smiled, too emotional to speak. Alisha quickly leaned forward and kissed him on the lips, the connection flooding through them with a surge of emotion that took both of them by surprise as well as their breaths. Alisha laughed emotionally and kissed him again, then threw her arms around his neck and held him tightly against her, Ailia between them. *"You have another daughter you need to meet,"* she said quietly and then rested her forehead against his, her eyes shut as she fought to control the overwhelming emotions enveloping her completely.

She wanted to kiss him again but could not move or open her eyes as he held her tightly. What words could she say and what of the many thousands of questions should she ask him first? She was totally overwhelmed and speechless. After a minute, Paul kissed the side of Alisha's head just as Philip stepped into view holding his chest in anticipation, Stewart following behind him. Paul looked over at his father and nodded with a welcoming smile. Philip clutched his chest with both *hands not quite believing what he was seeing. Slowly he began to walk toward them but then stopped just a few paces away as tears filled his eyes.*

"If I were to die this day, I would die a very content and happy man," Philip said, his voice shaking with emotion.

Stewart stepped beside him and smiled broadly at Paul.

"Always were one for making grand appearances," he joked and wiped a tear away quickly then laughed lightly. "Though only the Lord knows what miracle this is."

Paul raised his arm to Philip beckoning him to come closer. He did not move until all the others rapidly piled into the courtyard shaking him from his bewilderment.

"Father...I am home...home," Paul said.

Philip stood in silence for a few more moments as he just looked at him, Alisha and Ailia.

"Aye... that you are, my boy, that you are," he finally blurted out, stepped closer and put his arms around him and Alisha and hugged them. A tear ran down his face. "I fear my heart will stop this moment."

 1 – 16

Stewart patted Paul on the back and winked at him, Paul suddenly pulling him close so they all held each other. Ailia looked up at them from Paul's side and wiped her face quickly as tears of joy ran down her cheeks. Paul looked across the courtyard at the strange unfamiliar faces that stood staring at him until Sister Lucy stepped into view carrying Mellissa, who was rubbing her tired eyes. Ishmael and Percival came in and stood behind them as Sister Lucy walked over, clearly fighting to control her emotions upon seeing it was in fact Paul.

"Look Mell...'tis your father," Sister Lucy said as Mellissa looked up at him, tired, then simply rested her head against Sister Lucy's shoulder. "Worry not...you shall have plenty of time to get to know her," she said and smiled looking into Paul's eyes. "Plenty of time...and you certainly took your bloody time," she joked emotionally, the others all laughing at her comment.

෨ ෬

Standing upon the white stone circle where they had been married, Paul held Alisha in front of him, his arms wrapped around her waist as she leaned her back into him, her hair blowing in the early evening breeze. She wrapped her arms across his forearms.

He kissed the side of her face as they watched the sun set upon the horizon, Ailia stood by their side watching as Stephan lit the hanging lanthorn as he did every eve in memory of Arri, Taqi and all of Thomas's men. Paul had been introduced to everyone, Simon having been more than over enthusiastic in platitudes and comments how honoured he was to know and meet both Alisha and Paul. Gabirol swore to look after all of Paul's work entrusted to him, the Templar and Hospitaller both vowing to follow their commissions with great pride. There was much Paul had to catch up with, but for now, now he was home with his family. It had certainly been a journey. He sighed as he remembered Arri and all the others whom he loved and had lost...but he also knew his real work was only really just about to begin. But at least it would begin in safety surrounded by a loving and supportive family and friends he could depend upon with his life. He felt truly blessed.

Abi stood with Philip, watching them. Both were deep in thought when Sister Lucy came and stood with them.

"How in the Lord's name could he have survived his injuries...and the fall? 'Tis impossible and more than a miracle surely?" Philip asked as he folded his arms, looking at them with enormous love and pride.

"'Twas the power from the sword," Abi answered quietly. "'Tis the only explanation...and the healing staff. 'Twas fortunate Percival found it upon Paul and knew exactly how to use it...just in time. I also strongly suspect that before Paul threw the sword to Stephanie it must have done something to him. 'Tis the only answer for never in all my years have I known of such a thing as this...other than Kratos... so I strongly suspect the staff was and is indeed the same as the one used by Jesus himself. Kratos knew Paul would require it."

"I have already asked them, all three," Sister Lucy said quietly. "Percival tells me he fell from the caravan into what he can only recall as a ball of light," she began to explain, both Abi and Philip looking at her, puzzled. "He swears the next thing he recalled was waking up soaking wet downstream resting upon rocks with the small staff beside him. He did not have to look for it upon Paul. Someone, or something, placed it beside him. Percival swears he knows it is identical to the one Jesus supposedly likewise used, so you are correct Abi in what you state. He had no injuries but when he sat up, he saw Paul beside him...then Ishmael climbed out of the waters beside them. Paul was still alive but only just. Somehow, by means unseen, they were all put together. They managed to temporarily patch Paul up and carry him out of the ravine, some several miles downstream, but there was no sign of anyone else by the time they got back to the bridge two days later, just the fresh graves left by Al Rashid at the bridge on the other side."

"So where is the staff now?" Philip asked.

"Paul said they took a detour, another reason for their lengthy delay in returning," Sister Lucy began to explain, "via Mount Bugarach, or Mountain of God...a place you know well," she said, looking up at Philip directly as he nodded yes silently. "'Tis now safely hidden within it...for another time."

"But even then, why so long to get here?" Philip asked, still puzzled, rubbing his chin.

 1 – 30

"Percival said he believes he saw Kratos and another similar looking individual watch them from across the gorge, and several times since," Sister Lucy explained. "But I am of the opinion Kratos knew all along that day would come and made sure he was there to intervene. 'Tis the only explanation. Would also explain the healing staff. Though all mention of the staff the Church has tried to obliterate from history." She shook her head, sighing heavily before continuing. "Afterwards Percival led Ishmael and Paul on to Cyprus when Paul was well enough to travel... but they had to keep hidden for they knew by then that Lord Montferrat would seek him out and have him killed," she said then held onto Philip's arm and rested her head against him.

"Then I pray whatever our Lord has planned for their futures, it is worth it for many still do not learn the lessons of the past where the love of power, wealth and skill have become greater than morality...and power has taken over and all ethics are compromised until finally they utterly destroy themselves and very nearly this entire world along with them. The misuse of knowledge only ends in tragedy and I pray dearly that the message they take forward will not be forgotten. As Kratos told us, 'twas forgotten once before and why our ancient forefathers and those who watch over us placed certain restrictions upon the dissemination of knowledge. Those restrictions now form a system of instruction which many call mysteries, but is clearly visible and understandable to those who listen to that silent voice within," Philip explained just as the wealthy tailor approached them from behind. "'Tis why I agree it was wise the staff has been hidden, for now is not the time for its open use."

"Sorry to intrude...but all of what you have told me these past three days has...I believe...changed me profoundly already, so before I retire home this eve, would you kindly answer me just one question with a simple yes or no?" he asked politely, looking at Philip.

"Of course, please ask," he replied.

"I am prepared to dedicate the rest of my life to help bring about the Order of builders, of freemen, as you explained and as Paul wrote down...but I just need to hear it one more time," the wealthy tailor explained in a whisper. "Is everything you told us the absolute truth?"

Philip smiled as he looked at him. He then pointed toward Alisha and Paul silhouetted against the setting sun as they held each other, Ailia leaning against Paul, all stood looking at the lit lanthorn in front of them.

"Yes...absolutely....and there is your truth," Philip answered.

The wealthy tailor nodded and then simply began to back away slowly.

"Thank you...'tis all I needed to hear. I bid you all a good night and I am sure I shall be seeing you on the morrow," he said politely, turned around and began to walk toward the inn.

As he walked, the old lady with the gravelly voice who had visibly changed in Jerusalem stopped him gently with her old looking hand. She smiled at him then placed a small piece of parchment in his hand and looked deeply into his eyes.

"'Tis a simple fact that just because one believes in something, it does not mean that one has accomplished anything for our beliefs are nothing but a rigid, unchanging perspective on something you see or feel. This is a mindset you should not be proud of and one should seek to escape them because the more vehemently one believes, the less open one is to wisdom. Wisdom comes from questioning your ideas about everything. We grow, we learn and, hopefully, we also become wiser than we once were. 'Tis a simple lesson," she said softly, her voice not matching her appearance. She smiled, winked and then simply turned and walked away.

The wealthy tailor looked up toward the inn to see all the others talking and laughing, Stewart stood very close to Ayleth. In the fading light the wealthy tailor unfurled the parchment and read the small line of writing upon it. He scratched his cheek puzzled for a moment then looked up to see where the old woman had gone but she had vanished. He read again the single sentence.

 4 – 4

'Hebrews 13:2: Do not neglect to show hospitality to strangers, for thereby some have entertained angels unawares.'

As Paul held Alisha, the wind blew across the grasses and his gaze fell to the edge of the circle of stone his father had made and where they had been married. That time seemed like more than a life time ago, but as he looked at the circle around them he recalled what he had to do...and make encrypted notes of it all so that others would one day relearn and remember. He knew where he had to take his sword and hide it just in case mankind did not remember and should have cause to need it again. He would place the crimson rose and white lily upon the circle of stone. He smiled as he thought that one day in the distant future, people would learn of the reason and purpose why. A single rose and white lily would again be set in the future by those souls who would be touched by the truth...and remember. He kissed Alisha again, held her tightly and both smiled as they looked out across the sea.

෧ ෬

After all had retired to bed that evening, though more the early hours, Philip quietly removed the unopened letter from Princess Stephanie written for Paul many years previously. He opened it and read her words to decide whether Paul should ever read them or burn it. In it she professed her deep love she knew she had for him. That she knew they would become lovers for it was written in her parchments years before they had even met. But she wrote that she also knew he would not remain hers for long and that she would leave this world many years before him and requested that he have an inscription placed upon her eventual burial stone. It was a simple short poem. She also gave details of where two sound symbols would be hidden that would be key to unlocking all the later sound symbols to be set up in the new chapel in Alba. Philip sat down beside the fire, its embers glowing. The room was empty and quiet. He rested back into the chair, closed his eyes and smiled. A great sense of contentment and peace enveloped him...the first time in a very long time. For the first time ever in his life, he knew things were going to be alright.

෧ ෬

After the 'cutting of the elm' ceremony at Gizors in France, Princess Stephanie returned to Outremer with Count Henry. After some political manoeuvrings, Raymond, shortly before he died from an illness contracted at the end of 1187, and Balian orchestrated the divorce of her son Humphrey from his wife Princess Isabella. Humphrey having remained loyal to his stepfather Reynald and King Guy, which ultimately helped lead to the tumultuous upheavals in Outremer, Princess Stephanie was in full agreement with the divorce, though never publicly declaring her reasons why. Count Henry had always loved Isabella, and was shocked when he discovered she was to not only divorce Humphrey in a carefully calculated move, but was also to marry Lord Montferrat, who, through devious scheming, managed to finally realise his ambition and seized the Crown of Jerusalem, being crowned king in 1192. As soon as he was crowned king he immediately set about planning to eradicate all and any contenders or heirs to his throne, wherever they were in the world, Alisha and Paul being at the top of his list after discovering they and their children were still alive ... but true to his word, Al Rashid had two of his Ashashin infiltrate his ranks. On April 28th 1192, only days after his kingship was confirmed by election, Conrad was assassinated in Tyre. It is said that one of the two Ashashin responsible had entered Balian's household in Tyre some months previously, pretending to be a servant, in order to stalk his victim; the other, Taqi's colleague no less, having infiltrated Conrad's own household. King Richard was widely suspected of involvement in the murder but in truth he was not. Isabella, who was expecting her first child (Maria of Montferrat), married Count Henry only a short week later, his dream finally coming true. Balian in return became one of Henry's advisors, and later that year, along with William of Tiberias, commanded the rearguard of King Richard's army at the Battle of Jaffa. Later, he helped negotiate the Treaty of Ramla between King Richard and Saladin, ending the crusade. Under this treaty, Ibelin remained under Saladin's control, but many sites along the coast which he had conquered during the Crusade were allowed to remain in Christian hands. After King Richard departed the Holy Land, Saladin compensated Balian with the castle of Caymont and five other nearby sites, all outside Acre. Queen Sibylla sadly died before her time of disease in 1190 whereas King Guy lived out his days alone in Cyprus as a king without a kingdom until he died in 1192, his crown passing to Sibylla's sister Isabella. Princess Stephanie received word by secret code via one of Al Rashid's men that Paul had survived and had returned to Alisha. She was more than happy he had survived and was reunited with Alisha. She died in 1192, some say broken, for there was no visible ailment or sickness in her...others say she died peacefully and with great grace and smiling having said her time in this realm was done. Upon hearing the news of her death, Philip passed on the content of her letter to Paul, after which they arranged for the poem she had requested to be set upon her grave. Brother

Teric, who had remained the Grand Master of the Knights Templar before standing down in order to remain with and watch over Princess Stephanie, returned to France after she passed away and retired to live in Avallon and to help watch over and guard items hidden by Master Odo de St Armand, plus the two key sound symbols entrusted to him, the same as given in Princess Stephanie's letter to Paul. Gabirol did indeed take up Philip's offer and moved on to the city of Florence where he became one of the most influential and instrumental forces behind the start of the renaissance. Stewart married Ayleth and had four children by her and remained in La Rochelle. Attar became a famous Sufi mystic with great prestige and honour being bestowed upon him by both Christian and Muslim alike. The Templar married Miriam in the same spot and same fashion as Alisha and Paul had been married and when their time came to leave for England, they and his brother the Hospitaller accompanied Alisha, Paul, Ailia and Mellissa, and of course Ishmael, first to Balantrodach in Alba where the Templars had their first original headquarters in Britain for many years, then on to Glen Lyon before settling down. Peter went with them as their master stonemason bringing along his family too but not before carving a code in stone for the Genoese sailor to take to the New World (years before accepted history teaches us that the America's were discovered) along with the special acorns Alisha had looked after for so many years, originally taken from Abraham's oak tree, to plant and hide the stone within the island that would later became known as Oak Island in what is nowadays Nova Scotia in Canada. Philip retired to a place in what is nowadays called Cumbria on the Scottish borders accompanied by Sister Lucy after visiting and spending some time with Kratos near Tara in what is nowadays called Eire, Ireland. He also finally managed to visit the grave of his wife in Glen Lyon, and when he passed away, he was laid beside her. They lie there still. Thomas did indeed write many accounts of his adventures and released them under the guise of several pen names as Grail romances. He returned to his homeland where he married and went on to have many children. He died at the grand old age of 101. Simon became a great scholar and teacher of languages assisted by Philip. The Templar and his brother Hospitaller remained in Alba and their family grew under the adapted name of the St Clairs...the rest of their family tree is perhaps more widely known nowadays and their descendants built a chapel, as designed by both Paul and Philip together from older plans passed over to them, many years later, complete with all the sound symbolism and codes...except for two symbols deliberately omitted but hidden in Avallon in France. Everything hidden in plain sight. It was written in code that a single yellow rose would be laid within Balantrodach to let those who know, and see, that we have remembered that part of our journey as well as a single crimson rose and lily placed in La Rochelle on the 22nd day of July, Mary Magdalene's feast day. It was also foretold that the ancient male yew tree in Fortingall at the mouth of Glen Lyon would appear to change to a female tree and flower fruit berries if the presence of the sacred feminine returned to the area. Taqi's female partner turned up in La Rochelle with their son in 1193, Philip, after being notified, immediately taking them under his wing and protection when they moved to England to join with him. Alisha and Paul lived out their remaining years in peace in a small town in what nowadays is called Cumbria from where their many descendants would thrive and multiply, hidden from prying interfering eyes, their crimson line forgotten but shielded and protected as Philip had planned all along...until the day when that line would again step forward to remind us all of a choice we must soon make. The farrier after many years refusing to fully accept what he had heard, one day arrived in Cumbria with a train of horses and set up his own horse trading business and market, becoming a firm friend of Paul's, his sons eventually marrying Ailia and Mellissa...but their lives... that is another story. Paul and the farrier spent a year setting and sighting a marker tower on the island of Jura in Scotland and at a site not far from Balantrodach whereupon Rosslyn Chapel was later constructed, both aligned to a tower in what became known as Nova Scotia in Canada; just how they knew exactly where to site them so accurately still remains a mystery, but not to some. Percival returned to Georgia and became a senior trusted advisor to Queen Tamar. He went on to incorporate many esoteric teachings within Georgia's history and why it shares so much in common with England's. He never remarried, never fully getting over the loss of Nyla. Paul and Alisha managed to visit Queen Tamar in Georgia several times over the following years and saw Percival again. When Percival died, his funeral was attended by over a thousand people. His grave is hidden high in the mountains of Georgia...but not totally forgotten! In 1192, Saladin signed the 'Treaty of Ramla' alongside Count Henry as witness to formally allow Christians to be allowed to enter Jerusalem and worship freely and thus ending that Crusade, but also the formation of the Knights of Saladin – Muslim knights that would form a contingent of the Knights Templar themselves...Paul's commission by Saladin completed. Master Gerard was released from captivity after a ransom was paid by Henry but was again captured after the siege of Acre and chose to die that time rather than be ransomed. Stephan and Sarah remained in La Rochelle running their inn until the end of their years, becoming more like grandparents to Stewart and Ayleth's children. Stephan continued to light the lanthorn every night until his death, after which Stewart continued the tradition, and his son after him. Upside married the female Templar, her name being Ruth, and spent many years in Persia, where he served honourably. Upon his retirement he was visited by a tall enigmatic man who called himself Jaromir. He informed Upside that he was in fact the son of Theodoric and why they shared such a similar tattoo. He refused to reveal who his mother was. Consequently, accompanied by his wife and two children, he returned to Theodoric's former estate and vineyard in Rochfort, recovered several buried items, including a twelve string harp made from oak, and moved to Ireland, his intention being to make sure that the country adopted the harp as its national symbol, as it has indeed been. When Alisha passed away at a very healthy old age, Paul had her laid to rest within a hidden crypt not too far from where he had originally hidden the staff of Jesus. Shortly afterwards Paul was laid beside her, their full real names engraved upon the tomb. They still remain side by side, laid to rest within that secret crypt in Southern France, its location known to a select few, complete with the healing staff in their possession. But their family still thrives and its connection to apples and bees is as ever evident, again hidden in plain sight. One day soon, that light shall again be lit upon the point in La Rochelle, on Rue de la Stella Maris as it is still named, and the single crimson rose and white lily will again be placed upon the point in their remembrance...and it will be seen by those who promised to keep watch to know when we had remembered. For now is an end, but the voice within remembers...a new beginning is coming.

 17 – 2

Port of La Rochelle, France, Rue de la Stella Maris, July 22nd 2016

A young looking middle aged man wearing a simple yellow and black fleece, grey trousers and hiking boots walked along the stone covered path to where a circle of white stones had been positioned for many years overlooking the harbour to his right and the Atlantic Ocean to his front. He closed his eyes as he walked the last few paces across the grass that blew gently from the sea breeze. When he sensed a familiar feeling flood through him, he shuddered momentarily and sighed. Slowly he knelt down on one knee and placed his hands flat upon the few stones still showing through the grasses and he smiled. He half laughed lightly to himself and shook his head just as his female partner walked up quietly behind him. As her dark hair blew over her shoulders, she looked at him full of a mixture of emotions. Their journey to reach this point had been a long and emotional one…but they had found each other and they had remembered. The man opened his eyes and looked back up over his shoulder at her, her blue eyes full of love for him. She handed him a single crimson coloured rose and a white lily, which he took and very gently placed down upon the ground, the rose resting on top of the lily. He stared at them for several minutes oblivious to everything else around him as his partner placed her hand upon his right shoulder. As the laughter of children playing nearby drew his mind back to the present, he stood up and took his partner's hand then stood behind her wrapping his arms around her. She placed her hands upon his forearms and leaned back into him and smiled as he kissed her softly on the side of her cheek. They looked out across the calm sea at the sun just sitting on the horizon as it set.

"Do you think they will remember…in time?" she asked, her voice delicate and soft.

"Yes," the man replied and kissed her cheek again and paused. He shuddered again briefly and held her tighter as memories from a distant past echoed in his soul. "It will touch those souls it is meant to, and yes, most certainly yes…they will remember."

 3 – 4

Unseen by either of them, a tall blonde haired woman looking identical to Abi stood observing them intently. Her piercing blues eyes squinted slightly against the setting sun as she started to walk toward them but she hesitated and stopped when she saw the single rose and white lily. A great sense of pride and achievement swept over her as a recognition of souls flooded her entire body with almost overwhelming emotions that made her momentarily gasp aloud. She froze, thinking she had drawn the couple's attention as the man alone looked back in her direction. He simply looked directly at her, smiled briefly then looked back out toward the ocean. She nodded to herself knowingly, bowed her head slightly toward the couple, turned and silently walked away smiling.

THE END

(Or perhaps just the beginning?)

M IH M – LOVE CONQUERS DEATH

Epilogue: Author's Afterword
– The Choice

'Your beliefs do not make you a free thinker. The ability to change your beliefs based upon new information does.' Those words are what I was recommended to place at the beginning of Book I but I believe it would have been a wasted statement then. Having read this far it will perhaps make more sense now. My initial afterword read like some sermon where I found myself pontificating and by default being guilty of the very same thing I argue against. You should be free to see and understand what I have tried to reveal but in your own way...not necessarily my way. I have included quite a few bibliographic references already but if I wrote down every reference to check and validate all I have tried to convey then I would have another full volume of bibliographic references alone. But you can easily check and verify the validity behind what I claim by investing some time to research the facts yourself. It is all out there. However I do simply wish to add here a few facts that have indeed come to pass very relevant to Outremer.

Firstly, why apart from the mathematical values in the pillars of Joachin and Boaz, are twin pillars so important? Purely from a chemical and physical perspective, and as modern science confirms, two pillars set up can generate positive and negative forces essential to start that spark within the primordial soup that ultimately led to life being created. Also the actual measures given reveal the working formula for Pi. No engineering science can develop without first knowing the basic principles behind Pi. Our ancient forefathers certainly knew and understood it fully. The Giza Pyramids alone stand as an absolute physical proof of the high engineering standards employed.

In Scotland, there is a crimson coloured stone still hidden, carved with the same initials as those upon the later monument of the 'Shepherds of Arcadia' image at Shugborough Hall, a hall which just happens to be 2160 miles away from Oak Island in Nova Scotia. The image also has the same letters inscribed upon it starting with 'D'.

Historical records maintain that no reason has been officially given as to why Al Rashid, the leader of the Ashashin, gave over some 3,000 gold coins to the Templars. Having read *Outremer* then perhaps hopefully it has now given you an insight as to how and why. Likewise you can now understand how and why the green cross of the Knights of Lazarus became the universal medical colour for pharmacies and medical centres worldwide.

Within this story I have explained about another code hidden within the Bible but one that could not be understood until our modern era. That code, despite the contention surrounding it, is detailed within Michael Drosnin's bestselling book entitled *The Bible Code*. This particular code could only be cracked with the use of sophisticated computer programmes. It raises the question exactly how it was formulated in the first place nearly two millennia before computers were invented.

The cathedral of Reims, as well as Lichfield Cathedral, was constructed from red brick. Likewise Rosslyn Chapel, near Edinburgh, was indeed built and still stands today made famous by Dan Brown's *Da Vinci Code*. The ceiling has 213 cubes, each with sound patterns upon them. Two cubes are, however, devoid of any image...deliberately missing. The two missing and hidden symbols are secreted away within a Templar church near Avallon in France. Also present in Rosslyn is the statement carved upon a corbel 'Forte Est Vinum, Fortior Est Rex, Fortiores Sunt Mulieres: Super Omnia Vincit Veritas': 'Wine is strong, a king is stronger, women are stronger, but truth conquers all'. On the opposite corbel the figure of Melchizadek holding a chalice, the Grail, can be seen. The third missing bodyguard, as explained previously within *Outremer*, is symbolic of the line, connected with apples and bees, that shall remain separate and hidden, until it can be revealed again. The chapel in all its symbolism physically proclaims that God and nature are ONE, that every green shoot is a word of God; that, if there is any sacrilege, it is what man has done and is doing to Mother Earth. In *Outremer*, Peter the stonemason comes from the Lombardy region. This lintel or 'straight arch' bears the only writing in the fabric of the chapel that is in Latin: A stone with an inscription recently uncovered on Oak Island in Nova Scotia is likewise in the style of Lombardy.

Our actual physical earth is calling out to all of us! Listen and you will hear her. It is not some mystical nonsense but a real phenomenon and many people can now sense it and feel it. The animal kingdom certainly can already. I ask that you try to see with your soul...not your eyes, not your head and neither your heart. Changes are happening all around us and it is not simply down to so-called global warming. The reality is that there is a binary twin dark star within our own solar system with its own attendant planets...this is the true secret behind all the dark sun symbolism and Templar codes regarding it. This is not fantasy or hysterical conspiracy rubbish but fact; one which, despite the protestations of many agencies, will be proven to be correct. It affects directly our planet's very magnetic polarity and magnetosphere. Our world is presently going through the changes inflicted by this twin binary dark star. It is why our weather patterns are all over the place. But it is not the end of the world as so many doom merchants peddle to scare us. But it is the end of the fourth age of man as we now transit into the fifth age of mankind...though I really should say humankind. The fifth flight of the Phoenix as detailed within *Outremer*. We are entering the last phase of the end of the world we think we know and are familiar with. As we enter the fifth age, the old age will pass away as the world wakes up to a new dawn. It is not simply deluded wishful thinking and that nothing changes, as in wars will continue and disease and death will prevail as the poor remain poor etc....but our world was not always that way. Nor will it remain so. But in order for it to change, we have a choice to make.

We actively interact with our environment. If we are happy and positive it does have a very real effect upon our surroundings. In turn if we are depressed and negative, it adversely affects our environment. All the fear being generated now and orchestrated wars and poverty weaken our very planet. That is why it is so important to start being more optimistic and positive. You have a choice. You can accept what is peddled raising anxiety and fear and that we are all doomed or we can recognise that we have an alternative. We have not been allowed to destroy ourselves but guided and at times intervention has been necessary. This is something the mysteries of Mary Magdalene reveal to us, that love is the key. I will put my mark down as standing on the side of the fence which believes Mary Magdalene was, in fact, actually the first pope...not Peter! The present Pope and Catholic Church will in time come to admit this simple fact as a truth. It too will cease to exist as it presently stands and will, if the choices are made correctly, evolve into something far better and more universal than most people could possibly imagine. A balanced matriarchal Church of love unified with other faiths no longer constrained by dogma and ruled by fear. I would argue that the present Pope Francis, who as pope number 212 understands that he is the last one, and that he is playing out a part of a prophecy.

I also state on record that I firmly believe we will find irrefutable evidence of a highly evolved civilisation in what is now Antarctica. It is the only continent sized landmass past the Pillars of Hercules that is surrounded by all the oceans of the world as claimed. Look at the earth from directly above the South Pole and you will see it is so. The legends of Native Americans come from different cultures separated by vast distances and isolated from one another. However, all of them tell a similar story of a once fallen civilisation that existed in the distant past. In Central America, this ancient culture lived in Aztlan. According to legends, Aztlan was located to the south, on a white island, and perished without warning as a result of natural catastrophic events. Many researchers maintain that Aztlan means 'place of whiteness'. This is why it has commonly been connected to Atlantis and Antarctica, suggesting that Aztlan might have been the mythical Atlantis, the mythical place located to the south. Modern science is catching up in realising that Antarctica was not always covered in ice. New research sheds light upon geological facts that show it was in fact largely free of ice as little as 12,000 to 15,000 years ago. The science is readily available for you to read if you make time to do the research. The earth shifts upon its axis regularly hence how a continent now located to the south was once free of ice. Antarctica wasn't always located where it is today. It was once further north toward the equator and experienced a tropical or temperate climate, meaning that it was covered in forests, and inhabited by various ancient life forms. According to the mainstream theory of continental drift, the crust of our planet is in fact divided into several tectonic plates that literally 'float' over a molten inner layer. Over the ages, these plates slowly bump against one another. However, the theory of crustal displacement, which expands the theory of continental drift, says that approximately every 40,000 years, the entire crust of our planet shifts as a single unit. After each 'shift' all the land masses on our planet, including entire continents, are relocated to a new position on the planet. Many researchers believe that this happened the last time around 10,000 BC and caused the continent of Antarctica to move from its position near the equator to its current position...the South Pole. As detailed within *Outremer*, there is plenty of evidence that points to the undeniable fact that sometime between the 4th and 12th millennia BC there was an extremely advanced civilisation upon this planet, with great knowledge of navigation, cartography and astronomy. Their technological advancements were way ahead of other cultures that would appear after them. This 'lost' civilisation most definitely preceded our modern era by tens of thousands of years. Some claim Atlantis was in North West Africa as remnants of a vast ruin with concentric ring waterways just as described in myth, appear to be visible. I argue this is but a much later construction, perhaps to mimic or in honour of the former lost civilisation, for its location does not for the description of being surrounded by the major oceans of the world, not even by ancient knowledge standards.

Within *Outremer* I have explained that when the light returns to the Dome of the Rock in Jerusalem it would mark the beginning of the birth stages of the fifth age of man...the Age of Aquarius...the spiritual age. In 2014 many thousands witnessed, and caught on film, a bright sphere of light descend and rest upon the Dome of the Rock before shooting off vertically at great speed and vanishing. We are entering an accelerated phase of a spiritual awakening. The time of the fifth flight of the Phoenix and our very own physical planet and solar system are passing through what is known as the Photon Belt. In 2003, the earth itself and our solar system entered this belt. It is made up of light photons and it will take 2,106 years for our solar system to pass through. Also our actual planet's Schumann frequency is rising and has risen more in the past few years than in the last fifty years. This does, and is, having a very real physical effect upon us as individuals and ultimately collectively.

Great symbols of nature will appear across many lands. They will generate great interest and debate, but those who recognise them will hear and sense the past calling out again across time. Most people are by now aware of crop circles. Many ask why if other highly evolved beings exist out there in the vastness of the cosmos, do they not come and openly reveal themselves? The answer is simple really. Because we are in the process of changing as a species. If they revealed themselves now fully and openly we would want them to put right all that is wrong in our world... but that responsibility is down to us to correct and put right. Plus we would try to use their abilities and technologies when presently we are clearly not responsible enough to be trusted with such. But we are getting there and the change is happening. No, that is not some delusional wishful thinking again but a tangible reality taking place right now. People are remembering and recognising aspects of our true past and true potential. Despite what so many seem to believe, that humankind is too war like to ever know peace, I say that is wrong and is a mindset we have been conditioned to believe and accept. Humankind was not, and is not, made for war; that is why we fear it and are broken by it for it is not our natural state.

The Oak of Abraham detailed within *Outremer* is an ancient tree which, tradition says, marks the place where Abraham entertained three angels after pitching his tent for the night. It is said the oak is nearly 5,000 years old and has been venerated by Jews and Christians alike for hundreds of years. There is a long-standing tradition that prophesied that it would die just before the appearance of the so-called Antichrist. If the trunk remains dead, then the forces of evil and darkness would have prevailed...but if it re-grew, even if from its off shoots, then love and light will win. The tree did appear to die, but then re-grew in 1998 just after news broke in *The Sunday Times* that the ancient so-called Hall of Records in Egypt had been positively located. Acorn trees grow big around the large dolmen at Drauignan in France. Time will prove that those trees are identical to that of Abrahams Oak as well as the non indigenous oak trees deliberately planted on Oak Island in Nova Scotia in Canada. The trees being so different from the indigenous oaks stood out as a perfect marker, though most have sadly been deliberately cut down in recent years. Rare Templar coins have also been found on Oak Island.

Also the ancient yew tree in Fortingall in Scotland is reputed to be at least 5,000 years old but now believed to be even older. In 2015 it appeared to change from a male tree to a female tree, thus fulfilling one of the myths associated with it and the sacred feminine. Some myths claim the actual incarnation of Mary Magdalene would return to the tree. Glen Lyon is reputed by some to have been the actual birth place of Pontius Pilate with many connections to Druids, Joseph of Arimathea and a unique split standing stone known as the Praying Hands of Mary. In January 2016, during the height of Storm Henry, some would argue Hurricane Henry, when most people were inside sheltering as it raged cutting off Glen Lyon with sleet and snow, a dark haired female was seen at the tree and touched it, remaining there for some time. It was foretold that when the spirit of Mary Magdalene returns, the tree would give fruit for the first time. In the spring of 2016 the ancient yew tree bore fruit for the first time ever recorded. Just a coincidence perhaps?

King Richard the Lion Heart brought back the white flag with a red cross upon it and of course it became England's national flag. England also eventually adopted the symbol of the rose as its national flower as well as the unicorn upon its banners by King Henry VIII and in 2015 a young Scottish woman laid a yellow rose at the Balantrodach church in Temple totally unprompted. On the 22nd of July 2016, a young woman and man were seen to place a single reddish rose upon a white lily at the point of Stella Maris in La Rochelle at exactly 21:06 local time.

Many will continue to contest the origins of the Templars and most likely that which I have detailed within *Outremer*, but in short and to clarify, the Knights Templar came much earlier than 1119 as taught as fact. Think about it logically and from a practical point of view. You would not expect the Order, or any Order or organisation, to announce itself to the world with no prior detailed planning and forethought. Evidence for this can be seen in the close relationship of the first Master of the Temple, Hugues de Payens and his secular overlord, Hugh, Count of Champagne. The common factor in the origination of the Templars is always Godfrei de Bouillon, who appears to have set up a 'real' Order in the Holy Land. This is the Order of the Holy Sepulchre. The other details pertaining to how and when the actual Templars were created I have outlined within *Outremer*. It can all be checked and verified.

As for Ireland, it did indeed become known as Eire. It is also the true name of Ireland, correctly rendered 'Ariland' or 'Land of the Arya'. The term can be correctly spoken as Eri, signifying the earth goddess of the ancient Druids herself, hence nowadays known as Eire. I detailed the connections between Eire and Scotia and how it led to Alba being called Scotland. I am often pressed on the matter of the name Scotia, and as I detailed fully, it is indeed now confirmed as the name of Akenhaten's (Amenhotep III's son) daughter...just another connection between the 18th dynasty pharaohs and Scotland. (More on these details below.) I also detailed a scene showing when and how the pyramid at Abu Rawash exploded. Modern analysis clearly demonstrates that the large pyramid at Abu Rawash near Cairo was not simply abandoned mid construction as is claimed. It is often referred to as the 'Lost Pyramid'. But the damage and inwardly collapsed lower construction show that it was destroyed from within by an internal explosion of such force it threw debris several miles away and the remaining parts collapsing in and downwards upon itself. When complete, it stood higher than the Great Pyramid of Giza as it was set upon slightly higher ground. I also detailed how great stone crescents were constructed and hidden by the ancients, including one near to Stonehenge. I wrote this account back in 2005. In 2015 a great crescent was discovered still buried near Stonehenge, and coincidentally northeast of Stonehenge. Also there is new evidence emerging showing that Stonehenge was originally erected in Wales and stood for a countless period of time before being moved to its present location. A large buried crescent has also been found in modern day Israel and excavated to reveal its construction.

Islam did indeed eventually adopt the crescent as its main emblem. Many have given reasons when and why Islam adopted the crescent moon from being based upon the simple fact that in Arabia, travel along the desert trade routes was largely by night, and navigation depended upon the position of the moon and stars, the Moon representing the guidance of God on the path through life. The new moon also represents the Muslim calendar, which has 12 months each of 29 or 30 days. So in Islam the lunar month and the calendar month coincide, and the new moon is eagerly awaited, especially at the end of the month of Ramadan when its sighting means that the celebrations of Eid al-Fitr can begin. Some argue it represents the importance to the new moon phase but the moon depicted on many Islamic flags is the old moon, the reverse shape of the new moon, which is like a letter C backwards. However, even though the crescent is a very widespread motif in Islamic iconography, it is neither Islamic in origin nor exclusive to that religion. Most people are not aware that the emblem had been used in Christian art for many centuries in depictions of the Virgin Mary, for example. It is in fact one of the oldest icons in human history, having been known in graphic depictions since at least as early as the Babylonian period in Mesopotamia. The stele of Ur Namu, for example, dating from 2100 BC, includes the crescent moon to symbolise the god Sin, along with a star representing Shamash, the sun god. Later the moon became a female deity, typified by the goddess Artemis and her many counterparts, including Diana, who was celebrated as the moon goddess in Roman times and depicted with a crescent on her brow. The crescent emblem appears to have entered Islam via the Seljuk Turks, who dominated Anatolia in the 12th century, and was widely used by their successors, the Ottoman Turks, who eventually became the principal Islamic nation, and whose Sultan held the title of Caliph until 1922. Some argue that the Ottomans adopted the crescent to symbolise their conquest of Constantinople but this can be dismissed as inaccurate since the device pre-dates 1453. In the late 19th century the Pan-Islamic movement sponsored by the Sultan Abdul Hamid II used the crescent and star on a green flag as part of its propaganda, and from this were derived the flags of Egypt and Pakistan and many other Islamic states. The crescent moon (hilal) motif is featured with a five or six pointed star, the latter known as Solomon's shield in the Islamic world, on early Islamic coins circa AD 695, but it carried no distinct Islamic connotation. Five hundred years later, it appeared in association with various astrological/astronomical symbols on 12th century Islamic metal-work, but when depicted in manuscript painting, held by a seated man, it is thought to represent the authority of a high court official. Its use as a roof finial on Islamic buildings also dates from this medieval period but the motif still had no specific religious meaning as it decorated all types of architecture, secular as well as religious. In fact Ettinghausen (Richard Ettinghausen was a historian of Islamic art and chief curator of the Freer Gallery) argues that it was the European assumption that this was a religious and national emblem that led to several Muslim governments adopting it officially during the 19th century.

In *Outremer* I detailed the connections between King Arthur and the Isle of Man. In 2007 Queen Elizabeth II officially recognised Prince David, a cousin of the Queen, through her great great grandfather Baron John Sheffield, as the king of the 'Independent Kingdom of Man'. By royal assent he was legalised as a direct descendant of the Celtic Godred Crovan line through King William de Montague of Mann, and the lawful heir general to the Stanley Kings of Mann. He was also verified as a cousin and heir of the Scottish Dukes of Atholl from the John Murray line, whose heirs of the Lordship of Mann deferred to Prince David as having a superior claim through the Stanley Kings to be King of Mann. His Royal Highness Prince David thereby became King of the Independent Kingdom of Mann, an autonomous dynastic royal house legalised under the UK constitutional monarchy system, registered under UK law by force of the British Crown Office Act of 1877, Section 3.3. The British Crown remains the Head of State of the Isle of Man, which remains a British 'crown dependency' without its own sovereignty. However, King David of Mann holds full sovereignty of the ancient historical Independent Kingdom of Mann of his royal ancestors, as a nation-state without a territory, and an autonomous subject of international law. As a result, the Independent Kingdom of Mann fully represents and continues the medieval Celtic traditions from the Isle of Mann, the original territory of the legendary 'King Arthur'. In the 21st century so many questions have been asked about our true history and if we are alone in the universe. Perhaps the answers are even more relevant now because they have captured the imaginations of a whole new global generation that is becoming more fully interactive through the World Wide Web. The universal themes will not lie down. There may yet be new perspectives to add to the world's abiding fascination with King Arthur – and they may well be discovered in France.

It is said, and I am sure it will generate a lot of debate, that the so-called final pope will admit the sacred feminine principle. Part of the 'Third Secret of Fátima' says the Virgin Mary will appear at a ruined city, which some have claimed will be Rome when it is destroyed...but it is not for it will be the ruined city of Gamla near the Sea of Galilee. The Three Secrets of Fátima consist of a series of apocalyptic visions and prophecies apparently given to three young Portuguese shepherds, Lúcia Santos and her cousins Jacinta and Francisco Marto, by a Marian apparition, starting on May 13th 1917. The three claimed they were visited by a Marian apparition, or woman dressed in blue and white, six times between May and October 1917. The apparition is now popularly known as Our Lady of Fátima. According to Lucia, on July 13 1917, around noon, the Virgin Mary is said to have entrusted the children with three secrets. Two of the secrets were revealed in 1941 in a document written by Lúcia, at the request of José Alves Correia da Silva, Bishop of Leiria, to assist with the publication of a new edition of a book on Jacinta. When asked by the bishop in 1943 to reveal the third secret, Lúcia struggled for a short period, being 'not yet convinced that God had clearly authorised her to act'. However, in October 1943 the bishop ordered her to put it in writing so she wrote the secret down and sealed it in an envelope not to be opened until 1960, when 'it will appear clearer'. The text of the third secret was officially released by Pope John Paul II in 2000, although some claim that it was not the entire secret revealed by Lúcia, despite repeated assertions from the Vatican to the contrary. According to the official Catholic interpretation, the three secrets involve Hell, World War I and World War II, and the Pope John Paul II assassination attempt.

Part of the second prophecy states 'when you see a night illumined by an unknown light, know that this is the great sign given you by God that he is about to punish the world for its crimes, by means of war, famine and persecutions of the Church and of the Holy Father. To prevent this, I shall come to ask for the Consecration of Russia to my Immaculate Heart, and the Communion of reparation on the First Saturdays. If my requests are heeded, Russia will be converted, and there will be peace; if not, she will spread her errors throughout the world, causing wars and persecutions of the Church. The good will be martyred; the Holy Father will have much to suffer; various nations will be annihilated. In the end, my Immaculate Heart will triumph. The Holy Father will consecrate Russia to me, and she shall be converted, and a period of peace will be granted to the world.' It can now be argued that Russia has converted on many levels since the fall of the Berlin wall. Some say the lights seen were in fact the Northern Lights coming further south than ever before seen, all connected to the earth's magnetosphere being compressed and the planet's magnetic poles being affected by another celestial body other than our sun. The history and controversy surrounding the Third Secret of Fátima is prolonged and does fill volumes as the many books written about them testify.

In 1960 the Vatican issued a press release stating that it was 'most probable the Secret would remain, forever, under absolute seal'. This announcement produced considerable speculation over the content of the secret. According to *The New York Times*, speculation ranged from 'worldwide nuclear annihilation to deep rifts in the Roman Catholic Church that lead to rival papacies'. On May 2 1981, Laurence James Downey hijacked an airplane and demanded that Pope John Paul II make public the Third Secret of Fatima.

As recounted within this book, Theodoric buried a stone with details about Pontius Pilate. Well, a carved stone was actually found in the location given confirming Pontius Pilate's historical existence. It was discovered in 1961 and known as 'Pilate Stone', the only archaeological item that mentions the Roman prefect Pontius Pilate, by whose order Jesus was crucified. This at least gives validation that Pontius Pilate was real.

Modern astronomy has proved that Venus's orbit around our sun traces a pattern which creates a five pointed pattern identical to an apple cut horizontally in half. As for our hair...modern science now confirms that our hair is actually part of our nervous system and holds memories. It also holds our DNA, which can easily be extracted from it.

As foretold, the Cathars in southern France were indeed massacred during the purges of the Albigensian Crusade, from 1209 to 1244, a Crusade where more than 100,000 Christians were brutally murdered by their fellow Christians followed a few years later by the Papal Inquisition, the Plague, robber knights from Spain, the Hundred Years War with England, the Huguenots and the French Revolution.

The 'Cutting of the Elm' at Gizors in 1188 is a documented historical event though its reasons are shrouded in confusion as to why the Order severed its links from the Templars and why Gerard de Ridefort was branded as treasonous. Having read *Outremer*, perhaps now you know; though the controversy surrounding whether ceremony even took place still rages to this day.

The Chinon Parchment. King Philip IV of France had accused the Knights Templar of heresy and used that excuse to put many of them to death. On October 25th, 2009, the Vatican released the Chinon Parchment that acknowledged the Knights Templar were innocent of heresy (Vatican Information Service, 4th October). The persecution of the Templars began on Friday, 13 October 13th 1307, when the organisation was unjustly attacked and driven underground. It must be realised that the Templars were the special forces of their era. To believe they would all so easily surrender is somewhat farfetched. It is my contention they were in the main forewarned...hence their entire naval fleet just happened to vanish from La Rochelle prior to those remaining Templars being arrested. A very real physical treasure was likewise secreted away. If you can work out the code within *Outremer*, you can reverse the direction and clues to find a location that has been very obvious for years that still has much of that physical treasure. A letter to the Pope from so-called living descendants of the Templars appeared in the press in 2004. 'We shall witness the 700th anniversary of the persecution of our Order on 13th October 2007', the letter said. 'It would be just and fitting for the Vatican to acknowledge our grievance in advance of this day of mourning'. On 25 October 25th 2007, exactly 13 days from the morning of the anniversary, an official document was released by the Vatican absolving the Knights Templar and confirming their innocence.

Historically proven, we know that Balian of Ibelin, after surrendering the city of Jerusalem to Saladin, and the death of Sibylla at the Siege of Acre in 1190, led to a dispute over the throne of the kingdom. Balian's stepdaughter Isabella was now rightful queen, but Guy refused to concede his title, and Isabella's husband Humphrey, who had let her cause down in 1186, remained loyal to him. For Isabella to succeed, she needed a politically acceptable and militarily competent husband, the obvious candidate being Conrad of Montferrat, who also had some claim as Baldwin V's paternal uncle. Balian and Maria seized Isabella and talked her into agreeing to a divorce. There were precedents: the annulment of Amalric I's marriage to Agnes of Courtenay, and the unsuccessful attempts to force Sibylla to divorce Guy. Isabella's marriage was duly annulled by Ubaldo Lanfranchi, Archbishop of Pisa, who was papal legate, and Philip of Dreux, Bishop of Beauvais. The Bishop of Beauvais then married her to Conrad, controversially, since his brother had been married to her half-sister and it was uncertain whether he had been divorced by his Byzantine wife. The succession dispute was prolonged by the arrival of Richard I of England and Philip II of France on the Third Crusade: Richard supported Guy, as a Poitevin vassal, while Philip supported Conrad, his late father's cousin. Balian's and Maria's role in Isabella's divorce and their support for Conrad as king earned them the bitter hatred of Richard and his supporters. Consequently he has been much maligned since. I hope *Outremer* will go some way to revealing a greater truth behind the whole matter? Ambroise, who wrote a poetic account of the crusade, called Balian 'more false than a goblin' and said he 'should be hunted with dogs'. The anonymous author of the *Itinerarium Peregrinorum et Gesta Regis Ricardi* wrote that Balian was a member of a 'council of consummate iniquity' around Conrad, accused him of taking Conrad's bribes and said of Maria and Balian as a couple: steeped in Greek filth from the cradle, she had a husband whose morals matched her own: he was cruel, she was godless; he was fickle, she was pliable; he was faithless, she was fraudulent. But as detailed within *Outremer*, Conrad was assassinated just two days into his kingship, Count Henry then marrying Isabella.

As detailed within *Outremer*, several principalities were joined as one, as planned all along and so Switzerland was formed and still remains as an independent and neutral country.

Full details of John of Jerusalem's prophecies were finally revealed in 1992.

As leaders of the two opposing armies of the Crusades, Saladin and King Richard agreed and implemented the 'Treaty of Ramla of AD 1192', by which Jerusalem would remain under Muslim control, but would be open to Christian pilgrimage. After concluding the treaty, Saladin and King Richard continued to send each other many gifts as signs of mutual respect, although they never met in person. As a monument to this great historic friendship, a statue of Saladin and King Richard greeting each other on horses was erected in Old Jerusalem. In AD 1754, David Hume, the librarian to the Faculty of Advocates in Edinburgh, contributed to the core collection of the National Library of Scotland, including in the historical record some relevant facts about Saladin. 'This gallant emperor (Saladin), in particular, displayed, during the course of the war, a spirit and generosity, which even his Christian enemies were obliged to acknowledge and admire.' When Saladin died, he had left all of his money (much accumulated wealth) to charity 'without distinction of Jew, Christian or Muslim'.

However, an all too often overlooked documented fact is that Saladin was actually knighted into the Order of the Temple of Solomon himself (Knights Templar), c. AD 1190. One 13th century manuscript, the French work *Ordene de Chevalerie* (Order of Chivalry) written c. AD 1250, historically documented the event in which Saladin was given and received the secret induction ceremony of the Knights Templar. During the Third Crusade (c. AD 1189–1192), Count Hugo of Tiberias (of the Kingdom of Jerusalem) was captured by Saladin. Saladin announced that he 'admired the gentlemen of the Knights Templar', and expressed his desire to become one of them as a brother in chivalry. Saladin requested that Count Hugo perform the secret knighthood induction ceremony on him, promising in exchange the unconditional release of the captured knight. The sacred ceremony was performed, and Saladin, satisfied that he was now officially part of the Templar brotherhood, released Count Hugo as promised. It is generally believed by historians that Saladin wished both to better understand his nemesis colleagues in chivalry as well as to share an honourable bond with them in furtherance of emphasising their commonalities and making peace. It is also believed that the initiation ceremony he received, while official, traditional and authentic, was slightly modified so as not to violate Saladin's Muslim faith. Under the Treaty of Ramla of AD 1192, Muslims in membership as Knights of Saladin, Templars enjoyed strong support from Islam.

Within *Outremer* I detailed Gog and Magog and their connection to London. The images of Gog and Magog have been carried in the Lord Mayor's Show the second Saturday of November since the days of King Henry V.

Note that the actual chemical (Lananin protein molecule) formation that forms the basis for all DNA double helix configurations just happens to match the Cross from Corinthians. So when biblical statements claim that the cross holds us up, it is actually stating a very real fact

It is my contention and belief that the nine founding members of the Knights Templar were initially buried and secured in La Rochelle, alongside members of what can best be described as members of the Jesus and Mary bloodlines. They were then moved to Scotland and buried within the boundary of what is now named the small village of Temple not far from Rosslyn Chapel before their remains were moved on to Rosslyn itself. Several of those knights still remain but the rest have been moved to what we now call Oak Island in Nova Scotia in Canada. Incidentally, the City of David was built upon the original outline of Oak Island...not the other way around as some people are beginning to claim. Both Oak Island and the City of David share the same shape that replicates the bull's leg constellation of Taurus, identified in ancient Egypt as the place of 'those that came from above'. The sacred bull's leg depicted on Egyptian papyrus, is the same shape as the City of David perimeter, the seven stars of Taurus, and the shape of Oak Island itself.

Mary Magdalene. In 1968 the Catholic Church tried to remove the bad mark against her and she became known as the apostle to the apostles. Julius Africanus, a writer from Edessa, was the first to indicate the truth about the offspring of Jesus and Mary Magdalene or, to be more precise, the offspring of the Holy Family consisting of Mother Mary, Father Joseph and Jesus. But Jesus had, at least according to the highly respected author Laurence Gardner, three brothers, Joseph, Simon and Judas, and three sisters, Maria, Salome and Joanna. He stated that Mary Magdalene was married to Jesus, and that she left the Holy Land immediately after the crucifixion in AD 33 or later in AD 44, going to France, the second Holy Land. Where exactly she landed has caused much speculation and controversy. I hope having read *Outremer* you will accept where she initially landed as being at Roussillon? Others will always argue it could have been Marseilles, Stes-Maries-de-la-Mer or somewhere near Narbonne or Perpignan.

It is my belief that the Virgin Mary was of Phoenician royal descent as was Joseph. Mary Magdalene was likewise of royal descent and wealthy in her own right. In France she was visited several times by Jesus, who did not die on the cross, and in the Rennes-le-Chateau area, they established the Royal Houses of Acqs and Anfortas. From which sprang the Merovingians, the counts of Toulouse and Narbonne, the kings of Septimania, a Jewish kingdom and the house of Burgundy. Joseph of Arimathea went to England, to Cornwall and to Glastonbury, where he married princess Enygeusa. From that marriage sprang the royal Welsh houses of Powys, Gwynedd and Gwyr-y-Gogledd, the famous Fisher Kings, the emperor Constantine and the kings of Brittany, Cornwall and Scotland. The most famous bloodlines of Europe were started in Glastonbury and Rennes-le-Château. And even more peculiar is the fact that where these two bloodlines met, where they intermarried, some of the most powerful rulers in Europe were born. Like King Clovis and the emperors Constantine and Charlemagne. Some argue the search for the Holy Grail is just the search for the lost Sacred Femininity. Lost by the Church, which, during the last millennium, has been systematically putting women down, persecuting them and denying them any credence. That attitude is changing and will change further still.

It is my strong belief and conviction that our souls are created within a region we know as the Orion constellation. This is why Orion is held with such reverence and replicated in stone monuments, such as the Giza complex, sacred places and layouts across our entire world, as well as written into myths and legends. Modern science shows that within that region there is in fact a helix formation. Our ancient forefathers evolved and many physically left for a higher more spiritual way of life in the region we know as Taurus. It is why all four major religions hold part of the key which points us to this region.

People ask me about Freemasons and do they hold all the secrets? Initially they did when originally formed but I have to add, albeit sadly, that many have simply lost their way. Count Henry according to official papers did not visit the Holy Land until 1191. That is absurd to believe and I am more than confident to state that is not true as his position required him to be in Jerusalem. Plus he would not simply arrive in Outremer and then within weeks marry Isabella, which official records do confirm as being genuine and his subsequent actions over the following years.

I have heard the argument from many quarters that we as a species were made to be slaves, especially when connected to the myths and actual writings about the Annunaki gods…but if made to be slaves we would have been made so years before we became technologically advanced enough to fight back. Plus those who argue we are but simple slaves completely miss the inescapable fact that we are all following a spiritual path.

I make no apology when I state we are spiritual beings. I would class myself as spiritual…not religious for there is a massive difference. I believe that any religion that expects you to kill in its name, enslave or restricts free thinking, then it is perhaps time you changed religion. Religion has served its purpose. It has brought great comfort to many, but also great tragedy. I have learnt and believe that religion is a vehicle that has been used to impart certain moral rules and guidelines, sadly often grossly misunderstood or interpreted, but also to carry intact very real complex mathematical and harmonic codes, which to me at least clearly demonstrates there is a higher intelligence behind all of it. We are only now waking up to see those codes as our own scientific and technological knowledge grows; beforehand we could not recognise them for what they are. I believe my books explain this in some depth.

I believe from all the research I have done that there will one day be recovered books of plates of brass hidden in Alba, Scotland…a real physical treasure so to speak.

As outlined in *Outremer*, the chapel at Rosslyn was indeed built. At one end is an area known as the 'Lady Chapel'. The ceiling is supported by arched ribs reaching out and under it from the three pillars to its immediate west and the wall to the east. From these ribs hang what have become known as the 'Rosslyn Cubes' and among the 213 existing cubes (two are missing) can be found 13 uniquely different carved patterns. The markings carved on the face of the cubes match a phenomenon called Cymatics or Chladni patterns, caused when a sustained note is used to vibrate a sheet of metal covered in powder, producing marks. The marks produced by different notes can include flowers, diamonds and hexagons – shapes all present on the Rosslyn Cubes. If we assign a note to each of the 13 carved variations, and when played on medieval instruments *in situ*, they will resonate throughout the chapel unlocking a secret in the stone. But the secret of the musical score that the cubes represent is something called the Devil's chord, which is in fact an augmented fourth. A low frequency sound in the range of 80 to 110 hertz, the Devil's chord was outlawed by the Catholic Church in the middle ages under the belief that those exposed to the chord would begin to enter altered states of consciousness. Chladni patterns must have already been known by the 15th century and, on the basis of the layout of the 13 distinctly different patterns on 213 cubes, with only two cubes missing, are able to reconstruct the melody that has been hidden there for over 500 years. There were originally 215 cubes. Two of them have been broken off and lost in the past 500 years with no apparent explanation of why or how from Rosslyn. The number 215 does not make a significant number but 216 would. 216 is a cosmologically important number. We know that earth's polar circumference is 21,600 nautical miles, 'minutes of latitude' arc. It is also interesting that 'our' maths conventions use 21,600 arc-minutes as the circumference of 'any' circle or sphere. I explained the many references and connections within the Bible and other holy books, the significance of the value 2,160. It is therefore my suggestion that there should be 216 cubes/rectangles on the ceiling of Rosslyn (counting the two that are missing) because putting all the cubes together into one big cube would give us 216. Also a pattern will emerge when the correct sequence of smaller patterns are merged together. The final note of the music maybe?! The value 216 is also 6x6x6 and many other connotations.

To the medieval Catholic Church, Egyptian ideas of resonance were considered part of a pantheistic belief of God in nature and were a direct threat to the Christian belief of God outside of nature. As a result, the geometry of the pentagram and certain resonant intervals were considered unfit for use in the Church. This was especially true for the musical interval of three whole tones (six half-steps) known as the tritone. Known as *Diabolus in Musica*, or the Devil in Music, the tritone is very strongly related to this ancient understanding of resonance, sharing what we will call for now an 'inverse harmonic relationship' with a consonant major sixth. The Rosslyn stave angel emphasises this fact by pointing to the part of the tritone interval known as the 'leading tone'. As a matter of fact, the melody in the cubes emphasises the tritone in a way that would have been unacceptable to the Catholic Church in the 15th century. Banned by Pope Gregory IX in 1234, the tritone was and still is outlawed in Catholic music. As a result, the Freemasons hid their use of this forbidden interval by encoding it as Cymatic symbols in the chapel architecture. This was their way of preserving what they considered sacred Egyptian knowledge at a time when Europe was hostile to such beliefs. But there is another twist to this story that takes the concept of resonance to an even higher level of theosophical symbolism. While there are 13 angels corresponding to the 13 unique cube patterns, there are also eight dragons whose tongues wrap around the 'Tree of Life' carved at the bottom of the pillars in Rosslyn chapel. Together, the angels and dragons symbolically represent the Fibonacci ratio of 13:8 or 1.625. This proportion happens to be the first ascending Fibonacci ratio 'not' found as a resonant interval in the harmonic series. This begins the convergence of the remaining Fibonacci ratios towards the golden ratio (~1.61803) found in the pentagram and golden triangle.

It is a little known fact that the ratios of adjacent numbers in the Fibonacci series beginning with 13:8 = 1.625 create a natural damping effect in the standing wave of a musical tone or other coherent vibration. As each ascending Fibonacci ratio gets closer to the infinite golden ratio, the damping effect increases, thereby cancelling all fractional waves and leaving only the whole number harmonics to vibrate sympathetically. This damping effect is used extensively in the design of speaker enclosures and theatres, usually approximated as 1.62 x 1.0 x 0.62 to cancel reflection. Harmonic waves simply cannot resonate at or near the infinite frequency proportion of the golden ratio. The dragon, as the mythical serpent holding secret knowledge in the Underworld, represents this anti-harmonic damping effect in nature which is counterbalanced by the angel's symbolic resonance.

This brings us to yet another revelation about Rosslyn Chapel. In reviewing the chapel's dimensions, the length is exactly twice the breadth while the height-to-length ratio is equal to the golden mean. Furthermore, the length of the choir section taken as a proportion to chapel length is a 5:3 major sixth. Since a major sixth is the most resonant interval possible, the choir acts as a maximally resonant chamber in the horizontal direction while damping out reflected standing waves in the vertical direction. In this way, the chapel designers designed a perfectly attenuated chamber that amplified voice and music while minimising echoes. Perhaps this was also intended as an acoustical symbol that could 'thaw' the frozen music in the architecture. The architecture of Rosslyn Chapel blends the mythological symbolism of alpha–omega or good versus evil into a musical balance of harmonic resonance and anti-harmonic damping. The secret symbol for harmonic damping can be found today in the '007' moniker taken by Ian

Fleming from John Dee, a 16th century original secret agent to Queen Elizabeth I, self proclaimed 'angelic-alchemist' and hermetic mathematician very familiar with harmonic proportions. We also find it in the persistent negative symbol for resonance – the Christian 'number of the Beast' 666. But the chapel designers suggest a more balanced interpretation of this symbolism. The 215 musical cubes in the chapel total one less than 216, the ancient Hebrew number for God. It is said that finding the missing code for this number – six cubed or 6 x 6 x 6 – will trigger the Messianic Age of peace. With this, everything in Rosslyn Chapel seems intended to replace the misguided symbolisms of evil with truth and hope.

Opposing forces of resonance and damping are everywhere in nature: the spacing of electrons in an atom, averaged interplanetary orbits, branching patterns in plants and the joint spacing in animals that enable articulated movement. Without this duality, nothing could vibrate, move or even live. Passed down from Egypt and the Orient, driven underground into the esoteric brotherhoods, these fundamental harmonic principles are the very definition of sacred. What could be more appropriate for any sacred temple space than the harmony of nature?

Most people are aware of the Staff of Moses plus Aaron and Joseph. But very few are aware that Jesus likewise had a staff, too. It wasn't as well documented in the Bible as Moses's or his brother Aaron's, but he did have a magic staff. The ironic part about this is that his staff was much more powerful than that of any other prophet, prophetess or angel. Jesus was the divine presence incarnate. He was supposedly God in the flesh. His powers are the powers associated directly with the Holy Trinity…they are the powers that allow life to even happen. I can prove it because if you believe in the Bible, or at least that it has been a deliberately pieced together for our benefits in our time, then take the following verse, straight from the Bible, into consideration:

'The Lord is my shepherd; I shall not want. He maketh me to lie down in green pastures: he leadeth me beside the still waters. He restoreth my soul: he leadeth me in the paths of righteousness for his name's sake. Yea, though I walk through the valley of the shadow of death, I will fear no evil: for thou art with me; thy rod and thy staff they comfort me. Thou preparest a table before me in the presence of mine enemies: thou anointest my head with oil; my cup runneth over. Surely goodness and mercy shall follow me all the days of my life: and I will dwell in the house of the Lord forever.'

Notice that in the passage, the words rod and staff are mentioned. If you dig way down deep, you will also find that there are metaphors in this passage that tell the reader that the staff of Jesus Christ was packed with powers and mystical abilities. Further yet, the staff of Jesus holds the ability to grant these powers unto to others. Here's the history.

The original staff of Jesus, God the Son, was given to him by his paternal deification, God the Father. It was filled with the magic factor of the Holy Trinity, God the Holy Spirit. In this way, the trinity would be kept together at all times. When Jesus was very young, he was given the staff by his mother, who received the staff in a vision that she received from a host of Seraphim. At this age, Jesus was still kept in a mortal state of mind. He had no idea of the magic that was kept in his staff. It wasn't until he realised that he was the Messiah that the powers in his staff came to full fruition. After Jesus realised his full potential, and that he was sent to die as the Son of Man to save us from our transgressions, the power in his staff reached full capacity. He used it for many miracles including healing the blind, making the deaf hear, curing lepers, walking on water, controlling the weather, feeding the masses, opening up the sky to peer into the heavens, and much more. In his staff were stones from Heaven. Existent in the staff was anything from rubies to emeralds to diamonds and many other precious stones, which held no materialistic value other than the fact that it contained the magic of God. It wasn't a divination from God – it was the actual thing. It was the actual magic.

Upon his crucifixion, Jesus distributed the power of the staff to an island in the Etruscan Sea. It wasn't until over 1,000 years later that the staff was awarded to Saint Patrick by a hermit who had received the staff on the island in the Etruscan Sea. He told Saint Patrick that the staff shall be given to 'He that shall be called the Father of Ireland'. Lo and behold, Saint Patrick was sainted and became the Patron Saint of Ireland.

When Saint Patrick founded the Armagh Cathedral, he blessed and sanctified it with the staff of Jesus. He stored the staff, which he referred to as his sacred crozier, in his beloved cathedral upon its founding. The powers of his crozier have been emanated and used to make many religious relics including sacred crosses, grails, chalices and busts. It has been used to divine the gospels of Saint Patrick and many sepulchre alcoves.

After the death of Saint Patrick, the staff was burned on High Street in Dublin and given up as a sacrifice to the Lord by Archbishop George

Brown. The staff was stripped of its gems, which hold the powers of our Lord Jesus Christ and the Patron Saint of Ireland, Saint Patrick. These gems are the ones that have been venerated and continue to be venerated. These gems travelled with Jesus all of his life. They were there for every step of the journey. They hold the power of the Messiah. They were also with Saint Patrick for much of his life as a religious cleric. They hold all the powers of his sainthood and his devotion to Christ makes them even stronger.

For the record I firmly believe that Egyptian gold mines found in Australia are in fact the mythical and often debated fabled 'land of Punt'. I also state that they will also find within the Hill of Tara in Ireland that it is riddled with pearls from Egypt. Pearls of the sea show kingship, sovereignty, the true centre of kingship, a centre that rules over all. Tara is the site of queenship, the beautiful centre of the rose, which is not…located in England. The Goddess stands on Tara, in the centre, looking out over the Emerald Isle, Scotland and England.

In *Outremer* I explained how Queen Tamar had in her possession a manuscript…one that she vowed to have copied and placed back in the Churches vaults and archives or wherever the popes of the future would reside. It is an authentic manuscript that could turn the whole philosophy of the Christian Church upside down, for it details that Mary Magdalene was indeed the 13th apostle and that she was Jesus's fiancé and later wife. The manuscript describes her as Jesus's most trusted and closest disciple. It also describes her as the actual founder of Christianity. Tamar demanded the Church provide an explanation for this act of secretion but the Church responded that if these secrets were to be revealed, then the whole of society as we know it will collapse. It is why she allowed women to be ordained and hold offices in the clergy. Although women may be elected as Pope, none have been elected openly so far. She did much to change how women are perceived within the Church…and there will come a day when the Church finally admits that Mary Magdalene was, in fact, actually the first pope…not Peter! That document really exists and is presently still held within Vatican archives.

Within the Great Pyramid at Giza they will discover yet more chambers, one large one above the Grand Gallery. They will also discover that there is a pathway that weaves around the edges in a spiral format that was later back filled. The pathway was a passage used to ferry stone and material upwards as they built the structure from the inside out and upwards. The passageway was then back filled with lighter stones as they sealed it. People still argue that the Great Pyramid has quarry marks discovered by Howard Carter with the cartouche painted in the relieving chambers above the King's Chamber; but these are fake and put there by Carter himself. They are identical to the cartouche images he had within his journal, written incorrectly months prior to his entry into the chambers. But also keep in mind that the ancient Egyptians themselves state the Giza pyramids were already there at the very dawn of their civilisation as I detailed within *Outremer*.

Many Nordic legends speak of a shield put in place to protect the earth. They describe in detail what we would understand today as being ice meteors from space entering our upper atmosphere and exploding. But the shield was claimed to be in place and would remain so until the gods returned. NASA recently confirmed what appears to be a secondary protective shield that is not the Van Allen belt…but more surprisingly that this secondary shield appears to have been artificially constructed. Also there is much rumour regarding what is known as the Dark Knight, or Black Knight or Solar Warden, an artificial satellite that orbits our planet on a trajectory that requires it to automatically adjust its position in order to remain in orbit. If it did not, it would crash to earth and burn up; and should have done years ago. It is claimed by NASA and other agencies that this Solar Warden is an old solar panel that broke away from the space station years ago. If it was, then its orbit would have degraded a long time ago and it would have burnt up on re-entry. But also know that this very same Dark Knight was observed and documented by the ancient Sumerians and Babylonians thousands of years ago. Also by Leo Teslar in the last century. It was also observed that every time modern spacecraft attempt to get near to it, they malfunction. On July 22nd 2016 its position passed directly over La Rochelle at 21:06. This was also the time that a man and young woman were observed placing a red rose upon a white lily on the point of Stella Maris. Shortly afterwards several space observatory stations confirmed that a brief burst signal was detected transmitting from the so-called solar panel, toward Pluto.

So many people claim to know what the G symbol in Freemasonry means. From what I have studied and learnt, and as I have outlined within *Outremer*, I personally believe it is connected to the Egyptian princess

Scota, who fled from Egypt with her husband Gaythelos with a large following of people who arrived in a fleet of ships. They settled in Alba, Scotland for a while, until forced to leave. They landed in the Emerald Isle and formed the Scotti, and their kings became the High Kings of Ireland. In later centuries, they returned to Alba, defeating the Picts, and giving Scotland its new name. Scota's father is actually named as being Achencres, a Greek version of an Egyptian name. In the work of Manetho, an Egyptian priest, the translation of the name of the pharaoh Achencres was none other than Akhenaten, who reigned in the time frame of 1350 BC. Scota was in fact Meritaten, eldest daughter of Akhenaten and Nefertiti. I further personally believe that she was originally buried between Sliab Mis and the sea but was removed. She will be found one day in a glen located in Glenscota. As with many myths, as a real person she lent her persona and identity to the landscape of the land she became a part of, giving Scotland her name. [126]

And to conclude. The greatest code is actually hidden within our very own DNA and RNA. Not only does it contain the information that helps build our cells, but it also has a very clear message written within it...Very soon we shall be reading that message.

Appendix

Further information on selected aspects of the Outremer series

A major enigma surrounding the Knights Templar, is their reverence for 'Caput LVIIIm' which means 'Head 58m'. It has been argued the 'm' is in fact the astronomical symbol for Virgo. An important ancient Egyptian number that has many symbolic meanings is the value of 5. It is the number of the Pentagram and the 5-pointed star image that represented Sirius and 8 is associated with Isis, who was also represented by Sirius in the heavens. The numbers 5 and 8 are also present in the 'Brothers of the Ross Cross' known popularly nowadays as the Rosicrucians, their image logo being of a rose constructed with a centre of five petals surrounded by eight petals. Gerald Massey, the eminent Egyptologist states that the number is of a feminine origin and nature as METE was the BAPHOMET or mother of breath and that according to Von Hammer, the formula of faith, inscribed on a chalice belonging to the Templars is as follows: 'Let METE be exalted who causes all things to bud and blossom, it is our root; it is one (1) and seven (7); it is 'octinimous', the eight fold name'. Jesus is also associated with the number 8.

Another valuable number that crops up again and again is 64 which plays a multi functional purpose and is even connected with our very own DNA and RNA. Everything appears to be intrinsically linked by a universal mathematical pattern. The Giza complex is actually set out on an 8 x 8 grid square system, which equals 64. Not only do we find the important 64 value but also the Golden Mean proportion of the grid is based on a ratio of 5.8. Recall the Head 58 connection with the Knights Templar? These are two consecutive numbers in the Fibonacci sequence. It just so happens that each side of the Giza 8 x 8 square equals 1/2 a minute of equatorial latitude, as in 921.44 meters. 64 x 1440 equals 921.60 a difference of just 16, or 16 cm's. It is the 921 that is of importance. Jesus is linked directly with this number as his recorded ministry as detailed in the New Testament lasted exactly 921 days. Note that if you take a bearing from the Great Pyramids apex of 26 degrees, which the passages within it are angled at, leaving 64 degrees to make 90 and then travel in a north easterly direction for exactly 365 miles, 365 days in the year, you end up at Bethlehem. Note also that the Great Pyramid sits in the North Eastern corner of the grid on just four squares, or more correctly, 1/16th. That number 16 again. Finally, note that the Golden mean radius drawn from the North Eastern corner of the Great Pyramid passes directly through the Sphinx.

Atbash Cipher

The Atbash cipher is a basic encoding method known to be used in the Bible. Examples appear in the Book of Jeremiah which dates to around 600B.C. The simplicity of the code is perhaps why it was so successful. Atbash derives its name from the Hebrew language noted to use it. The first letter of the alphabet is exchanged for the last; the second letter exchanged for the next to last and so on. In the Hebrew alphabet, these letters are Aleph (first) and Tav (last), Beth (second) and Shin (next to last). Taking the first letter of each supplies ATBSH for the rendering of Atbash. Basically, it is a reversal of writing. In English, A to Z would equal Z to A. The process used for the Atbash cipher is the letters are all reversed to represent another.

It is also interesting to note that the infamous term 'Baphomet' has been found to render 'Sophia' by applying the Atbash cipher.

Eliphas Levi, who drew the full figured Goat of Mendes, translated 'Baphomet' as a reversed composition of three abbreviations: Tem. Oph. Ab, standing for the basic Latin *Templi omnium hominum pacis abhas*: 'The God of the Temple of Peace Among All Men.' Levi felt this to be a reference to King Solomon's Temple, which he believed had the sole purpose of bringing peace to the world. Also in Esoteric Tradition: Eagle, double headed Eagle: TEM OF AB ('ph' is the 'F' sound) meaning Duplex Avis Generation: spelled backwards the word is Baphomet/Bafomet. Also, from the Egyptian mystery portions: Tem: to name as in to proclaim: Tem is a title of Apep. Oph (again, the 'ph' is an 'F' sound as in 'foe'): winged serpent or dragon. Ab hearing, wisdom, and understanding; intelligence and Will. Again, Baphomet (Bafomet) spelled backwards. In short: Serpent of Wisdom, Serpent Knowledge. The word Baphomet is semi-Greek: Baphe Metis. It means initiation by origin of water (baptismo) and Wisdom of Measurement. In esoteric literature there is shown the far more ancient Babylonian version of the word: Bahu Mid. Unfortunately, this is not easy to come by. Bahu is Hebrew for The Waters (not the ocean). Elohim (God) moved over the face of Bahu (the waters).

The Knights Templar, were Roman Catholics that could read the Bible in Greek as the Apostles wrote it and the more educated members were also able to read the actual Hebrew of the Old Testament. 'Baphe' is pseudo-Greek, and 'Metis' is proper Greek. It is, in my opinion, conclusive that the Knights Templar, as Roman Catholics, used the image of Baphemetis to mean Sophia! Sophia is not just the Goddess of Wisdom from the Hellenic, Pythagorean and early Gnostic tradition associated with Gnosis; Sophia is also the Goddess and considered to be the Bride of God! Note also that Mary, Mar, Miriam, is associated with Water – as in the Babylonian/Hebrew word Bahu 'The Waters.' In short, with the Hebrew we have: Upper Shekina – and Lower Shekina – then Hochmah (a kind of Light-Word) In the Orphic and Pythagorean and in some early Gnosticism we have: Sophia – and Sophia Achamoth – then Logos (Light-Word) In the Catholic this would be: Sophia – and Mary – then Christos (The Light-Word). However, this would not be standard Catholic Doctrine, at least not at that time. It would be seen, it was seen, as heretical. This would be taking the literal story of the Virgin Mary, a woman who was the wife of Joseph and the mother of Jesus, and turning Mary into something quite heavenly, making Mary a Queen of Heaven and the Mother of God! It has been held by many that the Templars were followers of the Goddess Sophia or at very least instrumental in re-establishing the feminine aspect of divinity that had been excised by the Catholic Church. It should be remembered that the Templar patron, St. Bernard of Clairvaux, had an absolute obsession with Mary and was responsible for Her being named the Queen of Heaven and the Mother of God *in Heaven*, not just on Earth. Mary is today considered the Mother of God in Catholicism. Whether the Templars were devoted to the Goddess Sophia or simply respectful of Wisdom (Sophia), it cannot be disputed that Schonfield's Atbash cipher theory is among the most plausible, in our opinion it is conclusive, explanations of the etymology of *Baphomet*. Dr. Hugh Schonfield, one of the scholars who worked on the Dead Sea Scrolls, believed the word Baphomet was applied with the Knowledge of the Atbash Cipher: When the Hebrew letters that spells Baphomet is applied to this code, it generates the Greek word Sophia which is translated in English as Wisdom. The Greek Goddess Sophia is brought to mind here. 'Sophia' in the New Testament is also brought to mind as some Born Again Christians have pointed out: there is a Goddess in their Bible.

Hebrew Atbash Cipher and English alphabet construct from Templar cross:

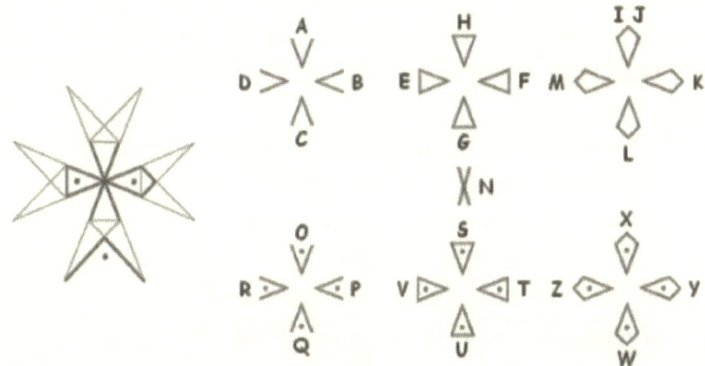

Hebrew Atbash Cipher

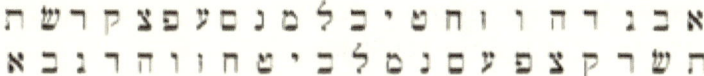

The word 'Sophia' in Hebrew is שופיא. The Atbash form of that is בפעמת or baf'omet. Both words are also written from left to right instead of from right to left. As early as 500 BC Scribes writing the book of Jeremiah used what we now know to be the ATBASH cipher. This cipher is one of the few used in the Hebrew language. The cipher itself, ATBASH, is very similar to the substitution cipher. A substitution cipher is one where each letter of the alphabet actually represents another letter. In the case of the Atbash cipher, the first letter of the alphabet is substituted for the last, the second for the second last and so on. I.e., for us (English speakers and writers) the letter A becomes 'Z', the letter 'B' becomes 'Y,' the letter 'C' becomes 'X' and so on. Schonfield became very interested in the charges of heresy levelled against the Knights Templar and the etymology of the word Baphomet. Schonfield decided to apply the Atbash cipher, which he was convinced the Templars were aware of, to the word Baphomet. If one writes the word Baphomet in Hebrew and remember Hebrew letters read from right to left, the result is shown here with our letters shown left to right. Applying the Atbash cipher, Schonfield revealed the following: The word Baphomet: Bet Pe Vav Mem Taf spells BAPHOMET. With the Atbash Cipher: Shin Vav Pe Yud Alef spells SOPHIA. Although written in Hebrew it reads as the Greek word Sophia that translates into 'Wisdom' in English. No matter what you use, 'Wisdom' is always coming up with regards to this word Baphomet, whether you use Sophia, Bahu Mid, or Baphemetis.

Schonfield's Atbash cipher theory and what it showed when he applied it, is just one more excellent explanation of what 'Baphomet' means – and we note that all the explanations yield the same meaning in the inner sense. In other words, Schonfield did not get a word that meant 'love' or 'war' when he applied it. He got SOPHIA! What does all of this show? Sophia is Upper Shekina! Sophia is also Wisdom. Baphe Metis means Initiation into Wisdom. The word Baphe is some kind of lingo jargon made from the either the word baptismo or Bahu. Water and Spirit (kundalini) are Bahu and Shekina! Most notable of all: Jesus said, "ean me tis gennese ex hydratos chai pneumatos, ou dynatai basileian tou theou." Literally: if anyone be not generated out of water and spirit, he is not able to enter into the kingdom of the god.Gospel of St. John, 3:5. (Note that the majority of English translations mistranslate this to read "unless you are born again." The original Greek says no such thing. The original Greek is specific and clear. The words "born again" do not exist in the actual Greek. The verses further explain, in literal English from Greek: "If anyone be not generated out of Water and Spirit, he cannot enter the Kingdom of the God. That which has been born of the flesh, is Flesh; and that which has been born of the spirit, is Spirit. Do not wonder, because I said to you, you must be born from above. The Spirit breaths where it will, and you hear its Voice, but you know not whence it comes, or where it goes; thus it is with everyone who has been born of the Spirit." Note especially that when referring to The Spirit, the pronoun 'it' is used. Nowhere does this call for a second Baptism.)

The Hebrew Scribes or Tanaim actually used to write manuscripts like this, and they called it 'ploughing the field' (a Hebrew name that means that) because when you read it you are supposed to read right to left on top line, left to right on second, right to left in third... etc. Like back and forth Reading like this is also called the SERPENT way. Sofia is upper Wisdom. Sofia Achamoth is Lower Wisdom or the "waters." The Waters (or Bahu, Baphe) is the root of the Christos (also called Logos). In a sense, it is the Mother of Christos, where this force in people springs out and up from. Who is the Mother of Christ? Mary. What does Mary mean? Sea. Hence, the waters. Layers of code are here. The Templars were Catholics – but they were HERETICS at that time for believing this. They were branded heretics. The name for this symbol was BAHU MID or Baphe Metis. The goat in the star is not the devil or satan. (Even the Wiccans know that.) It is simply the androgyne goat and might have been less goatish at the time. Ram heads were also used. In the Bible, satan, or Ha-stn, is not a goat or a horned headed being. In the Hebrew ha-stn is an adversary – any adversary or, at best, something God uses to test the faithful. In Catholicism and other forms of Christianity, Satan is a liar, a deceiver – but still a spirit -not an animal or man or animal-headed man. Satan is not a victorious rebel figure except in English literature, which is purely fictional.

I should point out that *Baphe* is not a Greek word, ancient or Biblical, that means Wisdom, Initiation, Holy Spirit, Cleansing, or anything normally related to Baptism in everyday speech. *Baphe* is a noun in Attic Greek that means 'dye' as in colouring. However, *Baptein* means the verb 'to dye' as in to colour something by dipping it. *Baphe*, as *a* word used to mean «Baptism» or Initiation» came after the word *Baptismo*, a word perculiar to these cults that practiced immersion into water, and it meant what we understand it to mean by Baptism – always by water. It is related to Bahu, but not linguistically as far as anyone knows. The Templars may have originated

547

the use of the word *Baphe* and stuck it on the word *Met* after they encoded Sophia with the Atbash Cipher. Not the other way around! If you know that they meant Sophia, you can figure out how they came up with the word Baphomet by using what Schonfield used.

In very late versions of the Set-Osiris myth, myths continuing well into the Roman Empire after Christ, Set was considered to have dismembered Osiris. Isis recovered all Osiris's fragments except his phallus; that was eaten by a letos fish. The symbolism here is: donkey cults (at that late time, they were considered this) murder esoteric mystery cults. There was always a war within the Semite groups between the dark mother cults and the patriarchal solar father group, (see *The Hebrew Goddess* by Patai for extensive detail). When Mother Goddess cults try to put the mystery cults back together, they are emasculated by the FISH: fish representing Christianity! Noteworthy also, a later Gnostic heresy of Clement of Alexandria's followers known as the Sethian heresy claimed that Seth was an earlier incarnation of Jesus. There were mystical Essenes in the First Century AD called Ebionites, who believed that the Holy Spirit was female. Some of these became Christians and developed into the Second Century Clementine Gnostics. They believed the Virgin Mary was a vessel of this Holy Spirit. It is well known that Christianity persecuted any mother goddess cults.

The mythopoetic telling of this tale continues on in some traditions: In Mahdia (pronounced MAK-tee-ah) the story goes that the cults managed to kill the fish, get back the phallus and plant it: and out of it grew the GOAT OF MENDES! BAPHOMET (Bahu Mid, Baphe Metis) was born. Mahdia was a place in Tunisia where the Fatimid Dynasty arose (Fatima, female line from Mohammed, was used for this dynasty). Assassins and others arose from this Dynasty. Hugh de Payens founded the Knights Templar; he was also a Master in the Order of Assassins. However, that is another subject. [127]

List of some of the books used for research

Gods Warriors: Dr Helen Nicholson & Dr David Nicolle. (Oxford, 2005).

The lost books of the Bible: Rutherford: H Platt. (New York, 1974).

A Brief History of the Crusades: Geoffrey Hindley. (London, 2003).

Perlesvaus + The high history of the Holy Grail: Sebastian Evans. (London, 1969).

Parzival: Wolfram von Eschenbach trans by Helen M Mustard and Charles E Passage. (New York, 1961).

Worlds in collision + Earth in upheaval + Ages in chaos: Immanuel Velikovsky. (London, New York, 1953, 1955 and 1957).

The trial of the Templars: Malcolm Barber. (Cambridge, 1978).

A history of secret societies: A Daraul. (New York, 1969).

The Sign and the Seal: Graham Hancock (London, 1992).

Who wrote the Dead Sea Scrolls: Norman Golb. (London 1995).

The House of the Messiah: Ahmed Osman. (London 1992).

The Murdered Magicians, The Templars and their Myth: Peter Partner. (London 1981).

Great Pyramid Decoded + The Jesus Inititaive: Peter Lemesurier. (London, 1976 and 1978).

The Atlantis Blueprint: Rand and Rose Flemath. (London, 1998).

Templar Revelation + The Turin Shroud, in whose image: Clive Prince and Lynn Picknett. (London, 1997 and 1994).

The Gnostic Gospels: Elaine Pagels. (London, 1980).

The Sword and the Grail: Andrew Sinclair. (London, 1992).

The Essene Odyssey + The Passover Plot + The Pentecost Revolution: Hugh J Schonfield. (London, 1984, 1965 and 1974).

Knight of Outremer: Dr David Nicolle. (Oxford, 1996).

Crusader Castles in the Holy Land: Dr David Nicolle. (Oxford, 2004).

Holy Bible:

Qur'an/Koran:

Egyptian Book of the Dead: trans Sir E A Wallis. (London, 1899).

Egyptian Virgin of the World: trans Sir E A Wallis. (London, 1899).

Holy Blood and the Holy Grail + The Messianic Legacy: Michael Baigent, Richard Leigh and Henry Lincoln. (London, 1982 and 1986).

The Holy Grail: Peter Gardiner. (London, 1996).

Knight Templar: Dr Helen Nicholson. (Oxford, 2003).

Knight Hospitaller: Dr David Nicolle. (Oxford, 2001).

The Knights of Christ: Terence Wise. (Oxford, 1984).

Armies of the Crusades: Terence Wise. (Oxford, 1978).

The Crusades: Dr David Nicolle. (Oxford, 1988).

Saladin and the Saracens: Dr David Nicolle. (Oxford, 1986).

Finger Prints of the Gods: Graham Hancock. (London, 1995).

The Magi: Adrian Gilbert. (London, 1995).

The Orion Mystery: Robert Bauval and Adrian Gilbert. (London, 1994).

Keepers of Genesis: Robert Bauval & Graham Hancock. (London, 1998).

The Hiram Key: Robert Lomas and Christopher Knight. (London, 1996).

New View over Atlantis: John Mitchell. (London, 1980).

Hamlets Mill: Santillana and Von Dechend.

A History of Palestine: Moshe Gil (634-1099. Cambridge UP, 1983, 1997).

The Armies of Islam. David Nicolle. (Men-at-Arms. Osprey, 1982). Saladin and the Saracens. Men-at Arms. Osprey, 1986. Armies of the Muslim Conquests. Men-at-Arms. Osprey, 1993. The Moors, the Islamic West. Men-at-Arms. Osprey, 2001.

Bibliography

113: Excerpts from The Woman with the Alabaster Jar: Mary Magdalen and the Holy Grail by Margaret Starbird. The Holy Place: Saunière and the Decoding of the Mystery of Rennes-le-Château by Henry Lincoln

114: De Expugnatione Terrae Sanctae per Saladinum, translated by James A. Brundage, in The Crusades: A Documentary Survey. Marquette University Press, 1962. William of Tyre, A History of Deeds Done Beyond the Sea. E. A. Babcock and A. C. Krey, trans. Columbia University Press, 1943. Chronique d'Ernoul et de Bernard le Trésorier, edited by M. L. de Mas Latrie. La Société de l'Histoire de France, 1871. La Continuation de Guillaume de Tyr (1184–1192), edited by Margaret Ruth Morgan. L'Académie des Inscriptions et Belles-Lettres, 1982. Ambroise, The History of the Holy War, translated by Marianne Ailes. Boydell Press, 2003. Chronicle of the Third Crusade, a Translation of Itinerarium Peregrinorum et Gesta Regis Ricardi, translated by Helen J. Nicholson. Ashgate, 1997. Peter W. Edbury [pl], The Conquest of Jerusalem and the Third Crusade: Sources in Translation. Ashgate, 1996. Peter W. Edbury, John of Ibelin and the Kingdom of Jerusalem. Boydell Press, 1997. Amin Maalouf, The Crusades Through Arab Eyes. London, 1984. H. E. Mayer, 'Carving Up Crusaders: The Early Ibelins and Ramlas', in Outremer: Studies in the history of the Crusading Kingdom of Jerusalem presented to Joshua Prawer. Yad Izhak Ben-Zvi Institute, 1982. Steven Runciman, A History of the Crusades, vol. II: The Kingdom of Jerusalem. Cambridge University Press, 1952.

115: After Wallyjack's 'Sieges Of History – 1187 Jerusalem'. Amin Maalouf, The Crusades Through Arab Eyes. London, 1984. "Crusades." Encyclopædia Britannica. Encyclopædia Britannica Online. Encyclopædia Britannica, 2011. Web. 24 Oct. 2011. James A. Brundage, The Crusades: A Documentary Survey. Marquette University Press, 1962. Kenneth Setton, ed. A History of the Crusades, vol. I. University of Pennsylvania Press, 1958 (available online). Peter W. Edbury, The Conquest of Jerusalem and the Third Crusade: Sources in Translation. Ashgate, 1996. P. M. Holt, The Age of the Crusades: The Near East from the Eleventh Century to 1517. Longman, 1986. R. C. Smail, Crusading Warfare, 1097–1193. Cambridge University Press, 1956. Steven Runciman, A History of the Crusades, vol. II: The Kingdom of Jerusalem and the Frankish East, 1100–1187. Cambridge University Press, 1952.

116: JOURNAL ARTICLE – Rush to Annexation: Israel in Jerusalem by David Hirst *Journal of Palestine Studies*, Vol. 3, No. 4 (Summer, 1974), pp. 3-31. Published by: University of California Press. Peter W. Edbury, 'Propaganda and Faction in the Kingdom of Jerusalem: The Background to Hattin', in Crusaders and Muslims in Twelfth-Century Syria, ed. Maya Shatzmiller, 1993. Peter W. Edbury, The Conquest of Jerusalem and the Third Crusade: Sources in Translation. Ashgate, 1996. [Includes Eraclius's letter to Urban III after the battle of Hattin (pp. 162–3: see also p. 47).] Bernard Hamilton, The Leper King & His Heirs, 2000. Benjamin Z. Kedar, 'The Patriarch Eraclius', in Outremer: Studies in the History of the Crusading Kingdom of Jerusalem presented to Joshua Prawer, ed. B. Z. Kedar, H. E. Mayer, and R. C. Smail, 1982.

117: Crusader Castles in the Holy Land 1192–1302 by David Nicolle. Osprey Publishing 2005. D. Nicolle, 'Ain al-Habis. The 'cave de Sueth', Archeologie medievale 18 (1988), pp. 113-40; H. Kennedy, Crusader Castles (Cambridge, 1994), pp. The Churches of the Crusader Kingdom of Jerusalem: A Corpus: Volume 1, A-K by Professor Denys Pringle.

118: After 'Gods Warriors' by Dr Helen Nichols. Osprey Publishing

119: Canons From 'The Council Of Carthage Against Pelagianism', May 1, 418. African Synods Catholic Encyclopedia. Schaff, Philip, The Seven Ecumenical Councils – Canons of Carthage. Godfrey of Bouillon, Encyyclopadeia Britannica (11th Edition), Volume XII, Cambridge at the University Press, Cambridge, 1910, pg. 172-173. Andressohn, John Carl. The Ancestry and Life of Godfrey of Bouillon. Indiana University Publications, Social Science Series 5. 1947. 'Godfrey of Bouillon'. New Advent Catholic Encyclopedia. Retrieved 2007-04-29. 'Godfrey of Bouillon'. Internet Medieval Sourcebook: The Crusaders at Constantinople: Collected Accounts. Retrieved 2014-05-18. Holböck, Ferdinand (2002). Married Saints and Blesseds. Michael J. Miller, translator. Ignatius Press. p. 147. ISBN 0-89870-843-5. Murray, Alan V., 'The Army of Godfrey of Bouillon, 1096–1099: Structure and Dynamics of a Contingent on the First Crusade' (PDF), Revue belge de philologie et d'histoire 70 (2), 1992.

120: Exposing Christianity. Macaca da Silva. https://www.academia.edu

121: 'Bloodline of the Holy Grail – The Hidden Lineage of Jesus Revealed' by Laurence Gardner. Element; New Ed edition (4 Nov. 2002) The Holy Blood And The Holy Grail by Leigh, Richard, Baigent, Michael, Lincoln, Henry Published by Arrow (1996) The Templar Revelation: Secret Guardians Of The True Identity Of Christ. Corgi; Revised edition edition (23 April 2007)

122: Virgin Mother Goddesses of Antiquity by M. Rigoglioso. Springer, 2010 George Hart. The Routledge Dictionary of Egyptian Gods and Goddesses. Andrew Gough. Article on sacred bees. https://andrewgough.co.uk. Ann, Martha, and Imel, Dorothy Myers, "Goddesses in World Mythology, A Biographical Dictionary," Oxford University Press, New York and Oxford, 1995.

123: Ronan, Miles V., "St. Patrick's Staff and Christ Church," Dublin Historical Record 5.4 (Jun-Aug 1943): The Annals of Ireland [from A.D. 1171 to A.D. 1616]. Translated from the Original Irish of the Four Masters by O'Connellan, with Annotations by P. MacDermott and the Translator

124: "ichthus". Oxford English Dictionary (third ed.). 2007. Los Angeles Times (1 April 2008). "Evolution of religious bigotry". latimes.com. The Merovingian Mythos And the Mystery of Rennes-le-Chateau, by Tracy R. Twyman. Dragon Key Press, 2004. Ben Zvi, Ehud (2003), *The Signs of Jonah: Reading and Rereading in Ancient Yehud*, Sheffield, England: Sheffield Academic Press.

125: The Dark Star- The Planet X Evidence by Andy Lloyd. Timeless Voyager Press, 2005. Nibiru and the Binary Twin Dwarf Star arrives to our Solar System as Planet X by Robert Mock MD. http://www.biblesearchers.com/prophecy/planetx/losttribes4.shtml

126: Kingdom of the Ark Paperback – August 6, 2001 by Lorraine Evans. Simon & Schuster. Scotichronicon, (Chronicles of the Scots) AD 1435 by a monk named Walter Bower.

127: After 'Guardians of Darkness' RC Priest and Tani Jantsang (from longer article).

Index

(Limited Index for Code*)

538-540 542 544 547 548 550-553 555-
559 561 564 566-570 573 575 578 580-
583 585-588 590 591 592 505 596-598
602 608

Castle. 1 5 85 127 131 139 140 144 156 157
159 162 191 192 197 199 217 221 225 226
227 261 283 382 405 409 441 443 449
453 474 475 490 501 502 509 526 535
537 551 573 574 577 581 583-585 587
590 591 595 596 601 610 630

Castle Blanc. 1 139 140 144 156 157 159 162
191 199 217 221 261 283 405 490

Catastrophe. 615 618 619 621 622 627 628

Cathedral. 4 5 124 127 131-133 136 138 177
180 295 364-366 378 379 380 382 389
406 409 410 412 413 461 463 534-536
579 580 616 619 629

Catholic. 2 38 224 226 263 315 316 435 522
620 623

Caucasians. 628

Cave. 74 126

Celestial. 122 172 384 387 434 435 458 459

Celtic. 33 101 102 116 117 125 176 389 612-
615 626 628-631 633 640

Ceremony. 23 32 34 35 50 54 55 63 72 199
207 271 290 302 308 316 319 320 321
323 325 326 348 369 379 462 539 569
570 626

Chain mail. 1 13 25 105 136 191 274 340
342 356 428 447 555 564 591

Chalice. 177 640

Chalki. 444 449 473 474 475

Chamber. 20 101-103 192 205 206 221 233
234 266 267 268 271 280 281 292 329
380 397 417 428 502 590

Chartres. 117 180 295 365-367 379 380 389
461

Chatillon. vi 6 136 142 200 226 227 501
503 508 537

Ching. 384 425 426 434-436 437 438

Chi-Rho. 521-523

Christ. 2 4 5 38-40 43 78 121 177 180 202 224
232 239 241 242 243 245 246 271 272 285

309 310-314 318 394 411 444 453 481 521-
523 525 554 603 619 620 636

Christian. 3 5 6 32 38 63 69 93 99 100 104
122 128 132-134 141 142 147 176 177
179 180 182 191 197 263 295 307 309
313 315 316-320 328 333 383 385 386
392 393 409 440 441 461 486 494 508
509 517 518 522 524 554 577 597 603
620 622 629

Cilician. 432 489 490 503 526 529 538 552
573 585 595 610

Circe. 444

Circle of Life. 168

Cistercians. 224 623

Clarendon Palace. 535

Coat of arms. 135 219 236 379

Cog. 12 21

Colchis. 380 576 630

Conroise. 1

Constantinople. 113 225 226 310 500 509
513 622

Constellation. 364-366 379 380-382 384
386 387 457 629

Cords. 18 36 37 42 183 211 270 385 451 585
586

Council of Clermont. 5

Count of Champagne. 9 224 260

Count of Troyes. 9 224

Covenant. 4 5 10 63 241 380 611 621

Crac de Moab. 1 138 226 501 537

Creation. 69 116 117 119-122 124 170-172
187 198 313 322 324 346 384 463 611
622 626

Crossbones. 35 61 62 113 461 516-523

Crossbow. 151-155 157 162 193 202 288
338 339 350 352 353 354 355 558 561
592

Crusade. 3 4 5 13 21 94 95 96 99 113 160
224 225 228 262 263 390 406 440 506
508 584

Culdeans. 622 623

Maverick. 447

Mebakker. 20

Mecca. 98 195 221 435 501 509

Medina. 99

Mediterranean Sea. 11 144 383 405 443 449 464 473 577 612

Megalithic. 3 11 101 370 621 628 629 633

Megara. 444

Melissae Inn. 12 33 45 55 63 76 85 103 110 126 139 158 188 196 210 221 239 254 266 276 294 326 336 345 376 389 406 426 433 440 447 455 487 500 516 532 550 570 583 593 607

Merkaba. 172 459 619

Merovingian's. 3 366 409 454 462 622

Mesopotamia. 460 520 521 574 575 576 632

Messiah. 124 176 241 294 295 315 366 367 377 383 455 464 468 522 524 619

Metatron. 170 171 172 176

Middle East. 5 6 98 172 176 180 182 242 315 365 458

Milky Way. 337 381 417

Miriam. 294 307 308 313 319 328-330 337 346 347 364 378 380 388 392-395 406-408 426-429 433 440 456 463 487 488 501 519 532 551 570 571

Mohammed. 189

Mohammad. 317

Monarchy. 457 613

Monism. 625

Montferrat. 534

Montgisard. 137 140 141 143

Moon. 34 44 2 72 73 122 287 339 417 420 445 458 461 465 568

Moorish. 174 263

Moses. 4 70 175 244 381 574 615 620 621 624 628 632

Mosque. 5 124 224 437 441

Moulins. 54 143 197 227 335

Mount Moriah. 380

Muslim. 1 3 5 16 21 32 35 38 44 48 55 63 67 71 72 93-99 113 127 128 133 134 137 138 140 142 148 160 176 195-197 199 201-203 206 212 221 225 255 263 270 295 302 307 316-320 326-329 332 335 346 355 364 368 377 386 387 412 431 440 441 486 494 496 501-503 509 517 518 531 577 591 597 598 600 602 603 629

Mystic. 3 4 41 70 123 172-174 180 188 189 365 388 457 518 595 611 626

Nautonier. 375

Navigator. 16 208 209 211 212 375 451 454 464 474

Nazarene. 63 402 403

Nephelim. 10

New Testament. 70 99 308-310 312 317 318 382 395 408 457 520 523 524

Niccolas. 66 67 71 73 74 82 84 93 94 96 100 114-127 164 167-175 177 179 181-187 207-211 213 229 231-239 247 252 258 260 267 271-273 278 279 284-286 294 298 307 316 318-326 336 344 345 348 349 351 354 360 361 365 370 383 384 388 403 435-438 444 446 451 452 460 480 489 507 524 545 550 593 608 612 615

Nicholas. v 36 38 39 40 41 135-141 144

Nile. 226 381 382 394 618 625 631

Ninhursag. 456

Nobis. 35

Nordic. 187 212 619 628 629

Notre Dame. 180 365 366 380 386 410 461

Numerology. 3 59

Oathing. 322 323

Odo de St Amand. 142 219 223 226 227 335

Old man. 13 14 15 16 18 30 33

Old Testament. 69 70 182 242 243 260 313 460 620 621

Thomas Becket. 534 536 537

Thorn. 178 180 204 332

Thoth. xii 158 172 189 385

Tiamat. 385

Tortosa. 25 64 84 85 127-129 131 132 137 139 141 143 144 151 160 161 205 220 258 269 432 465 600

Tree of Life. 172 180 619

Trigrams. 435 436 437

Trilithon. 18 101 103

Tripoli. 89 92 127 128 143 144 191 199 217 228 441 502 507 534

Troy. 224 460 461 462 614

Tuatha. 640

Turcoman. 22 87 104 106 108 135 145

Turcopole. 89 104 135 199 350 352

Tyre. 41 224 227 461 502 503 508

Tyrrhenian. 444 445

Urban. 5 95 96 98 126 263

Veil. 123 239 245 638 639

Venus. 173 176 178 179

Virgin Mary. 35 38 43 56 132 177 179 365 367 379 382 383 386 392 394 409 411 449 474

Virgo. 43 364 365 366 379 380

Vows. 37 42 43 88 138 197 205 224 261 263 270 271 273 293 314 322 323 325 416 542 554 586 591 634

Walter. 227 430 502

Ward. 430

Watchtower. 453 461

Wisdom. xi 2 52 61 62 68 70 78 100 101 110 117 121-124 141 167 180 211 219 241 243 318 322 344 380 384-389 392 394 451-454 459 461 493 494 515 523 546 572 574 614 619 623 629 640

Yahweh. 177 315 394 523 611

Yang. 436 437 519

Yarmuk. 95 96

Yataghan. 25

Yin. 436 437

Zähringen. 464

Zealot. 222 624

Zhang. 434

Zionism. 623

Zoroastrian. 174

Zurich. 464

*This is a limited index purely for the benefit of helping those interested in breaking and reading the code. It is all taken from just volume 1. Only the first few appearances are listed for some names and words but the number of times also fits the mathematical code.

List of illustrations

Fig 1: Stylised Bee Pedant.

Fig 2: Two-dimensional rendering of a sphere.

Fig 3: Arabic calligraphy.

Fig 4: Circle of Life pattern.

Fig 5: Egg of Life pattern.

Fig 6: Flower of Life pattern.

Fig 7: Flower of Life and Fruit of Life patterns.

Fig 8: 13 Circled Flower of Life pattern.

Fig 9: Metatron's Cube pattern.

Fig 10: Raja image.

Fig 11: Alisha side profile image.

Fig 12: Arabic calligraphy bird of Love and Peace.

Fig 13: Symbol of 'ichthys' for 'fish'.

Fig 14: Portrait of Alisha.

Fig 15: Architectural drawing of flying buttress and drawing of a rose window.

Fig 16: Drawing of an Islamic astrolabe.

Fig 17: Chinese Yin and Yang lines.

Fig 18: Chinese I Ching lines.

Fig 19: Two dimensional representation of equilateral triangle circumscribed by a circle.